Born in … varied career
include… in the RAF,
seven y… rder, hunting
the Lo… and brushes
door-t…

Othe… n Paperbacks
are *Hardacre*, *Hardacre's Luck*, … *ens* and *Sweet-hearts and Wives*.

By the same author

Hardacre
Hardacre's Luck

The Maclarens
Sweethearts and Wives

C. L. SKELTON

Beloved Soldiers

This edition published 1994 by
Diamond Books
77–85 Fulham Palace Road
Hammersmith, London W6 8JB

Published by Grafton Books 1986
Reprinted 1990

First published in Great Britain by
Granada Publishing 1985

Printed and bound in Great Britain

Set in Times

For
Alasdair and Justin

Book I

1

Naomi Bruce rapped lightly on the old nursery door, and a foreign-accented voice called, 'Come.' She opened the door, very quietly, and slipped inside, closing it carefully so as not to catch the trailing silken hem of her flowing, Ballet Russe-inspired gown. She waited patiently, just beside the door. She was a slender woman whose features, with their faint but unmistakable oriental cast, hinted at experience without admitting to age. Her skin was the warm colour of *café au lait*, and her hair, glossy black with only a few decorative strands of silver, fell loose over one shoulder in a manner quite revolutionary for 1914. Her eyes, a deep, un-English brown, surveyed the occupants of the room.

Rebecca Galloway was seated at its far end, in the clear light of the tall skylight window that faced the secluded garden of the house on London's Park Lane. She was completely naked, her hands crossed in front of her small breasts, posed on a small stool draped in grey velvet. There were no curtains on the window and even on this grey, rainy summer day, the strength of the light made her skin seem unearthly pale, and the stillness of her face, surrounded by rippling masses of recently loosened auburn hair, glowed with a romantic frailty. She stared at the opposite wall with trance-like devotion and seemed totally oblivious of both Naomi and the tall frock-coated, white-bearded man at the easel by the hearth.

'Excuse me,' Naomi whispered.

'Oh.' Rebecca looked up, her eyes bright with life, the ethereal image shattered. 'I never heard. Oh, do tell, what's the time? Am I free?' She did not await the answer, but went happily on, 'Oh, thank God, my neck's as stiff as a poker and I'm positively frozen. Rosie let the fire go out and Mr Leitner,' she spoke with refined distaste, exactly as if he were not there, 'never notices little matters like that. *And* I'm starving. I shall have sugar in my tea. *Two* lumps,' she looked with sly malice at the artist, under her lowered auburn lashes, 'and five crumpets.'

'Oh, be still, woman,' the white-haired man suddenly roared. 'One moment. One. Please. Soon enough you will be a big fat cow. There is surely no hurry.' Rebecca gave him another malicious look, but obeyed, finding her posture again, with the ease of long practice, and the ethereal shadow again swept her young face. There was a grunt of satisfaction from Leitner, and a few quick dabs of his long brush. Then he stood back, sighed, and said, 'Oh, very well. Be off and stuff your silly face. We'll finish next week.'

Rebecca sprang up, clutching her brown velvet robe, and hurriedly wrapped herself in it. Then she scurried to the hearth and leaned over the brass fender, warming her small, delicate hands over the dull ash. Naomi sank gracefully on to the blue brocade settle before the hearth, and affectionately gathered the girl's thick hair from inside her collar, stroking it out smoothly down her back.

Leitner, midway through washing his brushes, suddenly stopped and cried, 'Oh, charming. Charming. Wait. I will sketch.'

'You'll do nothing of the sort,' Naomi said sharply. 'Now go away. Rebecca is escorting Robert aboard the night train. They must be in Scotland tomorrow morning.'

'Scotland!' Leitner exclaimed with a prim wince. 'I make her famous, adored, art's creature. And all she thinks of is crumpets. And Scotland. Scotland! Philistines!'

'Yes, dear,' said Naomi mildly. 'Now go away like a good thing.' She turned her back to him. 'Art may wait a week.'

He shrugged, gathered his paintbox and brushes and made his way to the door, bowing beside the dappled grey rocking-horse and, as Naomi made to rise, assured her he would see himself out. The door closed behind him, and Naomi collapsed in a wave of giggles, her chin on Rebecca's shoulder.

'Oh, he's such a pet really. But really!' Then she got up and went to the fire, bending over it, and expertly rearranging the coals. She raked out the ash with the poker, and then with small brass tongs, piled a neat pyramid of new black coal on top of the glowing heap.

She turned away from the fire, saw the glint of something shiny on the floor by the rocking-horse, and bent to retrieve it. It was a child's pocket-knife, well made, with a bone handle and three blades. 'Oh thank goodness,' she said, 'Robert's damnable knife. He's been searching everywhere.' As she straightened, penknife in hand, there was a sudden impatient hammering on the nursery door, and she grinned at Rebecca and said, 'See?'

'Mother? Isn't Rebecca dressed *yet*? We're going to be frightfully late, and anyhow I must come in. I think I left something . . .'

'Stay out, you little beast,' Rebecca squealed. 'I'm *not* dressed.'

But the boy burst in anyhow, stuck out his tongue at her and said, 'Who cares? You're decent and, besides, who'd look at you? You're ugly as a pig.' Robert Bruce, at thirteen, was tall for his age, slim and unquestionably Naomi's child. His hair had the same eastern blackness, his skin and eyes were darker than her own. In his travelling suit and stiff-collared white shirt he looked like an Indian princeling packed off to England for his education. But his voice, when he spoke, was resoundingly British, as was indeed his mother's.

'You've found it,' he exulted, reaching for the knife.

Naomi withheld it, a warning look in her eyes. 'Not difficult,' she said, 'I had merely to follow the nicks in the furniture. Now look, young man, you're not taking this to Scotland . . .'

'But I *must*. Tenny gave it me. And I must show him my Gurkha knife charge, really I must.'

'Gurkha knife charges will be nothing compared to what I'll do to you if you damage a single stick of furniture in Culbrech House,' Naomi said. She proffered the knife. 'Go on, take it. Do us all a favour and lose it while you're there.'

'You're horrid, Mother. It's my absolute best possession. And *Tenny* gave it to me.'

'Yes,' said Naomi drily. '*Do* give Tenny my love.'

She dismissed the boy, sending him to the kitchens for his tea, with the warning that he must not mess his good suit or remove the stiff collar in which he was dressed for the journey.

'I think I'll murder him on the train and cast his body out to the wolves,' Rebecca said with dreamy satisfaction.

'There aren't any wolves left in Scotland,' Naomi replied, unperturbed.

'More's the pity,' said Rebecca.

Naomi laughed. 'Anyone would think you were brother and sister,' she said.

Rebecca's expression changed. She looked wistful and said, 'Sometimes I pretend he is my brother. Then you'd be *my* mother too. I should positively adore that, if it were true.'

She clutched the brown robe around herself like a lonely little girl, but Naomi only smiled and said briskly, 'Oh, thank God I'm not, dear. Your ancestry is quite enough of a problem as it is, I assure you. Quite enough.'

Rebecca Galloway's ancestry was more than a problem; it was a social disaster, and one which, upon her belated discovery of its true nature, had nearly proved fatal. For nineteen years previous to that discovery, Rebecca had rested secure with the rather romantic concept of herself as an orphan to the cause of Darwin. She lived in the London home of the man she believed to be her uncle, a certain Arnold Galloway, a respected, if not particularly notable, medical practitioner. Her own father was Arnold's brother, Justus Galloway, an eminent biologist, who had spent many years in Australia and the South Pacific researching Darwin's evolutionary theory. When he was quite young, Justus married a missionary's daughter he had met on Samoa. They returned to England for Rebecca's birth, but set out again on another year's explorations beyond the Cape of Good Hope, leaving the infant Rebecca behind in the capable hands of a nanny in the house of the good doctor. Alas, a shipwreck in the South Atlantic ended Justus's brilliant career and left Rebecca an orphan in the care of his devoted and mourning unmarried brother. It was a good story. Likely enough, too, considering that even Arnold Galloway was immensely interested in biology, evolution being a speciality of his. But in retrospect, the brothers' similarity of interests pointed neatly to a logical invention.

And it *was* all an invention. Rebecca had learned, in one shattering afternoon in her nineteenth year, that there had never even been a Justus Galloway or any missionary bride. Nor was Arnold Galloway any relation of her own. She was in truth the daughter of an Irish whore. The woman had gone into labour in the gutter outside Arnold Galloway's home. A compassionate man, bound by the Hippocratic oath, Arnold had the lice-ridden creature brought into his own spare bedroom, where, after a frightful three-day labour, the child was born, scrawny and half dead.

He put her aside and tended to the fast failing mother, who, victim of severe malnutrition and the conditions in which she had lived, died soon after. He pulled his fine linen sheet over the aged twenty-year-old face and wearily turned again to the infant. She was still breathing and he went through the formalities of caring for her in the feeble hours he believed remained for her and, amazingly, she lived.

It astounded him. Everything was against the infant, but she held on to life with extraordinary determination. She thrived in his care, and became a pretty, enchanting creature, a changeling of a child, fat and pink-cheeked, fair-haired and beautiful, hardly the offspring of the grey, wasted girl he had seen to a pauper's grave. The child captivated Arnold Galloway, partly by her beauty, but more by an appeal to his pride. He felt, after the weeks of struggle with the infant, as if he really were her father, and could not bear to see the product of his talent, skill, and luck squandered on an East End foundlings' home.

It was a gallant but foolish act. As a bachelor, getting on in years and used to living alone, he really had little vocation for rearing a young girl. But he kept her, and with a succession of nannies, raised her as his own. He invented Justus Galloway, his missionary bride, and the whole romantic story almost as a game to amuse. But the child believed him, and grew to be a woman, pretty, tempestuous, lonely, and very romantic. Then, in her nineteenth year, the whole foolish little play-act came crashing down on his head, and on hers.

Rebecca was introduced by chance to the student son of a well-known land-owning family. They sat side by side at dinner and were enchanted with each other. The next day a calling card arrived, the day after, flowers. It was all absolutely too lovely. When a shy, polite request came next for her attendance at a party at the young gentleman's Dorset home, Arnold Galloway decided things had gone too far, and must be set right before any social awkwardness might occur. With characteristic bluntness, he called his young niece to him, the invitation still in her hand, patted that hand apologetically and told her the truth.

She listened politely, a little unimpressed, as if the whole were another fairy tale. It was only when he took the invitation from her and quietly put it on the fire that the import of what he told her reached home. She went to her room, and sat alone, refusing dinner or any companionship. He heard her sobbing in the darkness, late at night, and assumed a little guiltily that this, like other childhood sorrows, would in that tearful way be resolved. He retired to his own bed and did not hear her rise, dress herself, and leave the house in the still hour before dawn.

Rebecca walked alone through the dark streets of London, too miserable to be frightened, and arrived at Waterloo Bridge with the first grey light of morning. She hoisted herself up on the parapet and seated herself with skirts flowing about her and legs tentatively extended to the grey, filthy water of the Thames. At precisely that moment a lone hansom cab clattered on to the deserted bridge. The noise startled her, hastening her decision, and she scrambled up, teetered awkwardly on the narrow parapet, and steeled herself to jump. The sudden move saved her life.

Naomi Bruce, the hansom cab's occupant, returning at a totally unacceptable hour from a tête-à-tête dinner with a titled gentleman, was curled contentedly on the leather seat, her mind on other things. A dreamy glance out of the half-shaded window was all the attention she gave the Thames. But her eye, in passing, caught a flutter of movement, the whirl of a skirt, and she sat up, stared, and then rapped with desperate haste on the roof of the cab.

The cabhorse clattered to a halt and the driver, turning his attention from the roadway, also saw the girl. He shouted, but before he could move from his high seat, his woman passenger had leapt down into the street. She ran swiftly towards the parapet where the girl hesitated, her eyes darting swiftly from the river below to the cab and its shouting driver. She seemed mesmerized by the man and the shying horse and only noticed Naomi when she was feet away.

'Leave me alone,' she gasped, drawing back as if the river behind her offered safety. She was suddenly an innocent abroad in the night world of London. Naomi, bejewelled and satin-clad in the dawn, was frightening, mysterious and awesome.

'Get down off there at once, you stupid girl,' she ordered imperiously.

Rebecca hesitated, hearing Nanny's authority echoing in the glamorous stranger's voice. She whispered, 'Go away.'

'Get *down*,' Naomi said.

Rebecca grew defiant. 'No. I shan't. I . . . I'm going to jump.'

'Jump? Ridiculous. Now get down before you fall, you silly ass.'

The cab-driver, having calmed his horse, hastened towards them, and his boot-heels thudded suddenly in the stillness.

The girl looked up and shrieked, 'Get away from me,' taking her eyes from Naomi who leapt forward with startling agility, caught her arm and wrenched her off the parapet. She landed, shrieking, on top of her rescuer and they both collapsed in a heap of skirts and petticoats at the feet of the amazed cabbie.

Naomi sat up, dismissing the cabbie's hesitant offer of his hand. She neatly brushed her gloved hands together and glared at the girl emerging from her own dishevelled tangle of lace and lawn. 'Well, my dear,' Naomi said, 'is *that* performance done with, or have I to look forward to a second act?'

'I want to die,' moaned the mortified Rebecca.

Naomi stood up, looking down at the girl with a faintly wry smile. 'Very well. Like all the rest of us, you no doubt shall. A little patience is all that is required. In the meantime, shall we have breakfast?'

After breakfast, wrapped in one of Naomi Bruce's gorgeous embroidered dressing-gowns, warm and snug before the morning-room fire with Naomi's white Persian kitten on her knee, Rebecca Galloway told her story. Over her protests, Arnold Galloway was summoned by telephone, and he, after hours of frantic worry following the discovery of her absence, arrived shortly afterwards in less than good humour.

'After all,' he said gruffly, 'it was hardly as bad as all that.' He looked across at his erstwhile niece for response, but she remained curled rebelliously on the pale green ottoman by the white Adam mantel, looking at Naomi Bruce for support.

So it was Naomi who said, with deceptive mildness, 'Oh? Was it not?'

Galloway had decided to bluff this one out. He was terrified of this elegant woman but he wasn't about to let it show. He stood, legs apart, feet firmly planted on the green and blue Persian carpet, head down, his hand rubbing his goatee and his moustache twitching. He looked at Naomi Bruce over his half-glasses in his diagnostic posture.

'It was hardly a disaster,' he said. 'Just a – let us say – a change. A change of plans. It wasn't as if she was being put out on the street like – like her wretched mother. Not at all. I never promised her anything. Social standing or any of that. I never said she could marry just any person she fancied. After all, what girl can?'

'Most girls,' said Naomi, again very mildly, 'can expect to marry into the circles in which they are permitted to move.' Her eyes were very distant as if she was thinking of something else, far off in time, beyond the pretty drawing-room.

'Well, naturally. But there *are* exceptions. Rebecca is, well, an exception. It does not mean she can't have friends, a good home. After all, I've given her that. And everything I have will go to her. She will not do without, materially.'

'There's a little more to life than that,' Rebecca cried suddenly in a choked, bitter voice.

Naomi waved her quiet with a jewelled hand.

'For God's sake, madam,' Galloway suddenly exploded, 'the girl's origins are not unknown, there's been no secret, no conspiracy. People are decent enough to ignore them for most purposes, but when all's said and done . . .'

'She may come to lunch but not to bed,' said Naomi.

'Really, madam, must we be so crude?'

'Oh, I suppose not,' Naomi said with a sweet smile. 'I do understand, you know. Mustn't taint the bloodlines, now, must we?'

Arnold Galloway felt distantly that she was talking through him, in some way, as if some other ghostly personage had entered the room and the conversation, and it was to that person that she spoke. It was a queer feeling and made him uneasy. He shuffled his feet and said, 'After all, the girl can take up an employment if she wishes something to do with her life. She could be a nanny, or a governess, and live in splendid style. Such people do, with the right families.'

'Oh, of *course*,' Naomi clapped her hands, her dark eyes brightening. 'The perfect solution. Of course.'

Rebecca Galloway looked up suddenly from the white kitten on her knee. Her eyes were full of silent distress and a deep sense of betrayal.

Naomi Bruce ignored her and walked about her elaborate room, her hands clasped theatrically before her and, smiling, repeated, 'How splendid. The perfect solution.'

Arnold Galloway smiled a little pompously, certain that he had put the silly woman back on her proper level of respectful admiration for his cleverness.

'Why,' Naomi continued, 'if she's really fortunate, and very well behaved,' she added as a careful aside, 'she might even end up in the very house that you forbid her to visit this weekend. She might be so lucky as to be nanny there, or governess to the children of her young man's future wife. I'm sure she'll be *so* happy.'

Rebecca collapsed in tears and Arnold Galloway stood open-mouthed. He doubted the sanity of this strange, beautiful woman. 'I'm not sure I understand,' he said at last.

Naomi lowered her folded hands, looked once at Arnold Galloway, and then crossed to a magnificent green velvet, wingbacked chair. It enveloped her when she sat in it, as if she were the heart of a strange green flower. She looked first at Rebecca sobbing over the wet fur of the kitten and then for a long thoughtful time at Arnold Galloway. 'No,' she said gently, 'I am sorry. I have been rather unkind. Forgive me, but I have rather a touchy temper on some subjects.'

'Madam, I . . .'

'You did not mean to offend. No. I doubt you've ever meant to offend. But nineteen years ago you did an extraordinary, adventurous act of kindness. I am sure it frightened you at the time. And now the result of that kindness is weeping on my settee, and I am being very harsh with you, as if it were all your fault. You've done something kind and now you're punished for it and it's all terribly unfair. It is. It's just as unfair as being punished for having done nothing wrong at all but be born.'

She slipped past his attempt to intervene and said, 'Actually, I can comfort you with the fact that it is not at all uncommon. People often do seem to be punished for kind acts,' she shrugged distantly. Arnold Galloway saw her as remote and foreign, eastern even. 'Perhaps it is God's will,' she said without expression. Then she moved forward from the depths of the chair, so the sunlight from the tall windows touched her face, making it animated and more friendly.

'Never mind,' she said, with a bright smile. 'What's done is done. You've done a fair job on her. She's pretty and pleasant when she isn't sobbing or throwing herself in a river. I can't expect you to understand what a woman might expect from life. Women do expect things, Mr Galloway, whether or not you want them to. But don't worry. She's not your problem any more.'

'I am afraid, madam, she very much is.'

Naomi shook her head brightly, as if perhaps the kitten's future were being settled. 'No. She's mine.'

'Madam, I . . .'

'Do not understand. I will be plain. I will take her, now, Mr Galloway. She is mine now. She will live with me.'

'Mrs Bruce?' Rebecca said, surprise, bafflement, pleasure and a slight concern mixing in her voice.

'You?'

Mr Galloway's voice must have reflected some of his shock, because Naomi, always a little touchy, said primly, 'Oh, don't be concerned. I am really totally respectable in my own way. All the best people call here; people who would not call on you. I am sorry, Mr Galloway, but it *is* true.'

Arnold Galloway would have liked to walk out in a huff, but a huff would have necessitated taking Rebecca as well. So instead he fussed, he worried, he accepted sherry, and he agreed. He had done his Christian charity, as much as he could stand, and now he bowed out willingly to await his reward in heaven.

Rebecca visited him dutifully every week thereafter with pots of Gentleman's Relish and dark Oxford marmalade, and she and Naomi Bruce were virtually inseparable from that day.

By the end of six months, Rebecca Galloway was almost unrecognizable. Not to look at, no; Naomi was too wise to make any transformations there. Rebecca had the face and figure to be the epitome of London's beauties, with the proper styling and enough money. And Naomi did have access to both. But that was not her intention with Rebecca. For what she intended, the girl was best just as she was, sweet-faced, unadorned, schoolgirlishly mischievous and devastatingly youthful. It was the perfect combination. Her mind, however, was another matter.

Rebecca had grown up in that most shielded and hypocritical of all societies, the Edwardian middle class. While the poor were dumped unprotected into the full torrent of life and the very rich and exclusive allowed to dabble toes in any interesting, aberrant backwaters they fancied, as long as they were exclusive enough about it, the middle class carried on its back the whole ark of the conventional covenant.

Appearances were everything; decency was external, propriety must not merely be done, but ostentatiously be seen to be done. The British middle classes were the vast crinoline of society. They shielded all the intimate parts of its body behind a suffocating wall of starched fabric. Naomi set about opening Rebecca's eyes and freeing her spirit.

She began with books, good, intelligent, unacceptable books. She went on to art, music, dance, the best but always with one foot beyond the bounds of 'taste'. She introduced Rebecca to all her friends, particularly her artistic friends, her unmarried friends, her friends set up in little arcadian *ménages à trois* (or *quatre* or *cinq*) in the Cornish countryside. Rebecca met her gentlemen friends who danced with the Parisian ballet and wore make-up in the street, and her lady friends who wore trousers and flew aeroplanes about the countryside. She met Aesthetes who had tossed more than their corsets over the wall of the fashionable garden in which Naomi freely moved. That was Naomi's world and Rebecca became a part of it. She was initially terrified, soon fascinated, and eventually accepted it as a natural habitat. She became companion to Naomi, secretary, occasional hostess, adopted big sister to Robert. She became Naomi's friend, and eventually, not only a beautiful young woman but an interesting one as well. It was, in six months, a startling transformation.

The sittings with Mr Leitner had begun rather by accident. An old friend of Naomi's, he had been quite taken with the girl's ironically spiritual beauty when her face was, rarely, in repose. Pre-Raphaelite in stylisfic inclination, he found her his perfect subject. The length of their mutual acquaintance, plus Leitner's advanced age and, above all, his Wildean leanings, removed any worries Naomi might have had. She knew the portraits might bring the girl money as well as notice, and might teach her grace. To Rebecca she said, 'Your face is a gift as much as Mr Leitner's hands. Use it before it fades. Money will buy you freedom; it's more than any man will ever give you. Besides, you will have to keep your mouth shut for as long as ten minutes at a time, a difficult lesson, my dear, and very valuable.'

Rebecca's shyness had vanished during the first sitting. That was important to Naomi. Women of the class to which she expected Rebecca to rise were accustomed to nudity in front of strangers, surrounded as they always were from birth to the grave by servants. Likewise the poor, of course, crammed in their crowded, multi-generational, mixed-sex flats. Coyness was a middle-class stigma, and Rebecca must be rid of it.

Mr Leitner portrayed her in all her charms as goddess and nymph and, more sedately, as Madonna and Magdalene, and she lost her bashful modesty. She became quite famous in a narrow aesthetic circle and there were other requests for her services, some from other artists and one from a gentleman of questionable theatrical connections, eager to see her on the stage. Most had been politely refused outright by Naomi, and one or two, carefully screened, had been allowed sittings in the converted nursery, secure in the feminine fortress that was Naomi's home.

Naomi Bruce scorned all the conventions. But she firmly knew their power. There was not a breath of scandal anywhere about Rebecca Galloway, and there never would be. There was much interest, though, much of it from highly attractive gentlemen. But Naomi knew the value of her charge, and the reserve price was going to be high. If Rebecca married, Naomi Bruce would write the marriage contract herself.

'But why?' Rebecca would ask in grateful astonishment. 'You're so kind. You go to such trouble, indeed, such expense. And I was a total stranger. You didn't even know me.'

'Oh, I knew you, my dear. I knew you. And it isn't kindness, I'm much afraid.'

'Oh, but it is. It is.'

'No, dear. Not precisely,' she would pat the shining-eyed young face and turn away, with just a trace of guilt upon her own. Revenge was not a word to use to one so young. But try as she did, she could find no other word for it. And now, by whatever name she chose to welcome it, the opportunity had arisen. The time to send Rebecca to Culbrech House had at last arrived.

'Oh, do tell me what they're really like,' Rebecca begged, slipping into the jacket of her tailored blue linen travelling costume and turning for Mary, her personal maid, to whisk away any lint. Mary put down the clothes-brush and turned again to the laden dressing-table in Rebecca's room.

'The tortoiseshell combs, don't you think?' Rebecca said to Naomi, as Mary's hand strayed over the selection.

'Naturally,' said Naomi, glancing at the combs. Then she said distantly, 'The Maclarens? I've told you what they're like.' She added mildly, 'Mary, you have packed Miss Galloway's walking shoes, no doubt?'

Mary nodded, but Rebecca demanded, 'Why?' like a suspicious child.

'It's *Scotland*, my dear.'

'You rotten thing,' Rebecca cried, indignant. 'You never said a word about walking shoes before. You said there was to be a ball, and tea-parties and . . .'

'And so there shall. But there will also be the August Bank Holiday picnic. It's a Maclaren tradition, my dear. Maclaren traditions are very important, lest we forget. No doubt, it goes back five hundred years at the very least. And no doubt, as on the last four hundred and ninety-nine occasions, it will rain. The Maclarens are very persistent, though, when they set their minds on something. There'll be no surrender. Though I do hear from Victoria that they're having a quite remarkable summer.'

'I hate picnics,' Rebecca moaned. 'Uncle Arnold always insisted I be taken on them. "Children *love* picnics, Nanny. Off you go, Becky. Have a *luvely* time." Bee stings and a wet bum. Oh tosh.'

Naomi smiled, looking over Rebecca's shoulder at the girl's reflection in her dressing-table mirror. Yes. She would do very well. 'There *will* be the ball,' she comforted, 'for good girls who don't moan at the picnic. And dozens and dozens of handsome young officers. You'll absolutely shine. If you don't fall flat on your face in the reels.'

'I'm a very good dancer,' Rebecca replied peevishly. 'Miss Morgan said I was the best in the class. Oh Naomi, you're just evading me. Please, what are they really like? They can't all be handsome young officers. Half of them must be women for a start. Oh, please play fair! I'm absolutely terrified.'

Naomi smiled at the reflected face in the mirror and turned her back and walked to the other side of the room. She settled herself on the edge of Rebecca's bed and then drew her legs up, tucking her satin-slippered feet beneath her, sitting cross-legged, as supple as a child, with her turquoise silk like a pool around her. She thoughtfully stroked the white Persian cat that was curled there like a fluffy pillow and it unwound, stretching its claw-trimmed paws. 'The Maclarens and Culbrech House,' she said at last. 'Well, let us say for a start that it's all *much* improved.'

'Oh, that's promising,' wailed Rebecca.

'Oh, but it is. You can't imagine what it was like when I knew it. To begin with, it's not a proper house at all. It's a fortress. God alone knows how old it is, but when it was built the major intention was keeping the savages outside away from the savages inside. The décor, as I first knew it, could be described as . . .' Naomi leaned her head back, eyes closed '. . . I think perhaps, Early Macbeth. A great deal of weaponry everywhere. One always suspected that any dinner-party might end in clashing broadswords.'

'How charming,' Rebecca said, making a sour face as she pushed a wisp of curling auburn hair into a ringlet at her right ear. 'No, Mary, not so high. It will only fall right over before we get to Euston.' Mary patiently unbound the long shining braid and began rewinding it more snugly about her mistress's head. 'You're making me ever so eager to go, you know,' Rebecca added to Naomi.

'Oh, never fear. It's all vastly changed. Victoria saw to that.'

'Lady Maclaren. Sir Ian's wife?'

'Yes,' Naomi said, quite softly. 'Really a very remarkable woman,' she added as a quiet afterthought.

'Is she pretty?' Rebecca asked.

Naomi looked startled, and then laughed, turning away and looking out of the window. 'Pretty? Oh, it is marvellous to be nineteen. Pretty. As if that were the beginning and the end. Of course she's not pretty. She's nearly fifty. She's past pretty long ago. She's elegant, graceful, all a lady needs.'

'But surely you're at least that old.'

'Oh, older.'

'And you're beautiful.'

'Thank you,' Naomi said with a small, surprised smile. 'If you think so. Some people have thought so, some not. Still, I was never pretty.'

'The gentlemen all think so,' said Rebecca bluntly.

'Oh, that. That is something else. No, dear, I was always different. That was all. Difference lasts, however, when prettiness is over, and it fascinates men because they are afraid of it. Particularly conventional men like the Maclarens.'

'What about them then, the men?'

'They're all quite magnificent, be assured. The Maclarens always bred men well. Just as well, I suppose. One doesn't make a Highland regiment with pretty women, does one?'

'Aren't any of the women pretty?' Rebecca said, trying her navy, pale-blue-trimmed hat in front of the mirror. Her sympathy was combined with faint relish.

'Oh, not so pretty as you, don't worry yourself. But you'll not be utterly without competition. Emma Maclaren has become really quite a beauty of late. But she's Tenny's sister, so she's no problem.'

'Who *is* this Tenny?' Rebecca demanded coyly. 'It always comes back to him whenever the Maclarens are mentioned.'

'And why should it not?' Naomi replied at once. 'Tenny is the heir. We wouldn't play for second best, would we?'

'Why, Mrs Bruce,' Rebecca flounced, blushing, away from the dressing-table, leaving the distracted Mary trailing after her, hat ribbons yet in hand. Rebecca stopped at the window, looking out over the street far below. The motor car, with Abbott the driver, was parked below, and Abbott was busy loading Robert's trunk within. 'That's quite dreadfully calculating, really. I mean, you'd think I . . .'

'I'd think what everyone will think, my dear, a splendid match for the both of you. The only thing is that I, unlike everyone, actually say it.' She turned her long, slender neck and looked rather harshly at Rebecca in the window, her dark, honest eyes full of adult mischief. Her mouth took a slightly sardonic twist, the smooth black brows raised. 'However, if you'd really prefer second place, there's always Tenny's younger brother Albert. He's a bit pudgy, but quite good-looking. Just about your age. He's considered a bit of a lost cause by the family but I've always thought him the best of the lot, certainly the kindest, and the best future husband for any girl. Or he would be if they'd let him alone. But they won't, not the Maclarens.' Her voice hardened subtly, 'No. They'll hound him and drive him and break him like they did my brother Donald, no doubt. And poor Harry probably as well.'

Naomi's voice grew distant, as it always did when her middle brother Donald was mentioned. Rebecca knew he had vanished in ugly circumstances in Africa during the Boer War, after his wife had been killed in Kimberley, and that Naomi blamed the

Maclarens who were, Rebecca was also aware, her distant cousins. That it was a kinship of illegitimacy was discreet common knowledge; a fact that forbade Bruce claims on the Maclaren estate, but had never prevented Maclaren claims on Bruce children.

'Families with power in their histories do not relinquish power easily,' Naomi explained. 'Particularly not in Scotland. The Maclarens are rich, aristocratic and land-owning. And a military family as well. A hundred years ago they were near feudal lords, and two hundred years ago virtually independent kings in a virtually independent country. They can recall in three generations the Jacobites who fought the King for his throne. True, they no longer control the lives of their lessers. But they are utterly ruthless with the lives of their peers. Oh, it's all very well for the adventurers like Tenny and Johnny Bruce. They're the stuff the regiment is made of, and the regiment is everything to the Maclarens. Everything. It's the others I pity,' she said.

She studied the girl's reflection in her mirror and added slowly, 'Actually, I imagine Donald took the best course, just stepping out of everyone's lives. Best for the children as well. They've brightened Mother's life no end, particularly now that Willie is getting on. Anyhow Donald was in no state to look after them, after his wife was killed. And he did provide for them, one mustn't forget. He did provide.' She shrugged. 'They've had a good enough home at Cluanie.' She paused, thinking. 'I dare say Harry might have been happier if he'd remained in South Africa. He hated leaving when Mother brought them home from Kimberley after Brenda was killed. He wept and wept. His first six months in Scotland he never left his room. Just sat, hunched up over the fire, with a rug about his shoulders, Mother said, just like a little old man. Bodachan, the servants called him. Poor little old man. Losing both his parents within a week didn't help, naturally. And Scotland's always been a misery for him, I think. The climate never suited his health, and all that hearty good nature up there mortified his whole being.' She shuddered delicately. 'Frankly, I understand completely.

'Johnny Bruce, however,' she said with a wry smile, 'simply thrives on it. He's a real Maclaren at heart, all adventure and daring. Poor Harry, it's a lot, living with a younger brother like that. Harry's rather like his father, I should think, rather read a book any time. And poor dear Albert Maclaren is only really happy by a warm fire with a good pot of tea. Sandhurst must be a misery for him. It's very hard, you know, being like that in such a family. I suppose even a Maclaren litter must throw up the occasional runt, but they'll never admit to it. The Maclarens simply don't understand anyone who isn't happy out in the drenching rain killing things.'

Naomi gathered Rebecca's light travelling cloak over her arm and escorted the girl out into the corridor. 'The odd thing, though,' she said, as they descended the first flight of stairs in the tall narrow house, 'is Tenny. After all, Tenny's practically a scholar compared to all the rest of them. He did superbly at school, and he reads. Really reads, and writes a bit, poetry and such. I would have thought that would have been practically heresy in Old Culbrech, but no, he's everyone's hero. I suppose he's just bold enough, and big enough, that he can do what he pleases, and no one dare cross him. Johnny Bruce tries from time to time, but he's only a close second. They're the best of friends, though, or so Ian says. Just as well, I imagine there'd be fur flying all the time if they were not.'

'What's Tenny short for?' Rebecca said suddenly.

'Alfred, Lord Tennyson, naturally.'

'Surely they didn't call him that.'

'What, his parents? Oh, never. Henry, he was christened. Lord Tennyson was what they called him at school. For his reading habits. It was meant to be an insult, but on Tenny insults come out as compliments. He's rather proud of it, I think. He's always got Keats or Browning in his pocket, rather like a badge. Or a chip on his shoulder. Anyhow, no one tried to knock it off, and he's never been anything but Tenny for years.'

'He sounds a bit awesome,' Rebecca said. 'I think, even without any competition, I'm not likely to make much of an impression.'

Naomi stopped short on the stairs and said, 'Oh, never you mind. I don't know the boy that well, but I rather knew his father. And I would say that Tenny, like any real Maclaren man, is likely to have one great weakness.'

'And that?'

'An absolute light-headed devotion to the prettiest face in the room, and an equivalently absolute inability to understand the mind behind it. Your looks will win his attention, and your wits are ample to hold it for ever. You'll wrap him round your finger,' she added with a satisfied sniff.

'I rather doubt it,' Rebecca said a little shyly.

'But I didn't say there was no competition,' Naomi warned. 'There is Susan Bruce.' She looked worried. 'I'd hate for her to have taken a fancy to Tenny, that would be a dreadful shame. You'd be such splendid friends otherwise. When last I saw her she had exhibited her feelings towards him by tripping him into the water-trough in the stables. But that *was* two years ago, when I was last at Cluanie. She may have grown up a bit. She was certainly a beauty, and a proper little devil. She got expelled from school some years ago for some perfectly unmentionable disgrace. Mother was in a positive flap, but Willie seemed to rather admire the girl. That was how he was with me, always,' she smiled, recalling. 'He always encouraged me to do my worst. I gather he'd been a holy terror in school himself, not that he went to school for long. He was in the regiment and under fire by his fifteenth birthday, I'm afraid,' she smiled again. 'In my case the whole thing rather went too far, even for Willie. Still, with Susan, it's more likely to have been dramatics than anything else. She's got a touch of the Sarah Bernhardt's, I'm afraid. She'll probably fall in love with you. So far Susan's fallen irrevocably in love with all her schoolmistresses, both her governesses, three ponies and a cat. I dare say she'll be moving on to men by now, though. She's nearly twenty-one. They'll have their hands full with that one. They'd probably have packed her off to a convent years since, if they weren't all so utterly presbyterian to the bone.'

'I don't think,' Rebecca said, glancing nervously at her previously assured features in the second-floor landing mirror, 'that I'm going to enjoy this at all. She sounds more formidable than *any* of them. Isn't there anyone plain and simple?'

'Oh yes, indeed there is. There's always Philippa, Tenny's younger sister. Now, it's a pity it isn't the other way round, and she isn't Susan. She'll be no competition to anyone. She would have made an excellent Maclaren man, actually. Pity she wasn't. If she isn't careful she'll end up like her Great-Aunt Jean, all horses and religion. She's got lovely hair but that's all, I'm much afraid, and every time she meets a man she either flings herself all over him or runs like a scalded cat. A most peculiar girl. Victoria is really quite concerned. It's hard to imagine her in the same family as Tenny, or Emma. Emma is so much a mistress of every situation. But then she is the oldest. Even Tenny looks up to Em, even if he won't admit it. So that's all of them then, Emma, Tenny, Philippa, and Albert. And of course little Jamie, but he's just a boy. And then the Bruces, Harry and Johnny and Susan.'

'Frankly,' Rebecca shuddered, 'they sound positively ghastly. Thank God they're not *my* family. I don't know how you bear them.'

'By living in London, my dear.' Naomi laughed, but then with a wry cynical smile added, 'They're hardly my family anyhow, are they?'

Rebecca looked at the stair-carpet and blushed and Naomi said, 'Oh don't be coy, darling. I know you know the whole story. My friends leave little to chance. Do tell, what's this year's version?' Rebecca paused and Naomi said, 'Come, come, speak up girl.'

'I try not to listen,' she said.

'Nonsense. You listen as if your ears were afire. Don't apologize. I'd do the same at your age.'

'Mr Leitner says you're really an Indian princess,' Rebecca whispered.

Naomi let out an unladylike shriek of laughter. 'Oh, he'd simply love that to be true. The dreadful old snob. A *princess*,' she repeated with scorn. 'No, dear, I am *not* a princess. No. Rather the opposite.' She raised the girl's chin with the fingers of her left hand, and their eyes met. 'I am, I fear,' she said, 'our family's little legacy of the Indian Mutiny. My unlamented father was a Sepoy mutineer. He raped my mother. Several times, I gather. It was not very pleasant for her, I imagine. But nature cares little for pleasure. She was young and very fertile, and I was the result.' She smiled again briskly and made a little turnabout on the stairs, showing herself off. 'The nuns in the Irish convent where I was born were quite convinced I was a changeling. Dear souls. The thought that a highborn English lady like my mother might produce a black child was quite beyond them.'

'Black?' Rebecca exclaimed.

'Oh, brown. Whatever. Figuratively speaking, naturally. My dear, I am clearly not white, am I?'

Rebecca gasped, amazed at so irreverent a concept. 'But you're beautiful,' she blurted out at last.

'Dear child,' Naomi whispered, 'do you honestly believe that beauty reigns only in England?' She was teasing, but her smile was sad and gentle. It was replaced in a moment by her familiar look of wise cynicism and she said suddenly, 'Tell me, girl, who's Robert's father meant to be?'

Rebecca was wide-eyed and silent. She was well aware that Robert Bruce was illegitimate. Naomi had told her, blithely, early in their friendship, and told her too that the married prefix to her name was a device she had adopted in her first days in London, in an era when a single young woman living alone was unthinkable. But the details of the story Rebecca had never dared to ask. 'Come on, child, they *will* have told you something.'

'Charles de Vere Smith,' Rebecca mumbled, fumbling with her hatbrim.

Naomi leant her head to one side and considered. 'Logical,' she said. 'The dates aren't right but who would notice?' London would not have forgotten her liaison with Lord Charles, a companionship of many years. 'Yes, quite logical. But not correct.'

Rebecca blinked, awaiting more. Naomi was terribly good at that sort of stunning revelation, often followed by weeks, or months, of silence on whatever the subject. This time she only paused for a moment before she said, 'I was only ever in love once in my life, only once, when I was very, very young. It was a charming but fruitless experience. I would not recommend it.' She started down the stairs. 'Still, you will enjoy Tenny. A delightful young man. Quite like his father in every way.' She paused, smiling distantly, her unruffable oriental smile. 'Oh, and do give Sir Ian my very best regards,' she said.

2

In the oak-panelled library of Culbrech House, that last masculine sanctuary that yet retained, in spite of the advances of the colonel's English wife, the old dark Scottish style, Sir Ian Maclaren was taking his ease. It was not something he was particularly accustomed to doing, having only a month before retired from active service as commanding officer of the First Battalion Maclaren Highlanders, a demanding enough post. Ian was still experimenting with the comparative leisure of running his estate, and was not yet sure he liked it.

Gordon Bruce, the man who had taken over his command, was also sharing the library fire, his stockinged toes extended to the snapping log blaze, the stretch of bare knee between hose-top and kilt reddening in the heat. It was August and not at all cold outside, where the sun poured down on the green lawns and the beech trees. But Culbrech House with its feet-thick walls retained the cold of the ages, like a cave. Besides, fires in the library were as traditional as whisky before dinner. And as there was plenty of timber yet on the Culbrech hills and plenty of hands to cut it, and maids to lay fires, fires there would be. An unlikely event like this startlingly sunny summer of 1914 was not going to upset tradition.

'Tenny thinks it will all pass over. Even now,' Ian said.

Gordon Bruce rubbed his greying moustache with his balled fist, and then chewed thoughtfully on the big knuckles of his hand. He said in his slow, calculated way, 'I would of course love to believe him right. You know I would. But I very much fear that's the happy optimism of youth. The thing's been like a snowball downhill, since the Serbian assassination. It's just got bigger and bigger, and everything it touches just gathers on to it. I don't think anyone could stop it now if they wanted. And I don't think they want. The Kaiser is determined to have this war, you know. Determined. And there's nothing like a Hun for determination.' He sighed.

'I don't know,' Ian said. He was looking a little desperately for a bright side, something to match the sunshine of the summer, rather than the black walls of headlines in *The Times* on the table by his drink. He felt for the first time a little too old, too secure, for a war. 'Tenny's quite the scholar, you know,' he said finally, 'I'd trust his opinion. I've often thought he's the only member of this household who really reads the newspapers. I mean beyond the rugby and the cricket. Albert reads the football too,' he said smiling and looking across to the leather wingback chair by the window where his second son was snugly ensconced. 'But that's only because he's determined to be a socialist.'

Albert looked up, blinking sleepily, emerging mentally from his book. Ian's smile faded as he noticed the whisky glass on the wine table beside the chair, and the way Albert's hand went to it, almost instinctively, before he spoke. He said only, with a pleasant nod, 'Breaking the rules, Father. You promised Mother.'

'Oh yes. So I did.' Ian looked at the floor, then up to Gordon Bruce, explaining, 'Promised Victoria no war talk this weekend. Spoils everyone's fun, she says. Dare say she's right. The August Holiday's really quite important to everyone; mustn't put a damper on it.' He rose, went to the decanter on the sideboard and filled his glass, turning to offer a refill to Gordon Bruce. Gordon shook his head, his face preoccupied, and two fingers of his hand flickering over the top of the glass in rejection.

But Albert said, 'Yes thank you, Father, don't mind if I do.' His smile was meant to be mischievous but it evoked momentary annoyance, and more than momentary unease in Ian. Still he crossed the room, and filled the boy's glass, a small fill, as he would to a guest of uncertain welcome. It was hard to know what to do with children, when they were virtually men and women.

'Anyhow,' he said, to close the discussion, 'Tenny is hardly likely to be over-optimistic; if anything, Tenny's rather looking for a scrap. You know how we were at that age. It's not as if he's hoping for peace like the rest of us.'

'At that age,' Gordon said at once, 'we were in the Sudan. War was a glorified stag-hunt. Oh surely, the stag could fight back, and bloody well too, and yes, we could get killed. But it wasn't European war. They were savages, after all. There wasn't a civilization at risk or anything like that. This is different.' He shook his head, looking into his glass grimly.

'That's just it, of course,' Ian said. 'That's the problem. There just hasn't been a European war for such a long while. Half the people in this country can't remember a time when there wasn't peace. And what they can't recall, they can't understand. Or fear.'

'Aye well,' Gordon said, 'they'll soon learn. Tenny will get his scrap all right. I thought, even until the spring, it would be in Ireland we'd be fighting if we fought anywhere. But not now. No. It will be France. And then on to Berlin,' he added, his lip tightening with satisfaction. 'To tell truth, Ian, in a way I'm just as pleased. We've all known it was coming one day, if we're honest about it. Sometimes it seemed it would be a long way off, but this has been coming for years. Ever since the Kaiser started building his navy it became pretty obvious. The Germans want to be put back in their place, and we might as well get it over and done with. By this time next year, we'll be glad we did.'

'Do you really think it will be that quick? You know, Berlin by Christmas, and all that?'

Gordon thought a moment and then looked up at the fire and said, 'Yes. Yes, I do. Why not? We've the best army in the world. And we'll have the Froggies and the Russkies to help. Don't know about the Froggies much, don't all that much trust any of them. But at least they won't be against us.'

'The Kaiser's made an army out of the entire nation,' said Ian uneasily.

'A lot of good it will do him. Conscript army. No bloody use. Fall apart the moment it's under pressure, if he ever manages to get the whole clumsy business mobilized. No training. No tradition,' he shook his head decisively.

'Yes, that's what Louis-Napoleon thought, until Sedan finished the French Army. And this German Army is much better armed than we are.'

'Oh, of course they are,' Gordon said bitterly. 'Our damned politicians will see to that. Kaiser Bill wants a war, so he gets a war. He wants an army, so he gets an army. No politicians getting in his way, are there?' Gordon finished the last of his whisky, and stood up, stalking to the fire. He was getting overheated with the discussion and Ian was sorry. Victoria would be wanting everyone in the drawing-room for tea shortly.

He sighed and then said slowly, 'I suppose you're right. It is best to get it over with,' his voice took on a wistful sadness. 'Still, it seems such a pity it has to be now, the children just growing up, the girls just having come out. I was rather looking forward to the next few months. Now I suppose everything will be postponed a year. Victoria *will* be distressed. She had such plans for the winter season.'

He walked to the window and stood looking over the tall back of the chair where Albert, lost in his reading, barely registered his presence. Turning back to the fire he said, 'Damn, but it's a shame to ruin this beautiful summer.' He shook his head. 'Rot the Hun. What do they want, anyhow?'

'Simple.'

'What's that?' Ian turned round to the voice. A tall young man was standing in the doorway. Brown-haired and fair-skinned, his drooping brown moustache gave his face an air of permanent sorrow. His voice still was lightly touched with the accent of his South African homeland. 'Simple,' he said again. 'The British Empire. That's what they want.' Harry Bruce stepped further into the room, the sun from the tall window lighting his faded tweeds. He looked rather like a schoolmaster and one was inclined to expect chalk-dust on his rounded shoulders. There was a severity, an uncompromising dryness about him, and it surprised no one when he chose to study Law. For all that, he was oddly handsome, his gentle features creating a deceptive mask for a sharp, cynically inquisitive mind. Women, certain women, found him both enigmatic and attractive, a fact which annoyed his young cousin Tenny Maclaren, and worried Tenny's father, Ian, for his own reasons. Gordon, Harry's uncle, was annoyed as well.

'Right,' he said with only perfunctory restraint. 'Right. And with your type around to just hand it to them on a silver platter, they're likely to get it, are they not?'

Albert looked up uneasily from his chair and Ian said softly, 'Gordon, please. That's a bit harsh, what?'

The young man however was quite unmoved. He said only, 'Don't bother about it, sir. Colonel Bruce and myself do understand one another. Besides,' he added coolly, 'he knows I'm right. It *is* the Empire. We've waved it at them for years like a red flag to a bull, and finally we've got them to charge.' He smiled the faintest, thin-lipped smile, and shrugged his bowed shoulders, looking over Albert's puzzled head at the green lawns beyond the window. Then he looked back at the two older men and said, 'Tea's about ready, I understand.' He smiled again to his uncle, said politely, 'Sir,' turned and walked quietly out of the door.

'Gordon, really,' Ian said. 'That was unkind.'

'Damn little snot gets on my tits.'

'Come, come. The boy's entitled to his beliefs.'

'Oh come on, Ian. All that talk of conscience. Just a bloody cover. The boy's a damned coward. It's my mother's fault in the end. She's pampered him hopelessly. Felt sorry for him always.'

'After South Africa, can you blame her?'

'Oh, I suppose not, but even so, if the boy had a hard time out there, it didn't help much to turn him into some namby-pamby . . . anyhow, look at his brother, damn it. Johnny lost his parents too, and look at Johnny. Couldn't ask for more in a boy if he'd been my own son.' He paused, and looked suddenly infinitely weary. He said in a quiet voice, so soft that Ian could barely hear, 'Damn it all, why the hell did it have to turn out the way it did?'

Ian looked startled. He had never heard Gordon refer before, even obliquely, to his childless state, and it took him a moment to realize what he was meaning. When he did he shook his head sadly and said nothing. There was nothing to say. He supposed it was this last miscarriage of Grisel's coming so late as it had, and offering so much more false hope, that had driven Gordon to his first words of protest.

Damned shame. Surprising too. The one thing they'd all said when Gordon had quite amazingly married a tenant farmer's daughter, broad-hipped and broad-handed, had been, well, she'll prove a good breeder anyhow. They'd laughed about it at the time: strengthen up the stock, add a touch of the Clydesdale, ha, ha. But Ian's highly thoroughbred Victoria had dropped five sturdy children from those delicate little hips. Grisel's ten pregnancies had each, with each year, ended in miscarriage. Funny things, women; Ian never would understand them.

The harsh burr of a two-stroke petrol engine suddenly shattered the peace of the library, as a motorcycle sputtered up the long, straight, beech-lined drive from the Beauly road, roaring through the open black iron gates and past the twin redwoods at the side of the house. Gordon Bruce jumped up and stalked, stocking-footed, to the window and stood with palms on the sill leaning against the glass, so that he might have a better view of the forecourt below. 'Who the devil will that be?' he demanded. 'Surely they haven't motorized Jimmy the Post?'

'Oh, no,' Ian replied resignedly. 'Nothing so simple as that. Didn't you know?' he asked.

'Didn't I know what?'

'Oh, wait. You'll see,' Ian's voice was touched with a mixture of resignation and bafflement. He joined Gordon Bruce at the window and watched as the sound of the engine grew louder, until the machine and its rider burst into view from around the curve of the west tower. Gordon watched fascinated until the motorcycle had been brought to a short skidding halt, scattering the pink gravel before the door.

'Good God,' he said. 'It's Emma.'

'The light of my life and the solace of my old age.'

'She's wearing bloomers, begad.'

'No doubt. At least if she's still got them on,' Ian glanced down at his eldest daughter again. 'And not got them hooked up in a bramblebush or such like.'

Emma was indeed wearing bloomers, navy serge and billowing about each leg, leaving the stockinged lower calf freely exposed. Her navy serge jacket was cut short, and neatly tailored, and she wore it with boyish flare. Her blouse, though, conceded to her femininity and cascaded ruffles of white lace beneath her chin, but its formality only emphasized the lack of it in the rest of her costume. On her head she was wearing one of her brother Tenny's stalking caps, with the earflaps at half-mast.

'Ian,' Gordon Bruce declared with hurt outrage, 'you've gone and let her bob her hair. Now Susan will be on about it too, and Mother will have a fit.'

'No, I haven't,' Ian shouted, his voice rising to a roar of fatherly fury. 'No, I most certainly have not. She better damn well not have.' But then he relaxed, red-faced yet with a small sigh as Emma removed the hat and her curling mass of brown hair tumbled over her shoulders, nearly to her waist. 'Thank God for that,' Ian breathed. That no doubt would be next week's little surprise. The bloomers had been last month's, and the motorcycle, last week's. Emma kept life interesting, he could not deny. She disappeared within the house and a few minutes later her light rap sounded on the library door.

'I say, Daddy,' she said as she entered, brushing loose strands of hair from her face, 'guess what silly old Tenny's done?'

Ian braced himself. 'Oh God, what now?'

'Broken his silly arm.'

'I say, what rotten luck,' Gordon Bruce said.

'Why in God's name did he do a pin-headed thing like that?' Ian roared. 'He's back to the battalion next week. Fat lot of good he'll be. How?'

'Fell off a rock, landing a salmon, can you believe?' Emma's eyes crinkled at the corners as she laughed delightedly. 'Or losing one rather, or so Sandy Gibson said.'

'I hardly think it's all that funny,' Gordon said suddenly. 'Broken arm's bloody sore.'

'Oh, Tenny's all right,' she said unperturbed. 'He's away down to Dr Robertson in the village to have it in a splint. Johnny's with him, anyhow, Sandy said. Besides he laughed like a crock when I fell off Bunty and broke my ankle.'

Ian grunted. 'He *was* ten, Em,' and to Gordon, and Albert who'd risen and was smiling rather broadly at his sister, 'Loving brothers and sisters present such a picture of charm, don't they?'

Emma shrugged happily. 'Turnabout's fair play. Oh, but Mother will be furious,' she said, suddenly much more concerned. 'Poor old Ten. He was meant to meet Robert Bruce at Inverness station tomorrow in the motor. And now he'll not be able to drive.'

'Damn. So he was,' Ian said.

'Shall I go on my cycle?' Emma offered brightly. 'He can ride pillion. He'll simply adore to.'

'And his mother will have simply fits, to say nothing of your mother. Besides there's a Miss Galloway accompanying him, if you recall. And no doubt a reasonable amount of luggage.'

'Oh, bother, so there is,' Emma said, rubbing a spot of Beauly road-dust from her chin with thumb and forefinger.

'She's probably ninety,' Ian went on, 'and not yet approving of hansoms, to say nothing of motorcycles. You'd hardly put *her* on the back. Damn Tenny. I'll have to go myself and I was hoping for an early start at the river. Who in God's name breaks an arm landing a salmon anyway?' he asked suspiciously.

'I say,' Gordon Bruce said suddenly. 'Why not send Johnny?'

Ian brightened visibly. 'Do you think he'd be willing? I'd let him take the Crossley,' he said encouragingly. 'He's been itching for a shot at it.'

'Of course he'll be willing,' Gordon said, 'Crossley or no. I'll speak to him as soon as I return to Cluanie.'

'Oh, capital. Grand of you. Grand of you both. Though I'll bet he'll accuse Tenny of setting it up. Johnny in Inverness with Robert and the maiden miss, while Tenny's in the drawing-room with every female north of the Border. Playing the wounded soldier, too. He'll lap it up.'

After his meeting on the Beauly road with Emma Maclaren, Sandy Gibson continued to Culbrech House. When he arrived twenty minutes later, he went directly to the vast, studded oak door at the front of the building. To a casual observer this would appear tremendous effrontery on the part of a common foot soldier. But that lordly door was not the main entrance to the house at all, merely the entrance to the kitchens.

The true main entrance, before which Emma Maclaren's motorcycle now leaned on its kickstand, was out of sight, round the towered corner of the west wall. It was a plain door, modest in proportion to the house, at the top of a flight of pink sandstone stairs, giving access to the entry hall of the first floor of the building which was also the first floor of familial occupation. The entire ground floor was devoted to servants' quarters and the kitchens and their associated workrooms, an unusual turnabout from the customary maid's-room-in-the-attic architecture of more normal houses.

It came simply from the fact that Culbrech, having been built hundreds of years before as a fortress, was left with the dubious gift of an entire ground floor designed to withstand an army of battering-rams. With four-foot-thick stone walls, and windows that were virtually gun-slits, it was clammy and sullen. Gaslamps burned there day and night. The family had emigrated upwards, and kept their top floor as a regal banqueting hall, rather than servants' quarters. The distant dining area caused innumerable difficulties, even though the banqueting hall was rarely used, which the servants did not forget quickly. Many also had memories of an earlier pre-plumbing era in which a near military operation was needed to have a bath in the high tower bedrooms.

Sandy Gibson knocked once on that vast door, and then let himself in, turning the heavy curved black handle with familiar ease.

'Sandy Gibson,' a voice called from the murky interior, 'you're no' coming in here to sell the laird his own salmon surely, the cheek of you. Yer as bad as yer faither.'

'Wheesht, woman, you'll have Mr MacLeod in here next and he'll chuck me out without my tea.'

'Tea now? You're expecting tea as well?' Mrs Murchison, the cook, put down the heavy black pot she was holding by the huge black-leaded range, and folded her plump red hands over her broad, billowing white apron. 'Surely, I'll never.'

'And why would I not expect tea?' Sandy smiled, turning sly and laying the leather sack with its two shining salmon on the broad pine table. He turned sideways to Mrs Murchison, his handsome lean face close to her neat-pinned topknot of brown hair. 'Surely ye'll no' turn down a soldier of the King, home from serving his country?'

'Away,' she said, a little captivated by his dark, narrowed eyes. 'The only serving you'll have been doing is yon loose women of Beauly hanging about the barracks where nae decent lass would show her face.' She giggled.

'Mrs Murchison!' Sandy sounded as shocked as a minister. 'And myself engaged to be married. Such talk.'

'Don't you be talking to me about marrying. I've quite enough of that with Fiona and her Ewan. You two will have to wait a bittie, till we've all recovered.'

Sandy laughed softly, 'Aye well. She's a grand lass. And a grand lad as well. Ye cannae blame them being excited, at the beginning of the best times of their lives.'

'I suppose no',' Mrs Murchison softened. Sandy had settled comfortably in a stick-backed chair by the central table and she recalled the salmon and was about to force him to take them away.

'Away, ye daftie,' he said laughing. 'They're Mr Maclaren's

salmon, and Mr Bruce's. I'm no' such a fool as that.'

She nodded relief, and put the big iron kettle on the range for his tea, saying, 'Och, yer no' the man yer faither was at your age. I mind how he'd been known to sell old Sir Andrew his ain fish more than the once.'

'Indeed he still does, I reckon.' Sandy wrapped his hands around the teacup that Mrs Murchison had set before him and relaxed into his chair, stretching his long, heavy-booted legs. 'But I dinna think there's quite room for two of us carrying on like yon. Besides, Sir Ian's right terrified of ma faither, what with him being RSM so many years. But he's no' scared a me, I can assure you.' Sandy leaned back, sipped slowly at his warm milky tea and then, his eyes on a row of pine shelves heavily laden with mixing bowls, he said, as casually as possible, 'And where's my lass?'

'Oh, Angusina. So that's it. D'ye ken, for a bittie there, I thought it was my own bonny face ye'd come to see.' Mrs Murchison had her back to him as she leaned over one of the open ovens, from which the warm smell of baking bread rose tantalizingly.

'Aye, there, gie us a crust,' Sandy said, and got the rejection he expected. Then he said, 'Och well, it was only that with the wedding tomorrow, and all, I was thinking to mysel', wouldn't it be grand if the two of us were to get away to the new croft barn and help with getting it ready for the wedding ceilidh.'

'Oh, would you. And how maybe Angusina would get an afternoon free to go with you, early?'

'Just a bittie, Mrs Murchison,' he sat leaning forward conspiratorially. 'Ye'll none of you miss her. She was certain now, she'd be allowed free.'

'Well, she won't. Miss Emma was late in, so tea's been held up a half-hour, and there are dinner guests tonight, Colonel Bruce, and perhaps young Mr Bruce as well, if he stays on, and Miss Susan as well. And young Master Bruce is arriving in the morning, with a lady. And there'll be a lady's maid as well, so an extra mouth to feed below stairs as well as another bed to be made up. I'll have plenty to do and so will Angusina. And half the household off to the wedding tomorrow. Then dinner upstairs in the banqueting hall, and the picnic to prepare for Sunday and then the ball on Tuesday, oh my, I don't know how I'll manage.' She rubbed her hands energetically on her apron, as if to rub some of the frantic business of the weekend away. 'These holidays are a terrible responsibility.' She was getting quite flustery and excited, something Sandy noticed more and more lately and assumed she'd reached 'that age'.

'Och away,' he said to calm her. 'Ye'll do fine. You always do.'

'And Fiona MacIntosh has been no use at all, tell truth,' she went on, as if not hearing him. 'Getting all the girls excited. This hall has been nothing but Fiona MacIntosh's parlour since the engagement. Yesterday, will you believe, she was dancing about the stillroom in her wedding bonnet. Poor daft wee Mairi was in tears because she wasn't getting married too and couldna have a pretty hat as well.' Her round face crumpled slightly, thinking. 'Och the poor wee thing. Ye wonder what the Lord thinks of sometimes, letting a bairn like that live, when there's many a fine, perfect wean dies afore it ever sees a birthday.'

'Wee Mairi's all right,' Sandy said, comfortingly. 'She's a good safe home here at Culbrech and she'll hae it till the day she dies. She doesna ken what a wedding's about any road. Buy her a bonny ribbon when next yer in Beauly and she'll forget all about it. Mind now, I'll do that mysel' and bring it tae her. Yon'll please the poor daft soul.'

Mrs Murchison smiled at his bent dark head. 'Och, yer no' bad, Sandy Gibson,' she said at last.

Sandy said nothing, but finished his tea, glanced to the door that led into the house and to the stairs, and said at last, 'So I cannae wait then?'

'Och you. All right then, but you must be very quiet.'

Sandy was quiet all of a minute and Mrs Murchison went back to slicing onions. Then she went through to the scullery, from which an almost continual dull clanking of pots and splash of water had emerged throughout their conversation. She was back in a moment, with her arm through that of a girl with wispy brown hair and a round, dull face. The girl stood, her slanted eyes drifting about the room and over Sandy's kind face, returning his friendly smile, as Mrs Murchison placed a wicker basket over her arm and said patiently, 'Carrots, Mairi. And beans, Mairi,' holding up one of each as she spoke. The girl nodded slowly and went out of the garden door.

When she was gone, Sandy said, 'I dinna suppose ye could maybe find out when she'll be ready?'

'And how?'

'Well, maybe nip upstairs.'

'Sandy Gibson, I am cook in this house. Cook does not "nip" anywhere. Certainly not upstairs. Unless of course I am sent for by my betters. Which doesna include yoursel' in case ye had any such notion.'

'Can ye no' send wee Mairi?' Sandy pursued cautiously.

'She's no clean enough to set foot upstairs. Besides, she'd most like get lost and end in tears. I wouldna dream of it.'

'Och, no,' Sandy said, and sank sourly into his chair, the empty cup before him. The woman he loved was but three floors above in the same house, but for all he could reach of her, she might as well be in London.

But if Angusina Munro, busying herself three floors above in Emma Maclaren's east tower bedroom, was not within Sandy's reach, it was not for lack of her wishing it. She had thought of little else but him all day, as most days, and stole every spare second to dash to the tower window with its view down on to the side lawns and the long straight drive, in hope of a sight of him. This rather uncharacteristic neglect of her duties had not gone unnoticed and was beginning to try even the affable temper of her mistress.

'Angusina,' Emma said quite sharply, seated in her silk chemise at her dressing-table, tapping lightly upon the rosewood surface with her comb, 'I'm quite sure my blue frock is not hanging at the tower window.'

'Oh yes, Miss. I mean, no, Miss Emma. Here it is now.' She dashed back, in a flurry of black skirts and starched linen, to the tall, mirror-fronted wardrobe, her fingers fumbling in haste on the polished brass doorhandles. Emma sighed, a small deliberate sigh that brought an equally small smile of approval to the face of her mother, Lady Maclaren, who was sitting at Emma's writing-desk, fussing over a piece of scribbled-on blue writing-paper.

It had been quite the perfect sigh, Lady Maclaren noted, not angry, but not to be trifled with either. She was pleased with Emma. Granted Emma was in a hurry now because Emma herself had been late out on her unacceptable motorcycle. But that was neither Angusina's concern, nor a justification for Angusina's dreaming; the sigh had made that point. The proper handling of servants was such a very important part of a lady's upbringing, and it had, in Emma's case, caused her much concern. Emma, with her sweet nature and that naturally egalitarian instinct which a childhood in the Scottish hills seemed to breed, had found this particular duty most difficult. There had been times when she had had to be reprimanded for sending off flustered servants and calmly doing their tasks with her own hands. It had taken some careful explanations to impress upon the girl that such action, far from creating a friendlier atmosphere in the house, only resulted in confused instability and even insolence. Servants of a weak master, as Ian Maclaren was at pains to point out in his military duties, are never content. Victoria Maclaren prided herself on running her house with the same blend of compassion and power that fired any good military establishment. Perhaps, being a barrister's daughter herself and not of military stock, she was always a little overconscious of the need to keep up the regimental standard. 'Guidance and order,' Ian would say and Victoria would echo, 'it's what all people want.'

Angusina Munro, hastening now to her mistress's side, the desired blue tea-dress spread out carefully over her extended arm, would not have argued. The stable world in which Emma had grown up had nurtured her as well. She would not willingly see it changed. It would shelter her, until she married Sandy, and then he would care for her, secure in the pay of His Majesty's forces, until retirement. His future was bright. He might, like his father, rise to the respected post of regimental sergeant major. Or even, like Willie Bruce, the old colonel-in-chief, rise from the ranks and surmount his crofting background, achieving a place among gentlemen's sons in the corridors of power. It was less extraordinary now; good men in the modern army could go far. It did not really matter to Angusina; she loved Sandy, desired him with awakening passion, and would happily bear his children and keep his home if he remained a lance-corporal all his days. His dark beguiling face drifted in and out of her consciousness, as she set about arranging her mistress's beautiful, difficult hair.

Emma watched her own self in the mirror as Angusina piled her long twist of hair up on her head, into a modicum of refinement. She frowned, but for no reason; she was an enchanting sight, as her mother was pleased to note. Her skin, bared by the slim little chemise, was milky white and perfect. Though she was forever out-of-doors, propriety demanded that she was always swathed in layers of pretty impractical cloth, even for tennis or golf. No skin but that of her face and forearms was ever bare, unless she was in the ballroom, or the bath.

The only concession to active youth was Emma's sporting little fringe of hair cut short over her brow in surrender to its own wildly curling nature. Victoria shuddered in her out-of-date grey lace tea-dress, recalling the summer-holiday struggles with her tempestuous eldest daughter, whose whole strong young being yearned to be out on the open hill with her wild brother Tenny at her side. The separation of those two had been Victoria's hardest task. Not that she resented their loving each other, no, but they influenced each other so outrageously. And on both of them, the beautiful open hills were the worst influence of all.

'You can't raise young people in the North,' she complained once to her own mother, in London, over tea at the Ritz. 'There's no controlling them, with all that space. The land's onlv fit for raising regiments.'

School had helped, though Emma had been in frequent trouble there for breaking rules. Thank God she had not, like Susan Bruce, been sent down in disgrace. Not that Susan Bruce appeared to care one tiniest whit.

'I do hope Tenny's arm will be all right,' Victoria said softly, out of a kind of formal concern. So many parts of her five children's young bodies had suffered temporary damage over the years that she did not worry overmuch.

'Tenny's quite fine,' Emma said, muffled inside the layers of blue silk that were lowered over her head by Angusina. 'Good heavens, girl, you're suffocating me.'

'Sorry, Miss,' Angusina said, glancing with distraction over her shoulder.

'On the contrary, Angusina, you are not sorry at all,' Emma said sharply, but her sweetly-turned mouth was gentle. 'You've hardly noticed. Oh go on, get away with you,' she said turning back to her mirror. 'Just do the buttons and get off downstairs.'

'Miss Emma?'

'Yes, you heard me. Just do the buttons.'

'Oh thank you, Miss Emma.'

'But,' Emma's voice hardened, 'if by Monday, when the holiday's over and Fiona is good and truly wed, *at last*, if you do not smarten up and come to your senses, I'll have another lady's maid within a week. It's a good position, as I'm sure you're quite aware, and there are a good dozen girls in the strath would be glad of it.'

'Miss Emma, I couldna bear anyone else being your maid,'

Angusina cried, her voice full of hurt.

'Nor shall anyone. *If* you kindly get over this wedding excitement, and settle yourself down.' She smiled brightly though and her hazel eyes met Angusina's in the mirror for a tiny conspiratorial instant. Angusina knew at once that the whole speech was for Lady Maclaren's benefit, and not her own. She smiled primly and said, 'Yes, Miss,' fastened each of Emma's forty-three mother-of-pearl buttons precisely, bobbed once to each lady, and was out of the door before either could speak or change her mind.

'That,' said Lady Maclaren, in the silence after the click of the door latch, 'was a mistake.'

'Oh, bother if it was,' Emma said impatiently, slipping her stockinged feet into blue silk slippers. 'She was hardly any use to me in her present mood.'

'Nor has Fiona been any use to me, since this rather hasty engagement, mind. But it does not mean she can have hours off whenever she wishes. Her wedding is tomorrow and she will be free to go away to her husband's croft. But I need her to do my toilette tonight, and she knows that to be her duty, and there will be no complaints. She will be free at eight, as agreed.'

'Really, Mother. Tomorrow's her wedding. Maybe she wants to help with the preparations.'

'Yes indeed. And next week it will be someone else's wedding, or christening, or God knows what. No, dear. Begin that and you will lose all authority. How, may I ask, will you manage to dress tonight?'

Emma stood up and turned to study the slim-fitting blue silk dress. 'If I can't manage to dress myself alone for an evening there must be something wrong.'

'A lady's dinner-gown, my dear,' Victoria Maclaren said primly, 'is designed with the assumption of a lady's maid's attentions. The frocks one wears demand it, dear. How would you do those buttons for instance? And if you plan on wearing your ivory silk, you'll have as many buttons on that.'

'Tosh. Philippa can do them, Mother. If the frocks we wear demand an army to get us into them, perhaps we are wearing the wrong frocks,' she said then with her perfect little eyebrows arching wryly. 'Has it never occurred?'

'No,' Victoria said coldly. 'It has not. Fine then, if you're feeling so inclined, you may come to dinner tonight in your bloomers like some suffragette. I'm sure Torquil Farquhar will be utterly charmed.'

'So he might,' Emma said mischievously, with a touch of malice. 'Perhaps he'd think I was interesting, or different, like Naomi perhaps. *She* doesn't dress like all the rest of you, and the men do seem to find her ever so enchanting.'

'What Naomi Bruce does to enchant men,' Victoria said in a whisper, 'is not something I'd expect a girl of your age to understand. Nor would a man like Torquil be interested in that. He's a proper young gentleman and he will be interested only in a proper young lady,' she added firmly.

'You make him sound positively boring,' Emma returned haughtily. 'I don't think I'm interested myself any longer.' But she was, and she knew it, and after a moment said, 'Will you help with my dress for dinner, Mother, please?'

Victoria shook her head with exasperation and then said, with a shrug, 'Oh, of course. But you *are* a silly fool.'

Lady Maclaren returned to her piece of paper, on which was listed, many times scored out and rewritten, a long tally of names, the guest list for the weekend. 'Bother Naomi,' she said at last.

'For her frocks?'

'No, dear, of course not. For sending her child. The trouble it has caused me. She must know that the house space is not unlimited. I've barely room to squeeze the boy himself in, much less this Miss Galloway, and a maid as well, mind you. Mr MacLeod was not at all pleased.'

'Oh Mother, he's only the butler. What does it matter if he's not pleased.'

'Only the butler indeed,' Lady Maclaren sniffed, scribbling something in the corner of the paper. 'The servants' hall is entirely his responsibility, and he takes it very seriously, thank God for that. It won't do at all to upset him. No. Naomi is quite unreasonable. She is a most awkward woman, really.'

'I think she's splendid, Mother,' Emma said dreamily. 'I'd positively adore to be just like her.'

'Indeed,' Victoria said icily. 'Oh, where shall I put this Galloway woman?'

'Oh heavens, put her in with me. I'll share happily enough. Or perhaps Susan Bruce could share with me, and Miss Galloway may have Susan's room. Or put the three of us up in the nursery.'

'A maiden lady of uncertain years might not be delighted with the nursery and the pair of you.'

'Well then, if she's frightfully old and proper, why not stick her up in the west tower with Great-Aunt Jean? They can call up the spirits together and scare the knickers off each other.'

'Emma!'

'Sorry, Mother,' Emma said, her eyes crinkling and her faintly freckled nose wrinkling between her brows. 'But Jean does make me laugh so, with her tarot and her seances and her tealeaves. No wonder she never married, she'd drive any sane man mad in a week.'

'Don't be unkind, dear.' Victoria leaned back in her chair, smoothing her hair, grey-tinged blonde now but still lustrous, with one tiny hand. She was a tiny woman, and had managed with something of a struggle to keep her small figure neat through advancing years. 'I dare say Jean would not have been like that at all, if she had married. It does something to one, being left on the shelf. I'm frankly sorry Philippa sees fit to spend quite so much time with the old girl. It's all very kind and all, but she's hardly a fit influence on an impressionable young woman.'

'I wouldn't worry,' Emma said, unconcernedly adjusting her haircombs, her eyes on herself in the mirror. 'It's mostly seances they have up there, not conversations, and besides Philippa's about as impressionable as old boots. It's just another of her whims. Last year it was that infernal poet she was forever quoting. It's midsummer madness, I think, with old Phil. She always goes starry-eyed when the moon's high. She'll come out of it, never fear.'

Emma's mind was on her own midsummer whim, Torquil Farquhar, that handsome young son of her father's old fellow officer and friend, Alex Farquhar, gentleman and horse-fancier, himself now retired to his Perthshire estate. Emma had remade the boy's acquaintance in May, after a gap of some years, during which they had both left childhood behind. Meeting each other again, she a young lady and he a serving officer now with the Maclarens himself, they were both equally astounded that the other had grown up as well. They had both hovered between embarrassment and overeagerness, and made rather a mess of that meeting, and each privately vowed to make up for it. However, they had not had the opportunity until this traditional weekend, and Emma's excited pleasure was tinged a little with nervousness in case he had concluded she was the fool she had undoubtedly appeared.

'Philippa will come out of it,' Lady Maclaren said wisely, 'when some young man brings her out. And not until.'

'There's always Harry Bruce,' Emma said quietly.

'Indeed.'

'He's a good sort, Mother.'

'Everyone's a good sort to you, dear,' Lady Maclaren said rather gently. 'He's a most difficult young man, really. I don't wish to talk about him.'

Emma shrugged, eyeing the neckline of her tea-dress in the mirror and holding one, and then another, necklace against her white skin. Eventually she chose one, fastened the clasp and turned, tugging behind her back at the soft bow at the nape of her neck.

'The dress is charming,' her mother assured her.

'No. The collar is still not right. I think I shall change my seamstress.'

'Very well, if you like,' Lady Maclaren said, not paying attention, her eyes fixed again on her guest list. She held it at arm's length, as she needed spectacles to read but avoided them out of vanity. 'Oh, bother Naomi,' she said once more. 'Really you'd think out of kindness to her mother she'd refrain from sending that child here. She must know what the very sight of him does to Maud.'

'Oh, come now, Mother, that's hardly fair. What's she to do with the child anyway? Keep him locked away in the attic because he looks like his own grandfather. *He* can't help that.'

'No. He can't. But she could have. She had no business . . . she should have thought of that sort of thing before . . . she should have thought of something.'

Emma laughed. 'I doubt Naomi's ever done much thinking before doing . . . that.'

'Emma!'

Emma only shrugged. 'Besides,' she said, 'he's a very handsome child really.'

'He's Indian,' Victoria Maclaren said with indignant finality. She stood up, folding her list crisply. 'Now, if we just get through this frightful weekend, and get that damnable wedding downstairs over, we just might be able to look forward to the Season in the south.'

'If there is one.'

'Of course there'll be one. There's always a Season.'

'This Season,' Emma said slowly, tapping her delicate wrist with her manicured nails and looking at the floor, 'if I understand Daddy right, there just may be a war instead.'

There was a long silence in the tower bedroom before Victoria, turning towards the door, said, moderately displeased, 'We all agreed, Em.'

'Oh Mother, this is such absolute madness. It's on everyone's mind. I dare say it's the only thing on Daddy's mind, or Gordon Bruce's. And yet we're all fussing about with picnics and balls and tea-frocks. Mother, I feel such a shameful fraud. We should surely be doing something.'

'What, dear?' Victoria said. 'Blowing the holy trumpet, and waiting for Jericho to fall? Come dear, there's enough fools in the world doing that already. No, we will get on with living, and if war comes, we will get on with that. In the meantime, we will have tea.' She glanced at the small gold-cased clock on Emma's dressing-table, a birthday present from her grandfather. 'If,' she added, 'we're not too late.' Then suddenly she shook her head, as if with an immense weight of emotional strain, and Emma saw there were tears on her lashes. Astounded, she gaped, mouth open. Her mother had never once been known to cry.

Victoria blurted out suddenly, 'Do you know, the foolish thing, it's little James I think about, night and day, and it's nothing to do with him. All the others, Tenny, Albert, Daddy, Johnny Bruce, even Harry perhaps; they'll go. And it's James I think of. It must be because he's my baby.' She blinked once, and turned away, forcing her grief into anger. 'Oh, that damnable Fiona. Why did she choose to marry now, just when I need her most? Surely she could have waited. It's all so dreadfully inconvenient.'

'Because she knows,' Emma said at once.

'Knows what?'

'That war is coming. Ewan will go too.'

'Nonsense. He's only in the Territorials. The furthest he'll have to go is Beauly to mind the barracks while the First Battalion is settling the Kaiser. They can't be sent abroad. It will all be over before they've ever heard a shot fired in anger. In a few years she'll have a houseful of children and a croft to tend for her haste, and be wishing she'd stayed in Culbrech in the first place.' Victoria sniffed. Marriage for girls of Fiona's class hardly seemed much of a bargain. 'She could surely have waited a month, seen the summer through.'

'Perhaps she couldn't,' Emma said suddenly.

'Why ever not?'

'Perhaps she's pregnant.' Emma said it boldly, but her very boldness was childish. The servant girls' lives fascinated her, with their dark undertones of experience. Emma, at twenty-two, did not know in any detail how women became pregnant at all.

'Emma,' was all Lady Maclaren said, the hush of her tone the same hush that had over the years veiled any question that might have provided Emma with the answer.

Victoria and Emma went, arm and arm, to tea in the drawing-room of Culbrech House.

Outside, in the soft early evening sunshine, Sandy Gibson and Angusina Munro ran hand in hand over the stubble of the hayfield, stumbling and laughing in the summer glory of Strathglass. At the flat bottom of the valley the river flowed broad and sunny, deceptively gentle before it reached its fierce gorge at Aigas. Sandy's father and brother were there, stringing a wire fence.

Sandy and Angusina released their handhold and straightened up with formality.

'Aye there,' Sandy said.

'Aye, aye.'

'And what are ye workin' at, at this hour?' Sandy said.

'Just a wee bit fence,' Frankie Gibson replied, and young Frank said,

'Aye. We've cleared the beasts awa' frae the picnic ground, and tidied up that bit, sae we're no' wantin' them back.' He carefully uncurled the roll of wire, with its regular sharp twists forming the barbs, and strung it along the top of the fence, handling its scraggly length with deference.

'That wee light fence will never keep the beasts away, surely,' Angusina said. 'Ye've nae a proper post of the lot.' She prodded one thin pole with her black boot.

'Well now,' Frankie said politely, 'you're right enough there, lass. But it's no' meant to stand but for the day, and we'd no' be driving proper posts for that. No, lass. It's this,' he ran his hand lightly over the barbed strand, so that his calloused palm just vaulted each barb.

Angusina studied it. 'Och, it's yon scratchy stuff, like I saw Ewan using once. It's not like proper sheep-wire at all.'

'No,' Frankie said. 'They use yon in America and Canada, tae keep in the cattle herds. It's gey clever, is it no'? As light as ye'd want and as easy tae string, but it'll dae the job better than any stone dyke.'

'Will it now?' Sandy said, with an outsider's eye, farming not being his occupation any longer. 'Surely they'll push their way through, it will no' do any real harm.'

'Aye, maybe not. But beasts are nae fools. Nae beast in its right mind will tangle up with the likes of that.'

3

Inverness, on the bright windy Saturday at the beginning of August, was a pretty and pleasant sight, as Officer Cadet John Bruce drove down the rough north road from Strathglass. The early showers of rain had died away, and as he roared along the edge of the Moray Firth, the smooth waters of the tide flats flashed and glistened in the morning sun. Johnny drove fast, pushing the gleaming dark green Crossley tourer to its limits, bumping and jouncing along the narrow road, past the Muirtown Basin and the distillery, blasting on the horn at every sharp bend. Fortunately for Johnny, considering that the motor car belonged to Colonel Maclaren, the roads were deserted except for occasional cheering children and scatterings of frantic hens, and he met neither farmcart nor motor car until he was through the village of Clachnaharry and well into the town itself, crossing the bridge over the lock-stepped waters of the Caledonian canal.

Even there, the town was quiet. It was a Saturday, of course, but it was the August Bank Holiday weekend, and many of the townspeople had closed up their neat houses and left their modest squares of green, rose-filled gardens for the more open green of the countryside. Country cottages in Glenurquhart or by the seaside in Nairn were a firm tradition among the shopkeepers and professional classes of Inverness. Still, there were plenty of people in town of lesser means, and as many country folk chose to spend their holiday away from the kailyard, savouring the pleasures of the shops. But if those visitors were there, something had hushed them. Only the seagulls wheeling endlessly over the wet shining slate roofs of the city made a noise, a mournful crying over the rumble of carriage wheels.

Johnny Bruce was too absorbed in his own problems to speculate on the concerns of Inverness. He was late. He'd been into Beauly the evening before, to Fort Maclaren, on some minor business of his grandfather's and ended in the company of a group of junior officers. Somehow the brief visit had resolved into a long evening in the officers' mess where war talk and cigars and brandy took equal measure of his time. He had arrived home at three in the morning, after a weary ride through the dark countryside, and slept in as a result. Rising late, he had barely time to fling his kilt on and leap into the Crossley that Ian Maclaren's chauffeur had deposited outside his grandparents' home the evening before, and proceed at once to Inverness to meet the overnight train. He had had neither coffee nor breakfast and was nursing a slight hangover, and aware from the time on the distant steeple clock of the Old High Church that the arrival hour of the train had already passed. He rounded a corner on a steep hilly wynd coming down into the centre of town, and found the roadway completely blocked by a bleating herd of sheep.

'Damnation.' The Crossley skidded to a halt, Johnny answering the sheeps' bleats with equally frantic bleats of the shiny brass horn. The sheep milled and their shepherd, a young Highlander in home-made tweeds and a flat cloth bonnet, looked faintly amused and whistled nonchalantly to his dog.

'I say,' Johnny leaned out of the open car, 'I'm in rather a frantic hurry.'

'Aye. I can see that.'

'I've got to meet the train.

'Aye,' the shepherd said again, and then nodding to his flock flowing around the Crossley said, 'And so hae they. Mind now, they're in no' so great a hurry themselves.'

Johnny leaned back in his seat, his solid, muscular body tense with nervous indignation. The clock hands on the church steeple clicked forward and the sheep milled again. Hamilton's stockyards at the railway station were their destination no doubt, and distant markets beyond. Johnny heaved a weary sigh and looked around. It was nearly ten o'clock. The train was long in, Robert Bruce and the maiden aunt would wonder where the hell he was and no doubt telephone Culbrech where Ian Maclaren would have a total fit over the misfortunes that may have befallen his splendid motor car. And Tenny, blast him, would be doing the rounds of the young ladies gathering in Culbrech's morning-room, Torquil and John Farquhar's sisters who had arrived the night before and sundry schoolfriends of the Maclaren girls and his own sister and no doubt a few local extras for good measure. Culbrech house-parties were well known for the sumptuous plenitude of female beauty. And everyone would have a dance card for the ball, and Tenny Maclaren would have his name at the top of each list; even one-armed, he was going to be cock of the roost.

'Will you kindly move those blasted beasts,' Johnny suddenly shouted. Two passing matrons, in sombre tweed suits, turned sharp eyes under their neat felt hats. But their attention did not remain on the striking sight of that handsome sandy-haired youth in his beautiful motor car. Instead they joined the small cluster of people on the narrow pavement outside a small, red-trimmed newsagent's shop. Johnny, engrossed in his sheep, and his visions of Tenny triumphant, had hardly noticed either the shop or the little knot of people. Now his eyes followed the offended matrons and found what held their attention. At first he could see nothing but the oddly quiet cluster of passers-by, looking downwards and talking with subdued voices. But then a customer passing out of the doors of the shop separated the crowd for a few moments, and revealed the object of their interest. It was the familiar newsagent's placard with its sheets of white paper held in by a metal grid, displaying the news of most immediate import. There were only two words, large and black: *Russia Mobilizes*.

Just for a moment, Johnny's world went very still. The sheep, bleating yet, receded down the road and only the gulls, wheeling over the buff chimneystacks, filled the town with their crying. He heard his grandfather saying, as if he sat on the polished leather seat beside him, 'Mobilization means war.' Not a declaration, not that posturing that Austria had carried out three days before with Serbia. That could yet be a device, diplomacy, or schoolboy's dangerous daring, whatever one wished to regard it. But mobilization. Johnny ran his hand through his coarse curling hair, studying the placard grimly.

'Yer gait's clear, the now,' said a small voice, which added, tentatively, 'Sir?'

Johnny looked up. The road ahead was empty, and a small barefooted boy was studying him curiously. 'Yes. Of course,' he said, and impatiently thrust the car into gear, but he was nervous, synchronizing badly, and the gears ground with a clashing that no doubt Ian Maclaren would feel in Culbrech House. 'Sorry, sir,' he said with a wince, and drove on into the town. He pulled off Academy Street in front of the Station Hotel entrance, leaving the car among a cluster of standing carriages there and bounding off into the station. It was empty, save for a few residual heaps of luggage and one or two idle porters. Cursing himself, he turned back to the hotel, hoping they had thought to await him there.

Once inside the double doors he stood, his eyes sweeping over the familiar curving staircase and the long room filled with gilded chairs and little round tables, at each of which sat a group of Invernessian matrons taking their morning coffee and gossip. His eyes searched among them for young Robert Bruce; Miss Galloway herself would obviously blend into invisibility against that background of other elderly ladies. He had almost given up, and was considering seeking out the house telephone and putting a call through to Culbrech House, in the hopes that they had already made contact, when a scuffle at the corner of the room sheltered by the staircase caught his eye. A morning-suited member of the hotel staff was apparently wrestling with a smaller person, seeking to procure some object from that person's hands.

'You cannot have it,' a boyishly shrill voice suddenly shouted, shaking the tranquillity of the pillared room. 'It's mine. Tenny gave it me, and it's mine.'

Johnny heard Tenny's name in the same instant that he recognized the dark-haired boy as Robert Bruce. He strode across the room angrily, an impressive sight in his Maclaren kilt and green tweed jacket, roughly tied ascot flying loose, his driving-goggles pushed up on to his forehead.

'I say,' he said sharply, 'leave the lad be. He's with me.'

The hotel person swung about, recognizing Johnny at once and, although looking puzzledly apologetic, made no move towards releasing his firm hold on Robert Bruce's arm. 'Mr Bruce,' the man said.

'Yes. That's my cousin you're handling, I'll have you know.'

'Johnny, he's trying to steal my penknife that Tenny gave me,' Robert shouted. Several heads turned and the gentleman in the morning coat recoiled visibly.

He said after a breath-gathering pause, 'I assure you, sir, I had no intention of thievery. It was merely an effort to protect hotel property from imminent destruction,' he added, glowering from Robert's indignant face to the penknife in his distantly held hand. 'I deeply regret, sir, but your cousin was carving his name on our pillar.'

'Robert?' Johnny said, his thick eyebrows rising slowly.

'It's absolute lies,' Robert said, his wide brown eyes as meltingly appealing as those of his mother. 'Honest it is. I merely took the merest tiniest insignificant little nick out . . .'

'You took what out? Of their pillar? Robert . . .'

'Just to see if it was proper gold, sir. It's not,' he added, looking disdainfully at the gentleman in the morning coat, as if the insufficiencies of his pillar were a direct reflection on his own truthfulness.

'Of course it's not, you silly ass,' Johnny said sourly. 'Now put your silly knife away.' He turned towards the hotel manager and shrugged suddenly and grinned. 'We'll make right any damage, of course,' Johnny said, smooth as milk, and at once was met with deprecation,

'Not necessary, I assure you,' the man tugged at his collar, thinking quickly of the numbers of Maclaren and Bruce guests that had passed through his portals, even this very weekend. 'Merely a matter of principle. Discipline, let us say. Very necessary for the young these days, would you not say?' he smiled nervously, patting Robert's head reassuringly. Robert ducked and glowered, fondly holding his knife in both hands.

'Of course, of course,' Johnny Bruce said, already impatient, and at once the manager faded from sight.

'I say,' Robert said, in his absence, 'you were stunning.'

'You,' Johnny said, leaning down and whispering, 'are a total blockhead. If you so much as touch anything with that knife again, I'll skelp your arse. Now where's the old biddy?'

'The who?' Robert said, curious.

'Miss Galloway,' Johnny said, pulling his watch from the little pocket in his green waistcoat. 'We'll be late back to lunch.'

'Rebecca's gone to the . . . you know. Where ladies go.'

'Oh. Splendid,' Johnny said sourly, forgetting by now that any lateness was the dual fault of himself and a flock of Invernessian sheep. 'No doubt she'll be hours.' He was thinking of his grandmother who could disappear for up to forty-five minutes within the gracious doors of the feminine retreats of hotels such as this.

'I suppose it's all those petticoats and knickers and things,' Robert said thoughtfully.

'What?' Johnny said, eyes opening wide.

'Those petticoats and knickers,' Robert said matter-of-factly in a conversational voice that carried with classroom clarity to a large ring of surrounding tables.

'Hush,' Johnny said, reaching to cover the boy's mouth.

'Well, it must take practically ages to get down to bare essentials, mustn't it. It's hardly like undoing your fly but—' Johnny's hand made firm contact and he decided to keep it there, over his cousin's mouth, until they were in open countryside. Which is why when Rebecca Galloway, trailed by her maid, Mary, emerged, her hair freshly done, feathered hat set at the ideal angle and linen skirts trailing prettily, she was met by the sight of Robert's frantically expressive eyes signalling to her over the firm hand of a kilted kidnapper.

'Let him go,' she said sharply. 'Let him go at once or I shall . . .' By this time the nearer ring of tables had taken a distinctly spectatorial approach to the unorthodox young people in their centre. Johnny let go of his cousin, astounded by the verbal assault falling on him from the sweet lips of the most extraordinarily beautiful creature he had ever seen. He stood staring, and fortunately Robert, his mouth in working order once more, blurted out,

'It's all right, Rebecca, he's come to meet us.'

Rebecca stopped still. Her own hand slowly rose to her face and touched one pinkened cheek. 'Oh my,' she smiled nervously, 'you must be Tenny,' she said.

They were a good halfway back to Culbrech House before Johnny decided to forgive her that. And then it was for no logical reason, but simply because the sheer prettiness of her, clinging delightedly to her bouncing seat like a child, her lovely face chaotically muffled with the borrowed gauze-netted driving hat he provided, made resentment of anything impossible. Of course it had not been logical being angry in the first place. She was totally blameless in mistaking him for Tenny, who was after all the expected person, and she had never met either of them before. But then, it was not the mistake that he resented, but her clear disappointment at the correction. Tenny's reputation had carried as far as London, it appeared, and even without his substance present, Johnny was distinctly overshadowed. It was rather much, particularly after the humiliation, yesterday, of Maclaren's Leap.

'Tenny would have come, naturally,' he said, breaking his silence, 'but he hurt his arm. Broke it actually.'

'Oh dear. I do hope . . .'

'He's quite all right. Nothing really. Just a clumsy accident while fishing.' Johnny chanced a smile. 'First Maclaren in history to break his arm with a fish.' She laughed and the joke was distinctly on Tenny. Johnny smiled again, a smile tinged with guilt. But then, he reminded himself, though it might not be the truth, there was no way he could tell her the truth. They'd both sworn they'd not tell a soul. It wasn't Johnny's fault that it was all suddenly so convenient.

Johnny's small verbal triumph over his cousin was perhaps understandable in the light of the events of the day before, which, for all their resulting in Tenny's injury, were but another example of the persistent humiliation that John Bruce had always borne in Tenny Maclaren's presence.

Downriver of Culbrech House, the broad meandering waters of the Glass narrowed, straightened, and tumbled into a black gorge through which they thundered in awesome haste. The banks of the river rose to form towering cliffs, and at one point the dark crags on either side of the water leaned so close together as to shut out all sunlight from the torrent below. That point, where the chasm narrowed so deceptively that it appeared to afford a crossing, was known as MacGregor's Leap for a certain legendary MacGregor who, fleeing from some hostile clan, made his escape by leaping the river. Or so the story had it; in truth it was a wide, dangerous gap above a forty-foot drop to the fierce, rock-strewn waters below. Anyone jumping it would have been a considerable athlete. But that was not the point of argument that arose between John Bruce and Tenny Maclaren as, returning from their fishing, they passed the dark gorge.

They had fished since early morning, upriver, at Ian Maclaren's favourite salmon pool, in the company of Sandy Gibson. As boys all three had been inseparable, but with the arrival of adulthood, class and rank had subtly divided them. Sandy, home on leave for a week, joined them now as ghillie and stayed quietly out of their conversation.

Conversation between Tenny and John Bruce was usually argument anyhow, one long persistent argument, in which Tenny attempted always to maintain, and Johnny to diminish, the undoubted superiority won him by his year's greater age. That superiority was underlined in a dozen subtle ways: three extra inches of height, and the proportional length of arm and leg that gave him the advantage in all athletic rivalry; a sharp academic wit that won him the last word in most debates; a grace and elegance about his six-foot-and-one-inch frame that commanded attention, particularly from the ladies. Even his hair, bright and eye-catching red, seemed designed to outshine the sandy-haired John Bruce. They were alike enough, though, to be taken for brothers on occasions, and John Bruce, rising to the role, displayed a greater degree of brotherly rivalry than either of Tenny's true brothers ever did. The year between them that ought to have placated Johnny, only enraged him. He saw himself running a race which time forbade him for ever the chance of winning. Whatever he achieved, physically or mentally, Tenny would still be that fatal year ahead.

Because of that perhaps, he took every opportunity to needle, to tease, to lower his rival, and Tenny, with a petulance left over from childhood, rose to the bait like the salmon, equally unable to admit himself ever wrong.

'Maclaren's Leap,' said Tenny, eyeing the chasm of the River Glass, as they passed

'Maclaren's?' Johnny returned, disbelieving. 'Maclaren's nothing. It's MacGregor's Leap.'

'Maclaren's,' Tenny insisted baldly.

'MacGregor's.'

'You're wrong, old man,' Tenny corrected pompously. 'It's Maclaren's Leap. Chap that jumped it was a *Maclaren*,' he paused and added gratuitously, 'They do still say only a Maclaren can jump it, even now.' He grinned. 'My grandfather told me . . .'

'Ballocks. You're making it all up. Besides, *my* grandfather always called it MacGregor's Leap.'

'Jealousy, I suspect,' Tenny answered, still grinning.

'You wish,' Johnny returned, glowering at the rocky crags. 'Sandy,' he said suddenly, 'you'll know. It's MacGregor's Leap, isn't it?' Sandy was silent. 'Well, isn't it?' Johnny persisted.

'I dinna ken, sir.'

'Of course you know,' Johnny said angrily. Sandy looked from one to the other of the two young men and then down at the box of tackle and the two salmon he was carrying home for them. His position was not enviable, forced to mediate between the son of his recently retired CO, and the nephew of that man's successor. He said nothing and Johnny, spurred on by frustration said, 'Well, maybe it *is* Maclaren's Leap, but the only man I know who's jumped it is a Bruce.'

'Your grandfather?' Tenny looked up, surprise brightening his pale blue eyes. 'I never heard that.' He would not have been too amazed, however. Willie Bruce had done practically everything in his long adventurous life and both boys had grown up in his beneficent but impressive shadow.

'No,' said Johnny smoothly. 'I've jumped it.' Tenny's jaw fell. 'Last summer,' Johnny added with calm assurance. 'I was late home off the hill, and it seemed a jolly good shortcut. Mind you,' he added, 'it wasn't easy.'

'Not easy?' Tenny returned at once. 'I should say not. It's ruddy well impossible. You're making it up. You've never jumped that,' he added with authority, glancing across to the opposite, crumbling crag. '*No one's* ever jumped that.' Johnny only shrugged. 'Come on, tell truth,' Tenny demanded belligerently.

'It is truth,' Johnny insisted. 'Besides,' he teased, 'what about that famous Maclaren?'

'That's all claptrap,' Tenny said brusquely. 'You know as well as I. Right, Sandy? No one's ever really jumped MacGregor's Leap, have they?' Sandy looked at the fish, and his feet.

Johnny just shrugged again and turned away. 'Come on, they'll be waiting tea,' he said pleasantly, walking off.

He first realized what Tenny was about to do when Sandy shouted with sudden uncharacteristic alarm, 'Sir, ye'd better no' . . .'

Johnny whirled and caught from the corner of his eye just a flash of tweeds and bright red hair as Tenny, his run-up completed, sprang from the edge of the precipice and launched himself into space. His green cap spun away in the wind, falling to the waters below, and the air seemed to hold him suspended for an impossible time above the noise of the river, and then the arc of his jump broke and he plunged downwards, arms and legs flailing for the far rock ledge. The bare toe of his leather boot caught the sloping granite crag. It slipped, but Tenny's momentum carried him forwards and his reaching hands caught a hold on a lithe bending spray of rowan branch. It bent like a whip, the bright berries stripping off in a shower like drops of blood. Tenny clung, his legs scrabbling. Helpless, Sandy and Johnny watched as he momentarily became simply a frantic animal clawing for salvation on the slippery rocks. Then hands found the trunk of the rowan, feet the notches of its roots, and then, quite suddenly, he was safe.

The struggle over, Tenny lay panting, face down on the crusty lichen covering the rock, a foot from the edge, his arms linked lovingly about the broad sturdy trunk of an ancient larch. It was a long, silent time before he moved. He raised his face then, his eyes not yet fully free of fear, but he grinned, sat up, companionably close to the old tree, and shouted over the roaring water, 'Up the Maclarens, you sod.'

John Bruce had only himself to blame. He had started it out of sheer devilishness and his persistent prideful inability to be bested in any argument. He'd never thought that Tenny would have believed him, and even less that he would so readily and recklessly respond to the challenge inherent in his extravagant and, as it was, utterly false claim. Now pride and conscience combined in deadly earnest.

With an uneasy eye he gauged the distance to the battered rowan tree. Like any athlete, John Bruce had a sharp awareness of his limitations. Tenny, who had bested him yearly at every event of the Strathglass Games since they were children, had barely made it. It was beyond him. He knew it. He also knew that the reward for seconding Tenny this time was not a smaller rosette, but a short, icy end to his cherished young life.

Johnny took seven careful paces back and again gauged the distance, with his eyes, and this time with the tense muscles of his sturdy thighs and calves. Sandy Gibson stood appalled and open-mouthed as Johnny began his run. At the edge of the ravine he let out a great shout like a Highland warrior and leapt, blue-green kilt flying, out over the Glass.

It was Tenny on the far bank, not Sandy, who saw that the leap was short; a matter of inches, but short. The instant he saw, he too leapt forward, and as Johnny's black brogue slipped past the landing-point and his flailing hands grasped for the hanging rowan, they found Tenny's bent arm instead. Tenny, his right arm and leg wrapped round the trunk of the old larch, felt them scrape and rasp nearly free. He clung desperately, with Johnny's eleven stone of weight bending his left arm back against his shoulder. He heard the bone break but felt nothing. For an instant Johnny's falling weight dragged them both towards the river, but then Johnny had the rowan branch in his left hand and his foot found a niche in the rock. He released Tenny's arm, and made the scramble to the tree himself, and was safe. Tenny sat down dully on the ground, cradling his arm across his chest as the pain caught him.

'Up the Bruces,' said Johnny, between panting breaths. He was lying flat on his back on the smooth granite, his eyes closed, his mouth widening into an exhausted grin.

'I've broken my arm, you blithering idiot,' Tenny muttered, attempting to move it and wincing sharply at the effect.

'Oh, poor thing,' Johnny said. 'What a shame.' He didn't believe him and was not yet looking.

'What the hell am I to tell them?' Tenny demanded. Johnny sat up. He turned round and looked at Tenny with considerable surprise. Tenny's face was white, his pale eyes furious.

'Have you really?' Johnny said, but Tenny's face convinced him. 'I say, what rotten luck.' He sounded as if he'd been a million miles away at the time, and in no way related to the event.

'Father will kill us both when he hears what we've been up to.'

'Oh. Oh yes.' Johnny was instantly serious. He sat morosely, his bare muscular legs crossed, the kilt splayed about him like a girl's skirt, conscious of Tenny's pain in a distant way as he was conscious of Sandy's shouts of concern across the rush of the torrent below. He was not callous, but casual. They had both experienced worse, over the years. But Ian Maclaren's wrath was quite another matter.

So that was when they concocted the story about the monstrous salmon, and Tenny falling off a rock trying to land it. Tenny was less than pleased; he felt their alibi made him look a fool. But the alternative was his father learning what they'd been up to, so he acquiesced, and joined with John Bruce in demanding loyal silence from Sandy, who, feeling he'd be held partially responsible if the real truth came out, was more than willing to agree. Of course, Tenny hadn't anticipated his rival's sudden opportunity to use the story against him. He hadn't anticipated Rebecca Galloway.

More fool he, Johnny thought gaily, grinning to himself and glancing sideways once more at the young lady in the passenger seat. Her profile, partly obscured from his vision by the rim of his goggles, was still perfect, the little nose turned up at the best of all angles, her nearside cheek dimpled when she smiled. A plan slowly began to stir in Johnny's mind. He relaxed a little, leaned back, glanced over his shoulder at Robert in the back seat absorbed happily in the scenery, leaning back over the folded canopy. The lady's maid, Mary, was sitting primly, her hands folded on her lap.

Johnny glanced again across to Rebecca Galloway and said casually, 'Anyhow, Susan will be relieved.'

'Susan?' Rebecca mentally covered the list of Maclarens and Bruces reeled off by Naomi, and then with a twinge of nervous recollection, placed Susan. 'Your sister?' she said, slightly uncertain.

'Hmm. She was quite frightfully nervous of Tenny going to meet you. Rather jealous is old Susan. Not that she's any cause. I mean, Tenny's quite head-over-heels and all. Still,' he looked again, barely taking his eyes from the road, 'I dare say if anyone could give her cause for jealousy . . . you certainly are most attractive, if you'll forgive me.'

Rebecca looked away quickly, picking annoyedly at her skirt with her hands. Oddly she felt a definite surge of jealousy herself, over a man she'd not yet met. It appeared Naomi's information was a little out of date. In her annoyance she almost overlooked Johnny's compliment, but it sank in gradually and out of politeness she smiled a small modest smile and said, still looking away, 'Thank you.' Then she did look at Johnny Bruce, for the first time, with care.

Four miles further up the same road, another, lesser Maclaren was also being outdone by a rival. He was in every way a lesser Maclaren: the youngest, the smallest, the last of a big family. A wiry, curly-headed boy, yet short for his age, he could never recall a time when there wasn't someone sufficiently bigger about to best him in any fight, as well as someone sufficiently bigger to protect him. He had gone through prep school and entered Fettes, always with an older brother a respectable distance ahead. He was Maclaren Minor, to their Maclaren Major, wherever he went. And he loved it. They bullied, protected, encouraged, and spoiled him, and consequently got him into all manner of trouble and situations ahead of his years. The effect should likely have been disaster, but it was exactly the opposite. At fifteen James Maclaren had every attribute that either his father, or his mother, might desire.

Like Albert, he was gentle and thoughtful, and like Tenny he was courageous and willing. Unlike either of them, he had a real sense of humour and saw his role in life lightly. Tenny carried the responsibility of being the heir, and he was heir to enough, both estate and family, and the regiment as well, to make it a heavy and limiting honour. Albert carried a different weight, that awkward burden of questionable usefulness of being second in line. His value was simply to be there, a second, a shadow, necessary but, it was hoped, never needed. He was too close to the lead to leave the race but still never likely to win it. He must remain always within reach, with any real purpose forever out of his grasp. But for James, there was neither problem. Tenny filled the first role, Albert the second. James had only to exist to bask in enough reflected glory to make a warm, well-lit life a surety. Unlike either of his brothers, he was often asked what he might like to do. The regiment was a possibility, naturally, but for him alone it was not a necessity.

It was ironic, because James, more than even Tenny, and certainly more than Albert, loved the military with his entire being. But at the moment, his love of the military and particularly of the Maclaren Highlanders had earned him a bloody nose from his erstwhile best friend, Jimmy Fraser, the son of the local postmaster.

James Maclaren, like all children of his class, had two separate circles of friendship. The first, starting in early childhood, was an egalitarian brotherhood made up of whatever workmen's sons were close at hand on the estate his father owned. The second circle began in his school years, and covered a network of people, geographically remote, whose parents moved in the same class as his own. They were naturally the circle in which, as an adult, he would move, work, and marry. And whereas he was positively encouraged as a small child to play with his lessers, he would be equally strongly discouraged in adulthood from continuing any but the most formal business relations with them.

It was an extraordinary system, if one thought about it. But no one did, not James nor 'Jimmy Post' nor indeed James's brother Tenny whose friendship with Sandy Gibson had followed the same evolutionary course. However, as James's youth and the physical distance of his school circle during the holidays made his childhood friendships both necessary and acceptable still, he and Jimmy Post would remain for a few years yet as close to each other as either would ever in future life be to any other man. In ten years' time, they would be acquaintances at best.

But if James, rubbing his bleeding nose against his sleeve, were to be asked at this instant, he would have been quite happy to declare the friendship firmly over already.

'Och, ye ken I didna mean it,' Jimmy Post said sourly.

'You did.'

'I didna.'

'Did. You did. You beastly hit me with your beastly knee.'

'Och away. You slipped. How was I t' ken ye'd ding yer great neb on ma knee?'

'It was on purpose. All because I said the Maclarens were worth any eight cavalry regiments. And they are. Cavalry's no bloody use anyway. My grandfather always said.' James's eyes squinted up, and Jimmy looked at his feet.

'Och well. Maybe yer right. Yer grandfather was a bluidy fine soldier. Everyone kent that.'

James softened as his nosebleed stopped and said, 'Of course cavalry's all right, in the right situation. Gordon Bruce rode with the cavalry into Kimberley and said they were super chaps, more guts than brains, but damned good soldiers.'

'Aye,' Jimmy Post said, dragging the word out deliciously, leaning back against his bicycle which he had retrieved from the roadside. 'Yon's the life for me. Muckle great horse, a white yin, and a sword.' He leapt on to his bicycle, snatching up a dead willow stick and brandishing it fiercely. 'At the gallop. Company, Char-arge,' he shouted, pedalling downhill, willow stick pointed, one hand clasping the centre pillar of the steering column as if it were reins. He circled round, skidding in the August dust, and pedalled back towards James. 'Clear off, or I'll run ye through.'

He stopped then, by James, laughing, and James said, 'Swords are for officers.'

Jimmy glowered. 'Aye. Yer right there.' He dropped the willow twig and kicked it disconsolately. His vision faded to the edge of his mind.

James said encouragingly, 'But if you join the Maclarens, you'll have a grand kilt, just like mine; officers and other ranks too.'

Jimmy Post considered. He lay the bicycle down and strode around with imaginary bagpipes over his shoulder, picturing the flutter of pleats about his sturdy young knees. There was something in that. The cavalry didn't have the kilt, true enough. The vision galloped gently along the edge of his mind, mane and tail flying, thundering hooves, white coat glistening, and the soldier with steeled eye, and flashing blade, as much a knight as a soldier; it was always the first picture in his mind when the word 'Army' was spoken. He shrugged. What use was a Highlander without a kilt?

'Aye there, Maclaren,' he said. 'Ye've got anither recruit.'

James cheered and slapped his friend's shoulder. Then they both mounted the bicycle, treating it with care because it was the property of His Majesty's Mail and Jimmy should not have been using it for pleasure, and they rode off, James sidesaddle on the bar in front of the puffing, black-haired Jimmy Post.

Where the road turned abruptly at the foot of a steep incline, they skidded sideways around a corner and were met by a furious horn blasting and a green flash as they missed Ian Maclaren's Crossley by inches. It screeched to a halt, and the driver's door flung open, and Johnny leapt down into the road, waving his arms and shouting.

'What in hell do you think you're doing, you little idiots . . . James.' Johnny went pale, a picture of himself explaining the flattened wreckage of Postie's bicycle and youngest son to Colonel Maclaren winging across his mind.

'Terribly sorry, sir,' James said, preparing for a thrashing from the infuriated John Bruce who, unlike his brother Tenny, really did terrify him. But then he and Robert Bruce saw each other in the same instant and Robert vaulted out of the back seat of the Crossley and was down in the road greeting James and Jimmy Post with enthusiastic punches and scufflings.

'Oh, to hell,' Johnny said suddenly, dusting his driving gloves one against the other.

A few minutes later, they were again on their way, Robert

Bruce squeezed in beside Mary, with the happy addition of James Maclaren beside him. In the road, Jimmy Post stood, wistfully lonely, watching the big car drive away.

4

Tenny Maclaren first saw Rebecca Galloway that evening at dinner. He had missed lunch because he had been in a one-handed way helping Ewan Grant sweep his chimney on his wedding morning. The couple had been given tenancy of a small croft that had lain empty on the estate for three years, and when Ewan lit the first preparatory fire on the morning of his wedding, he had discovered the flue blocked with birds' nests. He went to the Maclaren coalsheds to borrow the chimney brushes, where he had met Tenny, his broken arm in a sling and an expression of morose annoyance on his face. Ewan's frantic desperation, dressed there in his wedding suit and about to go off and do the dirtiest job imaginable, had won Tenny's heart.

'Look lad,' Tenny had said, 'I'll give you a hand as best as I can, and clean up the soot. I'm sorry I can't do the whole thing, but –' he shrugged his one good shoulder. Ewan grinned thankfully, and the two set off with the brushes in Tenny's Morgan three-wheeler, with Ewan driving haphazardly. Half an hour later, the chimney clean and a new coal fire flickering in anticipation of the wedding party, Ewan set off to the church in Beauly, full of gratitude and in the motor car of the heir to the Maclaren fortunes.

'Aye, sir,' he said, his young face warm with affection. 'Yer no' bad. I'll no' forget, sir. Never.'

'My pleasure, Ewan,' Tenny said grinning, a blackened sooty

grin, then he laughed and bent his voice into an imitation of Ewan's own and said, 'There's nae luck like meeting a sweep on yer weddin' morn, lad.' He laughed again and then walked off slowly for home, tall and handsome in his work trousers and open-necked shirt, his bright hair dusted to grey with soot and the chimney brushes over his shoulder. Just before he reached the gates of Culbrech House, the Crossley with his young brother and two other related young men roared by. Only Rebecca Galloway turned, her eyes taken by the oddly arresting sight of a man with the walk of a gentleman and a face black with coal soot. Then she turned back to Johnny Bruce. The sweeping of chimneys was no affair of hers.

At dinner Tenny was seated beside Rebecca and she had no recollection of ever having seen him before. But he had seen her, and one fleeting glance was enough to raise a new uneasiness when she entered the dining-room on the arm of Johnny Bruce.

Tenny grew more uneasy throughout dinner. He was increasingly aware of the plentiful attractions of the young woman beside him who was dressed in oyster silk, with her auburn hair piled high on her head, revealing a long sweep of neck with just a pale red feathering of hair remaining at the nape to hide the tie of the brown velvet ribbon about her throat. Tenny was disturbed that no matter what well-thought-out comment or discreet witticism he passed her way, her response was distinctly aloof and distant. He was convinced that her eyes were on Johnny Bruce the entire evening.

Actually, he was far from the truth on both counts. Rebecca's reticence was in large part due to the fact that she was overawed by her surroundings. Nothing Naomi had said, and nothing in the gracious femininity of Naomi's London dining-room, had quite prepared her for the baronial splendour of the banqueting hall of Culbrech House. Beneath the blackened roof-timbers twenty-five strangers, in the white gowns and brilliant tartans of Highland formality, mingled and talked in accents of Scottish gentility. Magnificent and vaguely antique, they were as far removed from London as they were, in truth, from the Scotland outside the door.

Rebecca felt overwhelmed by history and splendour. It was impossible to conceive that any of these people had real lives in the twentieth century. Tenny in his regimental finery was so clearly one of them that she hardly dared address him. Nor was she paying any attention to Johnny Bruce across the white linen and glistening silver and crystal. Two places away sat his sister Susan, her blonde hair glowing softly in the candlelight, her face animated with flirtatious conversation. Rebecca was more than a bit apprehensive at the prospect of sharing a room with her. Naomi was an absolute fool, she thought, stabbing her smoked salmon with the small two-pronged fork, to imagine such a young woman could possibly have failed to win Tenny Maclaren's heart.

She glanced up and down the table. Everyone was in animated conversation with their partners. Emma Maclaren sat, chin in hand, her eyes on those of Torquil Farquhar at her side and her dinner virtually untouched. Only that odd, plain girl Philippa was silent as she moodily watched her sister and her sister's beau.

'I do hope we will meet again after coffee,' Tenny said, half rising awkwardly and taking her hand an instant when Rebecca stood to join the retiring ladies.

'Oh, *do* sit down,' she said, her annoyance edging her voice. 'There's no need to stand. No, I've had a most tiring journey and I wish an early night. Good evening, Mr Maclaren.'

Tenny and Johnny Bruce spent the evening glowering at each other over the port, and later over liqueurs in the drawing-room. Not only Rebecca Galloway, but Susan Bruce and both the Farquhar girls had retired to their bedrooms before the gentlemen's return. The older men were grouped about Willie Bruce, listening to the old general's astute assessment of the worsening war news, and the older women gathered about the ottoman where Grisel Bruce lay propped up on pillows, in the convalescent's place of honour. Maud Bruce beside her wordlessly worked her needlepoint and said nothing; after ten miscarriages there was little left to say.

Victoria Maclaren sent young Robert Bruce and James off to their beds. Emma Maclaren and Torquil Farquhar, the latter with a newly grown drooping brown moustache, had retreated to a corner of the drawing-room behind a half-closed velvet drapery where they talked on the very edge of respectable visibility, as private as they ever would be until they were wed.

Philippa Maclaren, stark in unflattering dead white, sat beside white-haired old Jean and ignored her endless prattle. She watched the two lovers with strangely hungry eyes.

Tenny looked at Johnny, and Johnny looked at Tenny. The

evening had developed into a frantic bore. Tenny jerked his chin up in a beckoning gesture and walked out of the door, as if making his way to the water-closet. Once out in the hallway he waited until Johnny Bruce joined him. The hall was still and cold, away from the fires of dining-room and library and drawing-room. Even in August, the nights were cool. The two young men looked at each other with suspicion.

Suddenly Tenny grinned, and he assumed for a moment his dead grandfather's voice, 'Damned pretty little filly, wot?'

'You did all right, getting her seated next to you,' Johnny said accusingly. 'Thought you'd ruddy well be engaged by now. What say, the inimitable Lord Tennyson lost his touch?'

Tenny glowered a moment but then his grin returned and he said, 'Come on. Admit. She rather gave us both the slip.'

Johnny kicked at the foot-deep white baseboard of the hallway, with his silver buckled shoe. Grudgingly he said, 'I suppose she rather did. No doubt has some strapping great fiancé in the Irish Guards or something. Naomi will have fixed her up with something splendid; hardly fling her away on a couple of wild Highlanders.' His brow furrowed and then he looked up suddenly, a thought having occurred. 'I say, they'd not still be at that wedding party down at the croft?'

'Damn right they will. They won't finish till Tuesday morning. And it won't be coffee and liqueurs down there,' Tenny said sourly.

'What say?'

'Us. Oh never. We'd never get away. Mother would have a fit.'

'Whyever? The ladies all vanished soon enough,' he added accusingly.

'Well, of course. But they were tired. Travelling and all.'

'So, I'm tired too,' Johnny said. 'Oh dear, the vapours. I shall swoon.' He closed his eyes, one hand raised dramatically, and collapsed comfortably against Tenny.

'Get off, you brute,' Tenny said sharply. 'You'll break my other arm.' He dodged away and Johnny nearly sat, unceremoniously in his kilt, on the floor.

He caught himself against the wall and said, 'Come on, they'll never miss us. Bet you a month's pay I can get Sheena Buchanan's knickers by morning.'

'Not worth having, old chap,' Tenny said with an assured smile. 'They're greasy old flannel with a rip in the bum. But you're on. Come on, we'll lift a couple of hams from the kitchens as wedding present, and a bottle or two from the cellar. And if Mother raises the roof, laddie,' he said superiorly to Johnny, 'you'll bloody well stand by me, agreed.'

'Scout's honour,' said Johnny Bruce. He clapped his broad hand on Tenny's good shoulder, and with one backward glance at the drawing-room door they turned and strode off to the stairwell.

In her tower bedroom Rebecca Galloway undressed tiredly, helped by Susan Bruce's maid, her own having been allowed to retire early. Susan chattered happily about the evening, and the picnic the next day, and the ball afterwards, and plied Rebecca with a string of questions about London.

'Oh, it must be too too marvellous to be in London every day,' she sighed enviously, and wrapped her arms about the lace-trimmed pillow on her side of the wide double bed. She rolled over, her nightdress spilling about her like a white frothy pool. 'Oh, you are so dreadfully lucky. I've only been to London once in the last five years. And ever since I left school, I've not even been to Edinburgh more than twice a year. Oh, it's too beastly dreary for words.' She sniffed, cuddling the pillow, and then looked up with an engaging grin. Rebecca eyed her carefully. It was a pity they were going to have to be arch enemies, this Susan Bruce was extraordinarily likeable. She looked the picture of blooming health although Victoria Maclaren had said quite firmly that Susan had been educated at home because of her delicate condition. Surely, that wasn't what Naomi had said at all.

'If it isn't too dreadfully personal,' Rebecca said, 'what is the nature of your illness?' She would not have been so bold had she not been suspicious. And jealous.

'Illness?' Susan looked wide-eyed in amazement. 'I've never been ill in my life. Except childhood things, and even those I took lightest of everyone.' She was rather proud of that and could recall delicious nursery days when she could mock a spotted Harry, or a mumped Johnny Bruce.

'Oh,' Rebecca said slowly, 'I don't understand then. You see, Lady Maclaren said you left school because . . .'

'Oh yes,' Susan shrieked, rolling over, her loosened mass of blonde hair covering her shoulders and breasts. 'Oh, my delicate condition. I simply adore it. I always think it sounds as if I'm pregnant. No, darling, that's The Story. *You* don't have to know The Story. You can know The Truth, because you and I are going to be simply marvellous friends.' She extended her two smooth young hands to Rebecca, smiling happily, and Rebecca, feeling a positive beast, took them with reluctance.

Susan sat up. 'You see,' she said, glancing to the door, 'I didn't leave school. I was dismissed. Expelled. Sent home in shocking shame. Oh, it was positively glorious.'

'Was it?' Rebecca said, recalling Naomi and realizing this was more like the Susan she'd been told of. 'Whatever had you done?'

'I had a lover,' said Susan, her wide light blue eyes on Rebecca's face, calculating the full impact of her words. 'It was too marvellous for words.'

'A lover. A real lover. A man?' Rebecca recoiled. Such things she was accustomed to with Naomi, but Naomi was not her age. Lovers were as remote to her own situation as the grey in Naomi's hair.

'Of course not, silly. Not a *man*. I mean, that would be too positively sinful for words, wouldn't it? Oh no. No. Her name was Lady Moira Sinclair. Isn't it too gorgeous for words?'

'A woman. A woman lover?' Rebecca sat down on a chair beside the bed, trembling with mystery.

'Well. Not a woman. She was in the sixth form actually. Seventeen. She had pale, pale skin and brown hair and she wore it like Elizabeth Barrett Browning, you know, all coiled here, and here,' she pointed over her own ears. 'She would read to me, at nights when the lights were meant to be out. She'd sneak into the dorm and I'd meet her by the lavs and she'd read, with one candle . . .' Susan sighed and whispered, ' "how do I love thee, let me count the ways . . ." Oh, I did love her so.'

'Was that . . . all?' Rebecca said.

'Oh no. Oh, at first it was. But then . . . then I got the most marvellous idea.'

'Too marvellous for words, I imagine,' Rebecca said.

'How did you know?' Susan shrugged, and rolled back on the bed, clutching the pillow to her. 'Well, you see, the sixth-formers were in the next wing, on the top floor, the garret, just as we were, and the two wings of the building were side by side, and the roofs were joined, like that,' she made a sloping V-shape with her hands, 'and one day I realized that Moira's window was just across from mine. She had a room alone, you see, because she was a prefect. So one night, when the moon was shining and I could see, I climbed out of my window and went down our roof and up hers, which wasn't easy, I'll tell you, because it was slates and some of them were loose and would go slipping and crashing down to the gutter between, but anyhow,' she caught her breath, her lips parted with remembered excitement, 'I made it. And I rapped on the window. Of course my poor darling was absolutely scared to death, but then she saw it was me, and she was terrified for me and opened the window and practically dragged me in. And then she was all for taking me to the headmistress for risking my life, but I cried so that she didn't. And I was cold and soaked through so she took my nightgown and gave me one of hers and we climbed into bed a while to warm me up. And then I thought, wouldn't it be wonderful if I was her young man and I came to visit her in the night like that. Well, she was all against it, but I convinced her that it was safe, because it was really, and she agreed.'

'To what?' Rebecca said, uncertainly.

'To being my lover. Only I was the man, you see. We decided Victor; that was my name. And every night when I could get away, I would climb across the roofs. Sometimes I wore my riding britches, so I'd look more like a man. And then we'd greet like we'd not seen each other in years. I was to be like the Highwayman, you know, and one day she'd have to shoot herself in the breast to save my life. Oh, it was too delicious for words. So then we'd kiss, and I'd climb into bed and hold her in my arms, and pretend . . .' she stopped suddenly, her tongue wetting her lips. When next she spoke her voice was flat and low. 'Well then, one day another girl heard us and came bursting in and put the lights on and of course I had no nightgown because I'd been wearing my britches and taken them off to go to bed. And anyhow I shouldn't have been there. Moira just got hysterical and started to scream and was taken away. I don't know what she told them, but I was brought to the headmistress and she used a lot of words I didn't really understand, and I was afraid to ask. Anyhow, Grandmother was sent for, and I was sent home. Grandmother was terribly upset. Only Grandfather wasn't. He thought it very funny and all he'd say was something about heifers with no bull in the field. He just laughed and laughed. I was really rather frantically grateful because I was quite miserable really, with all the fuss.' She stopped suddenly and said, 'Do you think I'm terrible?'

Rebecca thought carefully, and said at last, 'I think,' she paused and Susan held her breath, 'I think you're too, too marvellous for words.'

'Oh Rebecca,' Susan squealed and flung her arms out, and when Rebecca leaned over she enfolded her and kissed both her cheeks. Then she fell back again on the bed and said, softly, 'I never saw Moira for years after that, and then I saw her in the spring, at a house-party in Carrbridge. She was married, and pregnant. She didn't seem to want to talk to me but I got her alone and I asked her, was it too, too wonderful to be in love and married, and do you know, she just cried. She cried and cried, and called me a silly fool. Her husband's rather fat and ugly, but he's got a title too, and too much money for words.' She sighed and clambered into bed. Rebecca slid in beside her and closed her eyes exhaustedly and then remembered Tenny and felt sour.

'Do you know?' Susan said, 'we had no idea what to expect of you? We all thought you were going to be frightfully old and stuffy. Tenny kept calling you the "maiden aunt". Silly old Ten, you rather surprised him no doubt. All of us. There I was expecting a grey-haired, stout old thing, and never knowing you were going to be my most delicious friend ever. You will, won't you?' She clasped Rebecca's arm in the dark.

'Well, of course,' Rebecca said, but her mind was on something else. 'Do you mean that *you* thought I was going to be old?'

'Oh yes. Ever so old.'

'Then you couldn't have been jealous over Tenny.'

'Why should I be jealous over Tenny?' she said, startled.

'But Johnny told me. You were ever so much in love with each other. Only you were a little jealous of him meeting me at Inverness.'

Susan squealed with delight, 'Oh, dear rotten Johnny. He is sly. Don't you see? He was throwing you off Tenny's scent so you'd fall madly in love with him instead. They're terrible, the boys. They always play the most perfectly rotten tricks on one another.' She laughed again, and wrapped her soft arms around the warmth of Rebecca's silk-clad body. 'Me in love with old Ten? It's too ridiculous for words.'

Johnny Bruce, her brother, also had his arms about a wealth of warm female flesh, clad not in silk but cotton calico, and not in so refined a place as an eighteenth-century Maclaren featherbed. He was also well on his way to winning his bet, though he could tell from his first tentative explorations in the dark loft of the haybarn, the music and singing wending up from below, that Sheena Buchanan had been slandered. Her knickers were lawn, not flannel, nor were they greasy, and though at present he could not swear to it, he was quite sure there was not a hole in them anywhere.

'Och away, Mr Bruce, ye know I'm nae that sort a girl.'

'Johnny,' he said, striking another blow for the brotherhood of man. 'Of course you're not.'

'Ye ken I dinna dae it wi' just onybody.'

'Of course not. I'm not just anybody, am I?' he grinned in the darkness, and undid another button at the back of her dress.

'We cannae dae it here,' she whispered. 'Some folk have ears like elephants.'

'You're right there. Where then?'

'Back o' the steading. There's two or three haystooks. Ye gae first, an' I'll awa an join ye.' Johnny was a trace reluctant to remove his hands from their warm sheltering, but he agreed.

'Promise you'll come,' he said, using his best hurt small-boy voice. 'I'll be most terribly distressed if you don't.'

'Och away, ye'll find anither. But I'll come. Just let a wee time pass, so nane kens.'

Johnny nodded, sat up in the hay and made his way to the lighted end of the loft and the open ladder leading down. He strolled round the back of the dancers and made his way inconspicuously to the open doors. A little while later, Sheena, her dress in modest array once more, followed, and a little later still went out of the door. There was none in the room who did not know exactly what was going on, but a small concession to formal morality was necessary, and they made it.

Johnny was lying in the August moonlight, his back against the soft hay. She saw him in the dimness and he opened his arms wide, grinning, and with a small moan of delight she fell headlong on to him, laughing as she did. Johnny rolled over, his mouth on hers, jerking free the side buckles of his kilt.

'Yer a terrible man, John Bruce,' she said.

'That's my lass,' he whispered in reply.

* * *

Inside, the wedding party continued until dawn. Tenny Maclaren danced, one-armed and awkward, with the young women who would one day be his tenants. He kissed the bride, and shook hands with the groom and whirled poor daft Mairi the kitchenmaid around in a one-handed Scottish waltz, she squealing with rapturous delight. Ewan and Fiona Grant stood together under the swaying cruisie lamp and sang 'Ae Fond Kiss', looking into one another's eyes, and Tenny took his turn and danced the Highland Fling, his good arm raised and the other bouncing, a little painfully, on his chest, aware only of the eyes of the women on his narrow hips, graced in swaying Maclaren tartan.

At three in the morning, when Johnny Bruce and Sheena Buchanan were launching into a second round in their haystack, the entire wedding party trooped out of the lantern-lit barn into the grey dawn, and across to the empty croft house and ceremoniously bundled the bridal couple through the door of their married home. The men then, drunk and excited, were all for bundling them into the bed itself. 'They'll no' find it without us,' they insisted. But Tenny intervened and said, leave off, and even with him drunk and dancing and singing amongst them, they obeyed. Ewan smiled gratefully and shut the door.

At four in the morning, when the day was already bright and Sheena Buchanan had scrambled home, dusting down her dress and thinking what to tell her mother, and Johnny Bruce had gone to sleep in the scruffy remnants of evening dress in the haybarn of Ewan Grant's croft, Tenny Maclaren walked home alone. He glanced back once to the silent croft house, where, with the daylight fussing at their windows, Ewan and Fiona were lying awake and silent, astonished at the consummation of their love. Tenny smiled and walked on. He stopped halfway up the drive, at the place where the fall of one beech tree had opened a vista of the tall pink stone house, backed by its big, pine-clad hill, and smiled again. He counted the tower windows up to the one where Rebecca Galloway would be sleeping in innocence. He had never been happier in his life.

5

When Tenny awoke at ten in the morning, with the slim, whisking figure of the upstairs maid, Joan, drawing aside the heavy draperies, that air of wellbeing remained with him, despite the soreness of his arm and a distant soreness of his head as well. 'Oh, surely it's not morning,' he muttered, but contentedly.

'I'm afraid it is, Mister Maclaren. Will you have your tea now, or later?' Joan settled the tray with a heavy clunk on the bedside table. 'Colonel Maclaren requests your company at breakfast in half an hour,' she added, thus making the choice irrelevant.

'I'll have it now, Joan, will you pour it, please,' he half roused himself in the bed, his hair over his bleary eyes, aware of the stale smell of sleep about him. He wondered briefly what servant girls like Joan thought, seeing people at their worst, doing unpleasant tasks for them like emptying commodes in the old days. Even today, where some were concerned. Old Aunt Jean always insisted on her chamberpot, despite the modern convenience down the corridor, as though it was a luxury reminiiscent of a richer era.

Joan poured his tea and smiled, a reserved smile. She had a thin young face with pale browny skin and hair of the same brown. Peelie-walie, Sandy Gibson called her. Still Tenny suspected he'd been her lover. Sandy had had lovers since he was thirteen, leaving Tenny far behind, and in considerable awe. He watched the neat bend of spine beneath the black cloth of Joan's dress as she bent away, lifting a fallen comforter on to the bedfoot. Like a humpy little snake, it would feel peculiar and interesting under the bare skin. He wondered, just for a moment, what she would be like.

'Will there be anything else, sir?'

'No,' he smiled privately, 'thank you.' He dismissed the maid, drank his tea propped one-handedly against the pillow and then rose, not waiting for his manservant to put in an appearance but dressing hurriedly, so as to meet his father.

'Ah, Tenny,' Sir Ian looked up from the newspaper beside his plate, glanced down again through his half-glasses, and then looked up again. 'I trust you slept well,' he said with irony.

'Oh, splendidly . . .' Tenny thought a moment, remembering the evening, and his failure to reappear at the party. 'I . . .'

'Went to bed early. So I gather. Shall we leave it at that?'

'Hmm, ra*ther*,' said Tenny, grinning. His father was really rather all right. 'Mother wasn't upset?'

'She wasn't pleased. Still, since the fillies had all bolted she turned a blind eye. A word of apology to Gordon and Grisel would not be amiss.' He took another bite of grilled kidney as Tenny cruised hungrily along the sideboard, lifting the lid off one tureen after another and from most of them spooning out a portion. Eggs, bacon, black pudding, kidney, lamb chops, fruit compote, porage; breakfast was in Tenny's view always the best bargain of the day.

'Hope you're not going hungry,' his father grunted, observing his son settling down luxuriantly before a vast plate.

'Always seconds if I am,' Tenny said seriously.

'How's the arm?'

'All right for a broken arm. Not much bother really.'

'Not much use, either, I wager. Damnable stupid thing, Ten.'

'Hmm. I know.'

'You know the battalion's likely to be moving out within the week?'

Tenny looked up, dropping his fork to his plate, quickly wiping egg from his drooping moustache. 'Has it come?'

'Not yet,' Ian returned, still eating, looking again at the paper. 'But I'm afraid there's no longer much doubt it will do. I haven't said as much to your mother, and I must confess I've been playing the angel's advocate to old Gordon, trying to keep this damnable weekend afloat if nothing else. But the writing is on the wall.' He tapped the interior page of the *Inverness Courier* which carried headlines of, by its terms, quite extraordinary magnitude, even though sandwiched between notices of local church and business affairs and the usual reports of last week's weather. 'The point is, m'boy, that I'll wager Gordon and the regiment will be in France by September.'

'And me,' said Tenny, offendedly.

'And you nothing. You'll be in Beauly patching the Territorials together to mind the fort. You've chosen yourself a spectacularly useful time to be an invalid.'

Tenny's mouth fell open. 'You don't mean – surely – I mean it's nothing.'

'Can you load your revolver?'

'No, but in a week or two.'

'A week or two may well be rather late. Oh well, your mother will be pleased, anyway.'

'Bloody damnation,' Tenny said, staring at his father in outrage.

'Mind your language,' Ian Maclaren said without lifting his eyes from his paper. 'One of the ladies might hear.'

Tenny fumed, silently, prodding his breakfast angrily. He poured coffee, drank it too quickly and burned his mouth, muffling another curse.

'Own fault,' said Ian smugly, apropos of everything.

'It wasn't,' Tenny said, having quite convinced himself of his own story regarding the arm. 'It's all so beastly unfair. I've been looking forward to this war all year and afraid it would all blow over, and now I'm going to miss it. Damn John Bruce will be beastly impossible, covering himself in glory before I ever see action.'

Ian leaned back and sighed softly. 'All over by Christmas?' he said.

'Well,' Tenny said, 'you're not expecting any more than that from the Hun, are you?'

'Tenny,' Ian said. He removed his glasses and leaned back in his chair and rubbed his eyes. Ian looked to his son older and more tired than he'd ever seen him. 'I don't know. I just don't know. Johnny's still at Sandhurst so if it's as soon done with as that, he'll not see action either.'

'Of course he will. They'll send them down early, I know they will. Better to have experience than studies any day. There's always a need for trained officers, and besides, I know Johnny. He'll go off and turn up as a private soldier if they don't let him in at the start. So would I, in his place.'

'Be damn stupid, for either of you.'

'But, Father. A real war. Not just minding the store in India or Ireland. Whenever might there be another?'

'Another what?' said Victoria Maclaren suspiciously, entering the dining-room trailed by her two daughters, Emma and Philippa, the two Farquhar girls, Diana and Elizabeth, and behind them Susan Bruce and Rebecca, Susan's arm through her guest's possessively.

'Another plate of haddock,' Ian said at once. 'Come in, my dear, join us, my, my, you look like Reverend Mother and the holy sisters.'

The girls giggled a little, except for Philippa who sniffed. Philippa was the only member of the family who took her church-going seriously, as indeed she took everything, and she was fiercely presbyterian, suspicious of the slightest trace of the Scarlet Woman in thought, word, or deed.

She seated herself beside Tenny, and took a single roll from a large covered bread warmer, broke it in half, and munched disconsolately. When she looked about the room her eyes flicked resentfully over the pretty face of her older sister. Philippa looked exactly like her father. Indeed, exactly like Tenny. With her hair pulled back flat, and a moustache, they would have had the same face. She had the same long, strong narrow nose, the same long upper lip and wide, slightly thin-lipped mouth. If she had smiled, it would have been as engaging a smile as his, for like her brother she had white, perfect teeth. But she, conscious of the wideness of her mouth, kept it prim. Her cheeks were flat, with a freckly reddish tinge, and her intelligent eyes, with pale lashes, were the same startling blue. Like Tenny's her eyebrows were white, and the complete absence of colour made her face all the more interesting.

Still, whereas Tenny's face was stunningly handsome, strong and virile, Philippa's was mannish and hard, unrelieved by any sense of humour, and in marked contrast to her extraordinary mane of red-golden hair which even now, bound up in a long, workaday braid, caught the sun that flooded through the four tall dining-room windows. She felt it was primarily a nuisance, a weight that custom demanded be balanced on her strong neck.

That a man might find it erotic had never occurred to her and would only have frightened her.

Men were a mystery to Philippa Maclaren, beginning, first and foremost, with her father, who had come into her earliest life with a fanfare of excitement at the close of the Boer War. He had filled her peaceful, woman-dominated childhood with new and overpowering sights and sounds and smells. Even today, loud male voices worried her and the smell of tobacco smoke made her as uneasy as the sight of a snake.

'Fasting?' said Tenny.

'We'll all stuff ourselves like pigs at the picnic,' she said sharply. 'There's no point in starting already.' She glanced with almost involuntary disdain at his laden plate.

'All right, old girl,' Albert said from across the table, where he had settled beside his sister Emma, 'I'll eat enough for both of us, so you needn't worry.'

'I shan't,' said Philippa, so sourly that Tenny reached to pat her offended arm but then Rebecca Galloway, seating herself on his other side, demanded sweetly, with a smile and a flutter of long dark eyelashes, could he possibly pass the butter, and he forgot everything else in the world. Carefully he collected the silver dish and handed it to her, as if it contained not butter, but his heart.

'I'm terribly sorry I missed you after dinner,' she said, spreading one small piece of toast. 'I was so dreadfully tired.'

'Of course, of course. I trust you'll be fit for the picnic . . .' he said, hope rising.

'Oh, I'd not miss it for the world,' Rebecca said, smiling shyly. 'I simply *love* picnics. I've loved them all my life.'

Rebecca certainly loved that one, anyhow, and Emma Maclaren loved it even more. So much so that, in later years and harder times, she would, lying alone at night, conjure the picture of it in her mind for comfort. She would begin first with the broad grassy field that the sheep had nibbled down to a velvety stubble, and that had later been swept and raked clean with the hayrakes. It sloped away, interrupted here and there by mossy rock outcrops, to the clear clean river. In later years the river alone was a soul-filling vision; clean water, Highland water, water that did not smell or swirl with mud, or worse.

Then she would imagine the trees, dark-branched tall Scots

pines, and scattered amongst them, light birches with their constant rain of dancing small pale leaves. There had been a rowan too, she would recall, dotted with circles of berries, an innocent bright red. Most of all she would recall those great pines, still and whole, blowing gently above the three long trestle-tables, white-cloth-covered, and dappled with summer sun. It was that rare thing in the North, a perfect summer day, when the clearness of the air and the brilliance of the sun outshone more common summers in more gentle lands.

The air was fresh enough that the food, platter after platter of smoked meats and fishes, poultry, chilled soups set in trays of last winter's ice, chopped this morning from the dark underground icestore, bowls of raspberries and early plums, bottles of claret, and a cask of ale, all stood outside, without fear of spoilage.

The ladies had dressed in frothy white almost without exception. Only Philippa Maclaren had ignored both romance and climate and appeared in a tweed skirt, barely calf-length and revealing solid walking boots, and a pin-tucked white blouse. She sat now on a rock by the river, watching Gordon Bruce and Ian Maclaren, thigh-deep in water, casting their fishing-lines over the deep river pool below the picnic site. Her legs were crossed mannishly and her face, beneath her sturdy felt hat, was a mirror of discontent. Just occasionally, when all other eyes were occupied, she let her own stray to that far rowan tree, fifty yards upstream, where Emma Maclaren and Torquil Farquhar sat talking.

Torquil was seated on a convenient rock, his knees apart, kilt draped between them, and his arms extended, hands folded thoughtfully, between his knees. His head was down as he listened to Emma. Her back was against the richly fruited tree that was as young and lovely as herself. Her knees were drawn up and her arms clasped about them. Torquil raised his head at something she said and laughed so softly that Philippa, still watching, could not hear the sound. He reached gently, took Emma's hand, and with a quick glance around, kissed it, and let it go. Philippa watched hungrily and then, unable to help herself, stood and began walking towards the rowan tree.

Albert Maclaren lowered his cricket bat while Philippa walked right through their game without a comment. Then he signalled again to the bowler, young Robert Bruce. Robert was glad of Albert's company; Albert had spent the morning leading the two youngsters, Robert Bruce and James Maclaren, through successive games of badminton, rugby, soccer, football, and now cricket and had promised to take them trout fishing (a discreet distance from where Gordon and Ian carried on the serious business with the salmon) in the afternoon. Albert had cheerfully filled for Robert the gap left by the unexpected defection of Tenny. For Robert Bruce's erstwhile hero reclined soppily on the green sward (Robert knew for such occasions grass became sward) and read aloud from one of his perennial poetry books to, of all people, Rebecca Galloway.

For her part in the treachery of Tenny, Robert had decided that Rebecca was going to pay a heavy price in ruthless teasing, not only all the way back on the London train, but for days, perhaps weeks afterwards, at home. Still Albert had been a fair substitute, and if not so glamorous, at least less likely to run off with some simpering fluff of femininity. Robert warmed up his bowling arm and let fly, but Albert, preoccupied as often with food, a pilfered chickenleg in this case, barely had time to lift his bat with his free hand before the ball went winging by. Robert sighed; he was beginning to think these Maclarens weren't half the men he had thought they were.

When General Willie Bruce arrived, in an open carriage in the old style with Maud Bruce, china pale in ecru lace, by his side, all those on the picnic ground came to unconscious attention. Even the two gentlemen in the salmon river turned briefly to face the arrival.

MacLeod, the butler, hastened to signal an underling to provide a wicker chair in the right spot of shade, between the tables and the river, and other chairs were quickly drawn about it. There was an unspoken rule at Maclaren picnics that the over-fifties were entitled to dry posteriors.

'Damned nonsense,' Willie grumbled, settling his solid bulk into the provided chair. 'Mak' a man feel he'd ae foot in the grave, soon enough. I'm nae deid yet, ye ken.' He dropped his silver-handled cane beside his chair and glowered at the women fussing about. Then he caught sight of the dark, slender figure of Robert Bruce, now whittling determinedly at a dried heather root.

He nodded to the boy, and called, 'Awa' here, laddie, I'll show ye something grand.' Robert came, shy of the white-haired man in his massive kilt, bright blue eyes sharp beneath overhanging white brows. He handed the root and the penknife to Willie Bruce. Willie turned it over and over and then, finding the right angle, said, 'Here now, lad, if ye'll tak awa' that wee bittie there, and that bittie, there, ye can mak' a wildcat o' it, are ye seeing now?'

Robert was warmed by the soft accent that was more like the servants' voices than anyone so terrifying as a general and came closer, leaning against the big, tweed-sleeved arm, and looked to where Willie pointed with the knifeblade.

'Yes. Yes, I do. There's the eyes, and that big knob will make the nose.'

'Aye, an' the wee flat ears there, wi' tufts o' hair. A Maclaren wildcat for ye. Awa' and get to work and mind ye show me when you're through.'

The boy left happily, but as he walked away, Willie called him back, 'Robert.'

'Sir?'

'How's your mother?'

'Very well, sir,' Robert stood waiting politely, his hands fingering the root and the knife.

There was a long pause and then Willie said slowly, 'I'm glad to hear that. And yerself lad,' Willie looked him over. 'Yer a big lad nou. Tell me nou, are ye after being a sodger?'

'Now sir?'

'Nae, lad. When yer grown.'

'Of course, sir. Mother doesn't know. But I shall join the Maclarens and be like Tenny. And Albert,' he added a little sourly, not wishing to give Tenny the benefit of too much hero-worship just now. 'Only I shall be a general, sir. Or at least a colonel, like Sir Ian, and Uncle Gordon.'

'Aye then, it's command yer after,' Willie said, his shrewd Highland eyes narrowing as he smiled.

'Of course,' Robert Bruce said. His thin dark oriental face was calm with assurance. 'I shall command the Maclarens, sir, just like you.'

Willie smiled again, a little sadly, and said eventually, dismissing the boy, 'Aye lad, ye dae that then.'

Robert ran off, to work on his wildcat, and Willie said, under his breath, 'Aye, perhaps you will, laddie, but ye've a gey hard gait tae travel, afore ye do.'

* * *

Old Willie's eyes now wandered across the vast scattered brood in their summer finery, lighting on his granddaughter and grandson, Susan and Harry, strolling arm in arm as if they were lovers. He smiled. It was only with Susan that Harry ever dropped that cold reserve of his and became the kind, gentle person that Willie was convinced was locked in the core of the boy. Willie's head nodded in the warm, river-fly-speckled air and he drifted into sleep.

It was Johnny Bruce shouting from the riverbank who woke him. 'I say, everyone, come along. Record it all for posterity, and all.'

'Bloody Johnny and his bloody camera,' Tenny whispered, and then covered his lips with two fingers, 'I am most dreadfully sorry,' he said at once to Rebecca Galloway. 'Quite unforgivable of me.'

'Never mind,' she smiled sweetly, 'Naomi says things like that *all* the time. And *she* doesn't apologize ever,' she added with another smile.

Tenny looked disturbed. 'I'm not sure what sort of influence our Naomi is for a young lady.'

'Dreadful, no doubt,' Rebecca said at once, 'except that she's the dearest soul in my whole world and I love her to distraction. Besides,' she added, dropping her eyes, 'she *did* rather arrange for us to meet.'

'In that case I'll forgive her if she swears like a trooper,' Tenny said, with feeling. He stood, and bent his good arm down to help Rebecca Galloway to her feet.

Emma Maclaren, on her grassy bank beneath the rowan tree, sighed softly, and she also then accepted a gentleman's hand and got to her feet, lightly brushing her moss-strewn skirt. Johnny would not be silenced, she knew, until he had recorded everyone with his camera. A photograph had long been as much a part of the traditional Bank Holiday as the smoked salmon and champagne. But until last year it had been done neatly and painlessly in front of Culbrech House, with the servants making a neat background to the scene, by Mr Fraser from Station Square in Inverness, who arrived, gathered everybody, and descended twice beneath his black tent, emerging each time to rearrange the company, and then finally clicked the shutter definitively open and shut on the August day.

But Johnny was intrigued by photography as he was by all

devices – motor cars, aeroplanes, electricity generators, telephones – and he was fatally driven to possess a camera of his own. Since then, all family gatherings had ground to the same frustrating halt, as Johnny, in poor imitation of Mr Fraser of Inverness, fussed and bothered, arranged and rearranged, while over-fed adults yawned and children squirmed, until finally he managed to record both Maclarens and Bruces frozen in eternal boredom.

This time would be no different. Emma stepped daintily and resignedly down the uneven riverbank to where the family was clustered together, in the company of all attendant friends, before the three laden tables. Her few idyllic moments alone with Torquil were lost already, anyhow, since Philippa with the bald insensitivity of the loveless had descended upon them, talking quite uncharacteristically loudly and foolishly, shifting from topic to topic, Aunt Jean's tarot cards, the cut of Miss Galloway's dress, the performance of a particular riding horse, and effectively dividing the two young people with a wall of irrelevant words.

Emma sighed again while Philippa trotted along at her side and Torquil trailed behind, a little shyly. She had so little time with him, surely her silly little sister could see to leave them be. She felt guilty in her heart then, and fought her resentment with a rush of kindness for Philippa, despite her thoughtlessness. Even when Philippa bossily rearranged them for the photograph so that Emma ended up beside her mother, and Torquil was partnered by Philippa who stood stiff and victorious, Emma suppressed her irritation with some difficulty.

Johnny clambered around behind them so that the sun was at his back, and then, looking out over the river, asked that Ian and Gordon move their fishing upstream so that they might be distantly included. They obliged, impatiently, and Johnny, under the black cloth, fiddled with the focus, then emerged to fuss and rearrange the group.

'Oh, get on,' Tenny shouted, fed up.

'Wake up, Willie,' Maud whispered, nudging him in his wicker chair in the centre of the scene.

'Damn,' said Johnny.

'Oh, what is it now?' Tenny fumed.

'That silly wire.' They turned, all of them, looking across the river to where old Frankie Gibson's string of new sheep-fencing continued on its opposite bank.

'Never mind it,' Albert said. 'It's to keep the sheep clear. Don't want them piddling in the champagne, what?'

'I know, I know. Only it's in the picture, any way I try it.'

'Turn round and take it the other way,' Tenny said, eager for any solution.

'Can't,' Johnny said with the expert's haughty disdain. 'Shooting into the sun the other way. Besides, he's strung beastly wire all along the edge of the wood there anyhow. It's all round us.'

Tenny looked around. Johnny was right, barbed wire fenced them in like sheep. The fence looked unnatural on the green land. He shrugged, annoyed in a deeper way than before, and said quite harshly, 'You'll just have to have it in then.'

'Looks like a washing-line,' Johnny said, muffled beneath his cloth. 'Ought to hang teacloths on it.'

'Take your picture or I'll damned well hang you on it,' Ian suddenly shouted from the river, 'and then go away and let us fish in peace.' He turned to look over his shoulder then, glowering, and Johnny clicked the shutter. Afterwards, it was the only way anyone could tell him apart from Gordon Bruce in that picture; they were so very alike, two slightly fuzzy figures in waders, thigh-deep in glistening water with a parapet of barbed wire behind.

After the photograph, they all gathered at the long tables and sat down to the lunch that Albert had been sampling since shortly after breakfast. Ian said grace, with gruff military solemnity, and Robert Bruce poked James and giggled, causing a sharp glance from the man who was, to his considerable unease, father to them both.

Tenny rose to seat his mother at the opposite end of the table, and turned round to discover that his shameless cousin, Johnny Bruce, had without a word of apology usurped his place at the side of Rebecca Galloway. His evident annoyance was totally ignored by Johnny, noticed with a flattered blush by Rebecca and, as he took his seat beside her, noticed with considerably more concern by Victoria Maclaren. She looked down the table, eyeing the girl carefully, then, with a slight catch at the beginning of the sentence, said, 'Miss Galloway is quite charming, Tenny.'

'Oh Mother, isn't she splendid,' he said at once, with ready delight.

The Maclarens had begun their first magnum of champagne when Jimmy Fraser, in response to his father's shout from the telegraph key in the small, shabby post office in Beauly, had rolled out his black bicycle and set out on the road to the west.

When the third magnum was empty and MacLeod the butler was carefully turning yet a fourth around in studied hands, gently easing the cork free with a silent wisp of blue vapour, Victoria Maclaren called her husband aside. She had seen him eyeing his waders and fishing tackle, and knew that if she was to speak with him before evening, it must be now. By evening the young people would be together again, gathered around the piano in the drawing-room, or down in the erstwhile billiards room with Johnny Bruce's phonograph filling the once sanctified air with ragtime. There were too many moments in such an evening for a young couple to be together. No, it must be now.

'Can it not wait, my dear?' Ian said patiently, but glancing with badly concealed eagerness at the river and the sky. Perfect weather.

'No, I'm afraid it cannot. But I will be brief. What do you think of Miss Galloway?'

Ian looked blank. Hardly seemed a question of such import, enough to interrupt a man's fishing. 'Perfectly charming,' he said quickly. 'Is that all?'

'Tenny certainly thinks so.'

'So I would imagine. Boy's got good taste. With you in a minute, Gordon,' he called as Gordon waded out, and upstream.

'Ian, that's hardly the point,' Victoria said, with such meaning that Ian looked at her carefully, noticing the appearance of the little pucker-lines around her small mouth that came when she was tense or concerned.

'What point?' he said then.

'Who *is* she?' Victoria said, glancing involuntarily to the young people, now engaged in erecting their badminton net on the flat ground between the tables and the little wood of bright birch. 'I mean, we have absolutely no idea. She just turns up here.'

'Come, come,' Ian said quickly, 'Naomi did say.'

'Of course she *said*. But that's all she said. No idea who the girl is. You'll recall we didn't even know her age, we weren't expecting a *young* person at all. Certainly not such a . . . socially accomplished young person.' Victoria subtly managed to make the last sound more criticism than compliment.

'Well,' Ian said, trying to bluff it out, 'we got rather a bonus. Better than another Aunt Jean, up to the knees in spirits and tealeaves.' He laughed loudly. Victoria's small, lightly powdered face remained calm, and displeased. Ian sighed. She wasn't exactly prim, no, indeed in her youth she had been vivacious to the point of flirtatious, and their intimate life had been rich and satisfying. It was only her sense of duty. Something about marrying into the family, rather than being born in it, always made a woman so much more concerned about those things.

'That is all very well,' she said at last, 'but it does not change the fact that Tenny is rapidly becoming smitten with a young lady who, for all her prettiness, has nothing to recommend her in the way of family, or . . .'

'For Dear's sake, Victoria,' Ian suddenly exploded into a gruff whisper, 'you are rather making assumptions. She could be a duchess for all you know.'

'If,' said Victoria, 'she was a duchess,' she paused again, 'you can be quite certain that Naomi would have told us. Naomi has been utterly silent about the girl's background. Silence is not a good recommendation, I fear.'

'Bother,' Ian growled. 'Naomi doesn't care fiddlesticks about such things. She'd never think one way or another.'

'Above it all, is she?' Victoria said airily. As she had grown older she had indulged, just rarely, in a touch of a waspish tongue.

'Yes,' Ian said angrily, and started to stalk away.

But Victoria caught his arm and lowered her head and said, 'No. That was unkind. I am sorry, truly. Please,' she looked up with that appealing softening of the blue eyes that had won him the day he met her. 'Please, I don't want anything to spoil this perfect day. The whole family together, why, it's not happened for years, quite so many of us, and quite so lovely a day.'

Ian was surprised to see her lashes suddenly wet, and he bent and made an embarrassed, middle-aged cheek-brushing attempt at a kiss, rubbing his moustached upper lip as he turned away, like an overgrown schoolboy.

'There'll be others, now,' he said, 'now that I'm retired. More time and all.' Still muttering he stumped off to the river and the salmon, waiting, restless in their shining pools.

Jimmy Fraser had reached the door of Culbrech House when Harry Bruce, standing alone, smoking his pipe at the edge of the picnic ground, saw Philippa turn away. He had been watching the two older men fishing, casting their lines, letting the flies trail a moment, then recasting, and, in another sense, had watched Philippa doing the same, all day. This time, she did not recast. Something Torquil had said, or Emma, or some look that had passed between them, had told her that whatever windows were in the sky, her lure would remain untaken. She walked, first slowly to the thicker wood of pine and larch beyond the picnic ground, and then, when sure she was not watched, more quickly, until she broke into a stumbling run.

He found her, alone, huddled like a child between two vast black, moss-wet trunks, her arms about her bent knees, her cheek against them, bright tears silently trailing down her strong unique face.

'Philippa?'

'Oh,' she looked up, startled and embarrassed. When she saw it was Harry, she was relieved. It was no one important. No one like Torquil. 'Go away,' she said irritated, turning her face aside.

He did not go, but sat on the damp mossy ground beside her, glad at the moment of the warm dry folds of his kilt. Usually a nuisance in hot weather, but it had its uses. He drew his tobacco pouch from his sporran (sporrans were handy, he had to admit) and filled his pipe, thinking about the regiment. He smiled to himself.

Philippa looked up puzzled and then angry. 'Go away,' she said fiercely, 'I don't need you to laugh at me.'

'Oh no,' he said quickly, 'not at you. Thinking about Uncle Gordon in his kilt in South Africa. Hot and sticky, and making excuses for it all the way. You know, if you ask him now, he'll give you a hundred reasons why it's the best costume for any possible climate.' He grinned. 'I recall, however, when he rode into Kimberley with the cavalry he settled for a pair of cavalry trews. Decided not to hold his manhood cheap, I gather.' He laughed again and Philippa grinned in spite of herself. Harry's cool eyes gentled and for once his smile lacked its sardonic twist. He was so like a brother to her sometimes; he could say the most outrageous things.

He leant forward and said, 'I'm sorry.'

She understood at once. He had not asked her what was wrong. She was glad of that. He knew, he always knew, he knew her so well.

Then Harry took her two hands and said, 'Damn, Philippa, he's not worth your tears. He's a good enough bloke and just right for Em, I reckon, but . . .' She turned away, crying again. 'Don't you see,' he went on gently, 'he's not enough for you. You'd be bored in weeks. You've so much intelligence, so much spirit . . .'

But she only buried her head in her arms, hiding from him, and reluctantly he rose and went away.

As he came out once again to the picnic clearing, he saw Jimmy Fraser, the postman's son, riding down the rough track from where the cars and carriages were parked, on his official bicycle. He looked so out of place among the light afternoon games of the gentry that Harry suppressed the urge to shoo him away for disturbing the artistic balance of the day. But it must be post-office business; otherwise he'd never intrude on James Maclaren in such a situation, nor would he have got past the chauffeurs and grooms above. No doubt they'd sent him on from the Big House. Harry walked more quickly towards the gathered company, but the black bicycle and its determined young rider spun by, intruding into the very heart of the gracious circle.

'Colonel Bruce,' Jimmy called, his voice yet high and boyish. Old Willie looked up dozily, hearing part of his name and then, realizing that messages of import came to younger ears these days, drifted as dozily off to sleep.

A moment, Gordon Bruce thought. Just a moment. He could see the fish. It was there, the sun glinting off its silver back, but inches below the golden surface of the water.

'Colonel Bruce,' the boy was at the water's edge. No. Silence.

Could not speak. Dear God, a moment, a moment more.

'Telegram for ye, sir,' the boy said. Damn. Never understood fishing, these townsfolk. The Gibson lads would never have interrupted. He jerked his head back a trace, hoping the boy would take the message. Ian Maclaren turned, facing him, having the sense not to speak.

'It cannae wait, sir,' the boy shouted over the rushing water. Damn. The fish struck, unreeling line, spinning, downriver, running away, beautiful, running, running. He played it joyously, a perfect balance, as if he had hooked the essence of that perfect summer, running free and bright down the Glass.

''Tis here, sir,' the voice, shocking loud, was at his ear. The lad stood beside him, waving the brown envelope, the water flowing about his hips. 'I must wait an answer,' he said, urgently. Gordon turned, his attention broken, the line snagged, pulled, broke. The fish vanished from his hands, leaving only its memory and the broken line floating on water.

Gordon handed his rod to the eager hands of the awestruck postman's son. Jimmy fondled its shining reel as Gordon slit open the envelope with a penknife from his pocket. He knew exactly what it would be and yet, as he read it, it jerked at his heart. He nodded his head once, twice, looked fleetingly at the river and then silently beckoned Ian Maclaren. Ian waded through the river, his face dark, took the buff paper in his hand and read the single word,

'MOBILIZE.'

6

On the thirteenth of August, 1914, the First Battalion Maclaren Highlanders landed in France. They were not by any means alone. Even as they were docking, a battalion of Coldstream Guards were marching off the quay in the growing heat of the morning. And as they themselves disembarked into the milling confusion of Le Havre, the *Cawdor Castle* was tying up, her load of Grenadiers waving and shouting to the crowds of women, children and, significantly, old men who cheered them in French. The Maclarens too had cheered and sung their way into harbour, after the smooth night crossing on a silken Channel, the men lying out on deck under the stars, so close together that their officers had to pick their way through rows of bodies as they went about their duties.

On the quayside their NCOs gathered them into a semblance of order and checked their kit. The First Battalion waited patiently while the officers' horses and the transport mules were carefully unloaded. The quay smelt of livestock and echoed with the thud of shod hoofs on wood and stone.

To Private Donnie Cameron, the Maclarens' newest recruit, the farmyard sounds were painful as they sharply recalled home. Donnie Cameron was part of the British Expeditionary Force of 1914, that small, beautifully honed professional army whose soldiers would one day, through the romanticization of a remark fancifully attributed to the Kaiser himself, proudly call themselves the Old Contemptibles. But Donnie's little corner of history, like most history, was scarcely clear at the time. During the landing at Le Havre, he felt two things: strangeness, and thirst.

He was nineteen years old, and for all his nineteen years he had never been forty miles from the croft where he had spent his childhood. Now, within one week he had for the first time travelled on a train, seen a proper city (two actually, Edinburgh by night as the Maclarens' train rolled through it at the very hour Britain declared war, and then London), travelled aboard a ship, set foot on foreign soil and heard himself cheered and acclaimed in a foreign tongue.

Now he stood in his field dress of kilt, and khaki tunic and apron, weighed down by his sixty pounds of active service kit, licking his dry, as yet unshaven upper lip, and trying to find something familiar in all the chaos. It was not easy. Beyond the wide cobbled street that served the quay there were buildings and trees, and he could see, through gaps in the crowd, a tram rattling by. But the buildings, four storeys tall with steep roofs and rows of chimneypots, though not unlike their equivalents in Inverness, were different in colour and their ground floors were occupied by shops and cafés, with long canvas awnings extended out over sidewalks, shading them from the lavish sun. Even the trees were different and foreign. Donnie shrugged and shifted the considerable weight of his pack and rifle, shuffling his feet, hot in their heavy kilt hose and khaki gaiters, on the dusty cobbles.

'What's wi' youse?'

Donnie looked up. It was Andy Henderson, an Inverness lad who'd joined up a few months earlier than himself. Donnie managed a small disconsolate grin. He liked Andy, they were mates and drank together, and sometimes Andy brought Donnie home for dinner at his parents' house on Celt Street, a special treat for Donnie who had never really had a home. On the train, when Donnie had let out a shameful involuntary yelp of alarm as the big steam engine had shuddered forward and the carriages crashed and banged and began to move, only Andy had not laughed. 'Ye dinna ken,' he said to the others. 'A train's a queer thing if ye've nae met one afore.' He'd stood next to Donnie then until Donnie was used to the thing and trusted it would stay on its narrow rails.

'It's awfu' strange,' he said at last. Andy was watching their captain, Colin Chisholm, supervising the unloading of his long-limbed black mare.

'What is?'

'Everything.'

Andy laughed, 'Ye'll get used to it.'

'I dinna ken what tae dae.'

Andy turned his face up to the sun, enjoying its warmth on his skin, a rarity in Inverness. He squinted his eyes shut, feeling oddly content. He said, 'You dinna hae t' ken what tae dae. Corporal will tell you.' He gestured to the edge of the quay where Lance Corporal Sandy Gibson, erstwhile ghillie to Tenny Maclaren, was reuniting another youngster with his misplaced rifle. The youngster was cowering under Sandy's verbal onslaught which more or less implied that the entire Cause of both British and French could well have been lost had the rifle not been found. But it was all a bit of an act. Sandy knew what it was like to be young, and confused, and lose things.

Donnie relaxed a little. That was the really nice thing about the army; there was always someone to tell you what to do. He began to brighten. He was a soldier of the King and there was adventure ahead. A soldier of the King. He let the phrase stride boldly through his mind. Och, it was great. It was great to be something. He decided he was going to enjoy this, and stopped feeling homesick and sorry for himself. After all, it had been entirely his choice that he was here at all. They were all volunteers. That was the British way. But how much choice of their own was really involved in their being there, was another matter.

Life hadn't presented Donnie Cameron with many choices. Even his name was not his own. His mother was a certain Mary MacGillveray who, at the age of seventeen herself, was already, in the local vernacular, 'on the game'. Her practice of that oldest profession had rather quickly resulted in Donnie whom she had kept in her own care, like one of the little china-faced dolls of her recent childhood, until he grew too noisy and demanding to be doll-like. Then she had abandoned him to the haphazard care of one and another neighbourhood woman until parish authorities had intervened and placed him in a Children's Home.

He had remained there until he was seven when he was fostered out to a crofter on the Maclaren estates, near Beauly. That man, Alastair Cameron, had bestowed his name, more by inference than any formality. His wife, Jess, was in her forties, and childless. She had good intentions, but had grown past the stage of flexibility that child-rearing demands. She too kept Donnie about the house until he grew too large to be cuddled, and then turned him out, like a stray cat, to work on the farm.

Alastair Cameron used him as he used the farm garrons, steadily, and with little compassion. At eighteen, Donnie had had enough. He joined the army. For his kind, it was the only way out.

He brought to it his half-educated mind, his work hardened body and a certain cringing obedience. The Maclarens took the first two willingly enough, and turned the latter into another kind of obedience, rooted in pride and schooled on the barracks square. Donnie loved the Maclarens. They'd given him everything he had. He loved his uniform, the first decent garments he'd owned, and kept his kit in perfect order with no need of the sergeant's encouragement, cherishing it all, spare shirt and socks, mess-tin, housewife or sewing-kit, towel, razor and case and lather brush; knife, fork and spoon; comb and toothbrush, greatcoat and cardigan, the little oil bottle even, and pull-through for his rifle, and the rifle itself, beautiful and heavy and powerful, the tool of his trade. They were the first real possessions of his life.

Donnie would be the best kind of soldier, loyal, unquestioning, tough and utterly devoted to his leaders. If they were good, he just might survive.

Unfortunately, officers and NCOs were also in the army for a variety of reasons, not all of them good ones. Sandy Gibson was typical of the best of the NCOs. The army was in his blood. His father, the retired RSM Frankie Gibson, the battalion's first VC, had behind him a lifetime with the Maclarens in which loyalty to his superiors was perfectly blended with Highland independence. His respect for his senior officers was in no way touched by envy, and his authority over his juniors in no way tainted with pomposity. He was exactly what he wanted to be. Those were the values that Sandy Gibson, and his younger brother Hugh, a private serving in B Company with Donnie and Andy, had been raised to respect. If Sandy Gibson could one day hold the coveted position of RSM, he would be a content man. If a better man than he held it, he would acquiesce. That one lesser than he should hold it above him was an occurrence he believed impossible since such decisions were in the hands of men who held his complete respect and trust, the senior officers of the Maclaren Highlanders.

In spite of Sandy's trust, however, they did make mistakes. Not many, but some. And Sergeant Ross MacDonald was one of them. He was a big, heavy-shouldered man, directing the unloading of the transport mules with a bellowing voice. His fondness for drink showed itself in the fold of belly pushing out the front of his tunic, and in the blotchy purple skin of his large, fleshy nose. The nose was his most dominant feature, set between small eyes and slung over a short, clipped black moustache. Behind his back they called him 'Nosey MacDonald' without affection.

Sergeant MacDonald had joined the army for all the wrong reasons. The only child of a successful local farmer, he had bullied his way through his schooldays, terrorizing other pupils and the dominie as well. His father had grown pompous with success and encouraged his son to throw his weight around. He joined the army for the chance to fight. His size alone got him in at fifteen. He looked nineteen already then, as he had been shaving since the age of twelve. By the time he *was* nineteen, he had attained the rank of lance corporal and possessed already a sizeable beer belly and the puffy eyes of a hardened drinker.

Indeed he had in early years risen to the rank of sergeant, only to lose it as the result of a brawl in an Inverness public-house in which a civilian was severely injured. But he earned his rank back again, and with it the grudging respect of his superiors. He had a subtle way of keeping his worst side invisible when there was anything resembling brass around. His men knew his underside.

He was quick-tempered and sadistic in his enjoyment of other men's fear. Perhaps he shouldn't have been in the army at all with any of those traits, but they were in effect the reverse of a coin. On the other side he showed experience, astounding accuracy with a rifle, and indisputable, if slightly brainless, courage. He was an expert at turning a rout into a victory by his bullish presence. In South Africa he had proved his worth again and again, and men under fire sought out his ugly shadow as a kind of devil's blessing. So the army kept him, but he was one of the few men in the Maclarens who went into action with an enemy force behind him, as well as in front.

Donnie Cameron turned away as MacDonald's heavy-soled

shoe connected with the sweating flank of a frightened mule that had stumbled and fallen on the slippery cobbles. The animal squealed and scrambled to its feet in panic, adding to the confusion.

'Steady on there,' Colin Chisholm called sharply, but MacDonald had already faded into a clump of milling men and animals and Captain Chisholm returned patiently to his task, supervising the cajoling of frightened horses down on the quay. It occurred to him briefly that, fond as he was of the beasts, their care, transport and feeding took up an inordinate amount of the battalion's time.

But Captain Chisholm was in charge of B Company and he did not involve himself with the army's policy decisions. The importance of horses, not just the cavalry's chargers but the legions of horses upon which the British Army relied for transport of virtually all its equipment including heavy guns, even while the civilian world was visibly abandoning them for motor vehicles, was a matter for his superiors. And his superiors, from the commander-in-chief, Sir John French, to Douglas Haig, who commanded the First Army Corps, were cavalry men. They had risen to their exalted ranks in earlier wars, wars in which victory had ridden on the backs of horses. Facing this great European conflict, they were hardly likely to turn from them now. Nor did they. So Captain Chisholm unloaded horses all morning, and the trains that would take them to the Front would carry eight horses to every forty men and half of their massive transport system would be, as always, devoted to fodder.

Colin Chisholm was not an innovator. In fact he was very like any of those exalted gentlemen would have been when young. For Chisholm the Maclarens were a solid, totally acceptable framework of an unchallenging life, filled perhaps with physical danger but socially secure. It was social rather than physical challenge that frightened men like Colin Chisholm. On this day in August, busy in the French sunshine, surrounded by his friends, he could not have been happier. Damn shame about Tenny Maclaren, of course, they'd miss him. But still, young John Bruce, newly commissioned from Sandhurst, was a welcome surprise.

Second Lieutenant John Bruce was surprised as well to find himself holding the King's Commission and setting out with the BEF landing in France that morning. Because Tenny Maclaren's broken arm had rendered him temporarily unfit, there had been a gap in B Company that had to be filled in a hurry. And there was Johnny Bruce, fit, able, and, in Gordon Bruce's judgement, genuinely untouched by any family considerations, the best man for the job.

Tenny would make a model soldier, he knew, but Tenny was out of action. And Johnny Bruce, his lesser in every respect, still had one indefinable quality that Tenny lacked, a sort of fierce determined flair for soldiering. By instinct Colonel Bruce knew that flair would never show itself at Sandhurst but would shine on the battlefield, and quite unexpectedly it was going to have a chance.

Gordon Bruce, without ever having thought it out, knew that what he was seeing in Johnny was the thing that had taken his own father, Willie, to the summits of military achievement. They were, both of them, military animals, natural soldiers with the kind of calculated courage that enabled a man to walk the narrow line between risk-taking and foolhardiness to perfection. He was a chancer, but a good one, and every battalion needed at least one of his sort.

As for Johnny, he accepted his totally unexpected inclusion with delight, confidence, and absolutely no remorse. True, he had caused the injury that had won him Tenny's place, and true, Tenny was understandably miserable and more than a little outraged. But he hadn't intended it. And having not intended it, he did not hold himself responsible. He loved Tenny Maclaren like a begrudged brother, but had Tenny's injury been fatal, he would still have felt no guilt, any more than he'd feel guilt for a man shot next to him in action. Guilt was for those who failed in their duty, and that was something that was not about to happen to Johnny Bruce.

A different kind of guilt afflicted Captain George Brown, as he formed A Company into marching order on the quay at Le Havre. Though he had to admit that the guilt was fading with every foot of distance he'd put between himself and Scotland. Indeed the commencement of hostilities could not have been timed better for George Brown if the Kaiser had expressly requested his advice. Captain Brown's guilt was directly linked to a certain Betty MacIver who had, until very recently, been an object of his affections. She was a bakery assistant in Beauly and her own extremely affectionate nature could, in truth, have been testified to by several other members of the battalion, a fact she had managed to keep secret from Captain Brown when she had confronted him with the news of her impending motherhood. He was after all tall, lean and handsome, and an officer, albeit one who had risen from the ranks. Marriage, that blessed state he had avoided for thirty-six happy years, loomed grimly in front of him, repeating ironically the circumstances that had brought him to the Maclarens in the first place.

For George Brown was not even a Highlander, but a farmer's son from Lanarkshire. When at seventeen he had got his father's dairymaid into the same unfortunate condition that now afflicted Betty MacIver, his first thought had been the army. That the Maclarens had won this sterling recruit had been due entirely to the distance of their regimental catchment area from Biggar in Lanarkshire. He could not have gone further without going to England. And an English regiment would have been a fate worse than marriage.

So the Maclarens got him, and were pleased enough with the bargain. He rose quickly through the ranks, a tough, no-nonsense soldier, and had been commissioned on the recommendation of his CO, Sir Ian Maclaren. The commissioning of competent men from the ranks, a practice begun in the Maclarens with the colonel-in-chief himself many years before, had gradually become more common. Brown was fortunate in that his farming background was not a poor one, and he found only limited difficulty in maintaining himself in the Officers' Mess. It was not a situation that would have been in any way improved by marriage to a bakery assistant.

'Fall the men in, Sergeant,' he said with a barely suppressed smile. He mounted his horse at the head of A Company and turned its nose inland, to the west and, he imagined, the advancing German armies, with a feeling akin to affection.

They marched through the docklands with pipers playing and the marching men's kilts swaying. The mounted officers, in tartan riding-trews, jingled along on their chargers in front of the columns of fours. When they entered the streets of the town they were mobbed by women and children waving little British flags and tricolours and shouting, '*Viva les anglais*', and then, '*Vive les kilties*'.

Lieutenant-Colonel Gordon Bruce, riding at the head of the battalion, felt oddly embarrassed. They were being greeted as a conquering force already, and the enemy had not yet been sighted. His destination, assigned him by an immaculately dressed staff officer at the docks, was a Rest Camp five miles outside the town, a modest enough march for a fit battalion. And yet it caused surprising difficulties.

The day was extraordinarily hot, and the milling crowds made the streets of Le Havre almost impassable. Donnie Cameron, marching in rank beside Andy Henderson, found himself suddenly confronted with the smiling face of a dark-haired, dark-eyed girl, her hands extending a jug of cider. She skipped along, laughing, and Donnie after a hesitant glance over his shoulder broke ranks and clasped the jug in his two hands, lifting it to his dry lips and drinking deeply. It was sour, but deliciously wet. 'Thank you,' he said shyly as his column marched past. She giggled, shook her head and broke free, running after another soldier with her jug. 'Jeez,' Donnie said aloud, suddenly realizing where he was.

'Sodger,' roared the voice of Sergeant MacDonald from far behind. He broke into a run, aproned kilt flapping, caught up his position and tried to vanish into the smooth ranks of dusty khaki. At the same time he saw another man ahead break ranks as well, and another to the right. The officers were having trouble keeping them in order, and it wasn't until they were beyond the perimeters of the town that something like true Maclaren form returned. It was mostly the sight of a battalion of Coldstreamers fallen out for a rest at the roadside that stirred an instantaneous swelling of regimental pride. Gordon Bruce glanced back over his shoulder and saw his battalion swinging along behind him with parade-ground precision, the rhythmic clash of their heavy soles ringing from the stone surface of the road. Somewhere within their ranks a voice sang the opening notes of Colonel Bogey, 'Bug-ger . . .'

'The Cold-Stream-ers,' a dozen Maclaren voices sang on, right in tune.

'Bug-ger,' sang a cluster of Coldstreamers.

'The High-land-ers,' their chorus picking up the tune in perfect key. It was a tradition, unfailing when marching regiments met.

'Silence in the ranks,' roared RSM Peter Leinie, less out of a desire for silence than from a desire to give voice to something. He grinned to himself, gloating over his delight in being here at all and having got the chance to cram one more scrap into his career before age forced a more sedentary existence. As it was he had just scraped through. He had narrowly missed being left to do the job of knocking the Territorials into some kind of shape as they moved into the vacated Fort Maclaren.

Leinie had come to the Maclarens over thirty years before, a youngster very like Donnie Cameron, shy, scared, and alternating between swagger and trembling as he approached his first action in the Sudan. He had survived that, though through no credit to himself, and gone on to survive an astounding number of grim situations, in the Far East and later in the Boer War. He now radiated a self-assured calm that was an immense comfort to the men under him. He was, as regimental sergeant major, regarded as both fearsome and indestructible. 'Picks his teeth with a bayonet and lights his pipe with cordite,' or something of the sort. Everyone was terrified of him because they wanted to be terrified of him; he was hardly a decent RSM if they were not. He knew that totally fanciful examples of his ruthlessness were held up as a matter of battalion pride before members of lesser regiments. It amused him because he recalled scaring the wits out of new recruits with his own tales of the ferocity of the RSM of his youth, old Frankie Gibson. Even now, approaching fifty, Peter Leinie was stunned to realize that he held the exalted position that had once belonged to the unapproachable hero of his youth. He looked ahead at the commanding officer, who rode at the head of the column, and wondered if he had felt the same when he took his father's place. They had been young together and now were almost brothers: each at a pinnacle of his career.

They swung out of the town and uphill towards the Rest Camp. Some men stumbled, weighted down by equipment and giddy from the heat in their heavy khaki and wool uniforms. Officers and NCOs propped them up and helped them along. Shouting at a man suffering heat prostration was pointless.

Lieutenant Bruce had already relieved one stumbling young Jock of his pack and rifle for the remainder of the march to the Rest Camp. Elsewhere, Colour Sergeant MacTavish was cursing his soft feet and the difficult French *pavé*, in equal proportion. Pavé du Roi, it was called, but the king was from long ago and his comprehensive road-laying plan had resulted in the antique but extremely solid French carriageways which they now travelled. They were constructed of stone cobbles, firm enough for wheeled vehicles but a difficult uneven surface for marching men.

Europe's plunge into war had come so quickly, particularly for men like MacTavish, a reservist since South Africa, who hardly followed the news in any depth. He was taken completely by surprise when he was called up. He barely had time to make arrangements for his plumbing business to continue under his brother's auspices, and for his family's care, before they shipped out. Indeed the day after he reported to the quartermaster at Beauly to be fitted out with field-service kit, he had taken his entire family, Belle, his wife, and the bairns, Calum, Hamish and Gertie, to Mr Fraser the photographer. He had posed, in his uniform, with Gertie standing on his knee and the two little ones leaning on either side, and Belle behind, all staring into the camera lens defiantly, as if it, not war, were about to separate them. But the real reason, they claimed, was that they were so proud of him, off to serve his country.

'Aye well, you never know,' Belle said afterwards.

'Och, no,' he said in reply.

He was glad they had done it, even though in a few days' time it would not matter; it would be like the old days in Africa, when he and Belle were still strangers and had nobody to miss. That was the best way. The damn thing was it was all so sudden, with the war being so close to home. A fortnight ago, all was normal. Even now, he could tell just what time of day it was there, and what she'd be doing. Midday. Bairns home from throwing stones in the Ness below Greig Street where they all splashed away the idle summer. Broth-pot on the big range. Belle, hair all sweaty from the heat, wee Gert on her hip like she were part of her, soup ladle in hand, smiling that quiet satisfied smile. Damn. War should be far away. Africa, the East, other worlds. Not like this, on your doorstep. He plodded on, his overweight body sweating and the blisters in his stiff new unbroken shoes a burning agony.

They reached the camp on the high ground beyond Le Havre in the late afternoon. The sun beat relentlessly on the mass of belltents. The men were allowed to seek what comfort they could. Most stripped to the waist and poured any available water over their heads. Some simply collapsed in the shade of tents or wagons. The officers worked on into the early evening. They supervised the setting up of field kitchens and made sure that the men and horses were fed and watered. Later in the evening, as the last baggage arrived, they were able to have the luxury of a change of clothing, and by eight o'clock Lieutenant Colonel Bruce was sitting before a well-laid table with his fellow officers, enjoying a good dinner and a cigar.

Donnie Cameron, satiated with brown stew and jam roly-poly, was stretched out comfortably on the beaten remnants of an erstwhile rye field, listening to a group of *poilus*, French infantry, singing softly in the dusk. He was cool at last, and better fed than he'd ever been in childhood.

'*Alouette*,' sang the French soldiers, a scraggy bunch of Territorials left to guard Le Havre, '*gentile Alouette* . . .' Donnie smiled to himself.

'*Alouette, je te plumerai* . . .' They drifted down the aisle of belltents, comical, like Charlie Chaplin, Donnie thought, their baggy blue coats folded back over bright scarlet trousers.

'Hey Donnie,' Andy Henderson called from where he too lay on his back, his hands folded over his open tunic.

'Aye?'

'See yon?'

'Aye.'

'Surely they'll nae gae t' fight like thot?'

'Dinna ken,' Donnie said propping himself up on one elbow, and watching as they passed. 'They sing nice,' he added, to himself.

'Bunch of jessies,' grumbled Andy with disdain.

Second Lieutenant John Bruce, having assured himself that his men lacked nothing, retired to his tent and withdrew a pad of writing-paper from his kit. He sat down then, with his back against a tent pole, and propped the pad on his knee. By the light of a candle he began to write,

> My dear Miss Galloway,
>
> I do hope you will not regard this letter as presumptuous, but I hope you will find it in your heart to forgive this boldness from a soldier on the eve of battle . . .

His pen paused and he tilted his head wryly. Well, maybe not the *eve* of battle, but after all they were *nearly* there. Besides, no one seemed to know where the Germans were. The French didn't. He suspected their commanding officer didn't either. So it might be the eve of battle after all. Anyhow, he could always postdate it.

> I have thought of little else but your charming person since that brief weekend of happiness . . .

He went on, getting well into his stride.

As it was, Johnny Bruce was not that far out, nor would he need to postdate his letter to such a great extent. The following day was actually spent in camp. But the day after found them moving, somehow with a feeling of blindness, towards an undetermined Front.

7

The same evening that Johnny Bruce sat composing his love letter, Johnny Bruce's recently retired commanding officer, Sir Ian Maclaren, Bart., was uncertainly climbing the main staircase of the Dolphin Hotel, Southampton. His Scottish soul was filled with characteristic Calvinist remorse at a late evening spent in quite uncharacteristic jollity over a bottle or two of Tallisker.

Ian Maclaren was experiencing something of the same feeling of startled displacement as Colour Sergeant MacTavish, the Inverness plumber, felt in Le Havre. Ian too had, as little as a month ago, hardly expected to find himself again in a genuinely military situation. He had, albeit reluctantly, accepted his retirement and had quite got used to the idea. He had begun to gear his life in a new direction, charting out the future development of the estate, and he had become familiar with it as a working entity rather than simply the solid, but little-thought-of background to his life that it had always been. He had been quite ready to make that his life; that, and his family, to whom he planned now to devote some of the time that events in the past had obliged him to deny them.

Ian reached the second landing of the wide, curving staircase and stood, swaying slightly. He found the electric lighting dizzily bright. He winced as he remembered the night's revelries, yet he was filled with a residual excitement at the gathering energy of an army preparing for battle.

Of course there wasn't likely to be any battle outside the Dolphin, in the busy and very English streets of Southampton. But the war wasn't far, and the English Channel had not yet assumed its mythic proportions of a modern Styx across which one might shuttle, in a matter of hours, between heaven and hell.

But Ian, despite his sorrow at parting from the family and his quite genuine dark concerns about the future, had reacted to Haig's summons to his staff with a certain joy. Granted he would not likely see action, granted his beloved First Battalion was already in advance of him across the Channel; but still he would be as close to them as a man his age could hope to be.

He pushed through a series of frosted-glass-panelled doors and found his corridor at last. He started down it, trailing the fingertips of one hand along the wall to steady himself. Passing a large mirror, he swayed back and caught sight of himself. Automatically he turned to face it and, leaning against the opposite corridor wall, blearily checked that all in his khaki service dress was in order. He straightened a pocket flap and brushed down the left side of his greying moustache, then straightened his shoulders and shifted his right leg to counteract a slight list to starboard. He was thankful that his room, if he remembered right, was just round the corner. But when he rounded that corner, he saw them: two ladies, and a dog.

The dog was a tall grey wolfhound with a long narrow head turned towards him. Its spindly tail gave a hint of a salutary wag. The two ladies were absorbed in bidding each other goodnight, in a way that only ladies of the proper class, with genuine affection, could manage. They clasped silk-clothed forearms with delicate jewelled fingers, and swayed their long necks to one side and the other as cheeks were kissed, their masses of beautifully dressed hair brushing together.

The hair of the woman nearest Ian, and with her back to him, was black and shining and done up in a smooth, wrapped braid. The other, young and dressed in a dark brown silk gown that set off her lighter brown hair and creamy skin, whispered something to her companion and they both giggled and clung close before they parted. Ian felt an erotic flutter at that secrecy of affection that women held amongst themselves. He watched, suddenly conscious of himself as a voyeur, as the young brown-haired girl turned and walked, straight-backed and graceful, down the corridor, the grey dog obedient at her heels.

The black-haired woman watched also, until the corner was turned, and then she whirled about, suddenly conscious of his eyes. The narrow skirt of her scarlet evening dress twisted like a vine about her feet and there was the faintest rustle of silk scraping the surface of the carpeted corridor. Ian heard his own breath.

'Good God,' the woman said, 'it's Ian.'

'Naomi.'

The silence of embarrassed strangers that had filled the corridor became at once a deeper silence of far greater import. Then, at a distance and out of sight, there came one sharp insistent bark as the wolfhound made his goodnights. Ian and Naomi, laughing, fell easily into each other's arms. They clung to each other like brother and sister and then responsibly straightened themselves up, exchanged cheek kisses, and stepped back.

'Two years, it must be,' Ian said.

'Oh I dare say. You haven't changed. You never do.'

'Nor you.'

'No,' Naomi giggled, 'we're both positively marvellous.' They embraced again, this time with more than sibling warmth, and both broke from it with embarrassment.

'But why?' Naomi asked and then finished for herself, 'Oh, naturally, You'll be with Haig's party. I had heard they were staying here. So you've been called back to the service of your King after all.'

'So it appears,' Ian said, smiling and rubbing his moustache with his fist, trying to keep his eyes somewhere other than linked with Naomi's. 'He seems to think I'll be useful somewhere anyway.'

'Of course. He'll need every man of your experience. He's hardly going to fight a war with children.'

'Mmm,' Ian said wryly. 'From the look of the company tonight I suspect he's going to fight it with a bunch of old antiques. Seems as if every regiment's cupboard has been emptied of what's been gathering cobwebs for years. I only hope we'll be able to shake our cobwebs off before we meet the Boche.' He grinned then, 'I must say I've added a few cobwebs of my own tonight. The wine flowed free, as they say. Do pardon, my dear, but I'm half sozzled.'

'Not at all,' Naomi said gracefully and then extended a tactful silken arm to improve his balance as they made their way, a little uncertainly, up the corridor. 'I must add that I think you're a bit unfair to yourself. You're hardly an antique; you've barely just left your own command.' And as Ian shook his head, she added, 'Oh I know you though. You've always had a bias for the young.'

'Not a bias, Naomi. Not a bias. Just a modest desire for them to get their noses in before they've all gone grey about the muzzle as well.'

He stopped short, causing Naomi to do so too, her hand firmly under his elbow as he swayed back, about to make a statement of military pontification. 'The thing is, my dear, I've never yet known a soldier who was willing to fight a war in any but the fashion of his youth. And I've never met a war that wasn't totally different from the war that preceded it. This one'll be different. Don't know how it will be different, but it will. Mind my words. If I can remember them tomorrow. Naomi, I love you.'

Her hand slipped, like a cat's tentative paw, from his arm. There was the slightest pause in which her dark eyes shifted from his shoulder down to the floor and up again and then she said brightly, 'Oh, but I must give you all the news of home surely. I was on the telephone to Victoria this morning.'

Ian knew why she said it. They both knew he'd only left home himself two days before and he doubted there could be much new since then. She simply wanted to remind him of his responsibilities. Nothing like hearing your wife's name, after all, when you were on the edge of an indiscretion.

He sighed. For all his having possessed her as a girl, and years later, again, as a woman, Naomi to this day remained tantalizingly out of his reach. Even when they were lovers, even when nothing, nothing at all lay between their joined bodies, even then he had never held all of her. There was always that remote, eastern part that belonged to no one but Naomi.

'Ah, splendid,' he said dutifully, suppressing another small sigh. 'Everything quite all right up north?' But before she could answer, he was suddenly struck through his fog of drink with a more immediate thought. 'I say, my dear, but really, you've not said. Whatever are you doing here yourself?'

'On my way to France, of course,' she replied at once, and appeared again about to launch into a report of news from home.

'France?' he said, astounded. 'You?'

'I have been there before, Ian. One goes.'

'Damn't woman, there's a war on now.'

'Yes. We have noticed. That *is* rather our reason, naturally.'

'Who's we?' Ian asked, suspiciously.

'Why, the Duchess of course, and myself. And the rest.'

'What Duchess?' Ian's voice began to rise.

Naomi shrugged her shoulder towards the now empty corridor, its dark red Jacobean wallpaper shadowy between the lamps. 'That Duchess,' she said.

'With the dog?' Ian said.

'With the dog. The Duchess of Westminster.'

Ian leaned against the wall and rubbed his chin sagely. The wall was very comforting and he was suddenly aware of being very tired. 'Seems too young to be a Duchess,' he said, slightly befuddled.

'Very well, but she is and she has a marvellous villa in Le Touquet, and she's every bit as practical as she's beautiful. So when war was declared she telephoned me at once and we've been gathering all the ladies who served in the hospitals in South Africa. We are all experienced, you see, even if we're not all trained. So we sail tomorrow and the villa will do splendidly for our hospital.' She paused and was more serious. 'There will be the need of course, Ian. No matter how well things go. Oh, I know it's all to be over by Christmas, but there's quite a few months till Christmas. I've seen war, Ian, as you'll recall. There are never too many nurses.'

Ian nodded, the boyish impetus of the evening leaving him. He gently put an arm about her shoulders, in such a way that even his wife could approve. 'You're as bad as me,' he said finally. 'You don't want to miss the fun.'

'Hardly, Ian,' she said, slightly offended until he added quickly,

'Oh, you do know what I mean. We've always been like that. We want to be in the middle of things, even if they're terrible things. It's never been either of our way to sit at home and watch.'

She nodded, smiling gently, and he stood looking down on the top of her head, at the spidery pattern of silver hairs wound like pearls into her black braid.

He said softly, 'Now do tell me, what is the news of home?'

Ian Maclaren's home, on that still August evening, had become an almost entirely female establishment, as had other homes throughout the nation. The library, hereditary domain of all male Maclarens, was empty and still, the stones of the big fireplace cold. No fire had been lit for days. Ian had left and Tenny was now at the barracks in Beauly hastily organizing the Territorials into a full-time military force. The war was very young and half the nation was yet to consider it more than a temporary interruption of a pleasant summer. The new Secretary of State for War, Lord Kitchener, had other ideas. He saw a long war, and a long war needed a large army. The Territorials were traditionally a home guard who filled in for the regulars. By right they could not be sent abroad without six months of training and their own consent. But the battalion of cheerful patriotic young men, pouring in from the farms and towns in response to the call, would need no persuading. Even Tenny, steeped as he was in regular army tradition, was obliged to admit that their sheer enthusiasm, added to their mental and physical quality, went a long way.

These were men to whom the army had been a glorified Boys' Brigade. Many had quite simply graduated from that church-run institution to the Territorials. It meant weekends of physical exertion and companionship for the townbound, and a chance to meet something other than the sheep and cows for the farm lads. For some, from the poorer quarters of Inverness, these venturings out under canvas and in uniform were the highlights of their lives. One of the few among them less happy than most with their sudden call-up was Ewan Grant who, after a brief week of marriage, was obliged to forsake his bridal bed before he was at all used to its comfort for a narrow metal-framed affair, amongst a row of twenty, in the barracks at Fort Maclaren.

Officer Cadet Albert Maclaren had returned to Sandhurst, as planned, though without the company of Johnny Bruce. Albert, squeezed a little uncomfortably into his uniform, his kilt on the last notch after this sumptuous weekend, had boarded the train with a mixture of reluctance and relief. Unlike Tenny and Johnny he had shown no great eagerness to be involved in the war any sooner than necessary. Tenny had seen him off, frankly mystified. When all the world was striving to get in on the chase, there was Bertie Maclaren, a paper sack of pan drops and a crossword puzzle for comfort, hunched into the corner of the railway carriage and concerned for nothing but whether or not the Highland Line would serve a decent tea.

'With any luck you'll soon be up to join us,' Tenny said encouragingly.

Bertie grinned, engagingly, pushing his silky hair aside. 'Oh dear, I hope not,' he said. 'I might end up serving under Gordon Bruce, and maybe even Father. I wouldn't stand a chance.' He paused, watching a group of the gathering Territorials clustered on the platform. 'Poor old weekend soldiers. Do be gentle on them, Ten.'

'I'll be a veritable mother to them,' Tenny had said, waving his good arm. His last image of Bertie, spreading out four pan drops for future consumption on the little shelf by the train window, remained with him for days. It was impossible to get angry with Bertie; he was still, even at nineteen, the nursery pet.

Two weeks later Tenny was the first to learn, through the military grapevine, that his quiet, comfort-loving brother had obtained a transfer and left Sandhurst and come north again to join the first New Army battalion to be raised in Inverness, as a private soldier. He never explained to anyone in his family why he did it, but by doing so, he won himself the brutally harsh life of the infantry with none of the rewards. It was an act typical of his generation in its sacrifice, and typical of Albert in its refusal of leadership. His father, Ian, remained permanently mystified. Tenny in time began to think he understood, and considered Albert's plunge into the ranks as an act comparable to his own leap across the gorge of the River Glass during the Bank Holiday weekend: a test of courage.

Philippa Maclaren, his sister, had no doubts. In her mind Albert's act was a redemption. She had suspected him of cowardice, just as she suspected Harry Bruce. When the news came she interpreted it by her own lights as an eagerness for the fray, and used his name shamelessly in her efforts to recruit others to that same New Army battalion. For Philippa Maclaren was fighting the war too. Kitchener had yet to call for his First Hundred Thousand, that mass of men with which he hoped to forge a whole New Army, bypassing the Territorials for the sake of expediency. But Philippa, and a selection of young lady friends, had been involved in recruiting for the Territorials ever since war was declared. On that summer night when her father was lingering outside Naomi Bruce's bedroom door, she was involved in another kind of seduction.

'*What* You *Can Do!*' was the title on the placard outside the Church Hall in Kirkhill. 'Woman and Duty' was the subtitle. 'Guest Speaker, Miss Philippa Maclaren of Culbrech House' was printed boldly beneath. The placard was decorated with two crossed British flags and a young girl in Grecian robes, carrying a sword.

The young girl, Victoria Maclaren thought from her seat in the front row of wooden chairs in the church hall, looked rather startlingly like Philippa. She had never realized quite what a striking face her daughter had until that evening seeing her on the raised dais, her eyes flashing with fervour, her marvellous hair glinting in the gaslight, one white arm raised to emphasize a stirring point. 'Women of the North, send forth your Highland lads . . .'

'She was marvellous,' said a lady of age and dignity, when the speech was done. 'If only I knew more young men, I'm sure with Philippa's help we could persuade an entire division. A marvellous girl. You must be so proud.'

But Victoria Maclaren, soldier's wife and soldier's mother, was not so much proud as she was afraid. She was afraid of the war and what it would do to her family. And she was afraid of her daughter and that fierce fervour, and what it might do to so many, many trusting young men. Of course it was right. Of course they should enlist. But who was she, so young and so loveless, to send them to war, those other women's husbands, sweethearts, and sons?

'If she had someone of her own,' Victoria had confided to Maud and Willie Bruce afterwards, 'surely she'd be more, what should I say, more understanding. More gentle.' Maud Bruce had agreed and comforted her with the thought that soon enough no doubt there would be someone for Philippa. Once she had thought her grandson, Harry, she added, but of course, Philippa would not think of him now. 'Perhaps that's it,' Victoria said, slowly. 'Perhaps she's speaking always to Harry with all this talk of patriotism. A woman will do that, and so will a man, talk to everyone, with the words meant just for one.'

'Aye, well enough,' Willie Bruce had mused, 'but she'll nae get a hearing frae that one. He's too much mind o' his ain tae be won round by a woman's tongue.' He had paused, sucking at his pipe, and finding it gone out, reached into his horsehair sporran for his tobacco pouch. He refilled the pipe slowly as they walked to the waiting motor car. 'I ken ae thing,' he said at last. 'There's ae kind o' woman wha'd mak' the warld o'er in the image o' the man she loves. If such a woman loves a sodger, then a' men maun be sodgers. A' for the sake o' one.'

'Surely not,' Victoria said abruptly. 'Besides, were that the case no doubt it would be Emma out recruiting all the men, so they'd all be like her Torquil. But all Emma thinks of is nursing. She's training with the Red Cross already. Surely that's the proper role for a woman who loves a soldier,' she added with a touch of reproachful anger.

'Ye'll mind I didna say all women. I said ae kind o' woman,' he said, nodding his old grey head in the direction of Philippa Maclaren. 'Yon's the sort wha'll set the whole warld afire the better to light her true love's face.'

Victoria turned uneasily towards her second daughter emerging now from the church hall, tall and severe on its flight of stone steps, and suddenly intensely beautiful in her severity, surrounded by a cluster of country women. She was handing out small slips of paper which Victoria knew bore the location of the nearest recruiting centre. She sighed and said petulantly, to end all discussion, 'Philippa is not in love with a soldier. Nor any other man. More's the pity.'

'That's as may be,' said Willie Bruce.

Emma Maclaren was in love with a soldier. She was really in love. There was nothing glorious in her vision of war; it was a very real threat to the very real young man she wished to marry. Words like honour and glory and duty that Philippa flung about with such ease meant nothing to Emma. The war meant two things. One, that a distant threat had become an immediate reality; that is, that Torquil's profession had emerged from its screen of drills and parade and showed its true face. He was a soldier. Soldiers, even officers, went out with rifles and artillery and shot at each other. And the other, that the proposal of marriage that they both knew was awaiting its private moment, would have to wait longer, perhaps much, much longer, perhaps indeed for ever.

'It was Philippa's fault,' Emma said peevishly, her hands stopped in their task of bandage-rolling. She was seated on the long wooden, chintz-upholstered settle in front of the drawing-room fire. On the other end of the settle was Rebecca Galloway. Susan Bruce, her blue tweed skirt pulled up above her knees revealing her knitted stockings, was cross-legged in front of the fire. The very informality of her posture spoke clearly of the absence of men in the house. The drawing-room, that domain of femininity, had come alive with activity just as the library had faded into darkness.

'However?' Rebecca said, eagerly curious. 'Do tell.'

'She was positively beastly at the picnic. You'll recall, no, you won't, you were all wrapped up in my silly brother.'

'Beast,' Rebecca cried, blushing. 'I was nothing of the sort. Still, go on.'

'Anyhow, Torquil and I were alone. At *last*. Mother does not make it easy, you know. She pretends to be terribly modern and liberal but she never lets us out of her sight. At last we were alone. And I knew. I knew what he was thinking. I always do. But at last he could speak. But it takes . . . oh, you'll understand . . . time. There's a rhythm to love, like music. And we talked and . . . and oh damn, then there was Philippa. She just arrived, utterly uninvited, sat herself down and . . . and stayed. We dropped all sorts of hints, at least I did. Torquil was too kind, he'd never embarrass a lady. But she stuck to us like glue. Surely you've seen that awful photograph of Johnny's. She's right in the middle. Between us. The silly girl. I haven't even a photograph of him and me.' Quite suddenly tears ran down her cheeks. She still sat, smiling, perfectly calm, but crying.

Rebecca embraced her, and Susan jumped up from the floor and the three clustered together by the settle.

'Oh God,' Emma whispered, 'don't let him die before we've ever even kissed.'

'Silly, he's not going to die. He'll be home on leave in no time. You'll be engaged. And when the war's over, you'll be married,' Susan Bruce said. 'Next summer even, you could already be his wife. *And* pregnant.'

'Susan,' Emma whispered, but she smiled. She looked down at her hands, and went back to her bandage-rolling. It was hardly a major contribution to the war effort, but Emma had been so intent on doing something somehow to make Torquil's way safer that immediately upon his departure she had enrolled with the Red Cross in Beauly to learn First Aid. It had all been a bit of a disappointment so far; their afternoon meetings had been spent in drinking tea and admiring the cut of the trained nurses' trim uniforms. One or two of the ladies had turned up in something resembling uniforms themselves, on no one's authority at all. It was all very romantic and a lot of time was spent bandaging each other's young and perfect limbs. Everyone made sure to wear their very best underclothes.

'I shall go to London,' Emma said suddenly. The two girls turned quickly at the firm determination in her voice.

'London?'

'I shall join the Voluntary Aid Detachments and nurse the wounded. At least I'll feel nearer Torquil, and I'll be doing something for all the boys. And perhaps he'll get leave . . .'

'But your mother . . .' said Rebecca hesitantly.

'I'm twenty-two.'

'Oh,' moaned Susan. 'I can just see you, in your uniform, all in white, with the red cross, and bending over this bed with your candle and there . . .'

'I do believe they have electric lighting in London,' Emma said sharply.

'Oh hush. With your candle, and there, in the bed, wounded . . .'

'No, stop,' Emma said sharply.

'Oh, not badly wounded,' Susan returned calmly. 'There is Torquil. And he opens his eyes and says, Emma, my love, is it really you . . .' She wrapped her arms around herself and sighed, 'It's too beautiful for words.'

'I shall go too,' said Rebecca Galloway.

'You?' Susan Bruce looked genuinely surprised.

'Of course,' Rebecca said. 'And why not?'

Susan shrugged. 'You're not the nursing type,' she said with finality.

'Of course I am,' Rebecca defended. 'I bring Naomi soup when she has a cold, and I'm perfectly marvellous with the cat when it has kittens and . . .' She giggled but then Susan Bruce said,

'I know. We'll all go. Together. And we'll train together and stay together, and nurse together. It will be too, too marvellous.' She stood up on the settle and spread her arms wide. 'This band of sisters . . . this happy breed,' she proclaimed.

Rebecca jumped up beside her, and raising one small clenched fist began to sing, 'Land of Ho-o-pe and Gl-or-ry . . .' She began to laugh but Susan joined in and followed Rebecca's beautiful contralto with her own soprano voice. Emma smiled at first and shook her head, but then she too stood, lower down than the two on the settle, and wrapped her arms about them both, her head at shoulder level, and sang with them until they reached the end.

Footsteps clattered outside the door on the polished wood floor and they turned as it was flung open. It was Philippa, her cheeks reddened by exertion, her solemn grey speech-making hat slightly askew on her mountain of hair. 'Oh, that was splendid,' she cried. 'I heard you as I came in the door. It was as if the spirit of the war were singing in this house.' She clasped her hands together, closing her eyes. Then quickly she opened them and said, 'Don't you want to know how well we've done? There were four young men who stood up, right there in the hall, right in the middle of my speech, begging to be told where they might join up. Wee Geordie Stirling was one of them. Imagine.'

'Wee Geordie?' Emma said. 'The laundrymaid's son?'

'Yes, he was positively elated. The last I saw the four of them were off up to Beauly, arm in arm. I dare say they'll wait outside the recruiting office all night. Just to be first in when the doors open in the morning. Isn't it splendid?' She flopped down in a pink flowered chair, removing her hat and replacing the long pearl-tipped pin in the crown. She began taking the hairpins out of her coil of ruddy hair, another informality only possible because of the absence of men.

'Philippa,' Emma said, 'Mairi Stirling's a widow. Geordie's the only one she had left. All the other grown children are away. And she's still two little ones to feed.'

'Mmm,' said Philippa, her mouth full of hairpins, not listening at all.

'But who will work the croft, Philippa,' Emma said harshly, 'if Geordie enlists? He's the only help she has.'

Philippa removed the hairpins from her mouth and shook down her hair. 'Oh that's better. It is *such* a weight. My neck's positively broken. I've been on my feet all night. Do be a pet and ring for coffee, Susan.'

'What will she *do*?' Emma said, rising angrily to her feet.

'Oh surely, Em. Someone will help out. After all, we'll all have to make sacrifices for the war. She'll just have to make more of an effort.'

'More of an effort,' Emma shouted. 'The poor woman works all day in our laundry, and all the rest of the time keeping together her pathetic little patch of kail and mangy sheep. She works from four in the morning until midnight. What possible more effort can she make? Must she never sleep at all?'

Philippa turned aside, clearly annoyed, rose and poked peevishly at the fire with the long brass tongs. 'Where's Margaret, anyhow?' she said. 'This fire's nearly out and there's no more wood. Really, this is too bad.' Then she looked back at Emma. 'I should think Mairi Stirling would be glad to have Geordie's army pay if things are as bad as that,' she said at last.

'A shilling a day,' Emma said. 'How splendid. I'm sure she'll be quite delighted.'

Philippa turned to round on Emma again with some new thought, but Victoria Maclaren entered then, with the maid, Margaret, on her heels with a broad silver tray laden with the coffee service. Victoria had heard the raised voices, in the corridor, and the faces of her two daughters spoke for themselves. She sighed. Her mind was still on the meeting at the church hall and that dreadful thing in the newspaper that Maud Bruce had shown her. She still had the paper, tucked into her large embroidered shawl. She laid it, still wrapped, on the table in front of the settee. She was not sure she wanted the girls to see it.

'Come, come,' she said, once Margaret had left, assuming maternal duty. 'What *is* this about?'

'Nothing, Mother,' Emma said, looking down at her feet. But Philippa was not about to let the matter drop, and the other girls were watching expectantly.

'Philippa?' Victoria said. 'Come, there must have been something. You were going at it hammer and tongs when I was coming up the stairs. I could hear you then.' She paused to pour coffee from the silver pot with its thistle-topped handle and lid. 'It was, I might add, not the sort of thing one wishes servants to hear. Whatever your disagreements, let us have them without shouting, please.'

'It was not me shouting, Mother,' Philippa said truthfully. 'Emma was objecting to my war work. She seems to think men are better looking after sheep than serving their country.'

'Philippa, really,' Susan Bruce said, astounded.

'It's beneath discussion,' Emma said coldly.

Victoria leaned back and closed her eyes, removing her hat as she did so. 'All right then, let us say we do not discuss it. I've really had all I can take of this war tonight.' She was thinking again about the article in the *Courier*, wishing she could put it from her mind. She reached for her shawl then, hoping to get rid of the thing quickly, before anyone else saw it, but Susan Bruce noticed a fold of the paper only half hidden and said,

'Oh Lady Maclaren, let me see the *Courier*. Perhaps they'll have written up Philippa's speech to the Women's Guild in Struy.'

Victoria made a vain grab for it, but Susan had already unfolded it and was poring over the columns of dull grey print. Her small gasp of dismay told Victoria when she had come to it.

'Oh Lady Maclaren, did you read . . .'

'Yes, Susan. I have seen it. I think we'll . . .'

'Oh, it's just too, too terrible for words,' Susan breathed.

Victoria looked up then, as the two girls gathered close. Susan's lips were parted, her feet together, as she sat straight up, her neck thrust forward, reading on with widening eyes. Victoria, watching the three girls, suddenly recalled her daughters at Cooks' travelling circus, that had come, two summers before, to the camp at the Northern Meeting Park in Inverness. The high-wire act, the lions, the trapeze, each had elicited that kind of excitement, small well-groomed hands on trembling bosoms. Why had she tried to hide it? she thought. The young loved savagery.

'Did you read the bit about the baby?' Susan gasped.

Lady Maclaren nodded, trying to shut the image from her mind, the image that melted into the image of her own babies, transfixed as that Belgian child, on a German bayonet.

'And what they did to that woman . . . of course it doesn't actually say,' Rebecca whispered. 'But you just know, don't you.'

Susan looked up from the paper, recollection lighting her face. 'Did you read yesterday about those poor priests? When the Germans took a Belgian village and demanded they ring the bells of their churches?'

'Oh yes,' Rebecca cried, 'I read it too. And the brave priests refused and they tied them to the bell-clappers. Head *down*. And used *them* to ring the bells. Oh, it was terrible.'

Victoria put down her coffee cup, her mind filled with broken skulls of Belgian priests. But Emma said from the far side of the room, where she had retreated from the newspaper, 'That's odd. I read about that too, but it only said they forced them to ring the bells. And they rang them. That's all it said.'

'That's only because they didn't have the full story then,'

Philippa said knowingly. Victoria shook her head. She preferred Emma's version, but honestly did not know what to believe. She straightened up on the couch and decided to take control, again a soldier's wife, tired or not. 'Very well, girls, let us now simply agree that the Germans are not behaving like very nice people. Daddy and the rest of the British will soon sort them out. Let us just forget all of this for now and have our coffee.' She smiled bravely and patted the settee next to her, and Susan Bruce came and sat down beside her. She saw two large tears roll down Susan's cheeks and was touched, but not too deeply. Susan, from the nursery days, had always held a remarkable talent for tears on cue.

But Philippa, not about to lose the last word, stood up and walked again to the fire, prodding the polished brass fender with the equally polished toe of her grey leather boot. She stroked down the smooth lines of her narrow grey skirt and turning over her shoulder said, directly to Emma, 'I would think any woman with a sweetheart facing an enemy like that would be the first to recruit others to stand at his side. Why, to leave him alone there, she might as well side with the Germans. A woman who doesn't stand behind her man now is literally shooting him in the back.'

Emma, her face gone quite white, stood, took two short steps towards her sister and then whirled about, and fled, crying, from the room.

Emma's tears were, unlike Susan's, quite real. She lay on her bed for an hour, sobbing and thinking of Torquil. Out in the corridor of her room James Maclaren was playing at soldiers with wee Robert Bruce. Their shouting and running feet drifted in and out of her tired mind until she slept. Then she dreamed of Torquil, in some empty place, surrounded by soldiers, all shooting at him. He turned and called for help again and again. But he was alone and no help came. She woke, calling, 'I'm coming, I'm coming,' and heard in reply only the sound of a woman's laughter.

'Philippa?' she gasped, in the darkness of the unlit room.

'No, darling,' it was Rebecca's voice. 'It's only me. Poor thing, you're all hot. You've been dreaming.'

Emma lay back on her bed, her face sticky from tears. 'It was awful,' she whispered.

'Don't think about it,' Rebecca said. 'I've brought you tea.' She leant over and switched on a small electric light by the bed.

'Philippa was a positive beast,' she said calmly. 'But never mind. I talked to your Mama about our plans, and she was terribly good. I think she believes it's just what you need. To be doing something positive for Torquil. She was really quite worried, you know, and frightfully displeased with Phil.'

'She needn't have been,' Emma said, sitting up sleepily, and sipping her tea. 'I'm quite all right. It *was* rather upsetting. Those gruesome stories, too. I wonder, do you think the Germans are really like that?'

Rebecca tilted her head sideways and said at last, 'Naomi says never to believe more than ten per cent of what you hear in gossip, fifty per cent of what you read in the newspaper, nor one per cent of anything whatsoever said by a politician. I suppose it's a bit exaggerated, if nothing else.'

Emma smiled gratefully and said, 'I do hope.' Then she drew her feet up and made room for Rebecca to sit on the edge of the bed. She glanced out of the window with its yet undrawn curtains. The long summer light of August in the North was slipping away.

'But what of our plans,' she said. 'Has Mother really agreed?'

Rebecca nodded happily. 'We're all to go together, down to London, when I take Robert down for his school term. I'd have to be going then anyhow; indeed I fear I've far outstayed my welcome. This was all meant to be a weekend visit, if you'll recall.'

'Not at all,' Emma said at once. 'We've all been delighted to have you, mother included. And particularly Tenny,' she said with a small smile. 'And it was totally logical for you to stay, and for Robert, since Naomi will be in France. But what of Robert in the hols if you become a VAD?'

'Well, there'll be the housekeeper,' Rebecca said practically, 'and no doubt Naomi will be back in a few months. She's only going to give a hand until they have time to find enough professionals. And who knows, like as not by the Christmas break, everyone will be home again. I've just written a letter to Naomi at her address in Le Touquet. No doubt she'll approve; I'm only doing what she's doing herself.'

'And Susan?'

'She'll have to ask her Grandmother when she's home next. By the by, does she always stay here half the time? She seems as much a Maclaren as a Bruce.'

Emma laughed. 'I dare say. We're all a bit mixed together, I'm afraid. We've lived in and out of each other's houses for generations as far as I can tell. No matter. I'm sure Maud Bruce will approve. She's led a terribly adventurous life herself, you know. She'll be all for it. Oh it's marvellous. I'll feel I'm really doing something at last. We must make inquiries at once, and find a hospital willing to take us on.'

There was a rap on the door. Susan Bruce entered in response to Emma's 'Come,' and stood there, her eyes bright, with a clutch of writing-paper in her hand.

'Listen,' she breathed, and began to read. When she had finished Emma was once again on the verge of tears and Rebecca was crying openly.

'Oh Susan,' she whispered, 'I wish you hadn't. It's all so terribly sad. That poor brave woman, kneeling down with the Belgian flag wrapped around her body, all dripping blood.' She sobbed, 'Oh, where did you find it? What newspaper was it?'

'None,' said Susan brightly. 'I wrote it myself.'

'You wrote it,' Emma cried. 'You mean it's not real?'

'No,' Susan said with a grin.

'You just made it up?' Rebecca said, growing angry. 'Just to make fools of us.' She was now ashamed of her tears and clutched one of the flounced feather pillows on the bed and hurled it at Susan. Susan sidestepped, a little shocked at her response, and stood open-mouthed.

'Oh no,' she said softly. 'I wasn't making fun. No, I meant it. It was all those stories. I had to . . . I had to *say* something back. It was a sort of tribute. Don't you understand?' She looked terribly hurt.

'Of course we do,' Emma said at once, comfortingly, her always soft heart touched. 'It's absolutely splendid. Like a poem, isn't it, Rebecca. It's as if Susan had written a poem for Little Belgium.'

Rebecca nodded, 'Oh yes, I do see. It really was terribly good, Susan. Terribly real. See, it made us both cry.'

'I shall call it "Little Belgium at Bay",' said Susan Bruce.

At breakfast, Emma said to Lady Maclaren, 'Mother, have you seen Susan's marvellous story?'

' "Little Belgium at Bay," ' said Victoria drily.

'Oh yes,' Rebecca said. 'Isn't it touching? It reduced Emma

and me to tears.'

'I dare say,' said Victoria, buttering toast.

'Don't you like it, Lady Maclaren?' Rebecca said quietly.

Victoria patted her hand. 'Of course, dear. It was very good. Susan is genuinely talented. But don't you think,' she said with a small smile, addressing both girls, 'don't you think rather a lot did happen to that one Belgian woman? Losing her husband, having her house burnt down, her poor old grandmother hung from a tree, her baby bayoneted, her toddler drowned in the well, and then being raped and bayoneted herself, wrapped in the Belgian flag, mind you, while her brother who just happened to be a priest is hanging upside-down from his own church bell. Really quite stunningly unfortunate.'

Emma giggled, finding perspective again. 'I suppose it is a little silly, when you put it all together like that,' she said. 'Poor Susan, she is rather romantic. Harmless enough though.'

'There's nothing harmless about a romantic, dear,' said Victoria primly. 'Ask your father some time.' Emma looked up, startled, but just then Susan Bruce appeared in the doorway of the dining-room. She was still in her long blue velvet dressing-gown and looked quite distraught.

'Has anyone seen "Little Belgium at Bay"?' she cried. 'I left it on the writing table in the drawing-room last night and now it's simply vanished.'

Philippa Maclaren did not join her mother and the other girls for breakfast that morning. She rose early and went to the stables and requested that her brother Tenny's grey hunter be saddled for her. She specified the side-saddle for although Emma had taken increasingly to riding astride, Philippa was more conventional and wore her skirted riding habit. She set off for Beauly at a canter. She was in a hurry, having not only an appointment to keep at the recruiting office, but an important letter to post.

She could, naturally, have waited for its collection by the postie who always obliged with that service, or simply have left it with the usual stack of mail on the hallstand for the butler, Mr MacLeod, who usually took care of such matters. But she was anxious about this letter; she neither wanted it delayed, nor its address displayed too openly to members of the household. Some things, Philippa knew, were best carried out alone.

She made an attractive picture, riding alone into Beauly, her neat little black veiled riding hat tipped over her forehead, and her heavy hair looped up in a double braid and held fast at the nape of her neck by a black net. People turned to watch her ride by, the lady from the Big House. She did not notice them, nor notice the tall, lanky figure in green tweed plus-fours and stalking cap who emerged from MacPherson's gun shop as she passed. Harry Bruce watched her as she trotted slowly up the street. She was oblivious of his presence.

Philippa herself was absorbed in a secret and girlish daydream in which Torquil Farquhar returned suddenly from France on leave and, upon his arrival at Inverness station, was attracted to a vast throng of cheering young men and women surrounding a slim, attractive figure who, from the little step below the plinth of a stone Scottish soldier, was exhorting her fellow citizens to rise in arms for the sake of Little Belgium. In her dream the returning soldier, overcome by emotion, strode through the parting crowd and mounted the platform as well, calling out to the crowd the justice of her cause. Only then did he turn and see it was herself. 'Philippa,' he would whisper, 'why did I never realize before . . .' A girlhood of romantic novelists had been no more lost on Philippa Maclaren than on Susan Bruce.

The voice that did whisper in her ear as she stood, with a moment's guilty hesitation, in front of the red metal letterbox set in the stone wall beside the door of the post office, was not Torquil Farquhar's. It was the voice of Harry Bruce, and he said, teasing, 'What's this then, secret love letters?'

She gasped, and her gloved hand came up so quickly to cover the address that he, for a startled moment, was quite convinced that it was a love letter after all. Then nothing would do but that he see it, a most ungentlemanly act only made faintly acceptable by the fact that, having grown up almost as brother and sister, they were accustomed to taking liberties. This was one liberty, however, she was quite unwilling to allow. There followed an unseemly little struggle that ceased only when Philippa, out of sheer embarrassment, allowed him his way. He unpeeled her fingers from the fat envelope and read, quite to his disappointment, 'The Editor, The Glasgow Herald, Glasgow'.

'A newspaper?' Harry said.

'Very good. You can read.' Philippa was standing straight as a poker, her thin cheeks reddening.

'So whyever all the secrecy, old girl?' Harry said, bemused.

'And what is it anyhow, some fearsome patriotic tract?'

That was a bit close to the bone and Philippa, foolishly, went quite out of character to throw him off track. 'No. Nothing like that. It's . . . it's an inquiry about an advertisement. A hat. A hat I saw advertised and rather fancied. That's all.'

Harry looked at her with dry disbelief and casually stroked the long flop of soft brown hair back from his eyes. He tilted his head sideways and lowered his upper lids, assessing her with an expression that had earned him the family nickname of The Dominie. Servant girls ordered hats from newspapers. The Maclaren daughters most certainly did not. Furthermore it was quite inconceivable that Philippa Maclaren, never a frivolous girl, would be thinking of hats in what the newspapers called 'these stirring times'.

'I don't believe you,' said Harry Bruce.

'Believe what you like,' Philippa said, snatching back the envelope. Guilt was gone now in her haste to get it safely away, and she thrust it hurriedly into the slit below the letters GVR. 'Now if you will excuse me, I have an appointment at eleven.'

'Very well,' said Harry Bruce, not moving, 'So have I. However, since it is now exactly ten-fifteen,' he had taken out his pocket-watch to underline the authority of the church steeple clock, 'I suggest you and I retire to the Priory Inn for coffee and discuss the state of the nation. Or,' he paused grinning, 'the millinery trade, if you prefer.'

'That would be very pleasant,' she said as unpleasantly as she could manage, turning away. 'However, Mr Bruce, I feel it the duty of every young woman to show where her true feelings lie. As mine lie, and I am proud to say it, with the brave boys in khaki going off to defend poor little Belgium, then it would be most unseemly for me to be seen in a café with a man of your . . .' she paused, her eyes cold, '. . . sensibilities,' she said at last.

Just for a moment Harry Bruce felt growing in him that real, deep anger that came upon him more and more these days. But he maintained, for the moment, his smooth control. He stepped back from Philippa, tilted his head sideways and smiled bemusedly. She took his smile for a softening, and when he said, 'Well now, that would never do. I would hate to weaken your cause, after all,' she took him at face value.

'Harry,' she said tentatively, 'you do know . . . you do know . . . I mean, how well I think of you aside from this. I mean, if you were to appear beside me in uniform, why, I would go anywhere with . . .'

'Thank you, madam,' said Harry. 'I would not sell myself so cheap if I were you. There are far more attractive cowards to be won for the cause. As for me, I might be persuaded, like others for thirty pieces of silver. But a cup of coffee?'

He turned and walked away, leaving Philippa alone before the post office and a recruiting poster of a Belgian mother in tearful distress.

8

On the twenty-third of August, Lieutenant Torquil Farquhar, that pleasant, unassuming young man who had quite unwittingly won the hearts of not one, but two Maclaren daughters, at last crossed the frontier into that country for whose sake, ostensibly, his own had gone to war. The picture it presented as he, and the rest of the brigade, approached the advancing enemy was hardly the same as the image being broadcast throughout the newspapers of Britain.

They had met with refugees, frightened women and children and old men, with carts and old prams, and even wheelbarrows loaded with possessions. But their language, the coarse and unattractive Flemish of the area, did not make for easy communications. Whatever they fled from remained only rumour. In the small farmhouse that had sheltered Torquil Farquhar and his brother officers last night, the talk had been of German brutalities. But no one could be precise regarding where and to whom these acts had occurred.

Torquil had kept an open mind. The countryside was peaceful enough, the fields rich with corn. The previous three days had been spent at the village of Grougis in France, near the Belgian border, and the men had been put to the task of harvesting the local crops. There was no point in seeing it wasted, and the hot sun was perfect. The CO had thought it best that they be working at something useful for the local population, all of whom were suffering from the lack of able men and the lack of horses. Idleness in a soldier, Gordon Bruce knew, bred introspection. And introspection before action was not wanted. Besides, many of his battalion were farmboys who had often enough in the past done the same work at the same time of year, back in the strath. Donnie Cameron for one had fallen gratefully upon this task, welcoming as all the rest an end to the daily marches on cobbled roads. Within half a day Donnie would gladly have stayed for ever in the hot French fields doing the thing that he knew how to do best. He felt quite proud showing town-bred Andy Henderson the best way with the sickle and the fork.

Then yesterday, orders had come through from Wassigny where the newly arrived General Munro had set up Divisional Headquarters, alongside the headquarters of First Corps itself. General Haig and his staff, Ian Maclaren included, were ensconsed there as well. On those orders they had marched again, towards the Belgian mining town of Mons, one more step on the way to their ultimate destination, to the left of the French armies. There they would form part of the left arm of the pincer movement that would envelop the advancing enemy. The agreement about their place in a European war had been made in 1911 at a time when a European conflict was far more diplomatic theory than fact. The agreement still bound them now.

'I would have thought,' Gordon Bruce had confided to his second-in-command, Major Jonathon Grant, 'that we'd be far more useful on our own. Perhaps even a Belgian landing, since Belgian neutrality is the issue after all. Something sharp and swift and a bit unexpected, instead of this business of attaching ourselves like a tail to the French dog. When Papa Joffre says wag, we're going to wag, mark you, and it's not what we're good at, these big massed attacks the French go for.' Grant had agreed, but there was nothing either he or Gordon Bruce could do about it. So they had marched instead northeastwards, from the railway station at Busigny on to Grougis, where they had awaited the concentration of their Division. Now they were marching again.

The men hated it. The cobbled roads were terribly hard on their feet, and twisted ankles and blisters were real if petty casualties. The heat, too, took its toll and many of the reservists were hardly fit. When they arrived in the village of Mons, a modest place of cobbled streets and small houses set down among fields and the odd coal-mine, it seemed too small and insignificant for its years of history in the eyes of the few, like Torquil Farquhar, who had absorbed enough from school to know about it. Mons was just a little market town, like Inverness with coalfields, Torquil thought. And a damned sight hotter than Inverness today, he'd wager.

Dusty and sweating, the men collapsed in exhausted heaps as soon as their officers allowed them. Donnie Cameron, his face sunburnt and peeling, slumped down over a water-trough and let the slimy contents wash his face and forearms. When he looked up, two young girls were offering a basketful of ripe red plums. He grinned and snatched a handful, forcing their wet sweet flesh into his mouth, one after another, as soon as he could spit out the stones. Andy Henderson, limping slightly from a growing blister, flopped down on the edge of the water-trough, lowering his pack and rifle to the ground.

'D'ye ken,' he said to Donnie, 'we've been in France nae as much as a fortnight, and I've had more smiles frae more lasses than in a' the rest o' the summer. I'm staying, lad.'

Donnie grinned, offering his friend the remnants of the plums. Despite the ache in his feet and the soreness of his shoulders weighed down with pack, rifle and ammunition, the day had much the atmosphere of a picnic. Along every roadside as they marched, flocks of young girls had waited, waving and cheering and ladening them with flowers. Yesterday they had been so decorated with bouquets and wreaths, even draping their rifles and packs, that they had seemed more a wedding party than an army. Still, as they left each village behind, they jettisoned their bouquets as discreetly as they could. They had so much to carry that even the weight of flower petals was a burden.

'D'ye mind those twa lassies yesterday, wha' had us halfway intae the café . . .' Donnie said.

'Aye.' Andy sucked loudly at a plum stone. 'I'd lay odds they'd hae us up the stairs as weel, if it werena for the RSM.'

'You were glad enough o' the sight of him, lad. Right scared you were, I could see it a' o'er yer face.'

Andy made to swipe at Donnie for that, but was too tired. He sagged instead against the water-trough and relaxed, his sun-reddened face broadening into a reminiscent smile. 'Jeez, but war is fun. If it werena fer the feet.'

'Och well,' said Donnie. 'Here's an end to it.'

'The war?' Andy said, his eyes closed.

'Nae. The fun. Awa' on yer feet. Here comes the sergeant.'

Sergeant Ross MacDonald strode towards them across the cobbled street, his big unappealing bulk parting the crowds of curious civilians. At his side was Lance Corporal Sandy Gibson, looking less than pleased.

'Right, youse lot,' the platoon sergeant addressed Donnie and Andy Henderson, and the five other private soldiers sheltering with them in the welcome shade of an apple tree overhanging the water-trough. 'Proceed to the railway-line beyond the town and await orders there.' There was a small moan from the Belgian girls surrounding them, quickly silenced by a black look from MacDonald, and the tired men scrambled to their feet and the girls scurried away.

'Where we gae'n?' Andy whispered to Donnie, and Sandy Gibson said quietly,

'There's a railway cut beyond the town. We're to entrench there. I ken the German cavalry are in the wood, just beyont.'

There was another, louder moan now that MacDonald was out of hearing and Sandy only said, 'C'mon lads, let's awa'.' They followed him, reluctantly leaving their shade. Halfway through the town they were met by a party of the Belgian girls who had served them the plums. With them now were a group of strapping twelve-year-olds, farm tools over their shoulders. The girls were grinning and in confused English managed to explain that, since the soldiers were so tired and so brave, the boys and girls would dig trenches for them.

'Och, thot's grand o' ye,' Andy Henderson said happily.

But Sandy Gibson turned on them angrily, 'Get awa' the lot o' ye,' he said, sounding as fierce as he could manage. 'Bugger aff. We havena time for bairns' games.'

Dejectedly, their erstwhile helpers left them, and Donnie Cameron said aloud, emboldened by annoyance, 'Why'd ye gae and dae thot? They're only wantin' tae help. An' I for one could use a hand, e'en wi' this bluidy pack.'

'Shut yer gob,' Sandy said sharply. 'They help us and the Germans line em up agin a wa' and shoot the lot.'

'The bastards,' whispered Donnie, but Sandy said at once,

'We'd dae the same if we caught them helping the Boche. We hae to. Wars nae place fer civilians, lad.'

For all that, as they set about entrenching themselves beside the railway-line, and setting up barricades of sandbags and uplifted paving-stones, they were hard-pressed to keep the local boys as well as the excited girls out of their way.

When they had completed their modest fortifications Andy Henderson and Donnie Cameron settled down in the shade of them and once again their brief rest was interrupted. This time it was the arrival of their platoon leader, Lieutenant John Bruce.

'Sergeant MacDonald.'

'Sir.'

'The CO has received word that German cavalry have been active just beyond that wood.' He pointed out over the heaped sandbags to the soft green of a farmyard copse beyond the village. 'Detail a section up to that farmhouse and see what you can find.'

'Right,' said the sergeant, 'Corporal Gibson . . .'

In a moment he was gone and Andy and Donnie were raising incredulous eyebrows, shouldering their packs and setting out, warily in extended formation, across the open ground beyond the town. Nothing occurred to justify their wariness. They reached the farmhouse and, finding it unoccupied, advanced beyond it to the edge of the wood itself. It was still and full of wildlife, and it became increasingly difficult to conceive of any force of men, enemy or otherwise, within miles. In the distance, the church bells of Mons were ringing. It was Sunday.

'Och, there's naething surely,' Andy whispered. Donnie had become so insolently calm that he was surreptitiously picking raspberries as they made their way through the cluster of trees. But quite suddenly they heard a shout, and then laughter, and just as they expected another group of village children to emerge, foolishly enough, in their midst, they heard the low beat of hoofs on soft, woodland turf.

'Horses,' Sandy Gibson muttered under his breath. There was a jingle of bridles and the creak of harness and then, with a wild, laughing shout they appeared, at a gay, hunter's canter, a half-dozen cavalry in German *feld grau*.

'Uhlans,' Sandy whispered, amazed, as the lancers halted before them in a clearing. They were still laughing and talking happily and it was quite evident that they were as convinced as he had been a moment earlier, that the wood was empty. They had blundered into war.

'Section, fire,' Sandy shouted. Instantly, their months and months of training took command. Rifles were at shoulders and men were firing, the incredibly rapid fire that only the British soldier with his Lee Enfield could manage, fifteen aimed rounds a minute, a volley of shots so fast and so quickly repeated that the reports blended into one storm of sound. German survivors of such attacks reported facing machine-guns. But there were no survivors of this attack and it was over long before the minute. It was over in seconds. The Uhlans lay messily heaped, a scattering of bloody *feld grau* on the ground amid the struggles of their dying horses.

Donnie Cameron stood with his mouth open, not believing what he had seen and what he had done. The spasmodic kicking of one frantic shod hoof dinned against the grey helmet of one soldier. Then Sandy Gibson shot the horse and the wood went silent, and then abruptly filled up again with natural sound.

'They're a' deid,' Andy Henderson whispered to himself, in amazement.

'Aye,' said Sandy. 'Come on.' He led his men back, knowing they were out on a limb, after all that firing, though he doubted there were any other Germans about. The small party they had met were just foolishly having fun, a nice ride in the summer sun, like the gentlemen at Culbrech were wont to do. No soldier expecting action or anticipating any meeting with the enemy behaves like that. Their lines must be far from here. Murder, he thought suddenly. We've done murder. He was stunned. That wasn't what his training told him. It wasn't what his officers would tell him. It wasn't true. He knew it wasn't true. But the day, the summer sun, the church bells still ringing, the beautiful wood were telling him. Like I'd done it at home. In the strath. Shot them down. In all their gaiety they could have been Tenny Maclaren and Johnny Bruce or any of the other young men.

'Are yer wantin' a raspberry?' said a shy voice beside him. Donnie Cameron was extending a hand with a pile of soft red fruit smearing the palm. 'They're awfu' good.'

'Get yer ass awa' hame,' Sandy growled and aimed a boot at Cameron's fleeing kilt.

The Maclarens had drawn their first blood.

When they returned to their own lines at the railway cutting, Sandy Gibson went at once in search of his officers to report on their encounter with the enemy. He found Johnny Bruce in conversation with B Company commander, Colin Chisholm, and dutifully related their finding of the six Uhlans, and his assessment of the situation in the wood. He was given a polite hearing and a minor congratulation on their success, but no one seemed particularly interested. The Battalion had received orders to march again, southeastwards this time, to the small village of Harveng to support the 3rd Division. Around them, the men were already forming up. Sandy Gibson collected his men and rejoined his platoon, feeling disjointed and confused, the brief violence of their summer morning already fading into unreality.

'Whar we gae'n nou?' Donnie Cameron whispered.

'Dear kens.' Andy Henderson finished cleaning his rifle and put away the small square of oiled cloth, shouldered his pack and, with the rest, set off once more. He was comforted by the knowledge that his officers at least must surely know what was going on.

A few hundred yards down road of him, Torquil Farquhar signalled to his own A Company commander, George Brown, as he rode up the side of the column. Brown slowed his trotting horse, and they paused in the dusty road. They had become good friends and now looked at each other with an exchange of wry shrugs.

'You wouldn't by chance have any idea what's going on?' Torquil said, glancing down the marching column of men.

'Wish I had,' Brown replied. 'Be nice to be able to answer questions without feeling like a liar.'

'The men all think we're practising for the grave-diggers' marathon. Dig three ditches, march four miles, dig two ditches, march four miles.' He grinned but said sharply, 'Damned disheartening.'

'It's that,' Brown said, turning his nervous horse. 'Wish we'd get a bit of action. Make them know what they're here for. Word is we're to move in beside the Coldstreamers and entrench east of Harveng. There's a big ridge beyond, where the Mons-Givry road runs. Boche are supposed to be in position there. Listen.' He went quiet, and over the sound of the marching feet they could clearly make out the rumble of distant artillery. Captain Brown grinned. 'More like it,' he said quietly, and turned his horse and rode to the head of the column.

'Hey youse,' Andy Henderson called to Donnie.

'Aye?'

'Hear yon?'

'Dinna hear onything.'

'Guns.'

Donnie shrugged, 'Sae what of them?' he grinned lopsidedly and rubbed his dusty upper lip with the back of his hand.

'We're gae'n towards 'em.'

Donnie shrugged again and rubbed his lip again. 'Maclarens'll sort 'em,' he said at last.

The Maclarens, it turned out, weren't asked to. They were moved into a support position at the base of the ridge Captain Brown had spoken of and found themselves between the Grenadier Guard battalion, whose arrival in Le Havre had coincided with their own, on their left, and the Coldstreamers on their right. Once more Donnie and Andy Henderson found themselves scratching away at the Belgian chalk with the light entrenching tools that each carried. Their tool cart was somewhere else, as it always seemed to be, and the more effective heavy entrenching tools with it. Over the ridge before them enemy shrapnel shells burst regularly, an invigorating sign that there really was opposition out there somewhere. Elsewhere their own artillery could be heard, pounding away at mysterious unseen targets.

There was a railway cutting that nipped across the southern foot of the big chalk hill, and in its limited shelter Gordon Bruce set up Battalion Headquarters. Over their heads there was a steady whistling of shrapnel but the shells, fired from beyond the crest of the hill, were overreaching them and landing an innocent distance away down in the valley. Gordon Bruce sent an aide in search of Major Grant, his senior company commander. Grant, a tall, dark, quiet-spoken Highlander, who had a way of listening to all around him before reaching a calculated decision, was his preferred adviser. When he arrived, Gordon Bruce offered the formalities of tea and as they drank it from tin mugs they discussed the state of the war. Although it was plain from the sounds of gunfire in the distance beyond Mons that someone was fighting a battle, they still knew very little. 'I spoke briefly with the CO of the Grenadiers,' Gordon said. 'There's a rumour about that Lanrezac's failed to get the Fifth Army across the Sambre. If it's true, we're a bit up in the air.'

'If it's true we'd better be getting out of here,' Jonathon Grant said mildly. 'But I think John French has committed us up ahead, from the sound of things. Are the Irish Rifles meeting with much up the ridge?'

'I don't know. I've sent a party out to see. Sent my nephew John Bruce. Time the boy were blooded. Might settle him down a bit.'

Jonathon Grant grinned, 'Bloody nepotism,' he said.

'Like to go yourself?' Gordon said. 'They've a machine-gun playing right down that road,' he gestured above them to the Mons-Givry roadway as it zigzagged, a slash of white, up their hill, hill 93 on their maps. Major Grant shook his head, assessing his commanding officer silently. He hoped he knew what he was doing, testing the boy so soon.

As afternoon tipped lazily into evening to the continuous sound of distant artillery, the men of the Maclaren Highlanders settled down in their newly-dug trenches and brewed tea in their mess-tins over the meagre heat of cakes of solidified paraffin. The trenches were moderate slipshod affairs, just indentations in the ground that provided enough shelter if a man kept his head down. No one expected to spend any time in them. They confidently expected to be advancing at any moment, and made the best of the rock-hard biscuits which they hardly planned to be eating for very long. It was with girded mental loins that Colour Sergeant MacTavish responded to Lieutenant John Bruce's order to accompany him up the Mons-Givry road.

'Aye weel,' he said with precisely the same sigh and the same laying of broad hands on broad thighs that would at home always precede his rising to go out to work. 'That'll be us awa'.' He heaved his bulk to his feet and nodded to young Donnie Cameron as he rose.

But John Bruce said, 'Just yourself, Sergeant. We're to see if the Irish Rifles are wanting a hand yet.'

'Och aye, puir wee things'll be lost wi'out us,' Andy Henderson said, dipping his biscuit into his tea with panache. He was feeling comfortable and sure of himself, like he knew all the ropes. He didn't, of course, and MacTavish the Inverness plumber, veteran of the South African campaign, did. That was why John Bruce had chosen him.

'Juist tell them t' wait until we hae our tea,' Andy called to his disappearing back.

Willie MacTavish laughed to himself and followed John Bruce with a certain eagerness. He wasn't eager for the fighting. Unlike the two lads behind in their snug trench, he had actually experienced it. But he wanted to get the job done. Soon they would engage, and once they engaged the sharp, swift retribution of British military might would, as it always had done, silence the opposition. But MacTavish could not tolerate this fiddling about on dusty roads. He wanted action, swift action that would finish this thing, and get him back to Belle and the bairns and the well-worn comfort of his trade. He hoisted himself up out of the trench, over the sandbag parapet, and followed Lieutenant Bruce into the narrow cutting through which ran the road.

'Someone's catching it somewhere,' he said to Bruce, jerking his head towards the distant sound of gunfire beyond. Someone was indeed. As MacTavish and Johnny Bruce felt their way gingerly up the sheltered left-hand bank of the road, some few miles away most of the rest of I Corps were engaged in what would be called the Battle of Mons. For the vast majority of the Maclarens it would pass as one more day of marching and confusion. For Willie MacTavish and Johnny Bruce it would be something more.

'Keep yer heid doun,' MacTavish roared suddenly, as a spattering of machine-gun fire snapped across the road. '*Sir*,' he added, retrospectively. Johnny Bruce was high on excitement, and his native courage was veering into recklessness. MacTavish, older and experienced, had shepherded young second lieutenants into their first actions before. And, he thought with humour, he wasn't about to be the NCO who lost the colonel-in-chief's grandson on virtually the first day of the war. No. Not even if it meant taking the wee sod by the scruff of the neck up to the CO of the Irish Rifles himself.

As it was, Johnny Bruce heeded his warning and kept himself in order, creeping up the roadside under the cover of its hedging of dried grass and wild chervil. There was meadowland to their left and up ahead a few trees. From somewhere beyond the trees there came an occasionally deliberate crack of a rifle shot, a more personal offence than the inconsiderate machine-gun bursts with which the Boche were covering the narrow road.

'Sniper,' said Johnny Bruce, 'I'll get the bastard.'

'Nae, sir. Ye'll ne'er see him. Come awa'. Never mind him.'

Johnny Bruce relented and they made their way upwards until

they reached the bend in the road that took it on a zag, back in a more northerly direction, uphill. The bend was exposed and they crossed it in two bounds. Then they were out of the line of the machine-gun and the sniper too seemed silent.

'Yon's the Irish,' said MacTavish.

Johnny Bruce nodded, and told MacTavish to remain where he was. He went on alone and met up with the second-in-command, a major who assured him that they were well in control of the situation.

'Any casualties?' Johnny asked.

'A few,' the major replied. 'Not bad. Highlanders, are you?' he said, rather than asked, nodding towards Johnny's khaki-aproned kilt.

'Yes. First Battalion Maclarens.'

The major nodded, satisfied. 'Glad to have you alongside,' he said with another sharp nod. 'Give my regards to your CO. Gordon Bruce, isn't it?'

Johnny nodded. 'My uncle,' he said, 'actually.'

'Do tell,' the major ducked down instinctively from the whistle of a high shrapnel shell. 'They're wasting those things,' he said, noncommittally. 'Ah yes. Your uncle, is he. Grand fellow. Saw him at the Northern Meeting. Charming wife. Do send my best.' Johnny nodded patiently, feeling more and more incongruous. 'Stay for tea?' said the major.

'Ah, no,' Johnny said. 'Must be getting back. Left a man alongside the road.'

'Mind that sniper,' said the major as he left.

'I will.' Johnny smiled to himself, scuttling down the road in a crouching run. He began, for no reason, to giggle. Oh do stay for tea. Oh do.

'MacTavish,' he shouted, as he reached the bend. An arm caught his leg, wrapped around the khaki gaiter and Johnny went flying, landing headlong in the dirt as the sharp report of a rifle filled the air.

'What the hell,' he shouted.

'Keep yer fucking heid doun, I said,' MacTavish roared, 'sir.'

'The sniper,' Johnny whispered, recovering his breath.

'Aye,' MacTavish said from inside his shelter of a bristling roadside thornbush. 'He spotted me while youse were awa'. What took ye sae lang? Are they needin' oor help?'

'No. They're fine. Sorry, the major was rather social.'

'Och aye, was he,' MacTavish growled to himself. 'That's grand. If we creep alang this bittie hedge, and then make a dash across that open bit tae yon tall skinny tree,' he pointed to a poplar that marked the edge of the road, swinging back down towards their position in the railway cutting, 'I think we'll gie him a miss.'

Johnny nodded. 'I'll go first,' he said. 'Give me some cover.'

MacTavish nodded. 'Right ye are, lad, but move it.' He raised his Lee Enfield and fired off shot after shot in the general direction of the invisible sniper.

Johnny made his dash over open ground and dived into the roadway, tumbling down the crumbling chalky bank. Then, thanking his Uncle Gordon for his unorthodox advice, scrambled back up the bank to provide MacTavish with the same cover. Fortunately for MacTavish, Johnny Bruce carried a rifle. Officers carried handguns, all very nice and proper but little bloody use at a time like this.

'Get yourself a rifle,' Gordon Bruce had said, and Johnny had. More and more officers he noticed did the same. Johnny now fired a few shots in the direction of the sniper until MacTavish was beside him. MacTavish grunted his approval. His young officer was shaping up. He was confident already of getting him back to his company intact. Then Johnny Bruce stood up and started to walk into the middle of the road.

'What the fuckin' hell,' MacTavish roared.

'Going to get that sniper,' Johnny said quietly, raising his rifle. He'd seen the tip of a branch move, in one distant dark green tree, when he fired his last shot. Someone up there had found that one too close. Someone had moved. In a moment he'd move again, taking aim. It was just a question of being quick, like stalking on the hills at home. He kept his eyes on that tree. He was quite safe, he was sure. The branch would move first.

'Doun ye bloody gowk,' MacTavish shouted, and then, as the machine-gun started up again, he dived for Johnny Bruce in the roadway. They both went down, MacTavish a deadweight on top of his young officer. Johnny lay flat as the staccato spluttering raked back and forth across the road. He'd forgotten it. He'd forgotten the machine-gun. It had been quiet. Jammed. Or the crew drinking tea. He had forgotten it. The sniper, like a stag on the hill, had had every ounce of his attention. He breathed a long throaty breath. Christ.

'Thanks, Sergeant,' he said. He twisted his head round. MacTavish's face was a mass of blood, his right eye a dark emptiness in his head.

9

At eleven o'clock that night, a night that had turned surprisingly cold after the heat of the day, Lieutenant Colonel Gordon Bruce was sitting and talking quietly with his second-in-command when a voice he recognized as that of Colin Chisholm called softly out of the darkness, 'Is the CO here?'

'Right here,' Gordon answered, getting swiftly to his feet. The men were sleeping around him in huddled heaps. They were stiff from marching and from the chill after sweating in the sun, and none of them had had a proper meal since they left their billets in the dawn. The last fifteen hours seemed impossibly long for the span of a single day. 'What is it?' he asked Captain Chisholm.

'Sorry to disturb you, sir,' Chisholm said, keeping his voice low in the eerie stillness of the night. The artillery had died away, and the dark was only broken by an occasional rifle shot that kept the camp from sinking into peace. Chisholm crouched down beside Gordon Bruce. 'It's young Bruce actually. He's taken it rather badly. I thought you might have a word.'

'MacTavish's death . . . was it his fault?' Gordon asked disarmingly.

There was a silence. Eventually Chisholm said, 'I don't imagine so. Anyhow, there's no one aside from Bruce and MacTavish who will ever know. And the Boche sniper. And the last two aren't going to tell us much. Not the point, anyhow. Point is the boy blames himself. He was there, he was the officer, you know.'

'Send him over,' Gordon said so quietly that Chisholm was obliged to ask him to repeat it. 'I'll talk to him,' he said, again.

As soon as Chisholm had left, he regretted it and sat leaning against the dry chalky bank, his knees drawn up and his chin on the dirty palm of his hand. Not an easy business at the best of times. Twice as hard when it was family. Damn though, he thought wryly, they were all family, one way or another, his regiment. He thought briefly of MacTavish, remembering him both as soldier and as good-natured plumber who spent his leisure time running the Boys' Brigade. Who'd have thought. War only a few days old.

'Colonel Bruce, sir,' the voice was so pathetically young, a child's voice suddenly, full of remorse.

Good Christ, lad, Gordon thought suddenly, I wish to God it were just another broken window back home.

'Yes, Bruce,' he said. 'Won't you sit down.'

Johnny Bruce found himself a corner of sandbag and settled on it, remembering the Irish Rifles major and wincing.

Gordon Bruce drew out his personal flask and extended it over a tin mug to his nephew. 'You'll have a drink?'

'No thank you, sir. I'd rather not. I'm quite tired and it will go straight to my head.'

Gordon Bruce shrugged and put his flask away. Worse than he thought. 'That never bothered you before that I can remember.'

'This is rather different, sir. Besides, there may be action. I need a clear head.'

'Of course,' Gordon agreed. 'Though I think we're about done for the night. Still, as you wish. Nasty bit of bother this afternoon, what.'

'Rather not talk about it, sir,' John Bruce said shortly, his voice tight with strain.

'Mr Bruce, I am your commanding officer and *I* wish to talk about it.'

'Sir,' Johnny Bruce said at once, straightening up to attentiveness, suddenly remembering his situation.

'Well?'

There was a long silence, and a faintly gulping sound from the young officer and his dim shadowy shape huddled up as his head bent over. 'It was all my damn fault, Uncle Gordon . . . Colonel Bruce, sir,' he gasped. He was suddenly just a boy crying, this brashest of the clan.

'I'd like to know how,' Gordon said, looking off at the dim outline of hill 93 above them. He waited while the youngster composed himself and eventually told his brief story.

'He saved my life, of course. He shouldn't have bothered. It was so damn damn stupid. I was just so certain I could get that blasted sniper. I just forgot . . . forgot there'd ever been a machine-gun emplacement up that road. He was quiet, you see. And that silly nonsense with the major took my mind off it. All I could think about was the sniper.'

'Why?' Gordon Bruce asked.

There was a pause. 'Why? I don't know. I . . . guess it was just because he made me so angry. Firing away at us from that blasted tree. Out of sight. Cowardly, sort of.'

'Indeed,' Gordon Bruce said. 'He wasn't "playing the game", was he? Mowing half a battalion down with a Lewis gun is quite all right, but we mustn't hide behind trees?'

'Well, hardly,' Johnny Bruce said angrily.

'Hardly *sir*,' Gordon snapped back. Then he sighed and leaned back against his chalk bank for so long that he sensed a restless embarrassed squirming on the part of the young officer. Like a schoolboy held by the bleak silence of the dominie. He said at last, 'Well lad, I can't give you lines, or the tawse or any other punishment that will clear the air for you. You're not at school any longer. And I can't bring Sergeant MacTavish back to life. You've learned a little lesson today. War's no game, laddie. It's a bloody nasty, unfair, cheating, ugly business. If you come through it with your sense of honour unsullied you'll have done a hell of a lot better than most. Now. Your little lesson has cost a good man his life, a good woman her husband, three children their father, and our battalion a bloody fine soldier.'

'I know that,' Johnny Bruce said with such obvious pain that Gordon Bruce softened.

'I'm not trying to hurt you, lad,' he said. 'You didn't do that badly either. You did your job and made one bad mistake. MacTavish did his job. Part of his job is looking after your lot until you've learned sense. Good NCOs make good officers. But it's good officers that make the battalion. As for MacTavish, I'll write his wife tomorrow, and you can dedicate the rest of your career to making yourself into the kind of officer he'd be proud of. Now get off and get some sleep,' he said, and as John Bruce rose to leave him he added, 'And Mr Bruce . . .'

'Sir?'

'Learn to concentrate. The Boche aren't going to promise to shoot from one side at a time. You can't make much of an officer if you don't stay alive.'

Johnny Bruce nodded a bit grimly and turned away, but before he was a yard from his commanding officer the stillness was again interrupted by a voice.

'Do pardon, but is Colonel Bruce about?' Johnny recognized the cultured tones of the major from the Irish Rifles.

'Right here,' Gordon said and then in the faint starlight made out the other's face.

'Ah, Gordon, what a pleasure,' the major said, smiling. 'So nice to see you. Just dropped in to let you know and all.'

'Let us know what?' Gordon Bruce demanded, mystified.

'That we're to withdraw, old man.'

'Withdraw?' Gordon said, astounded. 'But why?'

'Can't be sure, I'm afraid. But the Grenadiers are going too. I've just spoken to their CO. Seems our whole division is moving out. Thought I'd better let you know, though, 'cause we'll be leaving your flank up in the air. Hardly the thing, eh? How's your good lady?'

'When?' Gordon demanded, glancing despairingly over his sleeping men.

'Midnight,' said the major. 'Must be getting along. Do remember me to all at home.' He went out cheerily enough. His parting shot was, 'I'll wager the French have broken on our right, after all.'

Gordon Bruce took out his watch. It was eleven forty-five. God in heaven, he thought wearily. Who's running this war?

Private soldiers Donnie Cameron and Andy Henderson thought Colonel Bruce was running it, naturally enough. When Sergeant Nosey MacDonald awakened them with a roar and the toe of his boot, and when they had managed to shake off enough exhaustion to think at all, they concluded in Donnie's words, 'He's gane roun' the twist.'

But your CO was your CO, crazy or not, and you didn't argue. Instead you gratified yourself by laying silent curses on the head of the extremities of the long arm of military law that actually reached you; that is, your sergeant and your corporal. And then you did what you were told.

B Company had barely formed up and set out on the march when Lieutenant Colonel Bruce was confronted with a panting runner from Brigade HQ. He was glad to see him, having attempted to raise the brigadier on the telephone only to find the line, as was frequently the case, cut. Telephone wires strung out across a much trampled stubble field were invariably vulnerable.

'What's the word?' Gordon asked.

'No withdrawal sir. Division orders us to stay where we are.'

'Bloody *hell*,' Gordon said, looking painfully back over the columns of marching men. Then reluctantly he gave the order to turn round.

'Jesus Christ, what's he up tae nou?' Andy Henderson moaned.

'Och, shut yer gob,' Nosey MacDonald growled, and as he swung about the butt of his rifle connected with Henderson's shoulder, half knocking the heavily-laden soldier off his feet. 'Juist dae what yer told.'

'Bastard,' Andy muttered.

'Wheesht,' another soldier said at once, 'ye'll be for it, wi' that one.'

MacDonald swaggered up the line working out his frustration on the staggering boys in his command.

'Dinna mind,' Andy said, his voice hardening in an unaccustomed way. 'He's got nae right. I'll have that one. You mind me. I will. One day.'

'Cut the blether,' Sandy Gibson said sharply, but his eyes too were on the solid stiff back of Ross MacDonald, with cold anger. His men had enough to put up with, all this arsing about the roadways of France. They didn't need that bugger as well. Sandy sighed, marching northeastwards again, back to the spot of their interrupted rest. He seriously wondered if his officers knew what they were doing. The thought startled him. He had never had that thought before.

Lieutenant Colonel Gordon Bruce was having the same thought, at the same time, about his own superiors. In his case the thought was more serious because, unlike Sandy Gibson, he was in a position to do something about it. He had decisions to make, but he must use immense judgement, or the consequences could be dire.

As he considered the situation, the rumble of heavy, horse-drawn wheels came towards them out of the darkness ahead. It was the artillery, withdrawing. Gordon called a halt and fell his battalion out on the sides of the road to give the big limbers room to get through. The appearance of the Coldstreamers who had held the position on their right flank marching wearily southwards decided him. He spoke briefly with the CO of the Coldstreamers as they passed and then sent for his regimental sergeant major, Peter Leinie.

'Sir?' Leinie asked, clearly uncertain about the colonel's intentions.

'Sergeant Major,' Gordon said formally, 'we have been ordered to maintain this position, from Divisional HQ. In the light of the apparent general withdrawal all around us I fear we would be foolhardy to do so. Therefore I am disobeying that order in accordance with Field Service Regulations. I am satisfied that the issuer of that order is unfamiliar with the conditions in the field.'

'Sir,' said Peter Leinie. He paused just long enough for the moment of military formality to fade. 'If ye dinna mind me sayin', sir, thot's the best thocht ye've had all night. Sir.' He saluted and turned into the night, smiling to himself. He knew his opinion carried no military weight. The decision, and its consequences, were the CO's entirely. But even the commanding officer just occasionally can stand a bit of moral support.

Gordon Bruce turned his exhausted battalion round, again, and headed south.

'Bloody fucking hell,' said Donnie Cameron, summing up the general opinion of the ranks. 'Hae we lost?' he asked Andy Henderson.

'Dear kens.'

'Aren't we gonna fight?'

Andy shrugged.

'What we here for, anyhou?' Donnie demanded.

'Because we're here,' said Sandy Gibson with the bruised wisdom of experience. 'Because we're fucking here.'

They retired back into Harveng where the men were allowed a half-hour's rest. Instantly they were sleeping, scattered about the cobbled street, hunched on doorsteps, stretched full-length in the gutters. Then at dawn they moved out again. As they marched out towards Quévy-le-Grand, two miles further down the road, Gordon Bruce viewed the German artillery pounding hill 93 with mixed emotions. He felt vindicated, knowing that their infantry would soon be advancing over that ground, as he'd expected, and glad to have his battalion safely away and not out on the limb

Divisional HQ had provided for them. On the other hand, the enemy would have a splendid view of their gathered forces below the ridge. It was time they were out of there.

They got out. At Quévy-le-Grand they had orders to stand and fight, but were soon pounded out by shell-fire. They withdrew again and the retreat was gathering momentum. The roads were chaotic and crowded with the retreating army and also with hundreds of refugees, young and old, who blocked the roads with slow-moving farm wagons, overladen handbarrows and even little carts hitched to dogs. They were swamped with blankets and bedsteads and all the pathetic belongings of newly homeless people. For a while Andy Henderson was walking side by side with an ancient Belgian woman who was dressed in the customary black clothing of the district, and held in her tired arms a large parrot cage which imprisoned a highly distressed yellow tabby cat. The cat clawed at the cage. The cage latch had long since broken. Andy realized that the poor old soul was holding the door shut with her hands which were clawed raw and bleeding by her frightened pet. Andy glanced over his shoulder, looking quickly about for the bulky figure of Nosey MacDonald. When he didn't see him he shrugged suddenly and broke ranks.

'Where youse going?' Donnie called, alarmed. But Andy was already upon a broken wire fence, wire-cutters in hand. He was back in moments, a liberated length of stiff metal held out before him.

'Gie it here, ma'am,' he said and the puzzled woman stumbled away from him until, with the wire outstretched before her face, and fingers pointing at the latch, he made his point. Then he sat down on the roadside, heedless of his battalion marching past, and mended the cage.

The old woman was crying when he gave it back. She made the sign of the cross over Andy's head as he knelt with the caged cat in front of her, much to his amazement. He grinned then, patted her shoulder, extended a farewell finger to the cat and got it bitten for his efforts.

He was rubbing his finger and still grinning to himself when he returned. Nosey MacDonald was still nowhere in sight, and he slipped back gratefully into his place. MacDonald, like all the officers, had his hands full. Men were falling out left and right in the confusion, desperately trying to grab moments of rest. Then the confusion mounted when an unauthorized battalion advanced through their own and double-banked along the road, coming up to the left of the Maclarens and effectively jamming the narrow causeway so that neither could pass. It was bad discipline, and the Maclaren officers cursed them, but there was little they could do.

Torquil Farquhar observed that last bit of interference with a tolerant shrug. It had become a matter of survival of the fittest. His only concern was to get his own weary men to some point of safety where they might rest. He had spent the last hour picking up tired Jocks from the roadside, mostly with gentle persuasion. It worked better. Here and there he relieved a reeling man of his rifle and pack, and loaded them on the transport. The commanding officer, Gordon Bruce, was marching at the rear of the battalion now. He was collecting stragglers like a shepherd gathering sheep.

Torquil glanced back, watching him with some pride. He thought suddenly of Culbrech House, and the Bank Holiday picnic. As he bent to give a hand to a young soldier who had fallen, he saw himself suddenly with the same hand extended to Emma Maclaren below the rowan tree. He coughed in the dust, and spat on the ground. He could not believe he could possibly have been there just three weeks before.

They marched through La Longueveille and Maubauge and on to Pont-sur-Sambre where hospital trains were evacuating wounded in desperate haste. They went on. Late in the afternoon they stumbled into Landrecies. They had had no rest for thirty-six hours and no proper food for twenty-four. Landrecies was the headquarters of I Corps, and their commander, Douglas Haig, was there.

Gordon Bruce surmised that he would at long last find the answer to the two most pressing questions just now in his life: What the hell was going on? And, even more weighty, where in hell were the rations? He left the battalion in the charge of Major Grant and set off on foot through the crowded streets of the town. It was a sizeable place, and its population was greatly swelled by the troops of the Coldstream and Grenadier Guards, as well as the Maclarens. As they came in from the north the Maclarens had crossed both the railway-line and the wide, deep waters of the River Sambre by the town's single bridge. Instinctively Gordon Bruce mentally checked it off as a defensible point. But as he marched his battalion further into the town, defence seemed of limited importance, the place having rapidly become a British stronghold. He doubted the Boche would try anything.

He met an officer of the Grenadiers and asked directions to Haig's GHQ. The officer, with a cynical smile, pointed up a side-street to a large building, probably a hotel, Gordon judged. 'Just beyond there,' the Grenadier said. 'You can't miss it. Follow the shiny boots.'

When Gordon Bruce reached the building, a three-storey white stucco structure with green shutters, he laughed softly to himself. It was distinguished by a cluster of staff officers scattered indolently on the porch in the afternoon sunshine, marked by the red tabs on their collars as a breed apart. The very flashiness of their perfectly groomed uniforms told him of the unlikelihood of their ever seeing the Front. Poor old Ian, he thought, he'll go bloody bonkers among that lot.

Gordon entered the building, against the fussy protestations of a cluster of staff. He had found his way down several corridors before an officious-looking aide-de-camp stopped him.

'Your business, sir?'

'I wish to see Colonel Sir Ian Maclaren,' he said, rather than asked.

'I will see if he is free,' the aide replied. 'And who shall I say is calling?'

'The Prince of bloody Wales,' Gordon growled. 'If you'll kindly just show me,' but at that moment a door opened further down the corridor and another officer hurried from it. 'Colonel Maclaren is having his dinner,' he said in passing.

'Oh, just splendid,' Gordon said, and strode towards the door. But his anger cooled quickly. Ian wasn't one of this lot, he knew well enough. So he slowed and stepped quietly to the doorway and tipped it open with the flat of his hand, standing still out of sight beside the doorjamb. He began to sing, very softly and to the considerable consternation of the aide-de-camp:

We are Maclaren's army
The Highland infantry.
We cannae fight, we cannae sing
What fucking use are we . . .

There was the rough quick scraping sound of a chair flung suddenly back and two quick footsteps as a man strode, still with a young man's step, to the door. He poked his head out, amazement on his face, his tailored field dress flawless and immaculate. He looked the wrong way first, and then the right, where he faced Gordon Bruce in his road-filthy khaki. Just for a moment both of them were confronted with the appalling difference between them. They stood in embarrassed silence. The army in the field had met the army of command and they could not meet one another's eyes.

The moment passed. Ian Maclaren gave a whoop of delight and clapped a hearty left hand on Gordon's shoulder. 'I'll be buggered,' he said. It was, for him, a major display of emotion.

Like Torquil Farquhar, Gordon Bruce felt the uncanny length of the mere three weeks between their last meeting, and this. 'Good to see you, Ian,' he said at last.

'What are you doing here?' Ian asked.

'Running from the Boche,' Gordon replied grimly. 'God and perhaps your good selves know why.'

Sir Ian paused and stepped back, his hands automatically clasping behind him, a gesture familiar to Gordon Bruce as one of uneasy assessment. He cleared his throat, raising the balled fist of one hand in front of his greying moustache. 'Yes,' he said. 'Quite. I think you'd better come in.' He gestured lamely behind him to a small anteroom of the house that had been converted quickly into an office.

There were stacks of papers everywhere, giving rise to an oft-recurring thought in Gordon's mind that the army seemed to march not on its stomach as frequently held, but on its typewriters. Amidst the stacks on the desk was a tray, set with silver and laden with the unconsumed portion of Colonel Maclaren's dinner. A bottle of local wine stood on the table, and an abstemious half-glass was filled beside the plate.

'Pardon my dinner,' Ian said. 'Somehow can't seem to get used to sitting down with the whole company in style while there's all this going on. Rather mess alone and get on with my work. Do tell, have you eaten?' he said absently.

'A day and a half ago,' Gordon Bruce said and the sharpness of his voice caught Maclaren's attention.

'Good God, man, have my dinner. I didn't know it was that bad . . .'

'Ian, I've a thousand starving men out in the street. We haven't had proper rations since yesterday breakfast, our transport is God knows where, and my men have been on their feet since midnight. Can you do something?' Gordon Bruce suddenly felt his control cracking and heard the shaking of his own voice, less with tiredness than with frustration.

'Good God,' Ian repeated. 'Why didn't you say?' He didn't wait for an answer but was on his way out into the street, with Gordon Bruce trailing after, a little stunned. Passing a pair of lounging junior staff officers, Colonel Maclaren caught one by the elbow and propelled him as well out into the hot afternoon. 'Carruthers,' he said, as the startled young man struggled to attention. 'There's a ration dump down by the railway station. Find it. I want rations for a thousand men. I want them ten minutes ago. Move.'

The officer moved. Ian relaxed back on his heels with a small grunt of satisfaction. 'That'll get some dust on your boots,' he said to himself as Carruthers went off at a run. 'Now, Colonel Bruce,' he said, 'where are my Maclarens?'

As they walked back to the waiting battalion Ian Maclaren explained briefly that the French had suffered badly in the Ardennes. Their Fourth Army was driven back, and Lanrezac's Fifth on the British right had been obliged to fall back to keep in line.

'So we've got to fall back too, naturally,' Gordon concluded for him. 'Or they'll be around our flank.'

'Worse than that. Could bloody well cut us right off. If they got behind us on the Channel side as well, we'd have had it. John French promised to hold them, in front of Mons, and I gather it went well. But we daren't hold out any longer. Your lot seen any action?'

Gordon Bruce shook his head. 'None to speak of.' He wasn't about to mention their first casualty and John Bruce's part in it just now. 'What now?' Gordon asked.

Ian Maclaren, his attention drawn to the dusty mass of kilted men in the distance, hesitated before answering. He said then, 'I gather we're to regroup and make a stand when the French have got themselves together. Can't say when, or where. HQ is moving out tomorrow. Very much between ourselves I think old Sir John has the wind up. Damned uncertain fellow, half the time on top of the world, everything going splendidly, then just as quickly down so low you'd think we'd lost the war already.

Mercurial, as they say.'

'Comforting,' said Gordon Bruce drily. There was a ragged cheer from the ranks of his tired battalion. He looked up and smiled slightly, seeing that they had, quite suddenly, recognized their old commanding officer. Tired as they were they jostled forward to have a better look.

Sir Ian Maclaren felt a wave of humbling shame. They were exhausted and dusty, they hadn't washed for days, they were starving. They had been marching in heat and dust and unmitigated confusion for a day and a half, and were about to march a great deal further. And when all was done they would turn willingly, and fight to the death if they must. For a shilling a day. And for him. Ian Maclaren had more loose change in his pocket than most of them would see in a month, and had just risen from a well-cooked *coq-au-vin* and an excellent local wine. He shook his head, proud and diminished at once. 'Get your men fed and watered, and join me for dinner, Colonel Bruce,' he said, hiding emotion behind the gruff of convention. He walked stiffly away and, once more behind his back, he heard them cheer.

Colonel Bruce oversaw the issuing of a good ration of bully beef, biscuits and jam, and instructed his second-in-command to see the officers billeted in the neighbouring houses. The men would bivouac in the street. Then, his official duties momentarily over, he went off back to Corps HQ in the house up the side-street. Just for a moment he considered taking young Bruce along, but decided, family ties or not, it was not a good idea.

He went on then, alone, and gratefully accepted Sir Ian's offer of a bath. Transport had arrived, and with it the officers' kit, and he was even able to change his clothes. Afterwards he joined Ian Maclaren in the dining-room of the house, his 'office' already being packed away for the next day's move out. He had tasted one small succulent sip of steaming onion broth when a tremendous explosion flung the spoon from his fingers and showered them both with plaster dust. The German 7th Division had arrived in Landrecies.

10

'What da we dae?' Donnie Cameron whispered frantically to Andy Henderson at his elbow. He, like Andy, was lying flat out on the cinder embankment of the railway cutting, his Lee Enfield trained on the advancing shadowy figure.

'Dinna ken,' Andy whispered back, his own rifle muzzle following the man's form, hesitantly.

'Please. Do not shoot. Please. We are French,' the voice called, sounding flat and distant in the night air. 'Please. We are French.' The figure advanced. Sweat trickled over Donnie's shoulder from the back of his neck. His dirty face wrinkled with indecision.

B Company were spread out along the railway-line, facing northwestwards towards the Forêt de Mormal and the narrow roadway through it along which the enemy must advance. Fortunately for all of them, there had been a bit of early warning of their arrival, even before the sudden onslaught of shells that had ruined Colonel Bruce's dinner. A German cavalry party had ridden right into the town, quite unopposed, in search of billets. Only when they discovered that the British and French had got there first did they ride out, in a considerable hurry. Their appearance had caused great alarm among the French inhabitants of the town, and had brought the Maclarens and the other occupying regiments out into the streets, standing to arms. And although they had been later dismissed, for what turned out to be a temporary respite, someone had had the good sense to send the

Coldstreamers up northwestwards across the River Sambre and the railway to take up an outpost. They were there when the attack came and they were there yet, engaging the enemy, and the Maclarens, along with the Grenadiers and the Irish Guards, were sent up the road to provide support.

A and B Companies were spread out along the railway on either side of the level-crossing, while Headquarters Company fortified two unoccupied houses just west of the crossing. C Company was detailed to guard the side-roads, lest the Germans make an attempt to come round. There was considerable firing down the narrow front the road provided, though most of the artillery fire was aimed over their heads, at the town. Still, as Donnie Cameron hunched down among the cinders, machine-gun fire was streaking overhead. Off to his right the Grenadiers were bringing up their own Vickers-Maxims to aid the beleaguered Coldstream Guards.

Donnie peered over the bank for one more quick look, and ducked as quickly down.

'Hold your fire,' the voice called again. 'We are French.'

Donnie's finger slipped from the trigger and he turned round, looking for advice. It came in the form of a rifle-shot. The figure vanished and Corporal Gibson's voice roared out of the darkness, 'Fire, ye blinkin' gomerils.'

'Are they Boche, sir?'

'A' course they're fuckin' Boche. Fire.'

In a second Donnie had no choice, because the would-be Frenchman's companions had risen from their cover and were advancing at a dead run, flickering shapes in the near pitch-darkness. Donnie fired, half blindly, at everything that moved, and as fast as he could, paused, head down, to ram another clip of cartridges into the breech, and raised his head to begin firing again. There was no one left. The attackers lay in shadowy heaps across the open ground beyond the railway.

'Is that a'?' he whispered, awed.

'For the moment,' Sandy Gibson said, at his shoulder. 'Nae doubt they'll try again.'

They did, four more times, and each advance left another broken wave of dark shapes on the ground. Not a man came within reach of a bayonet. The massed rifle power of B Company had the precise effect of a machine-gun, a wall of bullets against which attack was virtually impossible.

Donnie relaxed. On the roadway a Field Howitzer had been brought up into the thick of battle. They were beginning to give the German artillery something to think about.

'Thot was simple,' Donnie said, surprised as much as pleased. 'Nae bother at a'.'

'Aye,' Sandy Gibson said. 'It was. That's the easy bit, lad. Defence. You wait till we're the ones trying tae attack.'

Donnie would have to wait a good while. They defended their section of railway all night, twice fending off German attempts to creep around their flank by firing straight down the cutting. It was an eerie battle, fought in utter darkness, with much confusion. But as daylight approached word came back from the defending Coldstreamers that the situation was well under control. At dawn the Maclarens were ordered to withdraw through the Grenadiers, and back into Landrecies. It soon became apparent to Gordon Bruce that the withdrawal was a continuation of their overall retreat. He was tired beyond caring. He felt only relief. There would come a time for the offensive, no doubt, but God willing there'd be sleep first.

Lance Corporal Gibson gathered his men together before moving back, and counted the toll. He had lost two of his section, killed outright. One young Jock was nursing a cut hand and he himself had just finished applying a field dressing to another's arm. Both were walking wounded, and well enough, and he directed them to report to the RAMC field-dressing station as soon as they were back in Landrecies.

'Weel, sodger,' a voice, low and growly, said at Donnie Cameron's ear. He turned quickly. It was Sergeant MacDonald, oddly conversational. 'What dae ye think o' fightin'.'

'It's a'richt, sir,' Donnie said, uncertainly.

'Ye dinna mind it then?' MacDonald seemed to be laughing in the dawn light. Donnie ducked instinctively as a shot whistled high overhead. 'Overs' they were, aimed far beyond them, but it took a cooler head than his to ignore them. For one thing, they had the occasional unpleasant habit of dropping short. MacDonald ignored them, swatting casually at his neck as if they were flies, Donnie thought.

'It was a'richt,' Donnie said again.

'Ye werena scairt?'

Donnie was, but he thought that wasn't the thing to say. He had an uneasy and defensive fear of angering the sergeant with a show of cowardice.

'No, sir,' he said as calmly as he could, his eyes on the back of the man ahead of him.

'Weel nou, isn't that grand,' MacDonald said, 'cause laddie, when ye reach yon brig,' he pointed to the road bridge across the Sambre which they were now approaching, 'ye've nae a snowba' in hell's chance o' gettin o'er alive. I'm richt chuffed yer nae afeart.' He laughed again and departed into the dimness leaving Donnie Cameron alone in terror.

After a few more yards he was conscious of the lean dark shape of Sandy Gibson beside him. Sandy said nothing at first, but eventually, ducking down under the noise of a passing shell, muttered almost in Donnie's ear, 'Yon's a bastard.'

'Is he right, Corporal?'

''Course he's nae right.'

'The bridge. They'll ken we hae tae cross it.'

'Aye. They will.'

'An' there's nae ither way across.'

Sandy shrugged. 'We'll cross it,' he said. 'Dinna fear. Maclarens hae crossed worse than a brig.'

Donnie sighed and relaxed a little.

'Ye juist stick wi' me, laddie,' Sandy said, feeling suddenly much older and much less afraid himself than he'd felt half a minute ago. 'I'll get ye back safe.'

The bridge, and the crossing of the Sambre, loomed ahead black against the brightening sky, and grew larger as they approached through the rough ground at the side of the road. Beyond, the roofs and rows of chimneypots that were the major part of Landrecies, still relatively undamaged by shelling, were also silhouetted. Even a man of most limited imagination could see that his own body, once on that bridge, would be equally outlined against an uncompromising sky, and a very easy target.

'Andy,' Donnie Cameron whispered.

'Aye.' The word was breathed, and shaky.

'D'ye mind on that wee howff doun on Pump Lane?'

'Aye,' Andy said again.

Donnie kept his eyes on the wiry figure of Sandy Gibson ahead of him for luck. He said softly, 'Ye ken. Yon wi' that lassie that wouldnae . . .'

'Aye,' Andy said again.

Donnie sighed. 'Och, she was bonnie, wasn't she.'

'Nae bad,' Andy said, cradling his hand-held rifle for comfort. He glanced across nervously at his mate. Donnie's lightly freckled face was screwed up in the grey light with an unclear expression. He shrugged, and they climbed up out of the ditch that edged the road into full view.

Donnie said only, 'Ye'll mind on her for me, lad, will ye no'?' Then he scuttled off behind Sandy Gibson, keeping his eye on the corporal's boots.

They crossed the bridge in small groups, at a dead run. The Sambre glinted menacingly below, and far above the malevolent whistling and whining of distant fire sounded. At any instant Donnie was sure that the rapid staccato of a well-placed machine-gun would make short shrift of his nineteen years. But it didn't. Nor, while the battalion was crossing, was a single shot fired in their midst.

They regrouped on the far side and made their way, light-hearted with relief, into the centre of Landrecies. The town itself was chaotic under shelling and high machine-gun fire, with hasty barricades of wagons and tangles of wire thrown across the main street. The inhabitants were hiding. The only activity was that of the military as they hastily gathered guns and horses for the retreat.

'Och, I never thocht tae see this place again,' Donnie laughed, turning to Andy once more.

Andy grinned. 'Never thocht ye wanted tae,' he said and then suddenly shouted, and staggered, and fell headlong into the street.

Donnie Cameron stood, quite mystified, looking down on him. 'Hey, what's wi' youse?' he said. He continued to just stand while Corporal Gibson came over and knelt down beside Andy, who by then had struggled up and was sitting on the dusty cobbles in his splayed-out kilt, holding on to his bloody calf with both hands. Then Sergeant Ross MacDonald lumbered over, took a disinterested quick look at the man in the street, and gave Donnie a hearty shove in the direction of B Company who were already moving down the street.

'Hey, he's my mate,' he shouted, shock emboldening him.

'Sae whit iv it?' MacDonald's upper lip twitched beneath his black moustache, and he rubbed the filthy khaki sleeve of his tunic over his big nose. 'Ye're nae marriet tae him, are ye? Move yer arse.'

Donnie looked desperately around, but there was no help. Still glancing over his shoulder at the diminishing shapes of Andy and the corporal in the dawn in this strange French town, he marched away. The loneliness that swept over him was like that of his first days away from the Children's Home, in the solitude of the tiny boxroom of Alastair Cameron's croft house. He began to cry silently and did not care if the colonel himself were to see.

Later in the day, when they rested briefly by the roadside just beyond Etreux, Sandy Gibson approached Donnie with the news that Andy Henderson had been seen safely aboard one of the final hospital trains leaving Landrecies, and in a few hours he would be safely on the coast in one of the new military hospitals at Rouen, Le Havre or some port town.

'An' anither week an' he'll be awa' hame in Inverness, tellin' his tale tae any will listen,' Sandy added with comforting assurance.

'Will he be a'richt?' Donnie asked hesitantly. 'Was it bad?'

'Nae bother,' Sandy said, 'I've cut mysel' worse shaving. I gied him a message for my lass at Culbrech House; as sune as he's gettin' aboot, he'll gae an' see her for me.'

Donnie relaxed about Andy. It was funny to think of him back in Inverness so soon. He wasn't sure if he was envious or not. It would be nice to be back in the pub in Pump Lane, and all. But he'd hate to think of the battalion going on in the war without him. Andy must feel the same, he thought, and asked, 'Will he no' be back?'

'Back. A' course he'll be back. Ye dinna get oot that easy.' Sandy grinned and wandered off puffing calmly at his fag.

Donnie Cameron watched him with admiration and thought maybe he'd take up smoking something, too, to get that look of self-assurance the corporal carried so well.

His loneliness gradually drifted away. He found new friends, and like a small lost puppy made his way surreptitiously to the patch of ground Corporal Gibson occupied, whenever they settled down at night to sleep.

They didn't settle much though. The march continued every day, through shuttered towns that but days before had laden the regiment with flowers and welcomes. There were no flowers now, and no welcomes either. The remaining inhabitants only watched bleakly.

'An army in retreat,' Captain George Brown said coolly, pausing by the roadside with Torquil Farquhar, 'is like a dog that turns its back in a fight. The whole pack's on it in a moment.'

Torquil laughed, his pale blue eyes surveying the backs of the marching men with candour. 'Come, come, old boy. Withdrawal. Withdrawal. That's the word we use.'

'Calling things by different names doesn't change them,' Brown said at once.

'Changes morale,' Farquhar replied. 'Retreat's not an idea that sets easy on the fighting Jock. Tell him he's withdrawing and like as not he doesn't know what the word means. Blind 'em with knowledge, old man.'

'They're not liking it,' Brown returned.

'No. I dare say not. But they're doing it and doing it well. Bloody tiring marching all day on these damnable roads,' he gave the *pavé* an annoyed kick with the side of his boot. 'And then digging half the night. And next morning, same again.'

Captain Brown nodded and mounted his horse again, with a creak of dusty saddle leather and a clatter of nervous shod hoofs on the stones.

'And as for them,' Torquil said, again with his engaging grin, his hand gesturing towards the group of black-clad women standing in front of a white stucco flat-roofed house, 'you can hardly blame them for not cheering. They know what's coming behind us.'

Brown narrowed his eyes, gathering the reins with one practised hand. 'I wonder,' he said at last, and then with a cynical twist of his thin mouth added, 'perhaps that's who they're saving the flowers for now.'

He turned his horse and rode at a brisk trot away to his place at the head of his company. Torquil Farquhar trotted on foot to rejoin his own men, past the silently watching women. He could not blame them, whatever they might do to win favour for themselves and protection for their children. He thought of Emma Maclaren in her white dress at the Culbrech picnic, and thought suddenly of her having to face an advancing, unknown enemy, alone. He set out on the French road again with renewed vigour, not withdrawing now, no, but in his mind marching on to the awaiting field of battle where those that might threaten his lady would be vanquished for ever.

Andy Henderson, by the time he finally reached the small base hospital to which he was sent, hardly cared any more who won the battle that Lieutenant Farquhar imagined in such heroic terms.

At first he hadn't felt too bad, at least after Sandy Gibson had applied the field dressing to his wounded leg, and the Regimental MO had had a look and directed stretcher-bearers to bring him to the waiting hospital train. That was a bit of luck, or so he thought, since it meant nursing care and relative comfort for the journey, as opposed to the fearsome jouncing of a horse or motor ambulance along the rough French roads.

But the train proved to be primitive and packed with the casualties of the battle at Mons and the other fierce engagements that the Maclarens had known only as the sound of distant gunfire. At the station Andy was relieved of his stretcher by a medical officer. A man who had lost half his leg needed it more.

'I cannae walk,' Andy had protested, though softly, because he saw the other's wound and his lolling head and the flies indolently flitting about his blood-speckled mouth.

'Oy mate.' Andy looked up into the face of a young Londoner, a corporal with the brigade artillery. He had a stained bandage around his head, but was standing. 'Oy'll give you a hand. We're on our own, the walkin' wounded.'

'I cannae be that,' Andy said. 'I cannae walk.'

'Can you hop?'

'Aye. Wi' a hand frae youse.'

'Then,' said the artillery corporal, 'you're walkin' wounded, if you can hop.' He extended an arm to Andy where he sat on the kerb edge, his throbbing bandaged leg stretched out in front of him. Andy took the arm, and with the help of a station pillar dragged himself to his feet. With the Londoner's assistance, he hopped dejectedly to the train.

The cattle cars were crowded with the badly wounded stretched out in rows in bloody straw. The nurses were fully occupied there. Andy and the corporal and six others were crammed together, sitting up, in a passenger compartment, without attendants, for the several hours' journey to hospital.

The train was of primitive design, and appeared to have no

proper braking system. With each halt, each carriage slammed into the one in front, until eventually, by sheer friction, the long train came to a shuddering halt. The first few times it happened, Andy and his companions fell into each other, and one injured man slipped painfully to the floor. Afterwards they got wise to it and braced themselves against the walls of the compartment, and each other, and the opposite seat. The space between them became a forest of outstretched legs. Once a boot brushed with accidental roughness against Andy's leg and he was surprised to hear himself cry out in pain.

They were all very kind to each other though, and the worse off were allowed to sleep on the shoulders of the more fit. Andy became conscious of a prickly hotness about his leg and a sharp central throbbing, like a splinter left too long in a thumb. He felt something rubbing underneath the field dressing, some bit of dirt or remnant of his shredded kilt stocking sticking to the wound. He would have liked to remove the dressing and look, but he could not replace it and was afraid that it would begin again to bleed.

Andy was hardly aware when the train made its last shuddering halt. He was dizzy and felt sick in his stomach and head. The artilleryman helped him off the train, a lurching painful process, and someone, he was no longer seeing too clearly and did not identify his next benefactor, helped him into a horsedrawn ambulance. There were several other men in the ambulance, some severely wounded and stretched out on the floor between the two benches where the fitter men sat, crammed together. One man was moaning continuously from a vast, messy stomach wound, and the sight, sound and smell, in the enclosed dimness of the jolting van, brought Andy near to retching. Fortunately the journey to the small volunteer hospital in Le Touquet was short.

Walking wounded or not, Andy was indulged with a stretcher upon his removal from the ambulance, and carried, for the first time in days and days, into the brightly lit entrance of a real building. It was a pretty building, set in a courtyard surrounded by apple and plum trees, and had until very recently, been a private villa, a holiday place for the rich. It was evening when Andy Henderson was brought in, and in the centre of the large hallway a young woman was standing below the glitter of a crystal chandelier. She was wearing a pale lavender evening gown and a diamond necklace. On her high-piled fair hair was a small, discreet tiara. As Andy was carried through into the billiards room which served now as a ten-bedded ward, the young woman smiled and said, 'Good evening.'

Somewhere, in another room, a gramophone was playing and Andy heard, distorted by the scratchy recording and his own feverishness,

> Do you remember the last waltz,
> The last waltz with me . . .

'Jeez,' Andy muttered, 'I've gane an' deid an' they've sent me tae the toff's paradise by mistake. Deil kens what they'll dae when they ken wha' I really am.'

It wasn't paradise actually, for toffs or otherwise. It was the Duchess of Westminster's villa-turned-hospital where the duchess herself was at that moment busily at work scrubbing out bedpans. But she was as aware of the need for high morale as was Torquil Farquhar, hence the music and the flowers and the lady in lavender at the door. It was early days yet, and the graces of the golden era they were all leaving had not yet fled.

Andy was so tired by the time he arrived in Le Touquet that he fell asleep while the two volunteer nurses stripped his filthy uniform from him, and did not even wake through the painful operation of removing the dirt-crusted field dressing and washing the now ugly wound. When he did wake up it was morning, and the Medical Officer and a slender dark-haired middle-aged woman dressed in a plain blue linen dress and long white apron were bending over him. He winced as they again uncovered the bullet wound in his leg. It had grown immensely painful and burned continuously.

The dark-haired woman smiled encouragingly and Andy, inspired by the close proximity of such an elegant creature, bent his wince into a smile as well.

'Maclaren Highlander?' she asked softly, handing the doctor a pair of scissors.

'Aye,' Andy said, surprised to hear his own voice as a scratchy croak.

She only nodded, and smiled again very gently.

'Is it a'richt me bein' here?' Andy asked suddenly.

'All right?' She seemed puzzled and straightened a little,

tucking a stray strand of hair under the white linen cloth that veiled her head.

'Is it bad eneuch?' Andy nodded with his chin downwards towards the injured leg. 'I'm nae funkin', honest, ma'am, the Corporal made me come. Only we'd nae been fightin' at the time. 'Twas no real battle wound. It just come out o' the sky, like.'

'I'm sure your corporal was quite right. And of course I'm sure you've done your best for your country.'

Andy smiled again; it was what he was needing to hear, the dark-haired woman seemed to understand everything. He drifted back to sleep.

Naomi Bruce walked down the ward with the doctor who attended to each patient. She held his tray of instruments and the white enamelled bowl filled with disinfectant. At the end of the ward they went out together into the small anteroom that served as Sister's office. The summer morning sun drifted through the many-paned window. The room had once been a small pantry, adjacent to the brick-floored kitchen. It was still pretty and pleasant. Naomi stood by the window as the doctor washed his hands. She said, 'The young Highlander, how is he?'

The doctor thought a moment, his mind jumping from one injured man to another. 'Henderson?'

'Yes. He's with my brother's regiment.'

'Mmm. Yes. The one who thought he mightn't be bad enough to be in hospital.' The doctor rubbed the top of his bald head. 'Gas gangrene. He'll lose the leg.'

Naomi sighed softly, and nodded. 'I thought so. It had that look.'

'You heard when I tapped it, that hollow sound?' She nodded again. 'That's the sure sign. Swells up like a balloon. And the smell, of course. Can hardly miss that, can you. Five in the ward with it today.'

Naomi sighed again, and shook her head, weary with sorrow rather than work. 'I simply don't understand,' she said. 'I nursed in South Africa, and of course men died, but not from a scratch like that must have been. They'd have been back and fighting in a month or two. It's not even touched the bone.'

The doctor studied her face seriously. He had been working with this lady at his side for only a week, and in spite of the shortness of time, he had grown extraordinarily intrigued by her.

He thought of his wife in Surrey with a totally illogical wave of guilt. Good God, he'd never even shaken the woman's hand. He smiled wryly, and stood and swung open the casement window, letting the rich scents of the garden drift in. Vegetables and flowers mixed in ordered sun-washed rows, leeks and onions, sweet peas and poppies, refreshed his eyes with colour. 'There,' he said. Naomi looked where he pointed. 'There's why.'

She looked again, mystified. 'There? The garden?'

He looked up, stroking his short brown moustache, and easing the collar of his tunic in the heat. 'Tell me, Mrs Bruce, have you seen a garden like that on the veldt?'

'Of course not, the soil's all wrong, and it's far too dry.'

'Exactly. Look at it,' he said, gesturing to the neatly hoed rows, black between the shining greens. 'Fertile and tended for generations, manured every year, year in, year out. Anything will grow in it. Anything. Trouble is, it doesn't stop growing, even when that soil's pulverized into a soldier's wound. All that fertility breeds corruption, and corruption eats flesh, and takes men's lives. And all I've got to fight it with is this,' he said, balling his fist around a bottle of disinfectant. 'And I'll tell you, it's damn all use.'

Naomi Bruce washed the septic wound in Andy's leg all day long, and all the next. He struggled against tears the while and always remembered to thank her. The next day was the same, and the next. On the fifth day Naomi came instead and sat beside his bed.

'Are ye no' gonna dae me, nurse?'

'In a moment.'

'Oh, shall I gie ye another letter tae write fer me?'

'Later, Andy.'

There was a silence. 'What is it, nurse?'

Naomi looked away from him, down the neat row of occupied beds, up to the ornate plasterwork of the ceiling of the converted billiards room, and eventually out of the window where the greens of the sunlit garden glowed beyond the leaded panes. Her eyes sought, shamefully, anything but the honest freckled face of Andy Henderson. She had walked for fifteen minutes around the brick pathways of the garden before coming here, but that gathered peace did not sustain her now. The green of the garden, shut off from her by the hospital ward, brought to mind the green of Hyde Park from the windows of her home. Four weeks ago, she thought. Mr Leitner and Rebecca, and Robert and the silly white Persian cat. In that moment, gathering courage to tell Andy Henderson he would soon be a cripple, Naomi Bruce caught an early glimpse of the world they were entering.

'I'm afraid it isn't really healing all that well, Andy.'

'But it will get better. Nurse? It will get better, won't it? Nurse?' Andy plucked at her sleeve with his stubby work-roughened fingers, for although her deep brown eyes were locked to his, he felt he did not have her attention.

Eventually she said, '*You* will get better, Andy. But without the leg. It's gangrenous . . . poisoned, Andy, do you understand. So we must let the surgeon take it away, and then you'll . . .'

'No. Noo,' Andy whispered. He had been watching silently all the while, and at the moment of comprehension he began to moan, like an animal.

'Andy, we must.'

'No, nurse. Ye dinna ken. Ye've got it wrang. Corporal said it was naething.' Andy turned his face away, dimly convinced that if he did not look at her, she, and the thing she was saying, would go away. But she did not, remaining instead by his side for half an hour, encouraging, pleading, comforting. Mostly he did not reply. When he did, he said only, 'Please, nurse, dinna let them tak ma leg awa'.'

Finally, perhaps out of exhaustion, he accepted. She knew he accepted because at last he looked at her, with eyes boyishly large in his pinched, undernourished face, full of resigned hurt. 'Ye'll nae tell my Mam,' he said.

Naomi thought instinctively to argue the hopelessness of that utterly illogical ruse, but then closed her mouth and agreed.

'Ye see, she's sae proud. She'd nae like a cripple for a son.'

Naomi nodded. Later, later, she would handle that somehow. Later, after the operation, the nursing, the dozen other operations this week, the endless bedpans and filthy, pus-encrusted dressings. Later, there would be a time for more compassion.

She went away, bemused that Andy solemnly intended to hide the fact that he was suddenly short of one leg from his mother for the rest of his life.

Even after the surgeon had sliced through putrefying flesh, and sawn through bone, and left Andy with but the stump of a thigh and a grim flatness in the bed beneath the blankets to tell the whole ward of his fate, even then, Andy stuck firm over the subject of his mother.

'Ye juist tell her I'm gettin' along fine, ye ken,' he would insist as Naomi took down his letter home. In a little while, a few days after the operation, Andy was actually well enough to write, but Naomi continued that task for him, having quickly guessed the boy was virtually illiterate, and saved him the embarrassment of having to admit it. Also, she knew he liked her company. He talked a bit, about his home, his joiner father and his three sisters and his mother's pride in the sight of him in his army kilt. 'She's got this bluidy great, pardon, ma'am, this big picture o' me, in a gold frame, right on the piano in the front room, and onybody comes through the door, ye can be certain they're drug awa' ben tae see it, afore they get awa'.'

Naomi was beginning to understand.

For a while he talked about the regiment a lot, about his special mate Donnie, wondering how he was getting on, and sang the praises of her brother, the commanding officer. Naomi made no mention of the relationship, knowing it would instantly freeze him into an awestruck silence through which she would never reach him again.

But he stopped talking about them altogether when the stump itself had turned septic, and the dressing of it was a twice-daily agony which left the young soldier so drained that Naomi would, in silence, pour brandy, drop by drop, down his throat until he could again speak.

'Ye'll nae tell ma mam,' he would whisper, as a daily benediction, and she'd agree. They were the last words he spoke. Naomi kept her promise. Nothing in her final letter tarnished his mother's image of the perfect body of her son. The maimed reality was buried in the churchyard of Le Touquet.

On the day Andy Henderson died, the Maclaren Highlanders turned with the rest of the hunted, exhausted British Expeditionary Force and made their stand on the River Marne.

11

On the Marne, at last, they checked the German advance. Then as the two armies raced each other towards the Channel, each attempting to turn the other's flank, they collided and clashed fatefully on the rising ground northeast of the town of Ypres. Again a British victory was proclaimed, but the French and British line was left wrapped around the town like a thin glove on a fist punched into the enemy's territory. A fatal salient had been created at great expense. The Maclaren Highlanders alone lost half their number at a place called Polygone Wood.

When VAD Emma Maclaren thought of them, the officers who had been her girlhood beaus, she did not picture them as they must have died, in torn and muddy khaki, but as she had last seen them, gorgeous in scarlet full-dress jackets and kilts, at one or another of last spring's Highland balls. When she thought of their names she could only envisage them scrawled in eager haste on her dance card, with a word of boyish flattery in the margin. It was impossible for Emma to believe them dead, and she struggled with the unreality of it even as she worked beside the doctors and trained nurses to save the lives of strangers.

Still for Emma Maclaren, as for all lovers, their deaths were always eased for her by the counterbalance of Torquil Farquhar's survival. No day, no matter how awful, was truly bad for her if she went to her bed in the VAD nursing hostel believing him still alive. Now, this brutally cold morning in November as she lay huddled for a last few minutes of feeble warmth beneath her two coarse army-issue blankets, she knew he was not only alive but that he was coming to London on leave. He was arriving tomorrow, and that fact, extraordinarily, was the cause of her sorrow.

'Rebecca?' she called softly towards the mound of blankets and tangle of auburn hair in the nearest of the two other metal-framed beds jammed into the tiny room. There was a rustle and then Rebecca's voice blurred by sleep, responded.

'Yes, Matron. I'm coming, Matron.'

Emma laughed. 'Silly goose, it's me. You're still in bed.'

Rebecca mumbled and then raised her head and looked blearily around the dim buff walls of the room. Then she flopped back down. 'Oh thank goodness,' she said. 'I was having the most beastly dream. Piles of dressings and bedpans and some poor Tommy haemorrhaging and Matron was making me walk *backwards* everywhere because I had a spot on my apron. Oh, it was ghastly,' she moaned. 'She's too awful for words. I shan't face today. I shan't.'

'Oh get up,' Emma said, rising quickly and hastening into her dressing-gown. 'And wake Susan, or we'll all be late and you'll really have something to moan about.'

'Whyever so cross, darling?' Rebecca said, stretching. 'I'd think you'd be delighted today.'

'Why?'

'Torquil's coming on leave, or have you forgotten?'

Emma sighed and sat down on the bed, feeling the hard metal frame through the thin mattress. 'No, I haven't forgotten.'

'What on earth is the matter?' Rebecca said again.

'I'm frightened,' Emma said simply. 'His letters . . . he seems so changed now. They were all so jolly over there in the beginning, everything sounded such a ball, I was practically jealous. Then of course when he had to tell me of one and another being killed or wounded, it was rather solemn, but you could see he was still Torquil. They're all soldiers and they expect deaths. But then, I don't know, I suppose last month, his letters changed. Quite suddenly really. I think it was when they first went to Ypres, though I didn't know then, since they aren't to tell us where they are. But later I realized it must have been then. Quite suddenly the letters got terribly short, like there was less and less to tell. Or less and less he wanted to tell. He never answered any of my questions. He never even congratulated me when I wrote and said I'd passed my First Aid and Home Nursing examinations and was proper Red Cross. And when we came here. Not a word. Just little things, like the weather out there, and seeing General Haig ride by on his horse once. Nothing else. As if I were a stranger, to make polite talk with.'

Rebecca was busy washing her face in the china ewer with the jugful of cold water they had brought in last night from the bathroom. There was one bathroom for the entire hostel of twenty girls, both VADs and trained professional nurses. And as the VADs were the bottom of the pecking order, they had soon learned to make washing arrangements in their rooms. Hot water was scarce in the badly plumbed old building and a proper bath, much needed and greatly longed for, was, despite the dirty work they were obliged to do, a rare luxury. 'Your turn to lay the fire,' she said, with a sideways glance to Susan. 'And don't you forget like last week, when we all came in freezing and had to scratch around for kindlers at eight o'clock.'

Susan nodded, still too sleepy to speak, and began scraping away at the cast-iron grate with a battered poker, still only half dressed.

'I wouldn't worry,' Rebecca said, drying her face on a coarse blue-striped towel. 'Johnny's letters aren't the same either, but I expect it's just being rushed and having nowhere decent to write. I remember one of his letters was quite peculiar, not like Johnny at all, the one he wrote telling me about that plumber, MacTavish, being killed. Quite strange really. Rather morbid. Which is hardly John Bruce, is it?' She fastened her apron ties and centred the red cross on her arm band. It was hardly red, actually, but a sickly much-used-looking pink, the result of deliberate ministrations from the bleach bottle. All the girls had done that in the first days, affecting an experience they had not yet undergone. Real experience soon vanquished such naïveties; they worked a twelve-hour day and in their spare time cooked, cleaned, sewed, laid fires, carried coal and wood, washed their own clothes, and did myriad other tasks that two months ago none of them had ever thought about.

Their days began at six in the morning and ended at eight-thirty at night, with minimal breaks for meals and no breaks at all if there was any kind of an emergency. They stood all day, every day. VADs must not be seen to sit down in a ward. Their feet ached, their hands ached, their backs ached, and their hearts ached over sights that made male orderlies turn aside with revulsion. But they did it with fervour and joy because for each of them it was not only a patriotic duty, it was a lifeline to the men they knew and loved at the Front.

'I should hardly think you'd care,' Susan Bruce said from the slate hearth, 'what Johnny writes. After all, you were thick as anything with Tenny Maclaren in September. And I dare say you answer all his letters too.'

'Well, of course I do,' Rebecca said, pinning up her hair, looking over Emma's shoulder at the small cracked mirror.

'I think you're quite unkind to my brother. We all know he's gone quite soppy over you. And there you are stringing him along when all the while it's really Tenny you care for.'

'But I care for both of them. I couldn't choose if I had to. I mean Tenny is too too marvellous, and September was paradise when we all had dinner at Brown's.' She sighed, wrapping the warm black cloak that completed the uniform about her shoulders. 'But then Johnny will write, and there he is out there at the Front, amidst all that danger. I mean, how can one not feel for him so?'

Emma picked up her little suitcase in which she carried spare apron and clean shoes and stockings in case the walk through the city streets to the First London General should muddy the ones she wore. 'I'm afraid, darling,' she said, 'you are going to have to choose, however difficult. If, God willing, Torquil and Johnny arrive safely, and if Tenny gets away with coming down to meet them as he planned, you are going to find yourself at Naomi's table square between the two of them. And I must warn you that poor old Ten is more than a little touchy about not being at the Front yet.'

'Grandfather said Tenny tried to get into the Second Battalion when Paul Grant brought them back from India,' Susan added, 'but no one would hear of it. Now they're in France too of course. That makes three battalions of Maclarens at the Front and Tenny's still in Inverness. Now it's the New Army needing him. Apparently they're just so drastically short of officers that they're writing to just anyone who's been to a decent school and begging them to accept a commission.'

'I do hope Johnny won't be hard on him,' Rebecca said as they left their little room and clattered hurriedly down the stone flights of steps to the street. 'You do know what a frightful tease he can be.'

Emma Maclaren was already hard at work scrubbing bed mackintoshes under the grim eye of Matron in her ward at the First London General when Victoria Maclaren, Emma's latest letter folded neatly before her on her desk, summoned Emma's younger sister to the morning-room of Culbrech House. It was a cold, blustery day. Hard grains of sleet rattled against the window glass, and the wind shook the old frames. Victoria felt tired and her head ached, a legacy, she was certain, of last night's dinner with the Bruces. Yesterday afternoon's news of wee Geordie Stirling, the laundrymaid's son, had rather dampened the evening.

When the telegram had come to Mairi Stirling's croft, she had fled the place, weeping, without even her shawl and run blindly down the road. Eventually she had turned up at the dark kitchens of Culbrech House, having homed there like a burrowing animal. Cook of course provided tea and a warm seat by the fire and Lady Maclaren had been summoned.

'The telegrams are so terribly blunt,' Victoria said later to her guests. 'Of course there'll be a letter from Gordon to follow.'

'Nae worry,' Willie Bruce had said. 'We ken whit sort o' truth tae tell. Ye'll nae find onything in Gordon's letter would gie a woman pain. He'll find a way tae say it, no matter whit happened tae the lad.' Victoria nodded.

'Do you know, the one thing that worried her most was what she was to do with the body. You see, she thought she had to go to France to bring him back. And she had nowhere to leave the bairns . . . quite brave really,' she sighed, stirring her cooling soup with little interest.

'Good on her,' Philippa said brightly. 'She's a good sort really, if a bit thick. I knew she'd come up trumps. I shall go and see her in the morning. Perhaps she'd like to join our little group of bereaved mothers and wives. They all get on famously.'

'So much in common?' Harry Bruce said quietly, with a nervous twitch of his head, tossing back the drooping forelock of brown hair.

'Of course,' Philippa had replied without looking at him.

'I do think,' Victoria had concluded, 'that it is perhaps just a little soon.'

'Quite right,' Philippa nodded briskly. 'I'll see her next week.'

Lady Maclaren looked up to the sleet-driven hills, tapping Emma's folded letter lightly against the leather top of her writing-desk. Next week. Next week there would probably be a half-dozen more for Philippa's little group. Philippa entered the morning room, dressed stylishly in a brown velvet suit with a lace-jaboted white blouse and a matching dark brown velvet hat. Victoria was struck again by the remarkable improvement in Philippa's appearance since her war work had begun. Of course it was natural for her to look her best when speaking in public, but there was more than that, as if the passions she aroused with her words somehow flowed back into herself, lighting her odd features with a stern beauty. Lady Maclaren was an honest mother, and had children enough to allow for variance in quality. Emma had always been her beauty. It was quite surprising to see Philippa now filling that role.

'Come and sit down, dear,' she said with the slight strain in her voice that talking with Philippa always engendered. 'Come, by me.' She patted the dusky pink velvet of the nearest chair. Philippa glanced at the marble mantel clock before crossing the room. 'I won't keep you long,' Victoria said with a hesitant smile. 'Would you like coffee?'

'Adore it, Mother, but I can't possibly wait. Sophia will be waiting at the Waverley. We're lunching with the provost.'

'Very well,' Victoria said. 'I will be brief. It's about tomorrow.'

'Tomorrow? I'm off to London tonight, Mother, have you forgotten?'

'No, dear. No. Quite simply, Philippa, I do not wish you to go. In fact, I am requesting that you not go.'

'Not go?' Philippa exclaimed, her cheeks reddening slightly. 'Whyever not? This is quite ridiculous, Mother. You know very well I've been planning a trip down since Naomi came back from Le Touquet. And Tenny's going down so I'll have someone to travel with. Everything is arranged. I can't possibly not go.'

'Naomi has been back for three weeks at least,' Victoria said quietly. 'You could have gone any day before now.'

'But I didn't, Mother. And I'm going now. Really I don't know what . . .'

'Go next week,' Lady Maclaren said, her hands unwittingly crumpling Emma's letter in her hand. 'Or the week after. Just *not tomorrow*,' she said at last, her voice cracking. She leaned back in her chair and covered her faded blue eyes with the back of her hand.

'Mother? Are you faint?'

'Of course not,' Victoria snapped. She softened a little, uncovered her eyes and leaned towards this difficult daughter. 'Oh darling, must you make me put it into words?'

'Put what into words?'

'I know why you're going, dear. I know.' The letter in her hand felt hot and sticky. Philippa shook her head, a gesture of impatience, and smoothed back the tumbling veil of her brown hat. 'Well, of course you do, Mother. I've told you myself. I'm meeting with Baroness Orczy to discuss the Active Service League. A Scottish branch is just what's needed, as I'm sure you'll agree.'

Victoria would not agree, actually. The Baroness, a popular novelist with a profitable grip on the public imagination, had formed her league of women for the express purpose of persuading every man who passed within their velvet clutches to join the army. Victoria, hardened soldier's wife that she was, regarded it, with its outspoken scorn of the hesitant man, as a form of patriotic blackmail. Still, it was Philippa's decision, and her dislike of the League alone would not have caused her to interfere. 'The Baroness,' she said drily, 'and the Active Service League,' she added, 'can surely wait a day.'

'Mother, time is of the . . .'

'I *know* Torquil Farquhar is coming on leave tomorrow. I know it, Philippa. Do I make myself clear?'

Philippa's face paled slightly and for a moment she was quite still. But she never made one expression, not so much as a blink of the eyes, that would give her away.

'Oh?' she said mildly. 'Is he? How pleasant.' She strode to the window and stared out at the sleet. Behind her, she heard her mother's voice saying,

'Oh darling, if you really love him, love him well enough to let him have his happiness. Let your sister have him. They do love each other. Accept it. Wish them well. And let them have their few short hours tomorrow. Alone.'

'Alone!' Philippa whirled about shrieking. 'What utter balderdash. Of course they'll not be alone. There'll be Naomi and Jenny and Johnny and God knows who else. What difference can

I make? Why is it always me who's . . . who's not welcome?' Her eyes wrinkled shut and Victoria, quite amazed, thought she would cry. But she did not. Victoria had not seen this daughter cry for years.

'Of course,' Victoria went on, as calmly as she could, 'of course they'll not be alone, really. That wouldn't do unless they were engaged, which of course they are not. Though, and I must be honest, I would not object at this point if they were to choose that course. It would be hasty, but the war rather does rush things. We . . . they . . . really don't know what time they have, do they?'

Philippa felt a weakness in her stomach, hearing her mother so calmly talk of the sword that hung over her love's head. The pain of it almost forced tears again, but she resisted them. 'They are not engaged yet, Mother,' she said, with a note of defiant challenge in her voice.

'No. But Naomi . . .' Victoria still hesitated over that name. 'As we all know, Naomi is rather liberal . . .'

'And does that please you?' Philippa demanded. 'So much that you'll relinquish your responsibility for Emma to that . . . that . . . whorish woman?'

'Philippa,' Victoria whispered, 'the shame of it.'

'And the truth, Mother. It's what you've always thought. You've called her that by a thousand gestures and expressions all through my childhood. Well, I've now called her that in words. Don't be such a despicable hypocrite.'

Victoria Maclaren waved her daughter away without another word. They were past discussion.

When Philippa Maclaren prepared, later that day, for her journey on the night train to London, she did so with iron determination, choosing the most arresting of all her garments, the emerald green, braid-bordered travelling suit with the swirling, silk-lined cape, and a hat trimmed with authoritative sweeping feathers that curled round almost to the sharp dimpled point of her strong solid chin. Her eyes in the mirror glowed softly from blue to green in the reflected light of the hat lining. Yes, she thought, toying artfully with one coil of her magnificent hair, I am different. He will see. At last, he will see. She knew it was her last chance. She was alone, all her friends, even her mother, even Harry, God damn him, were on Emma's side. An engagement, forced and hasty, would still be an engagement, an iron door shut on her dreams.

'Oh my love,' she whispered. '*You* know. You're not like them. You'll not turn from me now. Tomorrow, tomorrow, you'll be mine.'

12

The crowded night train carrying Philippa and her brother, Lieutenant 'Tenny' Maclaren, south was clattering through the outskirts of sleeping London when Pat McGarrity rose from his narrow, iron-framed bed. Pat regarded the faintly ill-smelling mattress and frayed coarse-striped blankets with distaste, and rose quickly into the cold air. It wasn't his own bed, or hadn't been until quite recently, any more than the garret room it occupied was his real home. Both belonged to a small, seedy boarding-house, smelling perpetually of cabbage from the sour kitchens and also faintly of urine from the cavalier use of the shared lavatories by its mostly young, entirely male occupants. The house stood in a decaying cobbled street in a small mining village just outside Glasgow, tucked in between two pubs and across the street from a chip shop. It was, all in all, not a bad location for the likes of Pat McGarrity.

Still, he thought, dressing hurriedly in his grimy black trousers, shirt and coat, he wouldn't mind it cleaner. Kathleen McGarrity, his mother, for all her other faults, was very clean, and Pat had been raised by her to a standard of decency comprised of hard work and a well-scrubbed household. He was nineteen, and had been working as a coal-miner since he was seventeen. For two years he had lived in the village with an aunt and uncle, the man also a pitman, but another, belated baby had ousted him from the room he had shared already with two cousins and forced him to find lodgings of his own.

He was just as pleased, actually. Now he felt more of a man, living entirely on his own wages, and contributing five shillings of them a week to his mother in the Gorbals. In fact, Pat McGarrity had had manhood forced upon him at the age of thirteen when his father died, crushed under a ton of coal, half a mile below the green fields of Scotland. Pat was the youngest son, the youngest child of Sean and Kathleen's fourteen. Of the surviving eight, all were married and out of the tenement flat that had been their most recent home. Some had gone back to Ireland where half of them were born. Others had scattered about Scotland, mostly down the pits.

Pat's childhood was tightly bound by family ties, by church, by ritual, by neighbourly tenement warmth. Its patterns were rigid; chips in the street waiting for Mam outside the pub, football on Saturdays, confession on Wednesdays, the Dance Palais on Saturday nights, and always, Mass on Sundays in the soot-stained Victorian Gothic church.

Pat had been bright in school, but so had all the McGarritys, and they had all, like Pat, left at fourteen. It was part of the tradition; a man's job, a man's wage. Pat worked in a fishmonger's until he was seventeen, sweeping up the floor, but the mines, in spite of his mother's quite traditional protests, were his real place, the place for any real man.

Once, for a brief few months at thirteen, he had dreamed of being a priest; a not uncommon dream, akin to his sister Maria's holy turning towards the veil at the same age. She'd slipped free at sixteen, her veil a wedding veil, cheap tulle from the haberdasher. And Rosie MacLennan, and what lay up her swishing skirt, turned Pat, too, from thoughts of holy vows. He had another girl now, a proper girl, the one he planned to marry when his wages and his nerve had both been raised. Theresa Kelly, blonde, brown-eyed, and Catholic as the Pope; his mother would no doubt approve.

Pat was happy with his life. He liked his work, being young enough to ignore both its dangers and its drudgery, and in fact involved himself further in his dark, risky world by enrolling in the Mine Rescue Brigade. His future lay before him, God and Theresa willing, marriage, weans, a house perhaps of his own, if only rented. It was a solid, ordered future, unquestioning and traditional, and on this icy November morning, dressing in the dark for the early shift, it was exactly what he wanted. Today too it was all spiced with an added enlivenment. He was on the early shift and had an afternoon free, this Saturday, which he would employ by joggling into the centre of Glasgow on the tram and meeting up with some old mates outside Parkhead football ground. The match, a few drinks, a visit to his Mam; it looked to be a perfect day.

But it was going to end in a way that Pat could never have imagined, and with it, the oddly cosy future he had always planned.

The first inkling of it came after the match. The spectators flowed out of the ground, into the street, a sea of dark clothing and flat, working-men's caps, full of cheer and song. Among them, half elbowed off their feet, swimming virtually through the crush, were Pat McGarrity and his mate Robbie Cadzow, a childhood friend from the tenement, now a driver of a brewer's dray. They were high on victory, their idolized team having provided the satisfying spectacle of a three-nil defeat of the opposition.

'Fancy a quick one?' Pat shrugged towards the frosted, decorative windows of the Black Bull.

'Aye, but I cannae,' Robbie said, turning up his collar against the cold wet wind and glancing with wistful longing towards the golden lights behind the engraved bull on the window. 'The wife'll be waitin'.' He said it self-consciously, having been married under a year.

'Och away,' Pat said smugly. 'Ye shouldna' hae married. Tied down tae her apron strings already.' But he said it with a smile and Robbie only grinned and said,

'Aye, but it's great. Fer a' that.' He turned to go, but as they were about to part, he for his home, and Pat for his mother's flat, their attention was caught by a small parade progressing unevenly up the cobbled street, between the yet milling football throngs. The parade was led by a couple of determined young women in the sort of severely practical dark suits, skirts a little shortened for striding about roads, and no-nonsense little hats and hairstyles that Pat McGarrity associated with suffragettes. Indeed they may well have been suffragettes, because the majority of those ladies had now espoused this new cause, for the duration. Between them, a solemn, slightly unshaven middle-aged man with the dazed look of a recently sobered drinker was bedecked in a large sandwich-board sign. Pat knew his type; various of the more esoteric religious sects regularly dragged them out of the gutter, dried them out and draped them thus to carry the message to the streets. But the message had changed. Before, at every Saturday football match in fact, sandwich boards had greeted his eyes, proclaiming in black, '*The End is Nigh . . . Repent; God's Time is at Hand*', and the like. He was used to them. But this one was different. It said, in letters of bold accusation:

'Are You Forgetting There's a War On?'

When the man turned his back, Kitchener's familiar moustached, military-capped portrait stared out, and the pointing finger pointed directly at Pat McGarrity's chest.

'Your Country Needs You'

The women were smiling, neat, middle-class, don't-touch-me smiles, and handing out leaflets at arm's length.

One of them approached Pat and Robbie, extending her leaflet from a long arm, with her fixed, certain smile. 'Won't you serve your country?' she said sweetly, like an offer of a cup of tea.

'Na fer me,' Robbie said, waving the paper away, 'I've a wife at hame, an' a wean on the way.'

'And won't you defend her from the German Huns?' the woman said with the same sweet smile, her determined eyes closing on Robbie's. 'Or,' she paused, a careful, trained pause, 'will you wait for some other man to do that?' With that her eyes swung to Pat. He looked down at his muddy boots and Robbie turned away. The woman waited, her patient smile never fading, then, after a discreet few seconds, moved away, letting her message sow its seeds on their stony ground.

After, Robbie said, almost querulously, 'An' whit's the army fer, anyway? Isna thot their job? Whit they need wi' us?' He'd gone off, shrugged a little belligerently into his coat collar, his flat cap making a silent lid on his thoughts. Pat McGarrity wandered alone through the Glasgow streets, ducking his head against the rain that was coming on with evening. The cheer of the day had gone, washed down endless muddy gutters with the clusters of discarded recruiting leaflets.

At the corner chip shop in his mother's street, Pat let the hot fat and vinegar smell that drifted into the street draw him inside. He stood on the sawdusted white-and-black tile floor, scuffing his boots about, making little mounds of the sawdust, while his order of fish and chips was fried.

The freckle-faced girl behind the counter reached down to a pile of old newspapers and wrapped the batter-fried fish and a scoopful of chips in a neat package, and handed them over. She smiled at Pat. He was a handsome lad, with fine strong features, shining coarse black hair and dark blue eyes under sharply defined black brows. His eyelashes were long and dusky, 'wasted on a lad' as his mother said with pride. He was gracefully built, though short, like most of his friends from the ill-fed Gorbals slums, and didn't think much about looks anyhow, which he regarded a lassie's concern. He smiled back at the girl, without thinking, as he paid her with coppers from his pocket and took the hot package, a comfort in his cold hands. Pat was used to female attentions. 'Ta,' he said, turning, and going out into the street.

He ate half the fish with his fingers, just standing in front of the chip shop and watching the 'talent', local girls on their way home from work. Then, still eating, he walked slowly up to his mother's close and turned into its familiar, urine-scented darkness.

Inside the building the smell increased and mingled with the cooking smells of a dozen families wafting down the six-storey stairwell. Pat plodded up, knowing each step, each worn place familiar from boyhood. On the third landing, his landing, a small dirty boy came casually out of the lav, pulled up his trousers and buttoning his flies as he did. He caught the passing scent of Pat's newspaper-wrapped supper.

'Gie us one,' he said, boldly grinning.

'Get away,' Pat said, but dropped a small cluster of chips into the grubby extended hands. He tapped once on his mother's door, and then went in, finding it open as it always was – no one locked doors here – and the flat empty. He expected that. It was not yet dark; old leerie only now lighting up the gaslamps in the street outside the kitchen windows. Kathleen would still be down in the wash-house in the yard where she spent most of every day, scrubbing other people's clothes with her great, accommodating red hands.

He recognized her footstep when she mounted the stairs by the heavy uneven thud. One step, then a lurch as she heaved the vast laundry basket up, then another step. Thud, pause, step. Thud, pause, step. Six flights of stone steps, a dozen times a day, right up to the drying loft below the roof in wet weather. Pat did not go to help, knowing she would not have it. So he waited, while her steps thudded by, and on upwards. Quite some time later they returned to her own door.

The door reverberated to the thud of her heavy-skirted hips and swung open, and Kathleen entered backwards, her arms wrapped around the wicker basket. It did not surprise her to find the flat occupied, gaslamps lit, and fire built up high, its light flickering about the aged yellow paper of the walls. Her flat, like those of all her neighbours, was open to one and all with family informality. 'Sae pit the kettle on, wha e'er ye be,' she shouted through to the kitchen.

Pat laughed softly to himself and did not move from the broad wooden-armed chair by the range. He had, some minutes earlier, already set the soot-crusted kettle on the black range. She heard the laugh, masculine, and hustled her bulk through to the open kitchen door.

'Och,' she cried, her face melting into her broad sweet toothless smile, 'it's my bairn.'

Pat winced. His mother could be counted on to undermine his newly achieved manhood faster than anyone. At least there was none with him to hear, this time.

'Aye, an' yer bairn's brocht yer houskeepin', wifie,' he said, slapping the five shillings down on the scrubbed pine table.

She settled herself with a vast sigh into a creaking chair, her cold red hands slapping down on the black cloth of her skirt. 'Och weel, laddie, ye'll ne'er amount tae much if ye bring every penny hame tae me. Nou the shilling will dae nicely, an' the rest is fer yer pocket.'

'Get away,' Pat said, firmly, 'I'll onlie waste it. Drink, and wimmen, ye ken.' He smiled and she looked shocked as if he meant it. Eventually, with real reluctance, she swept the five shilling coins off the table into her clumsy big hand. She rose and deposited them carefully in the old tobacco-tin that held her modest finances.

'Fancy a chip, Mam?' Pat said. 'I saved ye some.'

'Och no,' she said, returning to the table, but her sharp blue eyes had lighted on them and her nose wrinkled with interest. 'Ma stomach's tairrable bad, the nou, I cannae eat a thing.' She paused, eyeing them again. 'Och, mebbe juist the one.' She reached for a single chip, and Pat with a grin thrust the greasy paper towards her.

'There's a wee bit fish as well. Juist tae tide ye till tea-time.' He had left a good half-portion.

'Tea!' Kathleen exclaimed, nibbling a chip, 'I've no' had a proper tea in months. Cannae but sip a bittie soup, and now and then, a bittie bread. I've no' had the stomach fer food since yer puir faither . . .' She trailed off, munching chips.

Pat smiled. He'd never remembered the day when Kathleen had not protested about her bird's appetite. Nor had he known her not to eat everything in sight. He drowsed by the warmth of the coal-fired range, soaking up its comfort like old memories. Kathleen's cheeks, soft as a girl's, reddened slowly in the heat. She finished the last bit of fish and began, idly, to peruse the printed page in which it had been wrapped.

When the kettle began to spout steam, she was still reading and so engrossed that she only waved one distracted plump hand towards the range indicating he should see to it. While Pat poured water into the old stained white china tea-pot, she still read. He let it steep and then poured out two cups, black and strong, and sweetened Kathleen's with four spoonfuls of sugar. He set it on the worn table in front of her, and saw to his astonishment that her round cheeks were streaked with tears which ran from screwed up eyes down to the puckered corners of her mouth. Her chin, too, puckered as she cried out suddenly,

'Ach, this tairrable, tairrable war. How can our Good Lord allow it?' She sobbed openly and Pat cried alarmed,

'Whit's wi' ye, mither?'

She didn't speak but pointed to the printed page before her.

The newspaper was yellowed and old, as well as streaked with grease. No doubt it had sat for weeks at the bottom of the pile at the chip shop. Pat saw a smudged September date on the top of the page. The headline to which his mother pointed was bold and black. It read, '*Little Belgium At Bay*'.

Beneath, the editor's note explained how the sad story therein related had been sent to him by a Scottish lady from Inverness-shire, who had received it in turn from a Belgian acquaintance, a certain Mme Armand who, it was understood, was a witness to the terrible events. Pat read on. It was a long story, and quite extraordinarily grim. At the end he whispered, 'Jeez,' to himself.

'Och, the puir, puir woman,' Kathleen wailed, crossing

herself, her lips muttering prayers.

Pat tried his best to comfort her. She was a big-hearted soul, and her warmth, drawn from a life of many miseries, flowed from all directions towards the entire cast of the newspaper tragedy: the violated young widow and mother, the murdered child, the priestly brother, each of them was bound to draw on a thread of her own experience. Pat would just manage to get her mind off one, and she would wail afresh about another. He made another cup of tea, resorting in the end to a comforting dram from the whisky bottle kept for illness and the New Year. But by seven o'clock, long after the time he had hoped to be back in his local pub, she was still sniffling red-eyed into his large patched handkerchief and moaning, occasionally, 'Och Pat, where will it end?'

When Pat McGarrity left his mother's flat at ten that evening, he left with an embryonic conviction growing in his heart. Four hours later, when he had been drinking with Robbie Cadzow, coaxed by sheer determination from his marital hearth for three of those hours, the conviction had hardened to intent.

'I dinna ken whit ma lass will say tae it,' Robbie said doubtfully, his voice slurred as much by weary concentration on the issue, as by drink. He stared at the stained bar counter of the Black Bull, 'But I ken fine yer right. It's oor duty. It's oor country as well as onybody's, is it no'?'

The question, asked with the rising defiance of assured drunkenness, hung unanswered in the smoke-soured air of the Glasgow pub. As it was, there wasn't a soul in the place sober enough to reply.

Pat never went home at all that night, but slipped late into his mother's flat after parting with Robbie in the street. He could hear her snoring from her bedroom when he entered, and managed to clear her piles of neatly folded ironing from the settee in the kitchen-cum-living-room, and curl up, in his clothes, to sleep without waking her. She didn't seem surprised to find him there in the morning.

'Och lad, did ye miss the last tram then, wi' a' ma blether?' She handed him tea as he sat up, holding his head, the black hair tumbling between slightly grubby fingers. He took the cup and sat straighter, studying the fingers of his free hand. The coal-dust was so engrained in them that each line of his palm was marked clearly as if written in ink. He wondered how many days or weeks it would take to wear away, now that he would no longer be a miner.

Kathleen stood at the big range, energetically stirring the porage. She seemed quite cheerful now. Pat wondered, as he had wondered all his life, how she could manage such vigour on so little sleep. It was five-thirty, and her day had long begun.

'I was wi' Robbie Cadzow,' he said.

'Oh, aye.' It was a mother's reply, kindly and uninterested.

'We've baith made up oor minds tae jine the army.'

Kathleen turned slowly from the range, her wooden porage spoon trailing from the pot. She held it in front of her, mindless of the splattering of grey oatmeal down her apron. She let out her breath in a long, audible half-gasping sigh. Her face was a complex mixture of emotion, pride, fear and love, but uppermost was a sort of resignation, as if she heard what she had long, long expected to hear. That surprised Pat, who regarded his decision as spontaneous.

'Och son,' she said, after a long while. 'Yer faither would be proud.' Sentimentality was perhaps Kathleen's only sin.

The next day, when Pat met Robbie Cadzow outside the recruiting office in Buchanan Street, he found that the response of Robbie's young wife had been surprisingly similar. 'It was gey queer,' Robbie said. 'Ye'd think she was a'most pleased. Relieved at least. It was like she was waitin' fer me to say it, waitin' a lang while.'

So, that morning, when Robbie went off to meet Pat McGarrity in Buchanan Street, the young Mrs Cadzow was able at last to pass the rows of posters plastered to every bare bit of wall along her route to the shops without her customary guilty diversion of the eyes. '*Is Your Best Boy In Khaki?*' '*Women of Britain say "Go"*'. Perhaps worst of all was the one with the scornful Irish girl turning towards the flames of distant France and declaring to the shamed man at her side, '*Will You Go or MUST I?*' Jane Cadzow straightened her shawled shoulders as she passed the painted Irishwoman that morning, and her pretty young eyes glowed with pride.

Pat and Robbie had every intention when they entered the recruiting office of joining up, side by side, in one of Kitchener's New Battalions and serving, side by side, throughout the war. It was not impossible; indeed it was encouraged. The Pals Battalions, they were called, which gathered together men of one district, or neighbourhood even, or background or trade, to train together and serve in one exclusive battalion with the express promise that they would never be broken up or separated. Men flocked to them, joining up *en masse*, all the young and not-so-young men of one trade or another. In Glasgow there was a battalion just of office clerks, the City Tramways Department had formed another, old Boys' Brigade members had formed yet another. Elsewhere battalions formed of miners, of medical students, even of public-school boys. These were not, any of them, men dedicated to the military life, like the men who had formed the regular army. These were committed civilians, tradesmen like Pat and Robbie, with lives and futures in their cities and villages, who were loyal more to those home places than to the army.

They clustered together, and made tight units in which they could go off to serve their country with excitement and innocence. It was too soon yet for anyone to realize how such a grouping would create battalions full of men replete with a single, unadaptable skill, and eventually might leave an entire village bereft of its manhood and its future in one badly planned action at the Front.

However Robbie and Pat's military career was not destined for such an outcome, and their partnership came to a sudden end in the recruiting office itself. Robbie was pleased to find that the draymen were attempting to form their own battalion amalgamated with a group of joiners who had not been able to get up the near thousand men necessary. But there were no miners among them, and Pat McGarrity, miner of miner's stock, was not about to face the Hun with a pack of horse-drivers and joiners.

'Aye, an' they hae the undertakers as well, nae doubt?' he declared with immense scorn, intended to dissuade Robbie. But Robbie had met up with a couple of pals who drove for the brewery, and was intent on his course. He attempted persuasion but didn't get far and finally flew into a temper and said, 'Weel, I'm wi' them, whether ye like or no',' to which Pat declared,

'Aye, fine. If they'll hae ye, ye pigeon-chested wee runt. Mark, they're aye that bit peelie-walie in the joiner's trade. Nae doubt ye'll suit fine. But I'm awa'.'

'Aff wi' ye,' Robbie glowered. 'Wha's needin' ye?'

Pat turned to stalk off in a fury but then a voice said, 'We are,' in a genteel roar. That was how Pat McGarrity met the recruiting sergeant of the Maclaren Highlanders.

He stopped short in his tracks, his swagger, put on a moment earlier for Robbie Cadzow and his draymen pals, rapidly fading. The man was almost a foot taller than he was, massively filling out his khaki field-service jacket, his Balmoral bonnet crammed on to a stubble of hair as prickly as a thistlehead, his face marked by a sabre scar from some earlier campaign that cut right through his bushy moustache, making an island of its outer tip. 'Ye want tae be a Highlander, lad?' he roared.

Pat stepped back, eyeing the man's sharply pleated, blue-and-green Maclaren kilt, that symbol of his own nation that was as alien to him as a woman's skirt and yet which held his romantic awe. The kilt. A Highland soldier in the kilt. He'd never imagined.

'Ye mean I can? Ye ken I'm no' frae the North?'

'Aye weel, we're no sae fussy as we were like tae be, juist now,' the sergeant said, and Pat was not sure if that was meant as a joke or not. 'Ye'll dae, I reckon. The Inverness Highlanders they're calling them, juist the now, but they'll be taken over as soon as they're together, like the Territorials. Fourth Battalion Maclaren Highlanders, lad, dae ye fancy the sound o' it?'

'Oh, aye,' Pat breathed, like a delighted child. Then he paused. 'Inverness, is it? Where's thot, now?'

The sergeant narrowed his eyes briefly, but did not comment. After all, a good many of the crofters' sons he'd gathered from the west coast had had no idea where Glasgow was. He nodded sagely then and pointed one huge finger over his shoulder in something like the direction of north. 'If ye fancy joining us, lad, ye can count on us tae show ye the way. We'll even gie ye yer train ticket, nou hou's thot fer a bargain?'

It was the train that did it, actually. Pat McGarrity had never been on a proper train in his life. As a boy he had longed for the train ride that more prosperous children were given, to the Ayrshire coast, and later he had played dangerous games about the railyards, just for the company of the great steaming engines shunting with slow dignity in and out. A train ride. Four, five hours, the sergeant had said. That was what did it.

Pat McGarrity rode that train four hours later, with his face glued to the window for all the five hours, nose flattened against the glass, watching the beautiful unknown country that was, in all its awesome grandeur, meant to be his own.

At about the time Pat was stepping warily down on to the platform at Inverness station, a pair of thoroughly seasoned soldiers were also stepping off a train. Their train was the leave-train, homeward bound from France, and the soldiers, whose battered khaki bore the indefinable mark of experience, were Lt. Torquil Farquhar and 2nd. Lt. John Bruce. Surrounding them was a cheering crowd of Tommies and Jocks, faces alight with the frenetic joy of the newly on leave.

Not many feet away, at another platform of Victoria Station, a trainload of fresh drafts of Territorials, out to reinforce depleted battalions, was setting out in the direction from which the rejoicing soldiers had come. They were a remarkable contrast to the homecomers, fresh and clean, hiding nervousness in music-hall patriotism, waving their self-consciously battered caps at tearful girls.

But a close observer would at once pick up two far more significant differences in the returning soldiers. The first was the casual way, without stopping talking, that John Bruce scratched at his ribs with determined fingers, pursuing something that crawled contentedly beneath the khaki, and the other, more ominous, was the way, as the carriage door slammed behind him, Torquil Farquhar half jumped and ducked his head and then, slowly, nervously, and deliberately forced himself to relax.

'I'm glad,' Johnny Bruce said, 'it will just be Naomi meeting us. I honestly don't think I could face the rest, all at once.'

Torquil looked across to him, surprised. 'You feel it too?' he said, and added uneasily, 'It's madness, isn't it? I mean, Emma and all. Surely I should be happy.' He shrugged, and said finally, 'I suppose it just takes getting used to; no doubt tomorrow will be super.'

'No doubt,' Johnny said, feeling not only doubt but a lot of frustration. When you only had a week's leave, you hardly wanted to spend half of it getting acclimatized. Still, he was certain that time was the factor; time, and distance, or more accurately, the lack of both. It was so extraordinarily close. Ten hours ago he had been with the battalion at the Front. They were, granted, not exactly doing battle. They were in a quiet sector of the line, near Armentières, where they had been moved after their devastation at Ypres in October. Aside from the usual 'morning hate' session, and an occasional petulant volley at the evening stand-to, he'd hardly experienced rifle-fire for weeks. The artillery was more persistent, and unpleasant, being quite unpredictable, the Huns lobbing the occasional *Minenwerfer*, or even a heavy Jack Johnson from time to time for fun, but there'd been no proper barrage since they'd taken up the sector. There'd even been a bit of surreptitious light-hearted communication with their opposites in the German trenches; they were facing a battalion of Bavarians, good-natured and unwarlike, and there was no real hostility.

What there was plenty of was discomfort – cold and mud, lice and rats, a soldier's litany of misery – but with it the ironic awareness that the enemy had precisely the same misfortunes. It bonded them; it bonded them all, and it was the broken bond that was causing their present odd discomfiture.

'Do you think Jerry's still going to try to use that Observation Post?' Torquil said, laughing suddenly, the first laugh he'd managed in London. His mind was still back there, remembering the delight they'd had, sending out a scouting party to trim the branches off Jerry's tree. Of course, they could have simply fired on the observer the next day, once they'd spotted him, but he wasn't a sniper or anything. Live and let live. No harm in a bit of fun. 'What we should have done,' Torquil said, his face brightening, 'was just saw halfway through the trunk. So when he got up there the whole would have come right over.' He grinned. 'That would have been one astonished Jerry.' He laughed again, but the laughter died away. 'This is madness,' he said again under his breath.

They had reached the barrier, the moment that both had been unconsciously dreading. Beyond lay London and the real world. He braced himself for the awfulness of normality, but then he saw Naomi Bruce and realized he had no need.

She was not waving, she was not shouting. She did not call their names. She carried no flowers, and was not dressed in her stylish best, but in the drab cloak of a VAD nurse. She just stood quietly, waiting, her olive-skinned face impassive until each of them, in turn, caught her eyes. She smiled then, a small, quiet smile. Torquil knew at once; she understood. He was suddenly aware how much she'd aged.

13

An hour later, stretched out luxuriously in the immense copper bath in one of the three splendidly outfitted bathrooms of Naomi's Park Lane house, Torquil Farquhar re-entered the civilized world. What bright colours, he thought suddenly, noticing the pinks and pale purples of the wallpaper and the deep maroon of the velvet curtains in the adjoining dressing-room. He caught sight of one corner of the gilt frame of the large painting that hung on the far wall over the small flower-tiled fireplace, and leaned forward in the tub for a better view. It showed a Highland scene, a Shetland pony with two children mounted on it, a girl in a white frilled dress and a boy in a kilt. They were Emma and Tenny Maclaren. He gazed wistfully at their childhood caught forever in a moment of fleeting Highland sunshine.

Torquil lay his head back against the copper tub, sinking in the water till it lapped his chin, and closed his eyes. He thought of his own childhood, his own home in Perthshire. His father had volunteered to come south to meet him on this leave, on the pretence of saving him the long journey north. The real reason, he knew, was to allow him more time with Emma. Tentatively, very tentatively, he allowed himself to think of her, picturing her as always at the Bank Holiday picnic at Culbrech. The picture seemed faded, and try as he could, he could not, in his memory, hear her speak. She had become voiceless. He concentrated on the picture, terrified that she would grow faceless as well. He was almost as terrified at the thought that in a few hours he would indeed see that face again, his memory of it replaced by a new reality. What would he say to her, now, that pretty coy girl beneath the rowan tree? There was nothing left common to them; experience lay between, a private no-man's-land.

Torquil opened his eyes, gazed sleepily about the sumptuous bathroom. Naomi had forgotten nothing. Even a silk dressing-gown, a *man's* silk dressing-gown, was spread by the attentive maid across one of the Louis Quinze chairs in the anteroom. Shaving-kit had been provided, and Turkish cigarettes in a carved ebony box lay on the marble surround of the bath. He was particularly grateful for those, having taken to smoking more and more these past weeks. He stretched one wet muscular arm out and drew the box gently closer, and lifted the elephant-adorned lid. He drew one out, damping the paper slightly with his wet fingers, and put it to his lips, after first wiping soap from his moustache. He lit it with a match from the little silver box provided and noticed, with a small wincing grimace, that the flame danced in his shaking fingers.

He looked down at his naked body, blurred by soapy water, as he drew carefully on the cigarette, seeing himself at leisure for the first time in months. How young and soft those private regions of himself were. How then, he thought, would be Emma Maclaren, a thousand times softer, no doubt? He thought suddenly of her with sleepy lust, and started with an onrush of shame. It must be the war, making a man think such thoughts of a lady, common whore-thoughts. He closed his eyes, fighting tears, struggling for composure.

Dear Naomi. She was so wise. No questions, no chat, just the bath, and amongst all the exquisite soaps and lotions of Naomi's taste, a large obtrusive cake of the ubiquitous dark yellow carbolic. She had even provided for the damnable lice.

When he met her again in the drawing-room, she was wearing a low-necked flowing gown of magenta Chinese silk, embroidered with black dragons. 'Do forgive my informality,' she said softly, 'but I've been all day in that uniform, and it's hardly the most comfortable of garments. You'd think someone would realize that a woman who is scrubbing and cleaning and lifting patients might function better without several yards of fabric swirling around her ankles, but they haven't yet.' She shook her head, and then smiled quickly and said, 'But none of that for now. Come, shall I tell you of Emma?'

'Oh do,' Torquil said, trying to be at once both polite and enthusiastic yet hearing his voice filled with uneasy apprehension.

'Don't worry,' Naomi said, sitting beside him on the settee and touching his forearm with her small, work-roughened hand. 'She has grown up too.'

The door opened before Torquil had time to fully absorb what she had said, and John Bruce entered, clean and fresh, his hair still damp. 'Ah, Aunt Naomi,' he said, 'this is too, too kind.' He was smiling broadly and making a very good imitation of his old drawing-room self, but his eyes, like Torquil's, had that dull, aged look with which she had become too familiar. She poured whisky for him as well and rang for tea.

Over tea they talked, quietly. She related small details of London life, and accounts of family progress, Albert's surprise rejection of the officer's life for that of the common soldier, Tenny's continued frustration in his efforts to get to the Front, which brought an ironic, 'More fool he,' from John Bruce, her own son's progress at school, Willie Bruce's regular pontifications on the war scene from the distance of Culbrech House.

'He says you need a machine-horse for Haig's cavalry to face the machine-guns,' Naomi laughed.

'He's about right,' Johnny said. 'He should try telling Haig. The old man still seems rock sure we'll get the cavalry through somewhere next spring and wrap the whole thing up. But I wish I could be as hopeful.'

'There was one moment,' Torquil said, his pale blue eyes almost dreamy in remembrance, 'you know, at that place past Landrecies . . . Villers-Cotteret . . . there was one moment. It was a beautiful day, the sun shining, blue sky high up through the patches in the tall trees waving above us . . . it looked like that spot at the river where we had the picnic, at Culbrech. And we were stopped there, bunched up on the one narrow road where I suppose we shouldn't have been, but there was a lot of confusion. And the cavalry came through, one of the best regiments, all polish and style and glitter. We all stopped and talked. It was wonderful. Like a pause at a hunt somewhere. I remember thinking my father would have loved it; all that splendid horseflesh and the creak of saddle leather everywhere, and all the young officers so beautifully dressed. Some of them knew some of our boys. Bunty FitzJames, he was pals with a couple of the cavalry chaps, one of them was engaged to his sister. He's dead now, of course. Polygone Wood. But Bunty was chatting away, and we were all joking about stirrup cups. And the sun shining. I remember thinking, yes, this is war. This was what I'd always expected. I was sure that day it would all go well.' He stopped suddenly, nervously twisting the stub of his cigarette round and round in an ashtray. 'Damn. I have rather been going on. Do forgive me.'

'No, not at all,' Naomi said. 'Do go on.'

But Johnny Bruce had turned away to the darkening window, watching the silent maid draw the curtains. 'No, that was all, you see. That beautiful day. They were mostly all killed the day after. Some engagement along the road, where it all went wrong.'

He threw the stub of the cigarette over the brass fender where it lay glowing on the hearth. Torquil let his head drop into his open palms.

Naomi did not move, but stood looking down with dark compassionate eyes on the smooth brown hair of his head. Then she lightly touched it with her outstretched fingers, as the maid re-entered the room. She had heard the opening of the front door, and knew what the announcement would be.

'Miss Maclaren has arrived, Mrs Bruce.'

'Very well, Mary,' she said. 'Show her in.' Her fingers trailed from Torquil's bowed head. 'Come now,' she said. 'Here is your lady, at last.'

With great effort he straightened himself, and composed his face into a pleasant smile of welcome. The door opened again, and the maid's black-skirted form swished in, made its little turn, announced, 'Miss Maclaren,' and turned and swished out. Torquil rose, raising his face to the young woman standing there, and began, 'Emma, my dear . . .' his voice trailing suddenly to silence.

In the drawing-room doorway, tall and serene in emerald green velvet, her strong face bordered by two immense loops of red-gold hair, stood Philippa Maclaren. Only her faintly trembling upper lip revealed any emotion at all, as she extended her hand to him. 'Why, Torquil,' she said, her voice calm and assured, neither mannish, nor childish any longer. 'This *is* a most pleasant surprise.'

She was not the only one surprised, if she was surprised at all, which was unlikely. Johnny Bruce was genuinely surprised, first by her unexpected and unheralded arrival in London, and secondly, and more significantly, by her appearance. Like many dowdy women whose dowdiness is a product less of lack of style than lack of conviction, Philippa Maclaren, once blossomed, bloomed beautifully. Public appearances had enhanced her confidence. Her height dominated a room. Her beautiful hair, lavishly plentiful, was dressed with infinite care. She was a tall, lithe, unusual beauty whose body and face radiated strength.

Johnny Bruce, who had treated her always as a mix of boring big sister and maiden aunt, now rose and quickly went to her side, greeting her with the attentiveness she had seen him reserve for girls like Rebecca Galloway. She was flattered but turned even as she greeted him, her cool blue Maclaren eyes seeking Torquil. He too was standing, a little hesitantly, at the edge of the white marble fireplace, as if he feared to approach. Another, earlier Philippa would have hesitated, and then, unable to resist, she would have strode forward, arms swinging, face reddening with a girlish blush. This Philippa did not. Nor did she speak. She only waited, and showed no frustration when Naomi interrupted their silence,

'I'm afraid you've rather taken us unaware, my dear. I had no idea you were in London. I was expecting Tenny, of course . . .' Naomi trailed off, for once a little lost for words herself. She had planned this evening well, for Torquil and for Emma. Susan and Johnny Bruce, like any close brother and sister, would be glad of each other's company, a brief respite from wartime separations, and Naomi had her own plans for Tenny and Rebecca. But Torquil and Emma, teetering on the edge of engagement, needed time alone, forbidden, of course, but with the fierce acceleration that war put on all human friendships, she felt that custom might, for once, be waived.

She had already planned a strategic withdrawal from the dining-room that would have left the young couple an hour of privacy to use as they wished. Victoria, she knew, would not be pleased, but Victoria would never know. And Emma's father, Ian Maclaren, had, Naomi well understood, long ago and too late realized the value of grasping life's elusive brief joys. He would be with her in spirit, wherever he was, as she eased love's way for his daughter.

But what was she to do with Philippa? 'I'm not sure,' she

continued lamely, 'if there will be time to ready a room.'

'But I wouldn't dream of putting you to such a trouble,' Philippa smiled sweetly. 'I have taken a room at Brown's Hotel. I have an appointment there in the morning anyhow.' She smiled towards Torquil, 'My little war work; it's nothing much, of course, but we all do what we can and hope it will in some way ease the burden of you men at the Front.' She dropped her eyes with calculated care.

'Why, that's splendid,' Torquil stammered, 'I had no idea you were . . . I mean, of course, Emma and Susan are nursing.'

'Yes,' Philippa said. 'The finest work for a woman, of course. They wouldn't take me, I'm afraid. A little turbercular attack when I was at school. Quite nothing, of course, and quickly healed, but apparently they feel my health might break . . .' She looked wistfully aside, out towards the drawn curtains as if imagining herself in some distant hospital ward. The gesture showed her firm-chinned profile, courageously set. Torquil wondered suddenly if the thinness of her cheek was the result of that previously unheard of spell of illness. He said, 'I do hope you are not overtaxing yourself now.'

The girl smiled at Torquil gently and said, 'No, of course not. I'm as strong as an ox; it's just a bit of silliness.' Months of speech-making had taught her tongue flow, and her wit timing. She turned briskly to Naomi and said, changing the subject with assurance, 'Tenny and I came down together on the train. He went off to meet the girls at their hostel, while I booked in at my hotel room. I shall wait only long enough, if I may, of course,' she glanced, a quick fluttering of her pale-lashed eyes, 'to see my sister, and then I shall be off. I did so want to see Emma, of course, or I should never have interfered.'

'Of course you're not interfering.' Johnny Bruce rose quickly to the gallantry that the remark demanded, and Naomi said quickly, 'Of course not,' hoping the silly fool would drop it there and not offer an invitation to dinner. But he did not need to.

It was Torquil who said, extending one tentative, slightly shaky hand to the slim, erect figure before him, 'Surely Naomi, Miss Maclaren must stay and join us for dinner. Surely she must stay.' His eyes swept over her face, hungry for it, lest she leave. She radiated strength, and when he stepped closer he could smell a faint scent of lilac.

* * *

'How could I refuse?' Philippa confided later in a sisterly tête-à-tête with Emma Maclaren in the feminine retreat of Naomi's sumptuous boudoir.

'Of course you couldn't,' Emma replied a little too briskly, adjusting her hair in front of the white-and-gold-rimmed dressing-table mirror. She glanced with concealed envy at her sister's loops and braids of ruddy hair. Her own was lank and needing washing and she wished now she had been more insistent last night about her claim to a coveted bath in the hostel. But one of the trained nurses had bustled ahead of her in the corridor, towel over arm and determination in her eyes, and Emma had submitted with VAD meekness, as always. 'I'm sure Torquil was quite delighted to see us both,' she said as good-naturedly as she could.

'Well, one must do everything one can for the poor dear boys,' Philippa said, assessing her slim figure in the mirror, over Emma's shoulder. 'Familiar faces must be so comforting.'

'That is a most striking dress,' Emma said coolly.

'I think,' Philippa replied, with only the slightest downward cast of her pale, unreadable eyes, 'that we owe it to men back from the Front to look our very best. They must have every image of graciousness available to carry with them, when they return. Do you not think so?'

Her voice was mild and Emma could not hear in it any of the light mockery she was sure lay behind the words. Still she was sharp when she said, 'Well, that's all very well, but one can hardly be gracious when one spends one's days up to the elbows in dressings and blood and bedpans, can one?'

'But you look lovely, dear, that plain little dress looks positively charming on you. You always were the beauty after all. I don't know how you still manage. And I'm sure your hands will get better as soon as you're no longer nursing. One can always wear those charming little gloves, can't one?'

Emma suddenly whirled about, her temper flaring in her eyes and voice. 'Philippa, I have been working in theatre for half this day. I attended four amputations and later I watched two men die. I can't frankly care a damn about my hands or anyone's charming little gloves. Do you understand?'

'Why, darling,' Philippa said, 'don't be harsh, please don't. Why, we're all so terribly proud of you. I was only just saying to Torquil before you arrived that you've become the positive ideal of womanhood in all our minds . . .'

'And I don't need your recommendation, Miss.' Emma turned away from her furiously because Philippa's words had brought back the vision that had so startled her upon her arrival and haunted her now, of her exquisitely dressed younger sister, sitting by the fire, with Torquil in virtual adoration on the settle by her feet. He had, quite unconsciously, gathered one fold of her wide-spreading braid-trimmed hem, where it lay over the settle, and was holding it like a child holds its mother's hand. Even when he rose to greet her that image of him stood like a shadow between them and they had met with the formality of strangers.

'I think you're overtired, poor dear. I know you work so hard,' Philippa said smoothly. 'I'll leave you to compose yourself for dinner.' She swept coolly out, leaving a terribly uncomposed Emma Maclaren twisting her uncooperative, neglected hair into an angry coil.

In such a mood she rose from the dressing-table, straightened the poorly pressed hem of the one dinner dress her minuscule storage space in the hostel allowed, and went down to meet the tired, nervous stranger she had longed for since August with the longing of a bride. Later, seated beside him at dinner, she could think of not one word to say.

Tenny thought of plenty, perhaps too many. He was the mainstay of the conversation, and all he wanted to talk about was the war. He poured out question after question to the oddly reticent young officers, trying, as was natural for a regular army man, to get into his mind some picture of what was happening out there, some picture that would blend together the increasingly divergent reports that flowed from the Western Front.

'I can't understand,' he said sharply to Johnny Bruce, 'why the powers-that-be don't do something about straightening out the line. It's full of little salients, like Ypres, and every one of them is on our side, with our men pushed out into enemy territory. Damned stupid, if you ask me.'

'Then what do you suggest?'

'Well, withdraw maybe, behind Ypres at least.'

'We lost half our men defending Ypres.'

'I know that,' Tenny said touchily, 'but if you ask me, you'll lose the rest trying to hold an untenable –'

'You weren't *there*, damn it,' Torquil Farquhar shouted, his hand trembling on his soup spoon so it clattered against the china dish. His hair tumbled over his eyes and he shook it away angrily, and then pushed it back with a trembling hand.

'Torquil,' Emma said concernedly, 'are you all right?' He looked to her quite feverish, like a sick man.

'You weren't bloody there,' he said, and all the ladies froze. Even in the hospital when Emma dressed their agonizing shrapnel wounds, the men swallowed their blasphemies in deference to her. He shook his head, wiping a spot of spilled soup from the front of his jacket, looking around him as if uncertain where he was. Then he calmed and said, 'I'm sorry. That was quite out of order. Do forgive me, Naomi.'

Naomi patted his sleeve, from her place at the head of the table, and smiled encouragingly. 'I know Tenny is not questioning the performance of the Maclarens. Only the choice of the battlefield.'

'Forced on us,' Johnny Bruce said grimly. 'Can't give up Ypres or they'll go right to the sea and cut off the Channel ports. Or so they say. Same right down the line. They draw the line because every bit of land they take is stolen. The French hang on to every bit they can because it's their country. Don't suppose we'd be any different if Ypres were Inverness, would we? Anyhow we still do what Papa Joffre says, for better, or . . .'

'Or for worse,' Torquil Farquhar finished slowly, his eyes dull.

'For better,' Philippa Maclaren said, her voice ringing out over the table.

Emma thought it was a foolish thing to say to tired men so obviously failing in their conviction. But Torquil brightened under her brave smile, and when she said, 'Those who died defending Ypres will not have died in vain,' he actually smiled and summoned enough bravado to say,

'No. We'll see to that. In the spring, we'll see to that.'

Tenny nodded approvingly at his sister. Only John Bruce maintained a light cynicism, saying, in response to Tenny's proud promise of another full battalion of volunteers trained and ready by spring,

'Be sure they know how to dig, now. This rifle practice is all very well, you know, but today's Jock is first and foremost a trench-digger. Give me a good navvy any day, and you can keep your fifteen rounds a minute.'

'Oh, come now,' Tenny said smoothly, 'the trench system is surely a winter expedient. You don't expect to spend the whole summer keeping your heads down as well.'

Rebecca Galloway looked quickly from Tenny's face to Johnny's, waiting for a response. She had been struck already by the subtle change that had occurred between them. Once all the loud talk and bold gestures had been Johnny's, and Tenny had kept aloof, with a cool calm smile. Now somehow it was reversed. She noticed with an odd feeling of attraction the small recently healed scar across John Bruce's lean cheek. He had not even mentioned how he got it. She expected him to be riled and show outrage, as Torquil had done earlier, but he did not.

He said, instead, 'Oh yes. I'll keep my head down for the next ten years if the alternative is standing up in front of a machine-gun. All very noble, I know, but highly impracticable, old man. By the way, do try and teach your New Army boys a little something about warfare. Trench warfare I mean. The Territorials all come out expecting great flag-waving charges, "over the top", every ten minutes. I'm afraid they find us all something of a disappointment.'

'I'd . . . I'd teach them more,' Tenny said, struggling against frustrated blasphemy, 'if I had some equipment to teach them with. I'm out there drilling all day with a bunch of crofters' sons with sticks over their shoulders. How do I train men without rifles? Without ammunition? Without . . . damned all,' he muttered.

'Same way,' Johnny Bruce said with a small, eye-crinkling smile, 'as we fight the Boche without any shells for our artillery. And half the few they give us are dud. No, old man, give them warm boots and an entrenching tool, and the regulation issue of lice, and teach them how to keep their heads down. That's all they need to know.'

'I think,' Tenny said smoothly, his pale Highland eyes narrowing with well-thought-out disdain, 'that you, old man, have got the wind up.'

'Tenny,' Emma whispered, and Naomi quickly resolved that she was going to get through dinner in an ungracious hurry before anyone came to blows, but Johnny only laughed and said,

'Oh indeed. We've *all* got the wind up, mate. That's why we're still alive.' He laughed richly.

Rebecca thought how strange it was that in four short months this once childish boy had become so powerfully confident a man. She was quite content, when after dinner Naomi beckoned them from the table, to go out to the withdrawing-room on his assuredly offered arm.

Naomi herself escorted Tenny from the room, her other arm linked through that of Philippa Maclaren. She could feel a rigidity of tension through the velvet sleeve. She said lightly, 'Oh, I do love family gatherings. No need for all that formality. Come, let us have some music. Susan will sing no doubt, Tenny, if you play the piano for us. Oh, leave those two,' she said gaily towards Emma and Torquil who had found themselves suddenly abandoned in the dining-room. 'I've instructed Lucy to bring some Madeira. I know you'll have things to discuss, and we hardly need Emma's dreadful warblings to ruin our evening, do we?' She nudged Susan Bruce beside her and got the appropriate girlish teasing laugh, and then, quite suddenly, they were out of the dining-room, with the door shut firmly by Naomi's own hand.

Emma and Torquil sat silent as the maid entered, carrying a tray with the decanter of Madeira and two glasses. She set it on the table before them, and both of them were conscious of a dozen social rules broken at once.

'Odd Naomi doesn't employ a butler,' was all Torquil could think of to say.

'No. It's only women, you see. The whole house. Even the cats. It's rather like a convent, I suppose,' and then she giggled, 'only different.'

'Rather,' said Torquil. He managed a faint smile. Shyly he studied her face, as if remembering her from another life. 'Shall I pour?' he said, 'or do we pass it?'

She shook her head, 'I hardly think it . . . oh, dear God Torquil, what's happened to us?'

He shook his head, half closing his eyes, leaning back in his chair.

'Emma, Emma please,' he said. He paused and then said slowly, 'I wish you weren't nursing at all. I wish you were still in Scotland, in the drawing-room of Culbrech House, in that lovely frock you wore that day in August . . .' he trailed off, his hands opening and closing in frustration, trying to hold on to the past.

Emma was silent for a long time, then she said, conscious of the pettiness of her own words, 'I suppose you'd like me to flounce around all day in green velvet, war or no war, like Philippa.'

He looked at her pityingly, as if she were a child, and said only, at last, 'I'd like everything to be as it was, Emma, that's all.'

'And do you think I would not?' she snapped.

'Of course you would. Of course,' his voice was placating and his eyes distant. 'Only it's impossible, naturally. We've all changed. All of us,' he shrugged, not meeting her gaze, but smiling a little sadly at his still empty glass.

'Is it over between us?' she said.

He did not answer. Faintly, through the two closed doors between, they could hear Susan Bruce at the piano, singing to Tenny's accompaniment, with real music-hall panache,

'Goodbye-ee, Goodbye-ee, Wipe a tear, baby dear, from your eye-ee . . .'

'When Bunty was killed,' Torquil said suddenly, 'I was standing right next to him. It was a shell splinter. It took all his head . . . I had to pick . . . pièces . . . bone, brain . . . little pieces from . . . my . . . jacket . . .' He closed his eyes again, long streaks of tears marking his face. She rose mechanically, as she would in the ward, and stood next to him, holding his head against her breasts. She could feel his warm breath through her thin gown and was appalled at the incongruity of her own sudden shock of modesty. He pressed his head against her body and sobbed. They were still like that, she standing, he clutching her with desperate sad passion, when the door clicked open with a sound like a shot.

'Emma!' Philippa gasped in the doorway.

'Get out,' Emma returned at once. But Torquil leapt up from his chair, hurled Emma aside and ran to the curtained window of the room. He crouched there on the floor, his shaking body worming in behind the curtain, his arms protecting his head and his face turned to the wall.

14

Torquil Farquhar's entry, the following day, into the neurasthenia ward of the First London General Hospital, had the effect on the Maclaren household of an artillery shell landing in the drawing-room of Culbrech House. Reactions ranged from incredulity to embarrassed silence. Significantly, the people closest to the situation were by far the least affected. So, while a worried Alex Farquhar discussed his son's perplexing condition over the telephone with a sympathetic but uneasy Victoria Maclaren, Emma Maclaren, who had actually witnessed Torquil's alarming descent into insanity, felt only a kind of relief.

Now, at last, she understood. Shell-shock, as the condition was just beginning to be called, was a new concept in the first year of the war. It was wreathed in uncertainty and misconception but Emma was better prepared to understand it than half the generals commanding the army, because Emma, lowly VAD though she was, had spent almost a month attending its victims in the same ward where Torquil now lay. She had since been transferred back to a general ward, nursing the physically, not mentally, wounded, but she had not forgotten them. No one could.

Whereas a surgical ward would be forever fixed in her mind by its obscene smells of gangrenous putrefaction only lightly veiled by the counterstench of antiseptics, it was sound, not scent, that recalled the neurasthenia ward.

Silence was the first requirement of the nurse. Silence and

stealth and caution. Every gesture, be it the serving of a meal, or the making of beds, or the simple opening of a door of a cupboard must be done with elaborate care.

'Always let them see you first,' Matron would say. 'Don't speak until they've met your eyes. Don't *ever* touch them without warning. When you speak, speak softly, steadily, with no sudden change of tempo or tone. Never, ever slam a door or allow plate, or fork, or cup to strike the table with more than a whisper of sound.' Heaven help the unfortunate VAD who was so unforgivably clumsy as to drop anything, anything at all. Emma herself had seen one shell-shocked sergeant leap from his bed and run screaming down the ward because an incautious doctor had shut, with a sharp slap, the pages of a notebook.

For all that grim emphasis on silence the ward was not a quiet place. It was filled with the sounds of madness and distress, men moaning quietly as if in pain, men crying out suddenly at nightmares, or worse, visions that walked through daylight hours that they alone could see, men talking in high, excited feverish voices, laughing even, recounting again and again some event, sometimes traumatic, sometimes pointless, that held for them the key to a shattered world. Emma had learned to sit silently, smiling encouragingly, while some once fine young mind struggled to express to her the simplest reality.

In the officers' ward she learned to joke with the gloriously handsome young captain about the dances he would claim from her in some future carefree world of balls and tea-parties, ignoring the while the whiteness of his face and the trembling of his hands. She could not ignore, five days afterwards, the horror of his suicide, with a straight razor, in a solitary unguarded moment. It was hushed up, of course, and the official report read: 'Died of wounds, First General Hospital, London'. His was not the only suicide among the shell-shocked, but he was the only one she had known personally. To a military establishment wavering between uncertain sympathy towards a doubtful ailment, and harsh condemnation of 'nerves' and 'lack of moral fibre', suicide was an unspeakable shame.

Most of all Emma had learned, as all the doctors were learning, and the wiser, more compassionate of the officers were growing to understand as well, that shell-shock was not cowardice. Funkiness, the uninitiated said; got the wind up. Even Tenny, remote from the realities of this new warfare, had, against his kind-hearted will, been forced to that conclusion about Torquil and had turned in some distress from the spectacle of his collapse. Emma knew better. It was not the cowards who went that way, but the best.

And for Emma it was also a kind of godsend, a lover's dream. Here was Torquil, not in her ward but only two wards, a matter of yards, away down polished corridors. And yet he was unhurt, his body perfect, no wound or illness to threaten his life. That his light and totally understandable derangement could be any real threat to him in its own right was a fleeting thought quickly dismissed. Emma would never have rated her nursing powers so highly as to imagine herself a fair combatant to infection or illness in the body of a man. But his mind, the mind of one who loved her, and she him, so much that thoughts blended; that surely was in her power to save. Rest and care the nursing staff would provide, but love, great healer of the spirit, was her powerful and willing weapon.

She crept away in every spare moment to see him. She was, she realized gratefully, hugely indulged, both by the staff of the neurasthenia ward and by her own matron. Emma was the sort of young woman, emerging through back-breaking work from the chrysalis of ladyhood, who won the hearts of all around her, not only the young, but older people as well. She was hard-working and immensely willing, and Matron was accustomed to the sight of her, flushed cheeks shining, nose dabbled with sweat, her little curls of auburn hair managing to escape from her headgear. A lifetime of training for the peculiarly inverted self-sacrifice that the British upperclasses bred so willingly, together with an irrepressibly boisterous nature and sturdy constitution, made Emma Maclaren the ideal nurse. Add to that a distant and genuine love in the shape of Torquil Farquhar, and the picture was perfect. Here was an industrious young woman who always smiled, was always cheerful, and yet never romantic. She could love them all, all the boys, and their officers as well, without the danger that fluttered over other girls' heads, the danger of falling in love. Matron quite firmly kept the pretty ones, like Susan and Rebecca, in the wards reserved for NCOs and men. There, social standing would prevent hand-holding developing to liaisons, and worst and most forbidden of all, assignations after hours. Emma alone was trusted into wards where men of her own class might be met in the most romantically vulnerable of situations, that of patient and nurse.

Now Emma, ruthless as all lovers are, leant on her good reputation and tolerance of the staff at every opportunity, winning precious moments free with Torquil. She had even lied to win her way, having announced shamelessly to Matron that he was her fiancé. It was a passport, and Emma employed it, secretly, and yet knowing she must tell Torquil himself before it reached his ears from other sources. The shame of the idea made her blush in a way that the naked body of the patient she was tending at the time could not.

When she went to see Torquil again, in her half-hour lunch break, he was not alone. Tenny Maclaren was with him, and in the corridor beyond the ward John Bruce was waiting. They were allowed to see him only one at a time. Emma, her VAD's uniform allowing her free range of the place, joined Tenny at Torquil's bedside. It was an awkward meeting. Tenny greeted her too avidly, as embarrassed people will do, dragging a third party into a flagging conversation like a life-raft. Torquil looked away. Tenny chatted, too loudly, about what they would do when they were all, himself included, out at the Front having a go at the Boche. Emma watched his tall form with growing amazement, seeing his face that she had admired and respected since childhood grow fatuous, his sandy moustache twitching foolishly as his nervous upper lip curled over each little short uneasy laugh. When he said at last, 'Well, cheerio, mind yourself with all those pretty VADs,' and nudged her arm, she felt for him something very like hatred.

After he was gone, Torquil spoke for the first time. 'He thinks I'm a coward,' he said.

'Of course not, silly.'

'So does Philippa. I'll never forget the way . . . the way she looked at me.'

'Philippa's a baby,' Emma snapped, her anger not for him but for her sister whose behaviour in her opinion had verged on the despicable. Granted she was shocked by Torquil's collapse, but she had let the shock show so blatantly. And worse, she had done nothing to heal the wounds she had caused; she lacked even the courage to call upon the poor man in hospital. Philippa had left Naomi's house even before Torquil was taken away to hospital, while the attending doctor was yet calming him. She had given him no farewell, nor had she come to the hospital in the three days he had been here. She had kept her appointment with the

Baroness Orczy, sipping tea and discussing the nobility of war, Emma imagined. And then, with no farewell to anyone, she had boarded a train and journeyed north. She had arrived at Culbrech and, according to Victoria Maclaren, had not mentioned a word of what she had witnessed in Park Lane.

Nor did she ever again speak Torquil Farquhar's name to anyone.

'No,' Torquil whispered softly, 'Philippa is quite right. I am. I am . . . a coward. God, it's strange to actually say it when I've only just had the nerve to think . . .'

'Torquil, it's not so. It's an illness, like pneumonia, or dysentery, or any of the others. And you'll get better . . . and go back . . . and be very brave.' She fought against the tears.

He smiled and patted her hand, and she saw the now familiar wall of distance come up in his candid blue eyes.

She was thankful and relieved when John Bruce joined them. It had not taken her long to realize that there was a special communication among those who had been at the Front, that no one else could share. In John Bruce's company Torquil relaxed, even grinned a little, even joked that he had engineered it all for an extra couple of weeks in Blighty.

Emma dreaded the day, four days hence, when Johnny would have to leave for the Front, and would leave Torquil behind. Instinctively she knew it would be a challenging moment. She equally dreaded Tenny's return visits, for as much as she loved her brother, she saw him now, with his foolish inexperienced bravado, as Torquil's enemy.

Tenny of course hardly regarded himself as that. True, Torquil disturbed him, as would the vision of any perfectly fit man, a fellow Maclaren officer at that, who declined into childish madness. He was not callous by nature, but he had infinite faith in the military life and in the strength of military training. He knew the Maclarens had given Torquil, as they had given all of their men, everything that was needed to face death with equanimity. A man who failed was a blot on the regiment; there was no other way to look at it. And though he would never express such a thought to Torquil, or his poor sister Emma, he did in an unguarded moment express it to Johnny Bruce.

It was late the following night, when he and John Bruce were sharing a nightcap in the library of Naomi's house, which they had adopted as their base. Johnny had found one silver lining in the cloud that Torquil had flung over their leave, and that was the excuse it provided him to spend the rest of his leave in London, rather than travelling north. Attending his ailing friend had been the reason he had given his grandmother and grandfather. But the real reason was Rebecca Galloway, and the sudden chance to spend a week in near proximity to the creature whose lightly perfumed letters had wafted an odd eroticism over the muddy ditches and crude billets of France. For John Bruce, too, Torquil's shell-shock had provided something of a godsend.

Not to Tenny, of course; and that was no doubt part of the reason for his ungentlemanly attack on Torquil. He was seething with frustration after his long months in the North while those in France experienced the excitement and the glory. And now the infuriating, underplayed assurance of John Bruce made him feel like a schoolboy by comparison. And moreover, his war-worn look had entranced the ladies, Rebecca most of all.

Tenny and John Bruce had been thrown very much into each other's company these last six days. While Emma and Torquil were occupied whispering affection under the too-present ears of hospital staff, the two young men were, during the hours in which the other two girls were nursing, left to their own devices. And during those other, shorter, much prized hours when Susan Bruce and Rebecca Galloway were free of their duties, the four young people joined together, indulging themselves in what little quickly grasped pleasures they could find in their new, harsh world. London, of course, was virtually unchanged as yet by war, in fact to a degree that returning soldiers like John Bruce found a little frightening.

At night they went to the theatre or the music-hall, each with a young lady on his arm. To anyone else they would appear two happy couples, but it was hardly the case. Susan Bruce was happy enough. She was oddly childish in her affections, liking best the warm snugness of a group, like the snugness of the school dormitory. She adored her younger brother, and felt an equivalently sisterly fondness for Tenny Maclaren. Her major emotions could quite truly be said to belong to Rebecca. So she trailed contentedly behind as the two men quite openly vied for Rebecca's arm. More often than not, Rebecca, playing her uneasy balancing act between the two, linked arms in the end with Susan.

And so the foursome progressed, by day, from walks on the

Embankment, to teas in cafés and hotels, to shopping in the shops of the West End. Here Rebecca was unable to contain herself, purchasing one or another little comfort for the returning soldier; pots of Gentleman's Relish, a small earthenware jar of stilton cheese, boxes of sweetmeats, and a warm cashmere scarf. Johnny protested and Tenny glowered, but Rebecca would not be stopped. It was not so much that he needed such delicacies, but that they were the only talismans she could send back to the trenches with him.

Never once did it occur to either Tenny or John Bruce that they might, for half an hour, have Rebecca's company alone. Such a thought for any young couple not officially engaged to be married was an unacceptable social affront. And so they stayed together, locked in love and rivalry, until the girls were deposited at their hostel door, and the two young men shared a taxicab home to Park Lane, each sitting as far from the other as he might manage.

It was afterwards, over that last nightly brandy, for Johnny was to leave for France the next morning, that the subject of Torquil was raised. Tenny raised it himself, out of sheer frustrated perversity.

'Bloody shame about old Em,' he said.

'How so?'

'Torquil and all. I mean, she was really quite serious, don't you know. Nothing said of course, but there was an engagement in the wind, I'd have sworn by it.' There was a long silence in the book-filled room in which the spluttering of the flames on the coal-fire began to sound quite belligerently loud.

Johnny watched Tenny's face perplexedly, and then said, with caution, 'Well, they appeared to be getting on famously the last I saw them yesterday. Frankly, I left early, things were all so cosy I rather felt a third wheel.'

'Oh, of course,' Tenny said with the same perversity. 'Of course Emma's being an absolute brick. Wouldn't expect anything less. Until he's over the worst at least.'

'And then what?' Johnny's voice rose slightly, uneasily.

Now it was Tenny who paused, and watched the white fluffy cat that Rebecca loved so come stalking, tail high, into the room. Eventually he said, in a low voice, 'Well, there is simply no question of an engagement now, is there? I mean, after all, Emma's a Maclaren.'

It was despicable. He knew it the moment he said it. And in truth, poor Torquil was not his target at all. John Bruce and Rebecca Galloway, not martial cowardice, was the real issue at heart. Afterwards he wished that Johnny had committed the two logical, justified, well-earned aggressive acts at hand; that is, to empty his brandy glass in Tenny's face and finish it with a solid fist to the jaw. But Johnny did neither. He set the glass down untouched as if he no longer chose to drink in the present company. Then he stood up, said a short polite goodnight and walked out.

The next day he went back to the Front. Ironically, Tenny saw him off, because although they had not addressed a word to each other since that event, they were obliged to conceal their breach in front of Naomi. Neither was too sure of having succeeded, but thankfully she did not question them. It was only as they passed beneath the carved stone archway of Victoria Station, the Gate of Goodbye as it was being called now, where all the departing soldiers made their farewells, that the native decency in Tenny conquered his insufferably hurt pride.

He turned at last to make his apology, knowing he could not send this man who was almost a brother off to that dangerous world without a word of friendship. But just at that moment there was a shout and they were surrounded by a small group of returning officers of various regiments, three of whom were personal, if distant, friends of them both. Hand-shaking and laughter and nonsensical jesting enveloped them, and Tenny tried in vain to meet John Bruce's eyes, to speak his single word of regret. The train whistle blew, and steam puffed out along the platform, and a Railway Transport Officer began bellowing at the top of his voice. Someone, somewhere, struck up a chorus of Tipperary. Johnny disappeared beyond the gate, amongst the hordes of khaki, and although Tenny shouted his name, he heard no answer.

He stood a long while at the gate, after the train with its masses of waving arms had pulled out, and after the women, brave faces crumpling on each other's shoulders, drifted away, like mourners turning from a grave. Tenny still stood, looking at the coal-strewn gravel between the shining rails that led inexorably to France.

That same day Emma Maclaren, sitting in the stillness of

Torquil's ward, watching a dust-laden sunbeam light his soft brown hair against the pillow, confessed her secret lie.

'I must tell you, I'm so ashamed, but I had to . . . you see, to get to see you, I had to tell them I . . . we . . . I had to tell them we were engaged.' She gasped the last word on one ragged breath, her freckled face reddening with miserable embarrassment. He was silent so long she feared that he had not heard and she'd be obliged to repeat the whole humiliating thing.

Then he said, with the first real smile she'd seen on his face since his return, 'Oh, I am relieved. I've tried for six months to get up the nerve to ask, and never managed. I *am* relieved.'

'But I was only, I mean, Torquil, surely it was just a pretence . . .'

His face clouded. 'Do you mean you won't?' He sounded surprised but then quickly added, 'Oh Emma, forgive me, how could I ask even, how could I dream of it since this,' he shook his head against the pillow, 'this thing.'

'Of course I will,' she said so loudly that a nursing sister at the far end of the ward turned round with an angry gesture of her hand to her lips. 'Of course.' She leant towards him, as if to hold him, and then realized that she must not. So she took his hand, and he held hers tightly, his face beautifully, translucently happy. He drifted off to sleep that way and it was just on the edge of sleep that she heard him say, 'Oh splendid, splendid. We'll wed at Culbrech. I think I shall ask Bunty to be my best man.'

15

The first thing Donnie Cameron did when the corporal woke him was check his haversack to see that it was still there. The object he sought that Christmas morning of 1914, and found with such childish eagerness, was the very first Christmas present of his life. It consisted of tobacco and a pipe and a packet of cigarettes in an embossed tin decorated with a portrait of Princess Mary. Every man at the Front had received that little gift, much to their delight, and to the somewhat good-natured chagrin of officers such as Lieutenant John Bruce who had found it necessary to interrupt the serious business of maintaining an army in the field for its delivery. In the sector held by the Maclarens, this had led to rations being delayed on Christmas Eve because the important cargo had to be carried up through the communications trenches, to A Company in the front line, and B Company supporting. But the men had been delighted, even those who, like Donnie himself, did not smoke.

Donnie had not slept much last night, having been detailed by Corporal Gibson as part of a wire-cutting party. He and four others had spent the darkest hours of the night creeping across no-man's-land to within yards of the German trenches where, with hopelessly inefficient wire-cutters, they had hacked stealthily away at the rusty tangles of fiercely barbed wire. They could, throughout their work, hear the low German voices of their unsuspecting opponents going about their own trench existence.

It was an eerie time, punctuated with moments of sheer terror, when a white, soaring Very light went up from the Boche lines, lighting the ruined ground of no-man's-land as bright, momentarily, as day. They would freeze, cutters in hand, each limb in whatever awkward position the flare had found them, like children playing. *Simon says, 'Dinna move or ye a' gae west.'* The urge to fling themselves to the ground was as powerful as it was foolhardy, for the movement would invariably attract a burst of machine-gun fire that would make mockery of any safety the rubble of no-man's-land might afford.

In the few hours of night left after their return Donnie had lain trembling with fear and the all-pervasive cold, and sleep had been a restless visitor. He was glad of the corporal's waking him, and the dim bar of false dawn over his head where the trench mouth opened grimly to the sky. Day was always better than night. Now, as the dawn light spread from the east beyond no-man's-land, Donnie swung his curled-up legs down from his funk hole on to the duckboards, seeking an isolated corner in which to pee. He felt actually genuinely happy. All was well; he had his precious gift, although that he should not have it was quite an unlikelihood. Men did not steal in the trenches, nor did they ever expect to be stolen from. But there were other forces, rats perhaps, or an unkind hand of Fate that might pluck something, life, limb or a tin of tobacco away from a man in the night.

Still, nothing had attacked him, and his treasure was secure. Add to that the promise of a warm-hearted day, with an extra rum ration, a real cooked meal brought up from the field kitchens, something at least resembling Christmas dinner, and that special camaraderie that the regiment provided at such a time, and it began to seem almost like a party. And most of all, and moreover, Donnie had a new friend, a mate of his own at last, to replace Andy Henderson who had died at Le Touquet.

It was an odd friendship because it held elements of awe on both sides. Ewan Grant, his new companion, was a man of means by Donnie's measure. He was quite respectable, to begin with, coming from a solid Strathglass family whose menfolk often became elders of the kirk. And Ewan was a crofter in his own right, having been granted tenancy of some forty acres, half of them arable, by Sir Ian Maclaren of Culbrech House, who was not only his laird but had quite recently become their own brigade commander, with the rank of brigadier general. It was a thoroughly noteworthy background. Add to this the fact that Ewan was a married man with a child on the way, and Donnie was quickly ready to fall into a posture of subordination. But on the other hand Ewan Grant was not, like Donnie, a regular, but a member of the Territorials, that body of weekend soldiers that it had, until quite recently, been Donnie's express policy to scorn. But the Territorials had changed, or rather emerged from obscurity to fill the depleted ranks of the regular battalions with surprising distinction. They rapidly won respect.

Ewan was one of the first of them to come out to France. Later the Territorials themselves became a fighting battalion in their own right, the Third Maclaren Highlanders, who, along with the Second Battalion recently recalled from India, were serving further down the line at Neuve-Chapelle and Arras respectively. Since his arrival in mid-November, Ewan had seen very little fighting indeed, and experienced only one moderate artillery barrage, inspired by some wretched staff officer's over-zealous demand for a little action on their own part. The action had taken the form of a few of their scanty hoard of heavy shells being lobbed over the Boche lines by their divisional artillery. The response, as predictable as their own action had been pointless, was a two-day thundering of explosives and metal fragments resulting in several dozen casualties. The satisfied staff officer observed it comfortably from a pleasant château tucked well behind the lines, and wrote a glowing report home.

Aside from that brief, unpleasant interlude, Ewan Grant's introduction to the war on the Western Front had been essentially a baptism in mud, cold, and wry-humoured advice from his willing new pal.

'Thot,' Donnie would say as a heavy shell made a great whistling arc over their heads, landing behind them with a thudding crump, 'thot is yer Jack Johnson. Ye'll see nou, when we gae doun the line, a bluidy great hole in oor communication trench, sae ye'll fa' on yer ass in the mud. Thot's the purpose of yer Jack Johnson, as fired like yon.' He gestured in a sweeping arc over their heads. 'On the ither hand,' he said, getting comfortable in the clay niche on the friendly side of their trench, 'supposin' Jerry taks the notion tae lob yon on yer ain heid, then the purpose o' yer Jack Johnson is anither thing entirely. Houever, ye'll nae ken a thing aboot it, sae it doesna maitter tuppence.'

Ewan would grin and nod, scratching away at his wet face with a dulling razor as he absorbed this little piece of trench information. On another occasion when a lighter German shell burst in the next bay of their trench with no warning whistle at all, Donnie, raising his head cautiously after the pieces of earth and metal and God knew what else had finished settling, said in a hushed voice as the cry of 'stretcher-bearers' echoed down the line, 'Thot, on the ither hand, is Fritz's Whizz Bang, an' the Deil tak' it, and Fritz as weel. Ye see, he sends thot 'un frae close in, wi' a flat tra-ject-or-y.' Donnie stumbled over the recently learned word, 'Sae it hasnae time tae whistle or onything. I cannae abide them lot. I'd tak' twenty Jack Johnson's afore ane o' thot lot.'

Ewan learned, too, of the *Minenwerfers*, grenades mounted on a throwing-stick which the Germans could hurl for startling distances, sending them out of silence into their midst. They themselves had no equivalent, though Donnie instructed Ewan in the art of packing explosives into jam-tins to improvise a similar effect. Donnie had never thought much about that odd inconsistency, but Ewan, several grades up educationally and intellectually, quickly questioned why such improvization was necessary at all. He was not the only one to question the lack of hand-thrown grenades, and much else besides.

The list of what was needed, and was lacking, was as long as the face of a Jock who'd spilled his rum ration. At the top of the list was, naturally, ammunition and shells. But there were other things. Clothing was, as yet, only barely adequate. The Highlanders had replaced their traditional shoes and gaitors with the boots and wrapped puttees worn by the other infantrymen, but even these were hardly the right costume for a man spending hours, sometimes days, in icy muddy water often above his knees. Puttees soaked and shrank, constricting circulation. At night they froze, and the agony of unwrapping swollen feet for temporary relief was set against the agony of forcing them again into the constriction of boots.

Greatcoats were their only protection from the elements, though a few battalions had been issued with a motley collection of ill-tanned, evil-smelling furs. Their balmorals had long been rejected for woollen knitted balaclavas, at least by those who were lucky enough to have someone at home to knit them. A far more important item of headgear, some form of hard hat, equivalent to the sturdy helmets worn by their opposition, was yet two years in the future. For the present, the staff officers held that too much shelter or protection, be it steel helmets or reinforced dugouts, would be detrimental to the offensive spirit of the fighting men. So, clothed in their offensive spirit, the men of the Maclaren Highlanders settled down to spend winter in wet shallow ditches in the open, ravaged fields of France.

Donnie, on Christmas morning, was about to experience the day's one true warlike moment; morning stand-to. Stand-to-arms, the real and ancient phrase, seemed to deserve its present truncation. Stand-to. Stand to nothing. They stood. They climbed up, each man shoulder to shoulder with his mates on the wooden firestep that bordered the active side of the trench. There, in the dim light, they could peer over the parapet, rifles ready, in mild apprehension towards the opposing line, two hundred yards' distant, on the odd chance that Fritz had chosen this morning to make an attack, attacks being traditionally made under cover of the back edge of night. Donnie peered, and beside him Ewan Grant peered, and gradually the cold wet December morning brought proper daylight and, with it, the threat passed.

The second, intermittent little ritual of the day was omitted, in honour of the Christian feast. That was 'morning hate', a brief rapid exchange of small-arms fire from both sides, travelling down the line from some aggressive little starting-point like a wave of discontent. It would begin suddenly, die out as suddenly and rarely caused casualties. For all its effect, Donnie once thought, they might as well shoot up in the air.

Smoke coiled up over the German line. Sandy Gibson grinned and said, 'Och well, Happy Christmas Fritz, fall-out you lot.' He turned away towards his own breakfast, and Donnie and Ewan set about lighting their small coke fire and spreading their store of fatty bacon out in the lid of a mess-tin to fry.

There was real bread with the bacon instead of the usual hard Pearl Biscuits, and when the corporal came round with the rum jar there were three, not two, spoonfuls per man. Donnie, unused to spirits, had his in his tea. Those few moments, sipping the head-spinning hot brew, with his chapped hands warming around the mug and his knees warming over the little coke fire, were a brief paradise in which his world seemed utterly complete. Donnie could remember, but a few short weeks before, when fires in the trenches as well as smoking were forbidden on the comical grounds (less comical to the frost-bitten soldier) that they might reveal their position.

'Did ye e'er hear the like?' Sandy Gibson demanded to any who would listen. 'The lot o' us strung out here frae Belgium tae Switzerland, dug in twa, three rows deep, wi' support trenches, an' communication trenches, and saps an' machine-gun emplacements an' bluidy observation posts up ilka tree, an' aeroplanes flying awa' overheid an' observation balloons up on wee strings and every twa or three minutes a' the artillery in hell breakin' loose. An' they arena supposed to ken we're here? Deil tae the staff.'

Eventually a blatant near-revolution from the field officers reversed that directive. Fires were lit, and each side became quite cosily comfortable with the sight of the opposition's breakfast or dinner smoke going up at regular intervals along the line. Sometimes, as they sat around their little blazes and sang in the evening, an echoing chorus in only lightly accented English from the Jerry trenches served to remind them just how many of their enemy had, but a brief while before, been members of their own British community. The ranks of the Kaiser's conscripted armies were full of ex-waiters, shopkeepers, members of German bands, or just pleasant young men who had in pre-war years wandered across Europe to that other largely Saxon nation whose monarch was first cousin to their own.

After breakfast, Donnie sat and cleaned his rifle, a daily ritual that mud and general dirt made imperative even on Christmas morning. He was pleased now to have gun oil and rifle-rag to do it with. During the retreat from Mons they'd been tearing strips off their ragged shirts for that effort; a shirt was useful, but a clean rifle essential. He worked the rag contentedly through the barrel, enjoying this new luxury.

Donnie and Ewan were left in peace that morning, having served on the wire-cutting party during the night. Ewan settled down, seated on the icy rifle step, and with stiff cold fingers wrote a letter to his wife Fiona. He had received two from her yesterday; as always the mail came in intermittent, frustrating batches, with long gaps between. Each letter was a cheery account of how well she was managing without him, running the croft. He knew it was meant to set his mind at ease but it had an oddly opposite effect.

'Ye'd think she didna need me at a',' he said to Donnie, who, ignorant of marriage, said nothing. Ewan wrote the usual soldier's letter, recounting small details of trench life, acknowledging the receipt of her package of oatcakes and the home-baked black bun. He did not add that it had been sodden through with rain, after being mistakenly left out with other, less vulnerable supplies before delivery.

Donnie sat beside him and also wrote a letter. His was to Mrs Cameron, and he knew she would not answer. He'd fallen out of favour when he joined the army in the first place, depriving them of the hand-reared unpaid labourer they had expected as the reward for fostering him. He wrote anyhow, because everybody wrote home, and he didn't want to be different. He had got one letter, too, and that from Andy Henderson's mother in response to his own painfully formal little message of condolence. It was a sweet kind letter thanking him for being 'her dear boy's friend'. He kept it, always, in the pocket of his jacket and sometimes took it out when the other men were getting new mail, and read it again.

Ewan had just slipped his letter into its envelope and was about to hand it in to his officer for censorship, when there was a low shout from the sentry in his forward-reaching sap, and a commotion around the sentry point.

'Will yer look,' he said amazed. 'Whit's Fritzie up tae nou?'

Men gathered in the sap to peer warily through the loophole in the steel shield protecting the sentry point. Cautiously they awaited their turns. Any unprotected gap in which a man might choose to raise his head was well and thoroughly under observation by snipers. After the first handful of unwary victims were carried off with usually fatal headwounds, the survivors treated the rim of the parapet with deep respect. Even the loophole was slightly risky. Best yet was the trench periscope.

Lieutenant John Bruce had one. He had bought it in London, on one of his shopping expeditions with his sister and Rebecca Galloway and Tenny Maclaren. He had bought it in Harrods, in a special department wedged between the haberdashery and the delicacies with its trays of handmade chocolates and imported cheeses, a department labelled 'Trench Requisites'.

He raised the clever, lifesaving device over the parapet and peered into the viewfinder. The little picture provided was almost comical. Against the grey, snow-laden sky, three figures had appeared, standing in full view on the parapet of the German trenches. They were all half hunched over as if in readiness to jump back into their shelter, and the central figure was vigorously waving a huge white flag tacked incongruously to the branch of a broken tree.

RSM Peter Leinie, having come in beside John Bruce, took one quick look through the loophole and turned away, grinning and scratching habitually at his ribs. 'Och weel, thot's thot, then. They're gi'en up. War's over. Everyone awa' hame.'

He strolled leisurely away down the sap and Donnie stood open-mouthed. He plucked at the sleeve of another man and said, breathlessly, 'Is it true? Is it really over?'

' 'Course not, ye wee git,' the man replied with incredulity at Donnie's thick-wittedness brightening his beard-stubbled face. 'Hey youse,' he said to another, 'did ye hear the wee tink? Thinks the war's dune.'

'They're calling a truce,' John Bruce said in a voice mingling amazement and distrust.

There appeared to be considerable distrust across no-man's-land, too, on the part of the three really quite courageous peacemakers. They were advancing hesitantly across the shell-pocked ground, picking their way down a narrow alleyway between their own banks of wire, still vigorously waving their flag. Their voices, quavering slightly over the distance, called out, 'Hoppy Christmas Tommee. Hoppy Christmas Kiltie.'

Fully aware of their opposition, often knowing even the name of the individual regiment facing them at any one time, their action was doubly stout-hearted. A regiment of Bavarians themselves, they assessed the English Tommy as being a character rather like themselves. The Scots, the dreaded 'Kilties', were considered quite accurately to hold the same warlike qualities as their own Prussian compatriots. To advance thus, trusting in a peaceful response against the notorious 'Ladies from Hell', deserved credit. John Bruce thought so, anyway.

'Where's the CO?' he asked quickly of Peter Leinie.

Leinie, his little act over, had returned to stand with interested amusement at the lieutenant's shoulder. 'Awa' doun the line, talkin' tae the men,' the RSM replied.

Johnny had expected that. It was his uncle's policy to spend as much of the day as possible forward with the men in the front-line trenches, rather than in his dugout three lines back. 'See if you can find him, Sergeant Major,' he said, still watching through his periscope.

Peter Leinie hadn't far to go. Gordon Bruce was already making his way up the sap, aware of what was happening from the commotion and excited talk among the men. He peered through the periscope and then stood back, stroking the iron-grey stubble of his lean cheek. 'Blessed are the peacemakers,' he said at last, with what passed on his dour solemn face for a grin.

'Can we sort 'em, sir?' Sergeant Ross MacDonald, his Lee Enfield ready, demanded eagerly. His eyes were squinted up against the faint sunlight breaking the grey clouds in the east, and his lips were wetted by the tip of his tongue shining with an almost sexual urgency.

'For God's sake, man,' Gordon Bruce said, losing control. 'They're showing the white flag.' Ross MacDonald faded glowering into the background of spectators in the trench.

Johnny Bruce said then, his own different eagerness only faintly disguised, 'Perhaps I should make contact, sir?'

Gordon glanced once more into the viewfinder. They were still advancing, though a little more hesitantly having met only silence in response, and to the rhythm of their proffered flag of truce they still chanted, 'Hoppy Christmas, Hoppy Christmas.'

'I suppose you'd better see they don't come closer than halfway,' he said at last.

Johnny's face lit up with a huge grin. 'Sir!' he said at once, and in almost one movement, perhaps fearing a change of the commanding mind, he had divested himself of revolver and rifle and leapt over the parapet. There was a shudder of movement among the three as they came to an uneasy halt, but quickly recognizing his peaceful intent they made their way, a little more rapidly, across the barren space towards the lone figure on the British lines. Johnny walked out into no-man's-land with a dreamlike feeling of elation. The elation was dual in nature, inspired in part by the uncanny sensation of actually stepping out in broad daylight into the strip of land between the trenches, an area as unreachable in daylight hours as the surface of the moon, and in part by the imminence of a meeting with those equally unreachable members of the human race: the enemy.

'Friend?' the short central figure said, extending his hand, palm upwards as to a doubtful-natured dog, with a packet of cigarettes balanced there as offering.

Johnny grinned again, '*Kamerad*,' he said.

Then suddenly he was with them, all slapping shoulders and

smiling and chattering away in their reasonable English and his awful German as if they were long-lost brothers, which in a strange way, he sensed, they were. For each of them had one enormous thing in common – that he was quite unexpectedly spending Christmas of 1914 in a highly uncomfortable ditch in the snowy fields of northern France. And each, with monumental and equal longing, would have dearly liked to be somewhere else. Such were the ties that bind.

Gradually, as the little group in the centre of no-man's-land became involved in sharing cigarettes, showing photographs of home, peering curiously at each other's uniform and insignia – the three Germans utterly intrigued by Johnny's mud-encrusted, lice-infested kilt – other men on both sides came hesitantly out into the open.

Commanding officers on both sides watched with caution, instructing the participants to allow the enemy no nearer than halfway across. Sentries stood guard, in case the whole thing turned suddenly evil in intent. But in truth, no one expected treachery nor, with half their front-line troops in full view of the enemy, was either side about to commit it. Within half an hour the battered ground between the two zigzag lines of trenches was filled with little clusters of men, talking, laughing, singing, exchanging whatever little gifts they could find from their own scanty treasures.

Donnie and Ewan were astounded to find one handsome blond youngster who, having worked for two years waiting on tables at the fashionable spa at Strathpeffer, knew not only that place, but Inverness too, like the back of his hand. Within minutes they were comparing notes on particular pubs, and Donnie was delighted to discover a fellow admirer of his secret darling, the barmaid of the public house in Pump Lane.

The blond German sighed at the mention of her name. 'Oh yes, she was, how you say, so desirable, but alas, she would not ever . . .'

'Aye,' Donnie said with a wince of ancient frustrated memory. 'Thot's her a' richt. She wouldnae fer me either.'

Later in the afternoon, someone brought a football from the British lines, and a hasty formation of teams took place, and a game was soon under way. At one point, Gordon Bruce himself, having donned a greatcoat and an ordinary soldier's balaclava, had wandered into the truce zone himself and stood there, his furrowed brow wrinkled with bemusement, gazing up and down the line. For as far as he could see, until the natural turning of the Front and the slight roll of the French countryside broke the view, there was nothing but camaraderie, like a vast Boys' Brigade camp.

Had he been able to see beyond those bends in the line, indeed down the whole length of tortured ground that held the two sides locked together, and apart, he would have seen a sight almost chilling in its peacefulness. The truce had not begun with the Maclarens, at least not only with them. It had begun at certain points along the line quite spontaneously, like scattered sudden applause in a theatre. And then, again like applause, it had gathered and grown, spreading with stunning speed up and down the long twisted line. By nightfall, there was little in the way of hostility to be seen. Here and there a particular battalion held back, either in bitterness over some recent loss, or under the unrelenting command of its superiors. But they were the minority.

At nightfall both sides retreated, like the burrowing animals they had become, to the safety of their own dens. But there were agreements made, all along the line. The following day, Boxing Day, they met earlier, just after breakfast, each man going out in search of his new-found particular friends. Rations were traded, addresses exchanged, for 'after', and the footballers had a rematch.

It went on for four days. It went on just long enough to fall, quite comfortably, into a routine, that lullaby of the military man. It would, left to the men in the trenches, quite happily have gone on indefinitely. For on both sides they readily recognized something that their superiors would take years yet to understand; that they had quite enough war simply fighting the elements without the added complication of shooting at each other.

Gordon Bruce was not surprised when the order came, only surprised that it had not come sooner. And although a small part of himself regretted it, he was secretly relieved. There was the question of morale, and morale was, like it or not, based on hostility. The Us and Them unity that bound a fighting force with unbreakable loyalty was likely to fall down when the Them became so cosily entangled with the Us. He sent word down the line that hostilities were to commence the following morning and the opposition was to be duly informed. There were to be no exceptions.

John Bruce was genuinely saddened, though hardly surprised either. That afternoon he bade a formal military farewell to the young Bavarian officers with whom he had shared cigarettes and stories for four strange December days. They saluted each other, and walked apart back to their own lines and the making of each other's deaths.

But as much as he hated the appalling bloodshed, Johnny could never free himself from the aching desire for the exhilaration that only battle could give him. He ran to it, in his heart, as eagerly as he had run to the truce, the one as much as the other a part of his fierce, gregarious nature.

The following morning, his men beside him, he stood on the firestep and raked the opposing line with an enthusiastic burst of rifle-fire. The men did likewise, it not being in any of their natures to question an order.

'An' there ye are, Jerry,' Johnny heard one growly Scots voice behind him, 'an' a happy New Year tae ye a'.'

Hogmanay, that quintessential Scottish New Year's holiday, fell on a bitterly cold, sleet-driven day, and the Maclaren Highlanders were doomed to spend it huddled down against the frozen walls of their mud fortress warmed only by memories of years past. Their only comfort was the fact that the day after tomorrow they would be moved back to the supporting trench, out of reach of no-man's-land, and on their way down the line for a week's respite in billets.

Torquil Farquhar had been recently returned to the Front after his spell in the First London General. His company commander, Captain George Brown, although a man of little sympathy for anything approaching weakness, was not without understanding of the effects of shell-shock. He had observed early signs of it in Farquhar and was not too surprised to hear of the blossoming of the condition, ironically enough in the safety of London. However, medical reports, which Gordon Bruce had discussed with him because of his proximity to the man, indicated a mild attack and a quick recovery. Farquhar had returned a fortnight ago, seeming in excellent form and happy to be back with his men. Indeed he seemed in better humour than before his leave, and had been one of the leading lights of the between-the-lines football match during the truce, playing with schoolboy verve. Brown, as Gordon Bruce, concluded that the rest had been all that was needed. Still, he kept an eye on the man when he could, and with such a purpose in mind invited him, that icy New Year's Eve, into the dugout they shared for a talk and a precious sip of malt whisky from the hip-flask Brown always carried.

He was not the only officer to go thus equipped. There were times when every field officer felt the need of that particular form of spiritual sustenance; not for himself, naturally, but for some man in his charge for whom, for a brief moment, the whole thing, wet and cold, blood and misery, had proved too much.

On this evening it was Torquil Farquhar's morale he was most concerned with. He need not have been, actually, as he considered morosely afterwards. Farquhar seemed remarkably in control. As they huddled by the light of their well-shielded Kranzow lamp in the small, timber-roofed room cut into the earth, the 'door' of sheet tin shutting out most, if not all, of the cutting wind, talking over old times, it was Brown, not Farquhar, who began to grow moody and depressed. It was also Brown, not Farquhar, who refilled his tin mug with the warm golden liquid, and more than once. Torquil was bemused, and instinct told him to cut off this drinking session before Brown was any more the worse for wear. He dearly wished to object when his captain made the third refill, but his inferior rank made that impossible, even if Brown's now belligerent manner did not in itself make it unwise.

Torquil in the end excused himself, announcing his intention to have a word with the sentries, and went out, feeling a faint warm glow, distinctly pleasant, infuse his body as he made his way, head low, down to the next bay of the trench. It was nearly midnight, but most of the men were awake, rather pathetically determined to see the New Year in, despite the circumstances. A group was singing, softly and with real sadness, songs familiar from their own firesides at home. Someone rang a jam-tin gong to signify the entry of 1915 and a small ragged cheer fluttered down the line, jumped no-man's-land, and rippled off to the east along the German front. Slowly, someone began to sing 'Auld Lang Syne'. It was taken up at once by the entire company, and then B Company as well. Faintly, far away, the rest of the battalion could be heard in the support trenches and, sounding far too loud for their distance, the bells of the churches in the villages far to their rear tolling in soft disharmony.

Captain George Brown came out of his dugout, red-eyed and bleary, walking with a reckless rocking gait that adapted badly to icy duckboards. He slipped almost at once, landing at the shocked feet of a small cluster of Jocks brewing tea over a cake-paraffin flame. But he scrambled to his feet again announcing in a thickened voice, 'Damn it t' hell, I should hae married the poor lass. Damn should hae married her. Gane aff and leavin' her like thot. Bluidy shame, that's what it is.'

By this time, Torquil Farquhar, who had come upon this apparition, realized he was speaking of the unfortunate Betty MacIver with a refreshing, but quite unprecedented, remorse. But barely had he time to intervene on that subject, hoping to get Brown back in the dugout before his condition became apparent to the men, when the captain changed the subject.

'It's Hogmanay,' he said suddenly, as if having just discovered it. All around him, choruses of 'Auld Lang Syne' added to the conviction. Torquil reached for his elbow, but he shook free, grinning now, no longer the slightest bit morose. 'Wha's gane first-footin'?' he demanded, looking eagerly about the darkened trench. There was silence. He turned to Torquil, and pulled out his hip-flask and waved it in the air.

'Sir, I really think,' Torquil began, but Brown only shrugged his big shoulders and wandered off down the line. He suddenly jumped up, first to the firestep and then, with a gleeful shout, right up on to the darkened parapet, and lurched, flask held high, out into no-man's-land.

'What ye dae'in, sir?' an amazed young private soldier demanded.

'First-footin' old Jerry,' Brown's voice sailed back happily over the icy wind. 'What dae ye think?'

'Get down,' Torquil, himself dangerously exposed on the firestep, head and shoulders above the parapet, shouted to his reeling captain. It took more than a voice though to silence George Brown's celebration. It took precisely the first staccato volley of machine-gun fire, spattering systematically across the broken ground.

Brown hit the ground faster than a Glasgow drunk pitched from a pub door, but still not quite fast enough. Torquil Farquhar heard his sharp, almost annoyed yelp of pain, and knew he was hit. The next thing he heard assured him that the wound was relatively innocuous,

'Ye damn unsociable Jerry bastards. Fuck the lot o' ye, an' a fuckin' awful New Year tae ye a'.'

Another flare went up, and the machine-gun sought the prone figure uncertainly. They were plainly not in a mood to play. When Brown attempted to worm his way back to his own lines, a sharper, more accurate burst of fire splattered ominously close to his face, casting clods of earth over him as he lay. He was sobering up rapidly and feeling like a participant in a nightmare, the sort that left one suddenly illogically exposed, naked and innocent, in some all too public place. 'Shit,' he muttered to himself. 'I've gane an' dune it this time.'

He lay very still until the flare faded, and in the following darkness attempted once more to crawl to safety. Now he was aware of considerable pain in his wounded leg, and an alarming weakness. He was bleeding badly, though his as yet benumbed state made him only dimly aware of the fact. Still, progress over the ravaged ground was desperately slow, halted regularly by fresh flares, and bursts of fire, augmented now by the petulant sharp reports of a determined sniper. He dropped his face to the dirt, thinking with weary illogic of the warm, lost bed of Betty McIver.

Suddenly Torquil Farquhar called out over the din of the enemy's and their own covering fire, 'Right, hold your fire, I'm going out for him.' He jumped the parapet, almost in the same moment, picking his moment of darkness and running in short zigzag bursts of speed. The machine-gunner, soon aware of this new target, used the light of the next flare to concentrate on Torquil. But by that time he had reached the shell-hole in which Brown was sensibly seeking shelter. Brown half rolled over, wincing with pain, and Torquil said, anxiously, 'Is it bad, sir?'

'Bad? It's bluidy diabolical, man. The buggers hae smashed the bluidy whisky flask.' He waved the bullet-punctured object forlornly in the darkness. Then he said, 'Damn decent o' ye, old man. If ye gie me a hand, we can dash for it in a wee bit.'

They waited for the next dimming between flares, and then scrambled erect, Torquil jerking Brown's arm over his shoulder and virtually holding him upright by the gathered cloth of the back of his jacket. Brown groaned loudly with the pain but lurched forward, and like children in the three-legged race at school, they stumbled erratically through a whistling rain of bullets to the elusive dark safety of their lines. Torquil flung Brown headlong over the sandbags and leapt wildly into the trench landing heavily on a heap of waiting bodies with a bone-thudding jolt.

There was a great relieved silence, followed by the hasty arrival of the stretcher-bearers. As George Brown was carted away, Torquil, grinning to himself in the darkness, was tapped tentatively on the shoulder by a dim figure.

'Sir?'

'Yes, soldier?'

'Sir, as ye appear tae be the onlie first foot oor trench is gane tae hae, we a' think ye'd best hae this an' a'.' He was extending in his grubby hand a large slice of shortbread and a well-worn piece of black bun, the traditional fare of the New Year visitant.

Torquil took it, still grinning, and munched the moist fruity bun hungrily. He felt marvellous and exhilarated; all the ghosts of the past weeks laid.

Four days later, Captain George Brown was back in Blighty. His leg wound, as was so common, turned septic, and for a while he was in danger of losing the limb. When he recovered eventually he was quite satisfied with only the permanent limp that it left him. However, his military career was over as a result of that Hogmanay escapade, and when he retired with disability pension to a decent-sized farm near Dingwall, he accepted the firm hand of Fate as shown to him at Armentières. Miss Betty MacIver, eight-and-a-half months' pregnant, still made a charming, if rotund, bride.

As January plodded on its wet, cold way, Torquil Farquhar received command of George Brown's A Company which, with his newly achieved rank of captain, seemed proof enough to any who needed it that he was all one could want of a Maclaren Highlander.

16

The news of Torquil's act of gallantry, his promotion and new responsibilities, quickly spread through the Maclaren family like a wave of relief. Emma heard it in London, directly from Naomi who, her ally always, indicated that now was surely the opportune time to intimate to her mother her intention to marry. Victoria Maclaren and Torquil's father shared a quiet little exchange of notes of formal congratulation. And Tenny Maclaren, knee-deep in the New Army in tented splendour on the Northern Meeting Park in Inverness, would afterwards recall the news, delivered by his always better-informed brother, private soldier Albert Maclaren, as the one bright spot in an infuriating day.

It was the day he found James. Or rather the day he was presented with James, because actually Albert found James; and Tenny was, as with the news of Torquil Farquhar, the last to know.

The New Army held all the glamour, these days, next to the regulars themselves, and left the old Territorials in the shade. A man couldn't expect to become a regular army soldier overnight, but with luck he could make one of the New Army battalions, like the Inverness Pals, and to do so was the aim of all. But the organization was chaotic. They were poorly equipped and haphazardly screened. Health and age requirements were cavalierly waived. Uniforms were makeshift: a piebald mixture of tartans, kilts augmented with khaki or tartan trews for the less fortunate, balmoral bonnets a prized novelty.

'Ye look like a bunch o' wee Merkinch tarts, the lot o' ye,' declared Sergeant Major Robertson, a vast, iron-grey-haired Invernessian brought back hastily from retirement, surveying the gathering battalion in disgust. They grinned back at him, too green to know one doesn't grin at the sergeant major, and he, utterly bemused by the sight of them, was lost for words which, for a man in his position, was unthinkable. There was a giggle even, from a handsome young Glaswegian with shining black hair, which finally aroused the grey-haired old lion to a tail-tweaked roar. 'Silence, youse.'

Pat McGarrity was instantly silent, and stood, the very picture of military correctness, between his two new mates, James Maclaren and Jimmy 'Post' Fraser, until they were dismissed.

It was afterwards, as they made their way back towards their ring of belltents and the smell from some great cauldron of stew cooking over the open fire, that James, stumbling over a tent peg, literally fell upon his brother Albert who was sitting cleaning his boots in the pale January sun. Albert dropped his bootbrush and dropped his lower jaw. The gradual realization that he was facing not only the postmaster's sixteen-year-old son, but his own fifteen-year-old brother, both in a brave attempt at New Army uniform, stunned him to silence. James, of course, had prepared for this moment with all manner of patriotic 'I had to do it, don't you see?' speeches. He knew very well that he couldn't join a battalion containing both his brothers and not eventually run into one or the other of them.

'Good God,' Albert said at last. 'James.'

'Hello Bertie,' James said with an insane grin spreading to his slightly protruding, reddening ears. Every brave speech left him. He grinned some more and then made a little wave of his hand, and started to turn away.

'*James*,' Albert shouted, a tentative, still slightly pudgy hand reaching for James's shoulder. And then he said the one thing James was dreading. 'Does Tenny know you're here?'

It seems to be human nature to respond to the distant sound of one's name and Tenny Maclaren, striding in, smouldering, made a half-turn and then saw, as if spotlit by the January sun halfway across the field, the flaming red head of his brother James.

His direction turned, his stride lengthened, his speed increased and his head lowered. To James, glancing up as part of his effort to avoid Albert's challenging eye, his sudden appearance was akin to that of a charging bull. 'Soldier,' Tenny roared, to pin him to the spot of trampled grass on which he stood. Not that he would have attempted to escape a confrontation that was now inevitable.

'Sir,' James said, coming to attention, hoping wildly that an efficient display of military rectitude would aid his cause.

'What in God's name are you doing here?' Tenny demanded, and was not pleased to hear James's cheerful reply.

'It was easy. The chap ahead of us was seventeen, you see. And when he said so they turned him away. So we said nineteen, and there you were.'

'An' ten minutes later, the wee bloke wha' said he was seventeen cam' in ahint o' us and said he was nineteen tae, and dae ye ken . . .' Jimmy Fraser added.

'He's here as well,' Tenny finished for him grimly. He balled one big fist up and Jimmy shrank, wide-eyed, but all Tenny did was slam it into the palm of his other hand. 'It's not enough making an army without clothing, or food or weaponry. Now they're sending me children as well.' He said that to himself but got instant indignant outrage from his brother.

'I'm not a child, Tenny, that's beastly unfair.'

Tenny turned his face very slowly towards James. His pale eyes narrowed to their crinkly slits and he said in a hissing whisper, 'What's that, soldier?'

'Sir,' James gulped, remembering, then recovering he said formally, 'I assure you, sir, I will do my best to serve my country, even at my age. I swear it, sir.'

There was a momentary pause in which Tenny stood, glowering through half-closed lids, and then he said with emphatic finality, 'You, soldier, are leaving the army today. Tomorrow you're getting on a train. And the day after you're going to be at Fettes College where you belong. I will speak to the CO immediately.' He turned to stalk off but was followed by the quavering voice of Jimmy Fraser.

'Sir?'

'Yes?'

'What about me, sir?' That was when Tenny realized the dimensions of his problem. When he entered the small hastily erected wooden shack on the edge of the Park that constituted Headquarters, leaving a morose young brother waiting obediently like a chastened collie dog outside, he was met at once by the all-pervasive smell of mints that Lieutenant-Colonel Douglas Fraser, as he was now, sucked constantly to combat the pangs of his unhappy stomach. He was greeted warmly, having known Fraser in a family capacity since boyhood. Again, it was in a familiar manner that his case was put, and received.

At the end, the colonel merely chuckled, made some remark about 'a real Maclaren, eh?' and said, shuffling a loose pile of papers on his improvised desk into a neat squared stack, 'Of course. We'll just send the little cub home until he's big enough to be a wildcat, eh?' He was grinning beneath his massive moustache, and tapping the decorative regimental wildcat head on the silver paperweight holding down the stack of papers. He was about to dismiss Tenny, thinking the matter closed.

'Sir,' Tenny began, 'I'm afraid it's more complicated than that.' He went on to explain about Jimmy Fraser.

'Postie's son?' Douglas Fraser said, sucking on his mint. His face had undergone a subtle change and Tenny was aware of losing his cooperation. 'Too bad,' he said. 'Another damn little fool. Still, Maclaren, you can't expect me to patch up every mistake the recruiting boys make. Every third mother in Inverness-shire would be after me to get *her* son out. I'd be doing nothing else. What's done is done.' He seemed eager to close the conversation as if he felt, with some similar emotion, the blatant unfairness of the situation that had so outraged James.

'You can't, Tenny,' James had declared, forgetting his military fealty for a second time. 'You can't send me home and not Jimmy.' Tenny could. He knew that: the colonel had just made it possible. Torn between duty to his brother, and duty to the distant but vulnerable figure of his mother, he said with immense reluctance, 'Yes sir, quite right. What's done is done. I think, sir, James had better stay as well.'

Fraser looked up, surprised, wincing with a distant internal pain. He understood though and eventually said only, 'Are you sure?'

'Yes, sir.'

'What about your mother, lad?'

'I will inform her, sir,' Tenny said, and he left the office.

James, waiting, tail between legs, looked up with eyes full of miserably hurt pride.

'Get back to your unit, soldier,' Tenny snapped, 'before you're missed.' The meaning gradually dawned on James, and again the grin divided his face with spreading triumph. He ran back across the field half skipping, as over a field of play.

In the end, Tenny failed in courage and did not inform Victoria at all, leaving that odious task to his father, whose misfortune it was to be on leave in London when James Maclaren's elaborately arranged ruse at Fettes was eventually discovered.

'He said that he was at home,' Victoria explained to Ian that evening in Naomi's house in Park Lane when they next met. 'He got several boys to cover for him with alibis and of course I was told he was at school. It was only when the boys ran out of excuses that the Head telephoned me. Apparently he'd been told that James had contracted scarlet fever during the Christmas break and was in quarantine. He was most solicitous about his welfare. Most solicitous.'

'Little twit. I'll . . . I'll tan his hide.'

'That would do precisely no good at all,' Victoria said with unaccustomed coldness. 'There is only one thing that will do any good.'

Ian Maclaren sighed. It was not the first time they had been through this. He wished they were somewhere else, other than Naomi's, too. It had rather become the family GHQ since the outbreak of hostilities, far more convenient than Culbrech House to the field of conflict. Victoria had twice before come down to meet him on his brief leaves. Still, even with Naomi tactfully absent during this private dinner he would have preferred this scene of family hostility to occur on some less sweet-memoried field of battle. He felt vulnerable here, and Victoria, grown slightly less understanding as her own physical charms faded, grew faintly shrewish.

'I can't do it to the boy,' was all he said, opening his hands in a gesture of defeat. 'I can't break his pride.'

Victoria stabbed the linen of the dining-table with her silver sweet fork. 'What about what you are doing to me?' Her voice was low-pitched and filled with a sudden real anguish. She angrily shoved her sweet plate away, its sherry trifle untouched, and moaned softly, 'All of them now. All my beautiful sons.'

Ian Maclaren sighed, and patted her hand. 'Really, my dear,' he said, 'your position is quite enviable. After all, none of your sons is yet at the Front at all. As for myself, I've seen far less action than I'd like. Brigade HQ is hardly the field of battle.'

'Be that as it may,' Victoria said sharply. 'Your predecessor met with an untimely end, did he not?'

Ian shrugged, having walked into that one. His predecessor had indeed died in a shell attack on Hooge Château during the fighting at Ypres in October. His demise had rescued Ian from the sterility of Haig's staff, and brought him into direct command once more.

'More of an unlucky accident than anything, my dear,' he said. 'Shall we ask Naomi to join us for coffee?' She did not answer and he saw in her small, perfectly formed face, only slightly marred by a faint double chin, that obsessive look of unrelinquished discontent that meant more trouble. He sighed again and said, 'Really, my dear, there are men in some of the battalions who have four, maybe five brothers serving at their sides. These New Army chaps join up, arm in arm, whole families, villages, the like. Imagine their mothers, eh?' He was smiling at her, a bold, handsome, encouraging smile, as one would use to a child who had absurdly taken some foolish fright. She studied his face, lean and tanned once more from his new, more physically demanding life, and shining with an infuriating false optimism. She felt an approach of hatred, but it faded, more out of duty than love for him.

'Of course,' she said then, once more the army wife of a quarter of a century. 'How unpardonably selfish of me. I *am* sorry, my dear.' She rose from the table, instinctively checking her reflection in the mirror over the sideboard before they went through to the drawing-room, and Naomi.

He had shamed her, as he always subtly managed to do whenever she attempted to cross him. Her dignity and strength were her major weapons, and always had been, against that dark woman, now waiting for them, who had bordered their marriage for all its years, like a shadow at the edge of the sun. She would not let Naomi see her petulant. And so she set her pretty, ageing mouth into its familiar acquiescing smile, and relinquished the last of her boys to the regiment.

17

It was September 1915 before Victoria Maclaren's sons at last saw the Front. The war that Tenny had so feared would end nine months earlier, without him, was raging yet, its great trenches still open to devour men, like an ugly jagged mouth across the whole of Europe. The optimism that had carried the trench occupants through the misery of the winter soon met its end. In February a French offensive won five hundred yards in Champagne at the cost of sixty thousand men. The British tried in March at Neuve-Chapelle and broke through at last. But advancement eluded them. The broken line filled with reinforcements and the two armies ended battering each other like suicidal rams.

The fatal imbalance between offence and defence remained: Festubert, Aubers Ridge. Attack and you lost men in stunning numbers. Defend and you lost men in slightly less stunning numbers. Stand still and you lost men in handfuls, dribs and drabs like drops of blood. Wastage, it was called, the natural wastage of war. That was the fate of the Maclarens, through most of the spring and summer of 1915; while the attention of the world was focused on the growing fiasco of the Dardenelles, they awaited a September calamity of their own.

At home, flagrant patriotism solidified into bitter resolve. It changed people. It hardened some, disillusioned others. And some it simply drove to new excesses of an old hysteria. The change came in its own way to each separate person. It came to Victoria Maclaren on the day she visited the fourth bereaved croft house in two weeks. On that day, the end of the war, rather than victory, became her prime and central prayer.

For Emma Maclaren, that prayer had come even earlier. She could remember the precise moment, a day after Ypres, when she saw her first gas victim, and Matron's voice, frayed, uncharacteristically desperate, 'For God's sake, Maclaren, give me a hand with him.'

They did not see many; most never made it to London, but choked away their agonized lives in the field hospitals of France. This one had been a good one, saveable, or so someone had thought, and he'd made it all the way to Blighty to gasp and drool to death in Emma Maclaren's arms. His face was quite black, she remembered dully, swollen and black; she did not know if the gas did that, or the effort to breathe with lungs that would no longer hold air. Emma held him upright; he could not breathe any other way, and they prayed for him to die. He did, and with him died her last vestige of belief in the honour of war.

Ypres brought a lot else; a terrifying German breakthrough, later botched, like breakthroughs of their own. An upsurge of outrage in the press, conveniently ignoring their own long-standing preparations of gas warfare, and the cylinders of chlorine gas even now being readied for their own front lines; and a further loss of what innocence their world yet retained.

In April, Rebecca Galloway, at work in her hospital ward, wept for the death of Rupert Brooke on a hospital ship in the Aegean. Incongruous tears for one surrounded daily by dying strangers, but he had been the voice of their naïve, happy youth, now dying too, and no one could speak for them now.

Far to the north, the young solicitor Harry Bruce picked his increasingly difficult way through civilian life in the stiffening prejudice of the small village of Beauly, until on an August day, the war came home to him, too. His employer, a patient old white-haired man, Maxwell MacKay by name, had borne a lot in Harry's defence. But something about the gas attacks, and the lurid reporting of them in the patriotic press, broke through a chink in his wall of quiet decency.

'I'm sorry,' he said, quite brusquely really, 'and please do not think it is because of what others think. I am not driven by such interests.' He paused, angry with himself, but resolute. 'Damn the thing, Harry, it's making monsters of us all. I know you have to make your own decision. But I can't collaborate with you. Not any longer.'

'And my employment infers collaboration?' Harry said.

MacKay said nothing, knowing with a pang of moral guilt that Bruce would do the decent thing without the need of him speaking further. Nothing else was said until late afternoon. The young man completed the work on his desk, and piled up his files in a neat, ordered stack.

'Everything you need is there,' he said smoothly, at the close of day. 'I believe that Will for MacPherson is quite in order, perhaps you'd wish to check it.' He nodded briefly, and left the office for ever. Neither man said goodbye.

Outside, he clipped his trousercuffs neatly about his ankles, and climbed on to the Scott motorbike lent to him by Emma Maclaren for the duration. He felt very free, without the usual dossier of files to be buckled securely within the worn leather saddlebags. As the motorbike sputtered noisily away down the quiet August street and into the open countryside, silver and gold with ripening barley and oats, no one gave him a second glance. They simply ignored him and behind his back they cut him to shreds. Harry knew, and cared only for his grandparents' sake.

Harry's sense of irony, of cool deduction, indeed his sharp legal wit were his worst enemies in the North. In London he might have found, amongst the other disenchanted elements, even in Naomi's more rebellious circles of friends, some understanding. Here there was none. They judged him a coward and were infuriated at his inability to act like one, to grovel and apologize and wring his hands, to show any remorse at all for his failures. Harry Bruce was without shame, in his neighbours' eyes; proud of his cowardice if such a thing were possible. Harry allowed them their disgust. His own relationship with the war was so subtle, and so desperate, that he could not expect them to understand. The truth was he wanted desperately to go; he longed to go; were he a religious man, he would have prayed to go. But he could not go without one clear solid reason why he should, one pure justification of the cause of it all that was not a highblown fantasy of the lurid press. And search as he might, he could not find one.

Harry Bruce had seen real atrocities in besieged Kimberley, and overheard in family conversations meant for adult ears only the bloody fate of his mother, and more disturbing yet, the rumoured savage retributions committed in her name by his utterly British father. Of all those of his generation, Harry Bruce was one of the rare few who had had a childhood riven by war; he could never share the innocent fascination for its glory that was the inheritance of those around him raised in a golden era of peace. At times he yearned for the very simplicity of his friends, that patriotic faith that made sacrifice not only desirable, but obligatory.

At the village of Struy, halfway home, he slowed the motorcycle and came to a dusty halt in front of the Struy Inn. The day was sultry and he wanted a half-pint of the inn's good ale. Also, it would delay the time of arrival at home, which he dreaded. He swung his leg over the machine and started for the black wooden door of the inn. It was then he noticed a disconsolate figure in dark trousers, a seedy-looking tweed jacket and flat bonnet, leaning against the doorjamb.

'Ye've nae a hope, lad,' said the man.

'Frankie,' Harry said, recognizing the old retired RSM, Francis Gibson VC, Sir Ian Maclaren's head ghillie. 'Not your usual place, surely.' Harry managed a smile, nodding towards the closed door of the inn. 'Thought you'd be well ensconced. Don't say they've turned you out.'

'Nae, lad, worse than that. They've chucked us a' oot. The hale clanjamfrie.'

'Whatever?' Harry said, but his eye was caught then by the printed notice, resplendent with official authority, that had been nailed to the door. 'Defence of the Realm Act' was blazoned in large letters across the top. 'Oh Good God, I'd actually forgotten. The new licensing hours. So they've come to force at last.'

'Dora,' said Frankie, his watery old eyes crinkling with distaste. 'She's gane an' dune us nou. A man cannae get as much as a sniff o' the bottle stopper nou, atween dinner an' tea. Of a' the treachery tae a man wha's serve his country frae east tae west fer forty years an's come hame at last tae tak' his rest. I wouldna think they'd hae the hairt.'

Harry stood a long time gazing at the querulous old soldier and the shuttered pub door. 'The bloody damn pompous fools,' he said at last, and mounted his motorbike and rode away. Neuve-Chapelle, he thought, come home to roost.

The weather clouded as he approached Cluanie Cottage and

rain was spattering down on to the dusty road. The summer had been gloomy, often cold, and wet windy days had kept them all indoors around coal-fires for most of July. August had begun no better, and the traditional Culbrech Bank Holiday picnic had been cancelled. Of all the younger Bruces and Maclarens, only Philippa remained at Culbrech, and then only for short periods at a time since she was always travelling at short notice to Glasgow, or Edinburgh, or even London for recruiting speeches or meetings with the Active Service League. In a grim way Harry had to admit for her a hearty admiration; she did not lack courage, and her determination was frighteningly sincere.

On Bank Holiday Monday, Harry had taken his young cousin, Robert Bruce, fishing on the River Glass and listened with bemused frustration to his fourteen-year-old desperation to get into the war like James Maclaren. Even then Harry had realized with despair that he might well get his wish. The spring offensive of 1915 had come and gone, and another winter was looming in the trenches. Nineteen-sixteen would be decisive, with the might of Kitchener's Army thrown into the fray, everyone was certain. But what if it were not? He did not choose to think.

At the gateway of Cluanie Cottage, his grandmother was waiting. She had heard the sound of the motor and come to greet him. 'Oh dearest, I'm so glad you're early,' she extended her wrinkled throat like a delicate old bird, so that her cheek was ready for his kiss. 'I'm afraid Willie's rather bad again. I've had the doctor out, despite his protests. It's this weather, I think, he finds it so stifling. Do go in, dear, I'll ring for tea.'

Harry kissed her cheek, absorbing the ancient rose-petal smell that he had associated with her from the day he met her in the heat of South Africa, all those years before.

'The library,' she said, parting from him in the doorway of the house.

He made his way towards his grandfather. Cluanie was, as always, dark and damp inside, smelling of must. One room only, the morning-room with its southeast aspect, took the full sun, and had a light airiness more typical of England. It was Maud's room, and her Englishness permeated it. Willie preferred the library, and even the kitchen with its big range, always smoky and warm, and its floors worn more by tradition than poverty. They were not wealthy, in spite of Willie's inheritance from his philandering but honest father, old Sir Henry Maclaren, who had settled a fair amount on his bastard and favourite son, but they were not poor either. They lived more modestly than financial conditions demanded, in truth, because that was Willie's taste.

If there was a time in which Maud's taste was otherwise, as surely there must have been, Harry reflected, considering her childhood as the daughter of a wealthy East India company official before the tragedy at Cawnpore, it no longer showed. Harry often wondered what sort of woman she would have been, had she been allowed her way. He sensed that her daughter Naomi, free-living and shockingly unbridled, might embody Maud's long-lost dreams.

Harry smiled to himself as he entered the library. The old man seemed to have shrivelled and shrunk in the past year, his legs growing awkward and spindly, his forearms thin, and when they were bare, revealing folds of dry, wrinkled skin. Harry remembered his first vision of Willie Bruce. The man then seemed to fill the room, his head appeared to touch the ceiling, his kilted knees were as massive and hairy as the knees of a horse. Now Harry stood looking down on the balding, frail head of that once monster-man with a compassion that verged on pain.

Willie was asleep, bent over the map that he'd unrolled across the tartan rug that covered his knees. Without looking, Harry knew what map it would be, the much worn, tattered-edged, parchment-yellow representation of France and Belgium and the English Channel. Willie's frail shaky hand had drawn across in heavy black the line of the Western Front. Last August it had been drawn first, in pencil, ready to be erased and moved. Sometime in spring, tired of redrawing worn bits of pencil, Willie had grimly resorted to the permanency of ink.

Harry shrugged and gently touched the old man's arm. Willie woke with a sudden alertness reminiscent of his youth. He coughed once. 'Oh, it's yerself, lad. Guid nou. Sit yerself doun. I'll ring for a dram.'

He reached for the bell pull, just within his grasp by the pine mantel, before Harry could protest. He'd lost interest in his drink since leaving the Struy Inn, but knew he must keep the old man company. When the whisky arrived, he watered his freely from the cut crystal jug on the silver tray. Willie took his whisky neat and snorted at Harry's adulteration of his fine old malt.

'Gordon's at Bethune,' Willie said, as introduction. 'Or did I tell ye?'

Harry nodded. He knew he should discuss the likelihood of action, the long-awaited breakthrough, but he had not the patience today, with his own news hanging over him. He said quickly, 'I lost my job, sir.'

Willie looked up startled, his old eyes quizzical. His mind was sharp as ever and he said only, 'MacKay's gane pious aboot the war then?'

'Not really, sir, to be fair. He never could stick my attitude, you know. He just stood by me out of decency.'

'Decency's a gey wersh emotion, lad. Doesna stand up tae much.'

'His son was wounded at Arras, not long ago. I think that's something to do with it.'

'Willna mend his son, turfin' a guid man oot o' his job.'

'Lost his manhood, sir.'

Willie looked up. 'Is that sae then? I hadna heard.'

'They don't say, do they?' Harry pointed out, adding with a grimace, 'Wounded low down, is the way they put it, isn't it? I think it's the worst of all. Maybe worst too for the folks at home. Hardly heroic somehow, though God knows it ought to be, losing what we all hold dearest,' he almost smiled. 'But poor old MacKay, left with all that whispered sympathy, and no dream of grandchildren. Only son, you know. Only one to carry the name.' Harry shrugged, a sad gesture of sympathy.

'I dinna see what it's tae do wi' you, still.'

'What else has he to hit out at? The army? The Germans? His noble country? Poor sod, if hitting me helps him, then I'm almost glad. He's been good to me; it's the least I can give back. Anyhow, I'd not have lasted long there. Who wants to do business with a traitor?'

His eyes met Willie's then, and Willie saw all the haunted pain in them that he would never put into words. He said only, 'Nae, lad. I think not,' and smiled, extending his shaky old hand. Harry leaned forward, caught up the hand, and momentarily buried his face against the old man's neck, as he would once do as a child.

Later, as the rain pelted against the windows and Harry sat on the floor of the library, making slice after slice of slightly burnt toast for his grandfather and spreading them as messily as a child in the nursery, he explained how he would approach Lady Maclaren for a job.

'The head gardener's away, you know, young Stewart.' He had no need to explain where he'd gone. 'And she'll never find anyone now, staff are impossible to hold. I'm quite capable, I really rather enjoy it actually. Perhaps I can write a little on the side. There was that history of the Maclarens I've always wanted to do. No doubt I'll find time, if Victoria doesn't work me into the ground,' he grinned and said then, 'Or perhaps I'd better say Lady Maclaren, now, had I not?'

Willie sighed. He'd had such hopes for this brilliant young mind, and yet deep in his heart something old and cynical nudged him, saying, Why should he no' be a gardener, old man, colonel-in-chief and a croft-wifie's bastard? 'Wheels within wheels,' he said with a smile. 'The warld's a gey queer place.'

Harry Bruce took up his employment on the nineteenth of August, 1915. On the same day, at Douglas Haig's headquarters at Lillers, Lord Kitchener strolled in the garden with Haig and his Corps commanders and talked cautiously of the military-political issue of Compulsory Service that was threatening Mr Asquith's government and would one day threaten all those of Harry Bruce's pacifist persuasion. The door of choice was swinging slowly, but surely, closed. Later, in the privacy of Haig's writing-room the grim pressures on failing Russia were discussed and the need of a vigorous support of the attack planned by the French for September.

Two days later Lieutenant-Colonel Douglas Fraser commanding the newly formed New Army battalion known officially as the Fourth Maclaren Highlanders, and in the hearts of its men as the Inverness-Pals, received notice to prepare at last for embarkation to France.

The destination of the Fourth Battalion was the French town of Bimont several miles behind the lines, where they were to form part of the XI Army Corps, 24th Division, serving as reserve to a major assault being planned between the villages of Lens and La Bassée over the flat unpromising ground around the mining village of Loos. Pat McGarrity, James and Albert Maclaren and Jimmy Fraser linked arms and cheered as the ship slid out of Southampton into the Solent, with England, where they had camped and trained for weeks, behind them at last, and before them, dim with promised glory, the war.

Pat glanced with awed pride at the corporal's stripe on his

sleeve and wished his mother could see him. His rank had been achieved with amazing ease. Desperately short of NCOs, the battalion officers had simply selected likely men and made them corporals. In Pat's case, word of his service with the Mine Rescue Brigade was enough to deem him worthy of added authority. Still, Pat accepted not out of pride or wish for advancement but a quite humble sense of duty. The four decided his advancement would be considered a reflection on all of them, and lauded him mightily. But it frightened him, knowing now that small decisions of his own might one day save, or risk, all their lives.

Once in France, the Inverness Pals made their way by train and by taxing long marches on the difficult French roads towards the Front, in the company of a great mass of men, an entire division composed almost entirely of other New Army battalions like themselves. When, upon arrival at their designated destination, they could first hear the very faint rumble of artillery, they felt naïvely that they were on the very threshold of war. They did not know that the sixteen miles that lay between themselves and the front line contained within their measure the framework of a disaster.

First Army commander Douglas Haig knew it, just as he knew that the flat, largely featureless landscape, virtually devoid of cover, over which he was being asked to attack, presented a deadly obstacle for his troops. On the latter issue, he had been forced under pressure from Lord Kitchener to concede to the wide optimistic plan of Marshal Joffre. On the first issue he was in direct conflict with his superior, the commander-in-chief, Sir John French. Over it, the tactical rift growing between the two fellow cavalrymen and one-time friends yawned wider, until it was wide enough eventually to engulf the hapless 24th Division of which the Inverness Pals were part. They, and the 21st, and a division of Guards, were to be Haig's reserve for the planned advance; they were to be his ace in the hole. But the cards were not, unfortunately, in his hand, and French, in whose hand they were, was proving a reluctant gambler. He played them close, holding on to them to the last moment, hesitantly, perhaps fearing Haig would pour his men uselessly into the mincing-machine of the war and to no result. So he kept them snugly where Haig could not reach them, miles and miles behind the lines.

None of this, of course was known to Pat McGarrity or Jimmy

Fraser, or, for all their family connections, to any of the three young Maclaren brothers. Billeted outside the village, the officers in various farmhouses, and the men in freshly cleaned barns, they had a week of idyllic peace in the autumn countryside. Pat McGarrity, still his mother's good Catholic son, went to Mass at the village church, and lapsed badly in the afternoon, having found quite innocently that his classic dark handsomeness worked the same magic in France as in Scotland. Her name was Jeanne-Louise, her father's barley stack was the location, and had it been in Pat's power to award the Victoria Cross, she'd have had one for what she did for his morale.

It was returning from that happy place, glowing throughout with the young juices of life, and the dreamy tingling of the aftermath of love, that Pat McGarrity saw a sight that instantly took from him all the pleasure of that dying September day.

A general service wagon had been left standing, horseless, at the edge of a small orchard where a large number of other ranks were sleeping rough. Within the orchard the men, awaiting their hot dinners, were sitting about in groups beneath the mossy trunks of the ancient apple trees, but beyond the stone wall that enclosed the orchard, the wagon stood, unsheltered in the sun which had throughout the day been steady and hot. Against the large spokes of the offside wheel, a man stood, or rather, hung. Arms and legs were tied firmly, spread-eagled, to the spokes of the wheel. Though his feet were left, mercifully, in touch with the ground, his knees had buckled from exhaustion and he sagged against his bonds, his heavy tunic soaked with sweat, his face reddened from the sun, lips dried and cracked. His eyes were not closed, but followed Pat dully as he walked in numb shock past the wagon on the road. Pat, innocently naive, could not stand it, and approached the first authoritative figure he could find, a large, red-headed sergeant overseeing the stew-pot nearest the roadside in the orchard.

'Sergeant?'

'Aye, sodger?'

'Sergeant, I dinna ken whit he's dune,' he gestured to the spread-eagled figure, 'but dae ye no' think he's had eneuch?'

The sergeant glanced just once towards the suffering man, and then back at Pat. He was actually smiling, a not particularly unkind smile. 'An' dae ye think so, laddie?'

'Aye, sergeant, I dae,' Pat was encouraged by the mild tone.

'Sae mebbe ye'd fancy takin' his place, then?'

Pat stood dumbfounded, not certain if the offer was genuine, a cruel jest or a mocking threat. The sergeant, still clearly bemused by Pat's wide-eyed honesty, said quickly, a little gruffly, 'Field punishment number one, fer yer information, an' yon birkie,' he gestured towards the prisoner, 'is onerly gettin' his juist desserts. We'll get nae mair lip frae him. Nou get alang tae yer ain lot, sodger, and lea the army tae mak' its ain decisions.' He turned away and growled something to the young private stirring the stew. Pat watched him, and then himself turned, reluctantly, to leave. He looked back once at the punished man and the image froze in his mind: a crucifix. The French roads had so many, scattered wayside shrines at nearly every crossroad. What was one more?

Certain recurrent rumours occurred with such regularity as to demand to be ignored, among them the eerie and ever-present whispered certainty that one's own unit had been chosen for a suicidal mission of sacrifice which would no doubt save the war effort, but would also no doubt result in one's own demise. Johnny Bruce heard that rumour, that the First Battalion had been so chosen for the coming effort, but he ignored it. For a while Johnny had been certain that the attack would not take place in their sector at all, and shared his certainty with Torquil Farquhar on one occasion.

'Surely there'll be nothing here but possibly a diversionary effort. They can't honestly intend to attack across that. There's no cover for a start.'

Torquil had looked out grimly across the projected field of battle, overseen darkly by the twin slag-heaps or *crassiers* overlooking the town of Loos. Beyond was a huge double pit-head tower nicknamed Tower Bridge. Like the slag-heaps it was a marvellous observation point, and like them it was in enemy hands. Torquil thought of Ypres and the hopeless line drawn around that town facing always upwards to a ring of high ground in enemy hands. 'Oh yes,' he said slowly. 'Yes, they can.'

18

Long before the artillery bombardment began on the twenty-first of September, the rumour had gained the authority of certainty. Everywhere it was reinforced by the constant movement of supplies, the pounding of the dusty roads with countless feet of horses and men, and the great heavy wheels of wagons and limbers; the disguised, night-time movement of ammunition to secreted, camouflaged dumps; the night-time digging of new trenches, some for use, some, planted with dummy personnel, for ruses; and then, finally, the arrival of the gas.

Donnie Cameron and Ewan Grant knew there was a big push on, all right. They spent three nights on fatigues, trekking through the long, zigzag lines of the communication trenches, up to the Front, with gas cylinders carried between them slung from poles on creaking canvas slings.

'D'ye ken whit these are fer?' Ewan asked. Donnie did, and did not say. Later they carried the gas pipes. Long and awkward, they needed to be held over their heads to negotiate each corner of the zigzagged communications trench. At the end of the night Donnie had no feeling in his hands at all, and his shoulders crackled with agony when he attempted to move his arms. In the morning, Donnie woke in a front-line trench and saw, through the periscope, that a sign had been erected over the German lines at night. 'Time please?' it said. 'And Date?' The English was quite perfect.

'Sae much for secrecy,' Ewan said, watching the now-familiar sight of a Boche aeroplane, glinting silver in the dawn, winging high over their lines. It filled him with cold fear. They were like ants, scuttling about on the flat fields, and the Boche, secure in their Tower and *Crassiers*, had eyes everywhere, like gods.

Lieutenant John Bruce relaxed in the sun in the kitchen garden of the old red-tile-roofed farmhouse in which he and the other officers of his company were billeted, and wrote home. He wrote to his grandmother, a brief dutiful note. He wrote to his sister Susan, and to his maternal grandfather, Mr Wilson, the eminent London jeweller, with whom his relations were, as always, strictly a formality. His fourth letter, the one he saved, savoured for last, was slightly less conventional. It was his letter to Rebecca Galloway.

Time was running out for Johnny. As a romantic figure he would never match his cousin Tenny in any woman's eyes, particularly not Rebecca's. It was, quite clearly, only his status as gallant boy at the Front that had given him the slightest edge on Tenny throughout the year. In a few weeks Tenny too could be writing home of danger and modest gallantry, and his edge would be lost.

With that in mind, and with a slightly calculating wry smile twisting his sun-tanned upper lip, he spread two sheets of paper on the weatherbeaten wooden garden table, and wrote:

> My dearest Miss Galloway,
> Once again 'the shouts of war are heard afar'; once again, my dearest thoughts turn, as always, to you. Odd how the depths of adversity but deepen the sweetness of our memories. Ah my love, I feel so strongly now that time is shortening and soon it will be *only* memories. Men in peril do seem to develop an instinct, premonitory one could say I suppose. For some days it has haunted me, this vision . . . but enough of that, I would not trouble you with my concerns. Only, my dearest Rebecca, now that I see the nearness of the night, how saddened I am that our day was so brief and so,

he thought a long time and finally wrote,

> so incomplete. If only I had had true courage. If only I had

dared. Perhaps you would not have refused me, as I so feared you would. If only . . . oh my dearest, perhaps even now I could have been addressing you as my dearest wife. Forgive, if you can, my presumption, but the lengthening shadows do bring a certain reckless courage. Alas, too late. Even were you to consent at this moment, and send your reply with all speed possible, still I greatly fear I would never see that longed for, cherished letter,

Goodbye my dearest,
your always faithful
always remembering,
Johnny

He sat back and sighed, and then with hungry eyes re-read his masterpiece, his sandy moustache twitching with a moment's guilty humour. It really was good. She'd need a heart of iron to refuse that. Now, the *pièce de résistance*. He rose and wandered about the garden until he found a sprig of blue forget-me-not, which he carefully tucked within the delicate folds of paper. Then, grin broadening, he slid the letter into the envelope and sealed it with fervour.

'And the best of British luck to you, mate,' he said to the distant, unseen figure of Tenny Maclaren.

Torquil Farquhar posted Johnny's letter for him when he rode to Bethune to get his own letter to Emma Maclaren away as soon as possible. He had received her latest that morning, and it bore news that drove him to instant reply.

Emma was coming to France. She had at last circumvented authority and, despite her age, somehow gained permission to nurse at the vast military hospital at Le Havre. She had written, in her familiar bubbling style, with such joy at this sudden good fortune, in her eyes, that he felt real pain in writing his reply. For Emma saw only that she would be near him: 'Imagine my dearest, in a few short days we will stand on the same soil, parted no longer by sea. I am quite mad with joy.' The words had chilled him through. Emma in France, Emma on the same ground as the horror and devastation with which he, for one awful year, had lived.

No matter that the hospital was far, far from the Front, no matter that she had made no mention of the more dangerous Casualty Clearing Stations which did quite often come under attack, she would be in France where the war was, and he could not bear to imagine her in such danger. True, London itself, in their new terrible world, was no longer safe; zeppelin raids had brought casualties into the heart of the civilian stronghold. Emma herself had mentioned them. But they were rare. They did not deeply intrude on his imagined picture of her in safe, serene corridors, surrounded only by her loyal patients and wise medical staff, none of whom he was sure would allow a highborn lady into any position of real discomfort or danger. He had clung to that image, gently brushing aside her brave little protests, her brief descriptions of the harshness of her work, because he could not bear to imagine her other than as he wished her, safe, cherished, cared for and secure. And in England.

His letter contained a frantic plea that she at once abandon her foolhardy plan for his sake, if not for hers. Fortunately for Emma, for it would have caused her terrible guilt, she never saw that letter. She was, as Torquil rode back through the lovely, unspoiled countryside behind the war zone, already at sea, crossing the Channel in a party of six other determined young members of the VAD; and his letter, crossing her path, never found its way to her at all.

Torquil avoided the roads, choked as they were with dusty motor cars full of blustering staff officers, and roaring motor-cycles bearing messengers with the endless string of directives and queries that forever entangled the military in a net of its own unquenchable curiosity. Out in the open fields, a lovely string of horses, gunner horses, was being led by a single youngster, out for exercise. Horses, unlike motor cars, could never be simply left until needed. Torquil's own mare, exercised regularly by his batman, was still lively and spirited, needing the good gallop he was giving her.

Torquil returned his horse into the care of his batman and returned to his billet. He had received his orders that morning, and as a company commander had more idea than most of what was going on. They were moving up that night to the village of Vermelles. On the Thursday the bombardment would begin. They would advance, through the communications trench that began in Vermelles, up to the edge of no-man's-land. Then, preceded by smoke and gas, and with their way cleared for them by four days' thunder of artillery, they would cross the shell-pocked field and take the shattered remnants of the mining village of Loos.

It sounded so simple on paper. Gordon Bruce huddled in a front-line dugout with his company commanders, his altered and re-altered maps spread in front of him while overhead and all about and beneath his wooden bunk the ground shook and trembled with the might of their shelling. 'Particularly favourable,' Gordon winced, studying the terrain between Loos and the La Bassée canal, 'particularly favourable', those were Joffre's very words to describe the slag-heap shadowed plain. As if, Gordon thought slowly, stroking his stubbly chin, as if by the very saying of it, the land could be transformed from the deathtrap he knew it was into a stage set for victory. Torquil Farquhar came into the dugout from the outer trench. He had been testing the wind.

'It's in my face, sir,' he said.

Bruce cursed softly.

'Will we go anyhow?' Colin Chisholm asked. 'Without the gas?'

'We'll be cut to ribbons, if we do,' Major Murray, the adjutant, replied. Gordon nodded. Murray went off to find a runner to check again with Brigade Headquarters, the telephone line having been cut several hours before by a shortfall.

It was raining lightly, as it had been for most of the previous day. The gentle weather left them just when they needed it most. In the forward lines the men huddled under the waterproof sheets, waiting in misery, curled up against the hard white chalk of the trench walls, seeking some respite from the earthshaking thunder. The horizon flickered constantly, white to dark like heat lightning under the rain of shells. It was eleven o'clock on the night of the twenty-fourth of September, 1915. The Battle of Loos was about to commence.

At the forward Brigade Headquarters, a small farm shed still standing on the outskirts of the broken ruins of Vermelles, Ian Maclaren struggled to hear the static distorted voice on the other end of the field telephone line. The sounds of the bombardment had risen to such a crescendo, like a ceaseless surf pounding the tin roof of the shed, shaking through its frail walls, making any loose object rattle and vibrate, that it was virtually impossible to make out words. Ian covered his right ear with the palm of his hand, pressing it close till the sound of his own blood throbbing matched the beat of the artillery. His other ear pressed against the receiver at last faintly caught the words, 'Attack delayed one hour. Gas at 5.50.' He put down the phone.

Among those waiting for his message was the runner from the Maclaren Highlanders, sent by the adjutant, Murray. He was a tall, slender young farm labourer from Eskadale. In another world Ian had seen him twice defeat his own son Tenny in the hill race at the Highland Games. He gave him the message and added gruffly, 'Regards to your CO.' The young man saluted, took the written message and left the shed. Just after, the whole building was shaken by the impact of a heavy shell, 5.9 most likely, he thought, as the Boche were replying in kind. He hoped the runner had made it, less for his own sake than for the sake of the operation ahead.

He went out once more to test the wind. In the eerie mayhem of the night it was intensely difficult to concentrate on so subtle a thing as the shift of a capricious wind. He closed his eyes, held up a wetted finger, turned once around, a full circle. It strengthened briefly, blowing out towards the German lines. That was it. That was what they needed. A good stiff steady breeze, blowing from the south and west, to carry the gas out to the east-northeast, stifling all opposition. With that, all might indeed go well. But if it dropped, and left the deadly cloud hanging an unrelenting curtain before their own lines, they would be trapped themselves by it, unable to advance safely, and its deadly work would go undone. Worse yet, a sudden shift of the uncertain breeze could turn it back and gas their own men, forcing them to flee backwards, in the clammy misery of their gas helmets, before the attack could ever begin. 'Oh God,' Ian said with sudden fervour, 'give me a good wind. A good west wind.'

He thought suddenly, achingly, of Naomi, and heard himself whispering the words that, in the fury of the bombardment, he might as well have shouted,

> 'Western wind, when wilt thou blow
> The small rain down can rain?
> Christ, that my love were in my arms,
> And I in my bed again.'

At five o'clock, Gordon Bruce, standing alone before his dugout, felt the wind clearly in his face, blowing back across their lines from the east. He hastened back to the dugout and his recently restored field telephone and rang through again.

'The wind's against us, can we stop now?'

Ian Maclaren again contacted Rawlinson, as others were doing as well. He was told to await further instructions while, no doubt, Haig himself was left to decide, and while the fateful, fitful wind shifted insolently from quarter to quarter.

The message came at five forty-five. 'Too late to stop. Attack must commence.' The sheer clumsy impossibility of contacting so many scattered outposts of command, and relaying such a message down the miles and miles of trenches, made a reversal impossible. Like the commencement of the war itself, the Battle of Loos began under the sheer force of its own momentum.

As the dimness of false dawn spread over the sky, Gordon Bruce was left with the awful decision of whether or not to use the gas at all. Attacking without its cover, and the cover of smoke, would appear suicidal, but little less so than attacking into clouds of the deadly chemicals themselves. A last loyal shift of the wind decided him. With the coming of dawn it settled into the west once more, and strengthened. In his sector at least, there would be gas. He gave the order and out in their saps, the Royal Engineers attached to their battalion opened the valves.

The men, who had stood-to since three-thirty, having eaten their breakfast of hard biscuits and tea and swallowed eagerly their tots of rum, put on their chemical-impregnated flannel gasmasks, the flaps yet rolled up, and waited. The gas was released in bursts of ten minutes, alternating with ten minutes of smoke, since there was not gas enough to maintain the full half-hour's cover. As Gordon watched through the trench periscope, it rolled slowly away towards the enemy lines, mingling with the dim mist of the early morning. It was too slow, far too slow, but at least at first it was moving. By six-thirty it seemed to have stopped entirely, but in the fogged weak light it was impossible to tell.

At six-thirty-three, Lieutenant John Bruce checked with his platoon sergeant, Ross MacDonald, and fixed the bayonet on the rifle that he, like most surviving officers, now carried. MacDonald signalled readiness to Sandy Gibson, and Sandy nodded, looking down the crouching group of chalk-muddied figures that comprised his section. They were weighed down with their packs, their rifles, 200 rounds of rifle ammunition, sandbags, rations, grenades. One in four carried a pick or a shovel, making it virtually impossible even to crouch. Bayonets were fixed, rifles carried at the slope; the advance would be made of necessity at a walk.

The bombardment stopped ten minutes before the attack.

'Here we come,' Sandy Gibson muttered sourly, 'ready or no'.' Beside him Ewan Grant jumped at the sound of his voice. His face was white in the dawn, his eyes wild. 'Wait fer the whistle, sodger,' Sandy said with a grin, 'an' dinna fash. Jerry's no' in sae great a hurry as thot.' The sudden silence was thick and tangible after the days of unceasing noise.

At six-thirty-six Colin Chisholm blew the whistle and they went over the top, four feet apart and in perfect step. They scrambled up wooden ladders, crossed the open ground to their own front line and crossed that trench, by bridges thrown up by its occupants, and were out beyond, slipping quickly through the readied gaps in their own wire and out into the swirling haze and yet intermittent gunfire of no-man's-land.

There were four hundred yards to cover to where the German line snaked along before the outskirts of Loos, bordering the slopes of a small rise called, on their maps, hill 70. It was their destination, and in the murk of the smoke and mist-filled air, it was utterly invisible. Johnny dropped down into a shell-hole, took a compass reading, found themselves veering, instinctively, to keep in touch with the battalion on their right, who were also wandering. He rose up again, rallying his men, and keeping the dim bulk of Tower Bridge in sight for a guide. They crossed another hundred yards and the German fire began in earnest, small-arms fire, and the staccato beat of machine-guns dug in along the slopes of the hill and the slag-heap on their right. Johnny hit the ground again, thinking, so much for our artillery. Beside him a man fell, and then another. He could not, muffled in his gas helmet, have any notion who they might be.

The gas helmet was smothering him. Sweat and rain permeated the cloth, and the chemicals seeped in, stinging his eyes. He peered leftwards through the fogged mica eyepiece and saw, leading the charge, Colin Chisholm, his mask pushed up on to his forehead, his face exposed. It was all he needed, and he thrust his own mask up and gulped in air, thankfully pure and free of gas. With renewed strength he plunged forward after Colin.

Hill 70 loomed up suddenly, out of the mist, a dim rise, and in the same instant, with a sickening lurch in his throat, he saw the German wire. There were three rows of it, in all fifteen feet deep.

It was not only barbed and rusted wire coiled thickly like mats of hair, like that before their own lines, but an internally structured barricade, ribbed throughout with heavy crosspieces of wood. And their shelling hadn't touched it.

'Christ,' Johnny whispered, and instinctively hit the ground as a shrapnel shell descended, whistling, behind him. It shattered and shook the earth, but yards away, and he felt debris thudding painfully against his back. Face against the earth, he prayed it was only blasted mud. He lay still until it settled, and attempting to move, concluded he was unhurt. In the noise, vibration and excitement, it was often difficult to tell. He raised his head, studying the wire, searching frantically for a gap. An unexploded shell lay like an egg in a nest within its tangles. Duds; there were so many, no wonder the wire was uncut.

Johnny scuttled off, on hands and knees, with the whine of rifle-fire around him like the buzz of insects, and plunged into another shell hole.

'Lieutenant Bruce, sir?' a shaking young voice called. He looked around the crater. Several Maclarens were snugged in against its white chalk walls, trusting in the old adage that no hole created by a shell was ever hit by another. He recognized the youngster as one of his own platoon, Donnie Cameron. 'We cannae get through, sir,' he said.

Johnny nodded. 'I'll get you through,' he said, though he had at the moment no idea how. He peered over the natural battlement of the crater edge, trying to find some break in the blackened coils winding out into the dullness of the haze. Briefly he considered gathering his little group and returning to their own lines. It was better than getting them all killed. Still, it seemed early for a retreat. Another two soldiers leapt into their shell-hole, panic growing in their eyes.

'We've nae a hope,' one babbled. 'Nae a hope. I'm awa'!' Johnny leapt to intercede, but the man suddenly stood up, and his face showed clearly he'd passed that last point of rationality that made him controllable. 'I cannae stand it, I'm awa' hame. I want ma hame . . .' Johnny recognized him then. It was Ewan Grant from Culbrech.

'Get doun, man,' one of the older men in the shell crater shouted, and Donnie Cameron half scrambled up to capture him. But he was up on the rubble bordering the crater, and still shouting, 'I'm awa' hame . . .' His hands covered his ears, as if it was the noise alone from which he fled. In another moment he was out in the open, running, not towards their own lines at all, but as if by some native instinct running north-northwest up no-man's-land, straight through the hail of fire to where, far, far away, lay the brown heather hills of Strathglass.

'Ewan,' Donnie Cameron shouted, he too leaping up on the open edge of the pit.

John Bruce tackled him, dragging him down.

'He's my pal. He'll get bluidy murthured oot there.'

Johnny pinned the frantic youngster to the ground, in the same instant seeing over the crater lip the thunderous crumping explosion of a Boche heavy enfolding the fleeing figure in a towering column of blasted earth. In the comparative quiet as the earth settled, some of it thudding down around themselves, John Bruce said softly, 'You can't help him, Cameron. C'mon, lad, we've a job to do.'

Donnie slowly raised his head, peering confusedly off into the foggy air where Ewan had vanished. Dully, he followed the low-bent figure of his officer as he led them all away. In a series of sharp, desperate dashes they made their way, with Johnny in the lead, across the enfiladed front of the German wire. Fire poured down on them, not just from the trenches it protected, but from the shattered walls of the village of Loos to their left and the height of hill 70 beyond and to their right. A machine-gun was hidden in a dugout carved into a small chalk hill beside a minehead, or *puits*, just behind the Boche lines. Their own artillery continuously pounded the entire area, but it seemed to be having little effect.

Johnny gathered two more stray Maclarens from a ditch by the side of the Lens-Bethune road. They sheltered briefly, still assessing the wire, in the shattered stumps of the poplars that had lined the cobbled highway. Peering ahead, into the clearing day, Johnny saw the gap he sought. At just that moment, faint over the thunderous noise of constant fire, he heard the high skirl of the pipes. He took it as a sign, signalled his little band and advanced.

As they approached it, the German wire proved a heart-rending sight. The 15th Division of which they were currently a part was essentially a Scottish New Army division. Now, strewn across the vicious barricade, the bodies of those military innocents hung limp and bullet-torn. To Donnie Cameron, seeing those dark lifeless shapes, in their fluttering ragged kilts, the sight brought instantly to mind the image of the black corpses of hoody crows that old Cameron strung on the croft fences as fair warning to the rest.

Donnie fought the desire to tuck himself in beside the lieutenant like a lost lamb, knowing that the double target they'd thus provide would be irresistible. Again they went forward, passing numbers of wounded who held up hands and cried out for water, or stretcher-bearers. They were under orders not to stop, and could not, but Johnny called, as they passed, 'Hold on, help will be coming,' though he did not really know if it would. It was the traditional reply, and he was soon to learn himself that any human voice to a suffering man was comfort.

Throughout their intermittent charge, the sound of the pipes wailed bravely over the storm of artillery and small-arms fire, and he was yet to see the piper. It was eerie, as if a Highland ghost had chosen to accompany their advance into the valley of the shadow. But, as he plunged down into a disused Boche sap, just before the ragged gap in the wire for which he was aiming, the mystery was solved. Propped against the sagging chalk wall, his good leg braced against the opposite side of the trench, his other leg streaming blood, sagging beneath him, was the Maclaren piper, Major MacIntosh, alternately piping and cursing with equal vigour.

Johnny grinned suddenly and shouted, 'Up the Maclarens!' and heard behind him a ragged cheer, half-drowned by the constant noise of the guns. But it gave them heart and the piper gave a jerk of his head in acknowledgement and continued playing. Johnny looked back; his men were following, eager now, up the sap, renewed in vigour and ready for anything.

The sap ended in a crater, where one of their own shells had blown it in. A boot protruded from the shattered earth, and the decaying remnants of a leg. Johnny hardly noticed. Before them was the parapet of the German trench.

'Bomber,' he shouted, and a young soldier came up behind him and with deftly practised hand, tossed one of his cricket balls over the sandbags. The explosion was deafening, casting chalky earth back over them all. They waited only long enough for it to settle and then Johnny left the shelter of the crater and dashed for the low fortification. He leapt it blindly, rifle and bayonet ready, his men jumping down behind him. But there was no opposition.

Three dead Germans lay at his feet, torn by the sharp confined blast. Another was huddled in the corner, waving his hands to show his unarmed state and repeating in a babbling confusion, 'Kamerad, Kamerad. No fight, Kiltie. Kamerad.'

'Aye, a'richt then,' a grey-haired Maclaren regular growled. 'Nou where's yer pals?'

'There's a dugout here,' Donnie Cameron called, as other men fanned out down the trench, rifles ready at the corner of each bay.

'Awa', I'll chuck ane doun,' the young bomber said, waving another cricket-ball grenade. But Johnny insisted they be given a chance, stood by the dark entrance and called out for any occupants to surrender.

There was a scuffle and then a Scots voice shouted, 'Dinna shoot, there's naebody here but me an' Fritzie an' he's Kameradin' fit tae kill.'

Johnny laughed softly and answered, 'All right, Fritzie first, and nice and slowly, please.'

After another pause and more scuffling, two figures appeared at the dugout entrance. One was a young Highlander of A Company, with a roughly bandaged knee, and the other a small blond German who grinned engagingly, showing a wide mouthful of silver-capped teeth. 'Yer nae tae hairm him,' the Scot said, 'he's been richt hospitable.' He pointed to his bandaged knee and patted the field-grey shoulder of his yet grinning new friend. Johnny nodded, and gestured the German to the side of the trench where the other prisoner was waiting. There were rules governing conduct that protected them both, but it was their obvious care of the Maclaren prisoner that saved them, just then, rather than rules.

'Cameron,' Johnny said. 'You'll escort our prisoners back to our lines.'

'Juist me, sir?' Donnie said, hardly aware that he was questioning an order until Johnny's unamused sharp blue eyes settled momentarily on his face, and stunned him into a small gulping, 'Sir.'

But Johnny assessed the youngster quickly, and looking around, caught sight of Sergeant MacDonald. 'Find another man to help escort the prisoners and our wounded men, Sergeant,' he said, 'I'm going on.' He gestured over the parados towards a second trench line, guarding a row of fortified miners' cottages that comprised the outskirts of Loos. As he gathered his men, and headed for them, he heard a disgruntled mutter from MacDonald, but in another moment had forgotten him, the prisoners, and everything except the next coiling barrier of wire.

Donnie Cameron was left suddenly alone with the wounded man, the two prisoners and the detested Sergeant Ross MacDonald. The Germans picked up his unease and edged pathetically closer to Donnie for safety. Donnie waited for the sergeant to go in search of another guard, but he only gestured with an abrupt upward tilt of his heavily stubbled chin.

'Sergeant?' Donnie said, warily.

'Tak' the wounded man awa',' MacDonald said with another upward jerk of his chin, this time towards the parapet of the trench and the ground they had just covered. Donnie hesitated a moment, and then, with a glance at the two prisoners watching him with nervous intentness, he slipped his arm around the wounded man and slung the other's arm over his own shoulder and half-dragged him from the trench. Sergeant Ross MacDonald watched him go, and then turned in a slow, savouring circle towards the Germans, raised the muzzle of his rifle, and fired.

The sound was lost in the continuing fire from the village stronghold, as Donnie crossed the open ground to the shell-hole from which they had prepared their attack. Once there he let the man down into a sitting posture, his back propped against the crumbling chalk of the crater.

'I'm awa' back fer the prisoners. Sergeant'll hae found the ither man maybe.' He left the wounded Maclaren with some haste, and ran, only ducking slightly, across the open ground to the trench. Something, a kind of eerie fear, was growing in him. Panting with the effort of making such speed under his heavy load of equipment, he scrambled down over the parapet once more, into the well-dug, wooden-shored German fortification.

Sergeant Ross MacDonald was alone. There was no other man to help in the guard duty, nor was there any longer a need of one. The two prisoners, a minute ago grinning with the nervous relief of knowing that for them the war was over, were now only a chalky *feld grau* heap on the duckboard floor of the trench, with that discarded rag look that Donnie associated always with the dead. The wounded Maclaren's Good Samaritan lay on his back, his mouth open with the final, fatal surprise, the front of his tunic bloodied and blood seeping through his shiny silver teeth.

Donnie felt suddenly, unaccountably sick, and stopped his rising gorge with his hand, half turning away.

'Bastards turned on me, as sune as I was alone,' MacDonald said, without emotion. He was cleaning his rifle with quick surety. Donnie looked up then and met his eyes. At once he knew the man was lying. He stood open-mouthed. There was nothing in all his training to help him deal with this. An officer was lying. An officer had killed prisoners in cold blood, for no reason. And lied.

'Murthurer,' Donnie shouted, stunned by the ferocity of his own anger.

MacDonald said nothing. He finished cleaning his rifle, still with the same meticulous care, and then, quite slowly, turned it till the end of his bayonet was at Donnie's chest, the point just roughly scraping the middle button of his tunic.

'An' if,' he said slowly, 'juist if, it were sae, ye wee git, juist wha dae ye think onybody wad believe? Supposin' I saed it was yerself shot them? Or juist supposin' I shot ye as well? Yer word against mine?' He smiled a broad cynical smile, showing the gap in his lower teeth. 'Nou get yer ass awa' doun the line wi' your man, an' keep yer gob shut. Or,' he jabbed Donnie with the bayonet so it pierced his tunic and drew blood, 'or I'll juist dae ye mysel'. I'll hae yer wee balls aff wi' this an' a'.' He was still laughing, pleased with his parting sally, as Donnie scuttled in humiliated confusion back to his waiting charge.

'Where's Fritzie?' the man asked, raising himself up to see, when Donnie appeared alone.

'Gane,' he said, and jerking the man to his feet headed off to the Advanced Dressing Station just behind their lines at Vermelles. For all the long, painful journey, his mind in disarray, he would not say more.

John Bruce and his comrades had achieved the second line of trenches with moderate casualties, leaving him with a bare handful of men with which to make his way into the heavily fortified village itself. The houses, built in long terraces, had been efficiently loopholed at the windows, and possessed as well a cellar each. Those natural dugouts had been put to good use, and with machine-gun emplacements well-hidden among them, each house became a miniature fortress for which a separate small battle must be waged. As they worked their way up the cobbled street, clearing dugouts with grenades, and raking the broken walls with small-arms fire, they met a party of King's Own Scottish Borderers and scattered members of other battalions. Communications were appalling and most groups were already acting independently, totally lost from their battalion field headquarters, to say nothing of Divisional HQ. In the smoke and gas confusion of the dawn attack many had veered off-course, lost and disoriented, crossing the advance of other battalions and getting swallowed up by them, relinquishing their own objectives for adopted ones.

In the cemetery of Loos village, beneath the dark crucifix that hung over the graves and was visible from some distance, the young officer found his battalion commander and uncle, Gordon Bruce, sheltering in an abandoned German dugout amongst the crypts. He was attended only by his batman, the adjutant Murray, and a corporal of the Signals Corps, and was hunched over his outspread maps, peering at them with desperate intensity. As John Bruce approached, a forward observation officer came running in with fresh information, and the colonel hastily scribbled a message to the artillery battery behind Vermelles and sent it off by hand to the nearest field telephone with the corporal as runner. Only then did he look up and acknowledge his nephew. The acknowledgement was strictly military. John Bruce requested further orders regarding his small band of Maclarens and was told to leave the mopping-up of Loos to the Kosbies and move out towards the objective of hill 70 where, with luck, he would meet up with Colin Chisholm and the rest of B Company, and A Company under Torquil Farquhar.

Johnny acknowledged with a salute, and then for a moment let the formality slip, and taking advantage of his position said quickly, 'How's it going, sir?'

Colonel Bruce looked up, blinked once, and waved him away. Either he didn't know, or didn't wish to say, or most likely saw no need, in typical senior officer fashion, to share such information with a lowly subaltern. Johnny Bruce went on his way, unperturbed, and a few minutes later, his messages to the artillery acknowledged by a sudden series of loud crumps and a line of dust columns wiping out the point where a particularly irksome machine-gun had been plaguing their advance, Gordon Bruce grunted his satisfaction, rolled up his maps, and he too, with his attendants, moved on.

The casualties were already heavy, and it was but eight o'clock in the morning. In technical terms, the attack was going well, at least in the Maclarens' immediate sector. The 15th Division had captured Loos and were moving on towards the stronghold of hill 70, and heading for the Cité St Auguste beyond. They were well into the German lines. On hill 70, attacking uphill under heavy shelling and enfilade fire, they rapidly began to sustain the kind of casualties that were evident to the men in the field.

Johnny Bruce first approached the hill with his band of strays, three more of whom he had picked up outside the church in Loos, from the shelter of the one standing wall of a row of *corons* at the right-hand extremity of the village. Beyond was a railway embankment, and he was making for its protection when he was hailed by a shout from a row of roofless cottages.

Among the fallen timbers was Torquil Farquhar. Behind, systematically clearing the small nests of courageous German snipers working from the upstairs windows of the houses, was the remainder of A Company. There appeared to be roughly forty men, forty left of two hundred and forty.

'My God,' Johnny said, his voice suddenly weak. 'What's happened? Where are the rest?'

Torquil was remarkably calm and his voice, when he answered, was flat and smooth, unpassioned. 'We had a bit of difficulty with the wire,' he said. 'I think number two platoon are all right. They were separated from us at the start. I believe they're with C Company. They've lost all their officers, you see. I've lost all mine,' he added, still very calmly.

'All?' Johnny gasped. 'Craigie? Haig-Thomas?'

Torquil nodded. 'Dead. Both of them. Ferguson's copped a bad one, but he was still alive when last I saw him. Bushy Fox's dead too. Just outside of Loos. Mortar.' He paused, looking towards the hill ahead of them, seeming to be silenced by utter weariness. Johnny thought he should say something but did not know what. Torquil said then, 'And your lot?'

'Lost contact in the first charge. So much damned gas and smoke. It seemed to be getting us more than the Boche. Had damnall effect on them, anyhow.'

Torquil nodded, as if it were already an old story from long ago. Then without further speech he set out towards hill 70, stopping once and shouting to the stragglers, his voice suddenly vibrant with command, 'Come up, come up, on the Maclarens!'

They took up the shout behind him, and he was off, and running, into the rain of shells. John Bruce and his men followed after.

There was a German machine-gun emplacement at the foot of the hill and it was well-wired. Pinned down by it, both parties of Highlanders were temporarily halted, pouring rifle-fire at it and cursing their lack of artillery cover. Suddenly another party of Maclarens appeared to the left of the emplacement, and led by a wildly shouting, madly courageous officer, stormed within feet of it, and in spite of its raking fire managed to get close enough to toss a grenade. When the smoke cleared the German crew were dead and a half-dozen dead Highlanders lay in front of the shattered gun. The officer whose gallantry had driven them on sagged now on the wire, his kilt and tunic shredded by fire. Johnny ran towards him, and recognized the bloody face. It was his captain, Colin Chisholm, still alive, mortally wounded, bleeding rapidly to death on the wire.

Johnny went on, taking the lead now of his refound B Company, glimpsing the corporal, Sandy Gibson, his left arm dangling as if broken, charging at his side. Together, with the remnants of A Company, they made their way up the hill, learning to duck and dodge the heavy shells. They were surrounded now by masses of men, as the 15th Division ploughed determinedly upwards seeking the summit, all the while overseen by the grim black hulk of the double winding-towers of Loos. Johnny prayed they would soon fall into their own hands, and thus save them the pinpoint accuracy of the Boche heavy guns.

As the enemy moved back out of Loos, the shells began falling on the few standing walls of the town itself, and the great tower came under fire, indicating it was no longer in German hands. By that time, Johnny Bruce and his company were on the crest of hill 70. Beyond the crest the land spread out to the German second lines and the Cité St Auguste, flaming rosy-red in the wet morning light, set afire by their own shells. And beyond, Johnny thought, beyond. Beyond the land lay, open, unprotected, eastwards to Lille. And on, open, the way to Germany. His whole being was charged with incredible excitement, as if a doorway had been opened, or a curtain raised. The unapproachable was within sight. For a handful of seconds on the crest of a pathetic little rise on the flat Loos plain, Johnny saw the war's end within his grasp.

The moment passed with the stunning reality of a 5.9 shell thudding into the earth so close that as he flung himself flat on the ground, he could feel the earth leaping to meet him. He raised his head, assessing the ground before him, not an easy act with machine-gun fire raising little dust mounds, like angry summer raindrops, all around. Below, at the eastward foot of the hill, a heavy barrier of German wire, many feet deep and sturdily high, stretched uncut ahead of them. Spread out before it against the flank of the hill, they were like targets on a rifle-range. Johnny assessed it at once – untenable – and shouted, 'Back,' to the few men who had followed him down the slope. Torquil Farquhar appeared on the crest of the hill, and for an awful moment Johnny was sure he was about to make the sort of brave lunatic charge that had cost Colin Chisholm his life. But it would be pointless, and Farquhar in his odd, calm detached way was ruthlessly in control. He called his men back and they scrambled upwards and over the crest, until a shield of hillside lay between them and the German guns. They had done all they could alone; without their machine-guns and with their pathetic supply of grenades that had, often as not, simply refused to explode. Now they must entrench, and await the reserves.

Johnny set his men scratching ditches in the unrelenting white chalk with their inadequate entrenching tools, while he sent four soldiers back to their lines for picks and shovels, another two in search of machine-guns, and a third party for further ammunition. Then, sweating with exertion despite the cold damp rain, he flung himself into the work of entrenching, side by side with his men.

By mid-afternoon, they were well dug-in, and had filled the sandbags that each man carried and made a reasonable parapet of them. To their left Loos was being steadily pounded down by massive shell-fire, though the steel structure of the winding-towers proved highly resistant, and stood yet. The church was crumbling now, and the miners' cottages through which they had battled were reduced in most places to bare walls. As the rainy sky darkened, the burning glow of the Cité St Auguste brightened the sky over the crest of hill 70. The men were wet and cold and immensely tired, and their morale was not helped by the passage through their lines of numbers of confused and shaken men of other regiments coming back from more forward positions in a manner verging on panicked retreat.

Johnny and Torquil Farquhar attempted to calm them and entreated them to join in the Maclaren lines, but they had clearly had enough. Eventually the two young officers, with their NCOs, were obliged to concentrate on calming their own men, spooked by the sight of the retreat in much the way that sheep on their native hillsides would stir and turn to run at the sight of others running. Johnny went up and down the line assuring his men that relief was coming, they would soon have rest, hot dinners, rum, the rewarding trinity they all craved. As he spoke the words he silently prayed to the distant Presbyterian God of his childhood that it would be so.

In the early evening, Colonel Bruce appeared in their lines. His arrival coincided with that of half-a-dozen more B Company strays including Donnie Cameron, back from his mission of mercy, who scuttled into his company's trench with the eager enthusiasm of a lost puppy. Once more surrounded by the men and boys he knew, under the watchful eyes of his trusted corporal, Sandy Gibson, and able to glimpse from time to time his worshipped officer, he felt, oddly, quite safe. He was proud to be there, firing off a gratuitous few shots at the general direction of the Boche when his colonel came up the line.

Colonel Bruce conferred briefly with the two young officers, inquiring after the state of B Company's command.

'Captain Chisholm's dead, sir, and I'm afraid I'm the senior officer of what's left of B Company. There's a couple of whole platoons missing. They must be somewhere; I mean they can't possibly have all been wiped out.' Even as Johnny Bruce said it he heard in his own voice a slight question.

Colonel Bruce made no comment and only added gruffly, 'Appears you're in command, for now. Don't make a hash of it.' It was one of the rare occasions he let his façade slip towards the young man, and typically it came out as a dimly affectionate insult.

'No, sir,' Johnny said, chancing a small grin. Then he said, 'The way's clear beyond the hill, sir, if we can just get artillery cover and a couple of Maxims up. They've only a weak second line beyond and aside from the bank at the foot of the hill, there's no wire. My men are tired, but if we had some support I know they'd rally . . .' He stopped, waiting expectantly.

Colonel Bruce was silent for a long time, stroking the worn leather of his Sam Browne belt with the short broad fingers of his right hand. Eventually he said, in a voice barely audible beneath the sound of the persistent shelling of Loos, 'I know. The forward observation officer's been up the tower.' He gestured over his shoulder and Johnny glanced instinctively in that direction, with awed respect for whoever had dared to scramble up that stricken fretwork of bombarded steel. 'The way's clear to Berlin past there,' there was a slight trembling in his voice and Johnny was aware of a tremendous barricaded passion within the man, 'and I can't advance.'

'Why not?' Johnny demanded loudly, forgetting his place.

'We've no reserves.'

'Where's Haig? Where's Haig's reserves?'

'I've been on to Haig. He hasn't got them. French has them.' He shook his head suddenly, closing his eyes, fighting fearsome frustration. 'They're still in Bethune.'

Instantly exhaustion and pain came down on John Bruce like the fall of night. He felt he could barely stand. The day had been wasted, the day and its men. Colin Chisholm's brave bloody face rose in his memory. For nothing.

'Oh damn them. Damn French. Damn the idiots. Damn all of them,' he cried aloud.

'Mr Bruce,' the voice was as cold and as calm as if he stood on the parade-ground, 'that outburst was quite out of order.' His uncle's dark humourless eyes were on him, the greying brows descending in a discontented 'V'. 'You will compose yourself at once, and return to your duties. Goodnight, Mr Bruce.' He saluted, turned his back, and walked away, ducking low as a shell whistled over his head. Johnny Bruce, with one brief glance at the departing bowed shoulders of his uncle, turned back with a cheery Judas smile to his men.

The counter-attack came several minutes after midnight, in a sudden downpour of rain. Its ferocity was more than anticipated and for some time the two decimated companies of Maclarens, along with the accompanying segments of other battalions, were obliged to defend fiercely with continuous rifle-fire, to keep the attackers at bay. John Bruce's little company was much aided by the addition of a Maxim brought up, with much difficulty, to their hastily constructed line, and the British defenders profited most of all from the yet glowing firelight of the burning village beyond the hill. It lit the night sky, and silhouetted their attackers, who seemed unaware. It made them easy targets as, undeterred, they attacked again and again throughout the night.

The price of their courage was visible in the greying dawn, massed heaps of sodden grey dead, scattered the length of the line. With the first light, at four in the morning, they had been forced to cut off the attacks, and retreat, and fortify. A new no-man's-land would form between them, as always, in which the dead would quietly rot, and into which the living would creep, like rats in the night, to wire and mine and drag their own corpses back to their own muddy lines. John Bruce had seen it all before. Nothing had changed but the scenery. With the bemused rambling imagination of an exhausted mind he wondered how long they would be there, which small lumps and crags of the landscape would grow famous as snipers' points, which would carry odd names commemorating small events grown mythical with overextended time: Dead Leg Corner, Mule Alley, Sniper's Paradise; or familiar names to tease with memories of home: Academy Street, The Crown, Piccadilly, Rotten Row. Here they might well spend their winter, dreaming of Inverness, or London, or anywhere else in the world. Johnny sighed, and stood up, carrying his twenty years like eighty. There was a shattering loud drumroll of machine-gun fire, some hidden weapon brought up in the night, and Johnny Bruce, hit three times, whirled in a complete circle and dropped in a heap on the chalky ground.

Donnie Cameron, the shy little Inverness private, witnessed the whole thing from three feet away and for several seconds crouched behind the sandbags in stunned disbelief. Then with his pinched freckled face twisting with an emotion of alien power, he leapt up on to the parapet itself, in full view, and fired shot after shot in the direction of the machine-gunner, shouting and screaming abuse the while, until he'd emptied the magazine. Amazingly, he himself wasn't touched, and when he leapt down again to reload, he slipped to his knees, still dazed, and then slowly, forgetting his purpose, curled up in a ball, his rifle still clutched in his arms, and wept fiercely, his whole body shaking, and was still weeping when the stretcher-bearers came to take John Bruce away.

19

At the same dawn hour in which Johnny Bruce was carried from the new trenches on hill 70, his cousin Tenny Maclaren and his company of Inverness Pals were at last making their weary way in a ragged column of fours into the ruined village of Vermelles. They had had no proper food, nor fresh water, for two whole days.

The last two nights had been spent in forced marches, in rainy darkness, over foot-battering *pavé* roads packed with a confusion of men and vehicles, to advance from the too distant points of their encampments. For that matter, they had done little but march since their arrival in France a bare two weeks earlier, since they had crossed the entire distance to the Loos front on foot. Even their brief respites, like that at Bimont, had been marred by the ever-present need to search the countryside for the means of augmenting meagre rations. The occasional chicken, or basket of eggs or fruit thus gathered, did little to offset the energy spent when men should be resting. Now, with their cookers left behind, and each man labouring under the weight of pack, rifle, and greatcoat, all pretence of proper provisioning was abandoned. Extra iron and cheese rations, and a portion of cold pea soup, so salty that their meagre water ration was already sorely taxed, were their sole comforts.

Albert Maclaren, in spite of a brave face, was really suffering. Somehow, all through his life, at home at Culbrech, amongst his boisterous athletic family, or at school in those halls of hearty masochism to which 'for his own good' he had been sent, Albert had somehow managed to avoid the worst physical strains affronting his gentle, sensual, easy-going body. There were little dodges that always worked, at home, or on the playing field, little ploys that had always managed to get him somewhere warm, snug and comfortable, with a good fire, while others were indulging their delight in muscle-wrenching play. Even at the camp at Inverness, where his enthusiastic older brother had in record time turned weedy city lads and underfed crofters into fine examples of manhood, Albert had effected a few small escapes. He had done his share of square-bashing like the rest, but managed to twist an ankle once, and dislocate a shoulder later, and put himself temporarily out of action. He had emerged somewhat tougher than he went in, but it was not until reaching France that he finally came face to face with real, unrelenting, body-breaking physical hardship. There was no escape, on the miles of bitter French roads, and his pain was very real.

The pain of others was real as well. The *pavé* was narrow and bordered on either side with trampled mud, and the unfortunate man in either outside rank found himself hobbling along the broken edge, sometimes on stone, sometimes in the dirt, his swelling, boot-bound feet thudding blindly into the jagged edges of cobbles. Packs bore down on bent shoulders, straps chafing, and the fourteen pounds of a man's rifle became sometimes an unbearable load. Tenny Maclaren had long since abandoned his stumbling horse, the beast itself suffering from exhaustion, and loaded it instead with the packs and rifles of the stragglers of his flock.

Twice they were stopped by over-officious military police, demanding they spread out as if they were already in the front line. The request was ignored. There were other halts throughout the night, passes demanded, identification requested, and no proper traffic organization. No one would have imagined that the steadfast marchers were the desperately needed, already well overdue reinforcements of an army struggling in the field. The sense of urgency that impelled them forward, though written in their orders, was visibly denied by their treatment on every side.

But there *was* urgency, and when, with the misty dawn, the Inverness Pals finally tramped into Vermelles on the twenty-sixth of September, a body of men needing nothing so much as sleep and hot food, they were expected, within hours, to be at the Front.

Tenny Maclaren stood for a moment's rest beside the shell-battered walls of the village church. He had just completed the hopeless task of keeping his company intact through the night, after the almost unbelievable idiocy of the previous crossroads where they found themselves crossing directly through the path of a group of dismounted cavalry. He shivered in the dampness of the French dawn, unnerved by the chaos, memories of fabled military disasters passing through his mind. He wished he didn't read, didn't think, didn't do anything but eat, rut, and sleep, like half his men. Two of them sat in the street, back to back, knees drawn up, leaning on each other and sound asleep. Like patient animals. He was startled then to see that one of those simple men was his own brother James. The other, his young face smooth and untroubled, was the Glasgow miner, Pat McGarrity.

Pat was faring better than most. A man accustomed to a ten- or twelve-hour shift down the pit wasn't much bothered by a bit of a hike on a cobbled road. His feet were a bit sore, and his shoulders, and he could do with a good meal, but he'd gone hungry before this, more than once. The physical hardships really did not worry him. What *had* worried him, and worried him again in a nagging unpleasant way as soon as he awoke, was the confusion, the disorder, the uneasy feeling that his superiors did not know what they were doing. Pat had a mind every bit as sharp as Tenny Maclaren's and, born into Tenny's station, would have given him fair competition for a place at Oxford. The prime observation Pat made that night was simple: incompetence. All around him, but most of all, worst of all, above him. No competent leadership, be it army staff or mine management, would have allowed the chaos of the past two nights. Now, Pat was wondering, what other mistakes lay ahead? Being right square in the middle of their margin for error, he did not like to think. Pat McGarrity had been in France for two weeks of 1915, and already he'd made two firm conclusions. The army was cruel, unnecessarily cruel, and the army was at times a fool. Neither was a particularly acceptable thought for a soldier of the King.

Lieutenant-Colonel Douglas Fraser, like Pat, had also questioned those above him, silently, over the organization of the advance of the 24th Division. But as for what lay ahead, he had utmost confidence. The word from GHQ, when he was able to establish contact from Vermelles, was good. The German line was broken, and many of the first-day objectives had been met. There were some failures, but in the sector ahead of the Inverness Pals, all was supposed to have gone well, and the enemy front-line trenches were in British hands. To Douglas Fraser it was quite inconceivable that such green, untried units would be engaged in anything more than a most routine operation; and so when he was informed from above that the day would be a walkover, Douglas contentedly passed down the word to his company commanders and his men. It was a gullibility for which he would never forgive himself.

He mounted his horse and rode out of Vermelles, at the head of his battalion. His only concerns were his men, trusting and untried, and he prayed silently, as the tired horse plodded on, for a gentle blooding. The colonel dismounted at a crossroads beyond Vermelles. It was a place of incessant noise, as a battery of eighteen pounders was situated just behind it, in a sunken farm lane. They were shelling some distant point far beyond, probably the German reserve line, and although their missiles arched in high trajectories, far over their heads, the inexperienced men of the Inverness Pals ducked down into their collars, wincing with every thunderous blast.

Douglas called a halt there, conferring with his company commanders in the dim light, over their maps. Those they had lacked any real detail, and the points of reference that were to lead them into position were often simply not shown. Douglas Fraser and his second-in-command, Major Frank Grant, one of the several brothers of Colonel Paul Grant who currently led the Second Battalion, conferred at length, looking from the maps up to the confusion of the Loos landscape where the flickering light of shell-fire was giving way to the red light of morning behind the scattered pit towers and slag-heaps.

A group of transport officers, hurrying past with a laden ammunition wagon, shouted and waved their arms, pointing towards a white square nailed to the stump of a tree. Tenny Maclaren, attracted by the commotion, stepped towards the tree and read on a hand-painted sign:

Do Not Loiter on This Corner As It Is Being
Constantly Shelled

'You're on Suicide Corner, mates,' a voice called from the

transport wagon. 'Move yer arses before old Jerry moves 'em for you.' The speaker, mindless of military proprieties, rapidly disappeared up the road. A moment later the whining descent of a shell whistled down out of the grey sky, impacting fully on the general service wagon, its load of ammunition going up in a fearsome double explosion, casting men and mules into the air in full view of the terrified young soldiers. The Boche artillery had, quite ironically, missed 'Suicide Corner' for once, if only by a hundred yards, sending their benefactor into eternity and granting the Maclarens a brief reprieve.

'Did ye see thot?' one of them whispered in an awed, trembling voice.

'Are they dead?' James Maclaren said.

'I dinnae think they're juist pretending,' Pat McGarrity replied grimly. He was looking down at the ground where an oddly frothy piece of shining pink-and-red flesh lay yet quivering with instantly ended life. He did not even know if it was man or mule.

'Oh God,' James cried out, sickened, seeing it, but Pat just looked carefully, the image settling forever in his mind. As the men passed, unavoidably, the mutilated bodies by the splintered remains of the wagon, one young soldier asked, as if the innocent voice of his whole honourable age, 'Should we not bury them, sir?'

There was no answer, and as they moved on, he and others of these well-brought-up young men gradually absorbed the taste of the new world they were entering. Jimmy Fraser, the postman's son, searched for understanding in his mind and could fix only on the one other death with which he had been familiar, that of his grandmother, laid out in best black dress and white linen mutch in her coffin in the Best Room, the picture of Highland propriety. He shook his head and closed his eyes, stepping over the severed leg of a mule and sliding, on skidding boots, in a slaughterhouse mixture of bloods.

By the time, two hours later, that the Fourth Battalion took their allotted places in the front-line trench facing the village of Hulluch, they were already, in a small degree, hardened to such sights. They had worked their way up through the old front lines, crossing trenches by wooden plank bridges, finding paths through the old barricades of wire. Everywhere, the debris of yesterday's fighting lay scattered, torn tangles of wire, shell-shattered duckboards, abandoned weapons, remnants of blown-up wagons and gun limbers, and once, a great novelty, the burnt wreckage of a German observation aeroplane.

It was the wounded who most distressed the fledgling soldiers. The dead, after the first few dozen, were always rather alike. Unless one made the mistake of looking too closely, they blended uniformly into rag-doll heaps of cloth, bloodstains already blackening into mere dirty smudges. But the wounded, lying in full view in open misery, calling out for water or help or moaning with frantic pain, their wet sodden clothing testimony to the hours they had lain so, defeated every attempt at detachment. The men knew their orders; they knew they could do nothing, had other purposes, must of all things move forward. They knew that help was coming, and coming as fast as heroically exhausted ambulancemen, stretcher-bearers and medical officers could possibly manage.

'Jeeze,' Jimmy Fraser muttered still, 'I'd nae leave a sheep on the hill, like yon.'

They were crossing the last of their old trenches. Ahead lay the old no-man's-land and, if Tenny's maps were right, the line they must take. The mist of the rainy morning was breaking, quite suddenly, and as suddenly the sun came out, shining down on the strangely resilient cornfield before them where dead men lay like stones in the yellow, poppy-strewn grasses. Through the mist, a party of stretcher-bearers came, hugging the protection of an old road-bed, looking to Tenny like a mystical procession of ancient priests.

The Fourth Battalion reached their final assembly point, a captured line of German trench, at nine in the morning. They entered by a recently dug and sandbagged communication trench that extended backwards from the main trench into their own safe territory, so that, as always, the front line was reached below the level of the ground. A party of Gurkhas were leaving the trench, as they, the relief, approached, and the Highlanders stared wide-eyed at their dark-haired, dark-skinned forms as they passed. Many of them, having never travelled any distance from their remote homeland, had never seen a single man of a different colour, much less a whole regiment.

'Darkies,' one whispered, amazed.

'Are they wi' us or agin' us?' asked another.

'They're nae shootin' at ye, man, sae I suppose they must be wi' us,' said a third. Awestruck, they went on and into the trench itself.

At once Tenny set about posting sentries, and detailing small groups to find, and maintain, observation points on the small grassy ridge ahead of them, which should overlook the village of Hulluch. Hulluch had been reported to be in British hands, and the news from the CO that it was not, after all, was the first, uneasy sign that all was not as it should be.

Pondering that, he checked with his sergeant that their ammunition and supply of grenades was in order. The welcome arrival of the transport with dixies of hot food, brought up from their lagging cookers, was at least able to ensure that his company of men went into battle reasonably well-fed. Shortly after the food arrived, Douglas Fraser informed his company commanders that they would advance, with the Royal West Kents on their left and the East Surreys on their right, at eleven o'clock.

Almost immediately the barrage began, a scattering of shells from the meagre artillery support, without the benefit of their own divisional artillery, not yet in position. It all petered out after twenty minutes, and silence came down on the Front.

At eleven, exactly, the order came. Tenny rose up in the chalk trench, and blew his whistle, and primed with the perfect obedience of those weeks and weeks of square-bashing in the Northern Meeting Park, his two hundred and forty men rose as one, climbed from their shelter and went out into no-man's land.

They went walking. They went in extended order, in a long, perfect line, perfectly spaced. They went with full equipment, and packs on their backs, standing upright, each keeping his place. They went in broad daylight, with no artillery cover, where the day before experienced regulars had gone shielded by gas and smoke, in darkness, preceded by tremendous shell-fire, and been broken.

The shells began to fall, and the first casualties fell with them, and not a man of them wavered. Behind them, the second wave, with the remaining two companies of the Inverness Pals moved out, at four hundred yards' distance, and on either side of them, the second wave of Royal West Kents and East Surreys went too.

They crossed the Lens-Hulluch road, in the same splendid order, and the German shelling and rifle-fire and machine-guns began in earnest. They went on. The fire intensified as they approached Hulluch from the fortified houses of the village and from a flanking trench. Along the line gaps appeared as men began to fall. Tenny Maclaren ran out in front, half turning his back to the enemy, calling his men forward with voice and gestures of the hand. 'C'mon chaps, c'mon. Let's get at them now. This is it now,' the words came by rote, and he was hardly conscious of speaking them, just as he was only dimly aware that he was, for the first time, under fire. The imperative of leadership cancelled all other emotions. Bullets spattered at his feet, with a personal directness, and with the same distant consciousness he was aware of snipers somewhere, seeking out the officers. He realized soon that they were in the trees, by the road, but made no attempt to make himself any less obvious. Out in front, the colonel was even more obvious, signalling them forward with white-gloved hands. Miraculously he had not yet been hit, and the foolhardy courage reflected back to the ranks of following men. Jimmy Fraser advanced, trance-like, foot stepping after foot to the rhythm of the guns, his eyes seeing nothing but the colonel's white gloves.

Corporal Pat McGarrity had begun the advance just one place from Jimmy Fraser but now had drawn apart from him, and, oblivious of all around him, was striding towards his own objective, a winding-tower above the shaft labelled *Puits 13* on their maps. It had an hypnotic effect on him, almost as if it were, with its echoes of Glasgow, a personal talisman. He glanced about for the men of his section, suddenly aware of his position of leadership, but could see only three. He looked about wildly. Should he go back and look for them? For a moment he paused, but the impetus of the great crumbling line carried him forward. 'C'mon men,' he muttered, almost inaudibly, in echo of the lieutenant. 'C'mon youse.'

Albert Maclaren had begun the advance following his platoon officer, Second Lieutenant Farquharson. When Farquharson was killed he searched the remaining line and fastened his faithful eye on the platoon sergeant, a man called MacGillveray. When MacGillveray was obliterated by a direct hit, he sought out his corporal, Pat McGarrity, terrified that something might befall the little Glasgow Irishman and leave Albert as captain of his own soul. It was the one thing he feared most; to be left in that unreal hell, alone. He'd chosen a good lead to follow that day, because Pat, ducked down low as if once more in the back-breaking tunnels of coal, was rapidly becoming one of nature's survivors.

He was one of the few men to break the line and duck, from time to time, into a shell-hole, moving forward now in bursts of uneven, weaving speed from shelter to shelter. It was not the way he'd been told to do the thing, but his quick mind had rapidly assessed, in those early minutes, that the thing was not going as planned. 'Deil tak' the hindmost,' he whispered, dropping down again for shelter. 'We're a' for it.'

Albert followed him into his shell-hole, lying flat, panting, his still slightly pudgy body sweating heavily. 'Where now?' he cried, on the edge of panic.

'Over yon,' Pat said, gesturing to the remnants of a farmyard, where three large dung-heaps beside a low brick wall promised shelter. 'An' then forrard, awa' tae the right a bittie. It's yon trench,' he pointed over Albert's ducked head, 'causin' a' the trouble.' Another man, seeing them sheltering, joined them, and Pat felt grown upon him suddenly the desire to lead. 'Come awa', nou,' he said gently. 'We'll mak' it fine. Nae bother.' He set out for the dung-heaps, his two men in tow.

They advanced through the farmyard, passing several dead Cameron Highlanders, remnants of yesterday's battle. One man was propped against a broken wall and appeared as dead as the others, but as they approached he waved a weak, flapping hand, and croaked out, 'Go back, go back,' and as if that last effort had taken his last breath, toppled over, into the byre mud.

'Oh God,' Albert said. 'What do we do?'

'Naethin',' Pat said.

'He was still alive, and look,' he pointed, mouth open, to where another man lay, his rifle jammed bayonet-first into the ground beside him, left as a signal by some comrade.

'Stretcher-bearers,' the man called, twice, raising himself on an elbow, and then fell back. They had lain there since the day before, and, having cried the same word all night, he had long since lost any real hope.

'They'll die,' Albert said.

'Sae will we. Sae will everybody, some day. Move it, sodger,' Pat sounded quite gruff, and Albert Maclaren, whose father commanded an entire brigade, acquiesced quite willingly to the command of the Glasgow miner. Pat again found the winding-tower of *Puits 13* on the horizon and set out with his men towards his landmark.

The wood called 'Bois Hugo' lay on their right, and as they

neared it, they came under fire from that source as well, and Pat could see the depleted ranks of the East Surreys falling in droves. He veered to the left, advancing steadily towards the German second line. Albert followed. He could not get from his befuddled mind the conviction that it was all still a practice, and the dead would, like practice dead, rise up and go home to tea. He thought suddenly of Tenny and James. James. Where was he? He was supposed to look after James. He'd promised Mother, and in all the noise and terror, he'd forgotten. He plucked at Pat's sleeve and Pat shoved him angrily aside, forcing him to keep a safe distance.

'Where's my brother?' he cried.

'In Berlin, ye birk, haein' tea wi' the Kaiser.'

Albert stumbled on, and the other man with them screamed and fell. The German second line reared up before them, thick with wire.

A hundred yards to the left, Tenny Maclaren saw it too. He stopped in his tracks, his face whitening. 'Good Christ,' he whispered, stunned. 'They said it was clear.'

It had been, of course, at four o'clock the day before, the day of the first attack, but today they were facing not a fragile reserve line but a full-scale fortification, the result of the work of that terribly wasted night.

'Wire-cutters,' Tenny shouted, reaching for his own. He plunged forward, under the hail of fire, towards the forest of tangled steel. Around him his men were scuttling back and forth along the Front, looking for weak spots, like rabbits trapped in a burning thicket. Some flung themselves frantically upon it, clawing at it with bare hands. He saw wee Jimmy Fraser, the postmaster's son, racing back and forth in a panic, crying out loud, 'Oh Mam, oh Mam, oh Mam,' until a burst of machine-gun fire sliced across his middle, cutting his small familiar body nearly in half. Tenny gasped, mindlessly shocked for only an instant, and then was rallying his men, and attacking the uncut wire with cutters and their few grenades. Neither had much effect, and the carnage was unceasing.

They drew back, sheltered in shell-holes, tried again, and tried again. They tried five times in all, until, leaving mounds of their dead and wounded before the awful barricade, they began, at last, to retreat. Tenny turned once, as they went, looking over his shoulder. The wire was festooned with hanging, twitching bodies, and on their parapets the Germans were standing in clear sight, rifles ready, but not firing. They watched in silence as if they, too, had seen enough.

With a handful of men, Tenny Maclaren walked, upright, in one last long extended line, to the Lens-Hulluch road; they crossed it now unmolested, and moved back to the trenches from which they had come. Tenny thought of his company of farmers and clerks and labourers, who he had turned, in the Invernessian summer, into a fighting force, and who, in the space of two hours had been utterly destroyed. For them, those strangers, more than for friend and family, he felt the hot pressure of tears against his dust-caked eyelids and he rubbed his trembling mouth with the back of his wire-torn bloodstained hand.

At the side of the Lens-Hulluch road, where they stopped, sheltering in the trees now clear of snipers, Tenny caught sight of a familiar form walking alone towards his little group. It was a young boy, red-headed, his bonnet gone, his kilt torn in several places, his pack shredded and his rifle missing, but the boy himself was unhurt. He walked straight up to Tenny and saluted with sharp precision. It was James. His face was so white that the freckles stood out as if painted on, and his once bright blue eyes were bloodshot and darkened. Whatever private battle he had fought that day, whatever he had seen, Tenny would never learn, for James never discussed it.

He said only, 'I got through the wire, sir, but I was alone, and I felt I should be taken prisoner if I remained. I hope I did my duty, sir, there seemed no other course.'

Tenny stood silently amazed. He yearned to throw his arms about the boy and embrace him, but even had the situation allowed, the new agedness in James's eyes forbade it. He said only, 'Well played, Maclaren. Only sorry the rest of us weren't with you.' He was about to dismiss the boy, and then said gently, 'I'm afraid your pal Jimmy's gone West.'

James nodded slowly, so that Tenny was uncertain if he had seen Jimmy's end himself or not. 'Have you seen Albert?' James asked. Tenny shook his head. 'He could be anywhere,' he said.

They separated then, and continued to retreat. By evening they were once more in the trenches they had left that morning. In their sector at least, precisely nothing had been gained. They had lost over half the battalion and three-quarters of their officers.

When Tenny Maclaren reported to his commanding officer, he found Douglas Fraser alone in the solid German dugout, sitting upright on one of the wooden bunks, staring at the chalky wall, his sick old face streaming with tears.

He saluted and got no response, the man seemed entranced, and out of decency Tenny left and went out in the open trench. Overhead the sky was streaked with pink, and the men were busy preparing their defences for what counterattack might come. Tenny sought his company sergeant major, learned that he was dead, and then sought one after another of his NCOs, until he found at last the little Glaswegian, McGarrity.

'Corporal, we'll call the roll.'

'Willna tak' lang, sir,' McGarrity said coolly.

Tenny was taken aback and about to make reprimand, but only shook his head. You couldn't pillory a man for speaking the truth. Together with Pat McGarrity, while the stretcher-bearers plied their weary trade, he went up and down his section of trench, counting the cost. At the end, he sat down on the firestep and leaned his red head against the muddy wall. He had found no sign of his second brother, Albert, nor heard a word of his fate. His dry parched mouth twisted into a grimace of remembrance of all the day, and he whispered softly,

> 'Come brother, let us to the highest of the field,
> To see what friends are living, who are dead.'

'Sir?' said Corporal McGarrity, but the lieutenant made no reply, and regarding himself dismissed he wandered off in search of James Maclaren with whom he shared the stale remnants of a tin of bully beef.

Book II

1

'Pardon, is this London?'

The ambulance-driver swung round in surprise. His eyes swept the dim row of bodies packed stretcher by stretcher on the floor to the shadowy edges of the tented ward. Had one of them actually spoken? He was about to dismiss it, an imagining of his exhausted mind, when the voice came again, surprisingly strong, 'I say, man, *is* this London. I must get out at London.' No. That was real. If the place wasn't so hellish, he might have smiled. The voice had all the peevish impatience of a London bank clerk who'd slept through his station. He looked down. The man who had spoken was so caked with blood and chalk mud that his age, his hair colour, his facial features were all unfathomable. He was from one of the Scottish regiments; the kilt, what remained of it, said that. The tartan, in the uncertain light of kerosene lamps, flaring to brightness as gusts of wind penetrated the canvas shelter, was indeterminate.

'Take it easy, pal,' the ambulance-driver said, his big bulky body bent over the wounded soldier. It was all he could say. He didn't even add anything about help, or doctors or nurses, because he knew better. If the man asked, he'd lie, all right, but he'd not volunteer it. He straightened up, slowly. He was quite a tall man, tall enough to need to duck beneath the canvas to attend men at the perimeters of the ward, but his ponderous weight, the generous fold of belly over belt-buckle, made breadth, rather than height, his most noticeable feature. His was the body of a hedonist, he'd be the first to admit it, and to admit the irony of so pleasure-loving an individual finding himself in such pleasureless surroundings.

He had been four months with the Royal Army Medical Corps ambulance squad and this, the aftermath of Loos, was beyond question the worst he'd seen.

'Damned compartment, too damned crowded to move,' said the soldier, in a cultured, officer's voice. Scottie turned, with renewed interest. The man was flailing feebly out from side to side, his hand touching another still body each time. Those others just lay like the death they were approaching, without even a moan. The kiltie was a fighter, anyhow. Crazy as a bedbug, but a fighter. He opened his eyes wider and caught the ambulance-driver's glance. 'Do tell when we get to London, old man. Got to meet my aunt.'

The driver studied him, bemused. Man should know he was dying, for Christ's sake, and not go babbling on about railroad trains. He paused, and then, just as he was again about to leave, he caught sight of a shadowy figure moving slowly among the rows and rows of moaning, whimpering men, realizing with faint surprise that it was a doctor. Not many came here.

It was not out of heartlessness that the moribund ward was shunned, far from it, but out of sheer hopelessness. The numbers were too great. Even working twenty hours of every day in the surgical tents, the desperately overpressed medical officers couldn't manage them all. It was impossible, humanly impossible. So there must be some selection, some weeding-out of those with the fraction of a chance from those with no chance at all.

The latecomers were laid out beyond the ward in the open field, in the rain and wind. He thought of it as a kind of brutal mercy, like the custom in the place of his childhood of lifting the dying from the comfort of bed and laying them on the cold board floor, to ease and hasten their passage.

'Hey doc,' the ambulance-driver called from across the dark rows. The doctor looked up, recognizing the bulk, if not the face, of Scottie the Yank. He picked his way through the stretchers until he could hear over the distant thunder of the continuing barrage, seven miles beyond the Casualty Clearing Station, at the Front. He glanced down at the man at Scottie's feet, and raised his flickering candle. 'I think this one's worth a try,' Scottie said.

'Talking a blue streak, anyhow. Thinks he's in London.' A sudden gust of wind caught the candle and snuffed it out. Scottie turned to leave, having done all he could.

Behind him, Lieutenant John Bruce was carried out of the place of certain death into one of only probable death, convinced the while he was on a train to London.

The disaster at Loos was a wayward fowl, taking its time to come home to roost. Initial newspaper reports, gleaned from official statements, reflected initial optimism, an optimism held by all but those directly in the field, that the battle was going well. Even in the field, the same appeared so, at times. Objectives were being achieved; on paper things went well. The casualties were not, at first, on paper.

Soon enough, the long lists came rolling in, and close on their heels, the hospital trains. In the wards of the First London General, Rebecca Galloway saw how the battle had gone. On the first of October, at nine in the evening, as she stumbled into the hostel at the end of a full day nursing the wounded of Loos, Rebecca's eyes, glancing to the noticeboard at the stairfoot, found what they had each day dreaded. Her name was printed in large black letters on the outside of a pale blue envelope. It was unsealed, having been delivered by hand, no doubt by Naomi's chauffeur. She opened it with shaking fingers, mindless of their sores and cuts. The message was the one she feared most.

My car will meet you at ten.
Naomi

She did not stop to change, to wash, for anything. She did not even go upstairs where Susan, who had had the day off, might perhaps be waiting. She did not even leave a message. She stood on the rainswept stone doorstep of the hostel for the half-hour, until Naomi's car, with Abbott at the wheel, arrived. She got in the back without speaking, unable now to hold back streams of exhausted tears.

Abbott opened the car door for her outside the portico of Naomi's house, and held his large black umbrella for her to shelter under for the few short steps to the door. She ignored it and him, and the old man stood back sadly, watching her small thin back. He had taken the message to the hostel himself, in the afternoon, and suspected what it was about. The door swung inwards, letting golden light out briefly on to the wet pavement, and then, with Rebecca inside, swung closed.

Naomi was waiting for her in the drawing-room, alone, seated by the fire in the green high-backed chair, her hands on her knees and her whole body quite still.

'Mother telephoned this afternoon.'

'Tenny's dead, isn't he?' Rebecca whispered.

'Tenny? Good God. Of course not. Why would Mother be telephoning about Tenny? Surely Victoria . . . the telegram, I mean.'

For the first time in all the time she'd known her, Rebecca was aware of Naomi flustered. Her relief over Tenny flowed in like a tide, and like a tide receded. 'Oh my God,' she said. 'It can't be. Oh, surely he'd never . . .'

'No one's dead, dear. Johnny's had rather a bad scrape, that's all.'

Rebecca sat down slowly, her hand at her mouth. She was no longer crying. Her face was quite white. Eventually she said only, 'He said he'd keep his head down.' Then she looked up, plucking at Naomi's sleeve. 'Don't you recall, at dinner, he said . . .'

'He's in Rouen, now,' Naomi said smoothly. 'Emma tried to get away to see him, from Le Havre. But of course they wouldn't let her. Her letter came, just after the telegram. You'd think they could have been quicker. It's been days apparently. Things seem a terrible mess.' Naomi's voice ran on smoothly, scraping normality back into the evening. 'I think we'll have some tea, dear,' she added.

Rebecca looked up, her eyes widening. 'Where was he hit?' she cried suddenly. Would he come home a stumped, crawling, disfigured creature like the man whose torso, limbless but for one remaining arm, she had bathed this afternoon?

'Dear child, they don't tell such things in a telegram. We'll have to wait and see. Perhaps Emma will get word. At least he's alive, my dear. And Tenny, apparently, and the others. At least there's been no word.'

She rang for tea and was about to suggest that Rebecca go upstairs first and bath, when the girl looked up, with the same disjointed confusion, and cried, 'Oh dear, what of Susan? I didn't even check to see if she was in.'

'No,' Naomi said, her mouth grim again. 'I'm afraid Susan is yet to learn. She had an appointment with Mr Leitner at his studio, and the old dear promised her dinner. She's due back here shortly. I'm afraid she's a hard homecoming ahead of her. I thought you'd be able to help.'

Rebecca nodded again, still numb. She was experiencing the first truly adult emotions of her life. 'He knew,' she said dully. 'He knew. In his letter. He knew. I thought he was joking. You know how he is. But he wasn't.' She paused, straightening in her chair. 'I must go to France,' she said, in a firm strong voice.

Naomi looked up, her eyes widening with amazement. Before she could speak, the door burst open and Susan Bruce ran giggling into their midst. Her cheeks were flushed, from the wet cold night, and a little from wine. Her bright blue eyes sparkled bluer under her tiny violet hat. Her blond hair, elaborately dressed, glistened gaily. 'Oh darlings,' she cried, 'I've had the most marvellous day.'

It was past midnight when Susan and Rebecca returned to their hostel. They sat in the back of Naomi's car, holding hands, silent, as Abbott drove them back through the dark wet streets. Naomi had implored them to stay, but the girls knew that an early shift awaited them, and Matron's sympathy would not extend to allowing them time off. Other girls had their own worries and tragedies. Only last week Miriam Beveridge had appeared one morning with great puffy rings about her eyes and worked throughout the day with set mouth and trembling hands, which would stop, just occasionally, to forlornly caress her engagement ring. Rebecca had avoided her, not knowing what to say, having neither experience, engagement nor bereavement, to share with her. Now, suddenly, she was tipped into a new world. 'Really,' she whispered, weakly, 'we're lucky. At least he's still alive. Perhaps not even that bad.'

They had to ring the bell to be allowed in, and wait interminably until a disapproving nursing sister opened the door. She only nodded curtly to Rebecca's babbled explanation about Naomi, and Susan's brother wounded in France. Once the door shut behind them, the sister turned about, her heavy maroon dressing-gown snugged around her, and left them without a word.

Once in their room they undressed and climbed together into one bed, without bothering with the cold grate. 'Oh God,'

Rebecca moaned as she sat up briefly to wind the clock. 'We've five hours.'

Yet when they lay down together, neither could sleep.

'I wish Emma was here,' Susan said, sniffling a little. 'Emma always made me feel brave.' They both missed her, and since her place in the room they shared had not yet been filled, they had her empty bed to remind them of her absence. Susan's bed was usually empty as well; they had taken to sharing Rebecca's which was a fraction wider, to combat the unbearable cold.

'Oh damn, it's so beastly unfair,' Rebecca moaned. 'If only I had got to France, too. I could be with him now.' She thought with envy of Emma, forgetting temporarily that official rules, of which there were a multitude to govern the lives of poor VADs, had barred Emma, too, as effectively as the Channel. She felt, as they all felt, that once across that terrible watery divide, she was virtually in the arms of her love. Ironically, Rebecca was the sole reason Emma was in France at all.

They had gone together for their interview in August, having sent in their applications for overseas service simultaneously. Rebecca had been first, and she lasted barely a half-minute. She had entered a room, containing a desk and a single bare wooden chair, where she was told to be seated by a stern, portly woman in Red Cross uniform. The woman said, without looking up, 'And you are twenty-three years old, Miss Galloway?'

Rebecca said, 'Yes,' in a hasty, squeaky voice. Twenty-three was the minimum age for service abroad as everyone knew. One had no choice but to be twenty-three.

'What year were you born?'

'Pardon?'

'The year, Miss Galloway. What year were you born?' The sharp blue eyes came up and in Rebecca's momentary wild confusion read all they needed to know. By the time, counting back, she'd found the year, she was being ushered out of the door.

The door closed behind her discreetly for a moment, no doubt so that Matron could resume her fearsome presence behind the desk in time for the next entry. The next applicant was Emma Maclaren, and Rebecca swallowed her tears as she brushed shoulder by shoulder with Emma and whispered, 'Eighteen-ninety-two.'

'Whatever?' Emma looked startled.

But the voice behind the door called, 'Next please?' and she, still puzzling, went into the tiny forbidding office. When the question came, the puzzle was solved. Smoothly she spoke the appropriate new year of her birth, and then paused ever so slightly to add, with a smile, 'Of course.'

So Emma got to France, and Rebecca returned in defeat to the First London General and her poky shared room with Susan.

'At least you tried,' Susan said. She was whimpering openly, shivering with remorse and the cold. Then she burst out suddenly, 'Oh Rebecca, I'm so ashamed. I'm such a coward. Such a terrible, foolish, frivolous coward. All this week, while the boys have been fighting and being hurt . . . and dying even, all I've thought about is Mr Leitner and his foolish camera, and my own foolish face.' She buried that face against the flannel of Rebecca's nightgown.

Rebecca patted Susan's loose hair in the darkness and whispered, comfortingly, 'Don't be so harsh on yourself, darling. Of course it was exciting. And it *is* important too. Morale is as important as anything.'

'Oh rubbish,' Susan cried. 'It's all nonsense anyhow. Me all posed like an angel with some tea-towel thing on my head trailing halfway to my knees like a nun. And my hair loose. Can you imagine what Matron would say if she saw even *one* hair loose, much less the whole lot?'

Rebecca felt sorry for Susan because the chance to pose for Mr Leitner's series of patriotic postcards had come, naturally, first to herself and, determined then to go to France, she had passed the offer on to Susan. Susan forgot all about France in her delight. Her delicate fair features became Our Sweetheart, the VAD, pinned to trench supports and dugout walls up and down the Front, and an odd little flutter of anonymous fame came with it.

'You know,' Rebecca said, 'he gets letters all the time from the soldiers, sending their love to the postcard girls, asking marriage. I mean, it does *mean* something.'

Susan was so quiet Rebecca thought her asleep. 'All it means,' she said then, her voice alien and hard, 'is that all my life I've been frivolous and vain and thought of no one but myself. My brother is in France, suffering. I could have been there. I *should* have been there.'

'How could you know?' Rebecca said earnestly. 'You're only young,' she spoke as if she were, herself, much older. 'You have a right to be a little vain, and pretty, and foolish even. We all do,' she cried suddenly, bitterly, and repeated, 'We have a right,' again because she knew suddenly that, right or not, it was no longer relevant. Their pretty, harmless youth was already gone. There was no more time left to play.

In the morning, as they rose in the gloom with autumn rain slashing against the window, streaming down inside the one cracked pane, Rebecca said, 'I shall ask Matron for my leave. When your grandmother goes to France to see Johnny, I will go as well.'

Susan watched, her eyes wide, as Rebecca dressed with brisk determination. At last she said in a small, uncertain voice, 'But Becky, you're not even engaged.'

2

Victoria Maclaren stood a long time in silence before the tall windows of the drawing-room of Culbrech House, looking down, upon the green lawns, wet still with heavy October dew. The running of Culbrech estate had fallen more and more heavily upon her shoulders throughout the year. As time passed she became increasingly adept at it, which was as well, since new activities had arisen requiring new forms of management. Forestry was the chief of these; the trenches and their endless miles of wooden shorings were devouring timber at a tremendous rate. Forests and vital windbreaks were falling all over the North, and Culbrech was providing its share. On his visits home – rare since Victoria generally met him in London whenever he had leave – Ian Maclaren authorized which of the dark green acres should fall to the axe. But the rest, the hiring of lumbering teams, the shipping of cut wood to the sawmills, was Victoria's concern. She was sorely tempted to employ Harry Bruce's good business mind, surely wasted at his gardening, but was loath to thus offend Grisel and Gordon whose bitterness towards his pacifist nephew only increased with time. She looked down now, below the window, on his tall, rangy figure bent over the yellowing leaves of a standard rose. He was so patient, like an old man, with everything around him; roses, workmen, belligerent citizens, Philippa, most of all Philippa, whose sharpening tongue drew nothing from him but a wry ironic smile. 'As if the whole war was their personal battleground,' Victoria whispered to herself aloud.

Then she shook her head and reopened her diary. Should she see Philippa first, or Maud Bruce, who would be arriving within minutes? Victoria tapped the blotter gently with a dry pen-nib. She had lain awake most of the night, last night, re-reading Ian Maclaren's long, beautifully hand-scripted letter. She had never read anything like it, with its patient listing of dead friend after dead friend, its monotone description of disaster. He had obviously written it at a time of brutal reflection, for nothing of his usual vigorous optimism sounded in it. The letter had shaken her, his tone as much as the news within it. She folded it so that the small passage about John Bruce was uppermost, and awaited Maud's arrival.

There was a light tap on the door and Angusina entered, and announced, 'Mrs Bruce, ma'am.'

'I'll see her here, please,' Victoria said, her eyes distracted slightly by Angusina's waistline. The girl's apron was tied rather high, and the front of her skirt seemed lifted a surprising inch or two above her ankles. She said quickly, for the girl, conscious perhaps of scrutiny, seemed about to flee, 'Angusina.'

'Ma'am?'

'Has Sandy had leave recently.'

'Not since June, ma'am.' Victoria counted quickly in her head.

'Perhaps he'll be home at Christmas, Angusina.'

'I dinna ken, ma'am.' The girl was still standing half turned away in the doorway and Victoria, used to assessing female figures since this latest pregnancy of Grisel's that they all watched with fearful attention, her mind made up, said,

'Yes. I think he'll be home at Christmas.' She made a mental note to write to Gordon Bruce. The man must be due for leave anyhow, and, she thought, watching a definitely thickening Angusina disappear down the corridor, Christmas would be by no means too soon. She smiled slightly.

Maud Bruce entered then, and said, 'Before I forget, Grisel was on the telephone this morning, positively exuding good health. Says she's eating like two horses and has never felt better. Gordon's due home next week, on leave, and she's naturally thrilled to bits. I believe he's to stop off at Rouen on his way, and see Johnny, too.' Her face changed subtly as she spoke the last, as if the determined good cheer was a delicate mask, likely to crumble.

Victoria stood quickly and thrust the letter in her hands, saying, 'Here, now. Read that. Ian saw him two days ago, and says he's getting along fine.'

Maud clutched the letter in suddenly trembling hands, her wrinkled old mouth pursed up with concentration. Victoria rang for coffee, and turned, looking at the old lady, fumbling now with her reading-glasses and peering at the delicate script.

'Has Naomi told you?' said Maud, when she had finished reading the letter.

'Told me what?'

'About Miss Galloway.'

'No,' Victoria said slowly, as if she hadn't heard this news. 'What is it about Miss Galloway?'

Maud settled on the settee with a wince at the bending of her arthritic knees. 'It appears,' she said slowly, dragging out a pointed amazement, 'that Miss Galloway intends to accompany me to France.' Her delicate brows lifted as if that were further comment enough and she waited for Victoria's reply.

'Oh, has she got leave then?'

'Who knows,' Maud said sharply, then added, 'Of course she has got leave. That's not the point.'

'But Miss Galloway will make an excellent travelling companion, I am sure,' said Victoria.

'Fiddle-faddle.'

'Pardon?'

'Oh, please, stop being such an intolerable Puss-in-Boots, tiptoeing all around it. Miss Galloway is not going to France to be an old lady's travelling companion. She is going to France specifically to see my young grandson with whom she has absolutely no public understanding at all. It is simply not done.'

'Perhaps,' Victoria said softly, 'she simply cares for the young man and wishes to comfort him in his distress.'

'More fiddle-faddle. I know young girls. Let them get a man flat on his back in bed and they can twist him round their little fingers. And they do know it. All these VADs. Shameless the lot of them. Sitting on officers' beds, holding hands, half of them married men, as well. Shameless.'

'Maud, please,' Victoria whispered. 'I assure you, Emma . . . and what about Susan, your own granddaughter. Surely you'd not say such things of her.'

Maud sniffed. 'Susan is simply a child. A child doing woman's work. And Emma, well, Emma *is* engaged, and no doubt thinks of nothing but her Torquil. But this Rebecca Galloway . . .' she started in again.

'I think she's a very kind girl,' Victoria placated.

'Oh do you. And would you think the same if it were your son she was dashing off to visit in France?'

There was silence. Maud had hit right on the central truth of it; the whole reason why she was herself wildly disturbed and, conversely, why Victoria was so happily calm. Victoria paused a very long while, composing herself, and said at last, 'My son, thank God, is not lying ill in a hospital in France. If he was, I assure you I would be most happy if the company of a pleasant young woman, of whom he was fond, were offered him. I would be happy for anything that would give him pleasure.'

'Including marriage to Rebecca Galloway?'

Victoria drew in her breath, 'Such a possibility has not arisen.'

'Oh yes it has,' Maud said sharply. 'I've watched you, for over a year, whenever those two were together, watching like a jealous mother hen. Oh no, she wasn't to have your son. Not Tenny Maclaren, heir to Culbrech. Oh no. But my grandson will do, no doubt. Two birds with one stone. Ruin his chances so he won't inherit the regiment, and safeguard Tenny from an utterly *unsuitable marriage*.' She paused for breath, her old blue eyes bright with indignation. 'Because that, we both know, is what it is.'

'I don't know what you're on about.' Victoria was increasingly flustered, as much of what Maud said was so close to the truth. 'Unsuitable? What's unsuitable? She's a perfectly pleasant young woman. Her uncle is a decent, educated man . . .'

'Uncle be damned,' Maud sniffed. 'Her mother was an Irish whore.'

Victoria went silent, and turned away. 'So you know,' she said, at last.

'It's no secret. Half London knows. And don't tell me you didn't do your own little bit of investigating.'

'Of course one does wish to know one's children's friends' antecedents.' And before Maud could say anything, Victoria added shrewdly, 'But, my dear, your own daughter sees fit to give the girl every entrée to her own society. Surely that says something?'

'Don't throw my daughter up to me at a time like this.'

'My dear Maud, I hardly . . .'

'Oh enough,' Maud rose, brushing down her dress. 'I should have known I'd get nothing but sanctimony from you. Victoria Maclaren, the perfect Scottish wife. I know what you think of me, of us, all the Bruces. Oh surely, we're all the best of friends, just like family. Only we're never going to admit that we *are* family, are we? Oh no. We've all our places, and we all keep them, and that way, we're all happy. Only this time, Victoria, I'm not happy. I'm an old lady, but I've never forgotten what Maclaren pride took from me. I was born to better state than you ever were, I assure you. And I ended married to a croft-wife's bastard. Oh, I've paid for my nonexistent sin a hundred-fold. And so has my daughter. You're not to have payment from my grandson as well. Good-day, Victoria, I'll see myself out.'

'Maud . . .' Victoria whispered, but the old lady had turned her frail straight back and limped now, cane in hand, out through the drawing-room door.

Victoria was still standing by the escritoire, a tired hand pressed to her forehead, wincing at Maud's words, when she heard Angusina's light tap at the door, followed almost immediately by Philippa's voice out in the corridor.

'Oh coffee, jolly splendid. Do bring another cup, Angusina, I'll be joining the company.' She strode through the door behind the maid, glancing around the room, empty now but for her mother. 'Oh, thought you had Maud Bruce here. Quite sure I saw her car.'

'You did. I'm afraid she was rather in a hurry.'

Philippa shrugged, as always only half listening to any conversation that did not directly involve either herself or the war. 'Pity, but never mind. I'll have her cup. That will be all, Angusina.'

Angusina hovered, uncertain whether to accept the dismissal of this Maclaren daughter who seemed always to override her elders with impunity. Victoria, grateful for the loyal hesitance, turned directly to the girl and said, 'Thank you, Angusina,' and she, with a small bob, left.

Philippa's eyes followed her out of the door. 'Old Angusina's getting jolly chubby, what?' she said. 'Must be all Mrs Murchison's scrumptious baking.'

'It must indeed,' Victoria said with a private smile. Philippa at some times and on some subjects was as thick as a brick, a fact for which she was, at the moment, grateful.

'Do sit down, dear,' she added, automatically, for Philippa was already lowering herself before the low coffee-table, and reaching for the ebony handle of the silver pot.

'Shall I pour?'

Victoria sat as well, already exhausted by her daughter's draining presence.

'You wanted to speak to me, Mother?' Philippa was stirring her coffee briskly, glancing with undisguised restlessness at the clock. 'Only I . . .'

'Have an appointment. I am sure. No, dear, I won't hold you. It's just a small matter. About Fiona Grant actually.'

'Ah yes, I was planning to pop in on my way into town.'

'Yes. Actually, I'd rather you did not. That is what I wanted to say. I think it would be best if she were left alone. Just for a while.' Victoria poured her own coffee, since Philippa had forgotten to do that, and kept her eyes down, hoping that would be the end of it.

'Hardly seems the decent thing. After all, I visit them all. Everyone knows that. And I'm sure Fiona will need some bucking up, particularly with Ewan still in hospital in London. Must be frightfully worrying.'

Victoria thought that Philippa seemed able to use words like worry, fear, pain, grief as if they were cut from a book, printed and dry as paper. 'He's blind.'

'He's at the Eye Hospital, surely.'

'A formality. He's blind.'

'Oh, they do wonders.'

'Not for Ewan. There are no eyes, Philippa. They are gone. Completely. Gone.'

'Oh. I see. That is rather a blow, then.'

Victoria sighed. 'Fiona doesn't want to see anyone. Anyone.'

'Whyever not?' Philippa sounded offended. 'After all Ewan's quite the hero of the hour. We're to arrange a welcoming committee for his return.'

'She's had a letter. It distressed her. Angusina saw her in the morning, and she specifically requested that no one call.' The message had been blunter than that, and aimed more directly at 'Lady Bountiful' as the younger of the glen women called

Philippa behind her back. Briefly, Victoria considered allowing her daughter to go and learn for herself. But Fiona had enough to cope with, with her husband arriving home next week, shell-blasted and disfigured and blind, and raving in his dictated letters of the idiocy of the army and the war.

'You are not to go there. That is all,' Victoria said, and the conversation was closed.

Philippa left the house by the front entrance and was walking briskly around the east tower, on the pink gravel pathway to where the motor car and driver awaited, when Harry stepped suddenly, almost insolently, from the shadow of the holly tree, pruners in hand. 'Ah, my favourite Valkyrie. How goest the fray?' He was grinning, and looked oddly devilish with his skin now darkly tanned from outdoor work, his hair rough and untidy. He looked like a crofter, Philippa thought, mentally noting, *blood will tell*.

'Excuse me, Mr Bruce, I am late already.'

'Oh don't rush so, it will go on for years yet, I've no doubt.'

'What will?' Philippa looked blank.

'Your cherished occupation. The war.'

Philippa stepped sideways to avoid looking at him, her disgust was so great. 'I would think,' she said, lowering her voice with stylish consciousness learned on the platform, 'that you would be ashamed to so much as show your face in public, now of all times, with your brother lying wounded in France.'

Harry's grin faded. His eyes narrowed slowly and his hand on the pruning-shears tightened until the knuckles were tense and white. 'Don't,' he said.

'Don't what? Remind you of your cowardice?'

He lunged for her then and she was too taken by surprise even to move. The pruning-shears clattered loudly to the ground, ringing off the concrete edging of the path. Harry clasped both Philippa's elbows and thrust her up against the pink stone wall of Culbrech House. He whispered hoarsely, 'If you were a man I'd break your neck. But you're not, are you? Oh no, my flower of Scottish womanhood, safe in skirts, sending them all, decent men, all of them, out there, to get their balls shot off for your honour.'

Philippa's face whitened, and her stomach turned at his words. 'Let me go. I'll be sick.'

'Oh yes, you'll be sick, won't you. Since I can't use my fists on you, and madam, I'd dearly love to, why don't I use that bit you dislike the most? Because that's the truth of it, isn't it? You hate us. All of us. And you want us dead. Glorious, because we're sexless then, in our sainted graves. I should do you up against this sacred Culbrech wall, like the bitch you are. God, that would be justice,' he said laughing, and still laughing, he closed his mouth over hers, forced her squirming against the wall, forced every inch of his body against hers. She moaned and fought and kicked at him, and his tongue flickered insolently around the insides of her virgin mouth. When he was quite ready, he let her go, turned without looking at her, knowing she was too appalled even to speak. He picked up his shears and walked casually away to the far corner of the house. By the west tower he stopped, and remorse pained in the pit of his stomach. Philippa Maclaren was vomiting on to the flowerbeds by the doorstep of Culbrech House.

3

On the thirtieth of November, St Andrew's Day, 1915, the remnants of the First Battalion Maclaren Highlanders, now amalgamated with the Fourth, the short-lived Inverness Pals, had been in their new position on the River Ancre, east of the little town of Albert, for just over a fortnight. Already, Torquil Farquhar felt he had lived there all his life. Such was the grim repetitiveness of war.

Torquil was aware, as he emerged from his dugout that morning, of a persistent feeling of detachment that had haunted him since Loos. Part of it was, he knew, simply the deaths. There were so many of them, so many all at once. Whole sections of one's life, one's home life as well as life here, were just cut away. Again and again an event would come to mind, an event of the past, hoped to be repeated in some pleasant peacebound future, and with it the grey realization that it was no longer possible. No, one couldn't go fishing with Craigie down in Moy, or stalking with Haig-Thomas, or make up that party for golf with Collins and his two pretty sisters, because Haig-Thomas and Craigie were dead and lying somewhere in the brick heaps that were Loos, and Collins's whole head and shoulders had gone spinning off by themselves with a Jack Johnson shell and left nothing but his kicking kilted legs.

That was bad enough. But sometimes, worst times, one's memory was not so clear, one's recollections outdated or confused, and appalling as it might seem, one simply forgot. One forgot who was dead. A man would appear, big as life, who an hour before he had been quite convinced had gone West with the others. How could he make such a mistake? Or, worse, he would send a message through a friend to one or another, or make plans for a meeting, only to be informed, reminded gently, that that particular officer and gentleman was no longer with us.

Now that the two battalions were joined, the confusion was heightened. So many strange faces, and different kinds of faces too, Glasgow, Lowland faces like that odd Corporal McGarrity who Tenny Maclaren insisted on setting such store by, who looked as likely to kick you in the teeth as obey an order, half the time. And then suddenly to find the two young Maclaren boys, Albert and James, serving as private soldiers. While at the same time, there was Colin Chisholm's old platoon sergeant, Ross MacDonald, a right ruffian if Torquil had ever known one, suddenly commissioned in the field for his indisputable courage and leadership, in charge of the platoon that poor John Bruce had gaily led. Sublime to the ridiculous, Torquil thought, making his way past his stirring men, to the latrines.

Still, leadership was a hard-pressed quality on the Western Front, and the man was effective. Even Tenny Maclaren, who had been gazetted captain after Loos and given command of Colin Chisholm's old B Company, now so adulterated by New Army men as to be hardly recognizable, regarded MacDonald as a begrudged asset. Torquil mentally chastized himself for his snobbery, at the same time justifying his resentment of MacDonald with the undoubted fact that the men, for their own reasons, hated their new lieutenant. He wondered, was that his real reason, or simply a stylish distaste for the risen ranker? He dropped the thought, knowing the truth was closer to the old problem; change. He hated change and it was everywhere around him, pressing in upon him, shaking his values, his beliefs, everything he held dear. He remembered with dim sorrow the beautiful golden wood, on the retreat from Mons, and the jingling of cavalry harness, silver among the trees. And then, as always when at his darkest times, he remembered Emma in her white dress, beneath the rowan on the banks of the River Glass. That memory had become in his mind an icon, framed in golden nostalgia, his personal madonna.

A rifle-shot broke the picture, like a pebble in a still pool. Far off, a thin cry of pain arose where someone, somewhere, had been careless. Even in this quiet place, on the marshy edge of the small River Ancre, it did not pay to be careless. The cry for stretcher-bearers echoed relentlessly down the line. The day had begun.

As the morning progressed, Torquil relaxed a little, allowing the comforting patterns of trench life to lull and restore him with their familiarity. He should, after all, be delighted with life, he reminded himself from time to time. He was to go on leave, as from noon tomorrow, and by evening of that day would no doubt be in Le Havre with Emma Maclaren. And then, home, or London at least, and Naomi Bruce's peaceful haven overlooking Hyde Park. He assumed, naturally, that Emma would travel with him. He had written to her as soon as he learned of his leave, so that she could make her plans accordingly. Oddly, she had not yet answered, which was unlike her. No doubt she was too busy preparing for his arrival. He envisaged her, fondly, out somewhere buying a new frock, or hat, until he remembered that Emma was, like himself, in uniform.

He tried to keep the image of Emma foremost in his mind as he went about his duties, but it faded, under an onslaught of new insecurities. He would have to travel, to leave his company, leave his trench, his dugout, his men. He found himself clutching in his heart at those unlikely comforts as if they could save him from a nameless terror.

Yesterday some sadist in the Jerry trenches had tossed a mortar into their latrines, and aside from bringing one poor sod to a highly unheroic end, had scattered showers of human filth all over them all. That night an expedition, bent on revenge, had located the Jerry conveniences and retaliation was even now being planned. Torquil was sorry about that. Things had been quite decently peaceful since they arrived. There were a myriad of unspoken rules; 'morning hate' was slated for 8.00 a.m. and no earlier, transport was left, by both sides, unshelled, and the resultant calm made the wooded land behind the lines, and the gentle course of the river among its willow trees, a place of relaxation, even retreat.

In the afternoon Torquil went with a party of New Army boys down to a small stream that wound through clumps of yellow-leafed willow trees and past a ruined farm to its juncture with the Ancre. The sun beat down and the men willingly stripped in the soft air and plunged into the icy water. It was a rare luxury and they became quite drunk with the pleasure of it, splashing each other and shouting like children. Torquil stood at one side, mindful of an officer's dignity, watching the thin, vulnerable white bodies of his men. Although there was no danger, except from the ever-present threat of a solitary long-range shell, a threat they simply ignored, he still felt he was a kind of guardian. Something was entrusted to him, standing there, like a shepherd, watching over these playing boys. Quite suddenly, he was aware of tears in his eyes, and a shaking coming over him. Oh good Christ, he whispered, turning so that none would see, is it happening again?

He felt better as they walked back up the line and entered the communications trench, making their way back into the narrow sheltering world of their trenches. It was always better there, Torquil conceded. Out in the open, things, thoughts, happened. Last week, in fact, something had happened out there on the road to Albert that had shaken him to the root of his sanity. Out there, he had met Bunty FitzJames.

Had it been any of the others, he wouldn't have thought so much. Somehow, Craigie, or Collins, or Haig-Thomas, all casualties of Loos, were so present in his mind that he could dismiss a sudden resurrected vision of them as some kind of logical aftermath of battle, some clinical thing, akin to shell-shock. But Bunty died at Polygone Wood at Ypres. A year ago, back in the autumn of 1914. Surely, after a year, a man was really dead, and stayed in his grave in the Flanders mud. But there he was. Torquil had been alone, returning from the ruined town. It was evening, the light not good. The man had emerged suddenly, from behind the wall of a barn that flanked the roadside. He was marching along, as if in step with a whole invisible battalion. He passed but feet away from Torquil, and smiled, a big smile, young, and happy, and Torquil recognizing him had cried out his name, until, turning to watch his disappearing back, the shattering truth had hit him. The back seemed to break up, become part of the grey light in the small wood the marching man had entered. He had never spoken, or made any acknowledgement other than that heartening smile. But it was Bunty. He knew that. The vision, as it must have been a vision, had been so real, in fact, that he at first accepted it at face value. Its ghostliness came upon him only after it was gone. Trembling and sweating, he returned alone to his trench and his dugout, and an uncharacteristic solitary swig from his brandy flask. Later, alone in the darkness, he had walked up and down the front line, amidst the sleeping men. He found Sandy Gibson, Sergeant Gibson now, since Loos, tending the dying embers of a wood-fire and paused, ostensibly to warm his hands. He had a need to talk and somehow this quiet, businesslike man seemed the right person. Confiding in an NCO was hardly the thing, of course, but then, he sensed that Gibson, like all his class, might have some room in his philosophies for the supernatural.

'Did he look at you?' Sandy asked, curiously.

'Yes. Right at me. And he smiled. I mean it was Bunty, all right, no doubt about it. I'd know him anywhere.' He was conscious of sounding like a madman.

'Aye, they usually do. As if they kent something we dinna.'

'Usually?' Torquil said, eyeing the sergeant carefully. 'You mean there are others?'

'Och, no' a lot. Dinna pay any heed whit some folk will tell you. Aboot angels on white horses, an' hale battalions in auld farrant dress. But the odd ghaistie, och aye. We a' see 'em. Most willna talk aboot it, a' course. But they're there a'richt. Dinna fash, sir. They mean no harm.'

Torquil felt light-headed, balanced between relief and a conviction that not only himself but all his world was going mad. He thought then and said slowly, 'Does it signify something, I mean, a portent, do you think?' He asked the question so earnestly that Sandy grinned slowly.

'Whit did ye hae in mind? The end o' the war, like they say o' yon Virgin on the church in the toun? Or the resurrection day?'

'No, I mean about oneself. Does it signify something about oneself?' He searched Sandy's face in the firelight, but it had darkened into Highland privacy.

'Och sir, I wouldna pay it any mind. I would not.' He looked down at the wood-ash, and poked it until sparks flew like a miniature shellburst. Torquil knew then it was considered a portent of death.

The next day was colder than the previous one, and in the shadowy corners of the eerie and deserted town of Albert, the frost yet lay on cobbles and fallen bricks. Still, the sun was bright, and as Torquil handed the reins of his mare to his batman he glanced almost reluctantly eastward to the unseen and quiet Front. He paused a moment, running a gloved hand gently over the warm mane of the mare and smiled as she turned her head to him and blew soft breath over his wrist. Then he slapped her rump briskly, said goodbye to his servant and turned, walking sharply away, his boot-heels clicking on frosty stone. A Royal Engineers motor lorry awaited him on the other side of the deserted ruined square, his impromptu transport to Amiens and the train. As he clambered aboard the open vehicle, he glanced once, involuntarily, to the top of the shell-blasted basilica. The gilded statue of the Virgin, whose fall was Sandy's portent of the war's end, hung grotesquely from the tower, twisted horizontal by a German shell almost a year ago, now outstretched, impossibly balanced, child in arms, a tortured figure of peace. The lorry pulled away leaving the square more empty than before.

By mid-afternoon, Torquil was relaxing tentatively in a first-class compartment rattling through the French countryside past vast encampments of splendid cavalry regiments. The great breakthrough they awaited seemed now to hang as forlornly over the dim future as the golden Virgin over the empty streets of Albert. Torquil took out the gold watch his father had given him on the day he was commissioned from Sandhurst. Two thirty-five; it would be evening before he made Le Havre.

The Quai d'Escale Hospital of Le Havre was one of the better off of all such establishments, both in location and in physical structure. Its location, directly overlooking the quay into which the hospital ships came to berth and which was itself served by its own rail line for hospital trains; and its form, a rather splendid, many-windowed building with high-ceilinged wards looking out on to gracious balconies, were both due to its pre-war purpose. It had held once the first-class waiting rooms wherein the stylish passengers of the great liners awaited departure in luxurious comfort. The liners were gone now, and the glass-topped tables and wicker chairs and graceful palms. All that remained were the balconies where the occasional sentimental VAD might watch the departure, Blightywards, of a favoured patient before returning to the stench and drudgery of the ward.

Emma Maclaren knew the quayside building well, both in its new capacity and also in its previous incarnation. She had, in the summer of 1912, spent two afternoons here, drinking tea and watching the dazzling passage of the rich and elegant to their French resorts, at the beginning and the end of her Continental tour. She was seventeen then, and in the company of her mother and her maternal grandmother, both of whom were determined to use every moment of their month abroad to force some ladyhood into their unruly Highland charge. Sometimes, trying to remember where in the utterly changed room she had sat, Emma would recall ruefully the efforts of those two firmly intentioned ladies and how it had come, in the end, to this. Mostly, she did not think about it at all. It was another life, gone for ever, and besides, she rarely had time to think of anything at all beyond work.

Her working conditions at the Quai d'Escale, hard and steady as the work was, were luxurious by comparison to some of her compatriots, a fact of which she was well aware. At least she had solid walls about her, and a dry roof overhead, when so many were nursing under canvas, in dark wards lit only by kerosene lamps, and heated by smoking oil stoves, and in the case of the Casualty Clearing Stations, under the threat of shelling as well. Nursing sisters and VADs had died in France already. She felt rather a baby, safe in the great coastal base of Le Havre.

Sister called her to assist with a dressing and she hurried off, relieved by action, like the soldiers. It was an ugly dressing, a gangrenous stump of a leg whose odour sickened even its owner and filled his corner of the ward with its putrefaction. Every three hours it was unbound to be irrigated, while the soldier, a New Army Edinburgh lad, wounded at Loos, bit on his whitened, bleeding lip to stifle screams. Emma held the stump, her back to Sister who washed the pus-dripping wound with Carrel and Dakin Solution. Emma kept her eyes locked to those of the young Scot, and her smile of encouragement rigid as a mask. As always, he tried to joke, to say something flirtatious. As always, she tried to laugh. The washing finished, Emma relaxed as Sister rewound the stump in lint soaked with the solution, and wrapped it in waterproof Jackinette. The soldier was lying back with his eyes closed, savouring his next three hours of peace. Emma's hands were drenched in pus. She had never fainted, but sometimes, as now, allowed herself the luxury of thinking of something else far away, for relief.

She thought of Rebecca, blanking out the image of the

truncated leg with Rebecca's pretty face. She had had a letter that morning that both cheered and disturbed her, and as she cleaned up the soldier's bed she puzzled over it once more.

Rebecca had asked for her help: Rebecca, whose London assurance and social aplomb had been Emma's envy since they had met, was now begging for her assistance. And the person with whom Emma was to use her dubious influence was, of all people, Naomi Bruce. It seemed inconceivable, but Naomi, that outpost of feminine independence and bohemian daring, was now portrayed by Rebecca as a crusty bastion of established society.

'Oh, how wicked she has become,' Rebecca wrote, 'she knows how much he needs me and loves me, and how much he has suffered, and still refuses to grant me her blessing.' The letter had gone on to recount Rebecca's dutiful weeks of attendance at the bedside of Johnny Bruce, both in France and after his return to England, an attendance for which she had sacrificed her VAD work without a qualm. Emma had been a little shocked by that, and resisted the desire to disapprove. And now, with Johnny at last recovering at a convalescent hospital in Edinburgh, Rebecca wanted only to join him and become his wife. Emma could not recall if anywhere in the letter an actual proposal had been discussed, but it appeared that there must have been, as Rebecca was clearly intent on marriage. But not only had she to face the disapproval of Maud Bruce, a disapproval that Emma, ignorant of Rebecca's background, could not comprehend, as well as that of his commanding officer, and uncle, on account of his youth, but also of Naomi; her benefactor, her saviour, her patroness, and, 'until this day, I had thought, my dearest friend', came Rebecca's wounded complaint, refused even to discuss the matter: 'Dearest Emma, you are the only one they respect. I beg you to speak for me. You are my only hope.'

Late that evening, in the tiny quarters that Emma shared with Gerty Hill and Margaret Sutherland, she read the letter again and yet again, trying to sort out that which was truth from that which was Rebecca's perennial romanticism. 'Dear Emma, I am so changed, you would not know me. I know you always disapproved a little of my frivolity, but I assure you, that is all over.' Oddly, though she could picture Rebecca saying it, she could not picture her meaning it. She pondered the situation, full of unlikelihoods. Why would Naomi oppose such a match?

Everyone liked Johnny, and after all, he was her own nephew. Whom could she prefer? And why did Maud so resent Rebecca? She thought more about that and recalled her own mother's nervous concern when Tenny had seemed the more likely candidate for Rebecca's hand. She shrugged, and stood and opened the door of the tiny wood stove, adding another few meagre scraps.

'Oh don't,' Gerty moaned from her side of the little tin-roofed shelter, 'I've only just finished chopping wood, and you've burnt half of it tonight.'

'I'll chop more tomorrow,' Emma said calmly, and added another small log. She returned to her letter. Poor Tenny, she thought, remembering suddenly the day they had all met Rebecca, and how he had hung about her entranced the whole day of the picnic. She was the last to begrudge Johnny Bruce his happiness, after all he had endured, and yet, Tenny was her brother, and a more honest, decent man she had never met. The war, which had cost them all so much, had cost him now his love.

She set the letter aside, on the blanket-covered bed, and lay back wearily, putting her feet up and allowing herself, her duties to patients and friends alike over for the time being, the luxury of thinking of the man who was her own dear love, at last. Tomorrow she would see him. How, or where, she did not know. She merely trusted in Providence that the rules and regulations, the objections of authority and the scheduling of trains and boats would all be overcome, and an hour would be snatched for herself and Torquil. It was, she knew honestly, all they could be spared. It never occurred to her that Torquil himself expected a great deal more.

Emma had fallen asleep, still dressed in her uniform and apron, when a tap came at the door. Gerty had gone out again, on night duty, and Margaret was away home on leave. The little room, lit only by the bars of light that crept through the slotted door of the wood stove, was eerie. Emma woke to the sound, uncertain if it were real or part of her dream. Her dream had been awful. Men marching off to war, files and files of them, all carrying the bones of their amputated limbs, white and dry, freshly scrubbed and neatly gathered, like fresh-chopped kindling. The sound coming from them, as they rattled together, had mixed together the sound of hatchet and surgeon's saw. The sound came again.

Emma sat up, catching at her throat, 'Gerty?' she whispered.

'Emma?' The voice, a man's voice, was barely a whisper, but even as such, and through the closed door, she knew it was Torquil.

She leapt up, and then stopped, frozen there a few feet from the door. Here? He had come here? Surely he knew it was forbidden. But love and compassion overcame for an instant her deep respect for authority. She ran to the door, convinced something terrible had happened or he'd never have made so forbidden an approach. Her fingers fumbled on the latch, found it, freed it, flung open the door.

'Oh God, Emma,' he gasped, and in an instant she was wrapped in his arms. For a moment she acceded, dropping into the warmth and comfort of embrace as she did each night into the solace of her bed. He had never held her before; nor had anyone. She was stunned how natural it felt, and how, exhausted as she was, she yet felt passion.

Torquil, too, felt passion; he felt it as a drowning man feels a saving rope in his hands. He clung to her desperately, his face burrowing in her loosening hair, his hands clutching her garments, folds of cloth, and the muffled shape of her body within, with a husband's propriety, shameless. Even after she begged to be released he continued to hold her in desperate imprisonment until her voice rose, begging, touching hysteria and stunning him back to his senses. He released her, his hands floating off her body, still outstretched, amazed at his incaution. 'Oh God, Emma,' he whispered again.

She stepped back, brushing a confused hand over her forehead and hair. 'Torquil, this is impossible. You must leave at once. If anyone were to come . . .'

'Oh,' he said, reason returning. 'Of course, how foolish. I never should have entered, only it was so splendid seeing you. I'm afraid I forgot.' He stepped backwards, smiling shyly under the drooping moustache that still seemed too old for all of his face, except perhaps his aged, darkened eyes. 'Shall I wait for you outside, or around the front of the hospital?' He had moved out of the open doorway, into the darkness of the courtyard, and rain was now falling on his khaki greatcoat.

'Wait for me?' she said dimly.

'Or shall I book our rooms first, and return for you?'

'Rooms?'

'At the hotel, dear,' he said patiently, as to a child.

'Rooms at the hotel? What for?' Emma said, confusion making her voice sharp, annoyed with her own incomprehension. 'I have my room here.'

'But our boat doesn't leave till tomorrow morning. And frankly, I'm terribly tired. I've been travelling since noon, and it's been,' he paused, not wanting to open his dark storehouse of memories in the presence of his lady, 'it's been rather a sticky few weeks.' But Emma missed all that, her tired mind stopping at 'our boat'.

'Torquil,' she said, looking hard at him, as if he were suddenly unbalanced, 'do you think I'm going to England, too?'

He stood very still, silent, his mouth opening slightly as if to speak, and then closing. Like a small hurt boy he said, 'Aren't you?'

'I'm not due for leave for months, Torquil. I've really only just arrived. Besides, we're so overworked I'd hardly feel right taking my leave, unless there were some real need.' She stopped, knowing at once from his face that she was saying something terribly wrong.

'But I wrote to you. I said I was coming,' he protested, as if he'd heard nothing of what she'd said.

'I haven't got leave, Torquil,' she almost shouted, and then instinctively glanced about in the darkness, in case her raised voice had been overheard.

'Leave?' he said then, his voice indignant. 'Leave? What do you mean? You're all volunteers. They can't keep you here. Who are these people anyhow?' He was outraged now, and ready to defend her, as if she were indeed held captive. 'We'll simply go. They can hardly stop you.'

'No,' she said, her voice brittle with an anger she barely understood. She felt rising in her all her small resentments at his constant, sometimes almost deliberate misunderstanding of her role, of the role of all women, in the war. 'No. They would not stop me. But I would never be allowed to return. Never. I would be dismissed at once.'

He stiffened with resolve. 'Well, be dismissed then,' he said. 'In fact, I'd be just as pleased. I'll not have my future wife ruled by a bunch of petty tyrants in skirts.' He turned away.

'Where are you going?' she cried.

'I'm going to book two rooms at the Hotel Anglais and then

I'm going to the hospital,' he gestured angrily at the bulk of the converted building behind them where a dimly lit hospital train was shunting into the siding on the quay. 'And telling the biggest brass I can find that my fiancée is accompanying me to England.' Had he stood facing her, with his hurt, exhausted eyes upon her face, while the slow train clattered wearily to a halt, he would have won: she could not have refused him. But he did not, turning instead, with military precision, and stalking away. He had only gone a dozen steps when she, finding her voice quavery and unreal, called after him, 'Torquil.'

He hesitated, and she called his name again, and then he turned.

'Torquil, I'm not going.'

She was almost afraid of him, the way he came slowly walking back, measuring his paces, as though on the parade-ground. 'Emma?' he said, listening for her retraction.

'I'm not going to England, Torquil. I cannot leave here. I'm needed here, Torquil. Needed. Desperately,' she added, amazed at the truth of it. Ladies of Emma's upbringing were not taught to so value themselves.

'Needed?' he whispered, his voice breaking away beneath the rhythmic, funereal clicking of the slow creeping train wheels. Emma heard her dream again, the bones clicking. 'And I do not need you? I? I who have loved you so much that death, whom I know well, my dear, would be preferable to your loss?'

'You're not losing me,' she said, her voice conciliatory, pleading. 'And with luck you'll see me upon your return. Perhaps,' she was thinking quickly, 'perhaps we could dine together. It is absolutely forbidden, of course, for VADs to be seen with officers. But if I found a friend, and you found a friend, and we were to meet up at one of the hotels, I mean it must not look planned, but we could meet,' her voice was hurried and to Torquil it sounded like that of a naughty schoolgirl.

'Oh my dear,' he said, 'we could never do that. Why, Matron might slap your little hand, mightn't she?'

Emma froze into a surge of cold anger. She caught her words of sharp reply before they had time to leave her lips, but she could not totally hide her tone. 'I'm afraid, Torquil, we are both overtired. If you come to the ward before you leave, I will do my best to see you.' She wanted to turn, wanted to leave him standing there, to slake her pride, but kindness would not allow it.

'I love you, Emma,' he whispered. 'Please come with me.'

She wavered. The ward came instantly to her eyes, the rows of waiting, patient, brutally injured men, turning their desperate eyes to her for solace. Who would hold the Edinburgh lad's poor shattered stump? Who would know that she must dimple and smile as he strove to be a man? Who would speak for the brown-haired child in bed thirty-two that he might be spared the Front? The man before her needed her, she knew. But he was whole and well, and they were ill, and there was but one of him, and a hundred others beneath their red blankets this night. 'No,' she said, and he walked away, without another word.

In the morning, his ship sailed, and she hovered at the windows, stole scant seconds on the balcony, risked Sister's wrath, Matron's punishments. In the end, she was called away, and when the leave ship sailed from her berth, two quays away, Emma Maclaren was scrubbing a bed mackintosh and heard only her whistle of farewell.

4

The Channel crossing was rough and stormy, and the leave ship kicked about remorselessly on a grey, white-capped sea. The open decks, packed with other ranks, were awash with sleet, rain, and occasionally the tops of green seas. Early on, Torquil forsook the smoking lounge, crammed with too cheerful officers of every imaginable regiment, and made for the open air. It was not seasickness, that malady that had driven others to the rail, but a soul-weariness that resented all human companionship, that brought him, eventually, to a solitary point at the stern. From there he watched Le Havre, and then the lengthening grey coast of France, disappear rapidly into sullen morning rain. When at last he turned away, the kind salt spray had drenched his face, masking any signs of unmanly grief.

They were late into Dover because of the choppy crossing, and it was late afternoon by the time the leave train, packed with bawdily cheering soldiers, rumbled under the great glass canopy of Victoria Station. Jostled on every side by jubilant refugees from the Front, Torquil made his way, walking stiffly, face grimly set, to the ticket gate, and beyond; not glancing even at the near-hysterical crowds of waiting women; alone, to the taxi-ranks. No one would meet him, thank God.

The windows of Naomi's house shone golden in the early darkness of the wet December afternoon. The pavement before it was smeared with brown trodden leaves, and across the busy stream of motor traffic, the barren branches of Hyde Park clattered in a rising wind. He rang the bell, resisting the desire simply to open the unlocked door and enter unnoticed.

For all of them, the expanding circle of young men and women who comprised the sprawling network of Maclaren acquaintances, Naomi's house had become as their own, a halfway house, marvellously convenient in location, as it was now to Torquil, to their more distant leave-time destinations. For some, for longer spells, it became a haven from all stresses, where neither military nor family pressures could reach them. Naomi, unlike so many well-meaning bastions of the home-front, understood that what they, the returning soldiers of every rank, craved was peace, silence, warmth, cleanliness and most of all, quiet. The cheerful rounds of admiring relatives, the 'Oh we're so proud' tea-parties, the 'do say a tiny word' meetings of patriotic groups were, to all of them, like another petty war. Naomi, too, seemed to understand how the ferocious Hun-hating patriotism of the fireside chilled them to the marrow of the bone.

That patriotism was everywhere now, as recurrent losses and gloomy forecasts drove the armchair armies to near hysterical hatred of the enemy. Torquil had seen it in the newspaper placards, in the fierce, persistent smiles of ladies in mock-uniform who handed him flowers in Victoria Station; he had heard it on countless, muttering angry lips; taxicab drivers, newspaper boys, even flowergirls in the tatty streets where the boarded-up, smashed windows of foreign-name shops, daubed in paint with the bright words, 'Hun-Lover', 'Traitor', spoke of an often inaccurate home-front attack.

As Torquil waited on the doorstep, a distant newscrier's voice shouted, 'New Hun Atrocity, Read it Now,' as if not a moment could be spared.

'Northcliffe,' Torquil muttered in the teeth of the bitter rain. 'The bastard.'

'Pardon sir?' The door had swung open sharply as he spoke and he whirled to face it, and Mary, the maid, who waited inquiringly. God. Hope she hadn't heard, he thought instantly, his lifelong gentleman's schooling appalled at his own words.

'Nothing, Mary. I believe Mrs Bruce is expecting me?'

Mary ushered him in, and took his hat, wet greatcoat, and swagger stick, and, familiar as in his father's Perthshire house, he said that he would find his own way to the drawing-room, where, as it was tea-time, he would no doubt find Naomi.

With his hand on the brass doorknob of the white-painted door, he suddenly paused. A sound came from within, a sound utterly alien to this gentle house, the sound of raised voices. He waited, bewildered, his hand slowly slipping from the knob. They were women's voices, one he was sure was Rebecca Galloway's, slightly high-pitched with tearfulness, another, an older voice, he did not recognize, and the third, pitched low with quite uncharacteristic vehemence, was that of Naomi. He felt suddenly childlike, a boyish intruder in the secrets of feminine affairs, and turning quickly, he looked around, as if for somewhere to hide. With a nervous glance back to the hallway, he bolted up the stairs.

The house was a multistoreyed warren of passages and closed, mysterious doors. Like most military men, used only to the company of his own sex, he had a near religious awe of the private quarters of a female establishment and feared terribly that he might blunder into some womanly retreat, laden with frills and perfumes, and God knew what.

Three flights up, he came to a halt. Beyond would be the attic, and the maids' rooms. He'd better stop here. He went to the window that overlooked the street and the park, lit softly now by rainwashed streetlamps. Twitching the maroon curtain with nervous hands he peered down at passing hansom cabs and motor cars, glistening in the wet. Then he turned, determined to find a sanctuary, and boldly tried the first door he found, praying the room was not occupied. He was aware of a front-line caution come upon himself, and the eerie feeling that he was treating the house like a passage through no-man's-land.

Good fortune; the room was empty, unlit, uncurtained windows letting in the last of the light from the dying afternoon sky in a grey sweep across a multitude of dim shapes. Silhouetted against the window was the unmistakable curved form of the head and neck of a horse. He started, his heart pounding, confusion entangling him, threatening his sanity. Had he stepped through a doorway and ended back There? Then his eyes adjusted, his mind swung back to reality, and he laughed softly. A rocking-horse; a grey dappled rocking-horse. He had come by chance upon the old nursery, past abode of little Robert Bruce. Torquil stepped within, silently, and quietly closed the door.

* * *

He was wise. Three flights below in the green-papered drawing-room a battle was raging, and it was no place for children, or for men.

'And don't you attempt to tell me, my girl,' Maud Bruce was addressing her daughter in tones of cultured fury, 'that this wasn't all part of your little plan from the very start.'

There was a long silence. Naomi Bruce, unlike her mother, or Rebecca, was sitting down, in her favourite green velvet chair by the fire, with one green satin slipper tentatively toe-ing the polished brass fender. By instinct she chose places to sit or stand that flattered her beauty, as would, perhaps, one of her stylish cats. She was sitting very straight, her long slender body poised gracefully, her legs in their satin trousers (*unacceptable*, Maud thought, while awaiting her reply) crossed below the knee. Her two hands were laid one on top of the other, palms downward on her knees. When the silence had stretched to breaking point, and Rebecca's resumed sobs became audible, Naomi spoke. She had been remembering the while the morning of Rebecca's arrival, when Arnold Galloway had filled the role of fearsome blusterer that now her own mother played.

Now she said, very calmly, 'And if there ever was what you insist on calling "my little plan" regarding Miss Galloway, do you imagine I would be quite so furious with the silly fool now?'

'I'm *not* a fool,' Rebecca cried. 'He loves me.'

Naomi merely waved one hand in her direction, and returned it to its rest on her knees.

Maud Bruce said, with calculation, 'Yes. I do imagine. You're a clever one, my lady, and don't forget I raised you and watched you simper your way around your father and . . .'

'*Not* my father, dear. Let's at least be honest in private.'

'You're quite savage, aren't you?' Maud said coldly, and then continued briskly, as if uninterrupted, 'You've never made a straightforward action in your life. It would be just like you to arrange all this and then make a pretence of bewailing it with the rest of us, so no one would know your part.'

Rebecca left her lonely stance by the window for an isolated chair, far from the fire and Naomi, and sat and hid her face in her hands. If only, if only it *were* pretence, she wished fervently, then she would not be so hideously alone. Again, as so often in past weeks, she wished Emma were here.

'If,' Naomi said, her words measured out with tremendous

calm, 'if I have spent a life of pretence, which I might deny, can you, who were responsible for it all, after all, possibly tell me what else I might have done? What other doorways were there open to me? What doorways were there *ever* open to me?'

Maud bristled, stalked to the tea-trolley, fiddled with the ebony-handled pot, the Wedgwood china, making small tinkles of repressed fury. Then she said, 'How dare you accuse me? *Me.* What did I ever do wrong? Or will you blame Cawnpore on me, like others have? As if it were a sin to have survived. After all, those who died were heroines. But what was I? What doorways were open to me? Pretence,' she snorted, an old-lady sound, indulged in when the years of prissy control were past. 'If *I* had sought pretence I'd have left you in that convent in Ireland, and tried to salvage something of my life. It would have been possible, perhaps. People might have forgotten, if I hadn't insisted on raising the reminder.'

Naomi stroked her long, loose Eurasian hair with deliberate pride and smiled coldly. 'I would rather you had left me there. Perhaps today I'd be a holy nun, and no trouble to anyone . . . or to myself.'

Rebecca turned to her, startled, having never heard such an admission from Naomi before. A wave of love and pity swept her, but she remembered Johnny, alone in Edinburgh without her, and buried it. She sat silent; although it was her own future being clawed over, the argument no longer included her.

Maud looked a little ashamed at what she had said but she too remembered Johnny and the pride she felt in him, a pride that had to suffice for two grandsons because of Harry's strange lonely course through the war, and once again she was unforgiving. 'I know the games you play. I remember you on the day Ian Maclaren was married, coming in in that dreadful Indian rigout with that appalling actor you'd picked up somewhere . . .'

Naomi was silent. She looked up sadly and then said, 'Just playing court jester. My usual role. Amusing my betters on their nuptial day. It was the only role I was permitted, you may recall.' The eyes of mother and daughter met, those of the one so English china-blue, and of the other dark as a tropical night.

'I'm sorry, darling,' Maud whispered, in apology. She delicately dabbed her thin white nose. Naomi rose suddenly, and stepped towards her mother, and Maud crossed the drawing-room and the two silently embraced.

Rebecca rose to her feet. She stood alone, watching the two older women, and then, with the courage that being Johnny's protector had endowed her, found her voice. 'Don't you realize,' she said, 'don't you realize that at last you have the chance to undo the wrongs that all your lives were done to you?' She paused, aware of them turning, aware of having their full attention at last. 'And what are you doing with that chance?' she demanded. 'You are behaving exactly in the manner of all those terrible fools who did their best to ruin your lives, only now you are intent on ruining mine.'

Both older women were stunned into silence, each equally accustomed to a world in which elders spoke and the young, even when they were manifestly adult, listened and obeyed. Rebecca pressed her attack. She made her voice very calm, a great effort, and addressed Maud,

'You're quite right, of course, Mrs Bruce. Naomi did have a plan regarding me.' She almost enjoyed the sharp dark look of anger Naomi cast her. 'But I'm afraid you've rather misinterpreted it. It's all rather ironic actually, because if you'd only listen to what she's saying instead of trying to read your own answers into it, you'd realize that you are both quite firmly on the same side.' She paused for impact and to catch breath. 'Naomi,' she said, 'has no more desire for me to marry Johnny than you have yourself.'

Maud sniffed, 'I think I understand my own daughter's desires.'

'But you don't,' Rebecca returned at once. 'Naomi does not want me to marry Johnny because, although you are quite certain I am not good enough for him, Naomi feels rather that he is not good enough for me.'

Maud's mouth opened and shut, working with silent indignation, and she placed one tiny jewelled hand on the flowing front of her blouse. To Rebecca she appeared an ecru lace pigeon puffing enraged feathers. 'For *you*,' she managed to say. 'My grandson. My dear, you must be in no doubt that I am *fully* aware of your parentage. Fully aware.'

'Yes,' Rebecca said mildly, realizing suddenly that all that, and the same horrible truth that had once driven her to the verge of suicide, seemed pale and silly compared to the life she had come, in the last year, to lead. 'Yes, I was born out of wedlock. So was your daughter, and your husband, and for that matter, your youngest grandson upstairs, whose father's identity is the worst-kept secret in the family,' she added with a malicious smile. 'I would think you'd welcome me with open arms. I'm the stuff the Bruces are made of.'

Maud's mouth still worked, but she did not reply this time to Rebecca, employing instead that other Victorian device of speaking over the heads of children and young women as if they were not present. She said to Naomi, 'I fear, darling, your little private finishing school has had rather a failure here. Perhaps a little more homework.'

Naomi's earlier anger at Rebecca's apparent betrayal had eased, subtly, against her will even, into her own deep-rooted cynical amusement. She was not enjoying playing this role of outraged propriety in the slightest, sensing it as out of character as Rebecca had. She smiled and looked down at her green slippers, framed by firelight.

Rebecca caught her acquiescence and continued, emboldened, 'Actually, Naomi's little plan was rather grander than the second grandson of Willie Bruce. Naomi wished me to marry Tenny Maclaren.'

'Nonsense,' Maud exploded, finding her tongue in ridicule. 'And just how far would that little folly have got you? Do you imagine for a moment Victoria Maclaren would have permitted that match?' Again she was addressing Naomi who, again, did not reply.

'Very far,' Rebecca said to her. 'Right to the altar if Tenny had his way. He has proposed, you know. More than once.'

'Are you saying that you refused the Maclaren heir?' Maud's scorn was now utterly uncontrolled.

'No,' Rebecca said, sadly, almost to herself. 'I am saying that I refused one dear young man because another was dearer. It gave me no pleasure. But after all, I could not have them both, could I? Even the Maclarens and Bruces, as astoundingly friendly as they are, would hardly countenance that.'

Naomi laughed aloud, a giggling, delighted girlish laugh, and Rebecca turned to her, uncertain of her stance now.

'Victoria would never have permitted it,' was Maud's only comment.

'And when,' Naomi said coolly, with the certainty her life-time's rivalry with that distant delicate little woman had won her, 'when, since the day he said "I do", has Ian Maclaren taken

Victoria's wishes over my own?'

'Naomi,' Maud whispered, aghast.

'Truth, Mother. Between these unspeaking walls.' Her laugh that followed was hollow. She said then quickly, 'You buried your mistreatment in propriety, Mother. That was never my way. Yes, I had a plan, a little game. Yes, I took this lovely girl away from the stupid fools who'd toss her away because of the accident of her birth, the way I was tossed away, and yes, I groomed her and styled her, and despite what you say, I think I've done well. And yes, I cast her, a pretty bait, into Culbrech House. Yes, she was my revenge, and a charming one, you must agree. After all,' she waved one dark, delicate arm towards Rebecca, 'who was I harming? A lovely girl for a splendid young man? What more could anyone ask?'

'The right to choose,' said Rebecca Galloway. Naomi was silent and then suddenly Rebecca rushed towards her and dropped on her knees before the fire, looking up into Naomi's still, eastern face. 'Oh please, can't you see? You have succeeded. Maud thinks I'm not good enough for Johnny, and you think I'm too good. Isn't it possible that we are just good enough for each other? Just a man and a woman. Nobody special, just like so many others. But we love each other. Oh, please don't send me out without your blessing. I love you so, but I love him more and I'm going to him, no matter what you all say.'

Naomi leaned back in her chair, gazing over Rebecca's head into the fire for a long while in silence. Then she said softly, 'So I cast for a salmon, and I've hooked a trout. I wonder what Ian would say?' She smiled softly at the girl, and slowly stood, raising her to her feet.

She stood facing Rebecca, her long brown hands on either side of the young, fire-warmed face. 'So. Enough of little games. Now I *will* be serious. You loved another, before you loved this one, my girl. A change of fate has changed your mind. But Fate can change again. Are you certain it is love and not merely sympathy? Will you love him still when he is strong and well again, and has no need of you? Will you love him when Tenny Maclaren is lying as he did, at the door of death?'

'Oh God forbid,' Rebecca whispered, and a twinge of doubt rose deep inside her. But she had won so much, and would not now retreat. 'I am certain,' she said, her voice creating its own confidence, 'I will never love another.'

'Then he is yours,' Naomi said with a small, sad smile.

'Now wait just a moment, my good woman,' Maud began.

But Naomi overrode her at once. 'I will ask my *father* for his consent,' she said with another smile, a devilish one this time, and Maud knew, at last, that she had lost.

It was nearly dark when Robert Bruce returned home, that same evening. A long weekend break from his school in Cornwall had enabled him to spend four days in London, once anathema but now, as his body and interests had matured into young adulthood, his Mecca. Rhodes and Shaw-Schuler had joined him in the morning, and they had spent the day together, first in the Chamber of Horrors at Madame Tussaud's Wax Museum, and later through a succession of tea-shoppes where they lavishly indulged themselves in mountains of tarts and cream cakes as antidote to the term's boiled fish and cabbage monotony. His mother had provided the requisite finance, and turned a blind eye to what use he would put it to; she wanted him out of the house. Some sort of female confab, he gathered, of which there had been not a few since Rebecca had announced her engagement to Johnny Bruce.

He glanced up to the first-floor drawing-room windows, glowing softly behind their drawn green draperies. Still at it; must be a good one this time. He had suspected something monumental was in the wind this morning, from Rebecca's wan look and puffy eyes, and from his mother's somewhat cryptic announcement that old Maud Bruce was arriving at ten, from her rooms at Brown's, and Robert had better vanish.

Robert let himself in without formality, handed his grey school coat and hat to Mary, and made his way up the stairs, pausing long enough to hear the sound of female voices, calmer now, behind the drawing-room door and conclude that he was as well to stay vanished a while. He went on, up to the upper landing, and his own room. It was not, actually, the soft glow of gaslight creeping from beneath the old nursery door that drew his attention, but the sound of a voice, raised softly, in song,

'This is the way the ladies ride . . . clippa-clop, clippa-clop, clippa-clop . . .'

Robert's dark narrow face screwed up in a half-smile of remembrance and bemusement. Someone he knew used to sing that when he was tiny, and balance him on his knee. Willie

Bruce.

'This is the way the gentlemen ride, a canter, a canter, a canter . . .'

Surely not the old man; not away down here. He never travelled any more. Still the voice was high, and wavery, like an old man's voice. There was another sound, a creaking, slow and rhythmic.

'This is the way the cavalry ride, a gallop, a gallop, a gallop . . .'

The creaking increased in speed and volume, and the voice dissolved suddenly in soft, light laughter. Robert Bruce slid his hand to the knob and thrust open the door.

A man, incongruous in khaki field dress in the childish surroundings of the room, was seated, long legs dangling forlornly, upon the grey dappled back of Robert's long-forsaken rocking-horse. He rocked back once, his spurred boots scraping the wooden floor, as Robert entered, and his eyes met Robert's without recognition.

'Who the devil are you?' Robert demanded, incensed. Torquil stared, his mouth open slightly, the red leather reins of his wooden steed hanging limply over one hand. He could not fathom who this young man, materialized in Naomi's house, could possibly be. Tall, well-built, with broad muscular shoulders, a dark, handsome face, and the beginnings of an unshaven moustache, the stranger had challenged him with a man's deep voice, and challenged him with sharp, dark adult eyes. But then Robert's face relaxed into a wide, mystified, but happy grin. 'Good God,' he said, 'it's Captain Farquhar. I do apologize, sir, I didn't know you.'

Instantly, good manners overswept all Robert's doubts. So ingrained in him was the natural acceptance of the rules of respect for elders, superiors, any of his mother's admittedly unusual friends, that had Torquil Farquhar been swinging naked by one ankle from the drawing-room chandelier, Robert would have only smiled the same pleasant smile he smiled now. 'Topping to see you,' he added, extending his surprisingly large hand.

Torquil sat for an instant more on his commandeered mount. Then he rose, standing over it, straddling the wooden beast, and swung one leg over its back, reaching at the same time for Robert's hand. 'I'm afraid the failing was mine as well. I say, but you've grown, Robert. You were just a wee scrap when I saw you last. It must have been years . . .'

'August, 1914, sir. The Bank Holiday picnic.'

Torquil sighed softly, leaning his head back, remembering. 'Of course,' he said at last.

'Lot of water under the bridge since then, sir,' Robert said.

Torquil did not reply. He was looking behind him, at the bowed head of the dappled rocking-horse. 'We had one each, you know,' he said to Robert. 'Great horseman, my father, of course.' He nodded to himself as if that explained a great deal. 'Oh yes. My brother John and I. His was black, but mine was a grey, like yours. Called him Smoke.'

'That's funny,' Robert said. 'That's what I called mine.'

'Nothing original left in the world, old chap,' Torquil said, still facing the rocking-horse. 'Mine was bigger and I used to rag the devil out of poor John. Had him convinced mine was faster. How the hell one could tell whose rocking-horse was faster, God alone knows. But he believed me. Used to beg me for rides on Smoke. Wouldn't let him. Ever. He wanted it so bad, he'd cry. Because I said it was faster. You see, he rather looked up to me. I was older, three years. You know what it's like. No, guess you don't, you're rather on your own, aren't you.' It was a statement, not a question, and Robert nodded, a slightly confused acquiescence. The room seemed murky in the light of the single gas mantle. Torquil said suddenly, 'How old are you?'

'Fifteen, sir.'

'Ah yes. Big for your age, aren't you.'

'I suppose I am, sir. I'm forever asked full fare if I ride on an omnibus. Rather a nuisance.' He smiled, proud of his early manhood.

Torquil seemed to be thinking of something else, and he said, shortly, 'Damn. Wish I'd let him have a go.'

'Sir?'

'On the horse. I wish I'd let him have a go,' he replied impatiently. 'My brother. John.'

'Yes, sir.'

'He's dead now, you know.'

Robert nodded. He did know, having heard through the family and a letter from his mother of young John Farquhar's death in the spring, while serving with the Second Battalion.

'Nothing spectacular. Sniper. On his way to the latrines.'

Torquil's head shook back and forth and Robert, nervously misreading, chanced a small smile. Then he saw that Torquil's eyes were closed, wet tears on the lashes, and he reached out a blind hand towards Robert, touching, and then grasping his shoulder. 'I never let him. Damn. I never let him,' he cried, his voice an agony of remorse.

Then, quite suddenly, he straightened, brushed his eyes lightly, smiled at Robert as if nothing had occurred, and said, 'I say, you'd not have access to the decanter, old man, by any chance?'

Robert cautiously met his eyes, found them calm and lightly humorous, and chanced another small smile, which, met with approval, was rapidly extended to a grin.

'Just follow me,' he said, his doubts vanishing in the pleasure of being treated man-to-man by one of his heroes. Torquil Farquhar was, after all, what Robert wanted most in the world to be, a field officer on the Western Front.

5

In the dressing-room adjacent to her own bedroom in the west tower of Culbrech House, Philippa Maclaren turned sharply from her mother in anger. 'I will *not* ride with Harry Bruce,' she repeated. 'I will not. You'll simply have to send MacIlwraith, and your own car. And I do wish you'd arrange it now because I am running very short of time.'

She looked pointedly at her wrist, and the new-style man's watch that she wore there. Victoria bridled at the gesture, completed as it was by a prim tapping of the crystal, and at what she interpreted as haughtiness in the girl's voice. She had, quite wrongly, assumed that Philippa's reluctance to share a motor car with Harry Bruce for the journey to Inverness and the railway station, was a snobbish distaste for riding with the gardener, regardless of his parentage.

'MacIlwraith,' she said with deliberate slowness, 'is, as you know, not only my chauffeur, these days, but my head ploughman. I would think your ardent patriotism would demand that he be left to his ploughing, rather than making needless journeys to Inverness.'

'Hardly needless, Mother,' Philippa said coolly. 'I'm addressing the Aberdeen branch of the Active Service League at three. *If* I am taken to Inverness.'

Victoria shrugged. With conscription now looming visibly in the wings, Philippa's recruiting organizations had taken on an air of impending uselessness which seemed oddly only to increase their ferocity. 'Then I suggest, madam,' Victoria said, turning to the door, 'that Miss Philippa Maclaren lowers her standards for the sake of her noble cause. Harry Bruce is driving to Inverness, and as far as I'm concerned you may go with him, or stay here.' The door shut firmly behind her, leaving Philippa alone in resounding silence.

She stood in the centre of the room as anger, and courage, washed out of her. She glanced towards the mirror, startled by the sight of herself, suddenly slump-shouldered and oddly slight. Her mouth tingled, remembering that awful day in the garden. She had not spoken to him since, nor he to her. Her heart pounded and her breath shortened. She put her hand in front of her lips, fearing she would again be sick. But the sickness did not come, and down below, the thin petulant toot of a car horn told her that Harry was waiting. She straightened her back, and slowly, her eyes on the mirror, settled her hat in place, tucking in three stray strands of hair, and thrusting a pearl-tipped hatpin through felt, and hair, and felt. So, no doubt, with such deliberation, did soldiers go over the top. She took up gloves, calfskin handbag, and the notes for her speech. The horn blared once more, and Philippa Maclaren turned her face to the Front.

'You look charming,' he said. His eyes were straight ahead, looking through the windscreen on to the rutted Highland road. She said nothing.

'Have you heard from Tenny?'

'He is quite well thank you.'

'And Albert and James?'

'They are quite well thank you.'

'Are you going to Johnny's wedding?'

'If my work allows me.'

He smiled, glanced her way once, got a stony look and returned his eyes to the road.

'What will you do,' she said, unable ever to hold her tongue, 'if they bring in conscription?'

'Go to jail, I suppose,' Harry said, and then smiled, and was about to say, 'Will you visit me?' even as she was studying him coldly, trying to see if he meant it, when both their attentions were caught by a strange commotion in a field of barley stubble that bordered the road.

Midway up the rise of the hill, stark against the pale ground, were a man and a Clydesdale team, and a plough, strung out in a long dark line. They alone would not have brought a second glance; tenants and Culbrech employees alike were engaged in winter ploughing. But, where Angus MacIlwraith's rigg, which Harry's car had passed minutes before, was marked with neat geometry – a rich brown corduroy of furrows in a broadening rectangular strip – this field was scarred back and forth with dark jagged wounds of earth, zigzagging aimlessly up, down, sideways, as if a madman were ploughing.

Harry stopped the car and let the engine die. In the silence that followed, the ploughman's voice came clearly down the empty hillside, shouting and cursing at the horses, and answered by a frightened whinny of distress.

'What on earth is he doing?' Harry said aloud. 'Digging trenches?'

'He's mistreating that poor team, frightfully, for a start,' Philippa exclaimed, indignant. 'If my father saw that, he'd have him horsewhipped. Who is that man?'

Harry grimaced slightly, saying under his breath, 'I suspect the Crofting Commission would have something to say if he did.' Then he opened his door and climbed out, followed rapidly by Philippa. Harry was staring up the hill where the man was still wrestling with his plough and berating his staggering team with his voice.

'Get on, ye lazy buggers, get on,' the voice was high with a touch of hysteria, or maybe drink. Harry was mystified, and began trotting towards the gate in the wire fence, wondering who the wild ploughman could possibly be. He had realized with a jolt that the field was part of Ewan Grant's croft, and with Ewan only weeks back from his London hospital, blind and maimed, he would have expected to find no one working the croft at all. Fiona would no doubt have enough to do with her husband and bairn. He wondered then, as he swung the gate open, and stepped into the muddy edge of the field, if Fiona had hired some drunken tinker labourer, in desperation.

'Stop him, Harry,' Philippa commanded from behind, 'before one of those poor beasts breaks a leg.'

The team were plunging straight downhill now, the plough careening sideways, ploughman stumbling after. He had lost the reins and they flapped loosely on to the broken earth, slapping against the horses' flanks, frightening them still further.

'I say,' Harry shouted, starting to run uphill towards the crazed team, 'I say, ploughman . . .' There was no answer, the man seemed oblivious, unhearing, unseeing. Who the hell was he? Harry heard Philippa still barking sharp commands about the horses behind him, and then suddenly her voice was joined by another woman's voice and the high-pitched crying of a child. He turned in the mud of one of the field's vagrant furrows and saw, running up the road, awkward with the bulk of her pregnancy, and with the wailing child clutched in her arms, Fiona Grant.

'Ewan,' she shouted, the distance thinning her voice to a high wail, 'Ewan, please . . .' She saw Harry then and set the child down at the edge of the field and ran towards him, calling, 'Mr Bruce, Mr Bruce, can ye no' stop him? He'll kill himsel',' she sobbed. But Harry was already running towards the team.

He met them in the middle of the field, throwing himself in front of the plunging beasts, leaping up and catching the reins of the nearer bridle. The big horse skidded back on its haunches, flinging up its head, nearly dragging Harry off his feet. The plough flopped over, and Ewan, stumbling with his own momentum, pitched over it and into the furrowed earth. He was down just an instant, before he was scrambling wildly to his feet, turning his blind, eyeless, monstrous face towards the noise of the jingling harness, feeling wildly in the air for horse, or whippletree, or share. 'Damn bastards, I'll skelp yer fuckin' hides.'

The clutching hands caught suddenly the extended arms of Harry Bruce. 'Wha' the hell?'

'Ewan, it's me. Harry. Harry Bruce.'

'Ma team,' Ewan muttered, concerned, reaching around Harry.

'I've got them calmed. They'll stand. Ewan, what were you doing?' Harry said, his voice barely above a whisper. 'You can't plough, now.' He felt an idiot saying it, a fact which Ewan so obviously wished to ignore. Then Fiona caught up with them, flinging her arms around Ewan, sobbing, and begging him to come down, come away home, come back to his bed. Harry stepped back, unable to face their painful intimacy. Ewan turned his face away from his wife, towards the blank stubble hill, as if by instinct. It was as scarred and crisscrossed as the field he had ravaged, the dark eye-sockets like two gouges of the sharp steel plough. Against its ruin, Fiona's hearty pregnant beauty made a fearsome contrast.

'Come awa' hame,' she begged, tears running freely all over her face. The little boy, Willie John, had stumbled up from the foot of the field and was now clinging to her long white apron, sobbing frantically.

Harry, seeing Philippa standing silently a few yards downhill, was suddenly filled with anger at her inaction and shouted, 'Take the child, Philippa, for God's sake. Do something.' But she did not, and it was left to Harry to lift the crying boy and comfort him while his mother and father fought.

'I'll plough ma rigg, first, woman. You just awa' an' mak' the tea.'

'Ye cannae plough, Ewan. Yer blind. Yer blind,' she shrieked suddenly, losing control. 'How can ye do this tae yoursel'? And tae us. Have ye gane mad?'

'Awa' an' mak' the tea,' Ewan growled.

'I'll hire a man tae plough.'

'Wi' what fer money?'

'I'll plough it myself,' she cried. 'Just come home.'

'An' whit am I tae dae, while yer awa' on the hill all the day? Mind the bairn? An' look tae the dairy wi' yer old Mam?' He turned his awful face towards her as if he could still see. She faced him but closed her eyes, her hands balled into fists by her sides, swaying slightly back and forth. Harry, thinking she would faint, stepped nearer, but when he reached out his one free arm to help her, she turned on him angrily.

'Get away,' she whispered hoarsely.

'Let me help,' Harry said.

'Help!' she cried, her misery turning into misdirected fury. 'How can you help? Can you give Ewan his eyes back, that yer damned lot took awa'?'

'Just let me help him down the hill,' he said quietly, hoping Ewan would not hear. But Ewan did, turning his blind face towards the whisper.

'Whit are ye mutterin' aboot,' he cried, suspicious. 'Whit ye sayin' that I'm no' tae ken?'

'Nothing, Ewan.'

'Tell secrets wi' ma wife, will ye?'

'Oh, for God's sake, Ewan, he's trying to help us,' Fiona said, finding reason again.

'Och aye. I'm sure he is. I ken his kind. Stay safe at hame, while the rest o' us get blown tae pieces an' nou he wants tae help. Wants tae help himsel' tae ma wife, nae doubt.'

'Ewan,' she whispered, sickened. 'It's just madness,' she said to Harry. But Ewan was very close to that, just now, and he found the idea appealing and laughed bitterly.

'Nae doubt he's been helping a' alang. Ploughin' ma rigg for me, hae ye, Harry Bruce. Maybe then it's no' ma crop at a'. Maybe it's just anither Bruce bastard, instead. A guid crop o' those in the strath before. A guid crop.' He grinned grotesquely, his mutilated face twisting sideways. Fiona stood alone now, crying, her hands wringing her apron into a knot.

Philippa was still watching, wordless, as remote as the two Clydesdales standing flicking their long heavy tails. Harry stepped closer to Ewan, putting his left hand firmly on his shoulder, and handing Willie John to his mother at the same time.

'Ewan, that's not fair. We've always been friends. All our lives. And you know I'm not like that. I don't mind you calling me names, but it's unfair to your wife. She's good and honest. She deserves more.'

Ewan stood silent, shivering in the cold. Harry realized that the man wore no coat, had come out on the hill in his shirtsleeves, and he quietly slipped his own off and put it around Ewan's shoulders.

'Whit am I gonnae dae, sir?' he said suddenly, his voice normal, trusting, like of old.

'I don't know, Ewan, but we'll work something out. Myself, Lady Maclaren. I promise you.'

'You're aye a man o' yer word,' Ewan said, to himself, really. 'I ken that.'

He seemed calmer, and allowed Harry to lead him down towards the fence, while Fiona set about unhitching the team. Only at the gate did he turn, once, sweeping the lost hill with his sightless face, and resting his head against Harry's shoulder for an instant. 'Och Christ, why did I no' die out there?' he said.

Harry had got Ewan into the front seat of the car, and was helping Fiona and the child into the rear, when Philippa spoke.

'You're not going back to the croft, surely,' she said with that obdurate stupidity some women employ to mask a direct command.

'I am,' he said.

'Harry . . .' He knew at once what she would say, and turned, waiting for it, with growing amazement at her singleminded selfishness. 'Harry, I shall miss my train.'

In that instant in which she spoke, Harry felt drop away from him all the quiet sympathy his gentle nature held. He looked hard at her and saw a mannish, cold-faced woman whose determined features were already cast in the lines of disapproving maiden age. He smiled slightly and said, 'Get in, Philippa. Please.' She seemed uncertain, not knowing if he had agreed with her or not. Reluctantly she climbed into the rear seat of the car, straightening her grey tweed skirt quickly so it would not brush against the grubby knees and muddy shoes of little Willie John.

Harry cranked the engine and got in behind the wheel, and began, laboriously on the narrow road, to turn the car round. Philippa stared, disbelieving, looked wildly at her watch and cried, 'Harry this is absurd. My mother said you were to take me to Inverness.' She looked back at her man's watch for emphasis. 'If you must take these people, the least you could do is drop me off first, and take them home after.'

'Your mother,' Harry said, '*asked*,' he glanced over his shoulder, reversing the big car carefully up to the edge of the wire fence, 'if I would take you. If however you prefer, then I shall drop you off first.'

Philippa settled back, relaxing, until Harry suddenly slammed the brake on, got out and opened her door.

'Harry?'

'Out.'

She didn't believe him, but he jerked her down rudely by the arm and when she was standing, spluttering with outrage, he pointed calmly eastwards down the road.

'My dear,' he said, 'Inverness.'

Then he leapt back into his seat and the car roared off, splashing muddy rainwater on Philippa's lisle-stockinged ankles and high-laced leather boots.

Harry kept his promise to Ewan Grant, pursuing one avenue after another of potential solutions until he came upon an odd, but practical, scheme. With the agreement of Lady Maclaren, he approached Mrs Murchison in the Culbrech kitchens, and through her, the little feeble-minded kitchenmaid, Mairi.

Mairi was reluctant at first to leave the security of Mrs Murchison's kitchen, but a visit to the croft, where Fiona treated her like a spoiled baby sister, and Willie John, delighted with a companion of similar childish mentality, scrambled devotedly after her, soon won her confidence.

And though there was truth in her open admission that, 'I cannae dae onything, sir, I'm awfu' stupid,' she was able to do the one thing that was required of her by Ewan Grant; the one thing he could not do. She could see. Daft Mairi would be Ewan's eyes, leading him, like a wise, faithful dog, about croft and kailyard. Obviously, much would remain beyond him for ever; the ploughing would have to be done by others, and the harvest. But Harry, gently persuasive, convinced Ewan that men from the Culbrech fields could be, and would be spared, and managed to enable Ewan to accept his offer as if it were a reward for his service to his country, like his meagre pension, and not simply charity.

'I'll nae be needing them fer lang, ye ken,' Ewan said, assuring himself, more than Harry, and Harry agreed, leaving him the hope men need to live on, that one day he would again plough, with Mairi guiding his horses and his feet.

Mairi herself was thrilled with her role, feeling more important than ever in her life, and she became instantly and slavishly devoted to Ewan, waiting on his words, her slanted, happy eyes brightening joyously at his praise. In her innocence she was not the slightest off-put by his distorted face, and again in her innocence, she alone would speak of it to him.

'Yer like the bread dough, fu' o' cracks an' wee lumps,' she cried, delighted with her own image, clapping her hands.

'Aye,' Ewan smiled slowly, the first real smile since Loos, 'I ken I must be. Lucky fer me I dinna hae tae luik.'

'Bread head,' Mairi cried, clapping again. And then, coyly, 'Can I ca' ye bread head, Ewan, can I?'

Ewan smiled again, more broadly, knowing her audacious request was a statement of love. It, and her appalling candour, did more for him than all the gentle words of nurses, the reassurances even of his wife. He knew again that he could be, destroyed as he was, still loved.

'Aye, Mairi. But just yerself. Nane ither. It's just fer you an' me.'

Harry himself helped Mairi to move her small bundle of belongings down to the croft, and he left them there together one winter afternoon when the low sun was barely scraping the southern hills on its hasty way to night. They looked contented enough together, an odd little family. Fiona thanked him yet again, bending awkwardly over her bulging body to allow him to kiss her cheek. She seemed to sense the finality of his farewell, which was odd, since he had told no one.

He walked away to his car, looking back over his shoulder as Mairi, with Ewan's hand on her shoulder, led the way proudly to the sheep-fank, her moonface lit with her brightest of smiles. Harry smiled too, as he started the engine and got in the car. Yet as he glanced back once more, before driving away, and saw the pair silhouetted against the winter sunset the image of the blind man and the poor daft girl shook him terribly. He thought suddenly, there is Scotland's tomorrow, a nation crippled. Thinking about it, and the war that caused it all, a bitterness rose in him that only action could combat.

It was out of the same bitterness that, the day before, he had applied to join the Royal Army Medical Corps as an ambulance-driver. He had consulted no one, but after, he had told his grandfather.

Willie Bruce, frail and bedridden, had taken so long to answer that Harry had wondered if he had understood. Still Willie's mind was sharp, though all other faculties were rapidly failing. He said, his voice thin as his old face, 'Ye'll no' win Ewan back his eyes.'

Harry was amazed. Naturally the events of that day, and their consequences, had been spoken of, particularly Philippa's extraordinary predicament, but he had no idea the old man maintained such an awareness of life around him.

'I know that, sir. But I might save someone else's.' He paused and said in a rush, 'Don't you see, sir, it's the only way I can fight back?'

'Wha's it yer fightin', Harry? The Germans? Or the regiment?'

Harry was silent. He said finally, 'I think just the war. Just the war itself.'

Old Willie looked cannily at him and said, 'D'ye ken, thot's whit Johnny said once, in one o' his letters afore Loos. That he'd got the queer notion that the war itsel's become the enemy, fer a', Jerry an' Jock alike.'

'I think,' said Harry Bruce, 'it has.'

* * *

Harry was accepted by the RAMC at once, and left Culbrech within the week. He did not see Philippa again, after that day on the road, and was surprised to find that he simply did not care. She had closeted herself in her tower room, claiming to have contracted a severe chill on her long walk back to Culbrech House. But it was not that, but humiliation that made her hide her face. She had arrived at the house wet and bedraggled and in a towering rage, and had marched into her mother's drawing-room. Heedless of her mother's guests, a delegation from the newly formed Women's Rural Institute delivering supplies of knitted balaclavas, she had stormed lengthily about her mistreatment, demanding Harry's instant dismissal. Such a reaction would not really have surprised Harry himself; he had considered it a distinct possibility after his abandonment of Philippa on the Inverness road. Even before his decision to leave, he had regarded it as a worthy exchange.

However Victoria Maclaren was made of sturdier stuff. When Philippa had finally wound down to a normal shout, rather than an hysterical shriek, and at last paused for breath, Victoria, without a glance at her amazed WRI visitors, had said, 'Quite right, too. Good on old Harry. Go and wash your face.'

Whether she had, no one knew; Philippa had not shown her face, washed or unwashed, since that day. Victoria was unimpressed. She sent trays up regularly to two towers of Culbrech now, to Philippa and to Aunt Jean, and waited for maturity, or simply boredom, to overcome Philippa and drive her back down.

Harry was quietly relieved. He did not fear her anger but felt that had she taken the other tack, and come to congratulate him on his decision to go, in some capacity, to the Front, he might have done her harm. Might, but not likely; the angers in him were washed away by the new peace of his decision. He did not honestly know if he was triumphing over the war, or losing to it, but for the first time since 1914, his mind was at rest.

He left on the morning train, the second Monday in December. The day afterwards, Philippa Maclaren also left Culbrech, without warning, and descended unannounced on Naomi Bruce in London. It was the day Torquil Farquhar, his leave nearly over, returned there from his father's home near Perth, a fact of which she was quite ignorant. They met in the hallway by accident, he in the civilian clothes that those on leave loved to wear, tokens of normality. Whimsical Fate had granted Philippa what all her manipulative nature had never achieved. She was alone with Torquil Farquhar and Emma was far, far away.

Philippa stared. A tide of emotion rushed upon her, embarrassment, humiliation, her perennial jealousy of Emma, but not a drop of the compassion that might have saved them both. She found her voice in mundanity. 'But where is Emma?' she demanded stupidly. 'Didn't she know you were to have leave?'

Within Torquil Farquhar a small light of hope, a light that grew from a distant remembrance of Philippa in her green velvet suit, and a fluttering of unexpected romance, died out at once. 'Oh yes. Of course. Terribly busy of course, old Em. You know how these nurses are.' He brushed by her quickly, unable to speak further without his hurt showing, and she took the dismissal as one of herself.

They went to separate rooms; two who might have comforted each other, and instead only deepened each other's distress. They had so much in common; their mutual desire to hold on to a fanciful, vainglorious world that was already lost. But neither was able to speak from the heart. Safe behind protective shields of reserve, they smothered themselves in solitude.

At dinner, they barely spoke, exchanging only those pleasantries that pass for conversation among strangers. Naomi watched, as one watches unhappy children, with sorrow, and distance. The following day Philippa had a meeting with the editorial staff of *John Bull* magazine. Torquil watched her go from his bedroom window, seeing her brisk and assured once more, and wondering secretly what had happened between herself and Harry Bruce that made her so unwilling to discuss him or cheer his long-awaited entry to the war. Was it possible that she was in love with him? To Torquil, this day, love was equated with misery, and so, seeing misery, he assumed love. Yes, no doubt, a lover's tiff. He felt shut out by her, as by Emma, and indeed now, everyone else. None of them could understand. Not his father, surely, who had taken him stalking of all things, so that he had spent three days of his leave lying on a wet muddy hillside that might as well have been France. Poor old man, going on so about the old regiment, reminiscing about the old days, India, when war was fun. Couldn't expect him to understand. Still, he wished to God someone did.

A day of his leave remained. Halfway through the fortnight he had found himself positively longing for its end, and for his return. All he wanted now was to be back with his men, sharing their misery, and their dangers, back where he might perhaps protect them. It seemed indecent to be warm and clean, to go to the theatre, and to stop in cafés for tea. Still, in the early afternoon he went out, dressed in his plain clothes, trying to blend himself into the great city.

In Piccadilly Circus he met a sweet-faced girl with white-blonde hair and a flowing, mock-nurse's cloak. She smiled. Her smile lured him closer. She looked at his plain tweed suit and civilian hat, his young, fit body and face and smiled again. When he was close enough to hear her speak the smile came the third time and then she said, 'Coward,' and thrust a leaflet and a white feather in his hand.

For a moment, he mouthed a protest. She did not understand, he was a soldier . . . but the words did not come. Because she knew. He could see it in her eyes with their soft brown depths full of knowledge. She knew. Of course. How could she know? Here, so far away. No matter. If she knew, they all knew. He looked around, wild-eyed, at the crowds. They were all looking at him, furtive looks, quick turns away, and then staring again. Of course they all knew. The whole world knew. Coward.

He thrust feather and leaflet into his deep pocket and stumbled away, turning once to look at the girl before he broke into a terrified run.

By the time he reached Naomi's street he understood why Emma had not come with him, why Philippa would not speak to him. They knew too, of course. They were probably the first to know. He was sweating heavily and panting when he came to her door. He flung it open, not bothering with the bell, with any formality. Too late. It was over. In the open now. Over the top. No-man's-land.

'Torquil,' Naomi cried, scurrying to meet the commotion. 'Whatever is wrong?'

Instantly, Torquil calmed himself; training coming to the fore. Don't let them know you know *they* know. Mustn't act suspicious. Natural, calm. He grinned boyishly.

'Nothing at all, my dear, just getting a little exercise. Time I were back in shape, what?'

He drew his hand out of his pocket, as she reached to take his coat, and the leaflet and feather came, as if by their own volition, with it into the air.

'What's that you are holding?' Naomi asked curiously. He looked at his hand, the clutched paper, the matted feather.

'Oh nothing. Just this. Bit of nonsense some silly girl handed me. Imagine going around London handing people feathers,' he laughed strainedly.

Naomi was incensed the instant she saw the leaflet, recognizing the colours of the Active Service League handouts. The feather she crushed up and dropped in an ashtray. Her eyes searched his face, seeking upset. She was well accustomed to men under stress and knew well enough that he had had plenty. But he smiled, and she, seeing he wished to make light of it, laughed softly and agreed it was foolish and a trifle.

Her eyes studied his stiff back as he walked slowly, purposefully, up the stairs. She wished to follow him, but there was an aloofness in his posture that asked to be left alone. Yet she was not happy about it, and was still standing, hesitant, in the stairwell, her fingers folding, unfolding and refolding the leaflet Torquil had handed her when the doorbell rang. She jumped, realizing how nervous the meeting with Torquil had made her, and stepped towards the door as Mary rushed out from below stairs.

'Miss Maclaren, Mrs Bruce,' said Mary. Philippa stepped quickly into the hallway and strode towards Naomi, removing her hat and absent-mindedly thrusting hatpins through the crown, already talking.

'I wonder if I might dine early, tonight, my dear,' she was saying. 'I've promised to add a few lines to my essay on *The Lessons of Loos*, so I'm afraid I'll need to retire to the study quite promptly. And Mary, could you ask Cook if I might have a piece of plain boiled fish; I do get enough of these rich sauces. Naomi, I . . .'

'Torquil was handed this in the street today,' Naomi said, holding out the leaflet towards Philippa, but not close enough to allow her to see it properly. Philippa stepped closer, peering, and Naomi added, 'Rather ironic, don't you think.'

Philippa recognized it, stared a moment, and then said, her voice only slightly subdued, 'Well, he will go about dressed like a civilian. What are people to think? A bit of pride in the khaki would not be amiss. Avoid mistakes and encourage the others as well. Still, I expect he found it all a great hoot.' She laughed briskly and turned aside, and Naomi was about to speak, and in anger, when they both, at once, heard the singing.

'Whoever?' said Philippa, faintly indignant at the intrusion.

'Hush,' Naomi said, listening.

'Surely that's not Abbott?' Philippa continued. 'But who else?'

But Naomi, certain the voice came from above, and not from below in the staff quarters, was already mounting the stairs, at first slowly, and then with unreasoned haste. She paused at the first landing, hearing Philippa, still muttering querulously, climbing the stairs behind her. Over the thud of her sturdy walking boots, the voice, clear, and quite loud, drifted downwards, the words distinctly audible:

'The bells of hell go ding-a-ling-a-ling
For you and not for me . . .'

Philippa stopped on the landing âlso, hearing the words as well, and bristling visibly. 'Now that's a bit much really. *Who* is singing that ghastly song? I wish they'd ban the thing . . .'

'Torquil,' Naomi said quietly, to herself.

'Torquil? Singing that? Never.'

'Oh yes,' Naomi breathed and then began running, heart pounding, up the stairs. She made the second landing, but Torquil was not there, not in his guest bedroom, but above. The voice was louder and quite gay.

'Oh death where is thy sting-a-ling-a-ling
Grave thy vic-tor-y?'

'Oh God,' Naomi whispered, turning to the third flight of stairs, running, skirts gathered, as fast as she could, and yet, she was fifty and more, her breath short and gasping as she cried, 'Torquil! Torquil! Wait!'

'The bells of hell . . .'

He dragged the last lines out with broad, cheerful rhythm, and Naomi reached the last step, Philippa blundering behind her, and caught the railing, facing three closed doors.

'. . . go ding . . . a-ling . . . a-ling
For you and not for . . .'

The whole upper house shook with the tight confined crash of the pistol shot, perfectly in rhythm with his song. There was a clatter, a heavy thud, and silence. Then Philippa screamed. Downstairs voices shouted, there were footsteps running. But Naomi was alone, as alone as she'd ever been in her long, lonely life.

She breathed deeply and slowly opened the door.

He had been sitting on the old grey rocking-horse, and it lay now, overturned, like a fallen cavalryman's mount, half across his legs. He had wrapped a white towel around his head and shot himself through the mouth. The towel had done little to minimize the effect, and blood and shattered flesh was everywhere, and a piece of clean skullbone lay on the polished floor like a little shallow cup.

'Poor lamb,' Naomi whispered. 'A gentleman. Always a gentleman.' She shook her head at the pathetic bloody towel. Her eyes searched the room for something to cover him with as, deep within herself, she covered her feelings with the trained calm of her nursing years. She found a beautiful paisley shawl, left there from Susan's last modelling for Mr Leitner. She lifted it, stepped towards the awful mess on the nursery floor, and then she remembered Philippa, out there on the landing, and the leaflet of the Active Service League. She bunched the shawl in her hand, and her face hardened into ancient eastern lines of hatred.

'Philippa,' she said calmly as she stepped out into the hall.

Philippa was crouched in the corner of the landing, by the window overlooking Hyde Park. She was down on her haunches like a little girl, her knuckles pressed together in front of her mouth, her face as white as Torquil's riven bone.

'Come here,' Naomi said softly.

'No,' Philippa, like an animal, seemed to sense her intention. But Naomi would not relent. She stepped closer and when Philippa moaned, and made to scuttle away, caught her hard by both forearms and wrenched her to her feet.

'Come here,' she said again.

'No.' Philippa moaned, louder, and then screamed, 'No, no,' and struggled, but as big and strong as she was, Naomi's fierce anger gave her an overpowering strength and Philippa was dragged like a child to the nursery door.

'Don't make me look,' she cried, hysterical, 'I shall die, I shall die!'

'Oh no you shan't,' Naomi said bitterly. 'Looks don't kill.

Words do, but not looks.' She flung open the door and thrust Philippa in, and caught her turned face by its cleft chin and wrenched her head round until she could see, in the widening horror of the shallow pale eyes, that Philippa at last had seen. She let her go. The girl reeled away, shrieking, stumbled into another door, half opened it, and then stood, spewing vomit on the carpet, and finally collapsed in a silently shuddering heap. Naomi knew in that instant that she had gone too far, but could not bring herself to care.

She re-entered the room, covered Torquil with Susan's paisley shawl and went silently away.

6

Victoria Maclaren walked alone in the gardens of Culbrech House. The weather was mild for December, though not unusual in Strathglass, that sort of day that swung disconcertedly between rain squalls and wet sunlight, driving one inside to the fire at one moment and then calling one back to the garden. She could see the next squall coming and had not even a hat to cover her hair, but she remained, walking carefully down the long pathways of pink gravel amidst flower borders and rosebeds and clumps of glistening wet rhododendrons. Tatty and overgrown, the roses yet unpruned, the garden vividly recalled the absence of Harry Bruce. Victoria missed his sane, gentle self that moved so patiently through the hungry, impatient wartime world.

He was out there now, at last, in danger enough to satisfy anyone. He had written her one long, beautiful letter, and his descriptions of the sights, smells and scenes of daily life had chilled her through. She wondered if that sharp and sensitive mind would succumb to brutality, or to self-destruction like Torquil Farquhar. She sighed. Her mind had come back again to that which she'd sought the garden to escape. It was twelve days since Torquil's suicide, and today Ian was bringing Emma home from France.

The family would have gathered this week, anyhow, for Johnny Bruce's wedding, now put off by the tragedy into the new year. Rebecca's response, she readily admitted, had both amazed her and given her a new respect for the girl. She had left her lodgings in Edinburgh at once, leaving Johnny to journey north alone, and travelled to France to be with Emma in her grief. Now the three of them were returning together; Rebecca to be with Johnny until their delayed wedding, Ian but for a few days before his duties in France demanded his return, and Emma? Victoria sighed again, feeling the immense weight of her teetering family fully upon her shoulders once more. Emma. Emma who was always the strength, the brave one, the cheery one. Emma whose only communication with them since her fiancé's death had come through the matron of the hospital in France, a brief telegrammed message, WE ADVISE MISS MACLAREN'S IMMEDIATE RETURN HOME FOR REASONS OF HEALTH.

Reasons of health; it could mean anything, but Victoria, who had three days before endured the harrowing experience of leaving her younger daughter Philippa behind in a convalescent home in London when she returned to Culbrech from the south, could envisage only a similar descent into madness.

What had happened in Naomi's house on the day Torquil shot himself was a mystery to Victoria. She was led to understand that Philippa had not witnessed the suicide, nor had anyone. Why she had gone into the room afterwards had not been explained. The effect, however, of what she had seen was all too obvious. Naomi, who throughout the whole period remained oddly detached, indeed quite coolly uncaring about Philippa, reported only that Philippa had been taken from the house in a distressed state, and under doctor's orders been placed under nursing care. When Victoria visited her she found a room full of wealthy, senile old ladies, and her own young daughter, looking somehow frail and quite beautiful surrounded by her masses of ruddy hair, lying in bed and staring at the wall. She would not speak nor acknowledge anyone who spoke to her and in the end, with doctors' reassurances washing impotently over her, Victoria was forced simply to go away.

Now Emma was returning and Victoria prayed she would not appear like Philippa, at the same time knowing she must, for it was her lover, not Philippa's, who was dead. Victoria turned to the house. Johnny Bruce was standing on the steps, awaiting her, holding out a tweed cloak for her. He looked fit and well again, and even the cane he carried for his limp had begun to seem merely decorative. The sun came again and lighted his young face, his bright blue eyes, and his irrepressible grin. Not for the first time Victoria thought how lovely it would be to be a man, to go off and do, rather than wait at home for things to be done to oneself. No wonder men, strong men like Johnny and Ian, survived, and thrived on wars, while women at home were chipped away and diminished until nothing was left but a shell full of pain.

Emma was not like Philippa. Even in grief she allowed herself no self-indulgence. It would have been easy to collapse into hysteria, tears, a trance, to be petted over and put to bed and have her hands, so used to comforting others, held now by those who loved her. But she was too strong for that; too strong to allow herself a moment's relief from the guilt that overwhelmed her.

'I killed him,' she said to her mother, as she stepped off the train. And no one, not Victoria, nor Ian, not Rebecca nor Johnny, no one could persuade her that she had not. She let them try, all of them, because she was too dutiful a daughter to turn from her parents, too loyal a friend to reject Rebecca's love or Johnny's brotherly affection. She listened, white-faced and patient while Ian Maclaren bumbled through his explanation of shell-shock, and where it could lead a man, and how thinking leadership had grown to accept it as in no way a judgement on his courage. As if she cared about that. She lay long late hours on her bed in her childhood bedroom, while Rebecca assured her she had done all she could for Torquil and, had his mind not been affected by the war, he would certainly agree. She lay with her eyes closed, remembering years back to the dream she had had in that same room, of Torquil alone and calling for help with no one to answer. In the end she turned off the light so that Rebecca would not see her cry, and let Rebecca's gentle, well-meaning voice lull her briefly to sleep.

The following day Johnny walked about the garden, still limping slightly, with Emma on his arm, not speaking about Torquil's death at all, but instead of their experiences at Loos, and Torquil's courage and proficiency as an officer, as if those things could somehow overshadow his awful end. She listened most patiently of all to Johnny because she felt he had more right to speak than any, having been there. In the end she said, 'They don't understand, do they?' nodding towards the house, to show him she was understanding him, but then begged to be excused and walked off through the wet gardens alone. Johnny watched her go, knowing he too had failed.

She did not consciously think where she was going, and yet, she knew. Her feet found their way there relentlessly, across the road, and a field of bare stubble, and then the low river meadow, and at last she was within sight of the Glass itself, grey and full under a stormy winter sky. Her eyes sought the length of it for the familiar dark cluster of Scots pines that marked the picnic ground, and did not find them. She stopped walking, confused, sure she was on the right path, but yet unsure. Suddenly it became important to her, and her restless wandering towards the old river site where her one perfect day with Torquil had been spent, became a pilgrimage. She turned, began walking back along the water's edge, pushing through clumps of alder saplings, still holding bitterly to their last few crumpled brown leaves. How could a place so familiar be lost to her?

She stopped, straightened, and looked all round and then the outlines of the land slipped suddenly into place. She was standing in the middle of what she sought; the picnic-ground, overgrown and abandoned, lay all around her, and she saw now why she had not found it before. The great Scots pine trees were gone. Emma stared uncomprehending around her, searching vainly for their dark, kind shadows. She walked a few steps and found the first stump, sawn through but for the jagged tear where gravity had finished what the woodsmen began. She stumbled, benumbed, from one stump to the next, and finally sat down, alone, on one of the highest, and looked forlornly out on to the tumbling rock-strewn waters of the Glass. She felt as if some deliberate sacrilege had been wrought against her secret temple, and her heart filled with personal hurt.

She bent her head and began to cry, and for the first time since Torquil's death she was weeping not for him, but for herself. Frankie Gibson found her there, an hour later, sitting alone in the falling rain. She turned, saw him, and seemed to recognize him, but then turned away, watching the river again, without speaking.

'Sae ye've come home, lass,' he said, settling beside her and prodding curls of tobacco into his pipe. His old eyes went from the smooth brown tangles in his tobacco pouch to Emma's turned head, noting absently that her curly hair was quite the same colour. She did not answer.

'Sorry aboot yer lad,' Frankie said, again to no answer. 'Sandy told me. Says his men were richt stunnered. Not that he told them whit really happened. Ca'd it an accident, or some such,' he paused, lighting the pipe, but pursued relentlessly, 'but I'll nae lie aboot the lad. Taks a puckle courage tae dae whit he did. I'll nae lie aboot him.'

'Frankie, please,' Emma whispered.

'An' dinna let me catch you ever lyin' o'er him, lass. I'll skelp ye. Death's ae time fer honesty.'

Emma looked up, amazed, and finally managed to say, stumbling over her words in a mixture of anger and grief, 'How can you talk like this to me, you foolish old man? My fiancé killed himself. Killed himself. Because of me. Because I wouldn't listen when he begged for my help. Because I was too busy,' she began to sob.

Frankie nodded, sagely. 'Aye. An' whit were ye doin' then? Awa' wi' some o' yer lady friends haein' tea? Or oot dancin' wi' some brither officer?'

Emma whirled around to face him, suddenly furious. 'I don't understand why you've come here to torment me, but please, please go away. Of course I wasn't. I was nursing. I was nursing,' she repeated, beginning once again to sob.

Frankie stood up, and came closer to her and crouched down on his haunches in the heather. 'Aye, lass,' he said. 'Thot's whit I was waitin' tae hear. Nursing. An' whit finer thing could ye hae been daein'?'

Emma shook her head and looked away. 'Oh I know, I know. You're just like all the rest after all. Everyone tells me I was doing my duty, so it wasn't my fault. But I know I failed him. If it wasn't my fault, whose was it?'

'His ain.'

'No.'

'Yes, lass. His ain fault. You didna fail onybody. But he did. He failed his men, he failed his regiment, he failed himself, and he failed you. And you know it, in your heart, an' thot's why yer sittin' awa' oot here in the rain, a'cause the man you thought you loved has let ye doon, an' gane awa' wi'out ye, and left ye on yer ain. No, I willna ca' him a coward. I'll lea that tae yon braw folk wha' never cam near a battle. I ken whit it's like, fightin', and I ken frae Sandy yon's the worst fightin' oor warld's ever known.

Still, when a sodger gies way tae despair, it's no' his lass at fault, but his officers.' He leaned back, puffing at the pipe, and Emma turned, her eyes suddenly clear, and studied his lined face, and his lank, iron-grey hair. Suddenly she glimpsed how he must have appeared as a young man, and saw he had been handsome.

She said, in a voice gone strangely young, 'Frankie?'

'Aye.'

'I did love him. You said I only thought so. But I did love him.'

He replied at once, with a trace of a smile. 'Aye, lass. You did, aince. I remember, langsyne, the picnic, and yourself awa' there,' he pointed and she saw at last her lost rowan tree, surrounded by regrowth of cut alders. 'But I saw a lass and a loon, a wee girlie and a wee boy, in love there. And you went aff and became a woman, and the poor lad didna ken how tae follow. Thot's why yer grietin', lass, a'cause ye'd grown awa' frae him, an' couldna save him. But it wisna' fer ye tae do, lass. Aiblins it wisna fer onybody at a'.'

Emma sighed, looking around her slowly, feeling bits and pieces of her life beginning to grow real again.

'I ken whit it's like,' Frankie said. 'When ma wife died, a year ago, I didna want tae live. I'd wake every mornin' thinkin' "she's gane", and I'd no' want tae face the day. An' then, ae morning I woke an' thought o' the river, and just for a moment, wondered if the salmon were running yet. A'course I felt shamed, as if I'd forgotten her, but from that day on, I'd find ae thing, an' then anither wi' pleasure in it again. Ma pipe. The way the sun sklent aff the kitchen table, that I aye liked. Those things come back, e'en when ye'd try to keep them awa'. An' then one day, ye find yerself happy again. It doesna last, but ye ken it's possible. An' ye ken yer on the right gate at last.'

Emma looked across at him shyly, and with a little remorse. 'I didn't even know your wife had died, Frankie. I've been away so long, forgive me.'

'Och lass. We were nane o' us young, she and I. Yon's whit ye come tae expect at oor age. It shouldna be sae for yourself, but's whit comes o' lovin' a sodger, lass.'

'They're all soldiers now,' Emma said absently. 'Even poor Harry Bruce.'

Frankie puffed on his pipe, and nodded. 'Aye lass, changed times.' He stood up, and reached out his hand to Emma, and, hesitating for a moment, she extended her own and let him take it within his bent and calloused fingers. He lifted her to her feet, and she was startled by his strength. She left her hand in his and walked beside him strangely at ease.

As they turned from the river she said suddenly, 'Frankie, why did they cut the trees?'.

'Timber. Tae shore the trenches up. They've cut hauf the guid timber o' the strath.'

Emma looked sadly back at the river, where her rowan stood alone, without its dark brothers. So her trees, too, had gone to war. 'It won't ever seem the same without them,' she said.

Frankie was silent, trudging away with her through the wet bracken. Then, putting his pipe away in his pocket he said slowly, 'Lassie, when this war's o'er at lang last, I reckon there'll be naething left the same in a' the warld.'

He walked with her most of the way back to Culbrech, only stopping to turn off where the unpaved track leading to his croft separated from the long Culbrech driveway.

'Miss Emma,' he said thoughtfully.

She smiled. 'I think just "Emma" now, Frankie. Things *have* changed, everywhere.'

'Nae lass, we'll haud whit we can o' oor warld, while we can. Miss Emma, I'm wantin' tae ask a favour. I ken it's hardly the richt time an' a', but it's the only chance I'll hae. Ye see, it's aboot Sandy, an' he's only got anither few days o' his leave, afore he's back tae France.'

'What is it?' Emma said, forgetting herself at once, surprised by his request. He had never asked anything of her in all her life.

'Weel, lass, it's Angusina.'

'Oh.' Emma blushed, turning slightly away. For all she had seen for a year in the wards, for all the emotional havoc she had been through, she was yet a total innocent in matters of men and women. Angusina's pregnancy, however, was now so obvious that even a child could not miss it. So Sandy was baulking, and Angusina was an embarrassment. Emma felt anger rising. She said, 'I'm afraid, Frankie, that if anyone needs help, it's Angusina. You must understand my concerns are first for her.'

'Aye, lass, well they might be. Sae are ma ain. An' sae as weel are Sandy's.'

'Are they?' Emma turned to face him, amazed. 'Then whatever

is the problem?'

'Naething. Onlie she willna see him.'

'Angusina? She won't?'

'He's tried ilka way ye can imagine. Ca'd on the house. On her mither's house. Wrote tae her frae France, frae London, e'en frae oor ain hame. She willna answer, willna see him. Naething. Nou, yer a woman, Miss Emma. Can ye be tellin' me whit's wi' her, tae mak' her take on like thot? Ye see, Sandy kens aboot the bairn, a'richt, dinna see how he could not, a' else kens. Sae he's wantin' tae marry afore he's back tae France. Dear kens when he'll hae leave next, an' the way things are oot there . . . I dinna think he'd mind it bein' a bastard, as long as he'd get back ae day tae faither it, but . . .' he paused a moment, shuffled his feet and said, 'Ye ken hou it is.'

Emma did. Sandy's younger brother had already died in France.

'I'll see what I can do,' said Emma.

When they parted on the road Frankie watched her striding towards the house, long-legged and certain, and realized suddenly he'd quite accidentally worked a cure. 'Twa birds wi' the ae stane,' he smiled, a toothless, wry smile, and went on his way.

Victoria heard her come into the house and heard her voice, clear and young as she had not heard it since Emma's return, calling, 'Angusina? Is she down with you, Mrs Murchison? Very well, I'll not take a minute of her time.'

The following morning, Angusina waited, alone and reluctant, in the empty kitchen of Culbrech House. It had taken a lot more than a minute to persuade her, and all she had eventually conceded, and that only because she felt real sorrow for Emma Maclaren, was that she would, briefly, see Sandy Gibson, alone. She was aware that the kitchen had been emptied discreetly for her sake, and that the entire elaborate workings of the big house were held in abeyance, for her.

She tugged once more at her plain black skirt, pulling it down over the bulge, and arranged her apron so that it flowed over her front, disguising her shape as much as possible.There was no point; she knew that; but it had become a habit. Still, when Sandy knocked at the door, she forgot everything and stood up, and was standing there in the dark kitchen before the black-leaded range when he entered. He was in uniform, wearing the only good clothes he had, and he held his balmoral bonnet in his hands as he ducked his black head beneath the low dark lintel of the door. He saw her standing there, forgetting to hide the ripe swell of her body, her face and hair glowing with the special health of pregnancy, and was stunned by the onrush of pride.

'Och lass, will ye luik at ye.'

She turned away, ashamed. 'Juist say whit ye've got tae say, Sandy Gibson. I've work waitin'.'

He was silenced by amazement, and then suddenly exploded in frustrated anger. 'Right. An' I'll juist dae that. Whit's wi' ye, fer the love o' Christ, girl?' he shouted.

'Wheesht,' she whispered.

'The hell I'll wheesht,' he shouted louder. 'Nou ye can juist gie me an answer. Like ye didna gie tae my letters fer weeks an' weeks. It's nae a picnic out there, woman, an' I'd juist appreciate a wee bit Christian charity, nou an' again, like a letter fer ae thing. An',' he strode towards her and put his hands on her shoulders, 'an' like my lass being the one tae tell me I'm tae be a faither, no' the hale bluidy warld.'

She turned her face aside, biting back tears that came anyway, and her chin crumpled. Sandy let go, amazed again, and remorseful, and dabbed at her teary eyes with his hard fingertips and whispered, 'Och no, no. I didna mean any o' it.'

'Juist gae awa'. Please just gae awa'.'

He almost did, but anger overrode his remorse, and he stood his ground stubbornly and said, 'Aye. When I get an answer. No' before.'

Angusina was desperate. She had known from the start she should never have let Emma Maclaren persuade her to see him. Away from him, without his strong lean body to tempt her into the comfort of his arms, without his intense, unmasking eyes upon her face, she could be firm, and brave. But now . . . still she knew she had been right. She could not send him back there burdened down with a forced marriage and a child to support. She should never have let it happen, but having done so, she must now take the responsibility that she had abandoned for passion's sake. But how?

She looked about wildly, and then pulled back from him, and pushed back her heavy hair from her face and said, defiantly, as she'd once read in a book, 'It's no' yours, Sandy. Yer no' the faither. Now get awa' hame and lea' me be.'

In the silence that followed she read the success of her ruse on his face. He looked downward, shuffled his feet, suddenly smaller, as if his manhood was diminished by the words alone. Finally, as he turned to go, he said very softly, 'Ye didna tell me there was someone else,' his voice boyish and plaintive. 'I'd ne'er hae bothered ye if I'd kent ye loved anither.' He fumbled with his hat in his hands and then reached to cram it on to his head and then suddenly, at the door, whirled round and stared long and hard at her, and then whispered, 'Liar.'

'No, Sandy, no. It's the truth. Yer nae the faither.' But her confidence was shaken and she saw in the leap of light in his eyes that he'd outguessed her.

'Lassie,' he said with a slow grin spreading, 'I reckon it's either me, or it's the Prince o' Wales. Nou, he's awfu' busy these days, sae I'm thinkin' ye'd be wise tae settle fer second best an' marry me.'

She stood shaking her head, caught between tears and the infection of his humour.

'Nou dinna laugh,' he said warningly, 'or ye'll spoil it,' and he touched her face with his fingers as he said it, turning it up to his. She could not avoid meeting his eyes, and could not resist laughing when she did.

In an instant he'd wrapped his arms around her, with delight and passion, and as quickly let her go, terrified that he might have hurt her. 'Yer a'richt, I've nae squeezed ye too hard?'

'Och they dinna juist pop oot, like orange pips, ye daft fool.' She laughed again, and drew back just for a moment, still holding him by the arms. 'Are ye sure nou? Ye've sae much tae think aboot wi'out me an' a bairn.'

'Aye lass. An' most o' it I'd rather no' think of at a'. Dinna take frae me the ae thing that makes it a' possible tae thole.' It was the most serious she had ever seen him, and in a moment, it had passed. He grinned again. 'Aye, yer too bonnie fer his Royal Highness, any road. Whit's he ever dune tae deserve the likes o' ye?'

Miss Rebecca Galloway, wandering alone in the upper corridors of Culbrech House, was also thinking of both marriage, and her own remarkable good fortune. And yet, unlike Sandy and Angusina, she held within her the glimmer of a doubt.

It was a tiny doubt, a useless doubt, the sort that is always said to plague brides and grooms-to-be, and yet, she could not forget it. It had come upon her this morning as she had strolled aimlessly about the same upper corridor, awaiting Emma's company for breakfast. She had, quite by chance, found herself standing by the open door of a long disused bedroom, and, as if without her active will, had found herself drawn within. Something of its austere masculinity, coupled with a sad emptiness, had tugged at her heart. It was Tenny Maclaren's bedroom, and he had not slept in it for over half a year. She stepped in, and softly drew the door to after her, leaving it only slightly ajar. She went slowly to the window and stood looking out over the formal gardens of box and yew hedges, and the dark geometrics of winter rosebeds, and more distantly the ploughed fields and heather and bracken hills of the strath.

Thinking of him she turned and looked for a long time on his empty bed, imagining him lying there, so long, and bony, and masculine; he'd take up the whole of it, not just the tiny corner she herself filled when she curled like a soft cat at night. A rush of maidenly embarrassment startled her; it was not in her nature to think of any man like that. In spite of Naomi, Rebecca was as innocent as Emma, as all the girls of her station and times. Why then, on the eve of her wedding, she thought, did those imaginings come, not of her husband-to-be, but of Tenny Maclaren? She forced herself to transfer the thought to Johnny, but then the imminence of consummation frightened her into dismissing it entirely. She thought instead of her wedding dress, for which she had just had a fitting. The thought calmed her, and carefully avoiding looking at the bed, she turned to leave the room.

Johnny Bruce was looking for his fiancée. He had searched the whole house downstairs and upstairs and had tapped gently on the door of her bedroom, which took a surprising amount of nerve. At this late hour, guilt had defeated him. He had to tell Rebecca the truth about the letter. He knew it was half the reason she had agreed to marry him, and in spite of proving a startlingly accurate prophecy which his Celtic soul found disconcerting, the letter had been a pack of lies. Johnny had a high proportion of reckless scoundrel in him, something he'd not deny. And the fact that he'd won, by less than acceptable methods, his bride-to-be from the arms of his cousin Tenny did nothing but fill him with triumphant delight. It was the best hand of the game they'd played for years and he relished it. But where women were concerned, honour would come creeping in. He wanted Rebecca more than he'd ever wanted anyone or anything. But, at this late date, he had been forced to concede he wanted her fairly, that marriage was too serious a thing to treat as a game.

He was about to abandon his search when a door suddenly creaked open along the hallway and he stepped back a moment, startled. For it was Tenny's door and the room being unused was rarely entered. Perhaps Victoria had sent the maids in for its periodic airing. But it was not a maid that stepped into the hallway, turning to close the door silently and with great care, but the slim, auburn-haired figure of Rebecca Galloway. Johnny felt embarrassed, as if he had been eavesdropping and wished quickly to be elsewhere, out of sight, but she looked up as she drew the door to, and looked straight at him, for a moment without recognition, clearly preoccupied. When she did realize it was he, her small hand flew to her mouth and she made a near silent gasp.

'Terribly sorry, my dear, didn't mean to startle. Just been looking for you everywhere.'

'Oh. Oh yes. I . . .' she paused, conscious of a rising blush, as if she had really been caught doing something terrible, not merely standing in an old friend's room.

'There was something I wanted to say to you, Rebecca,' he said, and the solemnity of his voice brought instant attention.

She stared and then her eyes widened with the fear that everyone lived with these days. 'Oh God, don't tell me. No one's . . .'

'Oh, my dear, no. Nothing like that.' He reached for her arm, because she had slumped a little against a wall. As when the news of his own injuries had come to them, her first thought had been Tenny Maclaren. 'I'm most awfully sorry. I shouldn't have sprung it on you like that. It was nothing really. Only a little confession . . .'

Afterwards, they walked in the garden. They walked alone, each in a private world of thoughts, regrets and doubts.

'But why?' she asked again. 'Were you teasing me? Did you not expect me to believe you?'

'No. No.' Johnny found explanation painful, probing too deeply into the emotional abyss. 'Of course I wanted you to believe me. It wasn't you I was teasing.'

'Then who?'

'Tenny, I suppose,' he shrugged, regretting the words the instant they were spoken, as indeed he'd regretted the whole misguided conversation. He'd never imagined she'd take this tack, hurt and confused and resentful.

'So you asked me to marry you, for that is what that letter asked, Johnny Bruce, as a jest for the sole benefit of Tenny Maclaren.' Her eyes were bright, with tears or anger, or both, he couldn't tell. 'Oh damn Tenny.'

'Hardly his fault,' Johnny mumbled. But it was, for reasons Rebecca had kept to herself, reasons she dared not speak and hardly dared acknowledge in the silence of her heart. For, just for a moment, when Johnny had come with his mumbled confession, a most alarming thing had happened. She had thought he had got cold feet; was about, through nerves or genuine reconsidering, to call the wedding off. And for that brief moment, in the hallway by Tenny's bedroom, she had been glad. And it was that stunning realization that she was fighting and struggling with now, and her supposed hurt over the foolish letter but a convenient mask. Oh God, what was she to do? Was she in love with Johnny? Or Tenny? Or both of them, or neither of them? Her head whirled and she longed for Naomi, and remembered guiltily that Naomi, with her dark wise face looking down into her own, had been the one determined to dissuade her. She rebelled then, unable to face admitting she'd been wrong, and fought against her own wise uncertainties.

Johnny, however, had no uncertainties at all. Oddly, he had had, yesterday, even this morning. Thoughts had crossed his mind, thoughts of how complicated married life sounded, from all who spoke of it; how young he felt, suddenly, how unready to take to his shoulders the boring proprieties that in his world the word 'husband' implied. But those doubts had vanished the instant Rebecca turned away from him, the instant he saw her almost imperceptibly slipping from his grasp. Unlike his lovely bride-to-be, Johnny was no innocent. Society hardly asked that of a man, after all. And desire for that slim soft body, that was always shut from him by closed bedroom doors, rose suddenly to a frightening peak. He had to have her; he could not live on beyond that promised night without possession of her. Most of all, he could not return to that place of mud and shattered trees and slimy death underfoot without that longed-for moment of physical blessing made real at last. He felt, in her turning from his eyes, the gates of heaven swinging shut upon the sinner destined for hell.

'Rebecca, I love you. I love you. Isn't that all we need?'

It was not, but she said yes, too proud to retreat and unable, in their rushing world, to plead for a moment's reprieve. She opened her arms to Johnny Bruce and banished Tenny Maclaren to the darkest regions of her mind. They embraced, alone in the winter garden.

From the high turret window where Victoria Maclaren sat patiently reading *Gulliver's Travels* to the bedridden Aunt Jean, they were framed by the narrow sash as though in a painting, imprisoned in time. Victoria stared at the close single form they made, and thought, young as they were, the wedding could not, obviously, come soon enough. This war, undoing everyone's values; no one it seemed even remembered how to behave.

7

Over a thousand miles away, in the abandoned limestone farmhouse just to the west of the town of Albert that served as Brigade HQ, Ian Maclaren was also attending to duties, with as resigned an air. His duties were to that larger family of the regiment. But his surroundings were not totally without comfort. His booted feet stretched towards a pleasant fire on the plain terra cotta hearth, and a glass of malt whisky waited at his elbow. Beyond the room, the odour of garlic and chicken stock hinted at the dinner being prepared for himself and his fellow officers, by the young Frenchwoman hired from the neighbouring village. Resting on the small table at his side was a stack of regimental writing paper, and beside it, neatly aligned, another stack of letters and documents.

The brigadier had completed the worst of the task: letters of condolence and concern to those bereaved families whose rank entitled them to his attentions. Then there was that sad little matter of the widow from Moy whose desperation to find her husband's body, missing since Ypres, had driven her on a pilgrimage of the battlefields and an endless campaign of letters.

Ian stretched himself, and sighed, and sipped his whisky, pleased suddenly at the leanness of his own body. It was a young man's body again, and he'd never thought it would be. He thought back to the day, so long ago it seemed now, of his retirement. Short-lived. He grinned, and rubbed his luxuriant moustache, thinking young man's thoughts. As always, they turned to Naomi. He looked to his stack of correspondence. Must write to Divisional HQ again about those promised tin hats. A year and a half of war and they'd still nothing to keep the shell splinters off but a layer of cloth and a thatch of hair. And for all they laughed at the Hun with his 'jerry' on his head, they'd damn well be glad of the like. He reached for another sheet of paper, and then suddenly thrust it aside. He'd done enough. He rewarded himself with a sip from his whisky and an indulgence. His next letter would be personal.

'My dearest Naomi,' he began.

They were not love letters, his letters from France to Naomi Bruce, at least not in the conventional sense of the phrase. The days when she had been the lover of his body were now so far away, so discreetly veiled by decent time, that neither of them would ever breach their mutual entrusted silence to speak of them. But she was now, as she was always, the lover of his mind.

And so, whereas to his wife Victoria he wrote with optimism and vigour of successes and confidence, or at least of stern resolve, mixing concern for her welfare gently with assurances of his own, and never for a moment letting slip the noble cloak of paterfamilias with which he shielded her; when he wrote to Naomi, he wrote from the depths of his heart.

To Naomi he wrote his doubts and his fears, his pain over the fate of his men, his worries over their leadership, his growing disillusionment with John French's handling of the war. If Victoria had picked from his sternly self-censored account of Loos the bones of the truth, Naomi, in his first, heartfelt outpouring of words after that disaster, saw the intimate horror of the day. Day by day, month by month and now year by year, he had sent her an account of the world's descent into madness in the muddy ditches of France. His letters would have formed a perfect diary of the twentieth century's baptism of reality, had she kept them. But Naomi, wise as lovers must be, carefully burnt every one.

He concluded:

> Thank God, at least, that we are far from sodden Flanders this winter, and that misery at Loos, which dragged on until winter itself made it end. Some kind

immortal no doubt has smiled on my poor Maclarens, to bring us to this gentle haven by the Somme.

yours aye,

Ian

He had signed the thin paper with a graceful flourish and brushed the signature with an unembarrassed touch of his lips, when there was a sharp knock at the door.

He folded the letter quickly and slipped it within its envelope, and rose and called, 'Come,' turning to the fireside as he sealed the letter closed.

The door swung open on creaking unoiled hinges, and Major Munro, a staff officer from Divisional Headquarters, entered with a brisk salute.

'Yes,' Ian said, not pleased at being disturbed.

'Pardon the interruption, sir. But I thought you'd wish to know. The news has just come in. They've sent the Old Man home.'

'French?'

'Aye, sir. Haig's in command. At last.'

Ian Maclaren felt the news wash through him with the sort of relief that comes with a remembered nightmare; the awareness that the source of the fear haunting one has been removed. 'Thank God,' he whispered.

Outside in the roadway distant voices, British, were singing Christmas carols as a group of other ranks returned to their billets from the modest *estaminet*.

'Now we'll give them hell,' Munro said softly, his voice half swallowed by the quiet of the dusky room. The brigadier was not listening. He stared into the fire, and inclined his head towards the distant carol-singers.

'Noel, Noel, Noel, Noel
Born is the King of Is-rael . . .'

'Aye, and a Happy Christmas to you too,' he said aloud, and the astonished staff officer backed quietly to the door.

Pat McGarrity spent Christmas at home. When he was given that coveted leave he couldn't believe his luck, and when the day arrived he didn't stand around to argue. They were out of the line at the time, and he grabbed his pass and his kit and headed for the railway station before anyone had time to reconsider. By afternoon he was crossing the Channel, and by evening, boarding a train north. In the morning, he was in Scotland. At Glasgow Central he parted company with Jamie Maclaren with whom he shared the great good fortune of leave. Jamie had another train yet, and another half-day before he'd be home. He'd made a little world-weary fuss about the journey and asserted that he'd as well stay in London. But Pat knew he was lying. Jamie wanted to see his mother more than anything on earth. Pat knew because he, four years older and far wiser, wanted nothing in the whole world but to see his own Mam. All else, his mates, the pub, football, even Theresa Kelly, faded into the haze of that other world called peace.

The grey streets of Glasgow welcomed him as he emerged into a cold morning, full of grey sleet, and he could have knelt and kissed the grimy cobbles of the roadway and he drank in its sooty air as if it were wine. He strode out through falling snow feeling like a stranger in his own home, with his pack and his rifle and the Maclaren kilt swinging about his bare knees. Wherever he went, on the streets, in the tobacconist's where he bought a tin of Capstans, wondering guiltily what Kathleen would say to his new manly habit, even on the tram jolting towards home, he was met with proud smiles and encouraging words from the patriotic folk of his city. He grinned back out of shy politeness, but he was embarrassed by it all, and disturbed. From what he'd seen of soldiering and the war, he wasn't half as sure as they that it was a thing of which to be so proud.

In the crumbling streets and closes, crisscrossed with washing-lines, that made up his own corner of the city, barefoot children ran shouting after him through icy slush, begging to see his rifle and to hear of the Germans he'd killed.

'Get away,' he said, suddenly angry, and their adoration turned, with the sharp suspicion of slum childhood, to sullenness and then to mockery.

'Och, he's nae but a kiltie. Kiltie, kiltie.'

'Keek up his skirts, Jimmie, see his wee balls.'

'Get off,' Pat said sharply, giving one a light shove.

The shoved one wailed, 'I'll tell ma Mam,' but Pat ignored them, and strode on through the streets to escape. At the corner of his close a small tobacconist's shop displayed a newspaper placard declaring,

Pat looked for a moment and then shrugged, turning into the dark dampness of the close. He wasn't sure at all who Haig was, or what, for that matter, he commanded. The only commanding officer that meant anything to him was his own, Gordon Bruce, now that the Pals were part of the old First Battalion. And whatever he thought of the staff, those shadowy figures the front-line men disdained, he had for Colonel Bruce a wholesome respect lightly laced with a thin line of fear.

Kathleen McGarrity had been waiting for her son since the break of day, long before the train time. When the tiny neighbour child, posted on the doorstep to watch for him, at last glimpsed the kilted figure in the entrance hall, she went quite speechless with excitement and fled with a clatter of worn leather shoes up the echoing stairs, pounding on doors, gasping out only, 'It's him. It's the sodger,' to all she passed.

Pat mounted the stairwell of his tenement home to an honour guard of worn women's faces, toothless half of them, red-cheeked, wrinkled, aged early by hard poverty, but each beaming with pride as if he was their own son, as, in their crumbling vertical family, in a way he was. He was kissed, cuddled, cuffed and teased all the way up the stairs. They talked happily about him as he passed, as if he were a child, or simply not there.

'Will ye luik at the size o' him. I'd swear he's grown hauf a foot.'

'Och he's braw wi' the kilt, is he no'?'

'The pride o' the regiment, nae doubt.'

Pat reddened with embarrassment, but here, in the narrow sour confines of his childhood's home, he felt no resentment, no cynicism, only a humble pride in them, his own. They were his Scotland and for them, not for King nor Country, he would fight. For them alone.

Kathleen was weeping on their landing, before the old lavatory door, her hands clasped to her huge lace-draped bosom, her eyes squeezed shut in her soft wrinkled face. 'Oh ma bairn, ma bairn,' she moaned and Pat, half laughing, half crying, was swallowed up by her great washerwoman's arms.

And yet, the day, begun in such familiar warmth, did not go well. Well-wishers dropped in throughout the afternoon, and Pat's married sister, her husband Alec Dougherty and three restless, fractious weans joined them at their evening meal. Kathleen fussed shamelessly over Pat, and loaded his plate with uneatable amounts of food. His sister gushed on about his bravery and how handsome he was in his kilt, until her husband, a silent, shrewd-eyed miner with a belligerent look of experience about him, got up from the table with a grunt of disgust.

'Weel, ye can hae yer hero tae yersel', lass, I'm awa' tae the pub.' He slammed his cap on his head, while Kathleen and her daughter stared uncomprehending, and was halfway to the door when Pat suddenly arose also, as if to follow.

'Where ye aff tae, son?' Kathleen protested. 'Ye've nae finished yer tea.' She sounded so hurt that Pat wavered, looking back, slightly sickened at the unfinished portion of mutton stew on his plate. But suddenly he had to get out of the warmth, the endless praise, the question after question about the war which he had no wish to talk about. 'Och it was fine, Mither, it was grand. But I'm nae used tae such fare; thon army cooks are no' like yersel', ye ken,' he grinned, trying to make light to cheer her, and failing. Then with a muttered apology he strode through the door after his brother-in-law. Alec had not waited for him, and he had to run recklessly down the twisting stair to catch him. Once out in the street, he called after him, 'Haud on, will ye, I could dae wi' one mysel'.' Alec turned, Pat's tone of genuine annoyance slowing him, rather than the words.

He said nothing, but stopped walking, waiting only long enough for Pat to catch up and then continued, wordlessly, towards the glowing windows of the Drover's Inn. Alec paused on the grimy pavement outside the door, where the warm gaslight within outlined the beautiful window etchings of Highland cattle and clansmen in old-fashioned kilts. 'Ye ken we're nane o' us braw khaki laddies like yersel'. Ye'll no' mind drinking wi' a bunch o' conchies an' Hun lovers?'

'Whit's wi' ye, man?' Pat exploded suddenly in bemused outrage. 'Ye ken I'm no' like that. I dinna ken quite why I jined the army mysel' but it wisna tae be a hero. And ye can be damned assured I've nae become yin.' He raised his hands and then dropped them in a gesture of tired exasperation. 'I hauf wish I hadna dune it, or maybe thot I hadna cam hame at a'. The hale warld's gane gey queer. Yersel' included.' He turned as if to walk away, back the way they had come. But Alec's hand came down on his shoulder, and he whirled about, expecting a fight.

Alec was grinning, lamely and sheepishly. 'Och, dinna take on sae. I meant nae hairm.'

Pat shrugged, still confused, but followed Alec into the pub. Inside, in the rich smoky air, as they pushed their way patiently through the shoulder-to-shoulder ranks of men in dark coats and flat dark caps, to the worn bar counter, Alec said, 'It's nae yer fault, lad. Naebody's really. It's juist that wi' Molly and yer Mam an' all gaen on sae aboot yon blasted war . . . a man gets sae he cannae haud his heid up if he's no' in khaki.' He grinned again, almost boyishly, as if a little ashamed of his words. But in the next moment his face was hard again and his eyes under their heavy brows suddenly sharp. 'But mark me, lad, they'll no' get me thot road. I may be a coward, but I'm no' a fool.' Then, realizing perhaps what he'd said, he slapped Pat's shoulder again, and bought him a beer and a nip of whisky and assured him that he was as proud as the rest of the family's Maclaren Highlander.

Later, a man entered the Drover's Inn, and the whole room seemed to feel his presence. He walked among the standing men, speaking a few words with each small group. As he passed Alec and Pat he caught Alec's eyes with his own and said, 'Christmas Day, Dougherty, ye'll be there?'

'Aye,' Alec said with a slow grin. 'I'll be there.' The man passed out into the night, and the pub filled up again with noise.

'Whit was thot aboot?' Pat said.

'Naethin' much,' Alec said, and returned to his beer. Then apparently he reconsidered, and perhaps remembered that Pat was his brother-in-law, and not the enemy. 'It was aboot yon meeting, Christmas Day, wi' the shop stewards o' the munitions workers an' miners an' a'. The Minister's comin' tae speak tae us, aboot oor patriotic duty, nae doubt.' He was again grinning his slow secret grin, into his beer mug.

'Lloyd George?' Pat said, 'Munitions Minister?' He was impressed.

'Aye, himsel'.'

'Are ye gaein?' Pat said, still impressed.

'Och aye,' Alec said casually. 'We're tae gie him a richt proper welcome tae Clydeside, ye ken. Yon wee man,' he gestured over his shoulder to the closed door, 'he's wi' Maclean.'

'John Maclean, himself?' Pat breathed, much more awed by the name of the Clydeside labour leader than that of Lloyd George.

'Aye, the verra same.' Pat regarded his brother-in-law with new respect.

'Dae ye *know* John Maclean?' he whispered.

Alec looked wise and shook his head. 'Nae, Pat. I dinna. I'm no' the sort wha' knows folk o' import, ye ken. I'm juist a wee fella, a wee cog in the machine. But I tell ye this, lad, if I'm tae be a cog, I'll choose ma ain machine. And I'll nae choose the same yin thot's been runnin' ma ain folk intae the dirt sin' the beginnin' o' time.' He leaned towards Pat and tapped his corporal's stripe with care. 'Nae me, lad. I'm wi' Maclean.'

Kathleen had waited up for Pat to get home until late that night. She was sitting alone by the big kitchen table where they had eaten, in the dim light of one gas mantle. The table was scrubbed and bare now, except for a small, rectangular piece of card that lay exactly in the middle. Kathleen's eyes were on it when he entered the room. They raised to meet his as he stepped towards the table and lowered, once more, dramatically to the card.

'Whit ye daein' wi' thot?' Pat said, dimly annoyed.

Kathleen looked up, wide-eyed and innocent, the hurt of the tea-time argument still apparent and compounded now by a new hurt. 'An' was I no' tae see tae yer laundry nou? Are ye grown o'er grand fer yer auld mither?'

'Och, wheesht, woman,' Pat said, reaching for the card. 'First Alec, nou yersel'. Ye'd think I'd come hame a general on a big white horse.'

Kathleen's red pudgy fingers crept stealthily over the card.

'Come awa', Mither, gie it here. It's mine.'

'I ken thot, son. An' who will ye be tellin' me *is* she?'

Pat flopped into the kitchen armchair, giving up, and shaking his head in tired exasperation. 'Ye daft fool. It's juist a postcard. Onyone can buy it, tae gie tae onyone. I dinna know the lass. Hou could I?' He was faintly aware that what he said was not all truth. He did not know her, but he did know someone who did. And it was no accident he carried that one sentimental portrait rather than any other. It had adorned the trench support before his funk hole through his last week at the Front. It wasn't his, properly. Another Maclaren had hung it there; the wee Inverness-shire private, Donnie Cameron. But lack of ownership had not stopped him falling privately in love with 'Our Sweetheart, the VAD' and when Jamie had said, casual as could be, that he actually knew the fair-haired angel of mercy thereon portrayed, he had experienced an extraordinary thrill of vicarious delight. Nor had lack of ownership stopped him from spiriting the card away when they left the trench, and slipping it, like a talisman, into his haversack for the journey home.

Kathleen sniffed suspiciously and raised her hand slightly, still keeping one corner of the card beneath her thumb.

'Och weel,' she said with a fair imitation of sorrowful understanding, 'I suppose there's nane can blame ye. Awa' oot there wi' every temptation aboot ye.' She sighed. 'An a' the while, puir Theresa waitin' hame fer ye, faithful as a saint. No' thot anyone can blame ye, mind . . .'

'Fer the love o' the Holy Mother, woman, it's nae but a picture. An' as fer temptations . . .' he waved an angry hand, but then he stopped, torn between guilt towards the slandered name of those dear companions in misery left behind, and compassion for the innocent foolishness of home. Finally he said only, 'It's naethin' tae dae wi' Theresa, ony road.'

'Aye,' Kathleen said sagely, 'I wad think not.'

Pat shrugged off another wave of anger, and snatched up his postcard. Kathleen rose, lifting her bulky body with a small groan. 'I dinna ken whit things are comin' tae,' she muttered to herself, making for the black, soot-caked kettle. 'Nae decent lass wad let hersel' be pictured like yon, fer a' manner o' men tae see. Mind nou, she's most like a wee bit whore they paid tae pose . . .'

'No,' Pat suddenly shouted, slamming the table with his hand. 'She's no' that. She's no' that at a'.'

'And hou wad ye be knowin' whit she is?' Kathleen said, her eyes narrowed cunningly, 'seeing as hou ye dinna *know* the lass, at a'?'

Pat turned away, embarrassed, and muttered, 'One o' ma mates knows her. She's . . . she's a sorta cousin o' his.'

'A cousin? A sort o' cousin? An' whit sort is thot?' Kathleen was again giving him her cunning look, as if to say that she knew all about men's 'cousins'.

'I dinna ken,' Pat returned, frustrated, because the complications between Jamie and Albert's family and that of that revered distant girl called Susan Bruce constantly eluded him.

'A' I can say, Pat McGarrity,' Kathleen said, 'is wi' a good decent Catholic lass like Theresa Kelly stoppin' hame fer ye, ye've nae need tae carry pictures aboot o' some wee bit London fluff . . .'

'Fer the love o' Christ, Mither. She's the colonel's niece.'

The room went silent. Pat was standing with one hand half raised, as if to cover his mouth, knowing instantly that while a desire for a London tart would be offensive, but understandable, a desire for a lady of such stature was unthinkable.

Kathleen let her breath out with a long, cautious sigh. 'Och Pat,' she said at last, her grey head sinking down to her corseted bosom, shaking the while to and fro. 'Whit am I tae dae wi' ye?'

Pat took Theresa Kelly to the pictures the next night, and the following day, Christmas Eve, went with the gathered family, all that remained in Glasgow, together to confession and midnight Mass. Kathleen had begun to feel quite all right about him again. But on Christmas afternoon, when Alec Dougherty rose from the dinner table, praised Kathleen for her sumptuous feast, and kissed his wife and said he must be away to his 'little meeting', Pat too rose to leave.

'Och son, yer no' awa' as weel?'

'I'll juist walk alang wi' Alec. Keep him oot o' mischief,' he grinned and Alec nodded with an appreciative look. Against all protests they went out together.

In the street, Alec said, 'Sae ye've decided yer wi' us, after a'.'

'Like I said tae ma mither,' Pat replied carefully, 'I'll juist walk alang. I cannae know if I'm wi' ye till I've heard whit ye've got tae say.'

Alec looked at him coolly. Pat was dressed in his only good clothes, for Christmas dinner, the kilt and khaki tunic of the Maclaren Highlanders. 'If I'd a known ye were comin', I'd a seen ye dressed different,' Alec said.

'What's wrang wi' it?' Pat bridled. 'Any road, I've nocht else.'

Alec pulled his cap down over his eyes, acknowledging the truth of Pat's reply with a short nod. 'Aye weel, dinna gae wavin' ony flags,' he said.

Very quickly, as they left the holiday quiet of the tenement streets and went down towards the Clyde and the great shipyard cranes towering blackly over the rooftops against a pale ice-green winter sky, Pat understood Alec's discomfort with his uniform. This was Kitchener's Country no longer. Nor was it, necessarily, even the King's.

On bare stone walls, and wooden plank entranceways to factories and yards, the now traditional patriotic posters were torn and defaced, some ripped away entirely, others daubed with black or red paint. The initials of the British Socialist Party and the Clyde Workers Committee were splashed across every empty space. *Up Maclean*! proclaimed one boarded-over doorway, and down the next street red letters proclaimed the Irish slogan, *Home Rule*, jarringly unfamiliar on Pat's own streets. He bridled at that, and then felt a complex cross-current of loyalties. The name of the Irish labour leader, Larkin, was scrawled below for good measure. Pat glanced nervously at Alec, who was smiling quietly to himself and suddenly looking to Pat like a man of repressed power and anything but a cog in anyone's machine.

'Whit's thot tae dae wi' us?' Pat demanded belligerently, gesturing at the call to the Irish cause.

But Alec turned his head and drew his attention to the other side of the street. There, framed by two blank, boarded windows, the face of Kitchener stared out into the grimy street. Across his imperious finger was painted in letters of sharp, clear red, ARM THE WORKERS!

'Jesus,' said Pat, 'thot's a bit strong.'

'If ye ask me,' Alec said, his pace quickening as other men, all dressed like himself in dark coats and flat caps, all walking with the same quiet purpose, joined them in the street. 'If ye ask me, it's nae hauf strong eneuch.'

The meeting was held out of doors, within the vast gated confines of a shipyard, beneath the shadow of two great cranes, with the bow of a merchantman under construction looming over the dais built hastily of scrap timber for the distinguished speakers. The crowd swelled, pouring in from the neighbouring streets of tenements and low back-to-backs where the shipyard workers lived, and many from further afield, miners like Alec, and munitions workers from all over the city. Many, like Alec were shop stewards. All, it seemed to Pat, were electric with an unspoken excitement, an excitement that reminded him eerily of the few hours waiting at Loos before the Inverness Pals went over the top.

There were three thousand men standing in the icy December air when, amidst a commotion, a spreading wave of murmurings that rippled across the great crowd, a black motor car rolled into the yard. The figures, when they stepped from the car and mounted the dais, seemed so small and far away from where Pat stood that they looked as defenceless as bairns. Like the Germans look, he thought suddenly, with an odd shudder, across no-man's-land. He tried to shake off the feeling as the droning voice of some shipyard official introduced the speakers, but he could not free himself from the alarming similarity.

'It's Lloyd George,' the man next to him muttered, 'the wee Welsh bastard.'

In spite of Alec Dougherty's forbidding presence at his elbow, Pat could not suppress a small sound, almost a sigh which escaped his throat. He heard it echoed around him, an acknowledgement, a murmur of recognition. The form was familiar; the chesterfield coat and dark homburg, the white hair and bushy moustache. The crowd waited, tensing momentarily like a nervous dog, but the instant the politician began to speak, his high, queer Welsh accent thinned by the cold air, the dog began to growl.

Pat knew what the issue was; Alec had told him, but in a moment, had he any doubts, he would have lost them.

'Nae dilution!' a voice shouted, and a roar rose, swallowing the Welshman's words. Pat strained to hear, but most was lost in the growing noise of the crowd.

'Ye gie oor jobs tae women an' scabs. Whit's left fer us when we come hame again?' a voice shouted.

Pat heard Alec beside him fling back, 'Wha says yer comin' hame again, ye birk?'

An old man near Pat muttered, almost to himself, 'Fifty years we fight fer Unions an' nou they'll break us in ane.'

'Stuff yer Munitions Act,' someone else shouted and a few echoed it, laughing. The man on the dais seemed smaller and smaller as the crowd surged closer, held back now by buffeted police officers. The sound of voices was driven down by angry shouts on all sides and Lloyd George and his companions became small jerky dark shapes, waving and gesturing, like children's puppet dolls.

'Gie the man a hearin',' Pat spoke suddenly, sharply, and was cuffed from behind, a sharp jab to his ribs.

'Awa' tae fight the boss's war, sodger. We've oor ain.'

'Nae dilution,' a distant voice called over the heads of the crowd, a deliberate voice that Pat felt he'd heard before, 'an' nae conscription either!'

A roaring shout greeted that, and the sound of heavy applause, calloused hands slapping brutally together in the cold air. An official leapt up to the dais, raised his arms over his head, momentarily quietening the crowd with the gesture. 'Gentlemen,' the voice sounded reedy, English, and thin. 'Where is your honour? Where is your patriotism? Your country's at war!'

There was a silence, as the crowd considered, then a clear strong voice called, 'Nae, laddie. *Your* country's at war. Nae oors!' There was a cheer and the speaker was shouted off the dais and the man with the homburg and moustache and the chesterfield coat was gathered around by friends and hastened away. Pat was staring at the man who had shouted treason with disbelief; it was Alec Dougherty, grinning a broad, triumphant grin, and his eyes were wild. Pat, torn between reproach and admiration, found nothing to say until Alec slapped his shoulder and said, 'Come awa', laddie, I'm aff tae the pub.'

'Is it over already?' Pat whispered.

'Nae, lad,' Alec said, his grin hardening to a grimace. 'It's juist begun.'

As they made their way through the triumphant crowd, gay as after a football victory, a small unnoticeable figure darting through the moving men paused an instant and thrust a sheet of paper in each of their hands.

It wasn't until they were clear of the shipyard and making their way up the still crowded street that Pat paused to read the leaflet yet clutched in his hand:

Workers of the Clyde
Capitalism's War is Your Opportunity
Our Struggle is Here
Take Arms

8

'It's treason,' Jamie Maclaren said. They were aboard the Glasgow-London train, their leave nearly over, on their way back to their units and the Front.

'Aye,' Pat shrugged, 'I ken thot. But whit dae ye think o' it? Whit dae ye think it means?'

Jamie took the piece of paper almost reluctantly, handling it with distaste. 'It means, I suppose,' he said, 'that someone's full of balderdash.' He grinned engagingly, 'nothing more.'

Pat grinned also. He liked Jamie. He wished for a moment that Alec Dougherty could meet Jamie; it might make him feel different about the upper classes he so despised. But Pat turned from the thought; he knew it would make no difference to Alec; nothing would. Not even conscription that was rolling ever closer and with which Alec was going to collide with disastrous consequences. He'd go to jail, no doubt. But Pat was relieved. Better there than in the army where Alec's kind of talk would get a man shot. Jamie seemed to read his thoughts.

'I say,' he began, almost hesitantly, 'I do think it would be wise to get rid of that. I'd rather not be caught with it out There, if I were you. It is a bit treasonous and all, old chap.'

Pat nodded. He'd thought of that already. He had only wanted Jamie to see it. He had rather hoped Jamie would find some good strong argument against it that would ease his mind, and enable him to believe, as he wanted to believe, that his fine young officers, his courageous colonel and the handsome grey-haired brigadier who was, incredibly, Jamie's father, were not the enemy. He crumpled the paper up and dropped it to the compartment floor, kicking it into a grimy corner by the heating grille with the sole of his boot. By the end of the day, he had forgotten all about Alec Dougherty and the restless workers of the Clyde.

A week ago, on the journey from France, Pat had agreed to spend the last night of their leave with Jamie Maclaren at the home of Jamie's old family friend, Naomi Bruce. Had there been anywhere else in London for him to go, he would have refused. But there wasn't, and Jamie knew there wasn't; Pat hadn't a soul in London. He'd have still preferred to spend the night waiting for his early-morning train to Dover in Victoria Station, but Jamie would never hear of that. 'Come on, be a sport. You'll absolutely adore Naomi. She's a positive hoot.'

Pat had nodded numbly, like a shy child. Oddly enough, in France he commanded Jamie; Jamie recognized both his superior rank and his superior manhood instantly and without question, taking orders from him gladly and with complete trust. But here, everything was reversed. Without conscious thought on the part of either of them, they slipped at once back into their relative class roles the moment they set foot on English soil. Pat was awed by Jamie, his titled father, his grand castle home, and his glittering exotic family and friends. To mix socially with such people was unheard of, where Pat came from, and the thought was terrifying.

'Whit dae I call her?' he whispered to Jamie as they left the train, and headed for a taxi-rank.

'Mrs Bruce will do fine. Actually, she never really married, don't you know, but when Robert came along I suppose the family thought Mrs sounded better.'

'Wha's Robert?' Pat asked.

'Oh, her son. Wrong side of the blanket and all,' Jamie said smoothly, rather proud of that new knowledge he wasn't supposed to possess. Jamie had blundered into the old family secret one night in an *estaminet* with his brother Albert, when *vin blanc* had over-loosened Bertie's tongue.

'A bastard?' Pat breathed, aloud, in spite of himself, wishing at once he hadn't spoken. Amazement had overridden his usual awe.

'Yes, now that you mention it, I guess that's what it makes him, all right.' Jamie sounded as if he'd just hit on the idea himself. It didn't seem to disturb him in the slightest. Pat was speechless. It had never occurred to him that such things, common enough where he came from, happened among the upper classes as well. He wondered what Alec would think.

But nothing of what Jamie had said prepared him in any way for his meeting with Naomi Bruce. Looking back on it, he realized later, nothing could. For all he knew of Jamie's family, he still felt, when the motorcab pulled up in front of Naomi's door, that they'd surely come to the wrong place. The house was serene and white in the glow of gas streetlamps. A flight of stone steps rose to marble pillars and a gracious portico.

'I cannae gae in there,' Pat whispered to himself in the dark of the cab. Jamie was already swinging open the door and heaving his kit out on to the pavement.

'Come on, old man,' he called impatiently. 'We shan't want to miss cocktails after all.'

Pat McGarrity, who had faced the guns at Loos with consummate courage, sat frozen with fear. But, like at Loos, there was no escape. Jamie was tugging at his sleeve, the door of that lofty establishment was opening. Even the servant standing in the flood of warm light seemed a personage of forbidding elegance.

'Och, Mither, whit am I tae dae?' Pat moaned to himself. Then, physically bracing himself, he stepped down from the cab. For the first time in his life his tough, work-hardened body seemed not an advantage, but an encumbrance. Jamie's step beside him, lithe and springy, took on the assured grace of aristocracy.

Jamie, with the callous self-centredness of the young secure in their own society, immediately plunged off into the interior of the house, announcing his arrival, seeking out Naomi, Robert, Susan, anyone he knew who might be present. Pat was left standing alone in the entrance hall, scarcely daring to raise his eyes to the rich maroon-papered walls, or the glistening dark wood of the curving staircase that rose before him to the upper floors.

Beside him, the maid in her black dress and starched white apron, collar and cuffs, waited for him to do, or say something, apparently, but he had not even the sense to offer her his army greatcoat to take away. He imagined her laughing at him, behind her stiff waiting smile, and totally unnerved by the setting, Pat never thought to return that smile with his own, which in more modest places had won many a lass with far more charms than she.

'I hae tae be aff, nou,' Pat mumbled to the surprised English maid, who did not understand a word. He turned to the door, fumbled with the knob, and then a voice amazed him into inaction.

'Pat,' it called, from the far end of the hallway. 'How kind of you to come.' It was a woman's voice, clear and low and he turned, mesmerized, to face the stranger who had called him by his name.

He had never seen a woman like her before. She was very slender, and in an era when women's figures were embellished with weighty frills and folds and mountains of lace, so that even the lightly built had a majestic bulk when fully clothed, her unfashionable shape was further emphasized by her mode of dress. Incredibly, she was wearing trousers. Nor were they the bloomers, voluminous and every bit as figure-concealing as skirts, with which, from postcards of cyclists and cartoons of feminists, Pat was familiar. They were white silk trousers and they were, he was certain, the only covering of her body below the waist. Above she wore a loose blouse of green silk with a high, Chinese collar and her hair was smoothly braided and hanging down over one shoulder, as if she had just risen from her bed. For all Pat's childhood, he had never seen his own mother, even, with her hair down, or her body without its layers and layers of petticoats and skirts and apron. And yet, shocking as she was, the woman was both beautiful and kind. She stepped forward, held out her hand to him, and said softly,

'You must forgive Jamie, he's still such a child. I have only just now learned you were here. This is such a pleasure, Pat,' her hand lightly touched his which had risen numbly to meet it, 'I've heard such kind things about you from Albert Maclaren. We are all tremendously grateful for the way you've looked after him. And Jamie. I'm quite sure they'd both be lost without you.'

Pat listened, bemused, and yet, hearing at the root a truth which he believed. Out there he *was* their superior, they did look up to him, turn to him, both as officer and friend. It had never occurred to him that they might have families who worried about them as his mother did over him. Or that this strange, marvellous woman would so astutely assess their relative roles.

By the time he had finished marvelling at it all, he had been divested of coat and kit, in the proper manner, and led by his hostess into the drawing-room and the gathered company. With her beside him, he felt almost at ease. She thought of everything, all the things he wouldn't know, and the things he'd not know how to ask.

'The water-closet's right here, Pat, should you need it later,' she said openly as they passed a closed door. 'And later I will show you your bedroom and your bathroom. I'm sure a nice bath will be pleasant after dinner. I know how you men long for such things at the Front. Of course,' she was saying as they entered the drawing-room, 'we don't dress for dinner on occasions like this, when everyone's exhausted from travelling. And you *will* sit next to me, so we can talk.' He smiled gratefully, knowing that the awful ordeal of his first dinner with the gentry would be immensely eased by her wise company.

'Ah Pat,' Jamie said, from where he stood by the immense, candlelit Christmas tree, 'I wondered where you'd got to.'

'Pat,' Naomi said, with a private look of displeasure for Jamie, 'being the only person around here with enough manners not to simply barge into my drawing-room unannounced, was waiting at the door. Where you should have been.' She smiled again at Pat and said, 'Do have a glass of sherry with me. I'm sure you'll find it pleasant.'

Much to his surprise, Pat did find it pleasant; once he got used to balancing the tiny, cut-crystal glass in a hand much more accustomed to a pint of ale, he even found the taste was distinctly appealing. Not having eaten for many hours, he found too that the effect of the dark gold liquid was to infuse the beautiful room with a new and welcoming warmth that seemed to spring from somewhere within his lightening head. He refused a third glass, suddenly aware of the effect the first two had had. He was quite certain that even his gracious hostess would have little time for him if he suddenly emerged, in his own vernacular, 'roaring fou'.

In addition to Naomi, Jamie and Pat, and young Robert Bruce, the company included two older men, both of whom evidently had connections in the theatre, and one of whom dressed not dissimilarly from Naomi, and was every bit as beautiful, and an older woman, a Mrs Claude-Hamilton, who spoke in a refined and purified voice and amazed Pat with her conversation.

'Well my dears,' she said with that undefeatable confidence of the very highly bred, 'the answer is quite simple. The war is getting precisely nowhere and amounting to an unacceptable drain on the manpower and resources of every nation involved. Nothing is to be proved by further fighting. Negotiation should begin at once. If it's too late to prevent another miserable winter for all concerned, at least we'd be in time to head off another wasted offensive. On anybody's side.'

'Rubbish,' Jamie shouted and Naomi hushed him, so that he retreated to a corner and fumed. The conversation went on, and Pat watched fascinated as the beautiful theatrical man leaned on the shoulder of the older theatrical man, watching doe-eyed as that party embarked on his own theory about the war. Pat said nothing, but studied the tall, grey-haired lady who had spoken so treasonably. She was a million miles from Alec Dougherty, and yet she had spoken as his sister.

Pat was almost relieved when young Robert Bruce, having been dismissed by the sulking Jamie, turned to him with his endless worshipful questions about the Front. Normally, such conversation appalled him. Just now, it seemed a kind of anchor, a familiar security in a strange new world.

Robert had been permitted one sherry, and was now making do with cups of tea. The tea smelled wonderful and Pat longed for some, but would not ask. Instead he answered, with modesty, Robert's questions about his role at Loos, and Robert settled in a corner chair by the Christmas tree with Pat beside him, and a small table before him on which he set a whole plate of iced cakes from the tea-trolley. As he listened he munched through one, and then another. Pat stole glances towards the plate. It was laden with delicacies, iced in pale pastels, decorated with swirls of cream, nuts and glacé fruits, and he'd never seen anything like them. He longed to show them to Kathleen, and had he been on his way home, instead of to France, he honestly felt he'd have taken one and hidden it away to bring to her. To actually take one to eat himself seemed unthinkable. He only watched, as Robert ate them, and eventually they were all gone.

'I'm terribly sorry for the delay,' Naomi said, then, 'but I had hoped my niece would be able to join us. She's nursing, you know,' she said to the grey-haired woman, who murmured something appropriately laudatory. 'However, she must have been kept late on the ward. I think we'll dine now, and perhaps she'll be able to join us for coffee.' Then she took Pat's arm and led him into the candlelit splendour of her dining-room.

The sight of the table, its crisp white linen graced with richly coloured china, glistening silver and crystal, stately candelabra marching its length, brought from Pat an involuntary gasp. Perhaps Naomi heard, for her arm through his tightened a moment in a way that was distinctly motherly. Pat had a pal in the battalion, Fraser Henderson, who served as batman to Tenny Maclaren and had described to him the wonders of the Officers' Mess back home in Scotland. Until this moment he had regarded his stories as a good part invention. Now he knew they were true. Naomi said, as she seated herself at the head of the table, 'Do sit down, Pat, you needn't wait for the others,' by which he knew that to do so was what the rules decreed.

He grinned shyly and murmured, 'That's all right, ma'am,' and stood a little proudly behind his chair while the ladies were seated. He even leaned to help the grey-haired Mrs Claude-Hamilton beside him, and was rewarded with a surprisingly warm smile from that awesome-appearing creature.

He sat then and gazed a trifle wild-eyed at the array of silver spread before his place. Naomi said, 'I suppose it's a bit naughty of us to still be so formal with a war on, but since it's all here, we might as well use it, had we not, Pat?' She smiled encouragingly. 'It is rather pretty isn't it?' she added, almost girlishly.

'Oh yes, ma'am. It's lovely,' Pat whispered. He dragged his linen napkin surreptitiously down on to his kilted knees, as the others seemed to have done so.

'Do you know, Pat,' Naomi said, softly, just to him, 'when I was a little girl and was, just occasionally, allowed to have proper dinners with the family, that is the Maclaren family at Culbrech House, I used to be positively terrified.' Pat must have looked disbelieving, because she said quickly, 'Oh, I was, Pat. I was. I never knew which fork or knife to use, no matter how many times Mama had told me. You see, I ate in the nursery with Nanny and the boys and we were just little savages. Me most of all. I was quite unmanageable.' Pat grinned and she, as if reading his mind said, 'I dare say there's a good few who think I still am.'

She signalled to the shadowy figures in the corners of the room and they, silently, commenced serving soup. 'Anyway, one day, there we all were sitting around this vast table. I believe it was to celebrate the battalion's return from India or some such. And everyone was eating, and there was I struggling to manage some gruesomely awkward dish, with positively the worst and most wrong choice of cutlery, and suddenly this great, greasy lump of meat skidded right off my plate and hurtled down the table, and collided with Old Sir Andrew's prize candelabra. Gravy everywhere, Mother positively appalled, a deafening silence settling on the dining-room.' Pat was uncertain if he should laugh or not.

'And then, suddenly, Old Sir Andrew, that's the brigadier's father, and an old curmudgeon he was, too, Old Sir Andrew suddenly announces in this great *booming* voice, "I say, Maud, I really think that child would be jolly splendid at pig-sticking, don't you?" '

Pat laughed aloud, and covered his mouth with one hand, whispering, 'I'm sorry, but . . .'

'Oh Pat,' she laughed too, 'I really wanted to die. But afterwards, I decided something. Two things really. One, that it really wasn't my fault, not knowing how to do something I'd never really been properly taught. And the other was that I'd never again be really embarrassed because nothing, ever, would be quite so gloriously awful. And you know, nothing has.' She smiled gently and her eyes met his. 'One of the serving girls later took me aside and told me, "It's really quite simple, Miss. Just start at the outside and work in, with the silverware, and you'll almost always be right. And anyway who'll know if you're wrong? I've seen a proper earl drink his soup with his pudding spoon, I have." '

Pat smiled and tentatively reached for his outermost spoon with which to drink his soup, and knew then exactly why she'd told the whole story. He felt the kind of warmth within him that came when he found Kathleen had polished his boots in the early morning and set them to warm by the range.

Throughout the dinner Naomi talked with him, telling him little things about her own life in London, the few hours' nursing that she did in the week, the visits she paid to families of soldiers, the small garden she'd made behind this splendid house to grow her own vegetables for the duration of the war. She asked him about his family, and he found himself telling her about Kathleen, and Alec Dougherty and Molly and his brothers in Scotland and Ireland. Somehow, some deep male instinct kept him from even mentioning Theresa Kelly whom he was intended to marry.

At the end of the meal Naomi turned once more to him in that special private way and said softly, 'Now Pat, I will be taking the ladies out to the drawing-room for coffee. It is one of the things we do, and it has its purposes. You will be offered a glass of port with Jamie and my two friends, and Robert gets a half-glass only. I'd appreciate it if you'd see to that. Then in a little while you will all come in to have coffee too.'

Pat nodded, miserable again, knowing she would leave him. She said, 'I must go now.' Then the expression in her dark brown eyes became very direct and she said, 'Pat, they are all children in their own home, and you are a stranger. But you are more a man than any of them. You've nothing to fear.'

As she stood, he said quietly, 'Thank you. Ye've been sae kind.'

Naomi looked down at his earnest young face, the intense dark blue eyes full of surprising depth, and the smooth black wave of his hair falling forward over them. She leaned her head back slightly and gave her mysterious, oriental smile. 'Oh, it's been my pleasure, Pat. Do you know, for the first time I think ever, I'm just the slightest bit sorry I'm as old as I am.'

Whatever age she was, and he would not have known where to begin guessing, Pat McGarrity was at that moment severely in danger of becoming one of the many, many men from many and varied walks of life whose fate it was to spend their life in love with Naomi Bruce. But he didn't; not because she in any way lacked charm, but because another fate was, even then, awaiting him in the drawing-room of the house on Hyde Park.

Susan Bruce had only just come in herself, when Pat, in the company of the other male members of the party, entered the room. The night had turned from icy rain to snow, and the melting dampness of it sparkled on her face and her blond hair in the soft light of the Christmas-tree candles. She was standing by the fire, warming herself, her back to it and her hands, small and red with cold, crossed behind her, fingers outstretched to the flames. She had come, still in uniform, straight from her ward in the First London General where two sudden emergency operations had taken the time that had been intended for dinner with her aunt. Naomi brought her a glass of Drambuie liqueur, topped with whipped cream, and she reached her small cold hands to take it and smiled her gratitude as Pat saw her for the first time. The photograph had been a fine likeness, and even with her hair neatly bound to Matron's will, not flowing for Mr Leitner's romanticism, she was unmistakable.

'It's you,' Pat said, dumbfounded, aloud.

Susan Bruce looked up, startled, uncertain who had spoken, or to whom, and her eyes met those of the handsomest man she'd ever seen in her life. And incredibly he was staring right at her. She could not believe it, nor the passionate intensity of his gaze, and she had to suppress the very real desire to look about her for some other more worthy woman who would prove the true object of his devotion. But for once, there was no other. Only herself, Naomi of course standing at the doorway, and Mrs Claude-Hamilton, who, it had to be admitted, shook male hearts these days with her politics, not her face. There was, at last, no Emma, no Philippa, no Rebecca, to draw away that sought-after and fearful look that men at times bent on women. Susan turned to the fire, wanting to flee and yet yearning to hear his steps approach her.

When they did, she was trembling visibly as she turned to face him.

'Och, yer cold,' he said almost to himself, his voice full of a concern that overrode shyness. In the space of a brief hour in the dining-room Naomi Bruce had taught him an invaluable lesson; these were women, these fine and glorious creatures, for all their wealth, style, and manners. They were women. And women were his natural game.

From the beginning, they were right for each other. There was between them none of the nervous bickering or flirtatious jealousies that are so common to courtships. Pat had had many lovers, Susan none, but each seemed to have learned the same lesson from their divergent histories, that love was too fine to waste in foolishness, particularly when time itself was so rare.

He brought a chair to her at the fireside, and sat on the settle at her feet. He told her honestly about the postcard with her picture that he carried everywhere. She was genuinely touched, and found nothing embarrassing in his sincere devotion to her admittedly lovely face. She told him about Rebecca and Mr Leitner and what she regarded as her own childish vanities, and her shame at it all when her brother Johnny was wounded in France.

Pat considered, and said softly, 'If ye dinna mind me sayin', I think yer wrang. Ye see, those pictures, the songs, a' that sort o' thing; we ken a'richt it's no' real, it's all fairytale stuff. But fer a' that, we need it. We need something tae believe in, or, an' please don't take me wrang, I'll do ma duty like the next bloke, but wi'oot those things, I dinna think sometimes we could carry on.'

'It's very bad, isn't it?' Susan said softly.

'Och Susan,' he whispered, saying what he'd never said before, 'it's awfu' oot there.'

Their eyes met and instinctively their hands reached for each other's and a silence came down on the room. When they looked up, for the cause of it, there was not a pair of eyes present that were not focused on them.

'My dears,' Naomi said with a faint tremor of confusion in her normally smooth voice, 'I think it is time we all say goodnight.' But she knew already, it was far too late. Naomi knew men and women like she knew little else; she had spent a lifetime on the outside of everyone's lives and was a consummate observer. Susan and Pat were perfect for each other; she saw it at once. Both shy, late scions of large, overwhelming families, they shared a common placelessness in the world. They were very alike. Two perfectly matched souls, unreasonably imprisoned in lives so different as to be those of alien species. As well, she thought, as she sent them both, starry-eyed, off to their very separate rooms, as well for a swan to fall in love with a fish, or a tree with a bird in the air.

Later, with all the household asleep, Naomi sat alone in the silence of her empty drawing-room, sipping coffee by the dying fire. It was a time she was greatly fond of, the silence of the late hours. She looked up to the portrait of her mother, Maud Bruce, hanging above her writing-desk, musing how even portraits seemed to grow weary in the late hours, as if when she left the room, their eyes, too, would close in sleep. First Johnny, now this. Oh Mother, you'll never forgive me. Nor believe I never intended it at all. An accident. Chance. Isn't that what love is about? And life.

'Well, Mama,' she said, rising and settling the coals on the hearth, 'at least it's been interesting.'

She mounted the stairs alone, and as she passed Pat McGarrity's closed bedroom door she paused, a wicked thought bringing the faintest of smiles to her dark eastern face. Her fingers trailed across the porcelain knob and then dropped lightly away, as she turned, still smiling, and moved into the darkness of the hall.

9

Donnie Cameron twice slapped his frozen hands against the upper sleeves of his greatcoat, crossing them over his body, attempting to restore some warmth throughout before he lifted yet another sandbag to his shoulder. Then he turned once more down the line, the weight of the canvas sack full of freshly dug chalk chafing already. It was his fifth trip of the night and his fifth night on fatigues. He and a dozen others of his platoon had trekked the long way from the front line, down through the communications trenches, past the rear and support lines, to the distant camouflaged dump so often that his feet knew every frozen lump of mud, each duckboard of the journey. He thanked God for the cold. Bitter as it was, they had all welcomed it, because at last it was dry. For the three weeks since Christmas, snow, sleet and freezing rain had alternately drenched the Somme district. The trenches were quagmires; duckboards had floated like slick, useless rafts on pools of muddy water often as deep as a man's waist. Now, with the January freeze, came respite. The mud, rock-hard, was passable, the nights again bearable. Donnie knew that to be forever cold was a misery, but to be forever cold, and wet, was beyond endurance. Donnie knew the trenches. He was a veteran.

'Whit we daein' it fer?' demanded the exhausted and querulous voice of Hamish Drummond, a new young private, eighteen years old and fresh from the Ross-shire countryside, who'd come out with the last draft. He had attached himself to Donnie, finding the company of so experienced a man a great comfort. It would no doubt have surprised him to realize that the venerable Maclaren who'd served right through from the first days at Mons had himself only just achieved the age of twenty-one. In a way, it surprised Donnie himself.

He glanced about with old practised instinct, making sure that no officer was within hearing distance. Then he grinned in the darkness, shifting the weight of his sandbag slightly as his feet found a hole in the duckboards, and said, 'I see it this way. Staff hae decided we've nae a hope in hell o' chasin' Jerry oot o' France. Sae we'll be gey clever an' tak France awa' frae him in the night.' He joggled his sandbag on his shoulder for emphasis. 'When we hae eneuch o' her packed awa' in these wee baggies, then we'll juist heap her up on the shore at Dover an' thumb oor noses at the Kaiser. He'll hae tae come an' get her 'cross the Channel.' He grinned again in the darkness, glanced around to see they were unobserved and said, 'Never mind. Drap thot thing an' hae a fag.'

Hamish lowered his sandbag full of chalk earth to the ground and crouched beside Donnie in the communications trench. A third man came and joined them, but when a fourth tried, Donnie said, authoritatively,

'Awa', ye lot. This is oor funk hole. Fin' yersels yin o' yer ain.'

He drew out his army-issue tin of Capstans and they each took one. Donnie lit a match, shielded well from wind and the far distant enemy by his broad solid hand. He lit his cigarette, drew the smoke deeply into his lungs as if he'd been smoking all his life instead of a few months, and passed the light to Hamish. But when Hamish attempted to pass the dwindling light on to the next man, both Donnie and that soldier instinctively caught his wrist and snuffed the flame.

'Three on a match,' Donnie said, with sage condemnation, drawing out his matchbox again. He lit a fresh one and lit the soldier's cigarette, saying as he did so, 'Ane tae spot ye.' The cigarette glowed and he drew back his flame. 'Ane tae aim,' he blew it out. 'And ane,' he made a pistol shape with his hand, pointing the forefinger at Hamish's head, 'tae fire.'

'Third man's aye the one tae get it,' the other soldier finished, quietly, leaning back against the crumbling frozen mud of the communications trench to enjoy his smoke.

'Aye,' Hamish said, faintly argumentative, 'I see the sense in it a'richt. But wha' the hell's gonnae shoot us awa' back here. We're twa mile at least behind the line.'

Donnie and his companion were silent, the latter still nodding sagely as he puffed at his Capstan. 'Doesna maitter,' Donnie said at last, for he was not a thinker and had not quite comprehended that logical precaution had already slipped over the abyss into superstition and myth, in this as in so many other matters. 'You'll ne'er catch me bein' third man on a match, any road.'

They lifted their sandbags and resumed trudging down the line, talking then about a subject as dear to their hearts as grousing about the RSM; the web of fancies, myths, amulets and omens that overhung their ever-threatened lives.

'D'ye ken whit they sae o' yon statue?' Hamish asked Donnie hesitantly.

'The virgin o' the kirk?'

'Aye. Dae ye think it's true? That the war'll end when she fa's an' the yins wha' shot her doun will lose?'

'Win,' said the third soldier, supporting his version of the tale.

'Lose, ye gomeril.'

'Win, lose, whit's the difference? As lang as it's o'er,' said his opponent, trudging on ahead morosely.

Donnie Cameron laughed under his breath and said to Hamish, 'Och, no. It willna end. Aiblins they'll let a' the papists aff early, though. Seein' as hou it's their kirk.' Donnie didn't much care. He wasn't a papist, or a proddy either, any longer. Still, the night before they went over the top at Loos, he'd begged a Bible off the chaplain, to carry in his breast pocket, because one of his mates swore a man down the line had been saved from death by the printed pages of the Holy Word. And since Donnie survived Loos, he hung on to his Bible, and wore as well now a St Christopher that he'd got from Pat McGarrity. It was papist, but he didn't care. He'd wear a bishop's mitre if it would guarantee him safe passage. The trouble was, nothing would. And because of that, darker stories abounded, stories they did not share. Donnie believed them all, the tales of ghosts, and ancient warriors, and rats the size of dogs, grown monstrously hungry on human flesh.

He shivered, looking over his shoulder at the paling of dawn over the east that belonged to the enemy. Gentlemen in England mused in the comfort of armchairs that the war might last for ever, an unwelcome new wonder of the industrial age, passing from generation to generation; a permanent part of life. To Donnie Cameron, it already was.

When Donnie and his companions had emptied their sandbags in the prescribed place and trekked back through the zigzagging miles of ditches to their own piece of front-line trench, Captain Maclaren was again waiting for them, with a new stack of tightly packed sacks of chalk. Hamish began to think Donnie's theory of sandbagging France was right.

'Right,' Tenny said, 'shift that lot and you're done for the night. It'll be first light before you're back.' He was crouching at the mouth of the shaft sunk into the floor of a forward-reaching sap, peering at his watch in the light of a Kranzow lamp.

Donnie shouldered his next sandbag philosophically. He regarded the onset of dawn with affection, for a line of men with sandbags was as visible to the ever-more-present German aeroplanes as was the distinctive giveaway of unshielded heaps of the pale chalky earth.

No one liked laying mines. It was difficult and dangerous and trench life was dangerous enough already. The alternative, though, was to leave those subterranean regions to the enemy to make his own, and that was worse.

And the Germans were good at mining, and they'd started early, almost as soon as the war locked into rigid stalemate in 1914. That December, by blowing skywards a good part of a hapless Indian brigade at Festubert, they brought to the Western Front the unwelcome announcement that even the ground beneath one's feet was no longer friendly.

It was perhaps the most gruesome of all fears, and men who could face shell-fire with aplomb, dodge sniper-fire like rain-drops, lay trembling in their funk holes at night, listening for the faint and eerie chinks of scraping and mining far below them, like tappings from the denizens of the grave.

Countermining, quite apart from its strategic value, was an enormous aid to morale. At least, Tenny thought, peering down into the darkness within darkness of the shaft, at least one was doing something, not waiting helplessly for destruction.

The Maclaren mining party was a mixed bag, made up of selected members of the regiment chosen from all four companies with direct regard to anything resembling mining experience, and a scattering of Royal Engineers. Elsewhere the Engineers formed complete mining companies, and rumour had it that the brass were, in other parts of the line, importing civilian miners straight from the Welsh and Scottish pits. The Maclarens, however, with their growing lowland Scottish contingent, had a fair sprinkling of West of Scotland and Fifeshire miners to choose from, headed by a youthful but highly experienced one-time member of the Mine Rescue Brigade: Pat McGarrity.

Tenny was intrigued by McGarrity, finding his respect for the man's skill and fearlessness almost equally balanced by his concern over the miner's disconcertingly egalitarian attitude towards command. Unlike almost all his brethren, who positively welcomed being told, firmly, exactly what to do, Pat questioned orders. It was unthinkable, and had Tenny been a less thoughtful man than he was, McGarrity would have found himself strapped to a gun limber wheel for a day to think over the relative positions of a corporal and a captain in His Majesty's Forces. But Pat wasn't a troublemaker, Tenny knew, not yet, anyhow. He was simply intelligent and curious and oddly ingenuous. He wanted to know why he was doing what he was doing. If Tenny could give him a good explanation he became instantly the gamest and most willing soldier in the company. But it had better be a good explanation.

Oddly, for a man used all his life to army regimen, Tenny sympathized. But he also worried. He knew the day would come when no explanation would suffice. Indeed, if Pat started to do the kind of thinking Tenny himself had been doing since Loos, that day might be here already. And when that day arrived, there would be rebellion, and whether or not Corporal Pat McGarrity chose to acknowledge the fact, there was not one inch of room for rebellion in an army at war.

Tenny was glad of the mining, glad to keep that tough body and sharp young mind firmly engaged in action and purpose. Wear it out, exhaust it, spend it thoroughly, and maybe the mind would forget its questions. If not, Tenny knew, and with great regret because he liked the little Glaswegian immensely, the day could well come when he would be obliged to set Pat McGarrity before a firing squad.

But Pat, at the moment, had other things on his mind than the niceties of pleasing his officers. Over a hundred yards from where Tenny Maclaren waited nervously at the entrance shaft, Pat McGarrity knelt in the debris of their digging in a tunnel too low for a man to stand, lit only by fading, flickering candles whose flames threatened always to die in the failing air supply. The tunnel was ventilated only by a crude system of bellows and a hosepipe trailing from the distant outer air. Repeated requests by Tenny and his superiors had resulted only in ancient army issue ventilators last used in the Crimea which broke down at once. Pat's back ached from scratching away with his short-handled spade and his head ached from lack of oxygen. The man beside him, Private Tom Reid, breathing painfully as he stuffed loose chalk into a sandbag to be dragged out of the tunnel by the rope team, at its head, had twice last week fainted from lack of air and been himself dragged out with the same ropes. He was an older man, one of the New Army recruits like Pat himself, who came from Dennyloanhead and had a long mining career behind him. Pat suspected from his breathing he suffered from the beginnings of black lung, and marvelled he'd passed the medicals. But in those first heady days, medical officers like others on the recruiting side were lax, maybe criminally so, and many men sent out in the first flush of patriotism were now stumbling about hopelessly unfit, long-standing infirmities blossoming under hardship into real disability.

For all that Tom Reid never complained, and worked stoically, and brought from Pat that same pride that the sturdy women of his tenement home had aroused in him.

'Wheesht,' Reid said now, his scratchy voice barely a whisper. Pat was instantly silent. 'Bide nou, she'll come again.' Pat signalled to the rope team by shaking the line so they too would cause no sound. Silence came down on their narrow cavern and only the faint, persistent dripping of water sounded in the hesitant flickering circle of candleflame. The shadows of the roof supports loomed large, like the internal bones of a buried dragon. 'There,' Reid whispered again, 'd'ye hear?'

Pat shook his head, but then he did hear, faint and eerie, its direction intensely difficult to determine, a thin metallic chinking, a scuffle and scratching, and then silence again.

'Aye,' Pat whispered. The Maclarens naturally had chosen the narrowest point between the opposing lines to tunnel towards their opponents and lay their mines. If Jerry were mining as well, he'd choose the same area. Pat knew they might be digging side by side. The silence dragged long, and he wondered if they too were listening, lying also in the rubble of their digging, not many yards from himself, waiting, afraid to move, speak or even breathe. It was the third time in the day they had heard something, but this was the first occasion that was unmistakable. 'Aye,' he whispered again. 'They're diggin' a'richt.'

The chalk soil, solid and easily dug, was in some ways a miner's dream. But in others, it was treacherous. First there was the nuisance of its colour, making all waste a beacon proclaiming their efforts, unless carted far away. And, too, it conducted sound so well that at times, working close to the enemies' front lines, they were obliged to abandon their metal tools and claw away surreptitiously at the workface with their hands. Now, Pat knew, the sounds of digging he heard could well come from some distance, but the distortions of sound through solids could not be ignored.

At any moment the thrust of a spade could cast the underground opponents into each other's unwelcome company and a terrifying battle in their lightless, airless maze.

It was so long before the sound came again that Pat had begun to feel they had, in their perpetual edginess, simply imagined it. He had actually raised his grafting tool once more, to attack the wall of dripping chalk, when a crunch and rumble of metal against crumbling earth burst into the silence as if it were actually within their own tunnel.

'Jesus Christ,' Tom Reid muttered, 'did ye hear thot? He's richt here.' He pointed wildly towards the left wall of their tunnel. 'He's nae a foot awa'.' He clutched with shaking fingers suddenly at Pat's cuff. 'C'mon lad, awa' afore he's in here wi' us.'

Pat pushed angrily at Reid's nervous hand, and whispered, 'Wheesht. I cannae hear.' He was straining to determine the direction of the digging. But Tom was half in a panic. 'I want oot o' here,' he whimpered suddenly, and Pat, wanting the same thing very much, had sympathy. Still he waited, hoping the sounds would fade, indicating a turning-away of the unseen miner. 'He's gonnae blaw us,' Tom Reid cried, his voice rising dangerously, and Pat clapped his grimy hand over the other's mouth. But he was thinking, all the while. It was quite possible. Their own sounds of digging could well have been heard, and the eerie chinking beyond the chalk wall of their tunnel could indeed be the laying of charges to level their digging and bring their roof down on their heads. It was, after all, precisely what he'd do if he suspected the Germans were tunnelling towards his trenches.

He thought wildly, as the chinking grew steadily nearer. Was that it? Had they been heard? Or were the Germans themselves the unsuspecting, and should he send for explosives, pack this little gallery, seal it, and retreat to finish their opposition before they could finish him? Whatever, Pat thought, he couldn't do anything with Reid. At the end of an eight-hour shift, the poor sod was in no physical condition to start laying impromptu mines, even if his mental state were up to it, which Pat doubted.

'Aye,' he said. 'You awa' up tae the shaft-heid an' tell the officer we think we've got company. See whit he's got tae say.' Tom Reid scuttled off without waiting even to answer, making for the distant safety of the front-line trench; for compared to here, it seemed as safe as his own bed.

Pat crouched alone in the dimming light, waiting and listening. One candle died and he made no attempt to relight it. Were the ever-thinning wall of chalk between himself and the tunnelling German to be breached, he would do well with as little light as possible. He had no gun; his rifle, useless enough down here, was back in the trench with his kit. But he had his short-handled spade. The sounds stopped. Pat felt his heartbeat quicken, his body, shivery with cooling sweat, tense, waiting. The blast would be so close, he told himself, he'd be gone in an instant, that terror of live entombment would not be his. He clutched his spade closer, as if it were a holy object, and began to make an Act of Contrition.

'McGarrity?' the voice, even in a whisper, upper-class and unmistakable, leapt out of the blackness behind him. Pat spun about, on the heels of his boots, and, still crouching, raised his finger to his lips, signalling Tenny Maclaren to silence. Tenny, his height a great disadvantage down here, was half doubled over, feeling his way along the rope line. He came closer to Pat and he too crouched down on his heels, awaiting instructions. Down here, he regarded Pat as much more of an equal than up in the daylight.

'He's juist a yard or sae, thot way,' Pat whispered. 'I cannae be sure. An' he's stopped diggin'. He could hae gane hame. Or he could hae laid a charge. I hae tae warn ye, sir, we're mebbe sittin' on ane or twa sticks o' TNT,' he gestured towards the blank wall. 'Juist sae ye know.'

'Yes,' Tenny said, trying to keep his voice as calm as his corporal's. 'I see.' He paused again, looking charily at the wall of the tunnel. 'What do you suggest we do, Corporal?' he said then, wondering why he wasn't himself already suggesting they get the hell out. He supposed he wanted to hear that from McGarrity first.

But Pat said, 'Weel, sir, we can just bide here an' see if thot's the case. But I wouldnae recommend it.'

'And what *would* you recommend?' Tenny said, fighting annoyance and terror simultaneously. Hadn't the man any simple human fear?

'Och sir,' Pat said regretfully. 'We can blaw the tunnel, I reckon. But thot's oor workin' awa' tae.'

'I see,' Tenny said, and was about to suggest they did so, when Pat spoke again.

'Or,' he said, musing, 'I reckon we could break through, hopin' we dinnae walk right intae Jerry, an' gae awa' up their tunnel a bittie and chuck a grenade. Mebbe then oor ain will stand. Mebbe again it willna,' he added complacently.

'And if it doesn't?' Tenny said.

Pat looked at him, surprised, in the faint light. 'I dinnae hae tae spell it oot, sir, dae I?' he said.

Tenny felt a distant authoritarian urge to chastize the little corporal for his faintly insolent tone, but suppressed it. This was hardly the time, or the place. He thought quickly and said, with a decisiveness that again surprised Pat, 'We'll break through.'

He returned to the shaft-head and collected a couple of Mills bombs, leaving Pat with his revolver to guard the tunnel in case the Germans began digging again and broke through themselves. On his return journey, he half expected to hear the explosion of the German mine, but the silence remained, and he found Pat hunched over the candleflame, thoughtfully handling his handgun with the respect children give to someone else's choice toy. Pat handed it back reverently, and hooked one of the Mills bombs to his belt. Then he rose, still bent over beneath the low tunnel ceiling, and aimed his spade towards the side wall. He looked at Tenny, crouched beside him, pistol in hand. Suddenly he grinned, 'Dinnae luik sae solemn, sir. Maist like they're hauf way hame tae Berlin.' Then he struck the wall with his spade and the sound that rang back was loud, and hollow.

'Again,' Tenny whispered, but Pat was already hacking away at the crumbling chalk. Each blow brought an ominous unseen rushing of falling earth, as if a minor cave-in was occurring in the

German tunnel beyond the wall. Suddenly Pat's spade sank handle-deep into emptiness and in the same instant brilliant light burst through the wall, and chunks of earth fell about them as if blasted by the light itself. For a moment Tenny imagined an explosion had occurred, so stunning was the effect of that brilliance, but he realized quickly there had been no sound, no concussion; they were both unaffected and Pat was hastily slashing at his breakthrough, widening the gap in the wall, allowing more and more white alien light to pour into their safe darkness.

Mesmerized, Tenny watched, not comprehending the corporal's frantic haste. But then he too heard the voices, distant and shouting. In German. With his hands he clawed at the chalk earth beside Pat until the gap was wide enough and then he leapt over the rubble and into the white brilliance of the electrically-lit gallery, his revolver ready in his hand. Pat followed him at once, blinking as he looked around. The tunnel was solid and well constructed, wider and broader and higher than their own, reflecting in its efficiency the superior edge the enemy always had in all his constructions, trenches, dugouts, redoubts.

'Jesus,' Pat whispered, admiring the string of incandescent bulbs, disappearing around a bend in the tunnel. 'We havenae even got yon in Glasga.' But as he spoke Tenny snatched the spade from his hands and methodically smashed every bulb in sight, so that the end of the unfinished gallery was now as dark as any of their own.

Pat, feeling the faintest twinge of regret at the destruction, crouched now beside him in the darkness, waiting. The voices, querulous and loudening, grew nearer. Tenny strained to hear the German, could not decipher any, and yet instinctively knew the gist of the conversation. It was soldiers' talk, the same the world over. They were grousing; some officer had sent them to investigate a dim, distant noise which doubtless was nothing but a falling stone. Why couldn't it wait? They'd done their shift. He smiled wryly, levelling his revolver at the point their heads would be. He felt a bond of regretful understanding with their officer, as Pat had felt for the builders of the electrically-lit tunnel.

The grousing turned to sounds of surprise as they approached the bend, beyond which the tunnel was dark. But there were no sounds of alarm. A falling stone had severed wires. They came on, casting shadows that fell before them like their own fates.

Tenny fired the instant they appeared, perfectly silhouetted against their own brilliant lighting. The first fell, wordlessly, as the explosion crashed and echoed in the confined space, and there was a shout of panic from the second as he turned to flee, and Tenny fired again. The second man fell and the walls of the tunnel seemed to give a warning shudder. Behind them, loose earth from the broken wall slid down with a sound like running water.

'I wouldnae dae that o'er often, sir,' Pat muttered at his elbow.

Tenny said, in haste, knowing the shots would bring others, 'I want to close their tunnel with a grenade. Can I do that, or will it all come down?'

Pat thought fast, thudding a familiar hand against the wooden roof supports, feeling along the damp chalk wall for the distance to the next.

'Och aye,' he said then. 'Their's willnae come doun, if ye chuck it far eneuch. I dinna ken,' he added disconcertingly, 'aboot oors.'

Tenny glanced back nervously at the darkness of the gap and their own dark mine-workings behind. If he threw the Mills bomb, he would obliterate the German gallery, and cut them off from the advancing enemy. But he might, as well, block their own retreat and leave them both entombed here with the two dead Germans deep below no-man's-land, in an airless void. Shouts of concern echoed down from the lighted end of the German tunnel. There was no more time. Tenny clutched his Mills bomb, ran to the far reaches of the darkness where light from the first undamaged bulb showed, around the bend, the wood-propped earth corridor snaking away to the German trenches. Suddenly it darkened, as hastening forms blocked the end, and then blackness came down as someone thought to turn off the betraying electric light. A shot was fired at random, echoing down the tunnel. Tenny hurled his grenade around the corner and turned and ran blindly to where Pat, huddled by the entrance to their own workings, awaited him.

'Here, sir!' he shouted and then the blast of the grenade flung them both to the earth floor and flung cascading loose chalk over them. A beam split, a rending sound tearing through the deafening echoes of the blast. Pat scrambled to his feet, clutching at Tenny's arm, dragging him, dazed, through the dark gap between the tunnels. Earth was pouring into it, like sand in an hourglass, raining down on shoulders. Tenny plunged forward, blind in the blackness, and collided with the wooden shorings of the far side of their own tunnel. Behind him the wall between the two galleries collapsed with an earthy roar, like the distant explosion of a heavy shell. He was choking in the dust-filled air and claustrophobic terror yearned to engulf him. He remembered then he was in command,

'Corporal,' he called. 'Are you all right.'

'Aye, sir,' Pat said somewhere in the blackness. 'Juist fine, thankin' ye.'

Again Tenny heard insolence but found it hard to resent. 'I hae the rope here, sir, if yer wantin' it.'

'Yes,' Tenny said, determined to sound as damnably unruffled as his corporal. 'That would be nice.' He felt in the darkness for the guide-rope and made his hands clutch it with decent lack of haste.

'Ye ken she juist may a' come doun wi' the aftershock,' Pat McGarrity commented, blandly.

'Then, Corporal,' Tenny said, losing control, 'I suggest you get your arse the bloody hell out of here and I'll do the same.'

If Pat replied, he did not hear. A rumbling in the roof of the tunnel and another cascade of earth ended all conversation. They ran, as fast as was possible bent over in darkness, and frantically running a guide-rope through dust-caked hands. A roar of collapsing roof thundered behind them, and the timbers snapped and creaked through the constant rain of settling earth. Tenny's mind pictured the whole of the workings folding up, wooden roof props folding one on top of the other like a slithering pack of cards. He ran on, on the heels of Pat McGarrity, terrified, more than ever in his life, and yet determined that he would be the last man out. Once McGarrity tried to manoeuvre him ahead, but Tenny growled an obscenity followed by an order and Pat did not argue; if the captain was determined to be a hero, Pat would let him. If they stopped to argue about it, they'd both be dead.

They burst into the light filtering down the entry shaft in the instant that a great roar arose behind them and a section of roof twenty feet long came down intact, stirring the gentle grasses of no-man's-land with the subtle tug of subsidence. Then they were in open air, being dragged to the surface and into a clamour of voices and the pale light of a still, lovely dawn.

Half an hour later, having observed a desultory stand-to at first light, Tenny Maclaren was breakfasting on fried bacon, cooked by his batman over a sweet-smelling wood-fire, and considering the day's duties before catching a couple of hours sleep in his dugout. He rose, and out of curiosity, examined the ground between themselves and the enemy line through a trench periscope. Frost lay on the untrodden grass, and winter birds fluttered and picked and settled. There was no sign of the chaos that had occurred below, other than a slight indentation near their own parapet where the cave-in that had almost caught them had occurred. Mentally he noted that work must commence tonight on repairs. It seemed impossible that below that oddly gentle piece of ground two men had died but hours before and gunfire and bombing had thundered.

Pat McGarrity came past him, on the way to his own breakfast, and saw him studying the empty ground. 'Doesnae show, sir,' he said, 'does it?'

'No,' Tenny said. 'Odd somehow.'

'I mind when my faither died,' Pat said, 'in a cave-in in the mine. I went an' stood by the pit-head, looking out o'er the fields tryin' tae imagine him doun below; ye ken, sir, whit a faither is tae a lad . . . only fields, green wet fields . . . I couldna believe . . .'

'How old were you, Pat?' Tenny said.

'Twelve, thirteen.' Pat turned away, and Tenny sensed he had invaded privacy.

'I'm sorry,' he said.

Pat turned to face him, seeming surprised. 'Thank you, sir,' he said. Then he remembered something, and reached into the pocket of his tunic. It was a letter, which he handed to Tenny, as was customary, for censorship. Tenny took it with him to the dugout, and laid it with the others. It was only after his sleep when he had started on the peculiarly distasteful but necessary task of reading his men's letters home, crossing out any unacceptable references and resealing them for posting on, that he saw who the letter was for. In the past Pat's letters were simple; half to his mother in Glasgow, and the other half to a Miss Kelly. This envelope, written in the same scrawled unschooled hand, was addressed:

Miss Susan Bruce
The Nurse's Hostel
First London General Hospital
London

Twice, Tenny turned it over in his hand, certain he had read the wrong words, or held the wrong letter, but it was Pat's without a doubt. His mind leapt back to the darkened tunnel and the tough little Glaswegian trying to save him, first, from the falling tons of chalk. The warmth and pride he felt for the man warred with indignation. Susan Bruce, the colonel's niece. How dare he write to her? Where had he found her name?

He opened the unsealed envelope with stiff cold fingers, and began to read, striving to maintain a purely professional eye. No references to locales, work parties, plans, casualties, enemy action. No, none of those. Surprising for a man of McGarrity's character, no comments about his officers or the staff. Nothing out of order. Totally acceptable. Tenny refolded the letter with careful decency and slipped it into its envelope and sealed it. Nothing unacceptable at all. Merely a love letter from a corporal from the Gorbals to the niece of the commanding officer of the battalion. A love letter in reply, clearly, to one of the lady's. God in heaven, Tenny laid the back of his hand over his eyes as he leaned against the damp boards of the dugout, what could he possibly do?

He thought of Susan, sweet and pampered, the baby of the family, its one true innocent. He wondered abstractedly if he himself, had he not been so besotted with Rebecca Galloway, might not have fallen for her one day himself. His mind winged to Pat, his guttural Scots tongue, his canny sharp mind, that rebellious look that seemed always to say, I'll do it, but only because I choose to. How could it happen? They met at Naomi's, that was clear; damn fool Jamie bringing him there. It was all the fault of this blasted New Army egalitarianism, with boys like Albert and James deliberately wallowing in the lower classes. Christ knows where it would all end.

Tenny sighed and put the rest of the letters aside for later. He wanted fresh air, daylight. The dugout reminded him eerily of the tunnel he had escaped. Outside, in the trench, he stood alone in the shaft of weak sunlight that filtered down from the parapet, thinking of home. It was eleven o'clock on the morning of the eighteenth of January 1916. It was Rebecca Galloway's wedding day.

10

The marriage which took place in Inverness that morning was a subdued affair. A lavish celebration would have been unseemly when a goodly scattering of any company wore black armbands for private griefs. And the U-boats prowling the Atlantic shipping lanes had begun already to nip away at Britain's imported foodstuffs and although country districts like Strathglass were as yet lightly affected, a visible tightening of the belt was a patriotic necessity. Still, friends and family gathered, and with wine-cellars stocked yet from the previous generation, cold-stores and smokehouses providing venison and salmon, and root-cellars and clamps well filled from the summer, no one at Culbrech House was likely to go hungry.

Naomi Bruce had seen Robert off to his school and then travelled north for the occasion in the company of Arnold Galloway. That gentleman, beaming now with a quite unlikely pride, escorted Rebecca down the aisle of St Columba's High Church on the banks of the River Ness, thus completing in that surprising setting the odd fiction begun twenty years before in a London gutter.

Later, at the reception at Culbrech House, he drank a great deal of champagne, waltzed with the bride, and ambled cheerily from group to group of guests with such delighted avuncular beamings, that Naomi, quite amused, wondered if somehow he had convinced himself that a link of blood really did exist.

Naomi herself, having conceded to the marriage, had since that moment shut away her own feelings about the matter for ever. Rebecca had from her all she could ask of support and encouragement; her trousseau was provided, maternal advice was provided, some rather unmaternal advice, which had left Rebecca blushing, was also provided. On the wedding day Naomi dressed as matronly as such a woman ever might, and even Victoria was happily surprised. Since Sir Ian was a thousand or so miles away at Brigade HQ on the Somme, there was nothing to prevent cordiality, even friendship, between the two women. As it was, they passed each other with smiles, greeting with phantom kisses, asked kindly after each other's children's welfare. But that subject, like all others indeed between them, was charged with the same electric current of rivalry that had always held them opposed. In the end, at this occasion, as all others, the two women each privately conceded the wisdom of avoiding each other. They were both sorry. Each suspected that they could have, in another life, been excellent friends. Still, as long as in this life they shared the affections of one man, that would not be possible. Naomi was glad when, early in the celebrations, she could slip away with the totally justified excuse of spending the rest of her brief visit with her frail, largely bedridden stepfather, Willie Bruce. The visit depressed her; Willie's mind rambled now, and he had forgotten whose wedding she had come for, and recalling another, long past, berated her for arriving in an Indian sari, flaunting her origins in front of her mother, and her beauty in front of Ian Maclaren's bride.

As Naomi left the small house at Cluanie where she had spent her childhood, stopping once at the gate to look back at its steep slate roofs, and the now fading paint of its wooden gingerbreading looking worn and tattered in the dim of evening, she was filled with sorrow. She walked to the waiting car, certain somehow that she would not see her stepfather again. It was not an unlikely premonition; Willie was old and failing, and this visit, her first in years, was not likely to be repeated for years again. Even now she was not staying more than the span of hours between two night trains. She had not slept a night in Strathglass since she had born Ian Maclaren's bastard son.

She bent gracefully to step into the back seat of the car, and then straightened and looked back once again, unable to shake off the sorrow, deepening into grief, and as unable to explain the sudden power of it. As the car pulled away, her face behind its green veil was wet with tears.

Lost in private sadness, she did not even notice the bridal car, gaily festooned with ribbons and the usual prankster's motifs, that roared by them on the narrow road. So many conventions had fallen in the past two years, that it hardly struck anyone as unseemly for the groom to drive his bride away himself, in an open tourer, both of them casual in country tweeds and driving cloaks and Rebecca's going-away hat swathed in practical layers of muslin veil.

The day had been cold, but sunny, and the night that was falling was frosty and already filling with stars. After the days of preparation, Rebecca felt the wedding had gone by in a blur, and the sounds of it, fiddle music and dancing and toasts and applause, still swirled, like her dust veil about her head. She could hardly believe it was over, or that they were alone at last, or that her wedding night was but hours away.

Their destination was a hunting lodge in Glen Affric, property of Bruce family friends, kindly lent them for their honeymoon. Previously, in the world in which Johnny had been born, and into which Rebecca had been led, this would have been only the beginning. A week or two in London, or a tour of the Continent, or perhaps even the Americas, might have followed, and then long ritual visits to an ever-widening circle of friends, until the young couple finally returned to send out their cards and announce they were, at last, 'at home'. That, then, would be them settled; he to whatever gentleman's career awaited, she to the nursery which also awaited, and the next occasion in their lives, following most likely within the same year, would be the first christening. The top layer of the wedding cake, five-tiered and splendid despite the U-boats, was even now being carefully packed away for that event, but for Johnny and Rebecca that was the only part of the great wedding cycle that remained.

Their honeymoon would be four days in the modest though beautiful lodge towards which, with faintly indelicate speed, Johnny was driving, and after that he would return to his unit in France, and she to London and her interrupted duties at the First London General. If there was to be a christening this year, a lot would depend on the next four nights.

By midnight, on the first of them, the odds were not looking good. Almost the moment they had passed through the black iron gates of Culbrech House, Johnny was aware of a change come over Rebecca. She seemed to sink into herself, into quietness and strangeness, and he was reminded of the first day he met her, driving from Inverness to Culbrech, with Rebecca beside him a beautiful, preoccupied stranger.

Rebecca spoke suddenly. 'Isn't it strange, being alone?' she said. Johnny nodded. Of course, that was it. It was strange indeed. They had never before been so alone together, never before been beyond the range of family eyes and ears, even for a minute. Now suddenly, joined by a handful of words and a morning's celebration, they were abandoned, alone together for the rest of their lives, free to do whatever they would like with each other. It was terrifying.

Moray Lodge, set beautifully on a nearshore island in a dark loch, ringed with lofty Scots pines, was as solitary as a hermitage. No one seeking aloneness could find a more inviting place. Johnny, driving over the humpbacked stone bridge that crossed the narrowest point of lochwater and tied the island to the shore like a floating dinghy, wished dearly he was, instead, in London.

Of course, there would be servants, and windows were lighted throughout the tall grey stone building with its conically roofed towers flanking an arched doorway. But servants could, would, be dismissed. Servants would hasten away, embarrassed or smirking. Servants would direct all their attentions to the bedroom, lighting fires, setting out champagne, turning down counterpanes to reveal seductively-waiting pristine sheets. Servants would but add complicity to the event that yesterday had been a moral crime and today had become duty. Johnny's hand was trembling as he helped his bride down from the car.

They dined formally before a huge fire in the massive dining-room, immensely self-conscious and overwhelmed by the lavishness of the setting surrounding them, and the bounty of service. The staff were not from Culbrech, but members of the owner's household who generally accompanied his hunting parties and knew the house well. When dinner was ended they retired. Fires had been laid only upstairs; no one expected the drawing-room to be in use tonight.

The master bedroom overlooked the loch, and a rocky point of land with three picturesque giant pines, just faintly visible in the thin starlight.

'Shall I draw the curtains,' Johnny said, adding, 'dear,' in a self-consciously husbandly tone.

'I think not, the stars are lovely.' Only a handful of romantically placed candles vied with the starlight, and the room flickered with the flames of the hearth. Rebecca crouched down by the fire and warmed her hands.

'Are you cold?'

'No,' she said, still warming them.

'Do you wish . . .' he vaguely indicated the adjoining bathroom. She said no, then blushed and said yes.

'I'll go through,' he indicated the master's dressing-room, 'and get myself ready . . .' Somehow everything he said seemed to point to intimate ground.

She was standing by the window when he came out. Naomi had bought her nightdress and peignoir in a saucy French shop frequented by actresses. Rebecca had blushed and giggled and been delighted and they'd laughed together later over tea upstairs in Harrods. Now she was alone, wanting Naomi as if she were her mother, and wishing she had her opaque flannel nightshirt from the hostel to shield her from both the very Highland cold of the room, and her husband's far from cold eyes.

Whatever shyness had struck Johnny in the car, and at dinner, left him now. He was, unlike his bride, not an innocent and had led an active and satisfying sexual life since he was fifteen. Parlourmaids, crofters' daughters, camp followers in France; and when volunteers became unavailable, he indulged unashamedly in the company of professionals, that regular army of romance who'd always been the soldier's comfort. However, his period of convalescence, coinciding with the new moral strictures of his betrothal, had resulted in a long spell of enforced celibacy. That, plus the sight of Rebecca delicately silhouetted by firelight in her drifting gown, drove all reluctance from him in an instant. His body, if not his mind, forgot that she was Rebecca, his wife, and responded as it had done for every haystack consummation of his youth. Embarrassed, he shielded the rising evidence of passion, holding his folded day clothes in front of him.

'You can put those down, you know,' Rebecca said. 'I have seen men before.'

He was astounded for a moment, and then remembered the nursing. 'Oh, of course,' he was blushing and laid his clothes down on a chair, straightening to face her, aware that the thin silk of his dressing-gown had more or less come to attention. Her eyes fluttered over him for a solitary second and then turned away, to the fire, the window, anywhere. She had seen men, of course, but they had been helpless, wounded or ill, and their bodies passionless. Once, a disturbed shell-shock victim had clambered out of his bed, quite naked, and 'ready for action' as Matron had said with a grimace, and had advanced on Rebecca, thinking her to be his wife. She had been terrified, but only glimpsed him a moment before older, experienced nurses had overpowered the soldier and hastened the VAD's innocent eyes away.

Had that incident not occurred, Rebecca, in spite of Naomi's gentle attempts to instruct her in such matters, would not even have known now that extraordinary thing that men's bodies could do. The incident did not help; in her mind, Johnny and the blundering shell-shocked sergeant merged. 'I think, I think I shall get into bed,' she whispered. 'Could you . . . the candles . . .' she ran to the bed and slipped snake-smooth within, barely rippling the artistically arranged bedding.

Johnny blew out the candles, but when he came to the bed, he only sat on the edge and reached to touch her hand. His own, in the darkness, touched her cheek and she cried out as if in pain. 'Darling,' he whispered.

'Yes,' her voice was trembling.

'Darling, it's really not frightening.' He felt he should say they need not do it now at all, but his body undermined his kindness with its own hungers.

'How do you know?' she demanded.

'How?' he was puzzled.

'How do you know what it's like? You've just got married too. You don't know any more than I do.'

He laughed softly, delighted with that. 'Do you really mean . . .' he laughed again, less delighted. She did. He paused, thinking, and then began slowly, 'Rebecca, ah, you do know, I mean, a man, Rebecca. I mean, it's rather different, after all, isn't it?'

'What is?' her voice broke as confusion and fear brought her to the edge of tears.

'Surely you don't expect . . .' None of that worked. It was alarmingly obvious what she expected. He wondered if all men met such questions on their wedding night or if other brides simply lacked the temerity to ask. 'Rebecca,' he said at last, with dominie authority, 'life is different for men. We naturally, we all, well, we're simply expected to have a bit of experience.'

'Experience in what?' Rebecca demanded, her voice going dangerously short.

'Personal matters, my dear. Surely you understand. I assure you, all men are quite the same.'

Her next words were so soft as to be inaudible. He realized she was crying in the darkness. Then she said, 'Oh, how could you? How could you? And I've loved you so.'

'Rebecca,' he exploded, 'this is absolute madness. It has nothing to do with you loving me. Or me loving you. It's simply the way men are, and the way women are. Different.' He sank his head in an exasperated palm and slapped the bedclothes, conscious of his recently enthusiastic member beating a retreat.

'I trusted you,' she wailed. Then, slyly, 'Who was she? Oh, don't tell me she was one of my friends.' She sounded suspiciously as if she wanted it to be, so that she might wallow the deeper in the misery of his betrayal.

He turned and looked at her in the dim firelight. Her hair was mussed from her own distracted fingers and her eyes sparkled wetly in the dim light. Then he could not help himself, but laughed out loud. 'She?' he demanded. '*Which* she, for God's sake?'

'More than one?' she gasped, now totally disarmed.

'Rebecca,' he said casting caution to the winds of despair, 'I tell you solemnly, there have probably been a hundred.'

She howled, a great wail of disbelief.

'Since I was fifteen, girl, *fifteen*. And if you're going to insist I will sit here and try to recall their names. It seems as good a way to spend this night as any, at this point.' He got up and stalked away and she curled up in a ball of misery and sobbed into the feather pillow.

A moon rose out of the loch, and as midnight passed and the early hours crept by, it traced a path through the dark branches of the three Scots pines. Johnny watched it, mesmerized, torn between anger, regret and sheer boyish bewilderment, for although his body was experienced, his mind and heart were, in matters of real love and emotion, almost as innocent as hers. He heard her sobbing, and then breathing softly, in sleep. He slept too on the stiff velvet-covered settee that filled the window alcove, and woke to find Rebecca standing, looking down on him in the full moonlight. He muttered her name, sleepily.

'Is it true, Johnny?' she said, her voice composed now. 'Is that how all men are?' She sounded older, and she sounded too as if she had thought a long while before asking the question.

He sat up, straightening his stiff back, swinging his bare feet to the floor. 'Yes,' he said honestly. 'Most men. It's not considered wrong. Perhaps it should be. But it's not. My grandfather practically egged me on, and Tenny's father always turned a blind eye to him.'

'Tenny?' she whispered, for he had hit on the thought that had plagued her since he had first admitted his loss of innocence. 'Does Tenny also?'

Johnny felt anger rise sharply and he wished to curse and say he cared nothing and knew less regarding Tenny. But an odd loyalty arose also and he said only, 'I dare say. I wouldn't necessarily know, you understand. And I wouldn't say if I did. A gentleman doesn't . . . disclose.'

'I see,' she sighed, as if swallowing a year or two of age with her breath. Then she extended her hand to him. 'Well my dear,' she said, with a brave quaver faintly audible in her voice, 'I suppose it's time I learned what everyone else seems to know.'

She went to the bed with him, lay down beside him, opened her arms to him, and turned her mouth to accept his. She understood her duty, and found throughout the deep moonlit hours of the long winter night that her duty, as strange as it was, held the seeds of pleasure. At last he kissed her and went to sleep and she lay alone in the darkness, her body aching and exhausted, and yet pleasantly so. She stretched, yawned, trying out the feel of womanhood, a little proudly. But when she slept, she dreamed it was Tenny who had held her and done those things to her, and when she woke in the late dawn, with Johnny still asleep beside her, she was filled with anger. Tenny, Johnny, even Arnold Galloway; they were all men and all together had cheated and lied while she had been wrapped in ignorance from the day of her birth. She rose from her bed, a married woman, already chafing faintly at her new-won bonds.

11

When Ian Maclaren arrived in St Omer, on a cold February morning, he was met personally at GHQ by Sir Douglas Haig, commander-in-chief of the British Expeditionary Force. It was an occurrence that surprised and humbled him. Haig now held the fortunes of the British Army in his tough, neat horseman's hands, and Ian Maclaren, a soldier all his days, respected nothing like he respected military hierarchy. He would not have presumed, now that Haig had risen to such heights, that their own friendship still held. But Haig at once invited him to luncheon and it gave him a rare opportunity to hear the man's thoughts directly. For the sake of the men in his brigade he jumped at the chance.

His own business with the C-in-C was of a minor nature, and hardly merited more than a casual few words over an office desk. Were it not for Haig's natural hospitality, Ian Maclaren would have been by now on a train heading towards the Channel, and England. He half wished he were; the sooner away, the sooner back again. He was annoyed at being called away from Brigade HQ because the back-home boys, no doubt feeling the pressure of home-front frustration, had organized a new marvel, this time a kind of armoured landship to get the troops across the trenches. All very well, he grudgingly conceded, if the damned contraption would work, but from what he'd seen of boffin inspiration in the past he doubted it. If you asked him, if they'd just give them a decent supply of ammunition and shells, they'd break through all right. He shook his head, standing on the worn limestone doorstep of the old house, and knocking twice, sharply, on the door, mentally handed over the weight of such decisions to the man inside.

A sprucely dressed staff officer led him into a pleasant and functional room where a crowd of officers and a couple of civilians mingled before a blazing wood-fire, drinking spirits and talking in a mixed blur of languages. British khaki mingled with the *horizon bleu* of the French, and odd bits of tartan on officers of Scottish units. Ian thought the new French uniform at least an improvement on the gaudy red-and-blue with which they had entered the war, but still a long way from the fine camouflage provided by khaki or the German *feld grau*.

'Ah, Maclaren,' a soft Scottish voice called from the doorway to an inner room, and Ian turned and was confronted by Douglas Haig himself. 'Splendid to see you again.' Ian returned the greeting, mentally assessing the appearance of the man, a habit he'd developed of late as he had to worry more and more about the mental and physical condition of his officers. Haig passed the test. He was trim and tough-looking, his uniform immaculate, riding boots gleaming, spurs sparkling. His face, smoothly shaven but for the lushly groomed moustache, was rosy with the cold air, like that of a healthy boy. He exuded confidence, and stern Calvinist resolve, and the general mood of good cheer in the room seemed to flow directly from him. Ian Maclaren relaxed a little and accepted a whisky, relieved that the moody, excitable figure of Sir John French was no longer about. Determination and confidence, that was what was needed; and all the men about him seemed filled with both.

Ian was silent throughout the meal, eating little and listening hard to the several conversations around him. He asked no questions, well aware that his presence here was a social concession; his opinion was neither required, nor desired.

The conversation centred on the spring and summer and the coming offensives. No one questioned that there would be an offensive. Ian was already aware that a major joint effort was planned on all fronts, with the Russians and Italians playing their parts in the East, and the British and French in the West. Sir John French and Papa Joffre had drawn up the plan, but Haig appeared a willing inheritor. Throughout the meal the two French generals present repeatedly proclaimed, sometimes with a punctuation of fists slammed into open hands, or flat palms slapping the table, that this offensive must succeed; France could bear no more. Ian listened grimly; rumours abounded of the weakness of the French forces, their failing morale, but he had never before heard it so bluntly put. Haig's voice was so soft, so unruffled, that Ian, far down the table, could barely pick out his words of reassurance. The talk developed into a heated debate as to where and when the enemy himself might strike.

'He is in great force at Verdun,' General Castlenau insisted, his small beard trembling with concern. 'He will strike at Verdun.'

'My dear fellow,' Haig patted the tablecloth gently, 'surely not with but nine divisions in reserve. And tell me,' his sharp eyes searched the Frenchman's worried face, 'did you not yourself, but three days ago at Chantilly, insist that Russia would be his aim, just as Joffre insisted?'

'It is changed. Changed. It is all different now,' the Frenchman mumbled into his crumpled linen napkin. 'The Tenth Army must be relieved.'

'Ah, the Tenth again,' Haig said, a little coolly. 'I am 75,000 men below strength,' he returned, as if it were sufficient answer. 'Seventy-five thousand in thirty-nine divisions. It is impossible even to train.'

Ian Maclaren concentrated on his soup. The French Tenth Army was wedged between their own First, of which his brigade was a part, and their Third. Ian would be glad to be rid of them, even though it would mean a wider frontage for his own men. He'd still rather have the British beside him than the French. But Haig did not concede, and later, when they were once more in the anteroom, broken up into small groups, he heard the C-in-C insisting that Joffre's desired 'wearing out' attacks would not be attempted until the major attack was within a fortnight of commencing. Ian was relieved at that; the French had been insisting on these large-scale winter raids, to be carried out by British troops. But forays into the enemy front line were costly. Often they took a heavy toll of both lives and morale and resulted only in a stretch of enemy trench that was indefensible and must, within a day, be abandoned. And Ian suspected that any raids only caused the enemy to strengthen his line.

'We'll be attacking a fortress,' he said, aside to a junior officer who had queried the matter. 'A fortress we've helped to build. Better leave sleeping dogs lie, have a restful winter, plenty of training, and then hit them at once with all we've got.'

'So, you're a man of my own beliefs, Maclaren,' Haig said, later, when they had withdrawn for their own brief discussion, to Haig's upstairs writing-room. The general settled himself behind his desk and offered Ian a chair before it. Ian's eyes wandered the room as Haig shuffled through papers on his desk. The walls were covered with maps and aerial photographs and he resisted the urge to rise and examine them. He peered longingly at them from the distance of his chair. For the first time the immense value of those frail, papery-looking flying machines that floated high over their lines came home to him.

'Now, Maclaren. These landships.' Ian sat straighter, and Haig proceeded. 'There are to be trials or some such in Hatfield in two days' time. Kitchener will be there, and the King. I spoke to him myself about it when I was last in London.' He paused slightly, and Ian sensed, as he had before, that Haig, the border Scotsman, was a trifle proud of the close connections with royalty that his marriage had brought him. 'Their opinions are of course vital, but I want also the opinions of men experienced in the field. With that in view I have selected a small group of gentlemen whose opinions I have come to respect,' he looked up long enough for Ian to make a small courteous nod to the compliment, 'and I will very much be interested in your views upon your return.'

He paused again and then said, his voice subtly changed, less formal, 'I suspect that you, like myself, harbour doubts about this whole enterprise, but I'd like you to keep an open mind. I'd be a fool if I maintained that I haven't found conditions in France proving different from those anticipated in 1914. It is just possible different methods are needed, and that this will provide the key. Frankly,' he tapped his desktop with a pen-nib, 'if these landship devices can merely be made to function well enough to punch a hole in the enemy lines wide enough for me to get my cavalry through . . . the Western Front is the only possible scene of true victory, and yet the politicians won't be convinced, even after Gallipoli. You see, Maclaren, we have to show them it can be done; we have to show them that the enemy is not invincible on the Western Front. Which of course he's not, no one is. Perhaps these landships . . .' He trailed off, and then abruptly went quite formal again, shuffled papers and said, 'I will be interested in your report, upon your return.'

Ian realized he was dismissed.

Within five hours of parting with General Haig, Ian Maclaren was in London. Yet the city he found was in some ways so remote from the conflict it might have been in New Zealand. No doubt there were shortages in the shops, butter was becoming a rarity, but such things did not show. There had been zeppelin raids, but for all the outrage they engendered, their scale was small. The proliferation of uniforms in all public places was perhaps the clearest link with events across the Channel, and yet even they, clean and tidy in city streets, seemed to bear little relation to the mud-caked tattered khaki of the Front.

As Ian waited impatiently outside Victoria Station for his batman to find a taxi, a gentleman beside him grumbled loudly that there was no decent beef in the shops, and his companion bemoaned his low wine-cellar as if the war was essentially a conspiracy against the vineyards of France and their devotees. A well-dressed, over-fed lady in a huge feathered and fruited hat whined incessantly about the hopeless quality of servants.

'And then my best girl, really a gem of a girl, ups and decides she simply must be a VAD. It's all just to be with all those men and catch herself a husband, mind. I was positively ill, my dear. Ill. My husband insisted upon the doctor being summoned, against my wishes naturally, and he was quite livid when he arrived. Said if he saw the girl he'd give her what for, leaving a lady in such a hopeless predicament.'

Ian Maclaren rocked on his heels in the cold air, and only the sudden return of MacGregor the batman, taxi-driver in tow, saved him from bursting into an outraged, exhausted, and ungentlemanly diatribe that would have left the lady reason to feel ill indeed. Seated in the vehicle, he fought the embittered feeling that hit him, as always, when he set foot in Blighty, that his men were daily sacrificed for fools.

The taxi dropped him at the Savoy Hotel where he was to meet Naomi. They would go in together to the ballroom where his daughter Philippa was addressing a gathering of distinguished guests on the need for conscription. It was her first public appearance since Torquil's death, and her subsequent collapse. She was only three weeks away from the convalescent home and her doctors had advised against it. As ambivalent as Ian Maclaren was about his second daughter's war work, he was determined to support her tonight. She did not lack courage, he had to admit. Victoria was terribly worried about her, and from the first glimpse he caught of Naomi pacing restlessly among the ornamental chairs and tables of the magnificent foyer of the hotel, he knew that she was worried too.

Ian felt a tenseness all about her slim figure when she bent forward, arms extended, to greet him, and the kiss that brushed his cheek was without its familiar tingle of suppressed passion. He was surprised. When he had telephoned her from Dover her insistence that they meet here had surprised him too. He had half felt that there was something urgent on her mind, so determined was she to see him immediately upon his arrival.

If there was, she did not speak of it, only saying with uncharacteristic nervousness, 'We had best go directly in; they are ready to begin.'

Seats had been reserved for them at the front of the room, and they hastened up the aisle between the rows of chairs. Ian was self-conscious as always when publicly in Naomi's company. But he saw no one he knew among the crowd of well-dressed, serious-faced civilians, and silently they took their seats.

After a low-keyed introduction from a male dignitary, Philippa stepped quietly, head down, on to the small stage, and walked, still looking downward, to the podium. Ian Maclaren hardly recognized his own daughter. She had bobbed her hair, which two years before would have drawn forth a tirade of fatherly fury, but now he scarcely noticed. It was not the loss of that mountainous richness of hair that registered with Ian, but more what it seemed to signify. It was a deep gesture, like the shaving of a nun's head. Something had been shorn from her with her knee-length red-golden wealth. When she raised her head and met the waiting gaze of hundreds with her commanding pale eyes, he knew what it was. Before she began to speak, he knew, uncannily, what she would say.

The pale eyes never released their audience, as she began her speech with a quietly modulated formal greeting. And although there appeared a kind of trembling passion about her mouth, she spoke slowly, nor was one name or salutation missed. Her formalities over, she began, 'My dear friends . . .' Again she paused. Ian Maclaren saw for the first time the power she was capable of working over people and was stunned to imagine it in his child. 'You all know who I am,' she said. 'Indeed, I see among you many whose faces are familiar. We are a small band, after all, a small band of brothers and of sisters, who have served together since the commencement of hostilities. We are, in our own way, a regiment, and I, a soldier's daughter,' she glanced briefly at Ian, 'know the bonds of love and loyalty that hold together a regiment at war . . .' She paused again, seemed to take a deep breath, as if she had grown faint, and Ian, troubled with a father's concerns, yearned to run to her. But her head came up again and her eyes commanded him, as well as all others, into stillness.

'And now,' she said, 'we must part. Now, our paths have come to a dividing-place, beyond which, unless you choose to follow me, as dearly I hope you will, I must go on alone.' She let her eyes take in the whole room, where, puzzled and expectant, all faces were turned up to her.

'I called you into the fray when this war began,' she said clearly, her voice ringing out in the high-ceilinged room. 'I led you through dark days. Together we raised an army from a sleeping nation. Together we have helped to set in the field the greatest British Army that ever has been. The greatest of *all* armies. And now,' her voice dropped with finely controlled drama, 'and now, together with you if it shall be, but alone if I must, I must call them home again. It is time for the sons of our nation, the fathers of our nation,' again her glance swept to Ian, 'the brothers and the lovers of our nation, to return to the homes that love them, the homes that they love. Nothing further can be served by the continuance of their suffering. Nor can the suffering of the enemy cheer us, if we are of true Christian heart. This war, begun so nobly, has fallen into treachery. It has become merely a tool of those, in government and industry, heartless enough to use misery for private gain. The battle of the field has ground to an irreversible halt. Both sides have won, and both sides have failed. There will be no ending of it short of the day of resurrection, if we do not now, and at once, urge all in power to begin negotiations, to fight with words instead of guns, to win back with reason a world that reason has deserted.'

Around him Ian heard a growing mutter, first of disbelief, then, as her words truly sank in, of dismay, confusion, and then, of fury.

'This war must end!' Philippa shouted. 'It is become a juggernaut, a destroyer of nations. We have birthed a child that shall devour us. Negotiate now, today, and bring God back into our Godless world!'

She was done, turning her back, her winged hair flying, as the voices rose to a horrifying howl, crying, 'Traitor!'

Naomi sat between them in the back of her car, as Abbott drove them home. Ian thought numbly, she who had always before divided the peace of his family, by her distant presence, now divided its anger with her slim delicate body. Beyond her quiet dark shape, he could see Philippa's profile, strongly outlined by passing streetlamps, her bobbed hair reaching forward in little cheek-level peaks. She too was silent. She had barely spoken a word since she left the stage in the ballroom of the Savoy. Then, there had been little opportunity. Embarrassed leaders of her own League had hastened her out, through kitchen corridors and staff entrances, to an ignominious alleyway where, their duty done, they quite abruptly abandoned her.

Then they were left, the three of them, incongruous in their smart clothes, among bins and refuse. Ian looked at his daughter then, in the diffused glow of the distant lights of the Embankment, expecting to see insanity and seeing instead a very sane look of satisfaction and relief. 'Well,' she had said, lightly brushing imaginary dust from her hands, 'that's a start.'

Once in the car, Ian found his anger uncontrollable and burst out, 'Could you not, for decency's sake, have saved this, this . . . performance,' he spat the word from behind a moustache bristling with outrage, 'for an occasion when your own father at least was not present.'

'But, Daddy,' she said quietly, leaning her head back tiredly against the upholstered seat, 'what would be the point? To whom was I speaking, if not the military?'

That brought him up short. He wanted to say, 'But Philippa, I'm not "the military"; I'm your father.' But he did not, realizing that she very likely did not make any such distinction, any more than she ever had been able to distil the personal and individual from the great anonymous mass of her cause. Her late cause, he reminded himself. Of all people, for Philippa to turn thus against the war seemed most inconceivable. Had Naomi spoken so, or even Victoria in motherly grief, or poor Emma, deprived of her fiancé, he could understand. But Philippa, who had believed so heartily and lost nothing. He looked again at her and felt his fatherly love drowning in cold anger. And, ever so slightly, fear. For, whatever he had felt of Philippa's slightly ghoulish enthusiasm for sending fresh blood to the fray, he could not then, as a military man, deny that she was helping. And as a father he had chosen, perhaps conveniently, to regard her efforts as essentially harmless, if not in the best of taste. But now she was on the other side, and like all strong, begrudged allies, she would prove a formidable opponent. And there was nothing he could do to stop her. She could parade her new pacifist inclinations up and down the country, undermining the war effort and, as a sideline, disgracing her family wherever she went.

As the car pulled up in front of Naomi's house, he leant over Naomi's stubborn knees and said to his daughter, 'I ask you, for the sake of your mother and for the sake of your three brothers even now in danger of their lives at the Front, to cease and desist this traitorous course upon which you have set yourself. If you do not love me, which is painfully obvious tonight, at least perhaps you will act out of love for them.'

'Yes, Father,' she said, turning to face him, her face beautiful in anger, 'I have. Tonight, at last, I have. And now, if you will both excuse me, I will retire to my bed. I have an early rise tomorrow, and it's been a most exhausting day.' She kissed Naomi goodnight as they entered the hallway, and without word or gesture to her father, mounted the stairs with a spring of determination in her step.

Ian stood boiling with rage until Naomi's gentle hand on his forearm pointed him in the direction of the drawing-room. Twice he tried to speak but she put her slim dark fingers to his lips each time, as she busied herself, removing her hat, stirring the fire, ringing for the maid. Only when he was seated in front of the hearth, a brandy in his angry trembling hand, was he at last allowed to explode.

'The bitch. The sour-faced, spinsterish little bitch. How could she? How dare she? My God, I should take her over my knee and take a riding-crop to her.' Naomi only nodded quietly, expressionless. Ian roared on, 'I'll tell you, she's never been right in the head, that girl. No wonder she took on so after that nastiness in December. No wonder. She's unbalanced. Too much talk and women and books. If you ask me, what that girl's needing is a good man to take her and to . . . to . . .'

'Give her a good fucking?' Naomi suggested mildly.

Ian went a redder shade of purple and muttered incomprehensibly into his moustache. Finally he said, still reddening, 'Well, yes, actually, I do think she needs some . . . physical life . . . instead of all this womanish prattle and naïve politics. Yes, I do think . . . though I'd hardly have put it . . .'

'No. I dare say you wouldn't. Never mind how you'd put it, my dear, the active point is that you'd think it. No wonder the girl's turned out the way she has, with you for a father. The amazing thing is that Emma's quite normal, and even Philippa, after tonight, gives me some sense of hope.'

Ian's eyes batted at that. 'You're not going to say you're on her side.'

Naomi rose and walked to the fireside where she stood with her hands outstretched to the ends of the mantel, her back to Ian, her head inclined downwards towards the bright light of the fire. 'No matter whose side I'm on. At least for the first time in her life the girl is thinking with an element of compassion. A characteristic heretofore totally lacking. No, I doubt she'll ever be "normal" like Emma. Nor do I think that anything as simple as your sheepfank philosophy is going to make much headway with her. The girl happens to be wildly intelligent and no number of lusty male bodies, no matter how splendid, are going to undo that dreadful fact. Of course she's odd. Most political people are, they have to be. But she's powerful, Ian, people listen to her, heed what she says. And she's only just beginning. Once this war's over,' she sighed softly, abruptly thinking of something else, 'if it ever is, you'll see. Oh, you'll see.'

She still stood with her back to him, and Ian swallowed hard and was about to protest when she again spoke. 'Anyhow, there is nothing you can do about her, you know, so you may as well get used to her. And try to respect her a little, and stop thinking about her as if she were livestock.' She turned then and said, startlingly, 'Still, it was not to speak of Philippa that I brought you in here tonight.'

'No?' Ian said a little warily, for a moment expecting seduction. He had rarely in his life been further from the mark.

'No,' she said. 'Ian, I wish to ask of you a favour.'

'Anything,' he said at once, with fervent emotion. He was studying her face which was uncommonly serious, and even when she smiled, it was a smile without humour or real warmth.

'Answered like a man from whom little has ever been asked,

she said.

He was taken aback and said, a little hurt, 'That's hardly fair, my dear. Surely I've never denied you anything . . .'

'You have denied little,' she said, 'but I have asked nothing.' She paused again, and said, very softly, 'Nothing, Ian. In forty years. Nothing. Since we were little children, in Scotland. I have asked nothing. Now, I much regret, I must ask.'

Again Ian said, 'Anything,' for it was the answer that honour demanded.

She nodded gravely and then crossed the room to her writing-desk, from the inner drawer of which she drew a small, tattered envelope. She handed it to him without a word. He glanced up, and she nodded and he, somewhat reluctantly, lifted the torn flap and withdrew a small folded sheet of smudged paper.

The letter was a typically schoolboy affair, badly inked, smudged here and there, a word or two misspelled in haste. There were only a few lines; all slightly stilted in tone as if composed for a school essay. Ian read it through, knowing from the very first, 'Dearest Mother', exactly what it would contain. Like letters home from the Front, with which commanding officers, through their censorship duties, were all too familiar, letters of the newly enlisted were stylized in their sameness. 'Duty, honour, fight the good fight'; all good sincere Henry Newbolt stuff.

Ian sighed, and laid the letter on his knee. 'When?' he said wearily.

'I found it when I returned from the wedding. It was waiting for me when I got home. I still had that old fool Galloway with me, and I had to fuss about him, and see he had his sherry and his full allotment of entertainment before I could even . . . even . . .'

She did not finish the sentence, for the word 'cry' would no doubt bring tears. Ian's heart went out to her, coping alone, as always, with their son. 'Where is he now?' he asked.

'He was in Inverness, of course, when he wrote, but I dare say he's in England now, in one of the camps. Ready for embarkation.' Her voice broke and she turned away.

'Oh, the damned stupid little fool,' Ian said. 'If he'd only waited another couple of weeks, when conscription comes in, they'd never have taken him. No more volunteers.'

'Do you imagine he didn't know that?' she flung back. 'Oh,

he's clever enough. Got in just under the wire, when he'd look the oldest. Waited until I was away so that if his alibi broke down at school there'd be no one for them to contact. As it was, they were quite taken in. *I* had to telephone *them* and say he wouldn't . . . he'd not be back.' She sat suddenly on the settee, put her hands to her face and shook silently, crying.

He longed to go to her, to comfort her, amazed and aroused by her rare display of emotion. But he did not, knowing that if he touched her, he would be unable to refuse her anything. Already he was certain what she would ask. She raised her face from her hands and her dark wet eyes met his impotently comforting gaze. She stared, silent for a long while, and then turned her head sideways, looking towards the fire. 'You won't, will you?' she said.

'Naomi, I . . .'

'Anything,' she whispered coldly, her voice brittle with tethered emotion. 'Anything. But you won't.'

'How can I?' he whispered.

Her control broke and she began to sob, fiercely, angrily, not hiding her grief from him. 'Just a signature. A piece of paper and your signature. A handful of words. That's *all*. And then he'd be safe. Home. With me.'

'How can I?' he whispered again. 'Don't you understand what you're asking?'

'I have never asked anything, anything before,' she repeated fervently.

'But I refused Victoria,' he cried out. 'Don't you understand? I refused Victoria. For our own son, I would not do it.'

She stiffened and turned from him, and he realized what he had said. Too late. 'He is not then your son? Is that what you've always thought? Naomi's bastard. Nothing to do with you. Not worthy of your noble fatherhood?'

'Oh, no, oh no, my dear. It was never like that.'

'Was it not? I think, now, perhaps it was. I never thought so before.' She sighed. 'All right then, since we are no longer acting from love, let us try honour. I am asking one thing in exchange for all the ruination you have helped to cause in my life. Do you not, true gentleman that you are, pay your debts?'

'It would cost me my marriage,' he said simply.

She stood and stalked away, then whirled round, standing, hands balled into fists, her sleek hair slipping loose from its smooth braid, angry tendrils surrounding her face. 'Then let it cost your marriage. Let it cost you something. I stepped from your life without a word, lest I cost you your inheritance. I stood aside while you wed that pleasant little woman,' she made it sound intensely denigrating, 'lest I cost you the regiment. I kept silent while I bore your son, lest I cost you your honour, your home, your position. I have for all our years saved you always the cost. Now, once, let it be you who pays, before your damnable regiment costs me my son.'

She sank down on the settee, weeping uncontrollably, until, at last, gasping from her choked breath, she was able to raise her head once more and look hard at him. His silence, pathetic and broken, spoke shamefully for him.

Naomi rose and went to the door. She stopped there, turning to face him, her face once more set in its calm, distant smile that he had always loved. She gave a small laugh and said, 'I'll never understand, Ian, why it is that all the real bastards in your family are the ones born safe and snug between hallowed Maclaren sheets.'

Ian Maclaren left the house on Hyde Park the next morning, early, having breakfasted alone. At odds with his daughter, and estranged from the woman he loved, he had little heart for anything that morning. The taxi he had had summoned by telephone bore him away, very possibly for the last time, from the house he had always secretly regarded as his true home. Ahead lay a day of military and political stuffed-shirts lauding and exclaiming over this latest technical wonder that was no doubt meant to win the war in a day. These damned landships had better be good, or God help him, he'd walk out in the middle and get on the first train back to the capital and the Channel coast. All he really wanted now was to be back in France with his men.

Still truculent and cynical later that same morning, in a gentle English field modified by engineering ingenuity into an idealized image of the Western Front, Ian at last saw the key to the locked and frozen puzzle of the war. From the instant he saw it lumbering hugely across the frozen winter field, Ian Maclaren fell militarily in love with the massive machine whose modest pseudonym was 'the tank'.

Even on the train down to Hatfield where the landship trials were to be held, premonitions of import were all around him. He was surprised to find his carriage packed with officers of varying regiments and high rank. Indeed the whole of the train bristled with gold braid, interspersed with the sombre pinstripe formality of a number of members of the government. It appeared to Ian that there was no one on the train at all who was not in some way involved with the forthcoming military display. Which was just as well, he reflected, since the conversation, at least among the other occupants of his compartment, was open to the point of garrulousness on a subject that was, after all, meant to be a well-guarded secret.

Ian Maclaren learned among other things that the landship project was initially under the auspices of the Admiralty, and that the controversial First Lord, Winston Churchill, had been a major instigator, and was said, even now in his new disgrace after the Dardanelles, to be a guiding force. He felt both admiration and distrust for Churchill's undisciplined methods, but admitted a grudging respect for the man, that renewed his interest in the project.

The testing ground itself bore witness to careful planning. A full-scale trench system had been constructed, complete with four foot parapets and carefully sculpted shell-holes, differing from the real thing only in its precision and neatness and in its lack of the deep abiding stench of death.

On a covered dais, trimmed with a gratuitous little strip of red, blue and white bunting, Sir Ian Maclaren stood among a gathered crowd of underlings. They had been waiting for a cold half-hour when a long black Daimler arrived, followed by another and yet another. Surrounded by a phalanx of the brassier brass, the occupants emerged and made their way to their viewing stand, and only when they had mounted the platform was Ian able to see them clearly and recognized not only the tall, lean form of the War Minister, Lord Kitchener, but the belligerent little moustachioed Munitions Minister, Lloyd George, and the bearded figure of King George V. So. They'd brought out the big guns, just as Haig had said.

Ian turned now expectantly to the canvas-shrouded form in the centre of the field which, thus disguised, did indeed resemble an over-large cistern, and did justice to its code-name. Now the wraps were removed, smartly, by the team of naval engineers who had created the thing, and 'Big Willie', as they had christened it, stood revealed. It was, Ian thought, a stunning creation, worthy in its sheer magnitude of the small grunts and sighs of approval that passed over the crowd. Eight feet tall, and wider than it was high, its shape that of a vast rhombus, its thirty odd feet of length completely surrounded by massive caterpillar tracks, a great eyeless beast of a machine. Ian was intrigued by the mighty caterpillar tracking. He had seen lesser versions on French artillery tractors, but those had sat on top of their tracking devices, while this creature wore them like a girdle around its great metal body. The added stability was obvious at first sight. The prow of the machine slanted upwards as if disdaining the ground it soon would crush, the stern descended at a similar angle, and both ends supported a machine-gun turret.

'Wouldn't want to meet that in no-man's-land, eh?' said a staff officer beside Ian who clearly knew no-man's-land essentially from drawings in *The War Illustrated*. Ian made an appropriate half-swallowed grunt. All very well if it didn't turn upside-down at the first hillock, as so many mechanical vehicles and wheeled devices were inclined to do. The battlefield was always littered with upside-down transport lorries, gun-carriages, motor ambulances, like so many swatted flies. No wonder Haig kept his stern faith in the horse which at least didn't turn over at bumps in the road.

It was not fast, but armoured as it was it had little need of speed. Its angled front reared up, raising over the parapet of the trench, crushing it with its twenty-eight tons and then extended out over the broad deep ditch, bridging it easily and rumbling on by. It ploughed through tangles of coiled, cross-braced wire, as through summer corn. Glorious in the blue smoke of its exhaust it rumbled up and down the field before its King, pummelling all obstacles into submission. The crowd of generals and politicians, the leaders of the nation, cheered and hurrahed like boys in the nursery at the sheer delight of happy destruction. At last the great machine turned its eyeless front to the dais like the victor at a jousting tournament and Ian almost fancied it bowed its blunt and noble head. Willie Bruce's machine-horse had come to life at last in an English field.

Lloyd George was said to have been enthusiastic, the King was visibly impressed, and Ian Maclaren returned to France vindicated. No matter now that his daughter had turned against him, or that his love had deserted him, no matter that family and friends were unkind. For his other family out there in their cold bleak fortress, he at last had hope. No matter now the unpromising Somme landscape if that was indeed to be their advance. A dozen of those machines, two dozen, his mind leapt to it, a great mechanized cavalry charge across the tortured boundaries of the Front and then on, outward, his army led by those lumbering steel chargers sweeping at last into the great breakthrough to Berlin. The key was in their hands, the frozen lock would surrender to them, the end of the war was at last in sight.

And then, on the twenty-first of February, the Germans struck at Verdun.

12

It was an hour before dawn in the French railhead of Revigny and in a sky lit with ruddy intermittent flickerings of shell-fire, the morning star shone cold and timeless. Emma Maclaren, as she hurried from her belltent towards the ambulance depot, thought of it as the uncaring eye of God.

If Emma Maclaren had lost her faith, when she lost Torquil Farquhar, she had also lost much of her fear. She felt she had little to live for, and found the thought liberating. The muffled explosions of the fire-rimmed salient did not threaten her; they would find her, or not, as she pushed her battered Ford ambulance along the road to Verdun, and she did not particularly care. As long, that is, as the vehicle was empty of other than herself at the time. For Emma retained, when love and faith deserted her, her inbred need to serve, that peculiar altruism of her privileged class.

She had tried within weeks of Torquil's suicide to return to her nursing, but was stunned to find her mind, her body, even her knowledgeable hands, frozen by a kind of neurotic torpor. The instant she set foot inside the ward, the numbing misery of her parting with Torquil, and her terrible guilt, descended on her. Disgusted with herself, she fought hard to control it, but found herself again and again driven into corners, where she crumbled in tearful misery. Matron was remarkably understanding, and even at their parting insisted that Emma would be welcome back when she was well again. But Emma knew the wards were shut to her for ever, a place where her love of Torquil Farquhar would always lie, an unburied corpse.

She had returned home to Culbrech, confused and defeated, on the very day that Harry Bruce's eloquent letter describing the terrible state of the French *poilus* struggling at Verdun had reached her mother. Had she still believed in the Calvinist God of her childhood, she would have regarded the coinciding events as predestined Fate. As it was she shrugged, repacked her small bag and took the next train south.

This time, there was little difficulty getting abroad, or finding a place among the VAD ambulance-drivers attached to the RAMC. Two years of bitter warfare, and the frantic desperation of Verdun had wiped away rules, regulations and formalities like so many cobwebs. Satisfied, in a brief test around the peaceful streets of London, that she could actually drive, the RAMC equipped her with a variation of her VAD uniform, a dark skirt, wisely shortened, a shapeless, sexless tunic, and a flat, peaked cap, and shipped her off to Bar-le-Duc within the week.

From thence she was sent to the railhead at Revigny where she joined her unit, a mixed bag of British and American volunteers, mostly men but including one other young British woman, the twenty-five-year-old daughter of Methodist missionaries, a six-foot, broad-shouldered redhead with a sweet dimpled face and the incongruous name of Verity Heavenstone. She was, however, the best driver they had, which ability, coupled with her considerable musclepower, and a remarkably kind nature, made her everyone's favourite partner. Emma herself was partnered with a young American named Robert Spalding who called himself Bob and treated her like a kid sister.

The relationship suited Emma completely. There was no time in any of their lives any longer for anything else. Emma was faintly surprised to find in this new environment no trace of the deference to her sex that had always been present in her previous life. The only reference to her femininity that Bob ever made was a sorrowful muttering, 'I sure hope you're stronger than you look, ma'am. If you don't mind me saying, you sure look awful puny for the job.' Emma assured him she was not puny, and was totally capable, and went ahead to prove it by energetically cranking up the engine, and managing the crash gearbox with ease. In her mind she thanked her brother Tenny for encouraging her, in her fifteenth year, in the very difficult art of the internal combustion engine. She even understood how the thing worked which was more than could be said of her father. 'Yep, you seem okay,' Bob had observed. 'Bet you can't get her out of a ditch, though.'

Emma knew he was probably right there, and envied Verity Heavenstone her rugby player's shoulders. She determined to avoid the issue by staying out of ditches in the first place. They rode daily the tortuous miles between Revigny and the hospital in the converted château at Le Petit Monthairon that lay four miles from the disintegrating rubble of Verdun.

One road ran from Bar-le-Duc to Verdun, one road only left open to the beseiged fortress. They called it *la Voie Sacrée*, the Sacred Way, because it was the only way to a city whose existence had become synonymous with the existence of France.

Three thousand other vehicles made their way down that crumbling track every day, and turned, and made their way back. Most carried fresh supplies, fresh men. Ambulances were quite secondary. The wounded, and the dead, were the rejects of that awesome lady, Verdun; suitors from whom her seductive eye had passed away. No one in the great French war-machine seemed very much to care for them, or for their fate. At Le Havre, Emma had seen the massive casualties of Loos rolling in with field dressings on three-day-old wounds, the result of the breakdown of medical facilities well-planned but limited, the unimaginative meeting the unimaginable. Here, with Bob Spalding and a handful of volunteers, British, American, French too, naturally, Belgian, and colonial, she saw sheer incompetence risen to monstrous heights. It was unplanned, unorganized chaos. And through it all the brave tattered *poilus* plodding faithfully to the defence of their lady.

As Emma struggled with the wheel of the ambulance, Bob would brace his long western legs against the dashboard and puff laconically at his pipe, ready to leap out at any moment and clear the road of shattered tree, or broken remnants of some shell-destroyed vehicle, animal, or man. They worked side by side in lonely proximity to hundreds of strangers, his big leg a few inches from her thigh, his long arm braced around her shoulders when a falling shell shook the vehicle nearly off its wheels, and nothing passed between them ever but a smile of satisfaction when they reached the end of the road. Emma had abandoned the desires of the heart quite convinced she would live her life in uncomplaining maidenhood, like so many others, and if Bob Spalding had such thoughts he kept them for a better place, a better time. Personal feelings were, in this place, an intrusion on the anonymous suffering they sought to relieve.

Out here, men and women had only themselves to answer to in matters of what had once been called decency. But they had taken service upon themselves like the veil; in honour of the suffering, they lived like monks and nuns. Those like Emma who had abandoned Christ for abandoning the world, found Him looking out at them from the faces of the wounded, saw Him laden beneath the cross of pack and rifle, and watched Him daily crucified with the leaden nails of the guns.

Emma lived now beneath canvas, like those braver sisters she had once admired. She shared a small belltent with Verity Heavenstone and four girls who had come, unorganized volunteers from their boarding schools and village rectories, to pour tea and coffee and chocolate at the Cantine Anglais in Revigny. No one governed them with foolish rules, no one indeed seemed to notice them. Two of the girls were only nineteen years old, away from home for the first time, driven by private dedication and considerable courage to serve the pathetically mistreated French footsoldier scant miles from the Front. Clothed in white, their heads prettily veiled, they passed through the tattered ranks fed daily into the hell-mouth of the salient like literal angels. Yet they were just girls, giggling a little at their daring, excited by the great drama around them, shielded from its true horrors by the glorious blindness of youth. True to human nature, they could remain gently remote from the deaths of a thousand, if they were strangers, while the death of one, no stranger, could reach and change forever the quick of Emma's being.

Above Emma, the icy eye of God faded out into a wet daylight. She hastened her steps to a run, determined to be at the depot before Bob. The night crew were bringing her vehicle in when she arrived. They stepped down into the cold pool of washed-out electric light thrown out by the door of the corrugated-iron shed that was their headquarters. Their faces sagged in white folds of exhaustion and their uniforms were blotched darkly with bloodstains. They nodded and stumbled away and Emma wondered, did she look like that when, at the end of her shift, she handed the vehicle to its next crew? She had discovered that war, like childbirth in her mother's description, was in some ways worse to watch than to do.

She was in the driver's seat, the engine chugging and rattling the flimsy sides of the ambulance, when Bob Spalding came running, and leapt up to his seat as she pulled away. He did not, as she would have done, apologize for being late. Being male, she noted with irony, always seemed to be justification enough.

It was a ten-mile trip from the railhead at Revigny to the front-line hospital at Le Petit Monthairon, but the return journey would take up most of their day; a day that would see them fortunate enough to make two trips, and bring back a half-dozen casualties. As they drew nearer, the thunder of gunfire enveloped them. They pushed their way, inch by inch, through a long file of raggedly marching men and Emma waited as they parted. The braver of them grinned and shouted when they saw, amazed, a female face. Others were too benumbed by undisguised fear to make any facial expression at all. They were young, younger every day, she was certain, and each of them would resemble, fancifully in her mind, one or another child from the glen.

At the doorway of the château, their destination, a man was standing, balled fists against his eyes, crying with rage. He was a doctor; Emma knew him, a French doctor in military uniform. He would work for hours, and then go there, to stand by the door and pour tears on to his bloody hands, as another man might go out for a cigarette. Then he would return, to work again for hours. Emma never saw the château hospital, day or night, without him present. She could not imagine that he ever slept, other than standing, perhaps, like a horse.

The château was stone-built, graceful, two storeys with delicately peaked dormers, and small round turrets at the corners. To the right was an ancient dovecote, also round in structure, with steep conical slated roof. Two ambulances were drawn up before the single arched door of the château and stretchers bearing motionless mud-sodden mounds were carefully slid out from their open doors, and as carefully borne into the round building.

The dovecote was the first stop after the trenches; the wash-house, where uniforms stiff with frozen mud and dark with blood were cut away, and bodies were washed down with antiseptic solutions so that the surgeons in the main château could at least see the damage they must repair. To one side of the doorway, mounds of filthy clothing were stacked like manure heaps, and behind the cowshed beyond, endless fires burnt, day and night, consuming lice-ridden cloth, gangrene-infected field dressings, and what other horrors Emma did not choose to imagine. She stood watching the doorway of the dovecote while Bob Spalding went inside the main building in search of whichever three lucky soldiers, with wounds slight enough to ensure at least possible survival on the journey to the railhead at Revigny, would return with them.

Emma had been once inside the dovecote, by mistake, on her first journey to the château, and the glimpse of naked, savaged bodies, moaning in their stretchers as flinching attendants sponged their dirty wounds, remained with her. The floor was of great blue flagstones, like the kitchens of Culbrech House, and the cracks between them had become rivulets of blood. Emma recalled gruesome stories, of stacks of amputated legs, and of German charnel-houses where human corpses were rendered for lard; stories she had always dismissed. Standing there slapping freezing hands against her upper arms to thaw her fingers for the journey home, she realized they might be true. The snow outside the dovecote door was stained red-brown with watered blood. The horses shied from the smell of the place, as if it were a slaughterhouse. Emma could not take her eyes from it. Then the door flung open suddenly and a man came out, gasping at the icy air as if biting chunks of breath from it, and shook himself all over as a dog climbing from a filthy pool. He turned grimly, to return. Then he saw Emma, standing there.

The darkness of the dovecote had made the snow-reflected light of the late March day unbearably bright. He stepped forward to see better and then, his face yet unable to form the expression that emotion demanded, began running blindly towards her. He staggered to an exhausted halt before her, and stood still, a ragged figure in dirty and torn RAMC uniform and a badly tanned fox-fur jerkin. 'Emma,' he whispered, 'Emma Maclaren.'

A smile of astonished pleasure came and went on her face, like a patch of winter sunshine. 'Harry Bruce.' Then they were stumbling, laughing, into each others' arms.

'But how?' Harry Bruce asked, holding her at arm's length so that he might hungrily study her face, and then answered himself, 'But of course. Lady Victoria said you had joined us.'

'And you?' Emma said. 'Where are you based? I'm in Revigny. I haven't seen you.' Her words were little excited bursts that puffed her breath white on the cold air.

'Bar-le-Duc. How long have you been here?'

'Five weeks. I'm back and forth every day. I'm driving and nursing, and Bob Spalding, that's my partner, does the heavy work.' She glanced then to the château door in time to see Bob's long figure, bent over as he ducked beneath the old-fashioned low lintel, carrying his end of a laden stretcher into the open air of the courtyard. 'I'll have to be going,' she said numbly, stepping towards the ambulance.

'But wait, oh no, of course you can't.' He stood, puzzled, unable in his tired state to find a way to keep from losing her as suddenly as he had found her. 'We must have passed each other every day,' he added sadly.

'I must go, Harry.'

'Could we meet?' he asked. She looked startled, as if such an idea would never have occurred to her.

'I suppose we could. But where?'

'Revigny,' he said slowly, thinking. 'The Place de la Gare. There's the Cantine. English girls.'

'I know them. We've a tent. We share. They'd tell you where. If you can . . .' her voice trailed off as Bob Spalding returned to the château for another burdened stretcher.

She climbed up into the driver's seat, and Harry called over the sound of the engine that she had left running the while, 'I'll find you,' and then he turned his back and squared his shoulders visibly as he entered the dovecote once more.

Bob and a French orderly from the château carried out a second and then a third wounded man and secured the stretchers in the rear of the ambulance, and then as he leaned out of the rear door to signal to her, she drove out over the broken cobbles of the courtyard. He would ride in the back with the wounded, leaping down if necessary to push the vehicle through the mires of recent shell-holes.

Emma drove with great care, conscious that every bump and jolt was causing agony to the men in the rear. She was remarkably skilled; better than Bob who had thrilled her a week ago by saying so himself. After a mile he shouted through to her to make more speed.

'I've got a haemorrhage here,' he said, as calmly as he said everything. Emma speeded up, ignoring the bumps now, winding her way by sheer forcefulness through the lines of ammunition and supply lorries and occasional horse-drawn gun carriages making their way up the road. Horses shied and bolted whenever a shell fell particularly close and Emma thought of her father and what he'd said about Haig's persistent faith in the cavalry. 'He's mad,' she muttered to herself. After a while, Bob Spalding called, still calmly, 'No rush now,' by which she knew that the haemorrhaging soldier was dead. She sighed, slowing slightly, again seeking gentler portions of road. So often they arrived in Revigny with one or more of their charges already dead. Twice last week they had brought three corpses to Revigny.

Bob's next words were purely conversational, and would have seemed greatly out of place to an outsider, but he often chose to chat on the journey home. Perhaps he thought it comforted the wounded.

'Who was that you were talking to?' he shouted.

'A friend,' Emma shouted back, over the engine noise.

'You don't say,' Bob said. 'Someone special?' he shouted again. She knew he would be grinning, that broad open American grin.

'No, of course not. Just a friend. From home.'

'Well, I'll be,' he said, and she could picture his grin broadening.

'No, really. Just a friend from home,' she insisted. 'And don't you laugh, Bob Spalding.'

Bob didn't laugh. The shell landed in the gap in their conversation that should have held his laughter, and swallowed all sound in its huge throaty roar. It landed fifteen feet behind them, directly on the road, sending the lead mules of a supply-wagon flying into the air and shattering the back of the ambulance like a splintering orange crate. Emma was flung forward by the blast, into the tough glass windscreen which fortunately did not break. The blow to her forehead left her dizzily reeling on the edge of unconsciousness and when she shook her head free of spinning lights she noted absently that her left hand, wrist and forearm were bleeding from cuts inflicted by the shattered steering-wheel. She struggled to get free of the vehicle, finding at first that her ankle was caught beneath the seat which had broken from its moorings and slid forward. Numbly she jerked at her foot until, shoeless, it came free. Her ankle, too, was bleeding, but also without pain.

A great deal of time seemed to have passed, and yet when she flung the door open on its blast-twisted hinges, the voices of witnesses of the explosion were still shouting at a distance. Still numb, she made her way to the rear of the ambulance.

She knew the instant she saw it that no one within had survived. Bob Spalding had been flung out of the back of the vehicle, by some fluke of the blast, and now lay on his back in the road, eyes staring emptily at the sky, each limb twisted and broken. His face was unharmed, and his mouth slightly open, slightly smiling, at the edge of his last jest to her, now forever silenced. She looked down at him for a moment, turned briefly to the interior of the ambulance, just to be sure, knowing at once that the jumble of bloody flesh within contained no life. She dismissed them professionally, as she must, but suddenly found she was unable to do the same to Bob. She wanted to cover him, to find a coat, or a blanket, to straighten his broken limbs, to close his eyes, to make a small fraction of the decent gestures of civilization. She began to unbutton her bulky man's greatcoat.

'Now there's no point in that,' a voice said softly as she extended it out over the dead form on the ground. She looked up, startled; in her concentration she had heard no approach.

A big heavy man in RAMC uniform was standing at her shoulder. 'He won't be needing that, and you will,' he said. 'He'll not begrudge you it, lassie.' He helped her into the coat again, and she said only,

'He was my partner. He's dead.'

'I know,' the man said. Then he leant over, lifted the body below the shoulders and dragged it off the road, laying it down again on the verge. He knelt then, on the frozen mud, and muttered something, making the sign of the cross on the dead man's forehead with the side of his thumb.

He stood up, and Emma said, 'What was that?'

'Just a wee prayer.' He had an odd voice, she thought, she could not place the accent; Scots surely, but not Scots altogether.

'You're not a chaplain,' she said.

He grinned suddenly, turning to face her so that his big cold-reddened face was just above hers. 'Promise you won't tell him I've been poaching.'

She could not grin back. She said only, because he had paused at the back of the ambulance to whisper a few words over the carnage within, 'Do you always do that?'

'When there's time,' he said. 'Come on, lass, we'd best get this wreck off the road.'

Later, in the front seat of her rescuer's own ambulance, Emma cried quietly, and said, 'It's pointless.'

'What is?' the man said. His name appeared to be Scott or Scottie; she was not quite sure what his own partner, now riding in the rear, had called him, as they pushed Emma's ruined Ford off the road.

'Your little prayer.'

'Och aye,' he said and she knew he was really Scots, or at least had been, once, in spite of the occasional American inflection. 'He didn't need it. Died for the Faith, did he not, a holy martyr.'

'Died for the Faith?' she said, incredulous.

'For his friends. For others. For the Faith. It's all the same.'

Emma looked at him, coldly, through her tears. ' "Ah, what an old fool," she is thinking,' said Scottie. 'Here,' he drew a sizeable flask out of his inside pocket, 'have some of this. If the Holy Spirit's out of favour, maybe some ordinary spirit will help.'

'What is it?' Emma said, taking the flask instinctively with trembling hands.

'Hooch,' he said. 'Drink it. Our second saviour.'

Emma was shocked. 'That's quite awful,' she said, sipping tentatively at the unstoppered flask.

'You'd not look a gift-horse in the mouth, lassie,' he chided, and then she almost laughed.

'No, I meant what you said.'

'Ah. Yes, I suppose. Funny thing about unbelievers; they're always the first to cry blasphemy.'

Emma turned away. 'Habit,' she said.

'Och well then. Habits don't care what you call them,' he said. He took the flask from her, took a long swig and handed it back, and began to sing,

> 'Mademoiselle from Armentières, parlez-vous . . .
> Hasn't been fu . . . . kissed for forty-years, parlez-vous . . .'

'Besides,' he said suddenly, 'it was a priest that taught me to drink.' His voice had changed again, and that long-ago Irish priest echoed in it. Scottie was that sort of much travelled man who carried the accents of all his many abodes on his tongue. 'Jamieson. That was his tipple. It was years before I realized it wasn't essential to the Faith. By that time, it was rather too late

Grown rather fond of the stuff. Go on, lass, drink it up, drink to your friend in paradise.'

She pushed the bottle away. 'My poor friend,' she whispered, for the first time thinking of Bob Spalding as the friend he had become in his quiet and unassuming way, 'my poor friend is lying five miles behind us on the edge of the road. And it's so cold. It's so cold.' She sank her head in her hands and Scottie's big free hand came across and patted the soft hair at the nape of her neck.

'Poor wee thing,' he said. 'Poor wee thing.' Then he added to himself, looking back to the rutted road, 'So there's the wisdom of the modern age, lass. Is that really better than what I said?'

'No,' she sobbed, achingly, 'but it's true.'

'Bullshit,' said Scottie the Yank.

'I've met the most extraordinary man,' Emma Maclaren said to Harry Bruce. They were standing just to the side of the long serving counter of the Cantine Anglais in Revigny, hands clasped around mugs of hot chocolate, sipping luxuriantly between sentences.

'Oh?' said Harry Bruce, his voice, as always, carefully measured. It was eleven o'clock at night and the Place de la Gare was quiet, in a lull between trains. One was due in shortly, and the English girls behind the makeshift counter were bustling about with huge kettles, preparing for the hundreds of cups of free coffee, tea, chocolate and bouillon they would soon serve.

'Yes. His name is Scottie. I don't know if it's his first name or his last name, actually. They just call him Scottie the Yank.'

'American?' Harry asked.

'That's the odd thing. I don't think so. I think he's a Scot, actually, though it's hard to tell. His accent is most peculiar. One moment it's quite American, and then again it will be rather Scottish, quite Highland even, and once I thought he sounded Australian. And sometimes he sounds quite like you.'

'Like me?' Harry said.

'Yes. Or rather the way you used to sound, when you were younger.'

'South African.'

'Yes, I think so.'

'Why don't you ask?'

'Yes,' she said suddenly. 'Yes, I shall. I should have before, only we find so much to talk about. So much else.'

'I see,' Harry said quietly. He sipped his chocolate, looking idly about the mainly deserted square. The frost-covered cobbles were sharply outlined by the bright lighting along the front of the wooden building that housed the Cantine. Above their heads the British and French flags draped across the Cantine front rustled forlornly. 'You see quite a bit of him?' Harry said.

'Oh yes, of course. Since Bob was killed, I've been riding with him every other trip. Until they repair my poor old wagon. If they can, or find another. In between I ride with Verity. She's quite as strong as any man, so we make a good team. But I must confess, I do enjoy being with Scottie; he's so oddly cheering . . .'

'I'm glad for you, Em,' Harry said suddenly, his voice a little muffled. He cleared his throat and sipped his chocolate. 'You needed something like this.'

'I what?' Emma looked puzzled.

'I mean since Torquil. All that. You needed to meet someone. I'm glad, Emma. Really I am.' Emma stared. His face, severely outlined in the harsh light, looked tired and old and somehow resigned. 'Really I am,' he repeated, almost to himself.

Emma studied his face for a long time, not certain if she understood. Then suddenly she began to laugh, softly, and turned her head down so she was laughing into the remnants of her chocolate.

'What's funny?' he said. He was curious and not offended. He was never offended, she thought suddenly, unlike Torquil who rather often had been.

'Oh Harry. Harry, it's not like that.'

'I'm sorry. I've been rather forward about it. I wasn't prying, Emma, honestly.'

'Harry,' she laughed again, 'Harry, he's older than my father, I'm sure.'

A train came rolling in with a great clattering and hissing of steam, just then, into the station across the square. But even the noise of it, followed soon by the shouting and singing of French soldiery, could not mask the marked relief in Harry's voice when he answered her. For once his renowned lawyer's sang-froid was nowhere in evidence. 'Oh, I see, I see. Oh, I do understand. You'll think me a total fool, Emma, but I thought, I understood, I . . .'

'I know precisely what you thought, Harry Bruce,' Emma said

with a small smile. 'But I'm really quite astounded . . .' she stopped suddenly, feeling she'd gone too far.

'Oh, I would be happy for you, Emma. Honestly I would.'

'Of course,' she said. 'Of course you would.'

'Only to be perfectly sincere, I'm a little happier that it's not so.' He smiled almost shyly and set his cup on the counter as the swarm of approaching soldiers enveloped them. He took her arm and led her through the mass of *horizon-bleu*-clad Frenchmen that descended upon the open serving window of the Cantine Anglais, with obvious delight and looks of longing towards the handful of English girls behind it. 'We'd better go,' he said. He walked her to her tent, and she was glad of his company as they passed the eerie wreck of a downed zeppelin that lay beside her path. He was happy then to talk of Scottie and listened with relaxed interest.

'He has the most extraordinary religious faith,' Emma said. 'It's so earthy and practical; he really makes me believe that Jesus, if there ever was a Jesus, is right there, everywhere we go, in the ambulance, on the battlefield. It's so real to him, so unstuffy. I mean he's terribly bawdy. Not like religious people at home at all.'

'Catholic?' Harry said.

'Yes. Yes, he is. How did you know?'

'They're like that, the ones I meet out here. Their chaplains particularly. The front-line men say they're the only ones worth their salt. They do seem to be the only ones anywhere near the front line anyhow. They're right up there, too. A lot of them killed.'

'He's not afraid. I mean, he's really not afraid. The other day one of those frightful Jack Johnsons came whistling down, frightfully close; I really thought we were for it. I was terrified, after last week, you know.' His face clouded, imagining it, and herself in danger again. 'And as it came down,' she said, 'he just grabbed me with those big arms and shouted, "Here we go sweetheart," and then he started shouting his Hail Mary at the top of his lungs, and sort of laughing while he did. Then the moment it landed, and close enough to jolt us half off the road, he just drove off, singing one of those awful bawdy songs, changing half the rude words and forgetting to change the rest.' She smiled, remembering. 'Of course I don't believe any of that stuff at all, but when I'm with him, it gets rather convincing.

He's terribly good to talk with.'

They had reached Emma's belltent, and Harry paused with her outside. 'I'd like to talk to him,' he said.

'Seriously?'

'Yes. About his Church.'

'You're not thinking . . .' Emma looked amazed.

'Oh no. No battlefield conversions, not for me. I've *never* believed any of that stuff if you'll recall. No, it's about Susan.'

'Susan?' Emma was mystified. 'Whatever has Susan to do with Scottie? Or the Catholic Church?' It sounded as unlikely a combination to Emma as the Kaiser eloping with the Queen.

'She's under instruction. In the Catholic faith.'

'Susan?' Emma practically shouted.

'There's a man involved, I believe. Actually, there's going to be a hell of a row, I'm afraid. I've just had a letter from my grandmother and there are stormclouds over Strathglass. He's a Maclaren. A ranker. From Glasgow. A certain Pat McGarrity. A miner's son.'

'Oh my God,' Emma whispered. 'It can't be true.'

'I'll show you the letter, if you'd like.' He was reaching inside his RAMC tunic. She shook her head.

'No, no, not now. Oh, I must think.' She paused and said, 'Marriage?'

'She swears not. But she *is* seeing a priest. Grandmother found rosary beads and practically hit the roof. She's not exactly open-minded. Or maybe she just guessed there was something else at the back of it, something more romantic. Of course it's typical Susan, if you think about it. She's always done wild, romantic things.'

'A miner's son?'

'Yes. And a miner himself. Actually Tenny had to admit he's rather an all right sort. But still. I mean, it's just so extraordinary. I would like to see your friend Scottie. He might be able to explain a little of the Church angle. What they might, you know, expect from her.'

'Marriage?' Emma whispered again.

'I gather *his* mother hit the roof too. Rather funny actually. She's probably rather like Grandmama. In her own way.'

'I'll introduce you. If you come to the depot at the end of our shift, on Thursday. We could all talk. And then . . .'

'We could have dinner,' he said. She smiled, blushing a little.

'I wasn't really asking . . .'

'No. I was.'

'There's a café,' she said, 'behind the Place de la Gare. They're quite quiet. And open late.'

13

Victoria Maclaren was worried. Not about Emma's assignation with Harry Bruce, which she did not know about anyhow. Nor Susan Bruce's aberrations, which although essentially Maud's problem, she had taken on as her own. The mores of the young scarcely troubled her today, nor did the ever-present demands of the estate play on her mind. And the other, larger concern, the welfare of her three sons, her husband, and myriad others of the regiment, too great a concern to be limited to a small mental pocket of worry, never, ever left her. After two years of war the dangers in which her loved ones lived had so soaked into her being as to become part of her breath and the flow of her blood.

And yet, even she, well-informed officer's wife, knew nothing of the brutal reality of the Front. Her mental images were yet rooted in another century, updated only by magazine illustrations, sterile and cheery. She still imagined that all dead bodies were carefully buried, with chaplain's rites, in a row of neat wooden crosses at the rear of the line. It was not her fault. She was an army wife; and the army had taught her, as it taught all other ranks, neither to question nor to think too deeply. And above all, to carry out the duties of the woman's world.

Right now, those duties had presented her with a situation as testing as many her husband would face. Upstairs, in a hastily prepared guest bedroom, Grisel Bruce was about to give birth. Her history of ten failed pregnancies, and her age, had indicated a difficult birth and months ago the family had decided she would enter a lying-in hospital in Edinburgh and be attended by a carefully chosen specialist. Victoria had applauded the idea at the time. Although she herself had a quite legendary ability to produce babies in the natural lull between luncheon and tea, she did not expect the same from Grisel. And although outwardly Victoria held that every baby was as important as every other, nothing could disguise the fact that this was a child both long awaited, and irreplaceable. Grisel had already been informed there must be no other pregnancies. Too much rested on this birth for any chances to be taken. Everybody had been well aware of this, and even Gordon Bruce far away in France had been fully informed of every detail of the plan.

Unfortunately, no one told the baby, Victoria thought grimly, as she hurried down the hallway towards Grisel's room. Instead of waiting for Edinburgh, or even putting in a surprise appearance at home, it had chosen this weekend when Grisel had come to Culbrech, confident of three weeks yet before her time, to make its entry. Grisel had gone into labour after dinner, biting her lip at regular intervals throughout coffee, until she ventured to whisper to Victoria over the liqueurs, 'I think it's started.'

In the ensuing panic Grisel was put to bed and the local doctor hastily summoned. Unimpressed, he had announced there were many hours yet and he should be called in the morning. Thus Victoria spent the night mopping Grisel's brow, holding her hand, proffering cups of tea and accepting Grisel's profuse apologies.

'Oh Victoria,' Grisel moaned softly, as she entered the room, 'I am so terribly sorry. I'd never have come if I thought . . .'

'Yes, dear,' Victoria said, faintly pained. 'I know you didn't plan it. Let's just get on with it, shall we?'

'I do hope you're not angry . . .' Grisel's voice trailed off into a wince.

'I'll be positively furious if you say sorry one more time.'

'Oh of course, I'm sorry, Victoria.' Her eyes widened with apology and sudden pain. They looked suddenly frightened and young; the eyes at odds with the greying hair. Victoria was worried again. She remembered birthing Jamie at a younger age than Grisel, and finding that the youthful verve of her earlier labours was lacking. Grisel was forty-two and a first-time mother.

'Oh, I'm so old,' she moaned. 'The doctor in Edinburgh said I

. . . we never should have . . . but I did so want a baby.' Her voice trailed to a wail of despair.

'And you shall have one,' Victoria returned, 'if you'll just stop talking and start concentrating.' She signalled to the waiting maid, a prearranged signal that she was to telephone the doctor. The girl left and Grisel suddenly shouted and thrashed about in the bed with a new contraction and Victoria got worried again, thinking she'd left the summoning of the doctor too late. She attempted to lift the bedclothes and have a practical look at progress so far, but Grisel was so mortified with embarrassment that even through her pain she fought back modestly.

'Oh, don't be such a fool, I've had five myself.'

'Please, I couldn't bear for you to see.'

'Somebody will have to see, my dear,' Victoria said sharply.

But Grisel just moaned and shook her head back and forth on the damp pillow, her long strands of greying hair loosening and coming undone. She clutched the brass bedstead with her hands over her head and closed her eyes, her face screwing up with pain.

Victoria leaned back in her bedside chair, wishing Angusina Gibson were here. Such a practical girl, so unflappable. A surge of resentment passed through Victoria's mind; why of all times must she be deprived of her favourite servant now? The reason was obvious, of course, and iron-clad in its justification. Angusina Munro Gibson was at this moment at her mother's home, happily nursing her own firstborn child, a ten-pound boldly healthy son, born just a week earlier. A week ago Victoria had been positively delighted by it, particularly since she had been instrumental in ensuring its legitimacy. Now, however, she was highly annoyed with it, removing Angusina from her service just when she was most needed. Not that serving-girls weren't entitled to motherhood, she admitted. Only she wished there was some magic way of ensuring that they could achieve it without disrupting the stately pattern of Culbrech House.

There was a knock on the door, and Victoria rose quickly, expecting the doctor, and finding, instead, the pale, nervous face of Kirsty, Angusina's temporary replacement. She was a girl of sixteen from a neighbouring farm, an unimaginative, vaguely sullen child, with bland blue eyes and dark brown hair pulled tightly back beneath her white cap.

'Ma'am,' she began slowly, peering with irrepressible curiosity over Victoria's plump shoulder to the bed beyond.

'What is it, Kirsty? I said we were not to be disturbed.'

'Ma'am, there's a person at the door.'

'Oh, for heaven's sake, child. I'm not receiving today. Surely that was made clear to you.'

'But ma'am. It's a lady, ma'am,' the girl said. 'At the front door, ma'am.' That was meant to make all the difference.

'Send her away,' Victoria burst out. 'And you go away as well. Now.'

The girl turned, sullenly, sorry to leave the doorway, and murmured, almost to herself, 'It's a Mrs Bruce, ma'am.'

Victoria felt she could have shaken the lumpen child by the shoulders until she howled. 'Maud Bruce! Why didn't you say?' she demanded, glancing again over her shoulder.

'You didna ask, ma'am,' the girl whined.

'Oh go on, send her up. Immediately. Or . . . or I'll have Mrs Murchison take a strap to you.'

The girl's eyes widened and she vanished with a clatter of small, leather-soled shoes. Victoria stepped back into the room, feeling an onset of panic. Grisel's pains came so quickly now one upon the other as to leave hardly a gap for breath. She cried and thrashed about and gasped, 'Oh Victoria . . . something's happening . . . something's happening . . .' This time when Victoria made to lift the bedclothes, there was no resistance. Nature had overridden modesty, even for Gordon Bruce's gentle wife.

Victoria took one look, glimpsed a damp spot of crowning head and knew she was on her own. Unless the doctor was coming up the stairs, right now, he was going to miss the party.

'Never mind, dear,' she whispered to the frightened woman in the bed. 'You're almost there. Just a little push now, come, dear, just a little push.'

Grisel's face screwed up with concentration and her knuckles whitened around the brass of the bedstead, and she screamed out loud. The sound masked the click of the doorlatch but Victoria, without turning, was aware of someone entering the room and said, still leaning over the bed, 'Oh Maud, thank God, come and give me a hand.'

'A pleasure,' a voice said, low, soft and smooth. 'But let me first wash my hands.'

Victoria whirled about. A woman was standing in the doorway, in a plain dark brown woollen dress, sternly groomed, her greying black hair pulled back in a smoothly braided bun, fastened at the nape of a long, slender neck. Victoria's breath released in a little soft gasp. 'Naomi,' she murmured, stunned. Amazement at her sudden appearance was swamped at once in a flood of relief: Naomi was a nurse.

'Water?' Naomi asked; she was neatly and quickly rolling up her brown woollen sleeves. Victoria indicated the ewer and basin on the marble-topped washstand, and returned her attentions to Grisel.

'The doctor is late,' she muttered, her mind too numbed by the pressure of events to quite absorb the unlikely appearance of her long-time rival at this most fortuitous of moments. 'I think it's almost here.'

Naomi was then leaning over the bed beside her, and Victoria stood aside to allow her closer. Grisel moaned, and Naomi said at once, 'One more push, darling, you've almost made it. What a fine big head, come now, darling.'

'Oh I can't,' Grisel cried, 'I can't. I'm too tired, I'm too old. The doctor said . . . . too old.' She whimpered, defeated, and Naomi cried out,

'Bugger the doctor, darling, *push*!'

Grisel gave a gasp, half offended modesty, half effort, and a wet and shining baby son slithered gloriously into Naomi's waiting hands.

Afterwards, Grisel was to confide to Victoria that her son's birth was due totally to the sheer shock of hearing such a word on a woman's lips. Afterwards, too, when the doctor had put in a satisfactory if belated appearance, and the new arrival was washed and tucked into the Maclaren cradle beside the bed of his tired but healthy mother, Naomi had her own confession to make.

She and Victoria were sitting by a luxurious fire in the anteroom of Grisel's bedroom, talking in whispers lest they awaken the new mother. Victoria was voicing the immense relief that the sight of Naomi, an experienced nurse, had brought at that critical moment.

Naomi laughed, richly, her low throaty voice bubbling with delight. 'Oh my dear, how too, too comical!'

'But why?' Victoria said, her blue eyes blinking mystification. 'You *are* a nurse.'

'Of course, of course I am. South Africa, France, London. Amputations, gangrene, shell-shock; anything that can happen to a soldier. I've nursed them all. But I've never, ever until this day, nursed a member of the female sex. The only childbirth I ever attended was my own.'

Victoria blinked again. 'Oh Lord,' she sighed. 'Of course. And there was I, so confident, because you were there. Thank heaven you didn't tell me then.' Then she too laughed and they giggled over it together and stretched their toes to the fender, relaxing, and sipping coffee, feeling an immense triumphant warmth of companionship as if they'd been friends for years. So cosy was that mood of sisterly affection that Victoria was reluctant to put her next question, and yet curiosity demanded she must.

'But please, do tell,' she said, leaning forward confidentially, 'whatever brought you here?' She paused for a fragile moment and added, 'It has been rather a long time since last you called at Culbrech.'

Naomi was silent. Victoria surreptitiously studied her face over the rim of her huge Crown Derby coffee cup, a breakfast cup, the day having for all purposes only just begun. The mixed lights of rainy morning and glowing wood-fire played across features whose beauty had at last retreated to bony handsomeness. Naomi, who had always seemed young, looked old today. Victoria was surprised to find in her reaction to that less of triumphant satisfaction than of sorrow, such as she might feel if the beautiful cup in her hand were to fall to the hearth and smash. Something lovely irretrievably gone.

'I had not really meant to call,' Naomi said. 'But I was at Cluanie when you telephoned Mother last night. She would have come herself, but she daren't leave Daddy. I thought for Gordon's sake, I must come. I hoped,' she lowered her eyes, 'I would be welcome for Gordon's sake.'

'As it turned out,' Victoria said briskly, 'you were quite thoroughly welcome for your own.'

Naomi nodded, a reserved nod, acknowledging Victoria's rather brittle peace-offering. 'You see, I am going once more to France. With Robert gone, there's little need for me in London. I'd rather be . . . nearer to where he is. I have certain useful abilities. Just think,' she smiled wanly, 'I've added to my experience today. If any pregnant Maclarens turn up, I'll know just what to do.' She tried to laugh, but the laughter was swallowed by an underlying sadness.

Victoria, struggling with re-emergent jealousy, was unable to laugh either. Naomi in France. Naomi with Ian again, as in South Africa. She chided herself in her heart; they were old, all of them, for these children's games, but the jealousy remained, and grew bitter.

'How dedicated,' she said, between tight lips, drawing her feet back from the fender where they had rested companionably by Naomi's. 'I must remember to tell Ian. He'll be so pleased with you.'

Naomi seemed not to hear. She went on, unruffled, 'I came north to say goodbye to Daddy. I don't expect he'll be here, when I come back. Whenever that might be. It's odd, you know, but when I left Cluanie after Rebecca's wedding, I had the strongest sense of foreboding and sorrow, and I was certain I would not see my father again. I was certain it was a premonition. And yet, here I am and old Willie is still there. Still knew me. Still scolding me with his eyes.' She laughed softly.

'Stuff and nonsense, premonitions,' Victoria sniffed. 'Probably something you ate.'

Naomi smiled wisely. 'Oh no. It is not the warnings that are false, but what we choose to see in them. I sensed sorrow; a parting. Daddy was old so I assumed I would part from him. But the young can leave us as well, as Robert did, as he even at that moment was doing, running off to the regiment while I was away. And,' she looked carefully, and kindly, at Victoria, 'and others can leave us without any change of physical circumstances. They can leave us with a word, or a look, or a betrayal of faith. Such a parting,' she said slowly, 'is as real as a physical journey, and as permanent as death.'

Victoria understood then why Naomi was here, and why they could sit, side by side like sisters, two middle-aged women sharing the fireside. It was over. She sat silent for a long while, savouring this new situation. The relief that should have come, did not. Nor was there any of the smugness or satisfaction she had imagined when, over many bitter years, she had envisaged this scene of her ultimate triumph. She felt, indeed, no triumph, but instead a faint sorrow, as for the loss of Naomi's beauty, the broken cup. Her sorrow was for Naomi, and for Ian, whatever at last had parted them, and even for herself, as if something rare and wrong and yet still intrinsically part of their marriage had been lost. She shook her head slowly, without words, and then rose and extending her plump little arms embraced her husband's mistress in her husband's house.

14

'Nou, there's a rare sight,' said Private Donnie Cameron, looking up from the shirt he was mending and nudging Hamish Drummond with his elbow.

'Whit is?' Hamish demanded, his eyes refocusing on the distance after their painstaking concentration on his own sewing.

'Thot,' said Donnie. He indicated with his large grubby hand still miraculously holding the delicate little needle and thread, to where a slender, immaculately kitted-out major was making his way warily along their bay of the trench. 'The red badge o' funk amang us. A rare sight.'

'A staff officer,' Hamish said, staring, as the spring sun lit the red tabs on the officer's stiff collar. 'Awa' oot here?' He could not recall ever having seen one since his arrival at the Front, months before.

'Aye,' Donnie said sourly, 'I wonder if the war's o'er.'

The officer picked his way nearer, keeping his head well bent, so that there was a clear foot of safety between his hat and the top of the parapet. Donnie smiled to himself, but held his tongue, as the man was within earshot.

'Ah, soldier,' the officer said, and Donnie took the precaution of getting to his feet and presenting a passable salute. 'Looking for your commanding officer, soldier. Directions to HQ?'

'Aye,' Hamish spoke up with the reckless courage that standing behind Donnie evoked. 'It's yon muckle great buildin' wi' the flags on top.'

The officer straightened, looking dimly down the ditch in the ground. 'Flags, soldier? I'm afraid I don't see . . .'

Donnie jabbed a warning elbow into Hamish's ribs. An officer was an officer, 'Nae, sir. He means ye gae awa' doun this trench tae Dead Horse gap, an' turn back doun tae the support line, then ye gae left doun the High Street an' cut through the Kaiser's Arse.'

'Soldier?' A warning growl issued from the beautifully groomed walrus moustache of the major.

'Thot's whit we ca' it, sir,' Donnie said earnestly. 'There's e'en a signpost. It's yon wee cut back tae the HQ dugout. We a' call it thot, sir. E'en the CO.'

The officer garrumphed noisily, and slapped his swagger stick sharply against his mud-spattered shiny boot.

'Can't say I approve of such licensed obscenity, but that's as may be. Thank you, soldier.' He turned to leave, but paused a moment, looking back, 'And soldier . . .'

'Sir.'

'Get those boots cleaned. Disgrace to the regiment.'

He went off, and Hamish thumbed his nose at the ramrod straight departing back. Donnie watched, nervous that the officer would lose his way and turn back, but a chance intervention saved them further communication.

'Ah, Maclaren,' they heard the brittle voice crow, 'thank God I've found someone at last.'

Donnie smiled wryly at the inherent dismissal of himself and Hamish, as if their whole conversation with the major had been a dream. He was long accustomed to that tendency of certain members of the major's class to treat him as a blank spot on the paper of life. He shrugged and returned to his sewing, peacefully content in the beam of weak sunlight that warmed his corner of the trench.

'Good to see you, sir,' Private Albert Maclaren said politely. The major, Arnold Fleming by name, was an old friend of his father's, a fellow Maclaren, seconded to brigade headquarters, a man who, since his discovery of Albert in his lowly position at the Front, had made persistent efforts to get the boy to accept a commission. Albert had always declined, politely as he did everything, and with his usual self-deprecation, insisting that he had nothing much to offer his country other than a private soldier's broad back and solid loyalty.

'Glad I found you,' Major Fleming repeated. 'That pair of scruffs back there didn't seem to know one end of the trench system from the next. Looking for your CO, old man. Got some rather spiffing news for him.'

'What is that?' Albert asked tentatively. 'If I might be party to it,' he added uncertainly. But the major brought a hand down on his shoulder with familial warmth.

'Of course you may, m'boy. Family matter, anyhow, what? Seems the colonel's lady's foaled. Fine little colt, all well and all that.'

'Oh, splendid,' Albert said earnestly. 'That's topping news. There was rather a lot of concern. Uncle Gordon . . . the CO will be delighted.'

'Yes. Dare say. Always a bit of a worry such times, what? Not that I'd know myself. Not the family type,' he laughed with another hearty masculine clap on Albert's shoulder. 'C'mon along lad, show the way. Must deliver my message. Word came to Brigade HQ and your father honoured me with delivering it.' He said the last with a faint nervous tremor, as a distant petulant crack of rifle-fire reminded him where he was. Albert barely heard it. Things had hotted up in the last two weeks. The battalion of Devonshires who took over their stretch of line when the Maclarens were in billets had stirred things up with a couple of raiding parties. The colonel had called it a damn nuisance but the Devonshires had the backing of the staff who were nervous when things were left too quiet.

'Just down here sir,' Albert said.

A stray shell came whistling overhead, completely ignored by the clusters of card-playing, kilted soldiers snugged into funk holes in the trench walls. The major flung himself unceremoniously flat on the duckboards, covering his head with his hands. The explosion came, distant and innocent, and the major looked up cautiously to Albert Maclaren, who out of politeness had gone into a sort of companionable crouch.

'Bit of a close thing, what?' the staff officer said with a fragile attempt at a bluff shrug. It wasn't, but Albert politely agreed that it had been, and helped the now muddy major to his feet. Subdued, he continued on beside Albert down the twisting lines of ditches.

'I say, what a warren, how do you ever find your way?' The officer's voice still shook, but he was grinning idiotically.

'One gets accustomed. We *are* here rather a long time.'

'Hm. Yes.' The moustached face clouded. 'I do wish, Maclaren, you'd take my advice. This,' he waved his gloved hand to right and left with disdain, 'is no place for a lad of your . . .' he hesitated, looking with sudden emotion at Albert's pale-skinned, handsome, clean-shaven face, its once plump features grown gaunt now, from hard work and bouts of dysentery. 'Damn it, lad, you've such sensibilities, such breeding . . .'

'It's no place for anyone, sir,' Albert ventured softly, and still as polite as ever.

The major grunted something, looked preoccupied, and then burst out suddenly, 'I say, Albert, lad, I've known you since you were a boy. Watched you grow, been damned fond of you.' He hesitated, and stopped walking, better able to think when not sliding around on slimy duckboards. Albert stopped also. 'Fond of the whole family,' the major added hastily, as if something too personal had crept into the conversation.

'Of course, sir. They're all very fond of you.'

'When I think of you out here, Bertie . . . of something happening to you . . .' The major's large brown eyes were suddenly moist. 'Damn it all, lad. I could use a good secretary, at Brigade HQ. Your father could get you a commission in a trice. After all, plenty of men are commissioned from the field. All the time. Why not you, damn it?'

'I'm afraid sir, they commission only the best. I'm rather ordinary, sir.'

'Ordinary,' the major stepped closer, his voice low and his face so close to Albert's that Albert could hear, in the isolated stillness of the communications trench, each sudden little intake of breath. 'You're not *ordinary*, Bertie.' A spot of moisture trembled on the man's lower lip and his tongue nervously flicked it away. 'Please, Bertie, for me?' he whispered.

Bertie turned away, stumbling quickly through the mud of the ditch, fleeing the pressure of the major's dark hungry eyes on his back.

They reached the headquarters dugout without another word passing between them and stood for a moment before it in an embarrassed silence, forced once more to look at each other. The major was composed. 'Thank you, Albert,' he said gruffly, 'I'll find my way now. Appreciate the trouble, and all.'

'My pleasure, sir. Please offer the colonel my congratulations.'

'You won't come in?' Major Fleming indicated the corrugated-iron 'door'.

'Hardly the done thing, sir.'

'No. Of course. Well, Bertie,' he paused, 'do keep me in mind if you reconsider.'

'Of course, sir.' Albert Maclaren saluted his superior and quickly went away.

Robert Bruce, the colonel's youngest nephew, had arrived two weeks before with the most recent draft sent out from England. The battalion had been in billets at the time, and having been fitted into Tenny Maclaren's company, he had moved up into the line six days ago. He was quite inordinately happy.

He had seen no action, of course, nor any bloodshed. The condition of the trenches, ragged, crumbling-edged, water-filled ditches in which his idolized regiment scuttled about their daily business like tartan and khaki rats, had come as a shock compared to the idealized versions familiar from *The War Illustrated* but Robert quickly adapted. He had the immense flexibility of the very young, coupled with a rosy glow of romanticism that had brought him here in the first place. Regimental marches yet echoed in his head, and flag-waving charges that had never been part of this war still filled his expectation. But he learned quickly, and stopped, within a day, asking, 'When do we get at them, old chap?' because the laughter that evoked was humiliating. Still, he wrote postcards home to his schoolfriends, and pictured them, snug in old Weatherby House, green with envy.

The only thing troubling him, aside from an occasional twinge of guilt towards his mother, was loneliness. He was hardly among strangers. But Tenny's rank and authority effectively erased any familiar connections; the idol of his boyhood had become a hard, thin, serious-faced man, fraught with responsibilities and concerns. And Jamie, with whom two years ago he had played boyish games of imaginary soldiering, was grown years beyond him, a tough, experienced young man who played cards with the other rankers and shared short, guttural jokes with them as if he too had been raised in a tenement or croft. Only Albert, gentle and considerate, was still as Robert had remembered him. It was

Albert who brightened his first night in the trenches with a gift of a carefully hoarded piece of Fuller's walnut cake, part of his last food package from home. Robert ate it, feeling guilty, having been so recently in the land of tea-shoppes and comforts himself.

But Albert was quiet, studious and bookish. He spent long hours writing in his diary in a small, neatly rounded hand. For companionship, Robert would have to look elsewhere. And that was when the trouble started. At first he didn't understand it, the men all talked in the low guttural accents of working-class Scotland, half swallowing their short little bursts of words, dropping consonants altogether. When Robert passed and they grinned and winked to each other and made some quick, soft-voiced comment followed by laughter, he only grinned back uncertainly, hoping someone would choose to explain the joke. No one did, possibly because, as he was soon to learn, the joke was him.

In honour of the birth of his son, Gordon Bruce ordered that every man in the battalion be given an extra tot of rum. The men welcomed the suggestion with disproportionate delight; the daily rum ration itself being always the highlight of the day, to have it doubled was to have an ordinary day turn suddenly into Christmas.

Usually the rum was provided in the morning, just after the morning stand-to, just before breakfast. But on this occasion, the double measure was duly saved for early evening, to be followed by a particularly meaty MacConachie, and a lavish helping of hard biscuits and jam, a feast of celebration.

Robert's platoon sergeant dished out the rum, a thick, dark syrupy concoction, reeking gamely of alcohol, in two quick turns of his tin measure into each man's tin cup. Some poured it into their tea, others savoured it, and a few downed it in one glorious gullet-scorching gulp. Robert was sipping his uncertainly, not yet having grown accustomed to its fearsome strength, unlike that of any beverage he'd ever encountered, when a big quiet Lewisman with a blocky, solemn face leaned over and said, not unkindly, 'Och, darky, ye'll be after havin' my own. I do not permit alcohol to pass my lips.' Robert grinned. He was accustomed to teasing about his colour at school. Then he watched, startled, as the big man poured his double measure of rum into Robert's mug. He gulped and thanked his benefactor who smiled broadly, his small blue squinting eyes crinkling almost shut.

'Hey, Norman, whit ye dae thot fer?' a red-headed man demanded. It was evident that other members of the platoon, familiar with the island man's non-drinking habit, were accustomed to receiving his share of the rum. 'At least ye could gie it tae yin o' yer ain. No' a darky.'

'Aye,' someone else said angrily. 'Darkies dinna drink, either. It's agin their religion. Eh, darky, tell the man ye dinna drink,' he growled, approaching Robert.

'It is against my own religion to drink,' the Lewisman said mildly. 'But I may give my share to whom I choose. It is also against my religion to be hitting folk, but I have been known to fall from grace.' He lounged, still smiling, beside Robert, and the redhead, taking in his huge shoulders, his thick muscular neck, and the blond-haired legs as broad in the calf as most men's thighs, decided to hold his peace.

Robert relaxed, grinned at his protector, and drank the rum with flourish. He grinned again, more broadly, and had the sensation that steam was rising from behind his ears. He grinned once more, and the dark trench walls leaned in cosily. 'I say, this is good,' he said, his own voice sounding blurry and far away. He gulped the rest down, faintly aware of soft laughter from the big island man beside him. 'Here's to the colonel's son,' he said, and then, rum and good nature overriding good sense, he added, 'Here's to my new cousin, Donald.'

'Wha the hell's he?' murmured someone.

'My cousin. The colonel's baby. He's my cousin, you see. I guess I shouldn't say, but just between us, he *is* my uncle, you know, the CO. So that makes Donald my cousin.'

There was a long silence. Faintly, Robert heard the soft west-coast-accented voice beside him saying, 'Och aye, laddie. Of course. Now I am thinking you've had enough rum. Come get your tea inside you. It will be settling your head.'

'Don't you believe me?' Robert said, his words a little slurred. 'It's true, you know.'

'Aye, lad. I am sure that it is.'

'Will ye listen tae the darky sod,' someone muttered. 'No enough gettin' his wee black arse intae a fine Scots regiment. Now he's claimin' he's related tae the Old Man.'

'But he's my uncle,' Robert said. 'Look. My name is Bruce too, right? Gordon Bruce is my mother's brother.'

'Och laddie, do not be making a fool of yourself,' the island man muttered, trying to steer him away from the gathering crowd. But drink turned Robert both bold and pedantic.

'No, look here, let me explain. Explain everything. The colonel and my mother, brother, and sister. Makes me and Donald first cousins, right.'

'Nou thot's the limit,' the red-haired man exploded. 'First ye get oor rum, noo yer sayin' oor CO's the brother o' yer darky whore o' a mither. Shut yer filthy wee gob.'

This time Robert heard clear enough. 'Why, you wormy little cad,' he announced to peals of laughter, but he followed it with a good, professional right to the man's jaw that laid him out flat on the duckboards. There was a roar of delight, a scuffling in the mud, and Robert was instantly in the middle of a mêlée of fists and boots. He was a good fighter, and had he been sober he'd have finished two of his opponents at least. But there were five of them, and he was distinctly getting the worst until the island man, Norman MacArthur, with a resigned sigh waded into the battle on his side. Robert grinned through bloody teeth and got properly stuck in, forgetting everything in the rowdy pleasure of the fight.

'Hey, he's no' bad,' a viewer on the sidelines commented.

'Gie us some mair darkies, an' we'll finish Jerry as weel,' said someone else with genuine admiration. It looked to be Robert's hour of triumph, but at that moment the muddy tangle of khaki was frozen by a furious and authoritative roar,

'Youse. Whit youse daein'? Nae fightin'. Nae fightin', or we'll send ye o'er tae fight wi' Jerry. Eneuch.'

The cluster of arms and legs and muddy boots fell apart and as quickly fell to a semblance of attention. Corporal McGarrity, their section leader, and a man of whom each of them was thoroughly terrified, was glowering fiercely down the line of them.

'Richt,' he said. 'Idle hands mak' deil's work. Double fatigues, the lot o' youse.'

So Robert Bruce, in the company of five erstwhile opponents, and one kind-hearted west-coast defender, spent the night of their colonel's celebration in the communications trenches, hauling an endless supply of rations, mail, replacement gear, and a long-awaited supply of the new round-rimmed tin hats up to the Front. In the distance, the concert party they were to have attended could faintly be heard, a wafting of tinny music on the still spring air. By the end of the night, as they struggled and cursed authority together, Robert knew he would be 'Darky' for the rest of his military life. But he also knew he was not without friends.

The concert party was organized by the Sergeants' Mess at a venue two miles behind the line in the orchard of an abandoned farm on the road leading back into Albert. The slope of the land and the shelter of a broad brick wall of the ruined farmhouse made a rough amphitheatre for the transport wagon, lit with kranzow lamps, that they used as a stage. A surprisingly varied and talented selection of performers from the ranks of the Maclarens entertained.

Among the entertainers was Billy Kelly, the popular Glasgow comedian, Marco Marcello, the Scots-born Italian tenor, and the touring vaudeville song-and-dance team of Robbie and Sandy, the MacGregor Brothers, who, in spite of their stage persona, were neither brothers, nor even friends. They were a mismatched pair, Robbie tall and lanky, self-deprecating and good-natured; Sandy a pompous little man with Shakespearean pretensions; and other than on the stage they were rarely known to speak to each other. Both however were now privates in the Maclaren Highlanders, and both for the good of the regiment nobly put aside personal feelings and performed their act whenever asked.

Robbie and Sandy had just finished their turn when Tenny Maclaren arrived. He was nervous about leaving the line so lightly held, though reason told him that there was no cause for concern. That war would not be waged until summer, was a tacit assumption by now. The recent skirmishes in no-man's-land, the sporadic sniping and the occasional reminder shells, had not changed the belief that the Somme district was a district at peace.

Long may it last, Tenny thought. He watched Billy Kelly mount the stage with a vast tartan tammy on his head and his legs held knock-kneed beneath his kilt, to do a fair imitation of Harry Lauder. He clapped politely, glancing around as he did so to see if the colonel had arrived. He would stay for another act and make his way back. Officers were expected to put in an appearance, but not an overlong one, lest their presence put a damper on the fun. They were also expected to be here in the capacity of guests; that is, to ignore any rudery or flippancy aimed either at themselves, or, more likely, the ever-ready target of the staff.

The colonel's arrival was signalled by cheers and whistles, and Billy Kelly handed over the stage to the Italian tenor, Marcello, who sang 'If You Were the Only Girl in the World!' Tenny stole a glance at the CO, who sat the while watching as solemnly as if the whole performance had been grand opera. He tried to recall the last time he'd seen Gordon Bruce laugh. When Robbie MacGregor strutted on to the stage, dressed as an officer, kissed his 'wife' – Billy Kelly in a blonde wig – complete with bundled 'baby', and set about elaborately changing the baby's nappy, while the tenor sang solemnly on, the men fell about with delight. The CO watched, attentively, without the trace of a smile, as if hopefully awaiting a promised joke.

'By God, it's like pulling teeth,' a voice beside Tenny whispered. He turned, surprised, and saw Johnny Bruce standing at his elbow, and stiffened involuntarily.

'Mmm,' he said.

'Uncle Gordon's got as much sense of humour as an old maid with a padlock on heaven's gate.'

'At least he came,' Tenny said coolly.

'He could laugh. It wouldn't kill him,' Johnny protested. As he leaned forward to see better, Tenny caught a strong whiff of brandy on his breath which explained his sudden garrulousness.

Johnny was about to say something else when there was a commotion on the stage, and the bundled baby on Robbie MacGregor's bony knees made a little jumping wiggle, which evoked a startled yelp from the Italian singer, and shouts of glee from the men.

'Will ye luik, it's alive. It's no' a doll. It's a real bairn.'

At that instant Robbie stood up dramatically and flung aside the swaddling clothes, and a live, pink, and wildly squealing piglet leapt down on to the stage and clattered on small pink hoofs under the tenor's legs. He gave a great, melodious shout which indicated that he at least was not party to the joke. In another moment, with the frightened piglet running circles about his legs, the tenor crashed solemnly down on to his kilted buttocks on the stage. The audience roared, the piglet was duly caught and Tenny saw, out of the corner of his eye, Gordon Bruce convulsed in side-shaking, teary-eyed laughter.

'It's a bloody miracle,' Johnny muttered in amazement. 'C'mon,' he added, linking a companionable arm through

Tenny's, oblivious to the coldness of his response. 'Time to bea a retreat. The Old Man's leaving and the boys will want thei fun.'

On the stage an eightsome of Maclarens were dancing a respectable reel, the girls' parts taken with no self-consciousnes by hairy-legged lads, and the mood was growing jaunty an bawdy.

Johnny tugged at Tenny Maclaren's arm and Tenny wa peevishly tempted to call upon respect for his superior rank, bu stopped himself, knowing that would be, under the circum stances, faintly despicable. Also Tenny knew that Johnny wa more than a little drunk and could use an escort back to the line With an air of martyred decency, Tenny led the way back up th road to the trenches. Behind them, the raised voices of th Maclaren Highlanders echoed softly through the chorus c 'There's a Long, Long Trail A-winding'.

'Now that's really pretty,' Johnny muttered, still leaning o Tenny's arm. He started to join in, emotionally and far off key

'Oh, do shut up,' Tenny snapped, 'and just walk.'

Johnny did walk, humming clandestinely, for a short whil but then he halted, thought a moment, and then clumped heavil over to the edge of the *pavé* and seated himself on the high, gras grown bank. Tenny stood in the dark road and watched a dista white Very light mount in a fine arc over the front-line trenche briefly brightening the sky. He watched the darkness for anothe but apparently the first had revealed nothing suspicious in i ascent over no-man's-land. He wondered which side had sent up.

'Now *that's* really pretty,' Johnny muttered from the roadsid

'Beautiful,' Tenny growled. 'Are you spending the night o here?'

'Do you know,' Johnny began laboriously, as he held a da shape to his lips, 'how they'll signal the war's end?' He dra noisily from his flask.

'The combined ranks of Allied and German staff farti Tipperary in unison,' Tenny muttered. 'Give me that,' l reached for the flask. 'You've had more than enough.'

Johnny laughed, loudly. 'Very good, that's very good.' I handed the flask over willingly. 'Help yourself,' he said. 'Do.

'I'd rather not,' Tenny said, holding the flask out of Johnny reach. 'Now I suggest you get on your feet and try to sob yourself up, before you rejoin your company.'

'Oh, don't be such a prig, Tenny.'

'I may be a prig, but I'm not, fortunately for you, your company commander. Whatever you may think of Ross MacDonald, he's not a man to meet in your present state.'

Johnny nodded, much more soberly. He detested the new commander of Torquil Farquhar's old company, to which he had been attached, after Loos. And he was well aware that MacDonald felt an equal loathing for what he regarded as upper-class decadence among his officers; there would be no gentlemanly blind eye turned to drunkenness on duty. 'All right. But have a drink. For old time's sake,' he said with sudden maudlin gloom.

Tenny shrugged, and drank a restrained sip which slid unwillingly down his throat, like an unmeant apology.

'Four dark blue Very lights,' Johnny said, plodding on up the French road.

'Come again?'

'Come again? Come again?' Johnny mimicked. 'Four blue Very lights. Dark blue. That's the signal for the end of the war.'

'Oh really,' Tenny said, not listening. Then he stopped suddenly, and leaned closer to Johnny in the darkness. 'That's ridiculous,' he said earnestly. 'You'd never see them. Whoever heard of a dark blue light?'

'Oh well done, old man, you are quick.'

'Oh my God. I see. Where'd you hear that one?'

'From one of the Devonshires,' Johnny said. He stumbled in the rutted road, and cursed. 'Heard something else too,' he added.

'Aye, what was that?'

'The Bosche are down thirty feet.'

'Down where? What do you mean thirty feet?'

'Dugouts. Huge ones. Hold the whole front-line force if necessary. Thirty feet down in the ground. Safe as houses, even with a bloody 5.9 on their heads.'

'Impossible,' Tenny said.

'On the contrary, not only possible but true. The Devonshires saw them. When they took those few yards of line last week.'

'Aye,' Tenny said bitterly. 'Took them, and lost them within the hour and lost twelve men as well. Damn useless waste of life. Worse than useless. You know the wire's twice as thick at that point as it ever was. I had a recce party over three nights ago. Place is wired as thick as lice in the sergeant major's kilt. We're just giving ourselves work to do, come summer.'

'Damn it, man,' Johnny suddenly exploded, stopping still for emphasis on the deserted French road. 'You're as bad as the bloody staff. Did you not *hear* what I said? Forget your fucking wire for just one moment. I said the Bosche are thirty feet down. Thirty feet. Now there's a piece of information maybe worth twelve lives, even, if anything is. And what are you doing with it? What's anyone doing with it?'

'All right, all right. Calm down, point taken. Surely you're not saying that's their normal structure of defence?'

'Bloody coincidence if the Devonshire's little raid happened to hit the only piece of line so fortified.'

'They couldn't, surely,' Tenny said.

'Of course they could. So could we, if we got down to it. And you know as well as I why we don't. They,' he shrugged bitterly towards the dark countryside at their backs, where their superiors slept in safety, 'they don't believe in letting us get comfortable. *They* still believe we're going to climb out of these stinking ditches at any moment and make some bloody great charge back into the last century, bugles blowing, flags waving and everyone grinning his effing head off, oh jolly hockeysticks!' Johnny wavered, covered his angry mouth with one hand, belched abruptly and said, 'Pardon,' stiffly. 'Must be sick,' he added, and walked to the roadside and proceeded to vomit into the ditch.

When he had recovered, Tenny said, 'Did this information get anywhere? I mean, aside from trench gossip.'

'The captain of the company involved dutifully reported to his CO. And beyond that, mate, I do not know.'

'Yes, I see,' Tenny said. 'Well then, I assume it will be taken note of.'

'Oh yes. And somebody will write it all down somewhere and then wipe their damned arse with it. And come summer, you and I and every bloody Jock in the regiment are going over the top and Jerry is going to wait for us down in his neat little electric lighted palace in the ground, and come up just in time to blow our heads off. God rot the staff.'

'Easy does it, mate,' Tenny said casually, but with a hint of warning. Johnny took nothing back. They reached the mouth of the communications trench and Tenny entered the space between its low walls whose height would increase as they approached the Front.

'Stuff it,' Johnny said abruptly, his voice slurred now more by cynical ill-humour than drink. 'I'm sticking to the road. Sick of bloody ditches.'

'You'll be sicker still with a chunk of lead in your gut. Don't be an idiot, man.'

'Look,' Johnny said, facing Tenny sullenly, 'I've been two years out here now, in case you've forgotten, and with all due respect to your superior rank and age and all that, I do know what I'm doing.'

'I think,' Tenny said mildly, 'that the army ought to produce a rubber stamp of that phrase. For gravestones.'

'Ha, bloody ha. Anyhow, the road's in the clear for the next half-mile. It's just a shortcut. Joins up with the trench system behind that old ruined piggery. Off you go, mate,' he waved towards the trench entrance. 'I'll be in Scotland afore ye.'

He grinned in the dark and turned his back. Tenny cursed softly, shrugged, entered the trench, walked fifty yards, cursed again, and turned, running lightly back to the road. 'Where the hell are you, Bruce?' he shouted.

'Right here,' Johnny answered at once. He was sitting on the dyke at the edge of the road, a dim shape in the starlight. 'Thought you'd be back. Never could resist a dare, could you?'

Tenny muttered inaudibly under his breath, as they began walking up the grass-grown stretch of unused road. Finally he said, 'Actually, I happen to be rather fond of the young woman you just married and I'd not like to see her a widow. Even though her husband doesn't seem to care much one way or the other.'

'Now look,' Johnny said belligerently. 'Don't start that. And just leave Rebecca out, just clear out of all this. Nothing to do with her.' But he was well aware that every clash between them for the last two years had been essentially about Rebecca.

They walked on stiffly, Johnny fuming and Tenny watching carefully, side to side. He was aware they were approaching the point where the road rose slightly on to an embankment, and exposed its travellers to the view of the enemy line. The distance was great, an observer unlikely, but one attentive sniper was all that was needed.

A waning moon appeared out of the thin clouds and disappeared, leaving them once more with the thinner light of stars. An owl called, a soft lonely sound that reminded Tenny of home. He listened a while, as they walked, to the slow repeated pattern of quavering notes. After a while they stopped and he imagined the owl with its prey.

Johnny said suddenly, sounding quite sober, 'Bad luck, you know, hearing an owl before ten.'

In the silence, Tenny waited for the owl again, wondering if it was as distant as the German line. As they walked he was aware of the click of their boots echoing loudly. He tried to move more quietly, thinking of the hill, and stalking, and the sudden silence of birds. Then he heard the click of the rifle-bolt on the night air and shouted, 'Down,' and flung himself forward, his arms around Johnny Bruce's waist, bringing him down in a thudding tackle on to the grass-grown cobbles as the crack of the rifle-shot shook the darkness, and lead whistled over their heads.

'Good Christ,' Johnny whispered. 'You were quick.'

'Shut up,' Tenny said, listening, waiting for the next shot. It came at once, and the ground kicked up near them as something rang off the stone wall. 'He's still seeing us. Get over under the lee of the wall.'

They went snake-style across the cobbles. The unkind moon came out of the clouds, lighting the road and casting only the thinnest of shadows by the dyke at its side. They rolled into it, as the sniper fired again and again, with surprising accuracy in the faint light.

'Damn the sod, he can bloody well shoot,' Johnny whispered.

'Well, run across and give him a commendation. Blast you and your shortcut. I thought you knew it was safe. Out of sight, and all that.'

'Actually,' Johnny whispered, ducking at another low shot, 'I wouldn't know. Never used it before, old man. It was the Devonshires mentioned it.'

'You idiot, they lost two men to snipers last week.'

'Hmm, yes. Recall now they mentioned that as well. Sorry, old man, seems I've got you in rather a pickle.'

'Not exactly for the first time,' Tenny said, fuming, 'if you'll recall.'

Half an hour later, they were still there. The night had cleared, and the gibbous moon risen high lit the roadway and narrowed their protective shadow further. The distant sniper was in control. Tenny imagined him, snugly wrapped in a treetop blind, his eyes well accustomed to the dim light and the position of his prey exactly marked, so that their slightest move was instantly answered with a shot. He had only to wait until dawn.

'Will the moon be down before first light?' Tenny whispered.

Johnny turned slightly, on to his back, gauging its height and the hours until dawn. The sky was starlit and clear, the protective wisps of cloud had all deserted them. 'Doubt it. Should be quite low, in the last hour, maybe behind those trees. Suppose we'll have to break for it then.' He sounded discouraged and sober. The prospect of spending the rest of the night in the cold shadow of the dyke was not appealing. Nor, however, was the prospect of being shot. 'Sorry about this, you know,' he said, sounding genuine.

'I only hope,' Tenny said slowly, 'it doesn't occur to them to bring up a Maxim. Spray the whole roadway.'

'Think he'll do that?'

'It's what I'd do. No sense waiting all night. Finish the job and go to bed.'

Johnny was silent, studying the landscape as thoroughly as his prone position would allow. He crept a foot from the shadow of the wall and raised his head for a better look and was rewarded with the immediate explosion of a rifle-shot. He flattened himself, and crept back in against the dyke. 'Damned Hun efficiency. Regular as clockwork.'

'And effective,' Tenny reminded, with respect. He said then, 'Why don't you just stay still and wait for the moon to go down? Wriggling about's just going to get your arse shot off.' But then there was another shot, and with a sudden jolt Tenny knew lying still wasn't the answer. 'Blast,' he said.

'He's wasting ammunition,' Johnny muttered.

'It's not him. That one was from the other side. There's two of them, working together. Like,' he said, suddenly chilled, 'wolves.'

There was another shot, closer, as the new sniper found his range. The moonlight suddenly seemed brighter, the dyke lower, its shadow as flimsy and narrow as a ribbon of silk.

'We've got to run,' Tenny said at once. 'I'll try for that line of tree-stumps on the other side. There's almost always a ditch by these roads. Then I'll cover you from there.'

'What if there isn't a ditch?'

'Then you try somewhere else, after, mate. And the best of

luck,' he added grimly.

'I'll go,' Johnny said.

'Hero-time?'.

'Stuff it, Tenny. My fault we're here.'

'Precisely. And my command. Responsibility falls on the top.'

'Not in this war, that I've noticed,' Johnny whispered, and ducked as a third shot from the new sniper parted the moonlit grass.

'Well, let's start a fucking Maclaren tradition. Here I go, mate, kiss that pretty wife of yours for me.' He got up on his haunches, like a sprinter in a race, hunched down into the shadow. 'Fling a shot over the dyke, just to give them something to think about,' he said, and Johnny, revolver ready, waited.

'Here goes,' Tenny said, the sweaty palms of his hands flat down on the ground, his legs bunched under him. 'Hey jolly hockeysticks.' He leapt up and ran, stretching his long legs like a racehorse, feeling beneath his feet the memory of every finish of every Highland games, before him the phantom of a dozen winners' tapes. Johnny's pistol-shot cracked behind him, and was answered with a flurry of rapid firing, so rapid he thought for an instant they'd brought up their machine-gun after all. The cobbles rang with ricocheting lead. But he was not hit. The distance to the line of stumps and the imagined ditch seemed impossibly long, the cobbles dragged at his feet, like the quicksands of a nightmare. Another shot whistled by and then an explosion seemed to echo through his head. His left leg was slammed from under him as by a hammer. As he fell he envisaged the gorge of the River Glass, its grey and hungry water waiting for him, and he flung his body desperately forward, over the line of stumps. He tumbled headlong into the faithful ditch. 'Jesus Christ,' he whispered. He had never felt such pain; his whole leg went numb with it. Far, far away, Johnny was shouting,

'Are you all right? Are you there?'

He wanted to jest, through the pain, but only gasped out, 'Here. Here.' Then the first wave of agony receded, and his mind cleared. 'Wait, I'll give you cover.' He struggled to reach his revolver, and to turn in the ditch, deep and water-filled, to clamber to the lip. His leg was a useless, wooden thing he dragged after him. He realized he was a good half-mile from any safety, and he couldn't walk. Then he remembered that Johnny

Bruce had lost every race they had ever run. The day on the River Glass came back as he struggled to right his body against the crumbling wall of the drainage ditch. Johnny had missed his leap, luck and Tenny's flailing arm had saved him. Luck could not be so kind twice.

'I'm coming,' Johnny shouted.

'No.' Tenny found his voice alarmingly weak. He must be losing blood. 'No,' he shouted back. 'Not ready.' He raised the pistol, aiming high, knowing the sniper was totally out of range, and shouted, 'No, don't.' But the clatter of boots told him Johnny had not waited, and immediately on it came a rapid burst of rifle-fire. Too rapid, too many rifles. Oh God, he thought, more of them. Where had they come from? He waited for Johnny's cry of pain, and the sound of a body falling, but the footsteps kept miraculously coming, and with them an added burst of rifle-fire, from behind him. He froze. They were surrounded; they weren't on the road at all, but out in no-man's-land, and the Bosche had come out, a whole party surrounded them. Johnny's feet rang on the road kerb and his body loomed large, blotting out the moonlight and crashing down into the ditch on top of Tenny who cried aloud with pain.

'Damn you clumsy sod.'

'Sorry pal,' Johnny was grinning, crouching already in the ditch, pleased with himself. Then there were two more sharp reports behind them and the grin faded.

'Good God. Where are they?'

'Everywhere,' Tenny gasped, holding his leg. 'We've had it, mate.'

Johnny seemed to regain sense, easing out of the exhilaration of his run. He peered at Tenny in the moonlight. 'You hit?'

'Bloody leg.' Tenny shook his head. 'No matter. Nowhere to run to anyhow.' He drew himself up to a sitting position and braced his back against the ditch, his revolver levelled at its lip. 'You take that side, I'll take this. And keep count. Meet you in hell,' Tenny winced suddenly as the leg pained again. 'See if you're any better at Bosche than you ever were at grouse.'

Johnny stiffened, listening. Tenny's meaning slowly sank in, punctuated by another rifle-shot. The shots were high; they'd not found their new hiding-place yet. No matter, dawn would serve their interests perfectly. 'How in Christ's name did they get behind us?' he muttered, mystified.

Tenny shook his head. Answering was painful, and he had no answer. Somehow they must have blundered through their own line. He knew it was impossible, but it was the only explanation, and he believed eerily the superstition he'd heard the men tell: that in the night the lines of barbed wire sometimes mysteriously vanished, as though time and distance could come undone.

'Sorry I landed on you,' Johnny whispered suddenly. 'Must have hurt.'

'No matter.'

'I'm sorry.' He started to say something else, but stopped. 'Just wanted you to know I'm sorry.'

'I knew that,' Tenny said gently and the anger he had carried for months slipped away silently, like moonshadow. 'Wish they'd come,' he said.

As if in answer, there was a scuffle behind him, and Johnny instantly raised his revolver, bracing himself.

'Dinna fire,' a voice called, in Scots.

'Oldest trick in the book,' Johnny shouted back.

'Maclarens?' the voice called. Johnny hesitated. The voice sounded genuine. But the guttural Scots tongue was easy prey for the German imitator. And it was common enough for the Bosche to name the regiment they faced.

Johnny turned to Tenny, but Tenny, propping himself up against the wall, suddenly shouted, 'What's the name of the colonel's daughter?'

'He's nae got a dochter. Onlie a son.'

'Where the hell have you been so long?' Tenny shouted back. There was a mutter of laughter and a sudden running scuffle from the field beyond and a dark form launched over the dyke and into the ditch beside them with a dull splash of muddy water.

'An' whit, sir,' the voice said, 'were you doin' awa' oot here?'

'Keep your head down,' Johnny said. 'There're two snipers across the road.'

'No' ony mair,' said the voice and Tenny, through a growing dimness, recognized Pat McGarrity. 'Me an' five o' the boys hae seen tae them. We heard a' the shootin' on oor way back frae the concert. Thocht we maun hae a luik.' He studied the two officers, obviously seeking an explanation for their presence in this unlikely place. Realizing he wasn't going to get one, he set about applying a field dressing to Tenny's thigh, saying only, 'Juist as weel we did.'

'Mr Bruce,' Tenny said formally, 'I'd like you to meet a friend of mine. Pat McGarrity, Johnny Bruce.'

'*Pat* McGarrity?' Johnny said slowly, the name sinking in.

'Aye, sir,' Pat said, still bandaging Tenny's leg, 'I think I've met yer sister, yince or twice.' He was smiling to himself, his hands busy with his work, his sharp, cynical eyes masked by the dim light of the moon.

15

'Emma.' She awoke to the memory of the sound. Had someone really called her? She stirred slowly in her narrow campbed, and peered about the tent. The light was faint grey at the first trace of dawn, and she could just make out the sleeping shapes around her. She had dreamed so many times that Torquil was in a dark rain beyond her door, calling her name. And in the dream, she knew he was doomed, and yet she was unable to answer.

Emma swung her bare legs over the side of the bed, and rubbed her thick, tangled hair. She was unused to its new lightness. A few weeks before, finding it lice-ridden yet again, she had chopped it off short and had cast her auburn curls unceremoniously into the rubbish fire behind their tent. She drew on her dressing-gown, and sat, still dream-entangled. There had been a time when that dream had come every night. Lately she had been free of it, but its return plunged her back into her old sorrow.

She had dressed and was making up her flat mattress and three blankets when she distinctly heard the voice call again, 'Emma,' a little louder than before. A shudder ran through her.

'I don't believe in ghosts,' she said, aloud, startling herself. The voice again called her name, as if in answer. She trembled as much with cold as with sudden fear. She went to the entrance of the tent, and pulled the heavy flap aside to peer into the dawn. A man was standing at the gate in the fence that surrounded their little compound of belltents, ablutions hut, and tiny mess hall.

'Who is it?' Emma called in a hoarse whisper. 'What do you want?'

'Emma? Oh thank God, I thought you'd never hear.'

Emma's fear dissolved in sudden amazement, and she laughed and ran to him. With the gate yet between them, they embraced. 'Harry,' she cried, 'whyever did you stand away out here. I barely heard you at all.'

'I was so afraid I'd awaken everyone and give them all a terrible fright if I came any closer.'

'You gave me a terrible fright. I thought I was dreaming. I thought you were a ghost.'

He laughed and tousled her hair, delighted as before with the strange free feel of it without its guardian hairpins. 'Dreadfully sorry, I'm sure. Here,' he said, opening the gate, 'shall I come in, or will you come out?'

'I'll come,' she said, slipping through the gate and linking her arm through his. 'We'll get coffee at the Cantine,' and then as they walked she said, 'Were you on the night shift? Why are you here?'

'No. No, actually, this is my time off. I'm supposed to be sleeping. But I had to see you. You see, we're away tomorrow.'

'Away?'

'Yes, they're shifting the lot of us, three crews, and vehicles. Down to the Somme district. Looks like the rumours are right, and the big push is on for the Somme.'

'Oh,' Emma said, swallowing the word, 'I see.' She felt a great loneliness descend, as if he were already gone. She had not known until that moment what his presence at Bar-le-Duc and their occasional meetings had meant to her. 'I shall miss you,' she said.

'Oh Emma, shall you?' His arm, linked through hers, suddenly tightened, and he turned then to face her, taking both her forearms in his strong, long-fingered hands. He studied her face carefully, as if whatever answer she made must be assessed visually as well. She nodded, and felt, to her amazement, the pressure of tears. She turned away.

He was silent for a while, as if uncertain of what he had seen. He said, 'I'm sorry I never got to meet your friend Scottie.'

'Yes,' she said, preoccupied. 'He will be as well. I told him so much about you. He was very interested.'

'Can't see why,' Harry said, laughing. 'I've hardly made my mark in the world.'

She smiled. She wanted to say something complimentary, something that expressed what she thought of him, but found the words difficult and too intimate and said, instead, 'Actually, he was terribly interested in all of us, Bruces and Maclarens. Once I told him my name. You see, I knew him for three weeks before he knew my last name. And do you know,' she added laughing, 'I still don't know his.' They were in the big, empty cobbled square of the Place de la Gare, and walked with quickening steps towards the friendly glow of the windows of the Cantine Anglais. 'Everyone just calls him Scottie. It seems enough. I told him about Susan and her . . . problem. He seemed very understanding. I had the feeling he thought she should be allowed her own choice. I mean about the Church.'

'He would, wouldn't he?' Harry said, mildly cynical. 'They stick together.'

'Oh, I suppose. Still he rather jumped on me when I said I thought it was all because of this man, the ranker. He said only Susan and God could know that.'

'A logical deduction,' Harry said with his small quirky smile, 'if one didn't happen to know Susan. I'm afraid we all do. Rather too well at that. My God, do you remember that business with Moira Sinclair? And that other time when . . . oh no, Susan and God, that would be a deadly combination. Coffee, my dear, or chocolate?'

'Oh, coffee. At this hour. Nevertheless, I will pass on your regrets to Scottie. I am sorry, too. I know you two would enjoy each other. In the funniest way he reminds me of you. Oh, he's not so stunningly cynical about everything, but he does have precisely the same way of taking the stuffiness out of life.'

'Never,' said Harry with the same quirky smile.

Later, when it was time to go, Emma said, 'Will you be able to see Tenny?'

'I'll try. Unless they've sent him down to one of the base hospitals. The letter came from a Casualty Clearing Station, just behind their own lines. Sounded like he got off light. In fact, from what Johnny wrote Grandmother, I have the feeling getting shot is going to be the least of old Ten's troubles. Seems he and the boy were mucking about in a faintly inebriated state some place where they shouldn't have been in the first place. Gather Uncle

Gordon's less than pleased. Still, he may choose to overlook; apparently they were celebrating wee Donald's arrival at the time.'

Emma smiled. 'I'm glad he's all right. Give him my love if you see him. Silly old sausage, I do rather love him, you know.'

Harry only smiled that small, world-wise smile that she realized she had grown very fond of. They said goodbye to the girls of the Cantine Anglais and walked across the square to the Ambulance Depot, in the growing light. There were people about now, and the privacy of the dawn had left them. They no longer linked arms, but walked side by side, separated in the clear grey light.

They parted formally, with clasped hands and promises of letters, and Harry turned and walked away across the cobblestones, leaving Emma achingly alone in the dawn. He had gone thirty feet when he stopped, and swept by a rare sudden impulse, turned. She was still standing where he had left her, her hand still half raised from her farewell, seeming to lean towards him in the dim spring air. The impulse grew into a strong, illogical urge, a phantom intruder in his orderly life, that came as powerfully as it came rarely. He started to walk back towards her, and as she watched, unmoving, he broke into a run which startled her into response. She was stepping forward, both hands extended, when he reached her, wrapping her around in arms made bulky with the weight of his greatcoat. He pulled her close, his hands crossed behind her back, the breadth of them and length of the fingers covering her slender shoulders. He lowered his head over hers, his cheek against her soft hair, clinging to her with the breathless strength of desperation. 'Emma, I love you,' he said, realizing, in the saying of it, that it was true.

She never said anything, only nodded, smiling, wiping tears from her face, from his, and gesturing towards the railway station and the distant sound of hissing steam. The cry of the whistle saved them from the awkwardness of words. He turned, grinning, she laughing, and they both waved, as he ran, and flung useless phrases of parting like mementoes.

'Write!'

'Of course. Give Tenny my love.'

'Regards to everyone. Home . . .' He was waving from the station doorway, remembering her leave was due.

'Take care.'

'And you . . .' She blew a kiss on the last words, but the doorway was empty of him, and the train beyond was puffing away. Half of her hoped he'd miss it, and return, the other half, satiated with the sudden surprise of love, wanted him away, for now, so that she might, in solitude, absorb slowly this new unimagined pleasure.

He did not return. The train had taken him, and as she walked back to the depot her mind dwelt on the lengthening distance between her and this man who but moments before had held and touched her. If someone had asked her, right then, what was the meaning of the word 'war' she would have known the answer at once: it was that feeling, prickling over one's skin like the touch of a ghost, of parting; the few minutes when the touch, and sight, and smell of a person remain in their absence like the afterlight of the sun upon one's closed eyes. So it had always been with Torquil. So now, suddenly, it was with Harry. For the first time the memory of her dead fiancé was devoid of pain.

'I'm in love with Harry Bruce,' she said, softly, in her solitude. The thought stunned her, and filled her in its afterwash with glowing warmth that stayed with her throughout the long hard day. Even the sights and sounds of the château hospital could not divest her of her cloak of happiness, such, she acknowledged in awe, was the brutal resilience of the human spirit. She felt no shame; she had paid her share of tribute to misery and felt she owed it no more.

It was on the evening of that same, treasured day, that Susan's letter came. Susan's timing, theatrical creature that she was, was as always, perfect, if only by the chancy hand of His Majesty's Active Service Mails. It began:

> Dearest Emma,
>
> Oh how can I dare to approach you, you who have suffered such sorrows, with my trivial complaints. And yet, dear Emma, to whom else can I turn?

Emma read on, with a whimsical sense of *déjà vu* turning the corners of her wide mouth into a half-smile. She winced, patting the coldsore that the chill winds and poor diet had given her. She sighed, wondering why it was always to herself that her flightier sisters turned. First Rebecca, now Susan; she smiled again indulgently, enduring the small prick of pain. She accepted, with neither pride nor resentment, their tacit assumption of her superior maturity. It was true. She was, and always would be, years older than either of them. 'Oh Susan,' she sighed to herself, when she had laid the letter on the coarse khaki blanket of her campbed, 'what are we to do with you?'

'Perhaps,' said Scottie, the following day when Emma asked him precisely that question, 'perhaps nothing at all.'

'Nothing? Do you mean we should simply allow her to go ahead with it?' Emma was faintly incredulous. And then thinking quickly, trying to follow the circuitous route of Scottie's own thoughts, she said, 'Or do you mean that if we simply ignore her, she'll lose interest? Like a child campaigning for some foolish toy.'

'If,' Scottie said, swinging the wheel of the rattly Ford ambulance to avoid the wreck of a wagon, 'she is childish, then no doubt that will happen. If on the other hand she is a woman, and in love, then she will marry him.' He paused, negotiating a narrow space between a half-crumbled stone wall and a broken-down motor lorry. 'You've been in love, surely now you understand. Give her your blessing. And your support. It sounds as if she needs some.'

'Oh, but even if that were right, what good can it do? I'm only her friend. It must be up to her grandparents and they are dead set against it.'

Scottie did not reply, but lapsed into a silence which he did not break until they had reached their destination, accepted their load of wounded and were ready to start on the return journey. And then, as Emma climbed into the rear of the ambulance between the stretchers, he said only, 'Join me for dinner tonight. In that little café, near the Place de la Gare. And we'll talk.'

The café was nearly empty, when they met that night. To Emma its small tables with their red-checked cloths, and rough, home-made candles, and the rain-streaked windowpanes, instantly brought back memories of Harry. They were served a dish of chicken cooked with onions and carrots and Scottie ordered a bottle of wine, which they shared as they ate.

'Your friend, Harry,' he said later. 'He has gone?'

'Yes,' Emma said, smiling quietly to herself, looking down at her plate.

'You love him?'

'Yes.'

'How nice to be young.'

'In this awful time?' she said earnestly.

'In any time,' he said, 'and you know it. You said that because you are happy and are afraid I'd find it unseemly. Was that not so?'

'It was so.' Emma looked down shyly.

'Grasp your moments, lass. Time is flying. For you. For your Susan. For us all.' He refilled both their glasses from the bottle on the table, raised his own, and drank slowly. 'To love in the midst of war,' he said. Then he rose, and they went together out into the rain.

In the morning, he was already warming up the engine of the mud-splattered, road-worn vehicle when she arrived, and was singing to himself gaily over the noise of it. He nodded and winked when she climbed into the seat beside him, but immediately got down and wandered around to the back of the vehicle, securing the canvas, heaving something heavy inside, giving the narrow rubber tyres a kick. He was still humming when he returned, and when she shouted, 'Shall I drive?' he nodded affably. His mind seemed on something else entirely. Emma climbed down and walked round the vehicle and climbed back up to the driver's seat. Confidently she swung the heavy wheel around and drove out of the depot, cheered as always by her own mastery of the often recalcitrant machine.

Once out on the rutted, torn roadway, making towards Verdun, Scottie began to sing. He sang all of 'Tipperary', including some appalling sentimental verses concocted by the music-halls, and then launched, without a pause for breath, into 'Take Me Back to Dear Old Blighty', beating time with his hand on the wooden dashboard. Emma smiled and waited, and then when he had finished he began at once to tell her a long story about a trapper and a bear in the Klondyke.

A stray shell whistled overhead and they both ducked beneath their canvas roof, instinctively. It was distant, and not a threat. The road was safer these days, as the German offensive faltered under courageous French counter-attacks. German advances in early March had met fierce resistance; the appalling casualties that had racked the French defenders began to befall the attackers as well. The surety of capturing Verdun faded and the battleground was becoming, like others before it, a place of stalemate and attrition. The threat was not gone, but it was lessened, and already the fickle eye of the war was turning north and west, towards the Somme.

The change was almost imperceptible. There was a slight easing of the perpetual bombardment of the road, a barely discernible lessening of numbers at the château hospital at Le Petit Monthairon, a faint, ethereal flickering of hope in the eyes of the exhausted French soldiery. Yet all could be, they knew, wiped out at once, by a single fierce attack, and Verdun could yet fall. There was only one real hope, and that rested far away where Emma's father and brothers awaited their orders, on the Somme.

Another shell whistled over, and exploded in a nearby field, casting up a column of black earth and dust. 'Finding his range,' Scottie said, without expression. Emma opened her mouth to speak a question, but Scottie said suddenly, 'Next one'll hit the road.' She looked across nervously, forgetting what she meant to say. Scottie had such authority, she imagined he could even predict the fall of shells. What he could predict, actually, was a pattern of shortening trajectories. A third shell came screaming across from the German lines, and, exactly as Scottie had said, crashed down on to the roadway fifty yards ahead. There was another huge column of dust and smoke, but when that had cleared, the only apparent casualty was another ambulance, which, although not directly hit, had been blown off the road by the explosion, and rested now at a tilted angle against the blackened shattered trunk of a once mighty tree.

When Scottie and Emma reached the scene, the driver was standing supported by his partner, dazed, in the roadway, dabbing at his bloody forehead with the sleeve of his tunic. While Scottie attended to him, Emma hastened to the rear of the vehicle, where the cries of the wounded within were heart-rending. She climbed into the narrow space between the stretchers, checking each of the patients, whose old pains were renewed but who apparently had suffered no new injury. She spoke gently to them in her limited French, assuring them that they were safe and would soon be on their way once more. Then she climbed down and assisted Scottie and the still confused, concussed driver and his partner to tip the vehicle back on to its wheels, and carefully eased it once more on to the cobbled road. Scottie climbed up and started the engine, and the driver, his cut head neatly bandaged by Emma, climbed into the passenger seat insisting that he was all right, while his partner took the wheel.

They had pulled out on to the road and were some twenty feet away when Scottie suddenly ran after them, signalling to the driver, who, puzzled, slowed his vehicle to a halt.

'Take my partner with you,' he shouted. 'She's a nurse.'

'We're okay, pal,' the driver called, grinning a big American grin. 'But I'll take her anyhow, with thanks,' he added, the grin acknowledging Emma's pretty face. 'Thought you'd want to hang on to that one.' He was still grinning, still jesting, but Scottie was insistent.

'They don't need me,' Emma spoke up suddenly. 'And you can't manage alone.'

But Scottie had her elbow gripped in his big hand and he was hastening her towards the homeward-bound vehicle as if she were a sack of potatoes he wanted suddenly to be rid of. She was annoyed, and protested, 'Scottie, they don't need me. Now please let's be on our way.'

'You're going with them,' he said, and when she turned she saw his big jovial face set into surprisingly hard lines, as the image of another, earlier and far harder man emerged beneath his good-natured countenance.

'What's the matter with you?' she cried, embarrassed, because the driver of the other ambulance was laughing aloud now.

'In the back, lass. The lads have had a rough ride. Cheer them up a bit.' He was grinning again, but the grin was hollow.

'Scottie, I want to come with you,' Emma said suddenly, no longer angry, but oddly afraid.

But he had turned and was walking rapidly away. Emma crouched in the back beneath the torn canvas cover, patting the hand of one French boy who plucked at her sleeve for comfort, watching as Scottie's big shape dwindled as they drove away. She saw him climb to the seat, and turn, leaning out, and wave a big broad hand of farewell. Then he too pulled out on to the Sacred Way, and she could hear him singing,

'Then up the stairs and into bed, parlez-vous . . .'

She heard the whistle of the shell, gathering from far off, like the sound of a growing wind. Helpless, she crouched between the stretchers, as the French soldiers, who heard it also, moaned their fright. She clasped the white hand of the boy who had plucked at her sleeve. 'It's all right,' she said, with certainty. 'It won't hit us.'

The whistle rose to a shriek as the shell arched downwards, and it met the earth at the point where Scottie's rattly old ambulance chose to fly into the sky. Distinctly Emma saw the pieces of it take wing, soar over the trees, and then the whole vanished into a massive fountain of blackness and dust. Falling earth pelted the canvas roof above her, and a piece of splintered wood tore a hole in the vehicle's side. The ambulance shuddered to a halt, and Emma, still staring numbly into the swirling dustcloud, heard the sound of running feet.

'You all right?' The American driver, a thin boy with an overweight moustache, was peering into the dusty interior.

Emma looked about her, still wordless, her trained mind assessing the condition of her patients. They were babbling in French, but unharmed. She nodded.

'Afraid your partner . . .'

'I know.'

'Want to go back?' the American boy asked gently.

'No. There's no point,' Emma replied, calmly. There was a hole in the ground eight feet wide and three feet deep where the road, and Scottie's ambulance, had been. She remembered Bob Spalding, and Scottie's roadside prayers. She had no inclination to pray and was too honest to fabricate one. The American boy was already climbing up to his seat, and the vehicle slowly pulled away. Emma, still on her knees on the floor, stared at the empty hole in the ground that was Scottie's grave.

She wept, quietly, and did not disturb her charges, on the road home to Revigny.

16

Tenny Maclaren awoke, late in the morning, to the distant sound of a cuckoo calling in the hazel wood by the river. He sat up suddenly in bed. Sunlight was streaming thinly through a parting in the heavy draperies that moved in the breeze. The sight and sound were at once infinitely familiar, and tremendously remote. The faint pain in his leg, the one reminder of the Front, jogged his memory and brought him back to where he was, almost miraculously. He was home in Culbrech House, waking late on a sunny June morning, as he had done throughout his life, and had not done for two long years. He rose, testing the leg, and walked with a slight limp, barefoot across the soft carpet to the window where, drawing aside the velvet drape, he gazed out over the lawns and gardens to the greening hills beyond. He had forgotten how rich, green and lush it could be at the end of spring.

Tenny raised the sash further and leaned out and drank in the air. It no longer made him cough. It was almost worth the still painful wound in his thigh, just to be here, once more.

The leg wound alone would never have got him sent home. But although the leg healed, he developed, within days of arriving at the base hospital, a mild lung infection, as commonly occurred. Two days later, he awoke in the night gasping for breath, and the next fortnight was swallowed up by a life-and-death struggle against pneumonia. A further fortnight passed, and he was on his way home for convalescence. The incident had shaken him; both the closeness of death, and its sheer insidiousness. For the first time in his young life he was made fully aware that death could actually affect him, and like a sniper, it was unfair and unpredictable. Still, he was young and essentially strong, and after a week of home, rest and good food, felt so robustly healthy that he regarded himself as a shirker, and was already campaigning against doctor's orders to be allowed to rejoin his battalion. The spring was slipping by, and word had filtered back to all concerned that the big push for which they would be fully ready only by midsummer had been forced forward by the precarious situation at Verdun. The date, of course, was yet a mystery to a lowly company commander but Tenny knew it would be soon and wanted only to be back among his men and in readiness.

Still, when he dressed and went downstairs for a late and luxurious breakfast, he did so determined to hide his restlessness behind a cloak of demonstrative relaxation. His mother, he knew, could never understand his eagerness to be back in that place that he would not talk about, and her relief in having him briefly home and safe was obvious. No one at home could ever understand the complex guilt that shrouded every pleasurable act. How could one drink coffee from a glistening china cup, relax before a crackling fire, sleep, clean and louse-free, beneath crisply pressed sheets, while all the while one's friends, companions, brothers were still out there? It was one of the war's great ironies that while every waking moment at the Front was ticked off on a mental tally sheet as one moment closer to one's next leave, still when that leave at last came, each hour of it was eaten up by remorse, until the awful divide between civilian and front-line life threatened to rive one's soul in half. They had, all of them, taken misery for a mistress and found her a most unforgiving dame.

Tenny bluffed his way well through breakfast, allowing his mother ample scope to fuss over him, remembering to send special praise to Mrs Murchison in the kitchen for her sautéed kidneys, a dish whose richness had once delighted him but which now, after years of sparse diet, he found daunting. He smiled at the girl who served the meal, a stranger, as so many about the house now were, and she blushed appropriately. But after breakfast, when a chance remark by Victoria reminded him that today was the occasion of the christening of Gordon's baby son, a very major social event which had still completely slipped his mind, he felt himself descend into a kind of exhausted panic.

Once clear of the dining-room, he bolted for the door. He had to be outside and alone. Halfway down the drive he recollected that he had taken no coat, and worried about it, and then drew himself up angrily. If he started worrying about his health he'd be an old man in half a year. He felt far better anyhow, just out-of-doors, and realized with a jolt that he had become unaccustomed to a roof and found it restrictive and strange.

He walked down the half-mile-long driveway, and when he came to the road, turned westwards, towards Cluanie. In his haste to leave the house he had also forgotten to change his shoes, and those he wore were better suited to the drawing-room than to fields and moorland. He was sorry at first; the hills looked gentle and inviting in the strong spring sunlight. But the leg rather rapidly began giving him pain and he found himself weaker than he had expected. He turned and set out doggedly back towards the Culbrech driveway, limping again, and stopping occasionally to catch his breath. The sound of pony hoofs behind him, and the creak and rumble of a trap, were welcome. He did not turn. Although he hoped that a ride would be offered, he would not ask.

A young woman drove the trap. She was faintly puzzled by the sight of what she took to be an elderly man ahead of her on the road. For though he walked with the uncertain, shuffling gait of the old, he was tall and well-built, and was dressed like a country gentleman, not a crofter. The man paused again, raised his right hand to his forehead, and inadvertently knocked off his flat green tweed cap. As he bent to retrieve it, keeping one leg stiffly straight, she was startled by a sudden flash of bright red hair. He re-covered it, at once, with the cap, and started on his painful way and the young woman, with a startled cry, urged her pony into a trot. It closed the distance between them, but the man never turned and she, quite certain now, shouted out.

'Tenny, Tenny Maclaren.'

He turned slowly, recognition obstructed both by tiredness and the unlikely situation.

'Tenny, don't you know me?' she said, in a whisper.

'Oh my God. Rebecca. Rebecca Galloway.'

'Bruce,' she said with a small, cautious smile. 'Rebecca Bruce.' The correction passed by unnoticed. Tenny stumbled to the side of the trap, to embrace her, as she leaned down from the high seat. Each of them was so shaken by seeing the other that neither thought for a moment of the immense impropriety of their public greeting.

Fortunately, the road was empty and only the Culbrech rooks watched down from the bright green of the blossoming ash trees.

'Oh Tenny, you should never be out here,' she said.

'I'm all right,' he said with a gruffness meant more for himself than for her. Then he said, 'I wouldn't mind a ride home, though,' and grinned, 'Shall I drive?'

She nodded, relieved, and handed him the reins and whip as he climbed awkwardly on to the seat of the trap. He relaxed gratefully a moment, and then called up the small dappled pony.

'I didn't even know you were up north at all, my dear,' he said, studying her face, wanting to ask questions that he felt he mustn't.

She shook her head impatiently. 'Well, I shouldn't be here at all. I never would have come, but Matron insisted, and I'm afraid when Matron insists one has little choice.'

'Have you been ill?' he asked, concern overriding good manners. 'I mean, you look . . . of course, you're still quite marvellously lovely . . .'

'But I look like a washerwoman. I know. It was nothing, Tenny. A touch of bronchitis. As I said, I never would have come home on my own. But Matron rather panicked for some silly reason, and telephoned Mrs Bruce. Now that I'm a married woman, apparently I'm not bright enough to make my own decisions.'

'But if you were ill . . .'

'Tenny, we're *all* ill, all of the time. It's impossible not to be. There's infection everywhere. Our living conditions are medieval, and the hours are far too long. That's not a complaint, please, just a fact. If every VAD with a touch of bronchitis went home the hospitals would shut down. I think frankly Matron believes married girls are a waste of time. No doubt she thought I was probably . . .' She stopped suddenly.

Tenny, bemused by her rebellious impatience with bodily weakness, an impatience he was aware mirrored his own, said, 'My dear, you aren't?'

'Pregnant?' she burst out. 'No. Of course not.' She was so vehement that he drew back in confusion and apologized.

'No, it's my fault. Forgive me, Tenny. I'm terribly touchy these days. I really don't know why. Do tell, how are you? I wanted so to come and see you when I heard you were home, but of course . . .' She did not finish, and he, thinking that her touchiness was no doubt due to an illness that deserved more credit than she was giving it, said gently,

'Do you know, they didn't even tell me you were here. Now, why didn't Mother say? I'm frankly appalled. It must have seemed incalculably rude of me, not even telephoning, but I honestly didn't know. I shall let Mother know precisely how I feel, I assure you.'

'No.' She looked away from him. 'Please, Tenny. Don't. You see, I think,' she paused, embarrassed, not sure how to continue, and finally burst out, 'Oh, they're such awful fools. They still think I'm some sort of terrible threat to you. Even now. Even now that I'm a married woman.'

Tenny fumed, and maintained it was absolute rubbish, but she said only, gently, 'Please, don't let's waste our few minutes together being angry, even at them. It's been so terribly long.'

He slowed the trap and the pony ambled to a lazy halt beneath the rich dark light of the beech trees in the Culbrech driveway. 'Isn't it a laugh,' he said, turning to face her. 'We're out there fighting a war to hold their civilization together, and when we come home they still treat us like children. My God, I feel so old,' he added, his smile fading.

She reached for his hand. 'I know,' she said, anxiously studying his face. 'We all do. Oh Tenny, do you remember the day we met, here, and how I went sailing by you in Johnny's motor car, and you were walking with the chimney brushes, and I thought you were just a sweep?' She laughed, recalling, and then said, 'We were such fools.' Quite suddenly she began to cry and he quite naturally gathered her into his arms, stroking her hair, speaking words of comfort, kissing first her forehead, then her wet, closed eyelids and then her mouth, as if to do so were the only logical choice. Her kiss, already, was that of a woman no longer a girl. It lit passion in him, and jealousy, and then terrible guilt.

They fell apart, staring at each other as if they were strangers. Wordlessly he gathered the fallen reins, signalled the waiting pony, and in silence they rode to the tall pink stone house that awaited at the end of the drive, like forgotten duty.

'Will I see you at the christening?' Tenny said, his eyes averted, as he climbed down from the trap. She nodded, not speaking. He asked, cautiously, 'Are you coming in? There'll be coffee in the morning-room. Perhaps Mother . . .'

'No. I must get back to Maud. You know Willie is insisting on being brought across. Not to the church, but to the christening tea. It's madness, of course, all the stairs, but he was quite determined.'

'They should surely have held it at Cluanie,' Tenny said, finding relief from emotion in social trivia.

'Of course. But so many guests . . . and more than that. I think they wanted it in the Big House. Just to show it can still be; that the old life can go on, I suppose. It was Gordon's request, you know.'

Tenny smiled. 'Was it indeed. Now I understand. Just laying the foundations for the heir.'

'Heir to what?' she asked puzzled. 'Culbrech?'

'Oh no. That's mine. If I live long enough,' he added quietly. 'But the regiment. Our other inheritance. A Bruce son must also make his claims. Just a little reminder to those of us on the right side of the blanket, lest we think we'll have it all our way.' He grinned and waved, standing lame and war-weary before the lordly grandeur of his home, and she rode away behind her smartly trotting pony, cherishing that image of him.

Such was Tenny Maclaren's introduction to illicit love, an event so brief and mild as to pass easily under the innocent guise of simple warm friendship, should he choose to so allow it. But he was both honest, and still in love, and honesty forbade him disguise what he knew was passion on his part, and being in love made him hope that it was returned. He walked into the house, benumbed, forgetting both his tiredness and his limp, warm with conflicting emotions. Predominant, no doubt, was guilt, for when MacLeod, the ageing butler, met him in the inner hall with, 'Her ladyship desires your company in the morning-room, Captain Maclaren,' he started with instant embarrassment, convinced she had seen his arrival, and was preparing already an angry rebuttal to accusations as he entered the room.

No accusations came. Victoria was sitting at her writing-desk, with one of her many lists and schedules before her, and she barely looked up as he entered. 'Ah, Tenny. I trust you rested well?' She wore reading glasses, and looked over their gold rims as she spoke.

Tenny had forgotten he was meant to have been in his room, and blurted out, 'I had a walk, Mother, actually.'

'I trust it was refreshing,' she was again looking at her papers, barely listening.

Having escaped detection, he grew perversely self-righteous and said then, 'I met Rebecca Bruce. She drove me home in the ponytrap.'

'Oh, can Rebecca drive? I didn't know,' Victoria said, adding, 'I do hope Willie will manage the stairs. I suppose with your help . . .'

'Mother, I do think it would have been appropriate that I be informed of Rebecca's presence at Cluanie. We *are* after all very old friends.'

'Indeed?' Victoria looked up over the glasses, coolly.

'*And* she is married to a brother officer,' Tenny added, amazing himself at his sudden aplomb. 'Why, it was frankly embarrassing, meeting her on the road, having been totally unaware . . .'

'And *had* you been aware?'

'I would have telephoned, naturally. Or called. The girl has been ill, Mother. It was the least I could do.'

'In my day,' Victoria said, 'when a young woman was married, her previous gentlemen friends showed their respect by refraining from calling, *except*,' she looked firmly over her glasses at her eldest son, 'upon an invitation extended expressly by both herself and her husband. This seems hardly to have been the case.'

Tenny opened his mouth to reply, but Victoria gently reached for his hand, drew him nearer, and then patted the hand as if he were a child. 'Now my dear, I know precisely what you will say. It is no longer my day. The war has changed things, nothing is as it was. The old rules no longer apply. I know, dear, I've heard it all from Susan. The truth is, the more disrupting and difficult times become, the more we must rely on the old ways that the years have tested.'

'All I wished was to extend my good wishes.'

'And what harm could that do?' she finished for him. 'Has it never occurred to you, my dear, that every single indiscretion that blossoms into misery and social disgrace was perhaps initiated by some kind soul with his heart full of good intentions?'

'Am I never to see her, never to speak to her, ever again?'

'Of course you may. As you would speak to the wife of any of your brother officers. No less, and oh, my dear, no more.'

'She's not happy, Mother. I could tell. I know she's not happy.'

Victoria sighed, and stood up and walked away. She wanted to say, find me the wife who is, but refrained. She said only, 'Do not think her unhappiness has anything to do with you. I assure you it has not.'

'How can you know? I know her, Mother. I loved her. She . . . she loved me.'

'I know her too. I have known others like her, women, and men,' she said, pausing and turning slightly away from him, 'who can never save all their love for one person. It outruns them, goes off in one direction, then another, like a stream with too much water. Too *much* love, I suppose. So they love here, and there also, and whichever way they turn they are faintly unhappy, because they cannot turn both ways at once. Such people,' she said, slowly and weightily, 'cause those around them an immense amount of misery. I feel sorry for you, Tenny, but not half as sorry as I do for John Bruce. Not half as sorry as I would have felt for you, had you been her choice.'

'I am her choice,' he said.

She looked up, her sharp blue eyes turned quite hard. 'Never,' she said, 'never, Tenny, let me hear you say that again. They are married. You will put her from your mind and forget her, or you will leave my house.'

She turned from him with an abrupt squaring of her little shoulders beneath their shawl that made him realize she meant it. He suppressed a surge of anger under a heavy realization. In a week he would be back at the Front; Rebecca, his mother, Culbrech, all loved in their own ways, would be behind him. Before him would be the sturdy fortifications of the Somme, against which, within weeks, ill-prepared, they would advance. The entanglement of the heart, which a moment ago frustrated all hope of solution, would find its own settlement, no doubt. The life expectancy of a field officer on the Western Front had grown very short indeed.

'I'm sorry, Mother,' he said, gently. 'That was all terribly out of order. You must forgive me, I don't think I'm quite myself yet.'

She turned, smiling, accepting the pose he presented as the explanation they would agree on. 'Of course. Poor boy, you must still be quite exhausted. Why don't you have your rest now? We'll not leave for the church before one.'

'But what of Emma? And Susan? I thought I was to meet the train.'

'Emma has been delayed. A telegram arrived an hour ago. Apparently the Channel crossing was difficult. She will arrive tonight.'

'And Susan?'

'Susan,' Victoria said, 'is Maud's responsibility, thank God.'

'I thought Emma would meet her. At the hostel.'

'Susan is no longer at the hostel. Maud felt her behaviour warranted closer scrutiny, I fear. Susan has been in the care of her maternal grandparents, the Wilsons. I assume they will have seen her on to the train, and you can be assured that Maud will be personally in Inverness to see her off. Henceforth, Susan will remain at Cluanie.'

'My Lord. You'd think she was a criminal.'

'Susan is a very foolish girl, Tenny. I don't wish to discuss it further, as the man who is the root of it all is a soldier in your company.'

'You sound like it were in part my fault.'

'I haven't heard of your doing anything to dissuade him.'

'Mother, with all respect, that is not a matter within my province.'

'In our day, a soldier in your father's command accepted his guidance on all matters.'

'That may well be,' Tenny said with a soft cynical laugh, 'but I assure you none of them was Pat McGarrity. I consider myself doing well when he's obeying orders. I'm not about to muck about with his love-life.'

'Tenny,' she said in soft-voiced amazement, 'I would think if I didn't know better that you were afraid of the man.'

Tenny refused to be riled. He grinned and said lightly, 'No, Mother. I'm not afraid of him. There's just one of him after all. But I tell you, I'd not like to meet a hundred. He's a good man, a brave man. He saved my life, and John Bruce's . . .'

'For which, as I said before,' Victoria interrupted rapidly, 'I am most exceedingly grateful. But tell me this,' she added shrewdly, 'would you see him married to *your* sister?' Tenny was silent and she smiled a prim victory.

* * *

The christening was held at the Old High Church in Inverness where Rebecca and John Bruce had married. Half the principals were absent; Gordon Bruce was at the Front, and Tenny Maclaren stood in for his own father, as godparent. The baby's grandfather, Willie Bruce, for whom this late grandchild was a source of wondrous delight, stayed at home; the long journey to the church was quite unthinkable. And Maud herself remained behind at Cluanie readying her frail husband for the reception, which was to be his first visit to Culbrech House in nearly two years. She realized that the ostensible reason for Susan's return north, to aid her grandmother in the care of her ailing grandfather, was not a total fabrication. She could use that help, assuming that Susan chose not to sulk.

Actually, Maud was obliged to admit that Susan had grown, at last, beyond sulking. Indeed the serious and lovely young woman who had stepped from the morning train seemed far changed from the impetuous and unreasonable Susan of the past. Maud was visited by a flash of traitorous respect for the mysterious ranker who had won her heart; if he, and his much resented Church, could create such a change in the girl, perhaps there was something to be said for both. Maud buried the thought, both unworthy and inconvenient. Whatever Pat McGarrity's effect had been in the past, it had now, officially, come to an end. She herself would see to that.

When Willie and Maud arrived at Culbrech House that afternoon, in the dark green closed Lanchester tourer in which Maud had at last, and somewhat reluctantly, agreed to enter the twentieth century, the christening party was already well under way in the drawing-room. But Tenny hastened out, even before the driver had stopped, and with Maud on one side, and himself on the other, the withered, stooped old man hobbled slowly round the corner of the pink stone house to the broad entrance steps. His bald pink-skinned head, with its wisps of pale hair, that had once towered above Tenny, was now at the level of his shoulder. His smooth-skinned cheeks were rosy with excitement and he paused several times to point out one feature and another, the Indian stone carving brought back from a long-ago campaign, a beech hedge that he recalled was first planted by Tenny's great-grandfather, now as gnarled and ancient as himself, screening the whole eastern aspect of the garden. He exclaimed and beame over each remembered treasure like a child newly home fron school. Maud smiled patiently; he had become her child too now, no longer her husband. The years in which sex, anger parenthood and career had concerned them were as remote as time before birth. She no longer thought of him as the same ma who had shared an inconstant and passionate marriage bed.

'We must go in, they're all waiting,' she said kindly, adjustin the tartan rug about his shoulders.

'Let 'em wait. I havena seen the place in years. D'ye min Tenny ae day lang syne, nou, an' yersel' and Johnny rod steeplechase o'er yon hedge?'

Tenny laughed. He had not remembered for years. His fathe had been furious, he recalled. Strange how only the ol remembered clearly the days of one's youth.

They went in, and Willie was greeted with cheers and raise champagne glasses. A chair by the fire was instantly vacated, an enthroned there, the old man was presented with one and anoth guest. He seemed most interested in the children, rememberin their names when the names of old associates slipped his min The baby was brought and posed on his grandfather's knee for photograph, and as the brilliant flash filled everyone's eyes, ar left the children staring and blinking, Tenny imagined th photograph that would result, and how one day the tiny, sleepin infant would, a young man, be shown and reminded,

'That was your grandfather. Old General Bruce. Rose from th ranks. Born in a croft. Best of his line.' The young man wou nod, disinterested and polite, and turn the album page.

It was late in the afternoon when Emma arrived. The party h grown thoughtful and quiet, the infant for whom it was intended long since taken away to the nursery by its nanny, t older women talking in discreet quiet circles, remembering th own childbirths and christenings. The men were drinking in t library; Willie Bruce had drifted to sleep by the fire, with h delicate, still faintly lovely wife dividing her gaze between h peaceful face, and the striking countenance of her granddaught Susan.

Susan seemed remarkably serene for a girl who had receiv the sort of social ultimatum that had been laid down o luncheon by her grandmother. She, Tenny, and Rebe gravitated towards each other, almost defiantly, drawn by t mutual experience of the war, which melded their old friendship and simultaneously separated them from all others in the room. They were, each in their own way, participants, and even their own families had grown remote and dimly resented as members of the non-understanding home-front. Tenny answered politely all the questions, politely accepted the admiration, politely evaded the patriotic enthusiasm, telling himself always that in a week, none of this would matter. All the time his eyes rarely left Rebecca, following her about the room, feasting greedily upon the vision that must serve him for want of lover or wife. Twice his inadvertent glance met that of his mother, and slid away from her reproval. Emma's arrival, with resultant flurry of excitement, was a tremendous relief.

She had come directly from the train, and was still in uniform, and as she strode into the room, confident and strong, matronly heads turned at the calf-length skirt and the curly tangle of short-bobbed hair. Tenny's heart filled with love for her and as he embraced her he was dangerously aware of a protective emotion that would have him physically expel anyone, male or female, who passed comment about her appearance. Fortunately, all parties satisfied themselves with dramatic lifts of eyebrows and small, concealed clucking of tongues.

'Oh darlings, how marvellous,' Emma exclaimed, running from one to another of her friends and relatives, presenting Grisel Bruce with a huge pink velvet rabbit for Donald. 'I made it myself,' she said. 'That's why its ears are different lengths and its eyes are crooked.' As Emma turned to greet Willie, Susan Bruce, who had been temporarily absent from the room, entered, walked calmly to its centre, kissed Emma and announced in a clear and steady voice, 'Now that dear Emma is here at last, I have an announcement to make. I would like the attention of you all, if I may.' She looked around the circle of people and smiled with satisfaction, and a deep underglow of happiness. She turned once to Emma, and took her hand with sisterly pride. Slowly, Susan raised her other hand in the air, and Emma saw with amazement that her ring finger was decorated with a tiny, delicate jewel.

'It is my great pleasure,' she said, suddenly glowing with joy, 'to announce . . .'

'Susan,' Maud suddenly shouted, having risen from her seat beside Willie. 'Susan, what is the meaning of this nonsense?' She too had seen the ring.

'My greatest pleasure,' Susan said, quickly, regaining her stride, 'to announce my engagement to . . .'

'You will not,' Maud shouted with unladylike vehemence.

'To Corporal Patrick Joseph McGarrity of the Maclaren Highlanders,' Susan shouted back, and flung her arms around Emma's neck with a squeal half of delight, half of terror.

'Susan, this is ridiculous,' Maud shouted. 'Ridiculous.'

'I love him, Grandmama,' Susan shouted back.

'You will go home at once, and go to your room,' Maud declared, reducing Susan by tone to the age of six.

'No, ma'am,' a soft voice answered suddenly, 'I'm afraid she willna, wi' a' respeckt.'

A room full of elegant aristocratic heads turned, like the disdainful necks of so many swans, to the discordant sound of working-class Scotland suddenly emerged in their midst. There was a chilling, wide-eyed silence.

'Oh my God,' Tenny Maclaren whispered at last.

In the doorway, in the field dress of the Maclaren Highlanders, his black hair patiently combed, his hat in his hand, and his eyes calm and utterly in control, stood Corporal Pat McGarrity. 'Beggin' yer pardon, ma'am, but the lassie chooses tae come wi' me.'

The silence stretched to impossible limits, as if time might stop, reconsider, and remove this apparition from the very hearthside of Culbrech House.

Then Maud straightened her arthritic back, cast the glance that had withered servants for five decades and declared, 'Indeed. You foolish, improvident little man. You will leave this house at once.'

'Shut up, Maud.' She turned, staring. The voice beside her was a voice from the past, the long-ago Willie Bruce who had once, unknown to all present and all the rest of the world, turned her inelegantly across his knee and given her the flat of his hand.

'That's right. Shut up. Yer no' the mistress o' this house, woman. You never were, though it seems ye still cannae quite accept it. Lea' the boy alane, till we see whit this is aboot.'

'Wi' respeckt, sir, it's aboot yer granddaughter and me gettin' engaged,' Pat said ingenuously.

'An' ye shut up as weel,' Willie rumbled. He leaned back in the chair, deliberating, and then he beckoned to the young soldier waiting in the doorway. 'Nou, we'll hae a luik at ye.'

Pat advanced, still calm, his eyes fleetingly meeting Susan's with a look of gentle encouragement, his shoulder brushing with light tension by that of Tenny Maclaren, until he stood before the old man in the wingchair by the fireplace. Pat had an instinct for true worth, and the respect he showed the bowed old figure was utterly genuine.

'Sae yer Pat,' Willie said.

'Aye sir.'

'An' yer wantin' tae marry ma granddaughter.'

Coming from the yet imposing figure of the colonel-in-chief of his regiment, the question suddenly blossomed in import, growing terrifying.

'Wi' respeckt, sir, we were onerlie wantin' tae get engaged, juist the nou, wi' the war on, an a'.'

'Dinna shilly-shally. Ye meanin' tae marry the lass or no?'

'Yes,' Pat said, suddenly angry. 'I am. An' I shall an' a', whether ye gie permission or no'. Sir,' he added, glowering.

Willie laughed softly. 'Aye. Will ye now.' He laughed again, greatly amused, while Pat stood his ground, Susan fidgeted, and Maud Bruce fumed. Then abruptly he grew terribly serious and leaned forward in the chair. 'An' will ye be telling me then, Corporal Pat McGarrity, since ye're about tae marry intae this family, have ye e'en the slightest notion who we are?'

'Of course he hasn't,' Maud snapped, 'the impudent little . . .' she sputtered to a halt on the edge of vulgarity, and Susan began to cry.

'Then I'd best tell him, had I no'?' Willie Bruce growled. Maud waved one hand as if the matter were beneath discussion, but Willie only added softly, 'Aye. An' I shall. I shall.' Emma, glancing fearfully from where she stood at Tenny's side, was surprised to see a sudden flicker of humour cross his fierce old face.

Willie looked up, solemnly, and then he gestured with his chin to the settle by the fire. 'Ye'd better sit doun, lad,' he said. 'Some o' this may come as a wee bit o' a shock.' Pat wanted to remain standing, but Susan tugged fearfully at his hand, and Willie Bruce only glowered until, reluctantly, he sank down to the settle at the feet of the old man, and Susan huddled beside him. They looked suddenly like two small children awaiting a nursery tale, and Willie said, appropriately enough,

'Yince upon ae time, there was an old laird livin' in a bluidy great draughty castle, this yin, as a maitter o' fact, onerlie he wasnae old then, but young an' good-luikin' an' knowin' it as weel. His name was Henry Maclaren. Sir Henry tae the likes o' yersel', and he wasnae a bad sort exceptin' ae little weak spot an' that tae dae wi' the ladies.' He paused, glancing once up to Maud who was watching him suspiciously. 'An' at the same time an' in the same land, as they used tae say, there was a croft-wifie. She wasnae bad-luikin' either, and she was a guid enough lass exceptin' fer ae little weak spot, an' thot tae dae wi' the gentlemen.' He grinned at Maud and then leaned closer to the pair on the settle. 'Now, lad, ye'll maybe no' credit this, what wi' ye comin' frae a good decent household, like Susan's been tellin' me, but this pair fell intae the way o' all flesh, so tae speak, an' lo an' behold if the lassie wasnae soon rockin' the family cradle wi' a guilty air an' Sir Henry awa' aff tae his castle makin' excuses tae his wife.' He paused and looked up to Maud Bruce and said ingenuously, 'Dinna luik sae fashed, woman, these things dae happen, ye ken.'

He turned back to Pat. 'Sae thot, laddie, was where *I* cam' from. Now that would be bad enough, but I fear there's more tae tell.'

'That will do, Willie, I think,' Victoria Maclaren ventured boldly. Willie raised one bushy eyebrow and was silent for a long while. At last he said, 'Woman, when Our Lord did the like, he wrote it a' doun in the sand. Seein' as how we've no' a grain o' the stuff,' he gestured to the Persian carpet at his feet, 'ye'll juist hae tae put up wi' me speakin' aloud.'

Pat was shocked by that, but held his peace.

'Now where was I?' Willie said. 'Och aye. Now,' he glanced a Maud, 'ye've met ma wife, I see, but hae ye met ma daughter?'

'I have, sir,' Pat said clearly.

'An' whit dae ye think o' her?'

'I think she's a very fine lady,' Pat said, looking straight int Willie's sly old eyes. The eyes crinkled up as Willie dissolved i laughter.

'A fine lady,' he said at last, and Pat suddenly got to his feet, i anger.

'Sit doun,' said Willie, but Pat remained standing.

'Aye sir, as I said. A fine lady. Och, I'm nae a fool, sir. Y dinna need tae sae amuse yersel'. An' I'd a thocht any man, n maitter wha' his parents, wouldna mak sport o' his ain daughte I ken the things yer thinkin' of an' all. I said she was a lad because she was gentle an' kind. What mair is there than thot?'

Willie was serious again. 'Nae mair, lad,' he said at last. 'Nae mair than thot.' He paused. 'She wouldna fash fer ma laughter, Pat,' he said solemnly. 'I couldna gie her flesh and blood. Anither did yon. But I taught the lassie how tae laugh at the warld. Fer the likes o' hersel' an' mysel', that's no small thing.'

Pat still glowered but something in the old man's manner eased his anger, and slowly he sat down again, beside Susan.

'She's anither like mysel', Pat,' Willie said then, 'and a cross-breed as well.' He looked up to Maud and his face hardened. 'And yon lady,' he said suddenly, 'wha' would hae ye out o' here as if she owned the place, did surely try tae, yince. An' when she failed she settled fer second best, a thing no woman should ever dae. Nor any man tolerate. But I was young an' a fool wi' it. Aye, Pat, dinna think ever because we're old now, we always were. We had our time, tae, and we made as much a mess o' it as ever ye'll manage, I'm sure. An' tae tell truth, lad,' his eyes crossed Pat's face and settled on Victoria's, 'there's no' an end tae such goings on, even now. I'm no' the onerlie Maclaren tae hide behind anither's name. An' that's no' the worst we've done either.'

He paused, coughed and looked at the floor, his head shaking with the effort of his thoughts. Pat saw suddenly that the conversation was exhausting him. He moved forward on the settle as if he would go to the old man's aid, but Willie looked up, his eyes sharp, witty, and alert in the sagging lines of his face. 'We've done worse,' he repeated, 'an' I the worst o' all.' He pointed to Susan. 'Yon lass's faither, the yin we ca'd a coward, was a good man. An' I drove him out o' our lives fer the sake o' my own pride. Dear kens what became o' thot one, fer we never shall.' He shook his head, looking at Maud, the anger he had expressed earlier gone in remorse. He was silent then, for a long while, and the silence filled the drawing-room.

Then abruptly he said to Pat, 'And now, lad, ye ken whit we are, fer yince an' all. Are ye still wantin' tae marry this daughter o' a coward an' granddaughter o' a croft-wifie's bastard? Or will ye gae back where ye cam' from and find yersel' a decent lass tae wed?' He glared at the young man and Pat looked once to Susan who was sitting silent, her lashes wet with tears.

Pat got to his feet. 'Aye sir,' he said at last. 'I'll gae back where I cam' from.' There was an audible gasp about the room and Susan sunk her humiliated face into her hands. 'But,' said Pat,

'I'll tak' ma lass wi' me when I go.' He looked carefully about the room, cool and self-assured in a way with which Tenny Maclaren was all too familiar. 'I heard it a', sir, whit ye were sayin'. Maybe I even ken why ye were sayin' it as weel. But I'll tell ye something, sir. Ye'd no need tae speak. I ken I'm young an' I'm ignorant. That's neither thing a fault I've chosen. An' neither thing will last for ever. But still I've seen eneuch o' yer warld tae see there's plenty wrang wi' it. I didna need yersel' tae spell it out. An' I dinna care either. It's yer warld, sir,' he paused and looked from face to face in the room, to all but Susan. 'Nae ours.' Then he looked at Susan, and his smile softened his already hard young face. 'Aye,' he said on an outward breath, 'I'm aff now. An' yince I finish wi' this war o' yers, I'm takin' ma lass hame. No' to yer hame, but to ma ain.' He was still looking proudly at Susan. 'An' then the twa o' us, she an' I, we'll mak' a new warld fer our bairns. Aye, an' a better yin, tae, than any ye ever knew.' He took Susan by the hand and led her to the door.

Maud raised a now trembling hand to her granddaughter, as if to stop her, but Willie only said quietly, 'Aye, lad, I hope ye do.' He turned then to Maud, 'Nae, lass. Let them go.' His voice was very tired and very gentle and held a great authority. 'She's no' ours any mair tae haud.'

Maud was halted by the authority. She looked from the young couple, defiant in the doorway, to her husband. 'I'm sorry, lass,' he said, and then sighed and added, 'Dear Christ but I'm tired, Maud.' He leaned his head back in the wingback chair, craggy and ancient like an old bird of prey, and seemed to sleep.

He died late in the afternoon, just before six, without waking or stirring from the old armchair by the hearthside. Maud Bruce was at his side, a fragile, blue-eyed wisp of ecru lace.

17

Donnie Cameron's spade clunked dully against something hard buried in the earth. As he reached to shift the obstruction, Hamish Drummond said, 'Whit we diggin' *these* fer?' It was a hot June day and he was sweat-drenched and querulous at the edge of the large deep pit.

It was obvious to Donnie. They were digging mass graves in preparation for battle. But he only shrugged, looking at the puzzled innocent young face. 'Dinna ken,' he lied. 'Nae doubt yin o' them ration dumps.'

Hamish nodded, content. Donnie pried at the stone. It rolled free, to Hamish's feet. It was not stone, but dark yellowed bone, a human skull. They had unearthed one of yesterday's forgotten dead to make room for tomorrow's. Hamish recoiled, sick-faced. Donnie took it gruffly from the boy beside him and cast it spinning away. He made a joke to cheer Hamish. Donnie felt old, and strong, comforting and protecting the younger and weaker around him. He saw the officer watching him and bent his back to his shovel again.

Tenny Maclaren turned away and made his way back up the line to his dugout. There he sat at a rough table, busy with stacks of paperwork. For while outside and all around him the work went on, and the divisions gathered and preparations were made for the mightiest battle of the war, and of any war in all previous history, the army never forgot its delight in forms and lists and accounts, and Tenny Maclaren spent part of the twenty-third of June, 1916, answering urgent queries from some far distant office regarding a shipment of bootlaces that had somehow gone astray.

Later, he went out into the open air, and sat on the firestep, enjoying the sun, listening to the dreamy call of a cuckoo. It reminded him of home, and Rebecca, and when he rose to find something to do, other than think of her, he peered through a loophole in the parapet at the German lines, where yellowing weeds and bright red poppies blew in the soft June air. It too was like home, and wherever he went that afternoon Tenny heard, as an echo behind the day, the clip-clop of a pony's hoofs up the shaded drive of Culbrech House.

Brigadier General Sir Ian Maclaren arrived in the late afternoon. He had come for a tactical conference with the battalion commander, just as he had done previously with the commanders of the other three battalions of his brigade. He gave Gordon Bruce the final time of the attack, the twenty-ninth of June, at seven-thirty in the morning, and noted that Gordon Bruce involuntarily winced at the late hour.

After a moment, Ian said, almost placatingly, 'The French want good light for their artillery, and I dare say it will serve ours well.' He said nothing about what the same good light would do to their advancing infantry, and in true military tradition expected Gordon to say nothing as well. Then he went on to detail, once again, the method of attack.

As one of the lead-off battalions, the Maclarens would advance in waves on a single company front. As soon as the barrage lifted, A Company would lead off, followed by B Company, one minute and a hundred yards behind. There would be an interval of five yards between each man and they would advance at a slow walking pace, fully laden, into no-man's-land. They were to advance silently, without cheers or shouts to alert the enemy, and yet, were resistance to be met, they were still to continue at the same funereal pace to within twenty yards of the enemy, lest, laden as they were, they succumb to exhaustion in attempting to run.

As he spoke Ian saw reflected in the eyes of the man he faced the same grim, uneasy doubts he had fought so hard to quell in himself. He continued, 'Your third company should follow at another hundred yards, with mopping up and support platoons, and bringing up the rear, naturally, your carrying platoons, who will, of course, upon delivering their materials to the captured trenches of the enemy, become fighting platoons for the further advance.'

Again Gordon Bruce nodded, his eyes still reflecting the warfare within him between doubt and respect for authority. His mind was envisaging that advance, while remembering Loos. The ordinary infantry soldier was to be laden down with his full packs, his rifle and bayonet, a couple of gas helmets, his wire-cutters, his entrenching tool, two empty sandbags, two of the bombers' supply of grenades, his usual 220 rounds of ammunition, a flare and a miscellany of odds and ends that totalled over seventy pounds in weight. Some of those men, products of poor country farms and slum streets, weighed not a great deal more than that themselves. As for the carrying platoons, the list was marvellous and endless. Duckboards and scaling ladders, coils of wire, tied bundles of stakes, extra water, necessary in the heat of the dry land they'd cross, marker poles, even carrier pigeons in little wicker cages. He leaned against the dry earth of his dugout wall and momentarily closed his eyes.

'It's not an advance,' he said suddenly, 'it's a bloody emigration.' His tone, his closed eyes, were signals that the statement was personal, off-the-record.

'I am assured,' Ian Maclaren said slowly, 'that our bombardment will be so thorough that only minimal resistance, if any, will be met. We can frankly regard this operation as a mere shifting of position. A walkover.'

'Do you actually believe that?' Gordon Bruce said suddenly. His eyes were wide open and steady on Ian's face, in the closest to a bald challenge he had ever seen in them.

Ian was silent, tugging at the corner of his moustache, pulling down his thin upper lip. He said finally, 'I have had opportunity to survey the extent of the artillery cover. It is rather impressive. We estimate one gun to every twenty yards of the Front. It may be a trifle difficult to envisage, Gordon, but the kind of bombardment we are about to unleash is quite unparalleled in the history of warfare. Everything that has gone before will pale into insignificance. Anything that lies under the range of those guns will be simply pounded into oblivion. It is difficult to conceive of any organized resistance, by the time we advance.'

'All I can say,' Gordon replied, 'is that any resistance, *any* resistance at all, would have a field day facing a parade-ground advance of men at seven-thirty in the morning.'

'Be thankful for small mercies,' Ian muttered. 'The French, I understand, requested nine. Rawly drew the line at seven-thirty.' He was finding his display of confidence weakening. Every one of his commanders had shied from that daylight start. And giving even that much to the French had worried him deeply, too. The French had far more artillery, everyone knew, and wanted to use it to its best advantage. And more to the point, the brunt of the infantry advance would, since the bleeding of Verdun, of necessity fall on the British.

'Take the chestnut out of the fire with someone else's hand?' Gordon said with another humourless smile, adding, 'I'd be a lot more thankful if we attacked at dawn. The moment the barrage lifts, they'll know we're coming.'

'If there's anyone left to know,' Ian pointed out, loyal to his orders.

'If.' Gordon tapped a paper on his makeshift desk. 'A mighty "if" Ian, an awesome "if." '

Ian thought of going on, extolling their heavy guns, their careful planning, their air superiority that had guaranteed the safety of their artillery observation balloons and hence the accuracy of their fire. But abruptly he switched the subject. He knew better than to debate with underlings, even respected underlings, as if orders were subject to mediation and rearrangement. He said only, 'Seven-thirty, June the twenty-ninth, and the best of my luck to the Maclarens.' The rest, the detailed objectives, the secondary plans, were in the hands of Gordon Bruce.

'Sorry about your father,' he said abruptly, turning slightly aside with his customary avoidance of eye-contact in personal matters.

'Ah, yes,' Gordon said, his voice softening and his body relaxing, long legs thrust out under the wood-plank desk. 'Still he went out in style, wet the head of the wean, first. He had a good innings, after all, old Willie.' He was silent for a few seconds and added, 'Rather sorry he didn't hang on a month. Maybe see this scrap wrapped up.'

Ian heard the words as hollow, a kind of formality, much like his condolences. 'Indeed,' he said. 'How's your mother taking it?'

'Oh, her usual self. As you'd expect. Publicly stoic. No doubt some private tears.'

'How have the children taken it?'

Gordon Bruce lit a cigarette and passed his packet of Abdullahs to Ian who declined. He rose, and found a bottle of whisky tucked into a corner of the dugout and gave a shout for his batman who, when summoned, was instructed to produce glasses. 'Might as well toast our futures,' he said, without enough expression to indicate irony or patriotism. Then he said, before answering Ian's question, 'I hope you don't mind but I asked Tenny and Albert and young Jamie to stop by at four. Told them you'd be here,' he glanced at his pocket-watch as he spoke. 'Thought you'd like a word.'

'Indeed,' Ian agreed, politely, though his emotions at seeing his sons under the circumstances of imminent battle, were complex. Naturally he wanted to see them. But he was never able to find words, somehow, and such rather forced meetings balanced between kinship and the formality of military discipline were awkward in the extreme. 'The children?' Ian prompted then.

'Ah indeed. Harry of course I've had no contact with. Imagine he'll take it like he takes everything else. Couldn't ruffle him with the announcement that the entire *family* had suddenly succumbed.'

'Bit harsh, surely,' Ian said, forced as always to defend Gordon's aloof eldest nephew. 'Besides, thought you'd be proud of him, coming in with us at last.'

'Oh, he's not *in* with us. Not the way you mean it. Granted he's no coward, and if I ever said or inferred he was, well, I admit I was wrong.' Gordon paused, taking a deep breath; such admissions did not come easily. 'But he's no more in with us than ever. Still thinks we're wrong. Only now he condescends to help pick up the pieces . . . oh damn, Ian, I'm sorry. I don't know what it is about the boy; I can't make myself be fair to him.'

He poured from the bottle into the glasses the batman had set before them. Through the open sheet-tin door, sunlight streamed and birdsong drifted with afternoon laziness. Far away, a voice, rich with Glasgow vulgarity, sang,

'I wantae gae hame,
Please let me gae hame
Don't wantae gae tae the trenches no more
Where whizz-bangs an' shrapnel they whistle an' roar . . .'

'Johnny's all right, of course. Got drunk the night we heard, a little maudlin, blew up with his Jocks and gave them hell the next morning. Then forgot it. That's Johnny. Susan's still with Mother, of course.'

'Oh, is she?' Ian said, surprised. 'Thought she'd be back to London. Now that she's . . . won her point.'

'No. Quite the contrary. I gather she was all set to go off south, and . . .' he paused, not wanting somehow to name the man, 'the man involved, he said he wanted her to stay, look after her grandmother. And she did, too. Must say that for him; he's the first person to ever get Susan to do other than what she wants. Takes a certain talent, I dare say.'

'What's he like?' Ian said, cautiously.

'The man?' Gordon withdrew into himself, and said in a small flat voice, 'All right, I suppose. For a Glasgow keelie.' He sighed, and then, in a quick outburst said, 'It's absolute madness, Ian. I can't stop it, and I can't face it either. God help me, it's an awful thing to wish on a man, a good enough soldier too, but if on the twenty-ninth we do lose a few, well, I'd be a damned liar if I said I'd weep many tears if one of them were Patrick McGarrity.'

Ian said nothing, letting Gordon's outburst subside without comment. A tap at the door interrupted the heavy silence, to his relief.

Outside, lined up in order of both family and military seniority, stood his three sons. He stood without speaking for a moment, his eyes sweeping slowly from one, to the other, to the third. Three sons, born each of his seed, born each from Victoria's body, legal and sanctified in the same traditional bed, and yet, so different, so utterly different. Had he cast his seed as carelessly with each, as he'd done with his last, fourth, unacknowledged son, he could not have produced a more piebald, dissimilar litter.

Ian chose to address Tenny, rather than the others, because he alone faced him as the brigadier, instead of as a boy facing his father. 'Ah, Maclaren. I trust you are quite recovered.' A small nervous but loving grin twisted the brigadier's mouth, undoing his formality. It was sufficient to bring from Bertie a sudden,

'What a topping surprise, Father, we'd no idea you were about.'

Ian decided not to disapprove of either the interruption or the informality; there was no one about anyhow, but Gordon, who was family of a sort, and even he had retreated discreetly into the darkness of the dugout.

'Yes, indeed,' Ian said and Tenny, hardly noticing the interruption, replied,

'Yes, sir. Completely recovered, thank you. I trust your health is well, also?'

'Can't complain for an old man.' Ian laughed, shifting his feet and tugging at his moustache. 'Your mother was pleased to have you home, anyhow. Particularly considering what went on. Quite a barney from what I heard.'

Tenny nodded. His mind was on more serious matters, and he was fighting a desire to inundate his father with questions, the answers to which were, militarily anyhow, not yet his affair.

Ian shuffled some more. His eyes turned to Jamie, the youngest. Like Victoria, he regarded Jamie as the baby, even now, and felt a fatherly and unaccustomed desire to embrace the boy which he firmly resisted, allowing himself only an awkward, stiff-armed patting of the boy's shoulder. The feel of it, rock-hard as a man's, and the unresponsive new coolness of Jamie's eyes made him withdraw the gesture half complete. He said, 'All well with you, James?'

'Yes, sir,' the boy replied, and to Ian's amazement he saw that certain guarded darkness come across his face as he spoke, an image he associated always with the men who worked on his estate; a look that he always read as, 'I know who you are but I'm not afraid of you.'

'Regiment treating you all right?' He grinned, trying to draw childhood back into this stranger's face.

'Yes, sir.'

'Ready to show us what you can do?'

'I'll try, sir.' As Jamie spoke his voice shifted subtly, and the accent of his home and his schooling gave way to that of his trenchmates. He had that same restless look the rankers always had, and Ian knew suddenly that once released the boy would vanish into those khaki masses and joke in their guttural tongue of his ordeal, like any crofter's son.

'Good, good,' Ian said, turning to Bertie whose face, lit now by a grin, was a sudden relief. 'Best of luck anyhow,' he said. 'When the time comes,' he added, for though they were his sons, they would learn nothing from him. He avoided Tenny's eyes, for that reason, feeling those questions within them, and Tenny seemed to sense it, for he blurted suddenly,

'Sir, there are certain matters that have come to the attention of the men in the field. Matters of which you may not be aware. I would like . . .'

'I can assure you, Captain Maclaren,' Ian said abruptly, 'that my intelligence is quite reliable. I doubt there is any concern that has not reached me, and been dealt with.'

'In that case, sir, can I assure the men in my command that full consideration has been given to the depth of German fortifications . . .'

'Captain Maclaren, as I said . . .'

'Some of which are thirty feet into the ground and, as such, resistant to the effects of even our heaviest shells. Sir!' Tenny overrode his father's spluttered resistance.

Ian slowly, very slowly, drew in his breath, giving Tenny a little more time to remember who, and with whom, he was. When he replied his voice was so soft that the two others, who had stepped backwards down the narrow entranceway of the dugout, could barely hear. They huddled there, hoping to avoid the crossfire.

'Captain Maclaren,' he said. 'With all respect,' he paused again, and Tenny reflected that his father used that phrase in precisely the way Pat McGarrity did, with less respect involved than threat. 'With all respect,' Ian repeated, 'I think I am in a better position to judge the effectiveness of our artillery than you are.' Every word was underlined with a silent warning that his eldest son was trespassing and dangerously so.

Tenny refused to be warned. 'If you are, sir, you will no doubt agree with me that no bombardment of which either we, or the enemy are capable, will prove effective against dugouts of such depth.'

As with Gordon Bruce, Ian was far too experienced to enter a debate; and as with Gordon Bruce, he was at war with himself. Those rumours of the underground fortress of the Boche had reached him too; the response of his superiors had been, he admitted with shame, identical to that which he was giving Tenny. Not for the first time he cursed, silently, the stubborn hierarchy of their own command, where the unnerving custom was developing by which those who complained from below were 'degommered' by those above; sent home in disgrace. That was at his level. At Tenny's level they were reduced to the ranks. And a the level of the private soldier, they were shot. For all, it made resistance to decisions from above virtually impossible, regardless of one's doubts. And Ian Maclaren had enormous doubts. He would have given an immense amount not to have to overrule Tenny's expression of those doubts, lest, by sharing them, he found himself cut off from the men he loved and led, and sent away to leave them to their fate. Better at least to stay and fight for them from within. Still, it took more than many fathers had had to face to stand before the three sons he would send within a week into the maelstrom and deny them the very fears he felt himself. But that was what he did.

'Captain Maclaren, you will accept my superior wisdom on this matter. The issue is closed.'

'But Father,' Tenny protested, his strong young face quivering with emotion, 'you're asking me to send my men into . . .'

'You will accept the decision of your superiors. That is an order.' For a moment Tenny wavered, teetering on the pinnacle of disaster, then with a curse beneath his breath he whirled on his heel and stalked, undismissed, unacceptably away. Ian let him go. Another word could pitch them both into a conflict that would cost Tenny his commission. Jamie slipped away, with a nervous salute, at the instant of his dismissal. Albert vanished after him, with his sweet grin, trying as always to apologize for everybody else's sins. Ian stood alone then, between the sandbags, and whispered, under his breath, 'Goodbye.'

The trench was silent, filled with a golden late afternoon sun, empty of his sons. He felt cold and desperately alone. It was then, on impulse, that he turned back into the dugout and requested that a runner be sent to summon to his presence a certain private soldier, Robert Bruce.

He went out then, into the open, second-line trench to await the boy's arrival. He climbed up on to a bundle of stakes, aware that the exposed position it afforded him was a little unwise. Still, it was the rear line. He stood there, his polished leather boots slippery on the awkward footing, leaning on the sandbag parapet, looking forward, out over their own front-line trench, to the wire, and the untouchable ground of no-man's-land, beyond. Here, as all along this front, the land sloped upwards towards the German lines, giving the enemy everywhere the physical and psychological advantage of height. They tried to counter-balance it with the great artillery observation balloons floating at intervals along the line, and the aircraft, two of which even now were in sigh patrolling the sky they mastered like jealous dogs. But it was har on men, looking up always to the enemy, and hard, too, t advance upwards, even over that gentle slope.

He turned, his back to the enemy, looking out over their rea envisaging the hidden network of trenches working backwards t the empty villages, and all the back-up machinery of the arm the transport, and the munitions dumps, the mighty stores c bully beef and jam and biscuits, the lorries and ambulances an field hospitals, the horses and fodder, the waiting cavalry, th railways reaching back to the coast, the ships to England. What vast, mechanical and immovable thing it had become, this w that had started but two years before with a fast-marching an mobile army, setting out with horsemen and banners as armi had done for a thousand years. He sighed; mud, machines an misery; it was a sad substitute for the glamour of pennants an the thunder of steel-shod hoofs. And yet, Ian thought, straighte ing and turning once more to face that peaceful summ splendour so soon to be riven apart: the one machine he h longed for like he'd longed for his lover, that machine they h denied him. His beautiful landships lay yet in England, as uncertain authority deigned cautiously to produce but a fe without enthusiasm or hurry. Thirty-foot dugouts, wi machine-guns, God knew what; all would succumb to tho advancing steel-shielded chargers, if only they were here. I shook his head. He was thinking like Tenny. It would not do

He looked up suddenly, and the boy was standing there. I was startled, finding himself looking eye-to-eye with one he h remembered as a child. How tall he was now, how lean and har a man. And how handsome, that dark-skinned face, the de intense brown-black eyes, the hair as shiny and straight and bla as . . . as hers. Why did that astound him, he wondered, that t boy had become a man? After all, the years had passed for him well. Or that the man was handsome, and self-confident, a most of all that the man looked like her? Like them. The line jaw and the long straight nose; it was Tenny's and it was his ow Like Tenny, only dark, and if anything better-looking, a bolder.

'Private Robert Bruce, sir,' the young man said, saluting w assurance and grace, and oddly, addressing the man he'd alw called Uncle Ian, as a total stranger. For a mad moment I wondered if he'd forgotten who he was. No, of course not. Only this one, unlike his acknowledged sons, had learnt discretion from his cradle, learnt never to assume, or suppose, or mention even, his rightful place in the world. Naomi's lesson, taught to Naomi in her own childhood in turn. Ian paused, suddenly wordless, realizing he had sent for the boy on impulse and now had nothing to say to him.

Then the most obvious excuse leapt to his mind, so obvious that for an instant he could not imagine why he'd not thought of it at once. Perhaps because he knew, as few were meant to know, that Willie Bruce and Robert shared no blood. Still he said, 'Sorry about your grandfather, lad. Fine man, fine soldier. Be greatly missed.' He swallowed all the words behind his customary balled fist.

'Thank you, sir. I'll miss him too, sir.' The answer was honest, without deep or feigned emotion, a clear statement of fact. Those with life all before them could not be expected to grieve overmuch for those whose life was done.

'Yes,' Ian said again, reaching into his memory for what was disturbing him about those straight, honest brown eyes; where had he seen that look, that look that unravelled manners and pretence with its calm certainty? The answer jolted him; Willie Bruce. That was the way Willie Bruce looked at a man, be he great man or small man. How queer. No bloodline, and yet in his own bastard son, standing before him, he was seeing vividly the look of that venerable old soldier. It was as if inheritance passed from one generation to another like a salmon leaping the falls, electric and free from one soul to another. Queer. The boy was waiting to be dismissed. Ian wanted to hold him there a little longer, to feel a little longer the presence of the ghost of Naomi, but he had no excuse.

He wished him luck and sent him on his way, watching the straight young back disappear round a bend in the zigzagging trench. The last of his sons. He wondered dimly if, like his own grandfather, Sir Henry, he would one day weigh them all, and find that last child, the child of his love, the best. He turned slowly to re-enter the dugout and make his farewells to Gordon Bruce and leave behind him the men who held the line.

18

It was dawn on the twenty-fourth of June, 1916. The sky was clear and beautiful and green above the threat of no-man's-land, dark and still star-sprinkled in the safety of the west. From somewhere a Very light soared, white and skywards, a rising star. And then, with a sound that rose, like rising lava, like a sea within the earth, like all the thunders since the earth was born, the great guns opened up in unison and the barrage began. The ground shook, loose objects tumbled into the mud, men froze in amazement, with eyes widening into terror. The younger and newer flung their heads down to the shaking earth. The older huddled, like beaten sheep, into their holes. The sky brightened behind them with an alternative dawn, and over the land of the enemy a white, sepulchral dust began slowly to rise.

On the doorstep of the Dolphin Hotel in Southampton, Naomi Bruce, returning once more to the Western Front, pulled the door lightly shut and stood in an English dawn listening to the faint, far, ominous and shuddering roar. Then she stepped out to face the thunder that rolled westward from the Somme.

THE END